The Mammoth Book

Date Due	Date Due	Date Due
22/02/17		

Recent Mammoth titles

The Mammoth Book of the Mummy

Edited by Paula Guran

ROBINSON

ROBINSON

First published in Great Britain in 2017 by Robinson

A CIP catalogue record for this book
is available from the British Library.

ISBN: 978-1-47212-029-8

Typeset in Whitman by Hewer Text UK Ltd, Edinburgh
Printed and bound in Great Britain by CPI Group (UK) Ltd, Croydon, CR0 4YY

MIX
Paper from
responsible sources
FSC® C104740
www.fsc.org

Robinson
An imprint of
Little, Brown Book Group
Carmelite House
50 Victoria Embankment
London EC4Y 0DZ

An Hachette UK Company
www.hachette.co.uk

www.littlebrown.co.uk

Contents

Introduction: My Mouth Has Been Given to Me That I May Speak

Paula Guran

———

Any corpse with well-preserved flesh is considered a mummy. Mummification may be deliberate or accidental. Extreme cold, dryness, and lack of oxygen are all natural conditions that may result in mummification. Intentional exposure to chemicals—embalming—as practiced by the ancient Egyptians produced the "bandaged" mummy that is now iconic.

Human mummies, anthropogenic or spontaneous, have been found on every continent except Antarctica—and naturally mummified seals have been found even there. Some of the best-preserved mummies come from European bogs.

There are a handful of fictional non-Egyptian mummy tales, but the vast preponderance of pop cultural mummies in all media are based on the Egyptian model.

The Egyptians were not preoccupied with death; they loved life and wanted it to continue forever. For those with means to afford the expensive and complex process of mummification, it was a way of ensuring one survived in the afterlife.

The journey to the next life was fraught with danger. Spells, amulets, rituals, and funerary figurines were provided to assist the deceased to make his or her way to Osiris, god of the netherworld and the first mummy. There, the deceased would face the judgment of the Weighing of the Heart. The heart of the dead was placed on a scale balanced against the feather of Maat—the fundamental order of the universe, justice, and truth personified as a goddess. If the scales balanced, immortality was achieved; if not, Ammit—a monster part lion, hippopotamus, and crocodile—devoured the heart and one's chance for eternal life ended.

The Egyptian concept of spirit or soul was complicated (and not fully understood today). Very basically, the body was preserved to continue providing a host for the soul.

Mummification occurred in Egypt as far back as prehistoric times, but the earliest mummies were probably an accidental result of Egypt's hot dry climate. Around 2600 BCE, Egyptians began to intentionally mummify the dead. The process varied over the ages, but remained complex and expensive. Royalty and the elite were mummified, the average and poor had to rely on incantations and spells to reach the afterlife.

Sometimes pets were mummified, as were, for religious reasons, several kinds of animals.

Mummies have acquired meaning and symbolism quite separate from their value as a source of historic knowledge and tangible connection with the past. They are part of an obsession with the civilization once centered on the Nile River. This passion began with the ancient Greeks and, through the ages, continued in Western culture. Egyptomania has manifested in many ways: the fine arts, architecture, design, the beliefs of occultists, philosophy, politics, religion, science (both sensible and pseudo-), and society. It has played—for better or worse—a part in discourse of race and, according to some, even the national identity of the USA.

Two major waves of Egyptomania have washed over the West in the last two centuries or so. The first followed Napoleon Bonaparte's attempt to conquer Egypt (1798–1801). Along with some thirty-four thousand soldiers, the invader's ships carried more than five hundred civilians—biologists, mineralogists, linguists, mathematicians, chemists, botanists, zoologists, surveyors, economists, artists, poets, and other scholars. The campaign was a military disaster, but became a cultural triumph. The scholars produced the encyclopedic *Description de l'Égypte*, published from 1809 to 1827, and conveyed the glories of Egypt to the European public.

The French also brought back treasures from Egypt, but some of the antiquities gathered to study in Alexandria were forfeited to the British when the French occupation of Egypt was ended in 1801.

A hunger for objects, monuments, and more, developed. Unfortunately, during the nineteenth century many of the techniques employed to find pieces of Egypt's past were destructive and sometimes felonious. Nevertheless, they added greatly to the world's knowledge. Mummies were included among the many artifacts shipped back to museums.

In the 1840s, steamships made travel to Egypt feasible. Wealthy tourists brought mummies back as souvenirs and public and private "mummy unwrapping parties" became fashionable.

For those of lesser means, advances in printing technology resulted in larger and cheaper editions of travelogues, memoirs, and other literature concerning Egypt. Newspapers and periodicals covered the discoveries of Egyptologists. Europeans and Americans were enthralled with the idea of Egypt and fascinated by its mummies. The tantalizing thought of a mummy brought back to life began appearing, not surprisingly, in fiction.

During the nineteenth and early twentieth century, four main themes began fermenting in mummy fiction: reanimation, reincarnation, a love that lasts beyond death, and a mummy's curse that brought vengeance from the past.

As far as we know, the idea of a reanimated mummy would have never occurred to the ancient Egyptians. Mummies were still people of a sort. How can one bring life to the already living?

Mummies, their coffins, and masks are lifelike and seem to have the potential for reanimation. At the same time, these preserved remains defy what Westerners see as a natural cycle—"ashes to ashes, dust to dust." That which is not "normal," including mummies, can easily slip into the realm of the supernatural where the dead may walk and talk again. Reanimation of the dead can also be a result of "weird science," which prompts a cultural connection to the idea that humankind can not scientifically tinker with the unknown without facing dire consequence.

As handy a plot device as it is, the idea of reincarnation would also have been abhorrent to the Egyptians. The entire intent of mummification—and the belief system supporting it—was to preserve an individual's single life to enjoy eternity in the afterlife. Magical "backups"—in case offerings of food ceased or the body was destroyed—were provided by carved and painted representations on tomb walls and in sculptures that could provide a place of safety for the soul.

Despite all the magic (heka) that was commonplace to ancient Egyptians, they never connected curses with mummies. Perhaps the concept resulted from a combination of Western cultural taboos against disturbing the dead and an early Arabic (Egypt became part of the Arab world in 639 CE) belief: if one entered an Egyptian tomb and voiced the proper magical words, its treasure—made otherwise invisible by the magic of the ancients—would then be revealed.

As for eternal love, the Egyptians did expect their loved ones to be with them in the afterlife. They also assumed they would have sex there. Since divorce and remarriage were easy and fairly common, one can suppose "love that never dies" would be an individual choice, if it existed at all.

By the turn of the century the new medium of film took the mummy as a theme. At least three dozen films featuring mummies were made in the silent era. Fiction influenced film; film influenced fiction.

Howard Carter's discovery of Tutankhamun's tomb in 1922 and subsequent exploration and careful conservation of its contents—which took ten years—inspired a new wave of interest in ancient Egypt. The Western world was, once again, enthralled with Egyptomania. Many Egyptian-themed novels were churned out during the 1920s and 1930s. Exotic, mysterious ancient Egypt also became a staple of the pulp magazines that flourished in the USA during the 1920s and 1940s, so mummies occasionally showed up there, too. Like all pulp fiction, a few of the tales remain of interest, but most are best forgotten.

Film became the main manufacturer of mummy mythos for the masses. If horrific visions of the vengeful walking dead, pharaonic curses, and murdering mummies invade the public's nightmares, then the images probably came from the screen—and the Universal films of the 1930s and 1940s and their take-offs (including the Hammer Films of the 1950s and 1960s) are primary sources.

Although far from the first or last mummy movie, the classic 1932 Universal Pictures movie, *The Mummy*, directed by Karl Freund and starring Boris Karloff, is the most influential.

The Mummy's themes of romance, reanimation, and reincarnation are central to the twentieth-century image of the mummy. A doomed dark romance linking the present to the past can easily be seen as a metaphor for cultural fascination with ancient Egypt itself.

Karloff, in Jack P. Pierce's outstanding make-up, portrays a mummy only briefly—if effectively—early in the film. Although Karloff's short appearance as a wrapped mummy became an iconic "monster" as a result of the film, he's not really horrific. The mummy does not intentionally harm anyone; only in human form does the character kill. And, although it doesn't excuse his crimes, the revived human-appearing mummy is motivated by a profound love for which he has suffered a torturous death and centuries of unfathomable stasis.

The movie was successful enough that Universal exploited it during the 1940s with a series of plodding, unimaginative sequels that had nothing to do with Karloff's nuanced performance or much with the original mummy. They instead focused on Kharis, a mummy-creature resembling dirty laundry that shambled about with a stiff-legged gait trailing bandages. Kharis is always brought down by humans (and eventually revived). He is a creature serving human evil that "good" humans can defeat.

During the 1950s, stories featuring mummies became scarcer and often light-hearted rather than horrific. Movie mummies re-entered the horror realm in 1959 when Hammer Films managed to hit just about every theme/cliché in their remake of *The Mummy*.

The literary mummy remained alive in a few short stories and novels. One outstanding novel of the horror/thriller genre remains *Cities of the Dead* (1988) by Michael Paine, a chilling, well-researched, atmospheric novel written in the voice of Howard Carter. Supposedly excerpted from diaries written by Carter long before his famous discovery, the plot involves mummies, but not the walking dead.

By far the bestselling of all mummy fiction is Anne Rice's 1989 *The Mummy, or Ramses the Damned*. Rice returns to the theme of immortal love and lust with a heavy hand that makes this novel more of a steamy romance than a horror story.

Although mummies were seldom the theme, they do turn up in some mystery/thriller novels. Elizabeth Peters, a pen name of the late Barbara Mertz (a PhD in Egyptology), invented turn-of-the-century heroine Amelia Peabody, who is based very loosely on Amelia Ann Blanford Edwards, a real Victorian Egyptologist. Most of the nineteen novels only deal tangentially with mummies. Lynda S. Robinson (who holds a doctoral degree in anthropology with a specialty in archaeology) set a series of mysteries in Eighteenth Dynasty Egypt. In the first of the series, *Murder in the Place of Anubis* (1994) her "detective," Lord Meren, investigates a murder committed in a mummification workshop.

From the literary mainstream, an unusual novel *The Egyptologist* (2004) by Arthur Phillips involves a murder-suicide related to mummies, but no revived mummies.

There are numerous books for children and young adults—both fiction and non-fiction—with a mummy theme.

The movie mummy genre was somewhat revived with Universal's 1999 "reimagining" of their mummy with *The Mummy*, a big-screen blockbuster. It was followed by *The Mummy Returns* (2001), and *The Mummy:*

Tomb of the Dragon Emperor (2008)—the last set in China where the mummy of an emperor cursed by a witch centuries before is unearthed—all directed by Stephen Sommers.

Universal announced a reboot of the series in 2012. At the time of writing this, the most recent announced release date is 27 March 2017.

Although some of the stories in *The Mammoth Book of the Mummy* use earlier tropes, it's often with a modern twist. We offer three brand-new stories. Five tales employ non-Egyptian mummies: one Mesopotamian, two Northern European bog mummies, two American. Admittedly, the mummies may not all turn out to be mummies, exactly, but I think you'll agree the stories fit the theme very well. I hope you find these tales are a breath of fresh air in a subgenre that, too often, is as stifling as a sealed sarcophagus—if written in at all.

The history of anthologies (in English, at least) focusing on fiction related to mummies is a short one. In fact, there had never been a trade anthology of all-new, original stories from multiple authors on the theme until 2013 when *The Book of the Dead*, edited by Jared Shurin (Jurassic London), was published. It presented twenty new tales of the mummy. This volume owes a great deal to Jurassic London: four of our stories are reprinted from *The Book of the Dead*; they also published the novella *The Good Shabti*.

[Even in the realm of extremely limited editions, the only attempt at collecting original mummy stories was *Spirits Unwrapped*, edited and published by Daniel Braum, in 2005. Really a softcover chapbook (with no ISBN) of thirty-two pages limited to 250 copies, it included four original stories.]

Otherwise we have had—

The Mummy Walks Among Us, edited by Vic Ghidalia (1971, Xerox Education Publications), a compilation of pulp reprints, was—as far as I have discovered—probably the first mummy-themed anthology in the USA. A scant 151 pages, it contained five short stories that first appeared in issues of *Weird Tales* from 1930 to 1946; Théophile Gautier's *The*

Mummy's Foot, first published in French in 1840 (as *Le pied de momie*) and in English in 1871; and a story by August Derleth that first appeared in *Strange Stories*, April 1939. It was probably intended for what we now consider the young adult market.

Mummy! A Chrestomathy of Cryptology, edited by Bill Pronzini (Arbor House, 1980), appears to be the first hardcover mummy anthology. Nominated for a 1981 World Fantasy Award as Best Anthology/Collection, *Mummy!* contains seven reprinted short stories and five originals. The new stories were all based in non-Egyptian cultures, so I will note them individually: Talmage Powell discovers Mayan mummies in "Charlie," and mummies are found in Scotland in "The Weekend Magus" by Edward D. Hoch. "The Princess" by Joe R. Lansdale centers on a Danish bog mummy. Ardath Mayhar's "The Eagle-Claw Rattle" concerns an American Indian mummy. Mysterious (possible) mummies are chanced upon in a New England town in "The Other Room" by Charles L. Grant. The science fictional "Revelation in Seven Stages" by Barry N. Malzberg presents future aliens using Egyptian mummies on Earth long after humanity has ceased to exist.

The tales in *The Mummy: Stories of the Living Corpse*, edited by Peter Haining (Severn House, 1988), were all reprints published previous to 1940 except for two from the eighties. *Mummy Stories*, edited by Martin H. Greenberg (Ballantine, 1990) included five original stories—none memorable and two of which don't actually involve a mummy at all—as well as nine reprints.

Into the Mummy's Tomb edited by John Richard Stephens (Berkley Books, 2001) was another rehash of dated reprints.

Although mummies were not its theme, I'll note *Pharaoh Fantastic*, edited by Martin H. Greenberg and Brittiany A. Koren (DAW, 2002) since two of its thirteen original stories were mummy-related. The same with the *The Mammoth Book of Egyptian Whodunnits* (2002) edited by Mike Ashley. Its theme is apparent from the title, but since five of its eighteen original Egyptological mysteries include mummies, as does the single reprint—"The Locked Tomb Mystery" by Elizabeth Peters, which first appeared in the 1989 anthology *Sisters in Crime*—it, too, deserves a mention.

In 2004, *Return from the Dead: A Collection of Classic Mummy Stories* (Wordsworth Editions), edited by David Stuart Davies, again reprinted older stories as did Chad Arment in *Out of the Sand: Mummies, Pyramids, and Egyptology in Classic Science Fiction and Fantasy* (Coachwhip Publications, 2008). The latter is a print-on-demand publication.

Jurassic London published a companion volume to the aforementioned *The Book of the Dead*. *Unearthed*, co-edited by Jared Shurin and John J. Johnston, compiled eleven classic stories—one virtually unknown—for an excellent compilation of (essentially, if not exactly) nineteenth-century (1840–1906) short fiction. Both books were published in partnership with the Egypt Exploration Society and have introductions by John J. Johnston, Vice-Chair of the Egypt Exploration Society, that are the epitome of what I wish this introduction was.

Although there may be some anthologies among the many mummy-related fiction titles published for children and young adults in the last three decades, I haven't found them. Similarly, in the relatively new area of digital publication, *The Mummy Megapack: 20 Modern and Classic Tales* (Wildside Press, 2011), appears to be the single e-book-only anthology widely available. Despite its title, it consists of only three modern stories (two of which are by Nina Kiriki Hoffman) and seventeen public domain stories published before 1913.

Some final notes . . .

- A great deal of the above would, in a scholarly article, be footnoted. I'm not being scholarly.
- For instance, there should a footnote explaining the title of this introduction. It is part of Spell 22 in the Book of the Dead concerned with the Opening of the Mouth ritual. The ritual was needed so the deceased could breathe, speak, eat, and drink in the afterlife.

- I've retained the spelling of ancient Egyptian words and names as each author wrote them. Preferred spellings have changed over the years; stories set in an earlier era may well be employing what was "proper" then. English transliterations of hieroglyphs are dicey business to begin with, so we shall leave well enough alone.
- Similarly, any historical inaccuracies the authors may have used—intentionally or inadvertently—have been left. After all, this is fiction. Any mistakes made by me are unintentional, but I have no excuse.
- I use the term "steampunk" in a couple of story introductions. It occurs to me that there may be readers unaware of its meaning. In general, it is science fiction and fantasy that incorporates technology and aesthetic designs inspired by nineteenth-century industrial steam-powered machinery.
- Any historic Egyptian dates in my short story introductions come from *Ancient Egyptian Chronology*, edited by Erik Hornung, Rolf Krauss, and David A. Warburton (Brill, 2006).

Ankh, wedja, seneb!
(Life, prosperity, health!)
Paula Guran

When seeking stories for this anthology, I recalled "Private Grave 9" as one of the finest "mummy" stories I had ever read. A couple of other people mentioned it as their "favorite mummy story," too. When I reread Karen Joy Fowler's story, I realized Tu-api is not *exactly* mummified—but, even excluding the subtext of Howard Carter's famous discovery, this hauntingly powerful story is more than "close enough" to include here.

Private Grave 9
Karen Joy Fowler

Every week Ferhid takes our trash out and buries it. Last week's included chicken bones, orange peels, a tin that cherries had come in and another for peas, an empty silver-bromide bottle, my used razorblade, a Bakelite comb someone sat on and broke, and several early drafts of Mallick's letter to Lord Wallis about our progress. Meanwhile, at G4 and G5, two bone hairpins and seven clay shards were unearthed, one of which was painted with some sort of dog, or so Davis says, though I'd have guessed lion. There's more to be found in other sectors, but all of it too recent—anything Roman or later is still trash to us. G4 and G5 are along the deep cut, and we're finding our oldest stuff there.

I'd spent the morning in the darkroom, ostensibly to work but really because I was tired of the constant gabble of the expedition house. When I grew up, it was just my mother and me. I had the whole third floor to myself, and she wasn't allowed to come up unless I asked her. I've got no gripe against anyone here. It's just a question of what you're used to.

The photographs I was printing were all of infant skeletons. There's an entire level of these, laid out identically on their sides with their legs pulled into their stomachs. Davis had cleared each tiny skull and ribcage with his breath because they were so delicate, and it took a week because there were so many. That seemed very intimate to me, and I wondered if he'd felt any attachment to one more than another. I thought it would probably be rude to ask. My pictures were of all different babies, but all my pictures looked the same.

At lunch, I shared some philosophical thoughts—all about how much sadder finding a single child would have been and how odd that was, you feeling less with each addition.

Mallick, our director, said when I'd put in a few more seasons I'd find I didn't think of them as dead people at all, but as the bead necklace or the copper bowl or whatever else might be found with the body. Mallick's eyes are all rimmed in red like a basset hound's. This gives him a tragic demeanor, when he's really quite cheerful. The whole time he was speaking, Miss Jackson, his secretary, was seated just past him with her head down, attending to her food. Miss Jackson lost her husband in the trenches and her son to the flu after.

Remembering that, and remembering how each of her losses was merely one among so many they might as well have been stars in the sky, made me wish I'd kept my thoughts to myself. Women take death harder than we men. Or that's been my experience.

"No signs of illness or malformation." Davis has a face round as a moon and that pale skin that takes color easily; he's always either blanching or blushing. I watched him clean his fork on his napkin with the same surgical precision, the same careful attention, he brought to every task. Sunlight flashed off the square lenses of his spectacles whenever he looked up at me. Flash, flash, flash. "Best guess?" he said. "Infanticide."

Ferhid had carved us a cold lamb for lunch and had the mail lying under our forks. Ferhid has the profile of a film star, but a mouth full of rotted teeth. His mouth is a painful thing to see, and I wish he didn't smile so often.

We each had a letter or two, which was fair and friendly, though most of them mentioned Howard Carter's dig, which was not. Mine, of course, was from my mother, pretending not to miss me as unpersuasively as she possibly could. I missed the war as her sole support, but since that ended it's been more of a burden. Last month I wrote to her that a man must have a vocation and if nothing comes to him, then he must go looking. Today she responded by wondering if it was necessary to travel half a globe and forty-five hundred years away. She said that Mesopotamia must be about as far from Michigan as it's possible to get. How wonderful, she said, to be so unattached that you can pick up and go anywhere and never mind the people you've left behind. And then she promised me that she wasn't complaining.

Patwin read bits of *The Times* aloud while we had our coffee. Apparently reporters are still camped at the Tut-ankh-Amen tomb, cataloguing gold masks and lapis-lazuli scarabs and ebony effigies as fast as Carter can haul them out. These *Times* accounts have Lord Wallis and everyone else in a spin, as if we're playing some sort of tennis match against Carter and losing badly. Our potsherds, never mind how old they are, have become an embarrassing return on Wallis' investment, though they were good enough before. Our skeletons are too numerous to be tasteful. I'm betting Wallis won't be whimsical about paintings of dogs, nor will anyone else at his club.

As he read, Patwin's tone conveyed his disapproval. He has the darting eyes of an anarchist (and a beard like Freud's), but he's actually a stolid Marxist. So he'll tell you slavery was a necessary historical phase, but it's clear that shards of good clay working-class pots suit him better than golden bowls put by for the afterlife.

"We had a lovely morning in PG 9," Mallick said stoutly. PG stands for *private grave*, and PG 9 is the largest tomb we've found so far, four chambers in all, and never plundered—naturally, that's the part that has us most excited. A woman is laid out in the second of these chambers—a priestess or a queen in a coffin of clay. There's a necklace of gold leaves and a gold ring. Several of the colored beads she once wore in her hair have fallen into her skull. The skeletons of seven other women, presumably her servants, are kneeling in the third and fourth chambers, along with two groomsmen, two oxen, and a musician with

what I imagine, when Davis reconstructs it, will be a lyre. Once upon a
time Wallis would have been entirely content with this. A royal tomb. A
sleeping priestess. But that was before Carter began to swim in golden
sarcophagi.

Another American, a girl from Rapid City, has come to visit us in the
mud-brick expedition house. Her name is Emily Whitfield, and she's a
cousin of Mallick's wife or a second cousin or some such thing, some
relative Mallick found impossible to send away. She's twenty-nine, just
a couple years shy of me, flapper haircut, eyes of a washed-out blue, but
a good figure. Already there'd been some teasing. "High time you met
the right girl," Mallick had said, but the minute I'd seen Miss Whitfield
I'd known she wasn't that. I've never believed in love at first sight, but
I've had a fair amount of experience with the opposite.

Patwin had claimed to dread Miss Whitfield's visit, in spite of the
obvious appeal of a new face. "She'll need to be taken everywhere, and
someone will always be hurting her feelings," Patwin had predicted,
fingers scratching through his beard. Patwin prided himself on knowing women, although when that would have happened I really couldn't
say. "She'll find it all very dirty and our facilities insupportable. She'll
never have stood before." And then Patwin had a coughing fit; it was
such a rude thing to have said in Miss Jackson's presence.

But Miss Whitfield was proving entirely game. Davis took her to see
the baby skeletons, and he said she made no comment, lit an unmoved
cigarette. Apparently she's an authoress and quite successful, according
to Mallick who'd learned it from his wife. Four books so far, books in
which people are killed in clever and unusual ways, murderers unmasked
by people even cleverer. She was about to set a book at a dig such as ours;
it's why she'd come. Mallick told me to take her along and show her the
new tomb, so she was there when I took my picture. I'd been pointing
out an arresting detail or two—the way the workmen chant as they haul
the rubble out of the chamber, the rags they tie around their heads, their
seeping eyes—but she didn't seem interested.

We brought the smell of sweat and flesh with us into the tomb. Most people would have instinctively lowered their voices. Not Miss Whitfield. "I thought it would be grander," she said when we were inside the second chamber. Patwin had rigged an electrical installation so there was plenty of light for our work here. "I didn't picture mud." She lifted a hand to her hair, and when she lowered it again there was a streak of dust running from the hairline down her temple. It gave her a friendlier, franker look, but like Mallick's sad eyes, this proved deceiving. What she really wanted to know was whether there were tensions in the expedition house. "You all live in each other's pockets. It must drive you crazy sometimes. There must be little, annoying habits that send you right around the bend."

"Actually things go very smoothly," I told her. "Sorry to disappoint." I was taking my first photographs of the bones in the coffin, adjusting the lighting, dragging a stool about and standing on it to get the best angle. Miss Whitfield was beneath my elbow. Davis was in a corner of the chamber on his knees, pouring hot wax and pressing a cloth down on it. When the wax dried, he would lift out bits of shell and stone without disturbing their placement.

Miss Whitfield finally softened her voice. She was so close I could smell the cigarette smoke in her hair. "But if you did murder someone," she whispered, "would it more likely be Mr Patwin or Mr Davis?" She might have been asking this at the exact moment I took my first picture.

With her free hand, she reached into the coffin, straight into my second shot, ruining it. I watched through the rangefinder as she rolled the skull slightly away. I was too surprised to stop her. "Please don't touch!" Davis called in alarm from his corner, and she removed her hand.

"I heard Tut-ankh-Amen's head was bashed in at the back with a blunt instrument," she explained. Her smoke-filled disappointment wafted through the tomb. I came off my stool, tried to set the skull back the way it had been, but I couldn't be sure I'd done it right. I'd need to check my first photograph for that.

That night Patwin complained that I was blocking his light while he tried to read. I told him it was interesting that he thought the light belonged to him. I said, that's an interesting point of view for a Marxist to take, and I saw Miss Whitfield pull out her notebook to write the whole thing down.

Next day, a cylindrical seal was found on the bier, and Davis deciphered a name from it, Tu-api, along with a designation for a highborn woman. A princess, not a priestess, then. We also found a golden amulet, carved in the shape of a goat standing on its hind legs. There'd been a second goat, a matching partner, but that one was crushed beyond mending. Pictures of all the ornaments had to be finished in a rush and sent off to Lord Wallis. The goat is really lovely, and my photograph showed it well; no one will have to apologize for that find.

Even better were the stones and shells that Davis had impressed. Mallick believed they'd once been two sides of a wooden box, which had disintegrated, leaving only the pattern.

One side had shown scenes from ordinary life. There was a banquet with guests and musicians, farmers with wood on their backs, oxen and sheep. The second side was all armies, prisoners of war, chariots, men with weapons. Before and After, Miss Jackson called it, but Mallick called it Peace and War to clarify that it represented two parts of a cycle, and not a sequence, that peace would follow war as well as precede it. The unknown artist must have been remarkable, as the people were so detailed, right down to the sorry look on the prisoners' faces.

Patwin criticized me for taking more pictures of Tu-api than of the kneeling girls or the groomsmen or the poor musician. He said that I must fight the bourgeois impulse to care more about the princess than about the slave. It would be even harder, he conceded, now that the princess had a name. But Tu-api, he guessed, had the good fortune to die of natural causes. Unlike the others in her tomb.

"Does he always lecture at you like that?" Miss Whitfield asked. "How irritating that must be!"

Because I was busy developing prints of golden goats and verdigris bowls, because we'd already sent Lord Wallis plenty of photographs of skeletons, I left my pictures of Tu-api untouched for a couple of days. It was late at night when I finally put them through the wash and hung them up, and I didn't look closely until the following morning. In my first shot, Tu-api had a face. This wasn't part of the picture exactly, but a cloudy, ghostly spot with imploring eyes superimposed over the skull. It made my skin crawl up the back of my neck, and I took it out to the dig to show the others. It was a hot day and the air so dry it stung to breathe. I found Mallick, Davis, and Miss Jackson all together in the third chamber around the pit where the oxen had been found.

They were not as unnerved as I was. A human face is an easy thing to find, Davis pointed out, in the paint on a ceiling, the grain in a wooden board. "I once saw the face of God in the clouds," Miss Jackson agreed. "I know how that sounds, but it was as sharp and perfect as a Michelangelo. Sober and very beautiful. Thin Chinese sort of beard. I got down on my knees and watched until it melted and blew away."

This sudden display of fancy from solid, cylindrical Miss Jackson obviously embarrassed Mallick. He got scholarly in response, with his dry voice and those red-rimmed eyes. "I've heard of bodies preserved right down to the facial expression," he said. "In the Arctic ice, for example. Or at very high altitudes. I've always imagined those discoveries to be rather grim."

"Buried in the bogs," Patwin said. He'd arrived with Miss Whitfield while Mallick was speaking. He held out his hand for my photograph and looked it over silently. He handed it to Miss Whitfield. "I knew a man who'd met a man who'd found a thousand-year-old woman while digging for peat. He said you can't look into a thousand-year-old face and not find yourself just a little bit in love. You can't look into a thousand-year-old face and think, *I bet you were an annoying old nag.*"

"You've just put your thumb here on the print," Miss Whitfield suggested to me. As if I were six years old and playing with my father's Brownie.

I imagined myself with my hands around her throat. It came on me all of a sudden and shocked me more than the face had. I took my imaginary hands off her and gave her an imaginary and forgiving hand-shake instead.

In fact, I was angry with them all for refusing to believe the photo-graph even as they looked at it. Her face was indistinct, I grant you that. But you could see how beautiful she was. You could see the longing in those eyes. The fear. You could see she hadn't wanted to die alone, had surrounded herself with other people, but it hadn't helped her. I thought we all knew something about that, but maybe it was only me.

On payday there were forgeries to be exposed. A number of intriguing little carvings had begun to show up, all found by the same pair of brothers. The recent ones were simply too intriguing. Mallick made a show of dismissing the culprits as a lesson to the rest. It was all very good-natured. Even the brothers laughed at their exposure, left with a cheerful round of goodbyes. It was, no doubt, a great disappointment to Miss Whitfield, who had been looking forward to the confrontation ever since Mallick showed us the tiny forged bear.

None of the workmen would be back until their money ran out, which meant that we would start again in two days' time with a whole new crew. Yusef, who'd found the golden goat, had been paid its weight in gold and wouldn't be back for weeks. This was a shame as he was one of our most skilled workers and a natural diplomat as well. Diplomats were always needed on our mixed crew of Armenians, Arabs, and Kurds.

The site was quiet with everyone gone. I missed the rhythmic chanting, the scraping of stone on stone, the pleasure of dim and distant laughter.

Davis and I used the day off to drive Miss Whitfield to the holy shrine of the Yezedis. Davis said that the Yezedis worship Lucifer and represent him with the symbol of the peacock. We bounced along the road, the dust so thick I had to stop every fifteen minutes and wipe down the car windows. The last few miles can only be done on foot, but by this time you've risen into the pure air and walking is a pleasure. The shrine is breathtakingly white and intricate as a wedding cake. Streams pour through descending basins in the cool courtyard and acolytes tiptoe in to bring you tea. Clearly their Lucifer is not the same as our Lucifer.

Still, we'd done our best to work Miss Whitfield up with stories of Satan worshippers so that the tranquil, restorative scene would be a nasty surprise. I figured I was getting to know what Miss Whitfield wanted. I whispered to her that the priest, whom we did not see, was said to be kept drugged so that his aunt could rule in his name; I didn't want the trip to be a complete disappointment.

Davis sat holding his small, black cup of tea in two hands and smiling sweetly. The steam from the tea clouded his spectacles. I was across from him, growing sleepy from the sun and the sound of water. Miss Whitfield had knelt by the lowest of the fountain pools. She broke the surface with her hand, so her submerged fingers seemed larger than the dry hand to which they were attached. "Tell me," Davis said to Miss Whitfield. "When you come to a place like this, even at a place like this, do you find yourself imagining a murder?"

And I thought how easy it would be to push Miss Whitfield's head under and hold it. It wasn't even a complete thought, just a flicker, really, ephemeral as the steam from Davis' tea, no emotional content, no actual desire. I put it instantly out of my mind, which was easy enough since it had hardly been there to begin with.

"Would you think I was a ghoul if I said yes?" Miss Whitfield's black hair shivered in the slight breeze. She smoothed it back with her wet fingers, dipped her hand and wet her hair again.

"I'd think you the complete professional," Davis said politely. "But it's a ghoulish profession."

"So's yours," she answered.

And then to me, "So's yours," even though I hadn't said a thing.

On our way back we stopped in town to buy bread and chocolate to add to our supper of mutton and goat cheese and wine. Davis had gotten too much sun during our outing; he was as pink as if he'd been boiled. When he came to the table he sat on a chair that wasn't solidly beneath him and fell on to the stone floor with a loud cry of alarm. I'd never seen Patwin enjoy anything so much. He could hardly chew he was laughing so hard.

Miss Whitfield was too tired to eat. Ferhid took her untouched plate back to the kitchen, where he dropped knives and slammed pot lids to communicate his disapproval until Mallick went out to mollify him.

When I was sure no one was watching, I slipped away and took three more pictures of Tu-api, moving the light between each shot. If I stared long enough through the rangefinder into the coffin, I could conjure her face just the way my photograph had recorded it, floating over her skull. If I looked directly, then the face disappeared.

When I developed the new pictures, there was no face. I took another print off my original exposure, and her face didn't show up there, either. Perhaps this should have persuaded me that the image wasn't to be trusted, was a fault of the paper and therefore unreal. But I was even more persuaded in the event, which was proving so singular and so intimate. Tu-api had shown her face only once and only to me.

"I have a bone to pick with you." Patwin caught me as I came out of the bathroom. "You're always riding me about my politics."

Patwin didn't use American idioms, so I figured he was merely repeating what some native speaker had said to him, and I figured I knew who that would be. I was outraged by the collusion, but also by the sentiment.

"You must be joking," I said. "The way you lecture me . . ."

"Live and let live is all I'm saying." And he brushed by without another word.

I passed Davis on the way to my bedroom. "That really hurt when I fell," he said. "I may have cracked a bone."

"I didn't laugh as hard as Patwin did," I told him.

Miss Whitfield asked us all what it was about a dig that we liked. We were sitting in the courtyard of the expedition house and only Mallick was missing, trapped in town by a heavy rain that had turned the roads to mud. The air was washed and wonderful, and the sky an ocean of cool, gray clouds. Davis and Miss Jackson were playing a game on a stone board more than four thousand years old. Four thousand years ago they would have played with colored pebbles, but they were making do with buttons. Seven such boards had been found in Tu-api's tomb, and the rules were inscribed in cuneiform though not in our dig, but back in Egypt at Carter's. This same game had been played as far away as India. Ferhid was a demon at it.

"Not the fleas," Patwin said. He was scratching at his ankles.

"Not the dust." That was Miss Jackson.

"Not the way the workmen smell," I said.

"Not the way you smell," Patwin added, all loyalty to the working class. But then, placatingly, "Not the way I smell."

"I like a routine," Davis told her. "I actually enjoy picky, painstaking work. And, of course, we're all fond of a puzzle. We all like to put things together, guess what they mean."

"I like that it's backwards." Miss Jackson won a free turn and then a second. All six of her buttons were on the board now. "You dig down from the surface and you move backwards in time as you go. Have you never wanted, desperately wanted, to go backwards in time?"

Miss Whitfield paused for a thoughtful moment. "Of course. A person might want to erase a mistake," she suggested. "Or some stupid thing said without thinking."

"I like the monotony." Patwin had his eyes closed and his face turned up to the cool sky. "Day after day after day with nothing but your own thoughts. You begin to think things that surprise you."

Davis bumped one of Miss Jackson's buttons back to the beginning. "There you go backwards in time," he said, but Miss Jackson was speaking, too, only much quieter so it took a moment to hear.

"You have to be in love with the dead," she said. She took two of her stones off the board in a single turn and bumped one of Davis'. A third stone occupied a safe square, leaving Davis no move.

He shook his fist at her, smiling. "You're a lucky woman."

"Do you know how many bodies have been found on this site alone?" Miss Jackson asked Miss Whitfield. Her voice stayed low and colorless. "Almost two thousand. Just imagine writing one of your books with two thousand dead bodies to explain. And every single one of them left someone behind, begging their gods to undo it. Bargaining. Screaming. Weeping. You can only manage a dig if you already feel so much you can't take in another thing."

A long silence followed. "Excuse me," Miss Jackson said and left the courtyard.

Miss Jackson seldom made speeches. She never, ever referred to her losses; I'd always admired that about her. I only knew about them because Patwin, who'd worked with her three seasons now, had heard it from Mallick. Patwin had hinted that she was sleeping with Mallick, but I'd seen no signs and hoped it wasn't true. Miss Jackson was not a young woman, or a pretty one, but she was too young and too pretty for Mallick. I don't mean that Mallick's not a good guy. But honestly, few women wouldn't be.

I thought back on how she'd also told us she'd seen the face of God in the sky and how that speech, too, had been uncharacteristic. I hoped there was a simple explanation; I liked Miss Jackson and didn't want to see her handling things badly—sleeping with Mallick and rushing from a room in tears. Maybe we'd come up on some anniversary of something.

Or maybe Miss Whitfield was to blame. Miss Whitfield might make me edgy and snappish, but maybe Miss Jackson had finally melted in the sympathetic presence of another female.

"Well." The sympathetic female wrote a few words in her notebook. "I hope it wasn't something *I* said." She addressed me. "You're very quiet. Are you in love with the dead?"

Since I'd been thinking about Miss Jackson and not about myself, I had nothing prepared to say. I'm not good on the fly. "I'm not sure I do like a dig," I answered. "I'm still deciding." My heart was thudding oddly; the question had unnerved me more than it should have. So I kept talking, just to demonstrate a steadier voice. "I wanted to see some things I wouldn't see in Michigan. Mallick gave a lecture at the university and I asked some questions that he liked and he said if I could make my own way here, he could use me."

Miss Whitfield was staring at me through little eyes. From her vantage point, I could see how culpable I'd sounded, how unresponsive to the actual question. So I kept talking, which wasn't like me. "A photograph is simple. It's about the thing in the moment. I can take a picture of a dead baby and not be trying to guess why it's dead, when I'd never know if I was right. A photograph is never wrong."

She was still staring. "Rome wasn't built in a day, but every day we build Rome," I told her. I meant to use that to explain why a story was different from a photograph, but I stopped, because the longer I talked, the more suspicious she seemed. I felt unjustly accused, but also terribly, visibly guilty. "It's not a ghoulish profession," I said with as much dignity as I could find. There was a letter opener on a table by the doorway. I pictured myself picking it up and opening Miss Whitfield's throat in one clean swipe.

At that exact moment, I heard Patwin laugh, and the tension I'd been feeling vanished with the sound of it. "What?" Davis asked him. "What's so funny?"

"I was just remembering when you fell off your chair," Patwin said. He was still laughing. "How your arms flew up!"

I'd begun visiting Tu-api's tomb at night when no one would know. I'd like to say that there was nothing at all odd in this, but how defensive would that sound? I won't persuade you, so let's just skip that part.

In fact, I was disturbed by the murderous images coming over me, and the tomb seemed a quiet place to figure things out. I wasn't the sort to hurt anyone. People rarely upset or angered me. I'd never been a bully at school, didn't fight, didn't really engage much with people at all. Didn't care about anyone but myself, my mother had said once after my father died. She'd never said it again, but she hinted it. Buried it beneath the surface in every letter. Her own grief had been an awful thing to see for a six-year-old boy who'd just lost his father. If that was love, who could blame me for not wanting any part of it?

But I didn't think of myself as unengaged from the world so much as careful in it. Like many other people, I preferred watching to doing, only I preferred to do my watching within the spatial and temporal limits of the camera. A photograph is a moment you can spend your whole life looking at. I like the paradox of that.

A photograph isn't a narrative, so it's harder to impose on it. The only person who sees a photographer in a photograph is another photographer. And that's what I was doing in the privacy of the tomb. I was remembering those brief violent images of mine; I was trying to see the photographer.

They'd started up shortly after Miss Whitfield's arrival, and so they might have come from her. But they'd also begun shortly after Tu-api had shown me her face, a possibility I liked a lot less. If I remembered honestly, at the moment I'd taken Tu-api's first picture the word *murder* had been hanging in the air. The smell of smoke. The white light of the electric torches. "If you were going to murder someone," Miss Whitfield had been asking, "who would it be?"

No doubt Tu-api was herself a murderess. Patwin was always reminding me of this. The seven women in her antechamber, the groomsmen, the musician, the animals—all killed on her behalf. But I'd no wish to condemn her. In the context of those rows of dead babies, it didn't seem like much. In the history of the world, nothing at all.

What ruler in what land in what era has ever done otherwise? Name me one president, elected by and acting for us, who hasn't promised that we'll have peace just as soon as he's done killing people. Sixteen million soldiers (many of them killers themselves) dead in the Great War. Does anyone know why?

Does anyone believe we are done?

Besides, Tu-api was sorry. I'd been wrong to think that was longing in her face when it was clearly remorse. She'd wanted company in death, but that hadn't worked out. Was it possible she now wanted company in some unending world of guilt?

I found it easier to think Miss Whitfield was to blame than that Tu-api wished me ill. I'd begun to carry the print of her face in my pocket so I could pull it out and look at it whenever I was alone. I would sit on the dirt by her coffin and stare until her beautiful face floated up out of the darkness and we were, for a moment, together.

One night, walking back to my bedroom as silently as possible, I nearly collided with Mallick in the central hallway. He was wearing a night-shirt that left his saggy old knees bare. "Going to the lavatory," he explained unnecessarily, so that I knew it was true what Patwin had told me, that he'd been in the women's wing, visiting Miss Jackson. I tried not to judge her for it, but really, what comfort could sleeping with Mallick have been?

"Me, too," I said with an equal lack of conviction.

We stood a moment, carefully not meeting each other's eyes. "So Miss Whitfield leaves tomorrow," Mallick offered finally. "She's been a lively addition." I realized then that he thought I'd been visiting Miss Whitfield. As if that wouldn't be worth your life!

A woman's face appeared in a doorway, white and sudden.

When my heart began beating again, I recognized Miss Whitfield. She didn't speak, merely noted my suspicious, nighttime rambling, my covert meeting with Mallick, and disappeared as quickly as she'd come, no doubt to write it all down before she forgot. "Taking my pictures," she called it once, as if what she did and what I did were the same, as if her imposed judgments could be compared to my dispassionate records.

If I'd wanted to murder her, this would have been my last opportunity. Not that I wanted to murder her. Plus Mallick had seen me; I'd never get away with it. I went to my room and into a night of troubled dreams.

Miss Whitfield left the next morning. At Patwin's insistence, I took a group picture before she went. Patwin was always reminding me to document the work as well as the artifacts. "Take some pictures of live people today," he would say, fingering his beard with that annoying scratching sound. "Take some pictures of me."

Everyone lined up in the expedition-house courtyard, staring into the morning sun. Miss Whitfield was so eager to leave that she couldn't stand still and ruined two exposures before I got one that showed her clearly. It's a formal portrait; no one is touching anyone else in our strained little arrangement of bodies.

"Was there a curse on Tu-api's tomb?" Miss Whitfield had asked us shortly after her arrival. According to the newspapers, Carter had a curse; it was one more way in which we disappointed. Though Mallick, who had his own sources, said no one could find the actual site or text of Carter's curse. Other tombs had them, so, of course, Carter couldn't be expected to do without.

The very day Carter found the entrance to Tut-ankh-Amen's tomb, a cobra ate his pet canary. "Some curse," Patwin scoffed when we read this, but Davis reminded us how canaries in mines died just to warn you death was coming for you next. And sure enough, last week, we had a telegram from Lord Wallis that Lord Carnarvon, who sponsored Carter's dig, had suddenly died in Cairo. The cause was indeterminate, but might have been a fever carried by an insect bite on his cheek. Back in England his dog had also died—this curse was most unkind to pets.

It was the dog that put Miss Whitfield over the top. She cared little for mountains of copper, gold, and ebony. She was, as Patwin had noted, being nothing but fair, no materialist. But she did love a suspicious death. She left us for Egypt just as quick as an invitation could be wangled and transport arranged.

I believe we were all a bit disappointed to realize that none of us was to be the murderer or victim in her next book. All those murderous thoughts I'd obligingly had, all the probing we'd withstood, all the petty disputes we'd engaged in, all for nothing. The one to reap the benefit would, of course, be Carter.

We stood at the entry to the expedition house and waved. She was turned around to us, her face in the car window, smaller and smaller until it and then the car that carried her vanished entirely. "A dangerous woman," Patwin said.

"A terrible eater," said Ferhid. His tone was venomous. "A picky eater."

"I can't put my finger on exactly what it was about her," said Miss Jackson. "But there were times when she was watching us, taking notes on everything we said and did, as if she knew what we really meant and we didn't—there were times when I could have happily strangled her."

So we were all glad to see the last of her. It didn't mean she wasn't missed. It was hard to go back to how we'd been before; it was hard to stop being irritated with everyone just because she wasn't there asking us to be. There was a space left that no one else would fit inside. Ferhid kept setting her plate at the table for three days after she'd gone.

I've tried to tell all this as carefully as I could. Davis with the sunlight flashing off his spectacles. Miss Whitfield dipping her hand in the fountain. Mallick in his nightshirt. Ferhid's smile. Miss Jackson kneeling before God's face in the clouds. All that happened. All that was real. I'd rather you looked at that instead of at me. And yet here I am.

Some people are sensitive to exposure and some aren't. Miss Whitfield left her mark on me, but took no mark in return. Miss Whitfield was the sort of person who could touch Tu-api's skull, undisturbed, as it had been for centuries, and even move it and still not be changed by doing so. Me, I've always been the sensitive sort.

The night after Miss Whitfield's departure I went again to Tu-api's tomb. The silhouette of the ruined ziggurat shone in the moonlight.

There was the hum of bugs; a dog barked sleepily in the distance; my footsteps thudded in the dust. The wind was cool and carried the smell of cooked chicken. My relief was enormous. The only reason I'd thought of murdering Miss Whitfield was that she was an awful woman who often talked about murder. There was nothing supernatural at work here; it was all perfectly normal, and everyone had felt the same.

The moon had risen, round as an opened rose. I walked away from it into the perfect darkness of the tomb. I owed Tu-api an apology. How could I ever have thought, even for a minute, that she'd curse me into murder? I begged for her forgiveness. It was the first time I'd spoken to her aloud.

She was not the only one listening. Gossipy Mallick had apparently told Patwin his suspicions regarding me and Miss Whitfield, and Patwin, being more discerning and trained to read puzzles far older and more mysterious than I, came upon the truth of it. He'd followed me, and when I spoke, he was the one who responded. "What's this about?" he asked, and what could I possibly say?

"You can't be coming here any more at night by yourself." Patwin stepped toward me. "You can't be thinking this way." He took me by the arm. "Come back to bed."

I let him lead me over the moonlit dust to the expedition house. As we went, he analyzed my errors. I was guilty of romanticism, of individualism. I was guilty of ancestor worship. I had entertained the superstition of an ancient, powerful curse. I wasn't even bourgeois; I had barely made it to primitive.

There was no need to lecture me. I knew all those things. He put me to bed as if he were my mother, sitting beside me for a while, pretending nothing was wrong with me, just the way my mother had pretended. "You need a girlfriend," he suggested. "It's too bad Miss Whitfield has gone. It's too bad Miss Jackson is already spoken for."

I stopped listening. I'd just realized something about myself, something so unlikely, so unexpected, that no one would ever have guessed it. I myself would never have guessed it. Mother would never have guessed it, and she would be so surprised when she found out. The thing I realized was this: I was the sort of person who would do anything for love.

I'd never felt so joyful, so alive. Who could call that a curse? I'd never felt so serene. Mr Davis or Mr Patwin? Mallick or Miss Jackson or Ferhid? All or none of the above, and what if I got it wrong? But it had never been my choice to make. What I would do was whatever she asked.

Poor Patwin. I had only to turn to see his face. He'd believed so firmly in the march of history, it left him blind to the danger in the moment. Poor Miss Whitfield. Served her right, though, choosing Carter over us. How sad she'd be to have missed it all. Poor Miss Jackson. She'd never figured out that the secret is to love someone already dead. Then nothing can happen that doesn't bring the two of you closer together.

Serenity is, of course, a transitory state, just like living. Whatever Miss Jackson may wish to believe, humans being humans, eternal peace is found only in the grave and not always even there. I'm not telling you anything you don't already know.

But why spoil things with the long view? Let's leave me there in the moment, flooded with love. Patwin is talking and I am trying to make him happy by agreeing with everything he says. I agree that my infatuation with Tu-api is at an end. I agree that, circumstances being different, I would have considered Miss Jackson or even, God forbid, Miss Whitfield. I agree that when the weather grows too hot and we all go to our separate homes for the summer, I will put serious effort into finding a girlfriend who is alive. I agree that love can be usefully examined with the tool of Marxist analysis. I hand over my photograph and watch Patwin tear it up, both of us pretending there is someplace he can put those pieces where they won't last forever.

"The Good Shabti," an enthralling novella-length combination historical/science fiction thriller, was nominated for the Shirley Jackson Award. The words *shabti*, *shawabti*, and *ushabti* (along with variant spellings) are often used synonymously, which is not completely accurate, but all are small human-shaped figurines usually representing a person who would perform a certain task (agricultural labor, baking, brewing, various skilled crafts, etc.) for the deceased in the afterlife. As for the pharaoh depicted: Mentuhotep II had a lengthy reign (c. 2009–1959 BCE). During it, he reunified Upper and Lower Egypt leaving a prosperous kingdom. According to *most* (not all) sources, however, it was Mentuhotep IV (reigned c.1947–1940 BCE) who was followed by Amenemhat. A few of Mentuhotep II's bones have been identified, but no trace of Mentuhotep IV's mummy has been found.

The Good Shabti
Robert Sharp

"Oh, King Mentuhotep, he who has revitalized the heart of this land, the Divine One who wears the white crown, our benefactor, the One who unified the two Kingdoms, the being from whence all wisdom is derived, son of Hathor and the lady of Dendera, and to whom we owe our very breath . . ."

A breath is drawn, the voice continues.

". . . Giver of wisdom, bringer of the flame and the light, our guide, our ruler, our father! We thank thee for commanding us to come into Your Divine Presence and we beseech thee to bestow upon us the honor of doing whatever is your will."

This is the signal for the retinue to prostrate themselves before The Presence, and there is a rustle as fifteen men and three women place their knees, bellies, and foreheads on to the stone.

They wait. Three from the rear, Bak finds a pair of feet just two thumbs from his nostrils. The soles are cracked and variegated and they stink. Bak does not move.

Finally, the pure tone of The Presence washes over them.

"Get up."

They exhale and rise. A scrape of pottery, a light clink of metal, and a thud of wood as they pick up what they were carrying.

"Come," says the King, when fifteen heads have bobbed into his eyeline. "Take your places, let us begin."

The words unleash the retinue, and they billow out of formation to their spots around the room. The women pad over to the far wall, and sit. The scribes unfold their bundles and their tools. Bak nods to the two other handmen, and they scurry, platters in hand, to their post immediately behind the King.

Amenemhat, the Vizier, the one who gave the oration, is the only one who does not move. He straightens his robes and flexes his shoulder blades a little, and observes the activity around him. Looking into the room, over the King's shoulder, Bak can see that Amenemhat is taking great care to project calm and control. But little twitches give him away—Amenemhat is grinding his teeth.

It's not surprising. This is an unscheduled meeting. The King was supposed to be at leisure this evening, and yet, not ten minutes ago, just as the sun went down, a call had gone out to the compound that the Divine One wished to see the Vizier.

And so now they are here, and the King is breathing very deeply. His fists are clenched, as if he is spoiling for a fight. Bak snorts to himself at the very idea. The Vizier is going to get it in the neck now, thinks Bak. Better him than me.

Amenemhat takes the initiative. "What would you have us do, oh Divine King?"

"Summon my brother from the Western shore," says Mentuhotep.

Amenemhat looks puzzled, but nods anyway. "Of course, my . . ."

The King speaks over him. "And send out word to the administrators that the festivities following the Feast of Heb Sed shall be canceled."

In the corner, the women gasp. Amenemhat's eyes widen. Concealed panic, thinks Bak. But you have to admire the Vizier's control.

"And finally, muster a full company of men."

"As always, your wish is our destiny, my Lord. But may I . . ."

"Yes, Amenemhat, my wish is indeed your destiny. And you shall fulfill it, and I shall not justify myself further."

The room shuffles in disappointment. Is that all? Couldn't this have waited until tomorrow?

Amenemhat lowers his eyes and bows. I bet he's wetting his robes in relief, thinks Bak.

The King's body pivots, and Bak snaps out of his musings. In an instant, the eyes of the Divine One pierce him.

"Some water?" says the King. Bak and the two other handmen are suddenly the focus of the room.

They are well drilled. One holds the bowl, the other pours from the jug. When they are done, they pass it to Bak, and he passes it toward the King.

Mentuhotep hesitates for a moment, then reaches. The rings on his fingers chime against the rim of the bowl, and, just like that, it is in his hands. Success.

The King takes but a single sip, and then passes the bowl back. Bak sees that the Divine arm is shaking a little. Something is not quite right. Has anyone else noticed?

King Mentuhotep turns his back on Bak, and toward Amenemhat once more. "That is all, Vizier. Do what I ask."

"We shall. I shall."

The gaze of the King sweeps around the room, and alights upon the women.

"You, what is your name?"

One woman glances at the two others, to be sure it really is her that the King is addressing. She whispers. "Hena, your Majesty."

"Yes. Hena. You tonight. Let us go. The rest of you can leave."

Amenemhat makes an extravagant bow, bending from the neck, the waist and the knee all at once. It's a wonder he doesn't fall over, but, like a crane, he manages to keep balance, and rises once more to full height. His eyes are on the King the whole time.

But wait a moment. What now? Is the ritual continuing? The King staggers forward a step, and falls to one knee! He lowers his head. Is he bowing to his own Vizier?

Hena, the girl, gasps. Everyone else is silent, and her short squeak flutters about the chamber like a bird in the rafters.

Then it is Mentuhotep's turn to inhale. It's a horrible wheeze, the breath of an old man, but entering the body of a man in his prime.

At the peak, the zenith of the inhalation, a heartbeat. Then the King places his hands on the floor—like a dog, Bak thinks—and retches. It is a hideous noise, the sound of the throat screaming as it is pulled out of the body. A cup full of watery blood splashes on to the floor, in front of the King's hands.

Bak is the first to react. He abandons his post and his fellow handmen, and rushes to Mentuhotep's side. Without thinking, he thrusts both his hands under the King's armpits, and heaves the shaking body off the floor. But the King is limp, he's not helping himself. Bak cannot support the weight on his own.

"The King is ill!" shouts Bak, to the frozen retinue.

Amenemhat's eyes flare hot with anger. He strides toward Bak, pointing. "Blasphemy! Blasphemy!" he shouts. It is as if, for a moment, he has forgotten Mentuhotep's blood on the tiles.

"The King is ill!" screams Bak, again. "Somebody help me!"

"Let me in! Let me in I say!" The voice is confident and British. It expects to be obeyed. "Did you not hear me? Open this damned gate, you bloody jobsworth!"

Arabic voices are speaking now. First one, then another. There is laughter.

"Don't you give me that, you Neanderthal!" shouts the Brit. "Don't you know who I am?"

There is a rustling, clattering sound, a wire fence being shaken by desperate hands.

The group steps out of the facility and into the compound. The noonday sun is violent on the eyes, and Ruth's hands instinctively go up to her brow, so she still cannot see the owner of the voice on the other side of the barrier.

"Open. This. Bloody. Gate."

His verbal sparring partners begin chattering again. Ruth's Arabic is appalling, but she can make out the word *khedim* repeated over and over. She knows it means *servant*. The guards are claiming that they cannot possibly open the gate, because it is above their pay grade.

From the front of the line, Botha, the head of the team, speaks.

"Can I help you, bru? You lost or something? You don't want to be out this far into the desert at this time, yah? You'll catch sunburn." Botha feigns innocence. Ruth suppresses a smile.

"I am not lost," says the man on the other side of the fence. "I am merely here to retrieve my exhibit." He pushes his fist up to the wire fence and wiggles a finger through the hole. "In that truck there."

Botha, Ruth, and the guards turn to look in the direction of the waggled digit. There is indeed a large truck parked in the middle of the compound, one that had not been there this morning.

"And who might you be, bru?"

"I am Doctor Robert Ingle and I am curator of—" he corrects himself "—I am the Director of the Royal National Museum of Antiquities." He pauses for effect. Ruth can see that he considers that an important title. "And that truck has something that belongs to me."

"Really? Well, Doctor Robert Ingle, head curator of the Royal National Museum of Antiquities—"Botha also pauses for dramatic effect "—I am Doctor Frans Botha of the Emir Sharif Ali Al-Maud Institute for Research Sciences. And I'm pretty sure that whatever is in that truck belongs to me. It is in my facility now, isn't it?" Botha turns to look at Ruth, seeking approval. She nods. What is it that they say? Possession is nine-tenths of the law.

"That's ridiculous," says Ingle. "Look, that truck contains a major archaeological artifact. It was donated by the new government of Egypt to the people of this Emirate. And, as the head curator of the flagship museum, it is my duty to take custody of that item. I am in charge of its care. You cannot possibly have any business with him—" he checks himself again "—I mean, with it."

"I beg to differ." A new voice hovers over the compound. Ruth turns to see Mourad strolling across the gravel.

"Who are you?" asks Ingle.

Mourad doesn't bother answering. He keeps Ingle waiting until he has reached the security perimeter, and then answers a different question.

"You were wrong, Mister Ingle, to say that this 'artifact', as you call it, is a gift to the people." Ruth cringes at the use of the word *mister*, and she can see that Ingle is irritated too.

"In fact," says Mourad, "the little trinket in that truck was a gift to the Emir. The Emir, Mister Ingle. Not the people."

"Don't give me all that about the Emir, Mister . . . Mister, whoever you are. Look at my badge here." Ingle fumbles about in his pocket, and produces a plastic identity card. Ruth peeks at it over Botha's shoulder. She can make out some kind of seal on it, the symbol of the Royal family.

"My institution, the Royal National Museum of Antiquities, was established by charter with the explicit patronage of the

Emir. Not this Emir, mind you. His grandfather. But that doesn't matter." Ruth can see Ingle's eyes dart between Mourad and Botha. He is not sure which man to address with the final flourish of his argument.

"My point," says Ingle, "is that my museum is the rightful, lawful custodian of such gifts as are presented to the Emir."

"I see your point, Mister Ingle," says Mourad. "I'm afraid I do not have a smart ID card like you, sir. But look!"

He extends his wrist to reveal a watch. The strap is thick and gold.

"Do you see this watch?" With a deft flick he unclips it, and dangles it in front of the fence.

"My watch has the same emblem as your little piece of plastic. The flag of the Emir's House. This watch was given to me by my cousin . . . who happens to be Emir Sharif Ibn Ali Al-Maud. A lovely man. Very kind. Very generous."

Mourad steps right up to the fence, so his nose is almost poking through the wire.

"And the instruction to divert the truck to this institution was given to me personally, by the Emir himself. My cousin."

Ingle says nothing.

"We will take custody of this exhibit, Mister Ingle. And we will perform some minor scientific tests upon it. And when we are finished, I promise that it will be delivered to your museum. I shall deliver it personally."

Mourad turns his back on the Englishman, and starts walking back into the facility.

"In other words," adds Botha, "fuck off."

The men and women of the court seep slowly into the large reception hall outside the private chambers. They see a towering gold door, twice as high as a man, with carvings of Osiris and Horus set into the panels.

The assembled dignitaries cannot see the mighty Mentuhotep, so they are free to imagine him slowly ascending toward the other Gods. Or perhaps he is becoming luminescent like a torch, his skin whitening and glowing until he becomes a flash of light, one with the sun. Perhaps he is growing wings and flying through a window into the afterlife. Maybe he is simply walking through another door into a different world.

They are free to imagine whatever they please, whatever gives them comfort in this uncertain time. But they must not imagine crusted blood on the King's nose, or the hint of urine that now suggests itself to those who step into the final sanctum.

It is Bak's job to carry jars of water into the room, and to spirit away the bowls of mucus, phlegm, and blood, so that the growing crowd of family, courtiers and ministers gathering in the anteroom do not have to think too hard about the mortal parts of the King. Bak glides with purpose around the room, removing one vessel or adding another. He never stops moving. Now he is in the service rooms, discreetly depositing the humors. Now he is back again with fresh cloth or some fruit. Now he is by the window tweaking the curtains that keep out the flies.

Bak is a busy insect, scratching around the edges of a quiet tableau of death that has been composed in the center to the room.

King Mentuhotep lies on his back, foolishly clinging to life. A woman sits at his head, holding a damp cloth against his brow. Another kneels at his feet, holding a fan. Both females are dressed in the same simple robes, with their hair tied back in the same plain knots. Bak cannot decide if either of them is Hena, the one the King chose in the moments before he fell.

A scribe, plucked from the chambers of the civil service below, sits with his legs crossed and his tools ready. A stylus, some papyrus paper; wood and a knife if he needs it. It is not usual for utterances in the King's private chambers to be noted, but this is obviously a unique occasion. Yet Bak can see that the tools are still immaculately laid out. They have yet to be used. The King has not said anything for a while.

A thick wooden chair has been dragged to the bedside. Upon it sits the King's brother, fresh from the West. He stares straight ahead, and dares not look at the King's face, as if he is to be reprimanded for some boyhood prank. He is scared, thinks Bak. He is far too young and slight for this. Does he have a quickness of mind? Can he command the respect of Amenemhat?

Or, for that matter, of me?

No, he does not, thinks Bak.

Most of the ministers have been banished to the reception rooms, but Amenemhat has unfettered access. Though laden with robes and jewelry, he slips in to the chamber in near silence. Bak sees him enter, but the King's brother is startled when the Vizier materializes by his side.

"Anything?"

The brother shakes his head.

Amenemhat moves into the space between the prostrate King and his brother, and begins a whispered chant. Sticking to his wide trajectory around the edges of the chamber, Bak cannot hear the words, but he knows what is being said: "Oh, King Mentuhotep, he who has revitalized the heart of this land, the Divine One who wears the white crown . . ." Even now, Amenemhat retains his piety.

A gurgle from the King. All heads, Bak's no exception, are pulled toward the body on the bed.

"Vizier, is that you?"

"I am here, Majesty."

"You must begin making arrangements for my funeral, Vizier."

"I am entirely confident that your Majesty will soon recover from this minor inconvenience," says Amenemhat.

In response, Mentuhotep rolls over to the bowl by his bedside and coughs up a wad of black blood. A more eloquent response could not be imagined, thinks Bak, as he steps forward to clean the mess.

Amenemhat takes the point. "What funeral arrangements, oh Immortal One?"

Mentuhotep lifts his arm. It is pale and the blue veins are visible through the skin, but it is still as long and as thick as it always was. He looks at Bak.

"Help me up," says the King.

Immediately but carefully, Bak puts the clay bowl with its saliva and stomach debris on the floor, and places his arms once more under the King's. Amenemhat has to step back to move out of the way, which means the King's inconsequential brother has to stand and shove his own chair a few foot lengths toward the end of the bed.

"Prop me up," says the King to Bak.

Bak doesn't understand. He looks to Amenemhat for guidance, but the minister just shrugs.

"Prop, Majesty?" asks Bak. He does not remember ever asking Mentuhotep a question before.

"Just sit there," commands the King. "Just sit there and let me lean on you."

The women titter. Amenemhat's eyes widen. "Perhaps, your Majesty, I could . . ."

"Oh shut up Vizier!" croaks the King. To Bak, again: "Put your back there, and I shall lean."

Bak does as he is commanded. With caution, he lowers himself on to the edge of the bed and perches there, like a frog on the riverbank. The King sighs, and leans into him, and there they are, a God and his slave, back to back.

Bak remembers a time from his boyhood when one of the farmers brought a dead baby goat into the village marketplace. Only it was not one goat, but two, spliced together along the back. Two heads, eight hooves, but one skin. Bak remembers an argument between the farmer and the priests about whether this meant the Gods were happy or displeased. Bak cannot remember the outcome of the argument, but he guesses the priests probably took it to be a bad sign. He remembers they forced the man to burn the goat.

Mentuhotep's skin kisses Bak's own. The mass of the King weighs against him. He realizes he has to lean even closer in order to keep the equilibrium.

Now the King is comfortable, he looks up at his Vizier and begins to talk. The scribe begins to write, and Bak listens. Amenemhat's breath quickens as the King speaks.

The forklift is nowhere to be seen and the laborers have been dismissed. It has taken several hours, but the sarcophagus has been installed at the facility. The team assembles to behold their prize. Over the head stands Botha. Mourad to the East, and Ruth to the West. To the South, at the foot of the relic, Dr Stephano Lentini stands blinking behind thick glasses. Behind him, on the wall of the lab, hangs a portrait of Emir Sharif Ibn Ali Al-Maud in full ceremonial dress.

Ruth allows her hands to caress the slab of stone. It is cool to the touch. Her fingers explore the hundreds of naïf hiero-glyphs, carved into neat rows. They cover every plane of the block, giving it a dappled look. Ruth tries to picture the men who put the marks there, but they have no faces, just arms in the hot sun.

She finds it easier to think of the person who wrote what is on the slab. The author. He (probably, certainly a man) has had some thoughts. Some synapses have triggered, muscles have moved, words have been said. And now they are here on this block of stone. Her fingers are tracing the marks, and neurons have connected. But are the patterns in her brain the same shape as in the mind of that man, all those years ago?

"What do they mean?" she asks.

"Jesus bloody Christ, my dear," says Botha. "I know I have several doctorates but I can't be doing everything. You're the expert, ya!"

Ruth knows he is joking. She does signals, not linguistics. Statistics, cryptography, and the like. Botha knows this because it is the reason he hired her. And he holds precisely the same number of doctorates that she does, which is two.

"Hey, Mourad!" yells Botha. "Tell Ruth what the coffin says!"

Two feet away, Mourad consults a large ring-binder file, packed full of laminated cards.

"It's mainly orations," says Mourad, and reads off from a list on one of the cards. "He irrigated the land. He wore a white crown. He united the Kingdoms. That sort of thing."

"Thanks, Mourad! That's why we keep you around, eh, boyko?"

Mourad smiles and nods, while Botha rubs his hands together. "Right then: fire up the scanners. Let's see what sort of condition he's in."

The word is already bouncing around the palace that King Mentuhotep has made some spectacular demands on Amenemhat by ordering strange variations to the burial rituals. Bak has neither the permission nor any excuse to step out into the antechamber, so he puts his ear to the door. The tone of the murmurings from the assembly has changed. By his reckoning, there is more movement. They are unsettled.

A half-voice stumbles through the lamplight. "They do not understand." The King can barely speak now, his words blocked by mucus and saliva, and a ribcage that no longer rises and falls as it should.

"They are mortals. Mere people. They do not speak with the Gods."

Bak is not sure whether he should say "yes" or "no" to this, so he just nods.

"I know what they are saying," croaks the King. "'Oh, Mentuhotep must be mad with his sickness, Mentuhotep does not really mean what he says.'"

"I do not venture into the anterooms, Majesty."

"But this is not the disease. The people must know I formed my beliefs a long time ago, in my youth."

Bak feels out of his depth. Where is the King's brother? Where is Amenemhat? He proffers a bowl of water to Mentuhotep. A white hand grabs his wrist. It is cold and wet.

"They shall not disembowel me! I must submit to judgment as a whole man. I shall meet my brother Gods with my heart in my chest!"

"Yes, Majesty."

The Divine hand drops back on to the bed. Bak fights the instinct to wipe the royal sweat off his forearm.

Mentuhotep nods toward the window. "The curtains."

Bak is thankful for a task that involves moving his feet. He all but skips over to the window and draws back the sheet, revealing the twilight. A thousand torchlights glitter, as if reflecting the stars above. Beyond the city, Bak can make out the dark shapes of the monuments that mark the entrance in the great burial valley. The vast walls of stone have forever changed the mountains. They flaunt the power of the Kings who have been before.

And now there is Mentuhotep, who has not yet laid one rock on a mausoleum for himself.

The King raises his head and catches Bak looking at him. "You pity me?" he asks. Inside, Bak recoils once more. Why does Mentuhotep keep trying to engage him in conversation? Can't he just leave me alone to do my job, thinks Bak, and I will leave him alone to die? And where is Amenemhat?

And yes, if he is honest, Bak does pity the King, sunk into the bed, fading from life and from history. He would rather be a slave with his health than a God with bleeding lungs.

Mentuhotep is about to enter the next life, where he will reign again alongside Horus and Osiris with a thousand new slaves to see to his every need. But this bit, this gasping for breath, it looks painful. Right now, I wouldn't swap places with the King for anything, thinks Bak.

He is certainly not going to say that to his master, however.

"No, Majesty, I do not pity you. I admire your spirit. If I could take on some of your pain, I would do so gladly."

That should do it.

"Your concern for my condition warms my heart," says the King, coldly. Bak wonders if he may have been too enthusiastic. Perhaps the King really is of sound mind, if ill in body.

"But, do you not think I should have a great mausoleum, for my voyage to the afterlife?"

By the sun and the moon and the stars! Why does the King keep talking to him? Will this plague of the lungs not do its task and carry the King away? And if it will not, then let the heavens open and strike me down now, thinks Bak. And again: Where is Amenemhat? Where is anyone that is not me?

"You are a great King, Majesty. You should have a palace as large as that of Khufu . . ."

The King roars, then coughs, then inhales, then coughs again, and finally leans over his bowl. Saliva and blood seem to drip out of his teeth. Bak thinks he may have said the wrong thing.

"But I do not need another Giza! Those were Kings like me. I am of their line. Royal blood. Divine blood. When my people see those pyramids, they think of one word, and that word is 'Pharaoh'. I do not need to build more. Those monuments are already mine."

Lentini is ecstatic. He points to the ultrasound images. "I am not believe it. Look at definition in muscles. And here—" his thumb presses against the screen "—look at lobes in brain. Look at medulla, Ruth!"

Ruth is secretly aghast. She never expected the mummy to be anything other than mush in a dry skin shell. But now Lentini is saying that a four-thousand-year-old body is in good condition?

"How? How did they do this?"

"The body is covered in a sort of wax. It is an aldehyde . . ."

"Formaldehyde?"

Lentini chuckles. "Formaldehyde, this is too toxic. But this wax has similar to formaldehyde. It preserves in same way, locks in RNA strings. Younawhamsayin?"

Ruth has no idea how Lentini has picked up that idiom, but it sounds very odd coming from the lips of this anxious zoologist. Nor does she really understand what Lentini means when he talks about strings of RNA protein. That's not her department, and she gave up trying to decipher Lentini's private language a long time ago. Botha can keep up, of course, but she is sure that Mourad is as stumped as she is. The local Arab technicians stare at Lentini with dead eyes when he speaks. His instructions for them have to be filtered through Botha.

"So this aldehyde was put over this Pharaoh after he died, yes. And now there is preservation of each organs."

"Okaaaay . . . So what can you do?"

Lentini whispers his secret. "It will take time, yes. All cells require some Reinvigoration, a long time. Is not like with the monkeys or the horse. But I have already told Doctor Botha my answer. Our science is ready. We can make it happen, is my opinion. The Triple 'R' procedure. Even if is only for a short while, we can make it happen."

Mentuhotep is slumped back on the bed, yet still he insists on speaking.

"Are you trustworthy?" asks the King.

"Yes, Majesty."

"You will fulfill any task I give you?"

"Yes, Majesty."

"You will see your King's wishes done?"

"Yes, Majesty."

"And would you like your freedom?"

Is this a trick? Is this a joke?

"If your Majesty saw fit to grant me . . ."

Mentuhotep is restless. "Your freedom. Do you want it or not?"

This is definitely a trick question, thinks Bak. And if in doubt . . .

He prostrates himself before his wet rag of a King.

"You have heard of my request for burial?"

To be encased in wax? The entire Kingdom has heard the story, and two-thirds of them are appalled. The other third just think it odd.

"You must see it done, Bak."

This is just ridiculous. The King knows he has no influence. Why give this task to a slave?

"If your Majesty would honor me to dictate a message, I will pass it to the Vizier . . ."

"No, no. It is you who must perform the ritual. You must pour the wax and send me whole into my next life. I will leave orders that you will be part of the delegation."

More wet, hacking, royal coughs.

Bak gives in. "Yes, Majesty."

"Call Hena."

"Who, Majesty?" That is two questions he has asked the King, in as many days.

"Hena. The woman."

He remembers, and walks backward toward the servants' exit. Thanks be to all the Pharaohs that have gone before, thinks Bak. At last I have some respite!

Bak slips behind the curtain, ready for a hike down to the women's quarters, which will be fun because that place is usually off limits to the likes of him. But now he is on the King's business, so who can stop him? Bak is interested to see what the rooms are like. Will they have the same lonely squalor as the male slave quarters?

Bak stops in his tracks. On the other side of the curtain, the way is blocked. Hena, the woman he has been sent to fetch, is already there, sitting quietly on a low stool. Behind her, one of the scribes—the same man as yesterday, Bak notes—is slouching against the bare wall. How long have they been waiting there? They look at Bak, and then each other. Hena is calm but Bak can see how nervous she is. The scribe is more agitated. They are complicit in something. Is Bak being set up? Does the King know how long they have been waiting there?

Bak gathers himself. "You are wanted. The King has asked for you."

Hena says nothing, but just rises from the stool. It is a single, graceful movement, a levitation. She glides past Bak, slices the curtains apart delicately with her hand, and enters the Divine, if ailing Presence.

Bak says nothing to the scribe, but he pushes himself upright and strides after Hena. Bak can tell he is not a man working on his own initiative. He has orders from someone.

Bak follows them through the curtain, and bumps into the scribe, who has paused on the threshold.

Of the three servants, the scribe is the only one who is not a slave. That counts for little against the absolute power of the King.

Nevertheless, he is technically the most senior of the three. Bak leans over and whispers in the scribe's ear: "Say it . . ."

The scribe tiptoes forward. "Oh, King Mentuhotep, he who has revitalized the land, the one who wears . . ." he stumbles over the recitation ". . . the Divine one, who wears the crown, the white crown, I mean . . ."

Mentuhotep puts the scribe out of his misery.

"Enough. Stick to writing." He can manage only a whisper, but the scribe falls to his knees as if crushed under the weight of a boulder.

The reprimand seems to have sucked energy from the King. He takes a few deep breaths, before mustering enough strength to turn his head toward Bak.

"You shall seal my coffin. You shall deliver me to my brother Gods." He closes his eyes. Is that it?

No, there is more.

"You are my chosen one, Bak. This is my decree."

Bak watches the scribe take down what Mentuhotep has said. The King beckons Hena forward. "The gift?"

From within the folds of her cloak, Hena finds a knife. It is short and ceremonial, with a stubby blade no longer than Bak's little finger. There are bands of gold set into a dark wooden handle. She cradles it in both hands, and offers it to Bak, with as much deference as Bak would give to the King, when he presented water or fruit.

"Take it," commands the Divine One. "This seals the pact."

I do not remember agreeing to any pact, thinks Bak.

"Keep it with you," says Mentuhotep. "When the time comes, when the job is done, Chosen One, the knife will help you to freedom."

Bak turns the blade over in his hands. The King's emblems, the bird and the bread, are stamped into the gold banding.

"Thank you, your Majesty."

But Mentuhotep has already turned back to the scribe.

"See that this decree is copied a dozen times before daybreak. Take a copy to my brother, and another to the High Priest." The King gasps. His back arches against the bed, as if he is a cow straining in a harness.

"And one more thing. Do not show Amenemhat until after you have distributed it throughout the city."

The King waggles a finger at Bak. "And now, some water," he commands.

Bak conceals the knife within the threads of his tunic, and moves.

A pot of coffee sits brewing on the table, leaking steam, begging to be poured. Lentini cracks first, and plunges. He pours himself a mugful, leaving the others to help themselves. Ruth watches him take a sip and suck it through his teeth, like he is tasting wine. She half expects him to gargle it, or call for a spittoon, but eventually he swallows.

She reaches across the table, and retrieves the coffee pot for herself.

Botha is chairing the meeting, as always. Mourad sits at his right hand, leafing through ring-binders that seem to multiply before their very eyes.

"So the Reinvigoration is on schedule?" asks Botha.

Lentini gulps down his mouthful of coffee. "Is more intensive than we expected. I have changed way-points yesterday, now every six hours."

"Six? That is a lot of personnel time," says Mourad.

"Ya, ya," says Botha. "But you can afford it?"

Mourad shrugs. Of course he can.

"Good. Well, that means we can look at pulling Good King Wenceslas out of the tank in, what, thirteen days?"

"Mentuhotep" says Ruth.

Botha gallops past the correction. "Is that long enough for you to be ready, Ruth?"

"I think so. But this is orders of magnitude greater than what we've done previously. We're not working with a fresh CNS here. There would have been some degradation between death and the embalming."

Mourad quickly flips the sheets in his binder, then taps a page with his pen. "Several days," he says.

Ruth nods. "I've been thinking we should run the algorithms at a slightly slower rate, give ourselves some redundancy."

"But will that be stable?" asks Botha. "We've got to keep the top spinning, ya know."

Ruth is well aware of the technicalities. "Yes, it should be fine with just a little more power in the system. I would like to do at least three more test runs first."

Botha waves her away. "Fine, fine, whatever."

"Not fresh ones, though. And not from last year's vintage either. I need the originals."

Mourad looks up. Lentini raises his eyebrows. Botha groans. "But they're my last ones from Shenzhen, Ruth. You're betting my whole fucking zoo on this."

Ruth says nothing. Everyone knows she is right, including Botha, who throws up his hands.

"Ah, Ruth, you're killing me! All right then. Those orangutans will have a hell of a shock when they come out of the freezer!" Mourad and Lentini chuckle.

Will they, though? thinks Ruth. Will they even notice time has passed? Surely they just pick up where they left off? That's how

Reignition works. You do not need to know how a brain actually processes information or how self-awareness happens. You just need to connect the synapses together as they were before, and set the mechanism going again. Bypass all the theories of mind. You do not need to worry about concepts like "creativity" and "consciousness." That was her great insight, and that was why Frans Botha, who hates all that philosophy, turned up at her room in Boston one day and offered her an obscene amount of money.

Ruth wonders what it is like to be in the freezer. The monkeys are clinically dead, but a trace of the synaptic connections remains. Whatever the configuration of the cells at the moment of freezing, it remains while they are in storage. The thought persists.

What if, one day, it is Ruth in the freezer, and she is stuck with one thought for a week, a year, or longer? Better make damned sure that it is a good one.

She already knows what that thought will be. Little Esther. Only two years old, when she was taken from them, but still perfectly forrned, a complete thing.

She can still, if she tries, recall the last days, the last moments of Esther. The breathing becoming shallower, greater pause between each, until there were no more. She and Daniel fell asleep with Esther in their arms, and the doctor, God bless him, let them sleep together, and the thought, the dream, was of Esther breathing, hugging. She thanked the doctor for that, the extra hour of feeling her daughter was with her. By the time she woke up again, Esther was already under the sheet and getting cold.

Everyone steps around that moment, but it doesn't haunt her. It is but a single memory, a few weak synapses, and it is already fading. When she thinks of Esther, her mind goes straight to the stronger, earlier memories. A kinetic recollection of waddling, running and giggling. The unfettered beam that only a child who does not understand the world, her own mortality, could possibly wear. Ruth remembers Esther's delirious delight at discovering her hiding place behind the cushions in the living room. That's the expression Ruth remembers when she thinks of Esther. The curves of her cheeks, the parabola of her smile. The pain comes when she recalls, as she must, that the smile is no more.

Ruth retraces that smile in her thoughts every day, and she fancies the memory has become thicker in her brain. She has made up her mind. That is the smile she will picture if ever she goes into the freezer. If she is going to have one thought for a year, or a decade or a century or longer, then Esther's smile shall be it.

It's even worth hedging my bets, thinks Ruth. Even if I don't make it to the freezer. Who knows what technology Botha's team will develop in the next few years. Maybe a preservation process won't be necessary, and they'll find some other way to perform Triple R. Isn't that why we're experimenting with Mentuhotep?

I should still picture Esther's smile, she thinks. In moments of peril, if there are any, but also just when going about the day. Death creeps up at any moment. I could have a heart attack, she thinks. She has already made a habit of putting Esther into her head before she crosses the road. You never know when a careless moped or a runaway tram could end it all. Best be ready with a happy thought to see you through eternity.

"Are you with us, Ruth?" Botha's voice crashes into her awareness. "You were away with the angels, eh? I know it's too late and we're all tired, but just stick with us for a few more hours, ya? We need to be solid on this."

"Sorry, Frans," she says, and takes a big gulp of coffee.

A dark, serene service corridor behind the royal chambers, the soft pad of feet on flagstones, and a metal-clad fist that erupts into Bak's jaw with such force that the passage becomes a blinding red. The wall slams his other flank and seems to go right through him. The stone floor leaps into his face, and his mouth crackles like kindling on a fire.

A foot places itself on Bak's spine and presses down on his back. He cannot help but exhale. Pain shoots though his ribs, and he feels wet air rushing through a part of his cheek.

In just one ear, Bak hears the clink of jewelry. From the other ear, there is nothing, it is numb. His tormentor kneels down.

"So you want to be Vizier, do you, Bak?" sneers Amenemhat. "Or maybe you should just be the new Pharaoh?"

Bak emits a grunt that he hopes will be interpreted as a denial.

"The King has me riding out East with an army, all to go mining stone for his . . . his sacrilegious coffin. Imagine my surprise to hear that, in my absence, a new advisor has found favor with his Majesty."

Bak manages another grunt, this time an attempt at protest.

"You think that, because the King speaks to you now, that you are special? You are a deluded worm, Bak. He talks to you because you are there, nothing more. You were born a slave and that is all you will ever be. The King is dying, and when he goes, so will you. I will make sure of it, Bak."

Amenemhat stands, straightens his robes, and kicks Bak squarely in the groin. This time, Bak howls.

"You are not to say another word to the King in this life, do you understand?"

Bak nods furiously.

"Keep quiet, and I may just have you sent out to the mines in Siwa. A strong young man like you might find purpose out there. But if you continue this delusional partnership with the King, I will personally slit you open from your throat to your arse and let the rats feast on your organs, and you can journey into the afterlife without them."

Ruth is alone with a family-size bag of chips, a quart of orange juice, and a gilt-edged framed portrait of the Emir. Her office is actually a repurposed laboratory. The benches are long and have sinks sunk into them. Fifteen technicians could work here comfortably, but Botha and Mourad have given the entire room over to her project. So she sits at one end of this sanitized cavern with her laptop, perching on a tall wooden stool. If she were back at her penthouse she could have the ergonomic armchair she had Daniel ship over from the house in Boston. But she cannot directly program the Decision Array from her apartment, so she has to stay at the Institute and ruin her back.

She has a terminal window open, full screen. Back at MIT they coded an entire front-end to run the early experiments, but she has hacked the back-end of the system so much since she came to work with Botha that the interface has stopped working. Frans has offered to hire someone in to update it for her, but frankly, she prefers working direct with the code. It's easier not to have to second guess the Graphical User Interface, or worse, wait for the operating system to perform an elaborate animation every time she opens or closes a window. Once at FERMI, she remembers with a chuckle, they had to restart the accelerator at a cost of several thousand dollars because one of the computers crashed at a crucial moment, and that turned out to be the fault of an elaborate pop-up window. Far better to just type the commands into the machine and hit *enter* when you're done.

The only problem with her method is that she doesn't have a clock on the screen. Ruth realizes that she has absolutely no idea what time it is. The strip lighting is as bright in the middle of the night as it is at noon. She doesn't make a habit of pulling an all-nighter, and hopes she will be able to get out of here for a few hours' sleep before the embarrassing moment when the technicians, or worse, Doctors Botha and Lentini, start wandering in. She can do without Frans telling her she stinks again.

But for now, the entire facility is empty, save for the security guards, and she needs to get a new iteration of her algorithm done. That means reviewing the data from the latest Reignitions, the three orangutans from Shenzhen, which she has done twice already. But there remains one set of data that she has not yet dared to approach. The results from the only other time that the Reignition process has been applied to a viable human brain.

She knows that she cannot ignore this dataset. Lentini likes to wax about how all mammal organs are essentially the same, ninety-nine point nine percent similarity in the DNA, Ruth, yadda yadda, and if he can Reinvigorate a monkey's heart he can do the same with a human heart.

But for the task that Ruth is charged with, human brains and monkey brains are very different indeed. You cannot simply apply the same algorithms and expect the Reignition to go smoothly. The particular physiology of the human brain needs to be taken into account, and the frequency and pattern of the connections are unique to the species. The order in which the synaptic jolts need to take place is also crucial. If you start in the wrong area of the brain, the system cannot help but make mistakes that will multiply at an exponential rate.

Ruth remembers that first and only human Reignition. It had been another boring day of tests, and only really began in the evening, when Botha burst into her lab like a kid at Christmas.

"A donor, Ruth! We've got a donor!" he shouted, then ran off down the corridor to shout the same thing at Lentini.

By the time she caught up, Mourad was with them and was already explaining the circumstances. "A car accident. He lived for a while, made it to the hospital. He was in pain but we offered him a lot of money. It will feed his family for life."

"But hold on, did anyone explain—"

Botha jumped in: "No time to chew this over, Ruth. Get the kit set up. We're going straight to Reignition. We have a short window!"

Thinking back now, Ruth knows that was the point when she should have stood her ground, when she could have objected. But instead she did what she was told and rushed back to her lab to plug in her equipment. In truth, she was elated by the prospect of taking the Reignition to the next level. She believed in seizing opportunities, didn't she? Why else would she be here out in the desert? So she gave all the electrodes to the assistants, set the computer running, and made some on-the-fly adjustments to the algorithm. By the time she was confronted with the dead man's disembodied head, he was already rigged up to the machine, ready to go, and all she could think of was that stopping the procedure now would be like the time with the computer crash at FERMI. Once the machines are running, it wastes a lot of time and money if you stop them mid-cycle.

She is so ashamed that she said nothing. Sometimes, she is incredulous that she managed to keep working, that she had the focus to look at the diagnostic data displayed on her screen, and not at the bloodied head of the person whose synapses her computer was reconnecting, at a rate of sixteen and a half thousand decisions per second.

But she is always, always, thankful that when she saw the head mouth the words *Allahu Akbar*, she hit the kill switch immediately.

Botha was livid, of course.

"What the fuck, Ruth? We were nearly there! We could have got him stabilized!"

She screamed back at him as she walked out the door. "It's a head with no body. We went far enough!"

Three months later, they have never discussed where the severed head came from. Ruth knows that Mourad's story about a car accident was a lie, and she is sure that Botha and Lentini know the truth too. That evening binds the four of them together, and they persist with their work.

Ruth shudders in disgust, at Botha and Lentini and Mourad, but also at herself.

I need a break, she thinks, and types a familiar command into the prompt. The entire screen turns bright green. A moment later, rows of hearts, diamonds, spades and clubs appear on her screen. Ah, *Pyramid Solitaire*, my old friend! She snorts to herself at the simplicity of the game. The cards are dealt. The sequence is set. There is no skill to this whatsoever. Whether or not she will be able to solve this hand has already been determined. She just has to iterate, and the kings and the queens will fulfill whatever destiny fate has decreed. Just one game, Ruth, she says to herself, and then back to work.

After his exertions with the decree, the King is now sleeping, and may never wake. And while the Divine One is neither conscious nor dead, Bak may pause. So he is alone on the roof of the palace, and there is nothing between him and a King's sky, pale blue and unsullied by clouds.

He watches as the sun grazes the tops of the mountains, and feels the rays cool a little. Have the shadows of the peaks reached the palace already? Bak looks over his shoulder and sees his own shadow stretch many lengths behind him, like the train of a rich man's cloak.

He turns back and looks down at the city below him, already in the shade but still bright. If it were not for the swelling in his face, he might make believe that he were surveying his own kingdom. But whoever heard of a King with a black eye and a gash in his cheek? Through his good ear, he hears the chat of the city pick up as the laborers filter through the walls from a day in the fields, and the merchants begin to pack up their wares. Soon they will be home with their families.

Bak looks down at a yellow alleyway running toward the palace. He can make out a young man picking his way up the track, hopping this way and that to avoid the animal dung. His face is too far away to make out features, but Bak can see a purpose in the gait. He is walking toward a wife, probably, and maybe some children. Or maybe a drink at one of the communal houses? Either way, now that the sun recedes, that is a man who can choose where he walks. Bak watches until he disappears through one of the many gates in the city wall.

A long, low wail draws him back into the confines of the palace. A female drone, a single note, that is soon joined by another, and then another, and they unite in an ugly harmony. Male shouts join the composition. A percussion of footsteps urgently moving through the narrow alleyways between the palace buildings. Quite suddenly, a human yelp drowns out the chorus. "It has happened!"

Mentuhotep has left this life. He has taken his first steps toward his room in the palace of the immortals.

Now could be Bak's chance to abscond. Over the last few days, during the King's short illness, the palace has become a tightly wound spring. Arrangements for the funeral and the succession have been planned in increasing detail, and all the priests and laborers and artisans and cooks and slaves are poised and ready to act. In a moment, at word from one of the heralds, the Kingdom will burst into mourning. Everyone in the city will have some business up at the palace, and everyone in the palace will have some business down in the city. Right now, as it begins, thinks Bak, this could be the moment to hop quietly over the walls and disappear into the swarm.

But he is no longer the anonymous slave he was last week. Attention has been drawn to him. He has been entrusted with a task by the dead King, and thanks to that nervous scribe doing his job properly, everyone knows it. If he runs, he will be missed immediately. And his injuries, the great swollen bruise and the new scar that extends his smile, will make him easier to spot.

Bak reaches into the pocket of his tunic and runs his thumb over the handle of the King's knife. He can feel the grooves of Mentuhotep's emblem. The private gift that sealed a divine contract. If he plays his part in the funeral, if he can dispatch his King safely into the next life in one piece, then he might be able to walk out of the city without being harassed. And who knows what might follow? A job that he can choose. Perhaps even some livestock of his own. If only he can get this one last task right for the King.

A deep voice from the courtyard below: "Bak? Where are you, Bak?" It is the head of the household. He is required to serve once more.

Like a virtuoso pianist concluding a concerto, Ruth performs the final keystrokes on her laptop and locks in the algorithm. *Tap, tap, tap*. She hammers the *enter* key and hears the hard drive click. It is much less satisfying than a meaty chord in D Major, but the exhilaration of this conclusion makes her a little dizzy. "'Tis done."

At the other end of the lab, Lentini is checking his email. He grunts an acknowledgement, but Ruth doesn't think he was actually listening to what she said. She thinks of Daniel, who was the same.

"Never mind" she says, loudly. "I don't do it for the applause anyway."

Lentini looks up from his screen, puzzled.

It would be easy to ask for another few days to double-check everything again. If Ruth asked them, Botha and Mourad would definitely give her the time. It's not as if King Mentuhotep IV of the Eleventh Dynasty is in a hurry, he can stay warm and Reinvigorated in the tank for a few days without coming to any harm.

But Ruth knows that further delay would just be wasting time. They all have to stop procrastinating and do it. She will pilot the reconnections with certainty. Lentini will shrug off his infuriating nose-picking and nail-biting and turn into a dexterous surgeon. Frans Botha is already an assertive, decision-making machine, so he doesn't need to change. The local technicians will do as they are told, as always . . . and anyway, during the Reignition process itself, the only thing they actually need to do is handle bags of Botha's patented, customized saline solution, and it's very difficult to mess that up. And Mourad? Well, he will know when the time comes not to get in the way.

So, everything is completely ready for tomorrow morning. What now? Ruth contemplates checking her emails too, but she dare not in case there is a message from Daniel, and that might knock her off her stride.

It is too hot outside to leave the compound, and the vista is barren and boring.

More *Pyramid Solitaire*?

Ruth is rescued from the tedium by shouts from down the corridor.

"No way. No bloody way. Out of the question!" Frans sounds very agitated indeed.

Ruth slides out of the lab and eases herself down the linoleum toward Botha's office. She becomes aware of a presence on her shoulder: Lentini is also curious and has left his messages behind. Under the fluorescent strip lighting, they proceed in lockstep toward Botha's lair.

When they get there, both Botha and Mourad are on their feet. A thick wooden desk separates them. It is piled high with papers, several empty cardboard coffee cups, and a plastic replica of a skull. A ballpoint pen is stuck in one of the eye sockets. There's a portrait of the Emir on the wall of this room, too.

"Have you any idea what kind of a disruption it will cause?" says Botha.

Mourad is unrepentant. "It will cause no disruption. He will be here merely to observe. It is appropriate."

"I don't care if it's appropriate or not. He will distract the technicians."

Botha's eye wanders as he spots Ruth and Stefano lurking outside the door. Mourad turns to see who is there.

"Doctor Lentini, Ruth. I have some good news!"

Botha flops sullenly into his chair. "It's not good news, it's a bloody disaster."

Mourad ignores him. "I am delighted to announce that my cousin will be joining us tomorrow to observe the Reignition."

Ruth raises her eyebrows. Beyond, Botha throws his hands in the air, as if to say, *You see?*

"Your cousin, as in, the Emir?" She points to the portrait on the wall. Botha turns to regard it, and his shoulders flinch a little.

Mourad beams. "Exactly, Ruth. He will come to see the triumph."

"All those bodyguards in my lab?" says Botha. "Over my dead body."

Mourad flips back round to face Botha and slams his fist on the desk. One of the empty cups falls over. A single sheet of paper slips off the tallest pile, and floats down on to the floor.

"No, Doctor Botha. Over the dead body of Pharaoh Mentuhotep the Fourth! May I remind you, he is a king. He is of royal blood."

"Bollocks, the blood is all my saline solution."

Mourad scoffs. "But it is not your saline. It has been bought and paid for by the Emir, who has indulged your research for a good many years now."

"Indulged? I am about to bring him immortality!"

Mourad laughs. "Immortality? An immortal zoo of chimpanzees is what you have brought us so far. That, and twenty seconds of prayer from a decapitated traitor."

Ruth winces.

"We are nearly there," pleads Botha, "Look what we're doing with the Egyptian."

Mourad stands up straight and takes a breath. "Quite. Mentuhotep. But I say again: he is royalty and, when he wakes, he must be met by royalty. That is why the Emir will be here tomorrow."

"Royalty? You're being ridiculous. His empire has been gone for centuries. And don't your files say he was the last of his line?"

Mourad shrugs. "That is neither here nor there. A king is a king."

"You know what I think? I don't think the Emir gives a shit about royal protocol. I think he just wants to goggle at my mummy. And I am not bloody Mister Barnum and Bailey, Mourad. There aren't any spectator seats."

Mourad holds up his hands in mock surrender. "Let me put it this way, Frans. The Emir will be here tomorrow. Decide if you wish to be."

He turns and walks out of the office, and both Ruth and Lentini have to step back as he strides past.

At his desk, Botha puts his head in his hands and slowly deflates.

Interesting, thinks Ruth. For all his doctorates, Botha has only just realized that he is an employee.

The midday sun hammers down on the funeral procession, but it is Amenemhat's glare that is making Bak sweat. The Vizier's presence haunts him. As the train of people, animals, and the gilt cart carrying the King's body makes it way slowly out of the city and into the valley, Bak tries to keep his eyes firmly on the path. But every time he looks up, he finds Amenemhat lurking in the periphery of his vision. And every time he actually turns to face the Vizier, Amenemhat stares right back at him. The dark eyes are monstrous, beady things.

Bak tries to find comfort in his lack of power. He never really had a choice in any of this. Mentuhotep pushed this odd embalming task on to him, for reasons that he has taken with him into the afterlife. There have been no opportunities to escape. There is every chance that Amenemhat will charge at him at some point, and it is unlikely he will be able to get out of the way when that happens. I'm basically doomed, thinks Bak.

And yet . . . the King promised freedom.

Also, I have an honored job to do, Bak reminds himself.

Trudging up the hill, one foot in front of the other, avoiding the apple-sized pieces of rubble on the path, Bak runs over the options in his head. Performing this ritual may or may not mean I get to go free. But deserting means certain death, and always has. So my only option, really, is to follow the procession and hope it turns out in my favor. It is a cruel wager, but the only one available now.

And I still have the knife, he thinks. If the emblem does not save me, the blade might.

He looks back at Amenemhat, whose glare shows no sign of dimming. Bak imagines stabbing him in the throat, or maybe the eye.

The local technicians dance around the capsule like they're at an Irish wake.

Lentini declared Reinvigoration complete some six hours ago, and dialed down the flow of chemicals in and out of the unit. Now the assistants are doing diagnostics constantly. Some are using the remote syringe system, bolted on to the underside of the box, to draw small tissue samples from the corpse inside the sealed chamber. Others catalogue the tiny vials of flesh and fluid, for their colleagues to process. They move constantly and with purpose around the room, on paths that never seem to collide. One taps another lightly on the shoulder and the two colleagues pivot around each other.

Yes, like dancers, thinks Ruth. In the middle of the throng, she steps forwards, backwards, and forwards again, in order to keep out of their way. A do-si-do in the chaos.

Only it's not chaos, thinks Ruth. It is actually very ordered, and merely appears messy and random to her because she is on the outside of the system. Each technician has been given very specific orders by Lentini and Botha, and they are performing the steps they have been assigned. If only she had been sat in on the

Reinvigoration team briefing this morning, she would know what each of the lab assistants was doing, and this crowd, with its ever shifting center of gravity, would not seem so out of control.

Ruth reasons she could probably work out what each of the men is up to just by following one of them round for a bit. But to be honest she finds it difficult to even count how many there are. Fourteen or fifteen? Respectable hair and close-cropped beards, if they can grow them, each with a white disposable lab apron over jeans and flannel shirt—she suddenly realizes she can't tell them apart. Are they even the same technicians who were working here when she arrived last year? How has she not noticed?

Just beyond the foot of the capsule, a group of four assistants have congealed around a triptych of computer monitors. Each screen has two graphs plotted, plus a list of numbers that blink when they change. All the charts show smooth curves that rise quickly but level off after a time. Ruth knows that they measure the chemical make-up of the various types of cells and fluids in the subject. The smooth, shallow curves mean that the process is working.

Ruth looks over to the opposite end of the room, to the top of the unit. Her space. The dedicated computer she uses to pilot the Reignition sits on a table. It is switched off. Funny, thinks Ruth. If a graph on my screens showed a nice smooth curve, that would mean something had gone very wrong indeed.

Ruth's computer sits alongside a metal box, about two feet cubed, which is bolted to the table. Its sides are clean, brushed aluminum, but out of its back sprouts a bundle of thick black rubber wires, each about the thickness of her thumb. Her eyes follow the wires out of the box. They spill out on to the floor and slither over to the white fiberglass unit in the middle of the lab. As the wires reach the gurney they rise as one to pass through a plastic tie, and then burst away from each other, running to different sections of the capsule. Each wire finds its own customized hole in the fiberglass, and burrows into the unit.

They have taken to calling it the sarcophagus, an ancient name for something Botha ordered from his Chinese manufacturing team just a few weeks ago. Mentuhotep's body is too long for the capsules they use for the chimps, and it would not do to fold him up and squeeze him in. Botha mocks Mourad's reverence for dead royalty, but Ruth knows that he did not even consider recycling any of the monkey equipment.

Ruth peers through one of the portholes into the capsule. Her breath steams up on the glass, and she has to wipe away the condensation to see the cadaver floating within. The technicians keep the solution flowing, so there is a slight current inside the sarcophagus. Tiny shavings of wax, the remnants of the embalming aldehyde, float and dance across Mentuhotep's dark gray arms. Wrinkled flaps of skin hang off the body, wafting in the saline solution like seaweed. And inserted into the flesh at regular intervals, the access points for Reignition. Dozens of electrode spikes, driven deep into body, seeking out major nerve bundles.

Ruth tries to access that part of her brain reserved for trivia. Didn't she read somewhere that the Egyptians knew about acupuncture? Aren't there old papyrus scrolls that show all the points? Or maybe she is thinking about star charts, and the acupuncture thing was the ancient Chinese. She wonders if King Mentuhotep ever had acupuncture when he was alive.

An unexpected hush descends over the lab. Ruth is suddenly very much aware of herself, and looks up, but no one looks back at her. Instead, they are all staring toward the internal window, out of the lab to the corridor beyond. They look like a herd of livestock, carefully eyeing something that has disturbed the chewing of the cud.

Ruth follows their gaze. An entourage of people are walking down the corridor. At the head of the group are Mourad and Botha. Between them, another man, clad in traditional black and white robes. His headdress is a brilliant white, clamped in place by a gold headband.

It is the man in all the portraits.

The three of them arrive at the doorway together, and there is an awkward moment when Botha tries to hold the door open for the Emir, but it swings away from them, so Botha has to lean forward to keep it open, while his benefactor sidesteps into the room. Eye contact is avoided as personal space is violated. Botha follows the Emir into the lab. He doesn't hold the door for Mourad.

"This is Ruth, the one I was telling you about."

The Emir smiles with the lower half of his face. "Ah yes, the neurologist." That's not quite true, but no one corrects him. Ruth tries a sort of half bow, half demure nod—which doesn't quite work. I probably look like a narcoleptic, she thinks.

The Emir stares at her. His eyes are steady and confident. "Well, Doctor, what are our chances?"

Ruth was expecting small talk. She finds his directness makes her uneasy. She has not discussed anything so crass as the odds of success with Botha, and they haven't prepared an answer. She glances at her boss for help, but he just stares at her, too.

In fact, the Emir's question means that everyone is staring at her.

"There are many factors, sir. But we have the finest team and the best equipment. No one has a better chance than us."

The Emir nods, and immediately lets his gaze drift to the capsule.

"Ah ha! My fellow pharaoh." He skips over to the unit and claps his hands together like a boy at the zoo. "Let's see him! Let's see him!"

Ruth exhales, while Botha and Mourad follow in the wake of the Emir's robe. "Good girl," whispers Botha, as he drifts past.

The incantations are taking a long time. Three priests are leading this part of the ceremony, and they take it in turns to offer copious blessings and good wishes to the King as he begins his journey.

Bak feels himself swaying slightly, and has to will himself back into steadiness. Three of them, he thinks. That's the real menace of this ritual. It means they can each take a rest from chanting while another one keeps up the torture on the rest of us. And all the while, my moment seems to become ever more distant.

The cave is small. "Modest" is what Amenemhat called it. Bak thinks it is shameful. It is but a single chamber, and they have not even treated the walls. True, Mentuhotep died suddenly and early, and usually the Pharaohs take charge of their own funeral arrangements. But compared to the other tombs down in the valley, this interment is an insult.

Everyone in the contingent is male. Only one man is not standing, and that's because he is dead. The King is lying stiff and snug in the sarcophagus, already settled into his final resting place. The block of stone that Amenemhat and his soldiers ripped from the quarries in the East has been hollowed out, and its walls coated in ritual markings, the same words that the priests are now reciting. At the head of the coffin, the lid stands upright, waiting to be slammed down on the King's body at the designated moment. Bak imagines the noise it will make, the terrible slap of stone on stone. That will be the sound of his fate arriving, he thinks. The beginning of a new life as a free man . . . or the signal for Amenemhat to impale him on a spear.

There do not appear to be any weapons in the cave, Bak notices for the first time. True, there are some soldiers in the group, but they are in ceremonial dress, performing a role as a guard of honor for the dead King. No one looks like they're about to kill anyone, thinks Bak. Maybe I'm in the clear.

His eyes catch Amenemhat, still looking at him over Mentuhotep's corpse. The Vizier has the hint of a smile on his lips.

Spears or no spears, Bak shudders. He resolves not to let his concentration slip.

The rest of the entourage flank the coffin. The priests, the handmen who pulled the cart, and the King's pathetic brother, who hangs his head and sobs quietly as the incantations finally grind to a halt.

The priest at the end of the row concludes his prayer, annunciating the final words with a crisp confidence. Bak feels squeezed by the sudden silence, like the air is hugging him.

His moment has arrived.

The technicians have intubated the body. That's optimistic, thinks Ruth. The Reinvigoration may be working, but that does not guarantee Reignition will even get off the ground. If the corpse decomposed too far before it was sealed in the wax, then no amount of Lentini's chemical magic will restore the decayed connections. Her algorithms will be lost in a maze of synapses, searching frantically like a blind man who has mislaid his cane. In that situation, you might get some innate reflexes back online, where the nerves exist on a one-to-one correspondence with functionality and the signal barely has to enter the CNS. But to Reignite the cognitive functions, everything needs to be perfect. There is a very good chance that this experiment will result in nothing more than a perfectly nourished slab of dead meat. We may as well try Reigniting a sirloin steak, thinks Ruth. Or a carrot.

She has gnawed her fingernails down to their stumps, worrying about this, ever since the team received the go-ahead on this project. But at least if the worst happens she won't have to explain what went wrong to the Emir. Everyone knows that honor will fall to Frans Botha.

That was why he was arguing with Mourad yesterday evening, thinks Ruth. It was nothing to do with all that rubbish about the Emir being a distraction. The problem is that Reignition might not work, and Botha would prefer not to explain that to the Emir face to face.

But if Botha is worried about failure, he is doing a good job of not showing it. He stands behind her, hands on his hips, surveying the lab like it's a battlefield. The Emir has been sat in the corner, with Mourad perched by his side, murmuring explanations of the process.

"Are you ready, Ruth?" asks Botha.

"Of course."

"Good." He claps his hands, twice. "Okay, everybody, attention please! Moment of truth happening here." The Emir sits up expectantly, and the technicians make a point of looking alert.

Botha checks his watch. "It is four twenty-seven and forty-two seconds," he announces. "Stand by to commence Reignition, pass one, at four twenty-eight."

Frans is full of horseshit, thinks Ruth. She has done some cybernetics work for NASA in her time, and this is no rocket launch. She could hit the button now and the whole process would begin just fine. Frans is performing for his audience.

"On my mark, Ruth."

Yes, yes, get on with it.

"Mark!"

Ruth presses the button.

At the end of the cave, where the craggy ceiling curves to meet the floor, a cauldron squats over a fire. The molten wax, prepared to Mentuhotep's specification. Bak weaves through the other men in his way, and approaches the fire. All he needs to do is pour the wax over the King, seal him into the sarcophagus, and he will have done his duty.

The cauldron hisses smoke. The fumes tickle Bak's nose, but it is bearable.

It's odd, he thinks. He was forced into this. It is not as if he could say no to the King. But now he is here, it does feel like he is paying a debt, fulfilling a promise. He wants to do this. He wants to get this right.

No sense in delaying, then. He reaches for the wooden lid on the cauldron.

"Wait." Amenemhat's voice stabs him in the back. He turns around.

"This is blasphemy. This is wrong. Stop this at once."

Ruth's computer emits a single, lonely blip.

"Pass one complete" she says.

"Pass one complete!" bellows Botha. "Commence pass two."

All eyes are on Amenemhat, except for those of Mentuhotep's brother, who keeps his head bowed.

"My friends, this new method troubles me. It tears at my conscience. How can we let this happen?"

One of the priests clears his throat. "The King willed it. This wax, it was his wish."

"That is true," says Amenemhat. "But it is against the order of things."

The order of things is surely what the King says it is, thinks Bak.

"Are we to go down into the city and say, yes, we let the King go into the afterlife so ill prepared, the subject of a barbarian ritual?"

The entourage shuffles, but no one says anything.

"Are we to risk that this new apostasy becomes the normal way of things? When our time comes, shall you or I also seal ourselves in wax and hope that the great tribunal in the next place accepts our petition? Would you wish to come face to face with Osiris and explain this insult?"

No, they would not. They would rather have Bak break his vow.

"To save ourselves, and more importantly, to save the King, I think we should reconsider the burial procedures," says the Vizier. "For the sake of His Majesty, let us abandon this . . . this drowning, and replace it with something more traditional." He folds his arms over his chest, pleased with his own oration.

Murmurs of approval.

So that is how it will be, thinks Bak. The King's wishes shall be ignored. He shall arrive at the afterlife and discover he is without heart, lungs, or kidneys. His body incomplete and rotten. Everything he feared. And the blame on his ethereal lips shall be the word *Bak*, because it was I who promised the ritual would be completed as he specified. Worse, he will not have to wait long before Amenemhat's spear sends me into the afterlife too, and I shall be there, and I shall have to explain why I failed, why I was weak, why I allowed Amenemhat's forked tongue to persuade me. What shall I say?

"No!" A short sharp shout bursts into the cave. For a moment, Bak is surprised as anyone by the noise, and then his brain catches up with his ears, and he realizes it was he who shouted.

Amenemhat laughs. "You have something to contribute, Bak?" He turns to the priests. "It seems the slave is in disagreement with the Vizier!"

"I made an oath that I would perform the ritual," says Bak.

"Well, you must break it, Bak. But do not worry. The promise of a slave does not weigh much. We shall not hold your failure against you."

"I care only for the wishes of the King," says Bak. "When I meet him in the afterlife, do I have leave to tell him that it was you who forbade me from doing my duty?"

"The King will not be in the afterlife."

"In his divine wisdom, he thought otherwise."

The priests begin to talk amongst themselves. Clearly, Bak's theological puzzle cannot be summarily dismissed. Amenemhat's grin has disappeared, replaced by a glare.

"Perhaps I can offer a solution?" says Bak.

Amenemhat glances at the priests. One of them shrugs, why not?

"Talk, slave."

Bak speaks slowly and with care. "Your consciences are against this ritual. But the King has made a Godly decree that it should happen. So, why not let me perform the task alone? That way, you shall be without blame before both Osiris and Mentuhotep."

The priests collude, briefly. The eldest of the three addresses Amenemhat. "This is acceptable. We shall withdraw."

Amenemhat rolls his eyes. "Very well. Do the deed, Bak. But know it is without our blessing."

The three priests gather their robes and prayer scrolls, and leave the chamber as quickly as is possible while also walking backward. When they are out of sight, Amenemhat nods at the handmen, the ones who carried the sarcophagus into the cave. They are far more practiced at the art of walking backward, and scurry out of the chamber like crabs. Only Amenemhat and the soldiers remain. And the King's brother, who everyone has forgotten as he kneels in prayer at the foot of the coffin.

Bak turns back to the cauldron, and lifts the lid. The heat of the molten wax scratches at his face. A huge bubble, as big as a fist, rises slowly from the pot and pops, spitting specks of wax. Bak flinches as the heat pricks his arm.

Behind him, a rustle. The scrape of gravel that says that leather-clad feet are moving. The quiet clink of ceremonial garments being adjusted.

He spins. The four soldiers have removed the cords from around their waist, and are wrapping the ends around their fists. Beyond them, Amenemhat is smiling again.

"Pass two complete," says Ruth.

"Figures?" says Botha.

"They're OK," she replies. "Thirty-five percent on the second pass, with an average of twenty-eight percent intensity."

In the corner, the Emir turns to Mourad. "*Shou qasdha?*"

"The first number is how many extra synapses the computer reconnected on the second attempt, compared to the first."

"And this is good?" asks the Emir.

Botha interrupts. "Yes, Highness. In our other experiments, the figure is usually much lower . . ."

"About nine percent," says Mourad.

". . . but thirty-five is a good working figure for something so old."

The Emir looks reassured. "And the second number?"

"That is the average strength of the synaptic connections," says Botha. "The system becomes more and more sensitive on each pass. First we reconnect the strongest bonds. Then we go back and find the residue of weaker connections."

"So now you are finished?"

"No, your Highness. We are about to commence pass three."

Ruth types the command, and the metal box beside her monitor begins to buzz again.

So this was their plan, thinks Bak. An asphyxiation. Now I know why Amenemhat conceded the point so quickly, thinks Bak. All he wanted was for the priests to leave.

The soldiers edge toward him.

The beep sounds for the end of pass three, and instantly Ruth knows something is wrong. The figures are much, much higher than they should be.

"What's the story, Ruth?" Clearly, Botha can sense her unease.

"Something is not quite right."

"What? What's not quite right?"

"Just a second . . ."

"Talk to me, Ruth!"

"The numbers went up."

"Both of them?"

"Yes, both of them. The results for pass three were sixty-three on eighty-seven." Ruth grabs the monitor and points it toward Botha, who stoops to see the numbers for himself.

"Jesus, Ruth. I mean, fucking Jesus!"

Botha stares at Ruth, his eyes red and bulging. She can feel other eyes on her too: the Emir, Mourad, Lentini.

"I . . . I don't understand," she says. "If the Reignition fails it usually just goes to zero-zero."

"I bloody know that, Ruth. What I don't know is why your computer system . . ." he emphasizes the fact that it's hers, "your system is suddenly pissing off-piste."

"I don't know, Frans. I'm sorry."

"You don't know?" Botha lunges toward her, then checks himself. He diverts his hands to her computer mouse and grabs it. The wire goes taut for a moment, before the socket gives way. The lead whiplashes into his hand.

Botha throws the mouse toward the far wall of the lab, causing one of the technicians to duck. The plastic shatters.

"You stupid, stupid . . ." He checks himself again, and takes a breath.

Ruth protests, "It could be anything! What if the brain had some trauma just before it was put in the wax? Or maybe they waited too long, and it just decomposed? Or maybe, Frans, it's just too old?"

Botha just shakes his head in frustration.

In the corner of the room, the Emir speaks. "I do not understand? Has she failed?"

"The process is off-course," says Mourad. "She does not know why."

The Emir makes a strange sound, a sort of cluck. Then he leans forward, toward Mourad. He speaks quietly, but everyone can hear what he says. "Tell me again, how much of my money are we paying this girl?"

Ruth feels a pressure on her throat, like she is being choked.

The soldier nearest to Bak pulls tight on the rope between his hands. His bare arm muscles bulge. Bak feels his neck tighten, already resisting the strangulation to come.

The cauldron lid is still in his hand, a heavy wooden disk, a shield. It would not stop a sword or a spear, but he wonders whether it will help him against a rope. He's been in some fights in his time, of course, but he never had any kind of combat training. Four against one, plus Amenemhat, who Bak now knows can throw a mean punch. In fact, the only one Bak is confident he could beat in a fight is Mentuhotep's brother, but he still on his knees at the foot of the sarcophagus and looks in no mood to attack.

He hasn't forgotten the King's knife, wrapped into the layers of his tunic. Without looking down, he slowly lets his free hand wander into the folds. Layer by layer, he peels back the cloth until his fingers touch the unmistakable texture of wood and metal. He grasps the handle, making sure he has a good grip. Only then does he move his arm out of the cloak.

The soldiers take a step back when they see the blade.

"Get back," says Bak. "Step closer, and I will use it."

He watches them look at one another, and at him. They are weighing their chances. With just their ropes, there is no way they can make a clean kill, thinks Bak. And I have nothing to lose, which makes me dangerous. Will they risk a knife in their belly?

For a moment, they wait there. Bak with his knife and shield, the soldiers fingering their ropes.

Ruth is livid. "You're paying me what I deserve!"

The Emir recoils. Mourad raises his eyebrows.

Even as she speaks, she knows that screaming during Third Pass Reignition is not the best way to convey competence. But Botha started it, and right now, she hates him more.

She turns back to face him, righteous and taut. "You're right, Frans. It is my system. I wrote the program, not you. No one else could do it!" She hates herself for arguing like this, but now I've begun, she thinks, I may as well let it all out. But Botha is not calm either.

"But you haven't done it, have you?" he shouts. Ruth remembers the argument yesterday, where Mourad said much the same thing, and she is jolted out of the moment. She opens her mouth but says nothing.

Botha pushes it. "At least Lentini did his job!"

Out of the corner of her eye, Ruth sees Lentini's head bob up from behind the Reinvigoration monitors at the other end of the room. Then he ducks below the parapet once more.

Botha will not stop until he has skewered her. "I mean, just look at the mummy. It's in better shape than when he died."

That's true. Almost all the cells have been totally regenerated, puffing up King Mentuhotep like . . .

"Wait a moment," says Ruth. She rushes back to her keyboard, and begins to type.

"Look at him, Mentuhotep's most dedicated shabti!" Amenemhat bellows.

"I made a promise," says Bak. "If you want to stop me, then that is your choice. But I will not go quietly." He waves the knife. "And I will not go alone."

The Vizier smiles and shakes his head.

"You poor, deluded slave." He pushes past the soldiers and plants himself in front of Bak. The tip of the knife is a thumb's width from his nose. Bak wonders whether he is quick enough to slash Amenemhat's face.

"You do not understand, Bak. I care nothing for the wax or the burial. Mentuhotep can have whatever ritual he wants. He is welcome to try his luck at the reckoning without a heart to weigh."

He leans back against the sarcophagus and looks down at the dead King's face, pale and sunk in death.

"It's probably better for me if he fails the trial anyway. I do not relish the thought of seeing him again in the House of Kings."

"But you're a Vizier, not a king. You'll have your own place in the afterlife."

"You're right. I'm not a king. Not yet, anyway."

He readjusts his regalia, and turns his back on Bak.

That was not expected. Bak does nothing.

Amenemhat steps over to the foot of the pedestal, and puts his hand on the shoulder of the King's young, weeping brother. "It's time to go."

At his words, the four soldiers move as one. Well drilled, they surround the kneeling figure and haul him off the floor. His legs wobble and give way, but the four of them keep him upright.

The brother begins to wail. A steady drone. But he does not struggle.

In a moment, they have dragged him down the passageway, out of sight.

Only Amenemhat and Bak remain.

"You can put the knife down, Bak."

Bak looks as his shivering arm, still outstretched, still brandishing the useless little knife. No one is coming for him.

He allows his arm to flop down to his side.

Amenemhat acknowledges the gesture with a nod.

"What now?"

Amenemhat snorts. "Do as you please, Bak. I have more important things to address than you—" he looks down his nose at the corpse "—or him."

He turns on his heels and strides down the passage, out of the cave.

"Why don't you pour the wax?" he shouts, over his shoulder. "Do as you were asked. Then you will be free."

"The Reinvigoration" says Ruth. "How long did you say it has been going on for?"

"Long enough," says Botha. He is still seething. "What does it matter?"

"Maybe the cells are too healthy?"

He grits his teeth. "What do you mean?"

"The body looks . . . pumped. What if we've overdone the Reinvigoration?"

Botha opens his mouth to speak, but doesn't say anything. He doesn't know. Ruth turns and looks beyond the sarcophagus, to the other end of the room.

Lentini takes her cue. "Yes, this could happen. If original cells are being healthier when they go into aldheyde than our base calculations . . ." He pauses to think. "Then, yes, by now the cells are certainly being over-generated. This can explain why he is, as you say, pumped."

"So maybe he was embalmed closer to death than we assumed?"

"Is of course possibility. But, Ruth, this is not big problem for Reinvigoration."

"Not for Reinvigoration" says Ruth. "But what about Reignition? If the body was fresher . . ."

Botha picks up her train of thought. "Then the synaptic connections would be much stronger than we anticipated."

Ruth nods. "And we're running the algorithm too slowly. The stronger residual connections will just blot out the newer, weaker ones."

Botha is wide-eyed. "Well, shit! Ruth, we're erasing data! Shut down the pass and reconfigure it. Zip, zip."

The cauldron looks heavy. If he tries to lift it by himself, the wax will probably go everywhere. And there is fat chance that anyone is coming back to help him.

Thankfully, there's a small bowl lurking beside the fire. Probably left over from when they made up the mixture, earlier today. Bak grabs it and dips it into the ooze.

He remembers the communal pots of stew the foremen would put out, back when he worked on the construction sites, further down the valley. Large barrels of swill, old meat, and older vege-tables, but tasty enough after a long day toiling on some irrigation channel or temple. They would line up with their bowls and delve deep. The secret was to angle the bowl so the stew filled right up to the lip.

No more of that now, thinks Bak. Food on a plate, if I want it.

He carries the first bowl over to the sarcophagus. Mentuhotep, still lying in state. The King's soul cannot begin its journey until his body is comfortable in the coffin.

Should he offer some sort of prayer or incantation as he pours the wax? No one left any instructions or lines for him to recite.

He tips the bowl, and the thick, sticky liquid slides on to the body.

"On your way, your Majesty," says Bak. Then he returns to the caul-dron, to refill the bowl.

Pass four. Ruth never thought that she would ever wish for a progress bar, but she wishes now she had coded one into the system. Oh, for a Graphical User Interface! Instead, she has a cursor blinking by the word *executing*.

"How long, Ruth?"

"Soon, Frans."

For the first few pourings, Bak felt grand and important. The Chosen One. The King's Servant. Defender of the Ritual. Bearer of the Bowl. Pourer of the Wax. Head Shabti.

Now he's just a bored man in a cave, dripping wax over a dead body that does not seem to appreciate it.

Oh, for a bigger bowl!

Pass five. Ruth looks around the room. The Emir sits with his hands on his lap. Mourad checks some kind of grid in one of his binders. Lentini rocks on his chair with his arms folded, like he has a fever. Botha struts back and forth.

I've wasted far too much time with these awful, ungrateful men, thinks Ruth. She makes a decision right then. After this is all over, I shall resign. Tell Mourad that she wants to activate the escape clause in her contract. Forfeit the share options; take the lump sum.

Shake Lentini's hand, promise to catch up soon, then never speak to him again.

Tell Frans Botha to "fuck off." To his face.

Then get on a plane back to Boston and try again with Daniel.

The wax is up to Mentuhotep's head. The ears are already covered. With each bowl of wax in the coffin, the circle of liquid around his face grows smaller. Soon it will touch his mouth, then his nose. Then it will be done.

I'm going to sleep under the stars tonight, thinks Bak. No entertainment, or intoxication. No company. I will just find a tree and sit under it.

Just a few more bowls of wax.

Bleep. Pass six complete.

Ruth reads the figures off the screen. "Zero-zero. It's done."

"Well done, Ruth, you dodged a bullet there."

What a pig. It's not, well done, you just reconstructed the brain of someone who has been dead for four millennia. Oh no, not Frans. For him, it's just well done, you dodged a bullet. Botha really is an ungrateful, selfish, balding bully in a white coat.

But he is oblivious to his behavior. For him, she is just another step in the process, and now he is elsewhere: The third "R" in the Triple R procedure.

"Stephano? You ready for Resuscitation?"

Lentini reappears from behind his monitors. "Yes, Doctor Botha. We are ready."

"Very well. Open the capsule."

The cauldron is still half full, but this is the last bowl Bak needs. He empties the wax over the King's head, and the tip of the nose disappears into the opaque slime. That is the last anyone will see of Mentuhotep, thinks Bak. In this life, at least.

Now, how do I get that great slab of rock down without it falling on me?

It takes Dr Lentini the work of twenty seconds to undo the eight brackets that keep the fiberglass sarcophagus sealed. Ruth wonders why he does not delegate the task to one of the technicians from the Reinvigoration team.

There is a sound of a seal being broken, of rubber losing suction, as Lentini flicks the final bracket. The lid springs up an inch or so. A dribble of saline spills through the gap between the upper and lower portions.

Now the technicians are deployed. Four of them step forward and grab a corner of the lid. One of them leads the count: "*Tha, ith, waa . . .*"

The capsule is open. There is the sound of liquid moving around in the open container. Mentuhotep in his bath.

Lentini flicks a switch on the side of the unit, and the sarcophagus seems to gurgle as the saline begins to drain. Ruth edges forward.

As the capsule empties, the gray, shriveled skin of the pharaoh clings to the body like a wet paper towel in the laboratory sink. Ruth is sure that if she were to touch it, it would turn to wet porridge in her fingers. But where the ancient skin has split or detached, she can see the glistening bright red muscle, fresh from the Reinvigoration process. A transparent film of new skin cells keeps the tissue contained. Ruth thinks of sausages, packed with pink mince.

Ruth moves her gaze upwards to Mentuhotep's face. Here the skin is stretched tight over the cheeks. The jaw is closed but the lips are drawn back, and the brittle yellow teeth, untouched by Reinvigoration, are exposed. The Pharaoh grimaces, still dead, but on the verge of life. Healthier than Esther, under the sheet.

Lentini returns to the side of the capsule with a delegation of technicians, and an electric resuscitation device.

"Watch out, Ruth," says Botha, standing behind her. "You don't want a shock, do you?"

Bak balances over the thin, cold edges of the sarcophagus. With one foot on each edge, he is astride the molten pool of wax. He can see the submerged shadow of the King's body. How has it come to this?

It's a simple plan. He will grab the top of the lid, and pull it forward. As it moves, he will jump back, off the coffin and on to the floor. Nature will do the rest, and the weight of the stone will seal the King in place. Mentuhotep can set off to the afterlife, and Bak will take his freedom.

It just needs to be a clean, definitive act.

He takes a deep breath, and counts down, into the movement.

Three, two, one . . .

A new noise breaks his focus. A low rumble from outside.

What was that?

The high crack of the defibrillator makes Ruth blink.

"Once more, Stephano," orders Botha. He is studying a screen intently, and does not look up.

"Clear!"

Another crack.

Lentini holds the paddles apart, and awaits further instructions.

"That's good," says Botha. "Stand by for epinephrine, two hundred milligrams." One of the technicians nods.

Ruth looks over at the Emir. He is gripping Mourad's arm.

"Okay, deploy."

The technician presses a button, and immediately steps back away from the machine, as if that was his only task.

Botha steps back too, and puts his hands on his head. They wait for him to speak, but he says nothing.

"Well?" says the Emir. Botha stays silent.

Mourad shouts, "Tell us, did it work?"

Enough of this, thinks Ruth. She strides over to the resuscitation computers. The lines on the monitor trace a familiar pattern. Two peaks, one higher than the other.

"Yes, it worked," says Ruth. "He's alive."

Bak leaps down off the open coffin. Mentuhotep will have to wait a few more minutes.

He edges down the passage out of the cave. Dust hangs thick in the air, and Bak coughs. Has something fallen? He grabs the corner of his tunic to cover his mouth, and creeps further toward where the entrance is supposed to be. Thin rays of sun streak into the dirt cloud of the passageway. He is near the mouth of the cave, but boulders block the way.

Botha has regained the power of speech. He is taking the opportunity to tap the Emir for more money.

". . . No, Highness, it is all down to you. And just think what we could do with a bigger facility."

Mourad blocks access. "Steady on, Frans, you're not done here yet."

Botha chuckles. Touché. "Quite right, chum. Let's wake him up, ya."

He nods to Lentini, who mutters something to a technician, the same one who administered the adrenaline. The lackey nonchalantly types something on the keyboard in front of him.

Below the capsule, Ruth watches two of the automated delivery tubes wind into action. One moves slowly and deliberately, less than an inch. The other is more aggressive, and fires its entire payload through the cannula tubes and into the veins. It's all transparent liquid in the end, but Ruth knows that the hormones within will tug into consciousness whatever brain they are injected into. Synthetic smelling-salts, designed to disturb even a four-thousand-year slumber.

Ruth considers how much she hates her alarm clock. Anything less than a round seven hours and she is ready to throw it across the room. Thank goodness it is easier to shut up that hateful siren by pressing the snooze button. But she cannot sleep in any more. Anything past eight hours, and she feels guilty and irritable. Once you have a baby, something switches in your body clock. I wonder if that is a synapse I can track down? she thinks. I could find it, and switch it back. Then it would be like when I was at college, young and free.

"How are the signals looking, Ruth?"

Whoops. She is not supposed to be musing on the duvets she has known.

She flips over to the CT program that picks up the brain patterns. There is never a problem with Reignition at this stage. The connections through the brain have a kind of momentum. Once started, they keep going, so long as there is energy in the system. And now Mentuhotep's heart has started beating again, he's supplying that the old fashioned way. The electrodes are still sticking out of his body, but they are entirely superfluous. Reincarnation chic, she thinks.

And yet, these brain patterns are new. Angry lines oscillating. There is a lot of brain activity. Many synapses are firing. Perhaps the overload on the first pass has caused problems.

Or perhaps it is something else?

Botha is irate. "For Christ's sake, Ruth. Today, please!"

He probably should know about these fluctuations. They're unusual, and perhaps he experienced it before, in the Shenzhen lab.

"Frans, the patterns . . ."

"Speak up, my dear."

Ruth pauses for a moment before she speaks.

"All good, here."

Voices from beyond the boulders. Bak yells. He makes the loudest possible noise that his throat will allow. It makes his jaw hurt.

A question wafts through the gaps in the rock. "Is that you, Bak?"

Curses. It is Amenemhat.

"I'm trapped," screams Bak.

"So you are." The Vizier's voice lacks urgency. "That does limit your options." He sounds relaxed, like he is having a conversation.

"I need help to get out."

A moment of silence from beyond. Bak thinks he hears the clink of regalia bouncing off the stone. Then comes a question. "Do you really, Bak? Is your place not with your King?"

Bak leans his forehead against the nearest boulder. "I have done my duty. Now I go free."

He thinks he hears a sigh from outside.

"Duty does not end with the death of the Master, Bak. Every Pharaoh needs a shabti!"

What? Bak shifts himself so his ear is closer to the gap in the rocks.

"Mentuhotep needs someone reliable and strong to serve him in the afterlife. That is why we have sealed the chamber."

So they did it on purpose. Bak suddenly feels foolish for trusting the Vizier.

"Traitor!" he screams. "The King said I was to go free!"

This time, Amenemhat is quick to respond. "Not quite, Bak," he shouts back. "Did you read the proclamation?"

He and Bak both know that slaves cannot read.

"The King said, did he not, that the knife he gave you would help you to freedom?"

Bak thinks back to that dark conversation in Mentuhotep's private chamber. He cannot remember what was said. But how would Amenemhat know about that conversation? He was conspicuously absent, off at the quarry.

"Bak? Are you still there, Bak?"

"Yes, of course I'm still here."

"Use the knife to free yourself, Bak. It is what the King intended. That is why he ordered that you be sealed in his burial chamber. You are the Chosen One."

"He stirs," whispers Botha, as if he is stood over a baby's cot.

Fluid splashes on to the floor.

"Sorry, your Highness. We should have had that fully drained."

"Think nothing of it, Doctor."

Ruth looks down at her screen. The abnormal synaptic activity continues. And still, she says nothing.

Curse them all! Curse Amenemhat. Curse Hena and the Scribe. Curse the Priests. Curse the King's brother, who might have said something.

And above all, thinks Bak, curse Mentuhotep, to whom I gave everything, and received nothing in return.

Bak looks at the knife. Amenemhat is right. There is only one way out. Bak knows what he must do. It will be painful and it will take courage, but he has nothing else left.

The coffin lies where Bak left it, with the stone lid standing tall above it. The wax is already starting to set, but the outline of the King's corpse is still visible. A thin film of dust rests on the surface.

Two strong slave arms pierce the flat molten liquid. The heat rushes up Bak's arms like an animal bite, but the speed and purpose of the movement carries them further into the hot bath of the wax. He pushes his arms toward one another, and they hug the corpse. Two strong slave legs push against the side of the coffin, and the stiff body of the King is lifted out.

Bak lets go of the corpse. It hits the floor with a damp thud.

His arms feel cold and numb. He tries to make a fist with his hands, and they do as he asks, although he cannot feel the fingers bunched in his palms. No matter. He has no need for precision.

He grabs the knife, Mentuhotep's gift, and vaults back on to the top of the coffin, a foot planted either side. He looks beyond his toes, to the twisted body of the King, his enemy. Did he ever suppose, thinks Bak, that I might chase him into the afterlife?

He does not pause, he does not flinch. The blade sinks deep into the wrist and slides neatly up to the joint. Blood, brown in the torchlight, streams down his arm.

The knife falls. Bak steps forward, takes hold of the coffin lid, and leans back.

For a moment he is floating.

Then there is heat, and a bold deep noise.

I curse you, Mentuhotep.

Darkness.

The body writhes and jerks in the sarcophagus.

Botha smiles. "He is awake!"

The numbers on Ruth's monitor continue to rise.

The Emir leans closer. "A pharaoh stirs. Congratulations, Doctor."

He offers his hand to Botha.

For a moment, they look at one another. It is a mere glance, a moment of courtesy, to acknowledge what has been accomplished. A few seconds when they regard one another, and not the body lying before them.

But it is long enough. They do not see the red hand reach and tug at the electrodes that are still protruding from the flesh.

Ruth watches as the strong arms pull at the metal rods. She tries to shout, but finds she cannot. And by the time she has found the breath to scream, Frans Botha has a blunt piece of metal sunk deep into his eye, and the wet, red body has set upon the Emir with such animal ferocity that no one dare approach.

Evie Donnelly isn't exactly a hard-boiled detective—more soft-boiled—but she still walks some pretty mean streets in her steel-toed Mary Janes. Angela Slatter's story is set in an alternative world in which, back at the turn of the century, the events of Bram Stoker's *Jewel of the Seven Stars* weren't all fictional. Evie's 1950s San Francisco has echoes of Dashiell Hammett and a few other small literary references, along with more than one type of mummy.

Egyptian Revival
Angela Slatter

"Are you a follower, Miss Donnelly?" The voice was smoky and the question not one I'd expected.

People come to me because I find things, not because they care about which amulet I do or don't wear beneath my shirt. They don't give a rat's ass what sacred name's embroidered on my silky under-things, or whether a shrine does or doesn't light up the corner of my fifth-floor office. They come because I've got a proven record of locating missing people and items. Generally, the client goes home happy. Mostly, I get paid.

However, here was a possible patron, all blonde brass and Dior dress—blue and cream with a cinched-in waist and matching swing coat—wanting to know if I was a follower. I pushed a stray curl behind my ear, and played dumb.

"Of what, Mrs Kolchak? Fashion?" My functional green skirt and simple white blouse plainly said "no." My custom-made Mary Jane pumps with the steel caps in the toes said, "Hell, no."

"Of the gods, Miss Donnelly," she answered evenly. Her teeth were so neat they looked pressed. Then, as if I'd given an affirmative answer, she continued with, "And of which ones?"

She herself wore no talisman, giving no hint as to what I should say, so I went with the truth, which wasn't entirely a new thing for me, just not necessarily my first port of call.

"I don't follow a god, Mrs Kolchak. Didn't follow any of the ones around before the Egyptians came back into style; don't follow this latest crop; can't imagine I'll be following the next craze either."

"You're an atheist?" She arched one perfect eyebrow, but it didn't seem to make any of her skin wrinkle at all. Neat trick.

"Call me an agnostic realist. Whatever's out there probably has bigger things to worry about than the billion importuning prayers sent up—or down—every day."

My potential source of income bit at her pouty lower lip, as if considering my future, and I silently cursed the human mania for hitching hopes and dreams to invisible friends. Fifty or so years ago, when the dead-but-determined-not-to-remain-so Queen Tera managed to resurrect herself with the aid of the Jewel of the Seven Stars, Egyptian religion underwent a revival—how could it not? Forgotten gods found a foothold once again; prayers of the sometimes barely convinced faithful thundered from freshly erected temples, and the pantheon of Kemet made a place for itself among all the other belief systems as if it hadn't been gone longer than five minutes—especially here in San Francisco where outré is normal. Me, I think religion's like adding rocks to a body of water: the liquid just shifts around, displaces, to accommodate whatever's added. No one really notices when it disappears either, though most people don't admit that.

The restoration didn't matter one whit to someone like me, but to those further up the economic and social ladder it mattered a lot. If you wanted a certain job or promotion, membership in a particular club, the right house in the right part of town—then your choice of personal divinity could make all the difference. Small fry and ordinary folk mostly held to their Holy Trinity credos, Torahs, Buddhist chants, or what have you, but those with cash and position were happy to pay lip service to the new-old ways, and their willingness to do what was needed to prove devotion could, and did, open doors.

Still, Amun, Ra, Osiris, Isis, Sekhmet, Hathor, and all the rest held some sway over popular imagination. The pseudo-Egyptian-style portion of the Memorial Museum—torn down in 1929—had been rebuilt to house a permanent collection of ancient Egyptian artifacts, replicas, exhibits, papyrus, coffins, and, of course, mummies—both human and animal. Among the latter there was even an enormous mummified Nile crocodile. Cynics had noted, though, that since Queen Tera's show-stopping return performance no more ancient royalty had been revivified and there'd been precious few miraculous displays. The deities of the Two Lands were apparently unwilling to intervene on the behalf of those who were now devoted to their rituals, wore their amulets, and burned boatloads of incense in their worship.

Or maybe these gods just didn't make public spectacles of their divine works.

At any rate, Mrs Kolchak finally nodded and said, "Perhaps you're just what I need. No conflicting beliefs."

"I haven't said I'll take your case yet," I pointed out. She just looked smug.

"It's not even a case as such—more like simple information gathering."

Experience had taught me to mistrust the word "simple," but I managed not to blurt that out. I tilted my head: *Go on.*

"I'm a . . . collector. Mr Kolchak made a lot of money before he married me and I made a lot of money when he died. I do miss him, but the affluence helps me cope." She gave a girls-know-how-it-is grin. "But when you're so very prosperous everyone wants to take you for a ride— and I don't care to distribute my wealth unless I get what I want in return, Miss Donnelly."

"I can understand that," I replied, noticing that she'd not sat down since she'd arrived. I could have taken offense: I'd forked out more than I could afford to make sure the canary-yellow mohair-upholstered Danish modern lounge chairs were welcoming. But she stayed by the window, drinking in the lunchtime light, looking all Grace Kelly—if

Grace Kelly had started out as a showgirl and clawed her way up. I didn't know how Izolda Kolchak began her rise but I was willing to bet dollars to donuts it had involved high kicks in a pair of heels and sequined underwear. "So, how do you think I can help you?"

I thought I knew the answer: I'd worked before with antiquarians. It always cost them a lot and sometimes I didn't look too closely at the details of what they were doing and why. Even two-legged bloodhounds had bills to pay.

"There is a small exclusive auction house that deals with some very interesting arcane pieces. A specific lot that was sold two days ago to an anonymous buyer."

"And you'd like me to . . .?"

"Get me the buyer's name."

"You don't have a secretary? It's a matter of a phone call, Mrs Kolchak." I didn't usually talk myself out of business, but this seemed like an absolute waste of my time.

"As I said, Miss Donnelly, I'm a collector of note, a woman of considerable means—when my name is mentioned, the cost of something goes up in astronomical increments. My employees are also known in such circles, and I certainly don't want them using subterfuge in the course of their employment. That would send the wrong message."

"But hiring me doesn't?"

"Oh, Miss Donnelly, I think it's a long time since the needle of your moral compass had a spin." *Touché.* "You're a contractor, my dear, your actions are your own."

"What did they buy?" I asked, examining my nails and preparing to refuse, because no matter what she thought, I did have *some* standards.

"That's irrelevant. All I need you to *know* is the lot number—twenty-two, by the way—and all you need to *do* is get me the buyer's name. Then other intermediaries will begin negotiations."

"Well, Mrs Kolchak, tempting though busy work might be to some—"

"Ten thousand dollars.'

"Pardon? It sounded like you said—"

"Ten thousand dollars." She opened her handbag—creamy Chanel with the distinctive gold double-chain straps (okay, so I do know something about fashion, but my means don't stretch far enough to afford what I'd like) and pulled out a thick bundle of notes. "That's all of it, up front—don't look so surprised. You'll be earning your fee. The auction house won't give up information easily—do whatever you need to."

And I knew, then, that something was rotten in the state of California—no one's ever said Evie Donnelly was dumb—but I also knew that ten Gs could buy my sister Mamie time to get back on her feet, it could buy my niece Betty clothes that weren't second-hand, and it could take care of my rent for a quite a while, so I didn't have to worry whether work was going to materialize when needed.

It was a job. It was ten grand. It was a lifeline of sorts.

"Do you have a time limit, Mrs Kolchak?"

"The sooner the better, Miss Donnelly." She handed over that bundle of hundreds, every single one, and I realized it meant Izolda Kolchak owned a slice of me until I delivered. She'd judged me well enough to know that I regarded a contract as a bond, and my bills would ensure my sense of obligation kicked in. She knew what she was doing, and I knew too. But I took it anyway.

"I'll call as soon as I've got what you want," I said, carefully placing the cash on the desk in front of me.

"I'm counting on it." She passed me a single sheet of paper, inscribed with emphatic handwriting. "These are the details for Conville-Iredale. My number's on the bottom. And Miss Donnelly? Don't let me down.'

After she'd gone I stood by the window where she'd been, and stared out.

Usually what I do involves a lot of shoe leather, a lot of sitting outside places with a concealed camera, a lot of asking questions, and a helluva lot of being charming to men to whom I normally wouldn't give the time of day. But what Mrs Kolchak wanted was relatively easy; I just needed to be sneaky.

I checked my reflection in the glass; despite sleepless nights worrying about Mamie and Betty I looked OK. Better than OK—not in Izolda Kolchak's class, of course, but no one was going to kick me out of bed for eating crackers. As I reapplied lipstick and tidied my dark hair, a movement in the street caught my attention: a spick-and-span cherry-colored Chevy with a white roof pulled up outside the building across the way. Out jumped a tall figure in a gray suit. Even from my fifth-floor office I could see Detective Liam Murphy's bright red hair gleaming in the sun. He moved gracefully as he strode toward the entrance, and it was times like this I regretted walking away from him.

I made sure the seams of my stockings were straight, gave my shoes a little spit polish, shrugged on a jacket, hoisted my handbag, and locked Kolchak's cash in the wall safe. Her business could wait while I paid a quick visit to the crime scene; just because I'd left him didn't mean Detective Murphy hadn't remained of abiding interest to me. It didn't mean my heart didn't skip a beat every time I saw him.

Plus, I was nosy—there's no denying that.

I crossed Sutter Street and the patrol cops let me through like they always did, grinning, and saying "Fourth floor, apartment seven."

I paused at the top of the stairs to catch my breath, then made my way along the hallway until I found the open door. I darted in, smack bang into the back of Liam Murphy, who was standing just inside the threshold.

"Jesus, Evie!" Detective Murphy remained firmly on the side of Father, Son, and Holy Spirit and nothing was going to change that. Whether it affected his chances of advancement or not, he'd have no truck with new-fangled old gods. "What are you doing here?

And all of sudden I lost every ounce of confidence that, no matter what, he'd be glad to see me. Maybe he didn't cling to these moments the way I did. Maybe he wasn't interested in snatching at the crumbs. Maybe Liam Murphy wanted to move on without the shadow of his ex-girlfriend dogging his heels.

Maybe he saw that uncertainty in my face and his expression softened.

"Ah, Evie. Don't sneak up on me like that, makes me squawk." He grinned and lifted a hand to my cheek, oh so briefly. I felt his touch burning long after he'd turned away. "Here to see what happened right across the street from your office? What do you think?"

The corpse lay on a rug in the middle of the sitting room. The smell hit hard then, blood and death, and I covered my nose, coughing a little.

"I think someone's gonna need a new rug."

"C'mon, Evie, focus."

"You could have warned me."

"Well, maybe one day you'll learn better than to invite yourself to crime scenes." We crouched beside the body on the blood-soaked rug, which could only be identified as a man by its suit and tie. The dermis was dry and wrinkled as if all the moisture had been drawn from it, and the face was little more than a skull with a skin canvas stretched tightly over it. This guy's own mother couldn't have recognized him. "So, what do you think?"

"I think I gotta stop following you to crime scenes." I pointed to where the top of the head had been sliced off, neat as a boiled egg, a crop of thick iron-gray hair clinging on tenaciously to the skin-hinged skullcap. "But look at this: where's his brain gone?"

Detective Murphy shrugged. He hated with a passion the things he couldn't understand, they made him nervous. Give him a gruesome domestic murder, a Mafia massacre, a bloody bank robbery, and he was as happy as a clam. Give him something that smacked of the occult and he developed a rash. And this murder looked like it had "weird" in spades.

"And see here?" Murphy said. At some juncture the victim's shirt and pants had been torn open to expose the torso, which was slit from gullet to groin, the desiccated flesh and subcutaneous tissue peeled back like he was an orange. "Stomach's gone, intestines, too. And the lungs. But hey, the heart's still there."

"That's . . . odd." It was several steps beyond "odd," but no need to further agitate Liam's dislike for the uncanny.

"It's all odd." He paused, then changed the subject. "How's your sister doing?"

A month ago, Liam had taken Mamie's husband in for questioning on a racketeering charge while I got her and Betty out of the house and on to a train to a tiny town upstate where a former client who owed me a favor owned a farm.

"Still in hiding. When are you going to find something that'll stick to Louie the Louse?"

"I'm working on it." We both rose.

"I appreciate it, Liam," I said softly, hating that his name still tasted like honey on my tongue. I touched his arm, couldn't help myself, tilted my head back and watched him lean towards me, whether he wanted to or not. I pulled away.

"Dammit, Evie." His voice was raw. "This is stupid."

"I'm sorry. I am, truly." I glanced at the silver watch on my wrist; it had been a gift from him.

"Got somewhere better to be?"

"Not better, no. But somewhere to be. Goodbye, Detective." I felt him watch me as I walked away, but I didn't look back.

The building in which Conville-Iredale took up the ground floor was on Jessie Street between Market and Mission—an easy walk. I turned right on Montgomery and took another right on Market. I was trying to forget what I'd seen in the apartment with Liam. I had to concentrate hard, take deep breaths, and calm my stomach with a Tums. Pinching the inside of my upper arm helped a little.

The auction house looked like it had seen better days, but wasn't prepared to admit it. According to Kolchak's note, the original principals, Augustus Conville and Enoch Iredale, were long dead and the business had devolved by winding and mysterious paths of marriage and reproduction to one Adlai Constantine, who was great-grand-nephew to both men.

As I was about to enter, the brass and glass double doors pushed open and a short, fat, very angry man stood there, yelling over his shoulder. His black suit was so shiny it looked green. "And get those goddamned letters fixed before I get back. Get the goddamned filing up to date. And make sure my goddamned lunch is on my goddamned desk."

He charged past me; if I'd been a few seconds earlier he'd have knocked me down, but I doubt he'd have noticed. I watched him power towards a bar across the street, and felt something stir that might, in dim light, be mistaken for a plan.

Inside, the reception area was filled with antique sofas and chairs with legs that looked too thin to bear the weight of anyone but a small child. The oriental rug was threadbare and I wondered at Kolchak's description of the outfit as "exclusive"—maybe it was exclusiving itself out of clients. The front desk was a curved affair in mahogany with a black marble top, and the girl sitting behind it wore a cabaret troupe's worth of make-up. Though she must have been the target of the fat man's tirade, it didn't seem to have bothered her at all; I figured the Kleenexes in my handbag were unnecessary. No tears for Barbara Dain, which is what her desk plate dubbed her.

"Are you OK?" I asked anyway and she gave a combined nod-shrug.

"He'll calm down. Coupla shots of whiskey and he'll be a lamb by two o'clock, snoozing under his desk by three."

No wonder the business was sliding. "I'm hoping you could help me?"

"You buying or selling?" she said, sounding bored.

"Neither. Well, I guess buying: I'll give you twenty bucks and the chance to put one over that asshole."

She didn't say "no," or even look slightly suspicious. "That's a lot of money. You must want something bad." Babs gave a slow, sly smile. "Fifty bucks or nothing."

I paused as if considering, then nodded, just soon enough to let her know she'd bid too low. "Deal."

Resigned, she said, "What do you need?"

"The name of whoever bought Lot Twenty-two on Tuesday last."

"Mr Constantine hasn't given me those files yet." She tapped a pen against her teeth. "He'll be at the bar for at least another twenty minutes and I've got to step out to get his lunch, which might just give you time to find what you're looking for?"

I grinned and handed over the bill. It *was* a lot of money, but today I could afford to be generous.

The secretary stood, smoothed her pale pink dress, and jerked her chin towards the inner office. "You get caught and I never saw you before in my life. All the paperwork's in the top desk tray." She grabbed an Enid Collins purse—decorated with beads in the shape of tropical fruit—from under the table, then headed off, full skirts swinging.

The doorknob, shadowy silver shaped like a bird's head, took a couple of turns; I guessed it was one of those quirks an owner got used to, but drove anyone else nuts. Constantine's office seemed a little more upmarket than the room I'd just left: the seats were green leather button-back Chesterfields, and the Turkish rug on the floor was in a much better state than the reception carpet; I felt kind of bad walking on it. Behind the wide maple desk with its banker's lamp, big cut-glass ashtray, and fancy penholder was a series of windows, festooned with red velvet drapes that looked on to a narrow alley.

I found what I was after, third down in a disordered stack of about forty sand-colored manilas, the lot numbers written in an untidy red script in the upper right-hand corner. The first sheet had a range of details including items sold: four canopic jars; the seller: Estate of Audrey Schliemann, late of Vienna, Austria; and the name and address of the buyer: one Abel Mannheim of (the very wealthy) Hillsborough

Heights. All of which I copied into my notebook then, out of sheer nosiness, flicked through the rest of the papers in the file.

There wasn't much there except a brief history of the artifacts (found in a Ptolemaic period tomb in the old city of Shedet, capital of The Land of the Lakes, in Egypt), a proof of provenance certificate, which probably wasn't worth the letterhead it was written on, and a bunch of photographs that were not what I was expecting. Though the top one was just an image of the alabaster and gold jars—each lid a unique head: baboon, jackal, human, falcon—the photos beneath it were something entirely different.

And horribly familiar: shriveled bodies with the tops of their heads missing. But the images were old, I could tell by the victims' clothing, maybe fifty years out of fashion.

My stomach got unhappy again.

That's when I heard shouting from the reception area—Mr Constantine had returned early and was presumably yelling because no one was at the front desk to hear him.

I slid the file back into place and made for the windows, none of which wanted to open—if they had I'd have been gone like a greased otter down a slippery slide.

Nothing to do but brazen it out. I'd just got my backside in one of the visitors' seats when I heard the door being thrown open behind me.

"Who the hell are you?"

"Oh, hello! Are you Mr Conville or Mr Iredale? I'm ever so pleased to meet you, sir!" The chirpiness set my teeth on edge, but I threw some serious wattage into the smile and widened my eyes, all corn-fed innocence.

It confused him enough to make his stride slow. "I'm Constantine, Adlai Constantine. And you are?"

"Oh, how rude of me! I'm Minnie Smith. I'm here about my grandmother's diamonds—"

"Did my secretary let you in?" He took up his seat on the other side of the desk and I hoped he didn't twig that it had been warmed by a considerably smaller set of buttocks.

"Oh no, Mr Constantine. She went to get your lunch, sir, and I just thought to myself , why, Minnie-girl, surely no one would object to you waiting in the office! Things will move so much faster if you're all ready to do business!"

"Now look here, Miss Smith—"

"Oh, please. Minnie."

"Now look here, Minnie—"

"I'm here about Grandmamma's diamonds, you see. She left them to me and I, well, I just don't wear diamonds—I'm too young, obviously— but then I got to thinking that Grandmamma wouldn't mind at all if I sold them, would she? And they're just so elegant, why I—"

"Miss Smith!" he shouted. I stopped, blinked one, two, three times, all kewpie-doll like, gave him the big dewy green eyes, and watched him deflate. His tone was gentler when he said, "Minnie, honey, we don't deal with jewelry, at least not ordinary jewelry."

"Oh," I flustered. "I'm so terribly embarrassed, Mr Constantine. I'm sorry to have wasted your time."

"Not to worry, honey. Try Maxferd's Jewelry over on Market. Ask for Ferd Wolfson, tell him I sent you. He won't try to take advantage of you or anything."

I stood, leaned over the desk and shook his hand like I was pumping for oil. "Thank you for your kindness, Mr Constantine, sir."

"That's not a problem, honey."

"Just out of curiosity, what kind of items *do* you deal in?" I asked in hushed tones 'cause that always makes men imagine they're in bed with you; the perfect means of disarming almost every male with a pulse.

"Well, Minnie, we call it 'esoterica.' Specialized stuff, nothing to worry your pretty little head about." He guffawed, thinking we were friends, and I giggled and thought about how much I'd like to kick him in the crotch with my steel-capped Mary Janes.

"Well, goodbye, Mr Constantine."

"Bye, Minnie."

I barely breathed until I got outside, around the corner, and found a phone booth. Mrs Kolchak was going to be impressed, as well she should be: it was a fast result even for me. I'd done what she'd hired me to do and I wasn't about to give up the ten grand—but I couldn't shake the feeling there was something else going on and it wasn't a good something. So after I spoke with my very happy client, I made another call, to a somewhat less happy police detective, shared some information (though not all), and rashly agreed to meet him for dinner.

While I waited for Detective Murphy—who was late—at a corner table in Caesar's, I went to town on the bread and butter because my stomach was still a little displeased. I'd gone to a lot of trouble with my appearance—deep-cut purple shantung dress with wrap skirt and shawl collar, pretty but impractical kitten heel mules, a teeny silk clutch just big enough for my keys, lipstick, and some cash and coin, and more curl in my hair than usual—but none of that mattered if I looked green around the gills. The dinner rolls formed a calming raft, but I couldn't avoid thinking about the body in the apartment when I saw how many menu items involved marinara sauce.

"Miss Donnelly?" The waiter had crept up on me. In his hand was the chunky black phone he'd dragged across from the front counter on a very long cord. "A call for you."

Well, if that doesn't make a girl feel special nothing will. I waited until he'd departed. "Hello?"

"Evie, I've got a problem here." Though Detective Murphy's tone was even, he sounded strained, as if folks were listening on his end and he was remaining polite for the sake of appearances.

"What kind of a problem?"

"Well, that Mr Constantine you mentioned is somewhat dead and his files have been somewhat burned in his wastepaper basket."

"Oh. When you say 'somewhat' . . .?"

"Damn it, Evie!"

"Look, I'm sorry, Liam. If the photos are gone, then I don't know—"

"That's the least of my concerns. Constantine is deceased in the same way as the victim in that apartment."

"Oh."

"So, is there anything else you want to tell me?"

I thought fast. Secrets weren't worth more lives. "A woman called Izolda Kolchak hired me to get the name of the buyer of a particular lot at Conville-Iredale."

"Kindly share that information with me."

I did so; I might even have gone home, tail between my legs, except he finished the call with, "Right. Now stay outta this, Evie."

Which, of course, was the dumbest thing he could have said.

When the taxi pulled up at the wrought-iron gates, the driver asked me three times if I was sure this was where I wanted to be. Three times I said yes, each time with less conviction. I gave him a good tip for his trouble. Watching the tail lights disappear into the darkness, I wanted to run after him. Instead, I headed purposefully towards the gray metal intercom box. It'd be hours before Liam was free; with any luck I could begin tidying up my own mess, then find him back at the auction house, and we'd work out a plan together.

The twelve-foot-high fence with spikes on each railing seemed a little extreme for an estate hidden away in the hills, but what did I know? I could see the Italianate mansion from where I stood and Abel Mannheim's place put the palace in palatial. Out front was a fountain complete with gamboling copper nymphs pouring water from urns, surrounded by a drive of bronze tiles that reflected the spotlights on the eaves of the building. The entire house was lit up like a ship at sea; an enormous three-storied affair in sandstone ranging from dark ochre to pale pink. Three wings hugged a colonnaded courtyard scattered with flowering trees, benches, and sculptures of mythological figures.

I jabbed at the buzzer, which was answered quickly by someone I assumed was the butler. He was very polite, but really didn't want to let me talk to his boss. I dropped the names Conville-Iredale and Constantine, and mentioned Lot 22, then waited patiently while he checked to see if Mr Mannheim was available. Not long after, there was a clicking sound and a small person-sized gate I'd not noticed opened in the fence. My shoes were built for dining, not long walks up driveways, and a blister had budded on my left big toe by the time I reached the front door.

A tall dark-haired man was silhouetted at the entrance, the interior light making a kind of halo behind him. When he stepped aside so I could come in, I saw he was wearing a red polo shirt and khaki trousers with creases so sharp you could cut yourself. Probably not the butler.

"Mr Mannheim?"

He nodded and smiled. "My man didn't get your name, Miss . . .?"

"Donnelly. Evie Donnelly."

A strange expression shimmied across his face and he said, "Oh."

I raised a brow.

He was handsome in a kind of toothy way, which was fine if you didn't mind feeling as if you might get bitten at any moment. "How can I help you?"

"Well, it's more how I can help you, Mr Mannheim." He took my arm and led me through a foyer lit by an enormous chandelier, with taxidermied tigers and bears guarding the walls, and marble floor tiles in the shape of the Eye of Horus. If that wasn't sign enough Mr Mannheim was a follower, then the tattooed falcon with the Double Crown of Ancient Egypt on his right wrist was.

The sheer opulence was overwhelming and I was in danger of whiplash, trying to take everything in. It wasn't just the furniture, which probably once belonged to one of the French kings named Louis, or the paintings that sedately whispered, "Old Masters." It was the antiquities: statues and vases, scrolls and mosaics, jewelry and busts, weapons and armor that might have been Roman, some Greek, some Egyptian, some Persian. Mannheim noticed my interest and began a docent's patter.

"This breastplate belonged to Alexander the Great, that necklace to Nefertiti, this helmet was worn by Leonidas at the Battle of Thermopylae, Artemisia commissioned that sculpture."

We finally wound up in a room deep in the heart of the building, a cross between museum and library, books lining the walls, glass cases on shelves and tables filled with all manner of relics, curios, and fragments of the past. Mannheim gestured to the red velvet sofas and offered me a drink, which I declined though I felt in need.

"This is an amazing collection, sir, but I'm not here for a tour. I think you might be in danger." He laughed and, though it wasn't a pleasant sound, I continued, "You bought something from Conville-Iredale."

He nodded, giving nothing away.

"Four canopic jars, I believe. I have to tell you that, firstly, someone has shown an interest in that purchase, and secondly, Mr Constantine has recently become deceased in a very bad way."

"Are those two facts connected?"

"I fear so.'

"And this interested party would be?"

"Izolda Kolchak."

He gave a brief smile. "A parvenu if ever there was one. She's only been on the scene for a couple of months."

"She's not a follower, then?"

"Oh, she claims to be but never flies her colors. It's very important among people of position to let peers know where you—and they—stand. Mrs Kolchak married her money and, I believe, came to her 'faith' by way of convenience, Miss Donnelly."

"That's as may be, but she hired me to find out who bought Lot Twenty-two and I gave her your name. I'm so sorry, Mr Mannheim, but—"

"You think I'm in danger? From that chippie?" He shook his head, laughing hard. "Miss Donnelly, you're adorable. This place is laden with alarm systems. I have a staff of twenty. At the slightest peep, the police and a particularly heavy-handed private security firm will be on their way. I know there have been a number of artifact thefts among my circle recently—even Queen Tera's great ruby gem was reportedly stolen—but I and my collection are perfectly safe."

He was an idiot, but I'd found that speaking my mind to a particular kind of man to be counterproductive. Instead I smiled brightly and leaned forward. "Do tell me, Mr Mannheim, what's so special about these jam jars?"

He swept a hand towards something I'd missed: four alabaster vessels with gold heads, all lined up on a display table cut from a silky oak burl. Some private investigator.

"These," he said, "are reputedly the canopic urns of the last Petsuchos of Shedet."

"And who's that when he's at home?"

"The earthly incarnation of the voracious crocodile god Sobek, the embodiment of the pharaoh's warlike spirit—I believe its mummy is on display in the Memorial Museum."

"And inside those . . .?"

"The jackal has the stomach, the falcon the intestines, the human the liver and the baboon the lungs—all the things necessary for the journey to the afterlife.'

"Not the heart, though, not the brains.'

"No, the heart stays in the body so it may be weighed by the goddess Maat. The brain is irrelevant."

I wondered whether the corpse in the apartment had been missing his liver. "Mr Mannheim, you recognized my name. Why?"

"There's a man, a moneyed thug, who hangs on the edges of the community to which I belong. He's been trying to slither up the social ladder. Louis Jones drops your name every chance he gets to those who need something found, those he thinks useful to have in his debt."

Louis Jones, aka Louie the Louse, my brother-in-law. The biggest mistake I ever made was agreeing to work for him back in the day, the second biggest was introducing him to my sister. Mamie—who I love to death, but is not the sharpest knife in the picnic set—thought he was exciting. He threw money around. She got pregnant, they got married, and she got hit every second Sunday for five years until he turned on their daughter, and Mamie realized enough was enough.

Louie.

That asshole.

"I suppose someone new in town like Izolda Kolchak would have been the perfect target for him?"

He shrugged. "I couldn't say one way or the other."

But I could, and I was pretty sure Louis Jones was the guy ruining the rug in that apartment across from my office. I didn't know what he'd been doing there—maybe watching to see if I led him to Mamie—or maybe it was just one of the places he rented for his "girlfriends" who could be other men's girlfriends for a fee. Louie's demise solved more than a few problems for me and mine. Whatever had happened to him, he'd earned. I thought of Mrs Kolchak standing at my office window, looking out. "Mr Mannheim, I really think—"

The shrieking of an alarm cut me off, and my host leapt up.

"Stay here," he commanded, and I let him think I was an obedient girl.

As soon as he left the room I shot over to the urns. I couldn't carry all four so I grabbed the nearest one, which—even alone—was awkward and heavy, and tucked it under my arm. Already I could hear footsteps thundering along corridors and up and down staircases. I didn't know exactly what was happening, but I knew I'd had a hand in getting things rolling. Conscience is a great motivator and I felt more than a little guilty, so I wasn't planning on making it easy for whoever—or what-ever—was looking for these things.

Elsewhere in the house were the sounds of breaking glass, gunfire, and a whole lot of screaming. I kicked off my pretty party shoes and left them where they lay so I only had to manage my purse and the jar, and fled through a door at the back of the library. It led along a labyrinth of paneled hallways with doors that—if opened—would no doubt reveal luxurious rooms. I passed the glass doors of a greenhouse evidently devoted entirely to orchids just before I reached an enormous kitchen, with an exit into the cool air. I headed out through the manicured gardens and stuck close to the perimeter fence, circling towards the front gates, which hung loosely from their hinges as if they'd been blown apart. After waiting to see if anyone was on lookout, I'd tiptoed on to the still-warm asphalt.

Barefoot and terrified I did my best to disappear into the night.

I managed to hitch a ride back into town with an old guy in a truck who was kind enough to drop me near Jessie Street. Imagine my surprise to find Conville-Iredale in darkness, no sign of cops or coroners, and certainly no sign of Detective Murphy, which definitely put a crimp in things. I scrounged up change and called the police station from the phone booth around the corner. Tommy Maloney answered; he'd had a soft spot for me ever since I had, in a triumph of investigatory genius, found his mother's beagle two years ago.

"Hey, Sarge."

"Evie Donnelly, as I live and breathe. What mischief are you up to?"

"As a matter of fact, I'm looking for Detective Murphy. Any sign?'

"Naw, honey. The boys said he was going to interview some woman, weird name, a coupla hours ago."

"Izolda Kolchak?"

"That's the one. You wanna leave a message?"

"No, it's OK. You take care, Sarge."

"You too, Evie."

Well, that tore it.

I couldn't go home. I couldn't go to my office. But I still had a key to Murphy's apartment, and a fugitive with naked feet and a priceless funeral urn can't be too choosy. I needed a place to think and regroup.

The one-bedder was tidy and comfortable, but the bowl of wizened apples on the counter bore witness to how little the detective had been home lately. And it was empty, dashing any hope I had of finding Liam there, safe and sound. I helped myself to a whiskey and a bowl of cereal, then curled up on the old brown couch to contemplate the jar.

I'd souvenired the human-headed one, so I was in possession of a crocodile's liver. I figured a two-thousand-year-old liver was likely even more shrunken than the neglected apples. The lid was sealed with ancient wax, which felt brittle beneath my fingers, nothing like the smoothness of the candles I knew were in the kitchen cupboard in case of a blackout. I put the canopic container back on the coffee table and pondered.

Was it too much to hope that Izolda Kolchak had nothing to do with recent events?

That all of this was a coincidence?

Probably.

Definitely.

If she didn't, as Mannheim claimed, fly her colors, was it because she had something planned she didn't want anyone to know about? What if Mannheim had bought Lot 22 as much to keep it away from Kolchak as for the joy of collecting? What if she'd been behind the other thefts he'd mentioned? Was there a method, a pattern to what was taken? Were some robberies just distractions from the real goal?

While I thought, I helped myself to some of Liam's clothing. The trousers were a little long, the shirt a little snug, and the jacket didn't button over my busty substances, but I found a pair of my old Mary Janes in the back of the closet. Then I made the call.

She picked up on the first ring, as if she'd been expecting me.

"Good evening, Mrs Kolchak."

"Well, hello, Miss Donnelly. You've been busy." Her diamond tones could have cut glass.

"I could say the same for you. Whatever did Mr Constantine do to deserve that?"

"Once you'd charmed the information from him he had no further use, and I'm not above punishing those who get in my way."

"Did Louis Jones get in your way, too?"

"Horrible man, you should thank me. Claimed to be your brother-in-law."

"Alas, it's one of the few truths he's ever told."

"How unfortunate. Now, I've got something of yours. I believe you've got something of mine."

"Let me guess: we'll swap, then you'll let me walk away."

"What would it profit me to do otherwise?"

"I got in your way."

"That's very true," she answered. "Nevertheless, I don't see how you've got any choice."

Much though I hated to admit it, she was right.

Leaving Liam had been the hardest thing I'd ever done, but my family connection to Louie the Louse meant I had no hope of a future with a detective—or at least not one as clean and straight down the line as Murphy. Liam and I had argued back and forth: I told him I'd be a black mark on his record, he'd come to resent me; he'd denied it, swore it wouldn't happen. But the thing that had finished me was Louie telling me he wanted a cop on his payroll, that he could use me for leverage with my boyfriend. I'm not easily useable, but I figured whatever Louie's scheme was, it would wind up getting an honest cop who I happened to love hurt or worse. So I'd broken off with Liam.

But I wasn't going to leave him to die.

"Where shall we meet, Mrs Kolchak?"

"Why, the Memorial Museum, of course. Just let yourself in, the doors will be unlocked. Don't forget to bring your part of the bargain, Miss Donnelly, and don't *interfere* with it—I promise you I'll know."

I hung up. Part of that was probably a bluff. I was happy to call it a little.

Security guards' bodies were scattered along the way once I passed the Hathor-headed columns and entered the Egyptian wing—each and every one lacking the top of their head, torsos torn open. All presumably without their innards—I stopped examining them after the first few. The hair on the back of my neck prickled as I sensed myself followed, but all I caught were glimpses of dark formless things from the corner of my eye.

The corridor was set up as an avenue lined with sphinxes, and the walls held a range of reproduction weapons from the Nile Valley. A weird curved thing—the label advised it was a *khopesh*, a sickle-sword—looked handy, so I took it. The replica was so accurately rendered that the outer curve of the cruel blade was sharp enough to shave with, although you'd be a fool to try. Miraculously, I didn't cut myself, and I tucked the handle into the back of my trousers. Reaching the open gallery doors, I took a deep breath, then stepped into the breach.

The chamber was half the length of a football field and packed tight with *objets*. I passed sarcophagi of basalt, metal inlaid with enamel, others of painted wood; chairs and chests and chariots in ebony and gold; statues of jackals and winged women, of animal-headed humans. Obviously removed from their protective glass cases, small mummies of cats, mice, ibis, and larger ones—gazelles, bulls—sat in neat, attentive rows facing towards a carven throne decorated with lapis and other gems.

Two things stood out: Izolda Kolchak, a lot less glamorous now, draped across the broad golden seat; and the bulk of a huge Nile crocodile—*Crocodylus niloticus*—at her feet.

Mrs Kolchak looked well over fifty and maybe closer to a few thousand. She was finishing a meal, dipping her fingers daintily into the cranium of Abel Mannheim's disembodied head, and slowly changing from a wrinkled crone into the vision I'd seen less than twenty-four hours ago. Her skin plumped, whitened, smoothed; her hair became lush and shiny, lips reddening, eyes sparkling; her body filled out and did justice to the long white silk gown. A jeweled dagger hung around her waist on an intricate chain.

The crocodile was over twenty feet long, its torso thick as a barrel, tapering off at the head and tail ends. The armored skin was a mottled mix of bronze, yellow-green, and black; its teeth had turned sepia with age but were still long and sharp. It looked like a gigantic desiccated sausage with blue glass beads for eyes in its ugly head. The fact that it was also twitching, stubby legs scrabbling at the marble floor, was less a point of interest than a matter of terror. The movement seemed to increase the closer I got. I held the stolen urn a little tighter in my sweaty hands.

Oh, boy.

To its left was a table bearing the alabaster shards of three canopic jars. To its right, a canoe for the afterlife, and in it the glint of auburn hair. I froze until I saw movement, assured it was still attached to Liam's head.

"Good girl," she said, tossing the head aside and licking her nails as she rose. Kolchak crossed to the boat and effortlessly hauled Liam out. I heard him grunt and guessed she'd dislocated something, or nearly so. He had a black eye, a cut on his forehead, and the gag in his mouth was stained with blood. "This is yours?"

I put the jar on the floor and backed away. "Send him over."

"But of course." She gave Liam a gentle push, remaining where she was as he navigated his slightly concussed way past the squirming crocodile. I noticed a flash of red on Kolchak's right hand.

"Nice ring," I said, wondering what Queen Tera might pay to know where her missing ruby was.

"This old thing?" She fluttered her fingers so the Jewel of the Seven Stars caught the light on its points.

I pulled the gag from Liam's mouth and he stuck his tongue out, spitting bits of old linen. He leaned heavily on me. How hard had she hit him?

"So," I said, "a resurrection gem and a giant crocodile. What might you be doing with these?"

"What won't I do?' She laughed. "All the wannabes, all the snobs . . . all of them. Certain rewards will flow for nothing more than prayers. But what might a monstrous god like *this* do for the woman who followed it across thousands of years and offered a fresh start, and the chance to feed on all life in such a city?'

Liam leaned over and asked quietly, "Why are we not running?"

"Because she's not alone. Look at the doorway." From the intake of his breath I knew he'd spotted the columns of black mist that shimmered and shivered at the entrance behind us, crimson eyes flaring with hunger. "Besides, she'll only send that thing after us, and I'm guessing it is very fast.'

"You're a perceptive creature. It's a shame I can't leave you alive—or indeed him, he's so pretty, but terribly heroic. You'd be thorns in my side, and that gets old very quickly. But I thank you for bringing what I need."

"She poured blood from the guards on the organs from the jars then put them inside that overgrown alligator," Liam managed to say as we stepped backwards and Kolchak came to claim the last urn. The ruby ring began to pulse. She didn't notice the new wax around the lid, just smashed the vessel against a statue of Bast, then poured the contents into her hand.

The withered apple left her perplexed for a few moments while I dug into my jacket pocket and pulled out the even more withered liver I'd removed from the jar. Sure, I could have left it at Liam's but I suspected Kolchak would know if it wasn't brought into proximity with the great reptile—its increased mobility on my arrival seemed to prove me right. Now, the lump of flesh was dry and friable between my fingers as I held it up. "As I understand it, you need this too."

Izolda Kolchak screamed as I crushed the ancient thing and it crumbled from my palm, motes swirling like a dying universe.

She rushed at us. Much to Liam's surprise, I pushed him aside, then whipped the sickle-sword up towards Kolchak's throat. Kolchak tried to stop but her momentum carried her forward and that, as much as my swing, embedded the blade in her neck. Unfortunately for me she'd managed to unsheathe her dagger, and the very same momentum helped her ram it under my arm, sliding between the ribs.

I got to briefly enjoy her look of astonishment before we both fell. She crumbled to dust. Behind her the juddering Petsuchos shrank and then disintegrated; without its component parts and the driving will of its mistress there was nothing holding the crocodile together. The black shadow shapes at the door seemed to explode then dissipate. I found myself deep in a pile of sandy particles, hunched in agony, cursing, fighting for air, and clutching at something sharp beneath my palm.

Liam scrambled over and held me, kissing me as if that might help, rocking me like a baby. A big, sweary baby. "Don't you die, don't you dare."

"Will you miss me?" I stopped struggling to breathe and sighed.

He didn't answer, but tears dropped hot on my face as the pain in my side lessened. Murphy lifted my arm to try to stem the bleeding with his handkerchief, but, though the jacket and shirt were ruined, there was no longer a puncture in my skin, no welling blood. No wound. He checked the other side. Same.

"What the—"

I held up the now-dull Jewel of the Seven Stars I'd found in Izolda Kolchak's remains. "Resurrection gem."

He glared, but I noticed he didn't let me go. "And you let me worry?"

"In all fairness, I didn't know I wasn't dying until a second or two ago." I sat up, made myself comfortable in the circle of his arms, rested my head against his shoulder. "So."

"So."

"So, it's a good news-bad news scenario."

"What's the good news?"

"Well, for starters, I'm alive."

Though he looked as though the nature of that was up for debate, he tightened his grip on me. "And?"

"Plus we saved the city and maybe the world."

"And?'

"I've already banked a sizeable fee, plus I know someone who'll pay a pretty penny for the return of this." I slipped the ruby ring on my finger, waggled it a little. "*And* that first dried-out corpse was Louie the Louse, so he won't be a problem any more."

"Well, that is undeniably good news." He nodded. "What's the bad news?'

I glanced over his shoulder at the dead guards. He nodded in acknowledgement. While Kolchak and Louie definitely deserved what they got, and Constantine and Mannheim maybe had too, sadly the museum security guys lost their lives just trying to do their jobs—like good cops.

"There's one more bit of bad news-good news . . ."

"What?"

"One of us has to write up a police report on all this supernatural stuff—and it isn't me."

The late Kage Baker's The Company series of stories and novels involves a group of future scientists who master time travel and proceed to plunder the past for profit in their present. As it is impossible to modify the past, The Company must work sub rosa to acquire "lost" valuables they know have been destroyed. Company operatives find ways to preserve these vanished treasures and sell them in the twenty-fourth century. Since time travel is costly, The Company creates near-immortal cyborgs to act as operatives. Baker wrote eleven novels, four novellas, and a number of short stories set in The Company universe; it's all much more complicated and a great deal more fun than this description, but perhaps you'll get a hint of it in this story of the 1914 discovery of a Twelfth Dynasty royal burial by none other than Flinders Petrie, the Father of Archaeology.

The Queen in Yellow
Kage Baker

———

The lady waited in her motorcar.

It was a grand car, the very best and latest of its kind in 1914, a Vauxhall touring convertible with a four-liter engine, very fast. It was painted gold. Until recently the lady would have been waiting on a horse, by choice a palomino Arabian stallion. She preferred her current transportation system, because she did not particularly care for living things. She did admire machines, however. She liked gold, too.

Her name was Executive Facilitator for the Near East Region Kiu, and the sleek golden motorcar in which she waited was parked on a deserted road in the middle of a particularly ancient and historically significant bit of Nowhere. Not so far behind her, the Nile flowed on through eternity; above her, the white moon swam like a curved reed-boat across the stars, and it and they shed faint soft light on the rippled dunes of the desert and the green garden country. Lady Kiu cared no more about the romance of her surroundings than the Sphinx, who was her junior by several millennia.

She did not show her eleven thousand years, almond-eyed beauty that she was. She looked no older than a fairly pampered and carefree twenty-two. Her soul, however, had quite worn away to nothing.

Lady Kiu was impatient as she waited. Her perfect nails tapped out a sinister little rhythm on the Vauxhall's steering wheel. You would think such an ageless, deathless creature would have long since learned to bide her time, and normally Lady Kiu could watch the pointless hours stagger past with perfect sangfroid; but there was something about the man for whom she waited that irritated her unaccountably.

The man was standing on a ridge and staring, slack-jawed, at the beauty of the night. Moon, sand, stars, gardens, the distant gleam of moonlight on the river: he had seen a lot of moons, stars, sand, gardens and rivers in his time, but this was *Egypt*, after all! And though he too was a death-less, ageless creature, he had never in all his centuries been to Egypt before, and the Romance of the Nile had him breathlessly enchanted.

His name was Literature Preservationist Lewis. He was a slight, fair-haired man with the boyish good looks and determined chin of a silent film hero. He was moreover brave, resourceful, and terribly earnest about his job, which was one of the things about him that so irritated Lady Kiu.

He also tended to get caught up in the moment to such an extent that he failed to check his internal chronometer as often as he ought to, with the result that when he did check it now he started guiltily, and set off at a run through the night. He was able to move far more quickly than a mortal man, but he was still five minutes late for his rendezvous.

"Sorry!" he cried aloud, spotting Lady Kiu at last, sullen by moonlight. He slid to a halt and tottered the last few steps to her motorcar, hitching up his jodhpurs.

"Sand in your pants?" enquired Lady Kiu, yawning.

"Er—actually we've all got sand everywhere. We're roughing it, rather. The professor doesn't go in for luxuries in the field. I don't mind, though! He's really the most astonishing mortal, and I'm used to a bit of hardship—" said Lewis.

"How nice. Your report, please."

Lewis cleared his throat and stood straight. "Everything is on schedule and under budget. I guided the fellaheen straight to the shaft entrance without seeming to, you see, quite subtly, and even though it's been blocked with debris, the excavation has been going along famously. At the current speed, I expect we'll reach the burial chamber exactly at twilight tomorrow."

"Good." Lady Kiu studied her nails. "And you're absolutely certain you'll get the timing right?"

"You may rely on me," Lewis assured her.

"You managed to obtain a handcar?"

"All I had to do was bribe a railway official! The princess and I will roll into Bani Suwayf in style."

"The mortal trusts you?"

"Professor Petrie? I think I've managed to impress him." Lewis hooked his thumbs through his suspenders proudly. "I heard him telling Mr Brunton what a remarkable fellow I am. 'Have you noticed that fellow Kensington?' he said. Petrie impresses me, too. He's got the most amazing mental abilities—"

"Darling, the day any mortal can impress me, I'll be ready for retirement," said Lady Kiu, noting in amusement that Lewis started and quivered ever so slightly at her use of the word *darling*.

"I can expect you at Bani Suwayf at midnight tomorrow, then," she added. "With the merchandise."

"Without fail!"

"That's a good boy. We've set you up a nice workroom on the boat, with everything you'll need for the restoration job. And in your cabin—" she reached out a lazy hand and chucked him under the chin "—there'll be a bottle of well-iced champagne to celebrate. Won't that be fun?"

Lewis's eyes widened. Struck mute, he grinned at her foolishly, and she smiled back at him. She expected men to fall in love with her—they always did, after all—but Lewis fell in love with anything beautiful or interesting, and so he wasn't worth her time. Still, it never hurt to give an underling some incentive.

"Until tomorrow," she said, blowing him a kiss, and with a roar her golden chariot came to life and bore her away toward the Nile.

You will find the pyramid of Senuseret II west of the Nile, near Al Fayyum. It is an unassuming little twelfth-dynasty affair of limestone and unburned mud brick. It is quite obvious how it was built, so no one ever speculates on how on earth it got there or who built it, or argues morbidly that apocalyptic knowledge is somehow encoded in its modest dimensions.

To the south of Senuseret's pyramid is a cemetery, and on this brilliant day in 1914 it had a certain holiday air. The prevailing breeze brought the fragrance of fields, green leaf, and lotus surging up in the brief Egyptian spring. Makeshift huts had been put up all along its outer wall, and Englishmen and Englishwomen sat in the huts and typed reports, or made careful drawings with the finest of crow quills, or fanned flies away from their food and wondered plaintively what that furry stuff was on the tinned pilchards, or fought off another wave of malaria.

Within the cemetery walls, several shaft tomb entrances admitted sunlight. In such shade as there was, the Egyptian fellaheen sat sorting through fairly small basketfuls of dig debris, brought to them by brown children from the mouth of another shaft. Lewis, his archaeologist ensemble augmented by a pith helmet today, stood watching them expectantly. His riding boots shone with polish. His jodhpurs were formidable.

Beside him stood a mortal man, burned dark by the sun, who wore mismatched native slippers without socks, patched knickerbocker trousers, a dirty shirt that had lost its buttons, and a flat cap that had also seen better days. He was white-haired and gray-bearded but had a blunt powerful form; he also had an unnervingly intense stare, fixed not on the fellaheen but on Lewis.

William Matthew Flinders Petrie was sixty years old. He had laid down the first rules of true archaeology, and that made him very nearly a patron saint for people who invested in history as much as Lewis's masters did.

Though *invested* is not, perhaps, the correct word for the way the Company got its money.

Lewis never thought about that part of it much, to avoid being depressed. He had always been taught that depression was a very bad thing for an immortal, and the secret to happiness was to keep busy, preferably by following orders. And life could be so interesting! For example, one got to rub elbows with famous mortals like Flinders Petrie.

"So you think this grave hasn't been robbed? You have an intuition about this, have you?" Petrie said.

"Oh, yes, Professor," said Lewis. "I get them now and then. And after all, theft is a haphazard business, isn't it? How systematic or careful can a looter be? I'd be awfully surprised if they hadn't missed *something*."

"Interesting," said Flinders Petrie.

"What is, sir?"

"Your opinion on thieves. Have you known many?" Actually Lewis had worked with thieves his entire life, in a manner of speaking. But remembering that he was supposed to be a youthful volunteer on his first visit to Egypt (which was half true, after all), he blushed and said "Well—no, sir, I haven't, in fact."

"They have infinite patience, as a rule," Petrie told him. "You'd be astonished at how methodical they are. The successful ones, at least. They take all manner of precautions. Get up to all sorts of tricks. Sometimes an archaeologist can learn from them."

"Ah! Such as wearing a costume to gain access to a forbidden shrine?" Lewis enquired eagerly. "I have heard, sir, that you yourself convinced certain tribesmen you were mad by wearing, er, some rather outlandish things—"

"The pink underwear story, yes." Petrie gave a slight smile. "Yes, it sometimes pays very well if people think you're a harmless fool. They'll let you in anywhere."

As Lewis prepared to say something suitably naïve in response, children came streaming from the mouth of the shaft like chattering swallows. A moment later an Egyptian followed them and walked swiftly to Petrie, before whom he bowed and said: "Sir, you will want to come see now."

Petrie nodded once, giving Lewis a sidelong glance.

"What did I tell you?" said Lewis, beaming.

"What indeed?" said Petrie. "Come along then, boy, and let's see if your instincts are as good as you think they are."

The mouth of the shaft had been blocked, as all the others there had been blocked, with centuries of mud and debris from flood run-off, and it was hard as red cement and had taken days of labor to clear in tiny increments. But the way was now clear to the entrance of the tomb chamber itself, where a mere window had been chiseled through into stifling darkness. A Qufti waiting with a lantern held it up and through the hole, flattening himself against the wall as Petrie rushed forward to peer inside.

"Good God!" cried Petrie, and his voice cracked in excitement. "Is the lid intact? Look at the thing, it hasn't been touched! But how can that *be*?" He thrust himself through, head and shoulders, in his effort to see better, and the Qufti holding the lamp attempted to make himself even flatter, without success, as Petrie's body wedged his arm firmly into the remaining four inches of window space and caused him to utter a faint involuntary cry of pain.

"Sorry. Oh, bugger all—" Petrie pulled backward and stripped off his shirt. Then he kicked off his slippers, tossed his cap down on top of them, and yanked open his trousers. The sole remaining fly button hit the wall with the force of a bullet, but was ignored as he dropped his pants and jumped free, naked as Adam.

"Your trowel, sir," said the Qufti, offering it with his good arm as he drew back.

"Thank you, Ali." Petrie took the trowel, draped his shirt over the window ledge, and vaulted up and through with amazing energy for a man of his years, so that Lewis and Ali endured no more than a few seconds of averting their eyes as his bottom and then legs and feet vanished into stygian blackness.

"Er—what a remarkable man," observed Lewis.

The Qufti just nodded, rubbing his arm.

"GIVE ME THE LAMP!" ordered Petrie, appearing in the hole for a moment. "And keep the others out of here for the present, do you understand? I want a clear field." He turned on Lewis a glare keen enough to cut through limestone. "Well? Don't you want to see your astonishing discovery, Mr Kensington? I'd have thought you'd have been beside yourself to be the first in!"

"Well—ah—I'm certain I couldn't hope to learn as much from it as you would, Professor," said Lewis.

Petrie laughed grimly. "I wonder. Never mind, boy, grab a trowel and crawl through. And don't be an old maid! It's a sweat bath in here."

"Yes, sir," said Lewis, racing for the mouth of the shaft, and for all his embarrassment and reluctance there was still a little gleeful voice at the back of his mind singing: *I'm on a real Egyptian archaeological dig with Flinders Petrie! The Father of Archaeology! Gosh!*

In the end he compromised by stripping down to his drawers, and though Petrie set him to the inglorious task of whittling away at the window to enlarge the chamber's access while he himself worked at clearing the granite sarcophagus, Lewis spent a wonderful afternoon.

His sense of rapport with the Master in his Element kept him diverted from the fact that he was an undersized cyborg wearing nothing but a pair of striped drawers, chipping fecklessly at fossilized mud while sweat dripped from the end of his nose, one drop precisely every 43.3 seconds, or that he was trapped in a small hot enclosed space with an elderly mortal who had certain intestinal problems.

The great man's vocal utterances were limited to grunts of effort and growls of surprise, with the occasional "Hold the damned light over here a moment, can't you?" But Lewis, in all the luxury of close proximity and uninterrupted except for having to pass the debris-basket out the hole on a regular basis, was learning a great deal by scanning Petrie as he worked.

He was not learning the sort of things he had expected to learn, however.

For example, his visual recordings of Petrie were not going to be as edifying as he'd hoped: the Master in his Element appeared nothing like a stately cross between Moses and Indiana Jones, as depicted in the twenty-fourth century. He resembled a naked lunatic trying to tunnel out of an asylum. That didn't matter, though, in light of the fascinating data Lewis was picking up as he scanned Petrie's brain activity.

It looked like a lightning storm, especially through the frontal lobes.

There were connections being made that were not ordinarily made in a mortal mind. Patterns in data were instantly grasped and analyzed, fundamental organizational relationships perceived that mortals did not, as a rule, perceive, and jumps of logic of dazzling clarity followed. Lewis was enchanted. He watched the cerebral fireworks display, noted the slight depression in one temple and pondered the possibility of early brain trauma rerouting Petrie's neural connections in some marvelous inexplicable way . . .

"I must say, sir, this is a great honor for me," said Lewis hesitantly. "Meeting and actually working with a man of your extraordinary ability."

"Nothing to do with *ability*, boy," replied Petrie, giving him a stare over the edge of the sarcophagus. "It's simply a matter of paying attention to details. That's all it is. Most of the people out here in the old days were nothing more than damned looters. Go at it with a pick and blasting powder! Find the gold! Didn't care tuppence for the fact that they were crumbling history under their bloody boots."

"Like the library of Mendes," said Lewis, with bitter feeling.

"You remember that, do you?" Petrie cocked a shaggy eyebrow at him. "Remarkable; that was back in '92. You can't have been more than an infant at the time."

"Well, er, yes, but my father read about it in *The Times*, you see," temporized Lewis. "And he talked about it for years, and he shared your indignation, if I may say so. That would have been Naville, wouldn't it, who found all those rooms filled with ancient papyri, and was so ham-fisted he destroyed most of them in the excavation!" His vengeful trowel stabbed clay and sent a chip whizzing into the darkness.

"So he did," said Petrie, picking up the chip and squinting at it briefly before setting it in the debris basket. "I called him a vandal and he very nearly called me out. Said it was ridiculous to expect an archae-ologist to note the placement of items uncovered in a dig, as though one were to note where the raisins were in a plum pudding! Mark that metaphor, you see, that's all an excavation meant to him: Dig your spoon in and gobble away! Never a thought for *learning* anything about what he was digging up."

"And meanwhile who knew what was being lost?" Lewis mourned.

"Plays. Poetry. Textbooks. Histories."

Petrie considered him a long moment before speaking again, and Lewis was once more aware of the bright storm in the old man's head.

"We can never know," Petrie said. "Damn him and everyone like him. How can we ever know the truth about the past? Historians lie; time wrecks everything. But if you're careful, boy, if you're methodical, if you measure and record and look for the bloody boring little details, like potsherds, and learn what they mean—you can get the dead to speak again, out of their ashes. That's worth more than all the gold and amulets in the world, that's the work of my life. That's what I was born for. Nothing matters except my work."

"I know exactly what you mean!" said Lewis.

"Do you?" said Petrie quietly.

They worked on in silence for a while after that.

At some point in the long afternoon the auroral splendor of Petrie's mind grew particularly bright, and he cried out, "What the deuce?"

"Oh, have you found something, Professor?" Lewis stood and peered at the area of the sarcophagus that had just been cleared. There were hieroglyphs deep-cut in the pink granite. "The Princess Sit-Hathor-Yunet? Oh, my, surely that's a very good sign."

And then he almost exclaimed aloud, because Petrie's mind became like a glowing sun, such a magnificence of cerebration that Lewis felt humbled. But Petrie merely looked at him, and said flatly:

"Perhaps it is. It's damned unusual, anyway. Never seen a seal quite like that on the outer sarcophagus before."

"Really?" Lewis felt a little shiver of warning. "Do you think it's significant?"

"Yes," said Petrie. "I'm sure it is."

"How exciting," said Lewis cautiously, and turned back to chipping away at the wall.

By twilight, when the first blessed coolness rose in salt mist from the canals, it was still hot and stinking in the tomb. Lewis wiped his face with the back of his hand, leaving a streak of red mud above one eye, and said casually, "I suppose we'd better stop for today."

"Absolutely not," said Petrie. "I've very nearly cleared the lid. Another forty-five minutes' work ought to do it. Don't you want to see Princess Sit-Hathor-Yunet, boy?" He grinned ferociously at Lewis.

"More than anything, sir," said Lewis, truthfully. "But do you really want to rush a discovery of this importance? I'd much rather get a good night's sleep, wouldn't you, and start fresh tomorrow?"

Petrie was silent a moment, eyeing him. "I suppose so," he said at last. "Very well. Though, of course, someone ought to sleep in here tonight. Standing guard, you know."

"Allow me to volunteer!" said Lewis, doing his best to look frightfully keen. "Please, sir, it would be an honor."

"As you like." Petrie stroked his beard. "I'll have supper and your bedroll sent out to you. Will that suit?"

It suited Lewis very well indeed, and two hours later he was stretched out in his blankets on the lid of the sarcophagus, listening to the sounds of the camp in its rituals as it gradually retired for the night.

He found it comforting, because it was much more like the sound of mortals retiring for the night the way they had over the centuries when he had been getting used to them: the low murmur of a story being told, the cry of a dreaming child, the scrape of a campfire being banked.

Modern rooms were sealed against sound, and nights had become less human. In London, you might hear distant waterworks or steam pipes, or the finny clamor of a radio or a phonograph, or the creak of furniture.

You might hear electricity, if it had been laid on, humming through the walls. Humanity was sealing itself away in tidy boxes.

"But," he said to himself aloud, looking up at the ceiling of the tomb, "they used to do that, too, didn't they? Though not while they were still alive." He sat up cautiously and groped for his lantern. "At least not intentionally."

He lit the lantern and set to work at once, chiseling away at the last layer of mud sealing the lid of the sarcophagus. It went much more quickly when you didn't have to carefully collect every single chip and pass it out through the entrance in a basket, and Lewis felt certain qualms about the debris he was scattering everywhere.

"But we'll leave the professor a treat to make up for it, won't we, Princess?" he muttered. "And, after all, history can't be changed." Five minutes later he had freed enough of the lid to be able to toss the trowel aside and prise an edge up, and he yanked the granite slab free as though it were so much balsa wood.

"Wow!" he said, although he had known what he would see.

There was a mummy case reposing there, smiling up through a layer of grime as though it had been expecting him, and in a manner of speaking it had been. It represented a lady bound all in golden cerements, and painted about her shoulders was a feathered cape in every shade of lemon and amber, set here and there with painted representations of topazes and citrines. Her features closely resembled Lady Kiu's, save that there was a warmth and life in her eyes missing from the living eyes of Lady Kiu.

Under the dust, the whole case gleamed with a thick coat of varnish of glasslike smoothness and transparency. An analysis of its chemical structure would have startled scientists, if there had been any with electron microscopes or spectrographs in 1914. Lewis couldn't resist reaching down to stroke along the side where the case was sealed, and could feel no seam or join at all. It would take a diamond-edged saw to get the box open, but that was all right; it had served its purpose.

The chest at the top of the tomb had had no such treatment, and it had fallen to pieces where it stood, splitting open under the sheer mass of the treasure it contained: a crown of burnished gold, two golden pectorals inlaid with precious stones, coiled necklaces, armlets, collars, boudoir items, beadwork in amethyst, in carnelian, turquoise, lapis lazuli, obsidian, ivory.

"Let's get this mess out of the way, shall we?" said Lewis, and, reaching in, he picked up as much of the treasure as he could in one grab and dumped it unceremoniously into a recess in the wall at one side. Beads scattered and rolled here and there, but he ignored them. It was just so much jewelry, after all, and he was fixed and focused on his objective as only a cyborg can be.

"Now, Princess," he said, giggling slightly as he leaned down to lift the mummy case from its dais, "shall we dance? You and I? I'm quite a good dancer. I can two-step like nobody's business. Oh, you'll like it out in the world again! I'll take you on a railway ride, though not first-class accommodations I'm afraid—" He set the case, which was as big as he was, down while he considered how best to get it through the opening.

"But that'll be all right, because then we'll go for a sail down the Nile, and that will be much nicer. Quite like old times, eh?" Deciding the time for neatness had passed, he simply aimed a series of kicks and punches at certain spots on the wall. He did not seem to exert much force, but the wall cracked in a dozen places and toppled outward into the tomb shaft.

"Literature Preservationist Lewis, super-cyborg!" he gloated, striking an attitude, and then froze with an expression of dismay on his face.

Flinders Petrie stood in the shaft without, just at the edge of the lamplight. He was surveying the wreckage of the wall with leonine fury, and the fact that he was wearing a pink singlet, pink ballet tutu and pink-ribboned slippers did nothing to detract from the terror of his anger.

Nor did the rifle he was aiming at Lewis's head.

"Come out of there, you little bastard," he said. "Look at the mess you've made!"

"I'm sorry!" said Lewis.

"Not as sorry as you're going to be," the old mortal told him. "I knew you were a damned marauder from the moment I laid eyes on you." He settled the rifle more securely on his shoulder. "Though I couldn't fathom the rest of it. What's a *super-cyborg*? What the hell are you, eh?"

Lewis raced mentally through possible believable answers, and decided on: "I'm afraid you're right. I'm a thief. I was paid a lot of money by a certain French count to bring back antiquities for his collection. The Comte de la, er, Cyborg. He ordered me to infiltrate your expedition, because everyone knows you're the best—"

"Bollocks," said Petrie. "I mean *what* are you?"

Lewis blinked at him. "What?" he repeated.

"What kind of thing are you? You're no human creature, that much is obvious," said Petrie.

"It is?" In spite of his horror, Lewis was fascinated. He scanned Petrie's brain activity and found it a roiling wasps' nest of sparks.

"It is to *me*, boy," said Petrie. "Mosquitoes won't bite you, for one thing. You speak like an actor on the stage, for another. You move like a machine, mathematically exact. I've timed the things you do."

"What kinds of things?" Lewis asked, delighted.

"Blinking once every thirty seconds precisely, for example," said Flinders Petrie. "Except in moments when you're pretending to be surprised, as you were just now. But there's not much that surprises you, is there? You *knew* about this shaft, you very nearly dragged Ali to this spot and showed him where to dig. It was so we'd do all the work for you, wasn't it? And then you'd make off with whatever was inside."

"Well, I'm afraid I—"

"You're not afraid. Your pupils aren't dilating as a man's would," said Petrie relentlessly. "You haven't changed color, and you're breathing in perfect mechanical rhythm." But his own hand shook slightly as he pulled back the hammer on the rifle. "You're some kind of brilliantly complicated automaton, though I'm damned if I can think who made you."

"That's an insane idea, you know," said Lewis, gauging how much space there was between Petrie and the side of the shaft. "People will think you're mad as a hatter if you tell anyone."

Petrie actually chuckled. "Do I look like a man who cares if people think I'm mad?" he said. He cut a bizarre little jeté, pink slippers flashing. "It's bloody useful, in fact, to be taken for a lunatic. Why d'you think I keep this ensemble in my kit? If I blew your head off this minute, dressed as I happen to be, I should certainly be acquitted of murder on grounds of insanity. Wouldn't you think so?"

"You are absolutely the most astonishing mortal I have ever met," said Lewis sincerely.

"And you're not mortal, obviously. What would I see if I fired this gun, Mr Kensington? Bits of clockwork flying apart? Magnetic ichor? Who made you? Why? I want to know! What are you for?"

"Please don't shoot!" cried Lewis. "I was born as mortal as you are! If a bullet hit me I'd bleed and feel an awful lot of pain, but I wouldn't die. I can never die." Inspiration struck him. "Think about The Book of the Dead. All the mummies you've unearthed, Professor, think of all the priests and embalmers who worked over them, trying to follow instructions they barely understood. What were they trying to do?"

"Guarantee that men would live forever," said Petrie, with perhaps just an edge of the fury taken off his voice.

"Exactly! They were trying to approximate something they knew about, but couldn't ever really achieve, because they didn't have the complete instructions. My masters, on the other hand, truly can make a man immortal."

"Your masters?" Petrie narrowed his eyes. "So you're a slave. And who are your masters, boy?"

"I'm not a slave!" said Lewis heatedly. "I'm more of an—an employee on long-term contract. And my masters are a terribly wise and powerful lot of scientists and businessmen."

"Freemasons, by any chance? Rosicrucians?"

"Certainly not." Lewis sniffed.

"Well, they're not so clever as they think they are," said Petrie. "I saw through you easily enough. 'Sit-Hathor-Yunet,' you said when you saw that cartouche, without a moment's hesitation. And you'd said you couldn't read hieroglyphs!"

Lewis winced. "I did slip there, didn't I? Oh, dear. I wasn't really designed for this kind of mission."

"You weren't, eh?"

"I'm just a literature preservationist. Scrolls and codices are more my line of work," Lewis admitted. "I was only going to handle the restoration job. But my Facilitator—Facilitators are the clever ones, you see, they're designed to be really good at passing themselves off as mortal, one of them would never make the mistakes I did—my Facilitator pointed out that a woman would be out of place in a camp like this, doing all sorts of dirty and dangerous work, and that I'd arouse much less suspicion than she would. She said she was sure I could handle a job like this." He looked up at Petrie in a certain amount of embarrassment.

Petrie laughed. "Then you've been rather a fool, haven't you? You're that much of a man, at least."

Lewis edged slightly forward and the barrel of the rifle swung to cover him.

"Stop there!" said Petrie. "And you can just put Princess Sit-Hathor-Yunet down too, clever dick."

"Er—I'm afraid I can't do that," said Lewis. "She was the whole point of my mission, you see. Can't I have her? You wouldn't learn anything useful from her, I can promise you."

"There's something odd about her, too, isn't there?" demanded Petrie. "I knew it! Everything about the bloody burial was queer from the first."

"Suppose, a long time ago, you had something valuable that you needed to put away for the benefit of generations to come, Professor. You'd want to hide it somewhere safe, wouldn't you?" Lewis said. "And where better than sealed in a tomb you *knew* wouldn't be opened until a certain day in the year 1914?"

"So you've got one of Mr Wells's time machines, have you?" Petrie speculated. "Is that how you know the future? What's the princess, then? Is she another of your kind?"

"No! You can't really make an immortal like this," said Lewis in disgust, waving a hand at the mummy case.

"Then how is it done? I want to know!"

"I'm afraid I can't tell you that, Professor."

"You will, by God." Petrie cocked the rifle again.

"Oh, sir, does it have to come to this?" Lewis pleaded. "Just let me go. I've left you the nicest little cache of loot in payment, really a remarkable find—"

He gestured at the jewelry he had dumped into the recess behind the sarcophagus. Petrie glanced at it, and his gaze stayed on the gold in spite of his intention, only a second longer than he had planned; but that was enough time for Lewis, who fled past him like a wraith in the night.

He was a hundred meters away by the time the bullet whizzed past his ear, bowling over Ali and the other fellaheen in his passage. He'd have been farther if not for the aerodynamic drag that the mummy case exerted. Gasping, he lifted it over his head like an ant with a particularly valuable grain of barley and ran, making for the railway line.

"Damn!" he groaned, as he sprinted on, hearing the shots and outcry in his wake. "My clothes!"

They were still sitting in a tidily folded heap in the shaft, where he'd meant to put them on prior to exiting stealthily. Can't be helped, he thought to himself. Perhaps I won't be too conspicuous?

Lewis had a stitch in his side by the time he reached the railway line, and set the mummy case down while he cast about for the hut in which he'd hidden his handcar. Ah! There it was. He flung open the makeshift door and stared blankly into the darkness for a moment before the sound of approaching gunfire rammed the fact home: some-one had stolen the handcar. He tried looking by infrared, but the result was the same. No handcar.

He lost another few seconds biting his knuckles as the pursuit grew nearer, until he distinguished Petrie's voice, louder than the others and titanic in its wrath. Dismayed, Lewis grabbed up the mummy case again and ran for his immortal life, through the lurid scarlet night of Egypt by infrared.

A frightened cyborg can go pretty far and pretty fast before running out of breath, so Lewis had got well out of the sound of pursuit before he had to stop and set down the mummy case again. Wheezing, he collapsed on it and regarded the flat open field in which he found himself.

"I hope you won't mind, Princess," he said. "There's been a slight change in plan. In fact, the plan has gone completely out the window. You probably wouldn't have enjoyed the railway ride anyway. Don't worry; I'll get you to the Nile somehow. What am I going to do, though?"

He peered across a distance of several miles to a pinprick of light a mortal couldn't have seen.

"There's a campfire over there," he said. "Do you suppose they have camels, Princess? Do you suppose I could persuade them to loan me a camel? Not that I'm particularly good at persuading mortals to do things. That's in a Facilitator's programming. Not something a lowly little Preserver drone is expected to be any good at."

A certain shade of resentment came into his voice.

"Do you suppose the professor was right, Princess? Did Lady Kiu take advantage of me? Did she send me in on a job for which I wasn't programmed simply because she didn't want to bother with it herself?" He sat there a moment in silence on the mummy case, fuming.

"You know, Princess, I think she did. Mrs Petrie did plenty of crawling about in the shafts. So did Winifred Brunton. Granted, they were English. All the same . . ." Lewis looked up at the infinite stars. "Can it be I've been played for a fool?"

The infinite stars looked down on him and pursed their lips.

"I'll bet she weasels out of sleeping with me, too," he sighed. "Darn it. Well, Princess, you wait here. I'm going to see if I can borrow a camel."

He rose to his feet, hitched up his drawers and strode away through the darkness with a purposeful air.

Princess Sit-Hathor-Yunet smiled up at the sky and waited. It was all she knew how to do. She didn't mind.

After a while a darkness detached itself from the greater darkness and loomed up against the stars, to become the silhouette of Lewis, proudly mounted on the back of a camel.

"Here we are!" he cried cheerily. "Can you believe it, Princess, there was a runaway camel wandering loose through the fields? What a stroke of luck for us! I hate stealing things from mortals."

He reined it in, bade it sit, and jumped down.

"Because, you see, the professor was wrong about me. I steal things *for* mortals. Actually it isn't even stealing. I'm a Preserver. It's what I do and I'm proud of it. It really is the best work in the world, Princess. Travel to exotic lands, meetings with famous people . . ." He scooped her up and vaulted back on the camel's hump. "Dodging bullets when they decide you're a tomb robber . . . oh, well. Hut-hut! Up and at 'em, boy!" The camel unfolded upward with a bellow of protest. It had been content to carry Lewis, who if he did not smell quite right had at least a proper human shape; but something about the princess spooked it badly, and it decided to run away.

It set off at a dead run. The little creature on its back yelled and yanked on its reins, but the great black thwartwise oblong thing back up there was still following it no matter how fast it ran, and so the camel just kept running. It ran toward the smell of water, as being the only possible attraction in the fathomless night. It galloped over packed and arid hardpan, through fields of cotton, through groves of apricot trees. Lewis experienced every change in terrain intimately, and was vainly trying to spit out a mouthful of apricot leaves when the camel found water, and stopped abruptly at the edge of a canal. Lewis, and Princess Sit-Hathor-Yunet, did not stop.

The black earth and the bright stars reversed, not once but several times, and then it was all darkness as Lewis landed with a splash in the canal, though with great presence of mind kept his grip on the mummy case. Down they went, and then the buoyancy of the sealed case pulled them upward again, and Lewis gulped in a lungful of air and scanned frantically for crocodiles.

"Whew!" he said, finding none. He noted also that the tidal flow was taking them Nileward at a leisurely pace, and, settling himself firmly atop Princess Sit-Hathor-Yunet, he began to paddle energetically.

"Well, call me Ishmael! My apologies, Princess, but needs must and all that sort of thing. We'll be out of this in no time, you'll see. In the meantime, enjoy the new experience. I take it you've never been body-surfing before?" He began to giggle at the idea of bodysurfing and couldn't control himself, laughing so hard that he nearly fell off. "Whoops! No, no, you headstrong girl! This way!"

Leeches floated up eagerly from the black depths, sensing a meal; just as the mosquitoes had, they came into contact with the minute electromagnetic field surrounding Lewis's skin and changed their minds in a hurry.

About the time that Lewis spotted the lights of Bani Suwayf in the distance, he also identified a pair of crocodiles a kilometer off. Crocodiles take rather more than an electromagnetic field to discourage and so, splashing hastily to the side of the canal, Lewis pushed the mummy case out and scrambled after it. He paused only a moment to let the water stream from his ballooning drawers before picking up the case and resuming his journey by land.

"We're almost there, Princess, and we're not even late!" he said happily, as he trudged along. "I'll have a thing or two to say to Lady Kiu, though, won't I? Let's see . . . Ahem! Madam, I feel I have no choice but to protest your . . . mmm. Lady Kiu, this is a painful thing for me to say, but . . . no. Kiu, old girl, I don't think you quite . . . that is, I . . . I mean, you . . . right."

He sighed, and marched on.

Bani Suwayf was a small town in 1914, but it had a railway station and a resident population of Europeans. One of them, M. Heurtebise, was a minor functionary in a minor bureau having to do with granting minor permits of various kinds to other Europeans, and he deeply resented the smallness of his place in the order of things. He took it out on his wife, his servants, his pets, and once a week he also took it out on a person whom he paid for the trouble and who was therefore philosophical about his nocturnal visits.

He was returning from one of these visits—it had not lasted long— in his motorcar, and was just rounding the corner of the main street as Lewis entered it from the little track leading from the canal. He looked up, aghast, when the bug-eyed lights caught and displayed him: a muddy and sweating figure wearing only striped drawers, balancing a mummy case on his head.

"Stop!" cried M. Heurtebise on impulse, hitting his chauffeur on the shoulder with his cane. "Thief!" he added, because it seemed like a good bet, and he pulled out a revolver and brandished it at Lewis.

Lewis, who had used up a lot of energy on his flit from Professor Petrie, decided the hell with it and stopped. He set down the mummy case very carefully, held up his hands in a classic don't-shoot gesture, and vanished.

"Where did he go?" exclaimed M. Heurtebise. When no answer was forthcoming from the night, he struck his chauffeur again and ordered, "Get out and look for him, Ahmed, you fool!"

Ahmed gritted his teeth, but got out of the car and looked around.

He looked up the street; he looked down the street. He looked everywhere but under the motorcar, where Lewis had insinuated himself into the undercarriage as cunningly as an alien monster.

"He is not to be found, sir," Ahmed told M. Heurtebise.

"I can see that, you imbecile. But he has left an antiquity in the roadway!"

Ahmed prodded Princess Sit-Hathor-Yunet with his foot. "So he has, sir."

Muttering to himself, M. Heurtebise got out of the motorcar. He strode over to the mummy case and his eyes widened as he noted the excellence of its condition and its obvious value.

"This has clearly been stolen," he said. "It is our duty to confiscate it. We will notify the proper authorities in the morning. Put it into the car, Ahmed."

Ahmed bent and attempted to lift it.

"It is too heavy, sir," he said. "We must do it together."

Mr. Heurtebise considered striking him for his insolence, but then reflected that if the mummy case was heavy, it was possibly full of treasure, and therefore the issue of prime importance was to get it out of the street and into his possession. So between them, he and Ahmed lifted the case and set it on end in the back seat. They got back in the motorcar and drove on the short distance to M. Heurtebise's villa.

When they pulled into the courtyard and got out, Ahmed opened the door to the ground-floor office and they carried the mummy case inside.

M. Heurtebise opened the venetian blinds to admit light from the courtyard lantern, and he directed Ahmed to set Princess Sit-Hathor-Yunet on two cane chairs.

The office was a comfortable room in the European style, with a banked fire in the hearth, leather overstuffed chairs with a small table and lamp between them, and a formidable desk with a row of pigeon-holes above it. There was also a large cage in one corner, covered with canvas sacking. As Ahmed pushed the two chairs closer together, a hoarse metallic voice began to exclaim from beneath the cover. It said something very rude and then repeated it eighteen times.

"Silence!" hissed M. Heurtebise. "Bad parrot! BAD PARROT!" He took his cane and hammered on the side of the cage, creating such a racket Ahmed winced and put his hands over his ears. A stunned silence followed. M. Heurtebise nodded in satisfaction. "That's the only way to teach him, by the devil."

"May I go now, sir?"

"Go." M. Heurtebise waved him away. They left the study, and Ahmed drove the motorcar into what had formerly been the stables. Here he got out, closed the great door and locked it, and went off to the servants' quarters. M. Heurtebise paused only long enough to lock the office door, and then climbed the outer stair to his apartments on the second floor.

Alone in the darkness, Lewis uninsinuated himself from the under-chassis and fell groaning to the floor. He was now smeared with black grease in addition to being muddy and wet. He lay there a moment and finally crawled out from under the motorcar. He got to his feet, staggered to the door and rattled it.

He was locked in. He shrugged and looked around for a suitable tool.

In the office, however, something else was just discovering that it was *not* locked in.

In his enthusiasm, M. Heurtebise had beaten on the bars of the cage with such force that he had shaken the cage's latchhook loose, though with the cover being in place he had not noticed this. However, the cage's inhabitant noticed, once its little ears had stopped ringing. It cocked a bright eye and then slid down the bars to the cage door.

Thrusting its beak through the bars, it levered the latch the rest of the way open. It pushed its head against the bars and the door opened partway. There was a rustle, a thump, and then a parrot dropped between the cage cover and the bars to the floor. It ruffled its feathers and looked around.

It was an African Grey, all silver-and-ashes except for its scarlet tail.

"Oh, my," it said. "You bad boy, what do you think you're doing?" It waddled across the tile floor like a clockwork toy, looking up at the long slanting bars of light coming in from the courtyard.

"Oh, la la! You *bad* boy bad boy!" it said, and beat its wings and flew to the top of the window-frame rail. Laughing evilly to itself, it reached down with its powerful little beak and snipped the topmost venetian blind in half with one bite. The slat having parted with a pleasing crunch, the parrot then made its way along the rail to the cord and rappelled down it, stopping at each blind and methodically biting through, until the whole assembly hung in ruins.

The parrot swung from the end of the cord by its feet a moment, twirling happily, and then launched itself at the desk.

"Whee! Oh, stop that at once, you wicked creature! Stop that now! Do you hear? Do you hear?"

It made straight for the neat stack of pencils and bit them each in half too; then pulled out the pens and did the same. As though tidying its work area, it threw the pieces over the edge of the desk, one after another, and for good measure plucked the inkwell out of its recess and pitched that over too. The inkwell hit the floor with a crash and the ink fountained out, spattering the tiles. The parrot watched this appreciatively, tilting its head.

"As God is my witness," it commented, "if you don't be quiet NOW I will wring your neck! I mean it! Stop that this instant!"

It turned and eyed the pigeonholes. Reaching into the nearest it pulled out M. Heurtebise's morning correspondence, dragged it to the edge and, with a decisive toss of its head, chucked it over the side too.

The envelopes smacked into the mess already there, and spread and drifted. The parrot peered into the other pigeonholes and poked through them, murmuring, "Wicked, wicked, wicked, wicked . . . tra la la." Finding nothing else of interest on the desk, it backed out of the last pigeonhole, gave a little fluttering hop and landed on the nearest of the armchairs. It strutted to and fro on the smooth leather surface a moment before lifting its tail grandly and liquidly.

"*Allons, enfants de la patrie*—eee—eee!" it sang. "La la la!"

The parrot looked across the gulf of space at Princess Sit-Hathor-Yunet, but she presented no opportunities or anything it might get hold of. It contented itself with worrying at an upholstered chair-button. Snip! That was the way to do it. The parrot noticed there were several other buttons within reach on the chair's back, and crying "Ooooh! Ha ha ha," it carefully removed every one in sight.

Biting neat triangular holes in the upholstery with which to pull itself up, it scaled the chair's arm and stepped out on the lamp table.

"You're a naughty boy and you don't get a treat," it declared, looking speculatively up at the lamp, which had a number of jet beads pendent from its green glass shade. Straining on tiptoe, it caught one and gave it a good pull. The lamp tilted, tottered and fell to the floor, where it broke and rolled, pouring forth a long curved spill of kerosene.

It came to rest in the hearth.

"Oh, my," said the parrot. It looked at the broken lamp with one eye and then with the other. "Oh, what have you done now? Bad! Too bad!" With a soft whoosh flames bloomed in the hearth. They leaped high as the lamp tinkled and shattered further, throwing bits out into the room. The parrot ducked and drew back, then stared again as the inevitable tongue of blue flame advanced over its kerosene road across the floor, right to M. Heurtebise's scattered correspondence and the cane chairs whereon reposed Princess Sit-Hathor-Yunet.

"Oooh!" said the parrot brightly. "Oooh, la la la!"

*   *   *

Lewis had been carefully sliding the stable bolt out of its recess in tiny increments, nudging it along with an old putty knife he had slipped between the planking. He had only another inch to go when he heard the breaking glass, the roar of flames.

"Yikes!" he said, and gave up on any effort to be polite. He punched his fist through the door, opened the bolt, dragged the door to one side and scrambled out. In horror he saw the flames dancing within the office, heard the mortals upstairs begin to shout.

He was across the courtyard in less than the blink of an eye, and yanked the office door off its hinges.

"Good evening," said the parrot as it walked out and past him, its little claws going *tick tick tick* on the flagstones. Lewis gaped down at it before looking up to see the first flames rising around Princess Sit-Hathor-Yunet.

He was never certain afterward just what he did next, but what he was doing immediately after that was running down the street with the mummy case once again balanced on his head, in some pain as his hair smoldered. He heard the rattle of a motorcar overtaking him, and Lady Kiu slammed on the brakes.

"You're late," she said. Lewis tossed Princess Sit-Hathor-Yunet into the back seat of the Vauxhall and dove in headfirst after her, not quite getting all the way in before Lady Kiu let out the clutch, downshifted, stepped on the gas again and they sped away.

"I'm sorry!" Lewis said, when he was right side up again. "All sorts of things went wrong—most unexpectedly—and—"

"You idiot, you've gotten grease on the seats," snarled Lady Kiu.

"Well, I'm sorry it isn't attar of roses, but I've had a slightly challenging time!" Lewis replied indignantly, clenching his fists.

"Don't you dare to address an Executive Facilitator in that manner, you miserable little drone—"

"Oh, yeah? I've got pretty good programming for a drone, your Ladyship. I can perform all kinds of tasks a Facilitator is supposed to do herself!"

"Really? I can tell you one thing you won't be doing—"

"Oh, as though I was ever going to get to do that anyway—"

They careened around a corner and pulled up at the waterfront, where Lady Kiu's yacht was even now on the point of casting off. The Vauxhall's headlights caught in long beams three burly security techs, waiting by the gangway. They ran forward and two of them seized the mummy case to muscle it aboard. The third, in the uniform of a chauffeur, came to attention and saluted. Lady Kiu flung open the door and stepped out on the running board, as the motor idled.

"Take that to the laboratory cabin immediately! We're leaving at once. You, Galba, take the Vauxhall. Meet us in Alexandria. I want the slime cleaned off the upholstery by the time I see it again. That includes you, Lewis. Move!"

"Oh, bugger o—" said Lewis as he climbed from the back seat, his words interrupted as he found himself staring down a rifle barrel.

"Where's the damned mummy case?" said Flinders Petrie.

"How'd you get here?" asked Lewis, too astonished to say anything else.

"Railway handcar," said Flinders Petrie, grinning unpleasantly. "The fellaheen found one hidden away the other day and I thought to myself, I'll just bet somebody's planning to use this to get to the Nile with stolen loot. So I confiscated the thing. Threw a spanner into your plans, did it?" He had apparently traveled in his pink ballet ensemble, though he'd sensibly put on boots for the journey; his slippers hung around his neck by their ribbons, like a dancer in a painting by Degas. Nor had he come alone; behind him stood Ali and several of the other fellaheen, and they were carrying clubs.

"Look, I'm sorry, but you must have realized by now the sarcophagus was a fake!" said Lewis. "What in Jove's name do you want?"

"It may be a fake, but it's a three-thousand-year-old fake, and I want to know how it was done," said Petrie imperturbably. "I'm still wearing my insanity defense; so you'd best start talking."

"What is this?" Lady Kiu strode around the motorcar and stopped, looking at the scene in some amusement and much contempt. "Lewis, don't tell me you've broken the heart of an elderly transvestite." Petrie lifted his head to glare at her, and then his eyes widened.

"You're the woman on the mummy case!" he said.

Lewis groaned.

"And it's a smart monkey, too," said Kiu coolly. She began to walk forward again, but slowly. "Too bad for it."

Lewis scrambled to get in front of her.

"Now—let's be civilized about this, can't we?" he begged. "Professor, please, go home!"

Even Petrie had backed up a step at the look on Kiu's face, and Ali and the others were murmuring prayers and making signs to ward off evil. Then Petrie dug in his heels.

"No!" he said. "No, by God! I won't stand for this! My life's work has been deciphering the truth about the past. I've had to dig through layers of trash for it, I've had to fight the whole time against damned thieves; but if creatures like you have been meddling in history, planting lies— then how am I to know what the truth really is? How can I know that any of it *means* anything?"

"None of it means anything at all, mortal," said Kiu. "Your life's work is pointless. There's not a wall you can uncover that hasn't got a lie inscribed on it somewhere."

"Stop it, Kiu! Why should we be at odds, Professor?" Lewis said. "My masters could do a lot for you, you know, if you worked for them. Money. Hints about the best places to dig. All you'll have to do is keep your mouth shut about this embarrassing little incident, you see? The Company could use a genius like you!"

"You're trying to bribe the monkeys? That's so foolish, Lewis," said Kiu. "They're never satisfied with the morsel they're given. Better to silence them at the outset. Galba, kill the servants first."

Galba, watching in shock from the other side of the motorcar, licked his lips. "Lady, I—"

"It's forbidden, Galba. Kiu, you can't kill them!" Lewis protested. "You know history can't be changed!"

"It can't be changed, but it can be forgotten," said Kiu. "*Fact efface-ment*, we Facilitators call it." She looked critically at Petrie. "Mortal brains are so fragile, Lewis. Especially all those tiny blood vessels . . . especially in an old man. If I were to provoke just the right hemorrhage in a critical spot, he might become . . . quite confused."

She reached out her hand toward Petrie, smiling.

"No! Stop! God Apollo, Kiu, please don't damage his mind!" Lewis cried. "Haven't you scanned him yet? Can't you see? He's unique, he's irreplaceable, you mustn't do this!"

Lady Kiu rolled her eyes.

"Lewis, darling," she said in tones of barely controlled exasperation, "how many ages will it take you to learn that not one of the wretched little creatures is irreplaceable? Or unique? *Nothing* is."

"That's a damned lie," said Flinders Petrie, from the bottom of his soul, and took aim at her throat with the rifle, though his hands were trembling so badly it was doubtful he'd have hit her.

"OH!" cried Lewis suddenly, in a theatrical voice. "Oh, Lady, look out, he'll damage you!" He launched himself at Kiu and bore her back-ward. Before she had recovered from her shock and begun to claw at him they were both teetering on the edge of the pier, and then they had gone over into the Nile with a splash. Galba ran to see what was happen-ing in the water. He glanced over his shoulder at the mortals, and then made a conscious choice not to notice what they did. Killing wasn't in his job description, nor was taking the blame for a bad field decision.

Petrie looked at the Vauxhall, still idling.

"Khaled, you know how to work these machines, don't you?"

"Yes, sir." Needing no other hint, Khaled vaulted into the driver's seat. Ali and another Qufti lifted Petrie between them, as gently as though he were made of eggshell, and set him beside Khaled in the front. The rest of them piled into the back or jumped on to the running boards. Khaled swung the motorcar around and sped off into the ancient night, under the ancient moon, while behind them crocodiles scrambled hastily on to the banks of the ancient Nile. Like Galba, they knew when to stay out of a fight.

But as he rode along Petrie stiffened in his seat, for he heard a voice—or perhaps it would be more correct to say that he felt a voice, drifting into his mind from the ether, hanging before his internal eye like a smoke signal.

. . . *we'll be in touch, mortal* . . .

He looked over his shoulder, and shivered.

"Khaled, drive faster."

The stars were fading and the yacht was well downriver by the time Lewis was sitting in the laboratory cabin, completing the last pass along Princess Sit-Hathor-Yunet's case with a whirring saw. On the floor by his chair, a silver bucket of melted ice slopped gently to and fro with the motion of the river, and the champagne bottle in it rolled and floated.

Lady Kiu stood watching him. Both of them wore bathrobes. Lady Kiu merely looked damp and furious, but Lewis looked damp and battered. There were red lines healing on his arms where claw marks had recently been, and one of his eyes was still a little puffy and discolored, suggesting that an hour or two ago he had had a remarkable shiner. Some of his hair seemed to have gone missing, as well. But he was smiling as he heard a crack and then the faint *hiss* of decompression. The mummy case's inner seal gave way.

"Perfect," he said, and set down the saw, and with quick skilled hands lifted the lid of the case.

"Look! It's a remarkable body of work!" he chortled. Lady Kiu merely cuffed her lip, but there was a certain satisfaction in her gaze as she regarded the occupant of the mummy case.

On first glance it appeared to be a mummy, neatly wrapped in linen strips white as cream. It was, however, a great deal of rolled papyrus, cunningly laid out to approximate a human form.

Lewis reached in with a tiny, sharp pair of scissors and snipped here and there. He lifted out a single scroll, sealed in wax, and looked at the inscription.

"The complete text of the *Story of Sinuhe*," he murmured. "Oh, my. And what's this one? The *Book of the Sea People*, gosh! And here's the *Great Lament for Tammuz*, and . . . this is the *True Story of Enkiddu*, and this one appears to be—wait—ah! This is your prize. *The Book of the Forces that Repel Matter*."

He held up a thick scroll bound twice with a golden band, and Lady Kiu snatched it from him. She looked at it hungrily.

"You'll do the stabilization on this one first," she ordered, handing it back to him. "It's the most important. The rest is nothing but rubbish."

"My predecessor doesn't seem to have thought so," remarked Lewis. "What a lovely haul! The *Hymns to the God Osiris*, the *Hot Fish Book* (racy stuff, that), the *Story the Silk Merchants Told Menes*. And look here! *Opinions of all Peoples on the Creation of the World*!"

"Manetho was a pointless little drone, too," said Kiu. "It doesn't matter; we'll find private buyers for that stuff. But you'll have the scroll on antigravity ready to go by the time we reach Alexandria, do you hear me? Averill will be waiting there and it's got to go straight to Philadelphia with him."

"Yes, Great Queen," said Lewis, looking dreamily over the scrolls. "Care for a glass of champagne to celebrate?"

"Go to hell," she told him, and stalked to the doorway. There she paused, and turned; all the witchery of charm she had learned in eleven millennia was in her smile, if not in her dead and implacable eyes.

"But don't worry about the mission report, Lewis darling. There won't be a word of criticism about your performance," she said silkily. "You're still such a juvenile, it wouldn't be fair. There was a time when the mortals impressed me, too. There will come a time when you're older, and wiser, and you'll be just as bored with them as I am now. Trust me on this."

She took two paces back and leaned from the waist, bending over him, and ran a negligent hand through his hair. She put her lips close to his ear and whispered: "And when you're dead inside, like me, Lewis dear, and not until then—you'll be free. But you won't care any more."

She kissed him and, rising, made her exit.

Alone, Lewis sat staring after her a moment before shrugging resolutely.

He opened the champagne and poured his solitary glass. His hair was already beginning to grow back, and the retina of his left eye had almost completely reattached. And, look! There was the rising sun streaming in through the blinds, and green papyrus waved on the riverbank, and pyramids and crocodiles were all over the place. The ancient Nile! The romance of Egypt!

He had even been shot at by Flinders Petrie.

Lewis sipped his champagne and selected a scroll from the cache.

Not *The Book of the Forces that Repel Matter*, that was all very fascinating in its way, and would in time guarantee that Americans would rediscover antigravity (once they got around to deciphering a certain scroll, long forgotten in a museum basement), but it wasn't his idea of treasure.

He took out the *Story of Sinuhe* and opened it, marveling at its state of preservation. Settling back in his chair, he drank more champagne and gradually lost himself in the first known novel. He savored the words of mortal men; the Nile bore him away.

Both the mysterious military/political and supernatural goings-on here are products of John Langan's rich imagination. So is Skua Island. (There is an island of that name, but it lies between Argentina and Antarctica.) Skua birds do breed in the North Atlantic area of the story; mummies somewhat similar to the one in this story have been found in Northern European bogs; and, of course, people have gathered together and told scary stories since the invention of language . . .

On Skua Island
John Langan

———

I

The story had held us, round the dinner table, sufficiently breathless, but except the obvious remark that it was weird, as, on a February night in an old house with a strong storm howling off the ocean, a story should essentially be, I remember no comment uttered till the eight of us adjourned to the living room with our drinks. There Fiona, my fiancée, noted it as the first time she had heard anyone number a tale that could be classified under the rubric of the zombie story among his own experiences. Whereupon Griffin, the story's narrator, hastened to repeat, for the third or possibly the fourth time, that much of the substance of what he had related was as it had been related to him on the beach by old Anthony, the fisherman, when everything was over, and although he, Griffin, indeed had seen what he was sure was DeBoer's white body through the green trees, the local doctor had been unable or unwilling to fix DeBoer's time of death with any certainty, so that the glimpse of him might have been a last look at a doomed, but still living, man.

"But do you believe that?" Kappa, our hostess, asked Griffin, who shrugged and looked sheepishly at his port.

Jennifer, curled on one of the large wicker chairs, said, "You have to admit, most of the stories you hear in a setting like this—" She waved her hand for emphasis and, as if in response, the wind gusted to a shriek, rattling the windows and provoking a round of laughter from the rest of us. "Very nice," she said, "you see: I told you I had powers. You have to admit, the kind of story you tend to hear, which I guess means the kind of story people tend to know, is the ghost story. Isn't that true? Get my mother started, and she'll tell you about her Uncle Richard, who saw the woman next door two days after she died, when he was out behind the house, chopping wood. She was floating three feet off the ground; his hair turned completely white on the spot."

"What happened to her?" Fiona asked.

"The woman? Who knows? She floated away. The point is, it's a ghost story." She turned to me. "Come on, Mr Horror-story-writer, back me up on this."

"Ghost stories are popular," I said. "It does seem as if everyone knows one. Certainly you find more so-called serious writers trying their hands at ghost stories than you do stories about vampires, or mummies, or—" with a nod to Griffin, who returned it "—zombies."

"I don't know," Fiona said. "I just spent the past semester teaching Henry James—a lot of Henry James—and, let me tell you, there's a pretty fair amount of vampiric activity going on in old Henry's works, especially a book like *The Sacred Fount*."

"Granted," I said, "but he never wrote about mummies."

Bob, our host, said, "I wonder why that was," looking at Fiona, who answered, "It wasn't flexible enough: he couldn't adapt the idea of the mummy (mummyism?) to his type of story the way he could adapt the idea of the vampire, vampirism."

"Can anyone?" Jennifer asked. "I mean, how many big mummy novels have there been? It's not like the vampire: for a while there, it seemed like every other book, movie, and TV show was about vampires, for crying out loud."

"And frequently from the vampire's point of view," Bob added.

"I know, really, like I'm going to identify with this walking corpse that spends his nights sucking people's blood out of little holes in their necks. Hello! Whose brainstorm was this? Anyway, regardless of what I may have thought, they were very popular. And you've had God only knows how many of those zombie movies, those Dead movies, *Night of the Living Evil Dead from Hell Part III* or whatever, not to mention movies about the devil and possession and witches and toxic monsters—but we were talking about books, weren't we? Well, I'm sure you've had books about all those things, too, haven't you?" She looked at me.

"More or less," I said.

"And werewolves: this one—" she gestured at me with her wine glass "—is working on a werewolf thing. It's very good. Are you done with it yet?"

"Not yet," I said.

"He's been very busy with the semester," Fiona said.

"We've got the great werewolf novel—sorry, I know I'm not supposed to call it that—we've got the great werewolf story coming, too, but what about the mummy?"

"The mummy is different," I replied. "It's a relic from a different time, the imperial age, from when the sun never set on the British Empire. Has anyone read any of the original mummy stories, the ones Arthur Conan Doyle wrote?" Only Bob nodded. "I shouldn't call them the original stories; I don't know for sure whether they are or not. I assume they were among the first. Anyway, Conan Doyle's mummy is very different from what we're accustomed to when we hear that name; at least, from what I think of. His mummy is a weapon. There's an obnoxious student of obscure foreign languages at Oxford who buys one that he keeps in his apartment for use against his enemies. He can read the spell that animates the mummy and sends it to do your bidding, which in his case usually involves disposing of the latest person who's annoyed him."

"Talk about Revenge of the Nerds," Jennifer said.

"What happens to him?" Fiona asked.

"Fortunately, a fellow student figures out what's going on and forces him to destroy the mummy, cut it up with dissecting knives and burn it together with the papers that brought it to life."

"How does he manage that?" Jennifer asked. "You would think the guy would just sick the mummy on him."

"He goes armed, with a gun."

"Oh. I guess that would do the trick."

"Indeed. I haven't made any kind of exhaustive survey, but that seems to be how the mummy first enters English literature. I wonder if it doesn't express some kind of anxiety, or even guilt, about the whole imperial enterprise, particularly with regard to the museums. The mummy seems so much a creature of the museum, doesn't it? You imagine it shuffling through the museum after dark, one loose bandage trailing along the floor behind it. Where does that image come from? It must be a scene in a film, I suppose. But it's as if the mummy embodies a kind of doubt the British had about removing all those antiquities from their rightful locations and shipping them to London for display, as if they suspected the morality of their actions—"

"Or as if they were afraid of contamination," Fiona said.

"Mmm," Bob said. "Who knows what you're going to bring into the country?"

"Right, you have to be careful," I said. "That could be it, too, like Dracula. Watch out what you unload from the boats."

"Dracula?" Jennifer asked.

"There are those who see Dracula as sublimating a fear of rabies," Bob answered, "a fear of England becoming diseased through its contact with other, particularly very distant and very foreign, places."

"I see," Jennifer said. "Thank you, Bob. You're right about the mummy: we don't think about it in terms of the story you described. We think of it as a love story, am I right? It starts in ancient Egypt, with a priest who's in love with the wrong person: the Pharaoh's wife, or his sister—or weren't their sisters their wives? Anyway, he's in love with someone he's not supposed to be, so as a punishment for his *hubris*—see, I do remember something from Bob's class—he's mummi-fied. Could you say he's mummified alive?"

"Well, technically mummification was something that was done to you after you were dead," Bob said. "But hey—why not?"

"All right then: Bob has given me permission to use the phrase 'mummified alive.' So the priest is buried in the desert, where he's forgotten about for the next four to five thousand years, until a bunch of clueless archaeologists, or I guess they'd be Egyptologists, find him, bring him to the museum, and turn him loose."

"Which usually involves his trying to find the reincarnation of his lost love," I added.

"Yes, who just happens to be the woman the hero's in love with, too. Convenient, that. The mummy kidnaps her and carries her to the Egypt room at the museum, which he has set up for the ceremony that will return his lost love's soul to the heroine's body. Luckily, the hero has figured all this out, and he shows up at the museum just in time to foil the mummy's plans. And get the girl. The mummy winds up incinerated."

"That's Hollywood," Fiona said, shaking her head, "everything becomes a romance."

"What's wrong with romance?" I asked, receiving in reply a sour expression. "Well," I said, "certainly the film versions of the mummy story tend to rob it of the deeper implications you find in the earlier written stories. The mummy becomes another monster, his Egyptian origins so much window-dressing."

Bob said, "The Egyptian associations had no resonance for Americans."

"Not the same resonance," Fiona said. "For America, Egypt was just another exotic location."

"So that's it?" Jennifer asked. "The mummy is dead? There's nothing anyone can do with it? Him? It?"

"This is all very nice," Kappa said, "and very educational, I can assure you. But isn't it a bit off track? We were talking about things that actually had happened to people, not movies and books."

Bob nodded, and Jennifer said, "You're absolutely right, Kappa, we were talking about actual events."

"So," I said, glancing round the company gathered there in the living room, my eyebrows raised for effect, "does anyone have a mummy story they'd care to share?"

There was a pause during which the wind fell off, and then a voice said, "I do."

We looked about to see who had spoken, and our eyes settled on Nicholas, who had been introduced at the start of our stay at the Cape house as an old friend of Bob's from Harvard and who had maintained an almost unbroken silence in the five days since, departing the house for hours at a time on walks whose destination he shared with no one, but which appeared to take him inland, away from the beach and the winter-angry ocean. His face was buried under twin avalanches of white hair, one descending from the tangled mass crowning his head, the other rising from the tangled mass hugging his jaw, but his hooded eyes were a pale bright blue that I should have described as arctic. For dress, he favored a pair of worn jeans and a yellowed cable-knit sweater, which he supplemented with a long grey wool coat and boots that laced up just short of his knees for his jaunts outside. In reply to a question Jennifer had posed our first morning there, while Nicholas was out, Kappa had informed us that Nicholas was an archaeologist whose particular inter-est was the study of the Vikings, which was the basis upon which his friendship with Bob had been founded when they met at Harvard. Although they had maintained contact over the years, it was not uncom-mon for Nicholas to disappear on some expedition or another for months at a time, and occasionally longer, which was part of the reason Kappa assumed he never had married. He did not speak much: this we had witnessed ourselves as Jennifer, who prides herself on being able to have a conversation with any living human being, availed herself of every opportunity to ask Nicholas questions, about himself, his career, what he was engaged in currently, that he answered in monosyllables when possible, clipped phrases when not, his voice when he spoke the sandpapery rasp of one unaccustomed to frequent speech. Now he was sitting on a dining-room chair he had positioned at the group's perimeter, between the dining room and the living room, a long-necked bottle of beer cradled in his hands. We shifted in our respective seats to face him, and he repeated, "I do; I have a mummy story."

"You do?" Bob asked.

"Well," Jennifer said, "I'm sure we'd all love to hear your story, Nicholas."

"Why don't you come a bit closer?" Kappa offered, but Nicholas made no effort to move.

"You have a mummy story?" Fiona asked, to which Nicholas nodded vigorously in reply. "Yes," he said, "yes, I think you'd have to call it that."

Possessed by a sudden impulse, I asked, "Would you tell us your story, Nicholas?" which appeared to be the cue for which he had been waiting: he began to speak, his voice scraping like a machine that had been but seldom used for an exceedingly long time. It strengthened, his voice, as he continued speaking; at the end of the hour and a half, or perhaps it was two hours, his story took, it sounded almost pleasant, the kind of voice that would have been at home delivering lectures to large groups of students at a university. The story he told would not have found a home at a university, however: it was the kind of story that is suited to a February night in an old house with a strong storm howling off the ocean. When his tale was completed, we retired to bed without much comment. I do not think any of us slept soundly that night; I know I did not. In the dark, I lay beside my fiancée listening to the wind moaning at our window, to the ocean smashing itself on to the beach, and when at last I slept I dreamed of a dark island, and gnarled hands reaching up, out of the water, to choke me.

II

This happened twenty-five years ago (Nicholas said). Immediately after, and for years, I thought the memory of it would never fade. I was sure the memory would never fade: it was burned into my brain. But the surface on to which it was burned has worn away over the last quarter-century, and now the memory doesn't seem as deeply engraved.

I was at the University of Aberdeen on a faculty exchange program. I was supposed to be delivering weekly lectures and meeting with students for tutorial sessions, but I was able to pass the bulk of those duties off on a bright young assistant someone at the university, probably the department chair, had decided to assign me. His name was Bruce; as I recall, he was from Greenock, a town on the west coast. Bruce delivered my lectures, which was to say he gave lectures he had researched and written and I told him I had read and approved, and Bruce took care of my tutorials. He was very eager. I was, too: I was using the free time Bruce allowed me to make trips all over the country to do research for a book I was writing on the Viking presence in Scotland, a subject I considered, and still do, vastly understudied. I would leave the university for anywhere from a day to a week at a time—well, I was away for a week only once, and that was to take part in a dig on Skye that an old friend of mine from undergrad was running. Nothing disastrous ever happened while I was gone, and I thought Bruce would benefit from all the experience.

When I returned from a trip, I spent a day organizing my notes, then another couple of days writing. I wrote from eight in the morning till four in the afternoon, stopping for a half-hour lunch some time between eleven and one, depending on how the writing was proceeding. At four, I pushed my chair away from the typewriter and left my cold flat for a warm pub, usually one just down the street called The Tappit Hen. Most days, Bruce would join me to fill me in on how the latest lecture or tutorial had gone. I would nod at whatever he told me, not really listening to him, and say, "Sounds like you're doing fine." This pleased him what seemed to me an inordinate amount. I was flattered, yes, but I was also annoyed, maybe more annoyed than flattered. A number of significant discoveries concerning the Viking role in British history had broken in the last couple of years, and I had not been involved, not even remotely, in any of them. I had only been aware one of them was in progress. The picture of myself I saw in Bruce's broad freckled face reminded me acutely how far my reality was from his ideal.

Bruce was with me when the man from MI-5 pulled up a stool at the table. I assume he was from MI-5; I didn't ask and he didn't volunteer the information. He was affiliated with some type of intelligence operation, of that much I was sure. His skin was bad, his teeth were bad, and he wore his hair in a crew cut. He was carrying an old briefcase that he swung up on to the table and unsnapped, but did not open. He verified my identity, did not bother with Bruce's, and gave his name as Green. There were no handshakes. He had sought me out, Green said, because he thought I might be able to help him. He propped open his briefcase and withdrew from it a large envelope which he slid across the table to me, asking me to have a look at its contents and tell him what I thought.

The envelope held a dozen or so large black-and-white photographs. The first few were of an island, not a very large one from the look of it, a rocky beach and a couple of hills. There was a shape on top of one of the hills, the one to the right in the picture: what looked like a stone column. My guess was correct: the next photos showed a tall, narrow column that was covered from top to bottom in runes. A couple of the pictures were clear and close enough for me to have a good look at some of the runes, and when I did my heart started to knock in my chest. I had not seen runes like these before: there were certain family resemblances to runes I knew from parts of Eastern Norway, enough for me to be able to read a couple of words and phrases here and there, but there were also striking variations, and more than a few characters that were completely new, unprecedented. You may be surprised to hear that not once did I doubt these pictures' authenticity, but that was the case. I looked at Green and asked him where this was.

"So you're interested?" he asked. I said I was, and he told me that the island in these photographs was located north-northwest of the Shetlands, an hour and a half's boat ride from the nearest human habitation. The place was called Skua Island, and if I thought that arti-fact of any archaeological significance, he and his employers—his term—were prepared to send me there to study it within two weeks, as soon as school let out for Christmas holiday.

Of course I was suspicious. People don't just approach you in a pub and offer to pay your way to unearthing a potentially historic find. Did I say unearthing? Yes: that was what one of the segments of writing I could read said, that there was something buried underneath this column, something I immediately thought might be the remains of a nobleman or hero. Even if what lay below the column wasn't that excit-ing, the column itself was: among the runes were characters that I thought I recognized as ancient Greek, and a couple that resembled pictographs I had seen on scrolls on display at the Met, in New York, in the Egyptian wing. I saw myself invited to lecture at Oxford, at the Sorbonne, on my earth-shaking discovery. And if that discovery had been arranged and financed by an intelligence organization, what difference did that make? I had heard of such partnerships in the past; it was impossible to go very far in the field in any direction without encountering them: a team was provided generous funding to go to Peru, or Morocco, or Indonesia, and in exchange all they had to do was answer a few questions on their return, plot out the route they had taken through the mountains on a map, share their photographs of the capital, the airport. It's been the way of the archaeological world since at least the Victorians, probably longer. Undoubtedly, I was needed on the island as a cover, a front for whatever operation required its use. Perhaps they wanted to monitor the movements of Soviet submarines in the North Atlantic. If we could help each other, I saw no harm in it.

So I agreed, and even engaged to have Bruce accompany me as a reward for his slave labor. The morning after the last day of classes, the two of us were flown in a small plane from Aberdeen to the Shetlands, where we were introduced to the rest of our crew, eleven men whose posture and crew cuts bespoke their military associations as well as any uniform would have. I don't remember most of their names, only the leader's, Collins, whom I later heard the men address as "Major," and another, Joseph—I'm not sure if that was his first or last name—and a third, Ryan. Collins was older, by ten years at least, than his men, in his early- to mid-thirties. He was short and stocky, and his eyes were green and sharp. All the gear I had requested he had procured and had stored on board the fishing ship that had been hired to ferry us to the island. One thing I will say for the military: they are efficient. We ate lunch on the ship as it rode out of port.

By then it was three o'clock, and already the sky was darkening. I don't know if any of you have been that far north in the winter (Bob, I know you've been to Iceland, but wasn't that in the summer?), but the sun only puts in an appearance for a few hours a day, the fewer the closer to the Arctic Circle you venture. It goes without saying that the sea was rough. Rough! It was a heap of grey slabs heaving around us. Despite the pills we had swallowed with our lunches, Bruce and I were soon hanging over the ship's side, our lunches offerings to the sea. None of our companions seemed much affected. I remember that trip as a succession of flights and drops, the deck see-sawing beneath our feet, the ship's engine throbbing as it scaled one grey hill then slid down another, the waves striking the bow with a great hollow boom. We made better time than the season should have allowed, and it was just over an hour after we left port that Skua Island rose to our left. Ryan pointed it out to me, but my eyes already had found it. It wasn't more than a couple of hills that seemed barely taller than the waves swelling around us. Even given the hour and the failing light, the place seemed unusually dark. I searched the hill crests and located the column on the hill to the left, which meant that the photograph Green had shown me had been shot from the other side of the island. It was to there that we made our way. Seen from above, the island resembled a horseshoe, the opening facing north and forming a bay that was only a little less choppy than the sea. The ship dropped anchor in the bay, and Bruce and I and the eleven soldiers packed our gear into bright yellow inflatable rafts that we rowed to shore. As we approached the beach, a great cloud of black-backed gulls, really, a surprising number for so small an island, rose into the wind, shrieking furiously. It's an enormous bird, the black-backed gull; as we pulled up on the beach, the flock hung there overhead screaming at us for what seemed a long time, before veering away.

The ship waited for us to land, then raised anchor and headed for home. In a week, it would be back to collect us. I had wanted longer, two weeks minimum with the possibility of a third should the need arise, but seven days was the best offer Green claimed to be empowered to make. So once we had carried our rafts across the beach, up and over a rise, up to the relative shelter of one of the hills, while Bruce and the men struck camp, I dug a flashlight out from a bag and set off for the column. I wanted to see it. The ground was soft, spongy: peat bog, covered with moss. The hill wasn't especially steep, but there was what felt like a hurricane-strength arctic wind blowing against me as I climbed, and by the time I reached the summit, such as it was, and the column, my face felt as if it had been peeled off.

The column was as tall as I was, a foot or so wide, struck from what appeared to be grey granite. I traced the flashlight beam up and down it, over the tightly bunched runes descending from its rounded top to a point beneath the ground's surface. I circled it, slowly, not caring that my face was not even numb any more, thinking about the men who had raised and carved it, about whatever they had buried underneath it. I knew little of them: I could venture a few educated guesses but I would remain largely in the dark until I had deciphered these runes and seen what the column covered; even then, there would be much I would not know. But standing there in front of their handiwork, the stars already glittering in the sky, I felt close to those strange men to an extent I had not experienced before, so much so that I would not have been surprised to have turned around and found one of them standing behind me, wrapped in a great fur cape. The secrets I was poised to uncover filled my head, as did the lectures waiting for me to deliver them at Cambridge, Berkeley. The wind was finally too much for such revelry, however, so I quickly made my way back down to camp.

As I did, I thought of my father. I don't know if I ever told you about him, Bob; I don't think so. He had owned a hardware store in Ann Arbor when I was a child. Never terribly successful, he had slid into bankruptcy not too long after my mother died, my first year at Harvard. He had held a series of low-paying, low-skills jobs over the next couple of years, then wandered in front of the minister's Chrysler one unlucky Saturday afternoon. He had lingered in the hospital long enough for me to make the trip out to Michigan to sit by his bedside as he died. My older sister—her husband, actually—had to pay for the funeral and the tombstone. At some point in the next two days of standing around the funeral home, shaking the hands of people I hadn't seen in ten years or didn't remember, I had promised myself, pledged myself, that my life was not going to follow the same trajectory as his. I was not going to struggle at society's margins until the designated car arrived to strike me down. At other people's funerals, especially the funerals of those who are close to us, it's natural to think of our own funerals, our deaths, and I vowed that mine would be different from this drab, sparsely attended affair with which my father was sent to his eternal reward. When I died, people would sit up and take notice at my passing. I would be remembered. Sliding into my sleeping bag that first night on the island, on the brink of discovery, I thought I was at last on my way to realizing that pledge.

We were up and at the site early the next morning, while it still was dark. The wind had abated from the night before, but only somewhat; we stood with our backs to it as much as we could. Green had told me I could have seven men at my disposal, and seven men I had. I didn't see where the others went, nor did I care. I had decided to push ahead and excavate the column and whatever lay beneath it, a move I described to myself as bold but which was really premature, if not foolish, before I had deciphered the runes. But it was a move I felt Green's time constraints compelled me to. The men worked swiftly and well, including Collins, mostly under Bruce's supervision, as I copied down the column's inscriptions into a notebook that I pored over in our tent later that night, surrounded by all the dictionaries of ancient languages I owned or had been able to procure in the time before our trip. The first order of business was to remove the column, which the men accomplished with what seemed remarkable ease within a day and a half. Among their other skills, they appeared to have had some training as engineers; perhaps that was why they had been selected for this trip. Perhaps it was part of the reason, anyway. The column descended another two feet into the ground; when it was out and lying on a blue tarpaulin, I spent the end of that afternoon and the beginning of the following morning inspecting the cavity that had held it before giving the go-ahead to start digging. Within five minutes of that command, none other than Bruce himself made our first discovery.

It was a sword, wrapped in the remnants of a cloth that melted when the air struck it. It was unlike any Viking weapon with which I was familiar, and I knew them all. Its rusted blade was easily a yard long. The hilt had been struck in the shape of a bird, its opened beak holding the blade, its outspread wings forming the exaggeratedly wide guard, its body the grip, and its talons the pommel. Through the peat clotted around the pommel, I saw bright green: scraping it clean with my fingers revealed an enormous emerald, clutched in the bird's claws. The style of the metalwork was completely foreign to me, as was the bird it was supposed to represent. It was no bird of prey, which is what you would expect for a sword. Joseph recognized it, however; it was a bonxie, a skua, the seagull-like bird from which this island had taken its name. Dreadful fierce birds, he said, especially when they were nesting. They would fly straight for you if you wandered in among their nests, peck your eyes out.

You can imagine my excitement, which, to be fair, seemed to be shared by all the men, and not just Bruce. Each of them wanted to see the sword, to hold it. Here was history come up from out of the ground, and they had been present for it. Although the sky was clouding over with the advance forces of a storm that had been approaching steadily from the south since sunrise, we continued the dig. Down a foot and a half from our first find, our second took almost another hour to come to light; once again, it was Bruce whose shovel uncovered it. His work had revealed part of a human body, a shoulder, the skin dark, shrunken, and leathery from having been held for who knew how long in the peat bog. The rest of us converged on Bruce's find, and I began directing the excavation. In a short time, the shoulder was revealed to be connected to an arm and a torso, and that torso to a head and another arm and to two legs. We did our best not to handle the body, clearing out space on either side of it so that we could stoop to examine it. By now, the sky was completely dark, and our flashlights out and on. The rain was spattering, and threatening to do worse imminently. The men shining their flashlights down into the hole, I knelt to see what we had, Bruce to my left.

It was a woman, her skin dark oak in color and pulled tight around her bones by the relentless action of the bog. Her throat had been cut, that was the first thing I noticed; you could see the ragged space where a knife had been dragged across it. Neither very tall nor very big, she was wearing a short, plain, coarsely woven tunic. Her arms were bound together behind her back, and her feet were bound as well, both with leather straps that had worn well. Her face—there was something wrong with her face; even allowing for the effects of the peat bog on it, her face appeared to have been disfigured, particularly around the cheeks and eyes, where dull bone shone through, as if she had been struck by a knife, or a club or axe. Her nose was largely gone, apparently torn off. Her jaws were slightly parted; her eye sockets filled with brackish water, her braided hair woven with peat fibers.

Years after this, Bob, you sent me a collection of Seamus Heaney's poems, *North*. Your inscription said that I would enjoy the poems because Heaney, too, was doing archaeology. I didn't know he had written about the Irish bog mummies, so until I read the book, which wasn't for months, I resented what I thought was a too-glib comparison on your part. Once I opened the collection, however, and started reading, I found I couldn't stop. I read and reread those poems. There was one in particular I kept returning to, called "Strange Fruit"; I read it until I had memorized it, and then I mumbled the words in my sleep. It was a description of a girl's decapitated head, which it compared to "an exhumed gourd." Heaney wrote of the head's "leathery beauty," its "eyeholes black as pools," and his words returned me to that hole in the peat, to that woman's body lying slightly curled, seven flashlight beams wavering on it. I wasn't sure what she was doing there: she might have been a sacrifice sent to accompany an important personage on his journey into the afterlife, but in that case she should have been both better dressed and closer to the man she was to join. Her garb, her bound hands and feet, the damage to her face, strongly hinted that she had been executed, punished for one crime or another, possibly adultery, possibly witchcraft, possibly murder. Yet if that was the case, then why had she been buried under this monument and strange sword? You wouldn't mark a criminal's grave in such a way.

Before we could investigate any further, the hole we had dug and cleared began to fill with water. It welled up quickly; from where I was crouched, I could have sworn it started from the gash in the woman's neck, pouring out of it in a thick stream. Bruce and I scrambled to escape the hole, the soldiers catching our arms and hauling us up and out. In a matter of seconds, our find was submerged in water so brackish our flashlights could distinguish nothing beneath its swirling surface. At almost the same moment, the clouds assembled overhead unleashed a deluge so fierce it left very little beyond Bruce, who was standing next to me, visible. There was no recourse: we would have to retreat to camp and wait till tomorrow to continue our work. At least, I reflected as we trudged down the hill, heads down against the rain, the water would preserve the body for us.

That night, I worked at further decoding the column's text, but found it difficult not to become distracted speculating on the sword lying on a towel beside my sleeping bag, or the woman lying underwater at the top of the hill. Bruce and I spent quite a bit longer than we should have trading suppositions, imagining explanations, and when I closed my notebook and sank down to sleep, I had accomplished much less than I had intended. With the possibility of more awaiting our discovery, however, I was less distressed over my lack of progress than I otherwise might have been. As long as the site continued to yield results, the translation could wait; if it came to that, there was no reason for me not to work on it when I returned to Aberdeen. It was a history, dating from when I was not sure, but guesstimated some time before the first millennium. It recounted a terrible plague that had afflicted the communities of all the islands, a geographic vagary that seemed to encompass at least the Shetlands, the Orkneys, the Outer Hebrides, and possibly the Inner Hebrides and parts of mainland Scotland itself. This plague was no mere ordinary sickness, but had especially malevolent associations: it had either escaped or been set loose or been sent from a place deep under Middle-Earth, a place connected to a god or person, perhaps a sorcerer, with whom I was unfamiliar, but who was or was associated with the worm. His name was represented by a pictograph of a circle broken at about two o'clock, for which I could find no reference, however tentative. The plague's effects were reported as horrible, but left unspecified.

The next morning, the rain had passed and everything changed. Bruce shook me awake to tell me that something terrible had occurred during the night and the storm, and Collins wanted to see me. In reply to my questions, he answered that he didn't know what was the matter, but the Major seemed agitated, quite agitated. I dressed hurriedly, and found Collins standing beyond our cluster of tents, on the other side of the rise separating us from the beach, beside a pair of blue tarpaulins like the one on which we had laid the column two days before. The tarps had been weighted down at their corners with large rocks to prevent them from fluttering away from the shapes they stretched over. There was a pair of large brownish birds standing beyond the tarps that I thought I recognized as skuas. Greeting Collins, I asked him what the problem was. "There are two of my men under there," he said, jerking his thumb at the tarps. "They're dead." He made no move to pull back the tarps, nor did I request him to.

I was shocked, and said so. Aside from the fact that both men's necks had been broken, their heads wrenched almost backwards, and their eyes gouged out (although that was probably the birds, the skuas, which had found the bodies before he did), Collins didn't know what had happened. He assumed that the aggressor, his word, had ambushed the first man while he had been standing guard, then waited by his body for the second man to come to relieve him. He himself had not heard a thing, although given the storm blowing that would have been more difficult. Of course I hadn't heard anything, and told him so, which didn't seem to surprise him. Who could have done this? I asked him, and despite his reply that he hadn't the faintest idea, something in his answer, the way he gave it as if it were a scripted line he had been forced to deliver without having had sufficient time to rehearse it, made me think that he had a very good idea who was behind this. Perhaps the specifics were a little dim, but I realized that he thought we had been discovered, or I should say that he had been discovered, he and his men, by whomever they had come up here to observe. If that were the case, then whoever had assassinated these two men was most likely still on the island, waiting for night's early fall to finish his—or their—work. When Collins told me that he was going to have to ask me to remain by my tent for a little while this morning, until his men had had a chance to scour the island, I did not protest but said of course, I understood. If this man and his orders were all that was going to be standing between me and a team of Soviet commandos, I thought it wisest not to antagonize him.

Thus, I was back at my translation much sooner than I had anticipated, while Collins sent out two two-man patrols to sweep the island, one heading east, the other west, from our camp to meet on the opposite side of the island, where they would advance together to sweep the hills before returning to camp. Throughout, they would maintain radio silence. Collins, the men, were not dressed any differently than they had been the day before; they had not changed into camouflage and berets at the first sign of trouble; but there was something different about them, and it was only after I had been seeing the hands held in the large jacket pockets, or inside the jackets to one side or the other, that I realized they were all armed, with pistols and submachine guns, and were keeping those arms close at hand, ready for use. They were more tense, but I could hardly fault them for that: I was more tense.

Bruce kept with the men, watching for the patrols' return, while I did my best to apply myself to the column's strange characters. When the patrols were not back within a couple of hours, I was not worried: even islands as small as this one could contain hidden caves, gullies, chasms, that might lengthen a search of it considerably. When the patrols had not shown by lunch, Bruce was noticeably anxious; I told him to relax, it might be hours yet. The translation was no less difficult, but I began to find the rhythm of it, so that even though large patches of it remained unclear, the broad outlines were beginning to swim into view. During this terrible plague, the peoples of the islands had sought high and low, near and far, for relief and found none. There was a considerable list of all the important people who had gone to their graves with the thing, denied the glory of a warrior's death in battle through the machinations of the one who had unleashed it. At last, the leaders of—I thought it was the Shetlands, but it could have been the Orkneys—had decided to seek the aid of a wizard whose name I couldn't quite fix; the characters appeared to be Greek but weren't yielding any intelligible sound; who lived in the Faroe Islands and who was something of a dubious character, having dealings with all sorts of creatures—human, divine, and in-between—whom it was best to give a wide berth. Driven by their desperation, the leaders dispatched an envoy imploring his aid. Twice he refused them, but on the third request his heart softened and he agreed to assist them. He journeyed to the islands on a boat that did not touch the water, or that moved as swiftly as a bird across the water, and when he arrived he wasted no time: disclosing the supernatural origin of the plague, he told the leaders that strong measures would be needed to defeat it. He, the wizard, could summon all the sickness to himself, but he could not purge it from the earth. In order for that to be accomplished, he would require a vessel, by which, as the leaders quickly saw, he meant a human being.

By now, the sun had set, and neither patrol had appeared. I was uneasy; Bruce appeared to be barely containing a full-fledged panic attack: he ducked in and out of the tent half a dozen times in fifteen minutes, until I closed my notebook and went with him to join Collins and the others. Collins and two of the men, Joseph and Ryan, were crouched outside his tent; I presumed the other two were standing guard somewhere off in the gathering darkness. The weapons were out and on display now: each man carried a black submachine gun slung over his shoulder. They were engaged in a quiet conversation that ceased as I drew near. Squatting beside them, I asked if there had been any sign of either patrol, and was not surprised when Collins shook his head from side to side. Were we going to continue to wait for them? As of now, that was our plan. Should we perhaps think about radioing for reinforcements, that kind of thing? Collins fixed me with his sharp green eyes. "Reinforcements?" he repeated. "Why, Doctor, you make it sound as if this were some kind of military operation. My men and I are out here to assist you in your excavation and analysis of objects of priceless value to our national heritage."

"Then why those?" I asked, pointing to the guns.

"No harm in being prudent," Collins replied.

"Ah, yes, prudent," I said. Well, if we weren't going to call for reinforcements, since, I hastened to add, we were only an archaeological expedition and, as he had said, what possible need could archaeologists have for reinforcements? Perhaps we could shorten the length of our expedition?

That was a decision Collins would leave for the morning.

In that case, I said, would he be so kind as to provide Bruce and me with samples of the prudence—I gestured at the guns—he and his men had seen fit to exercise? Things being what they were, it seemed prudent for all of us to be prudent.

He did not think that was prudent, Collins said immediately. If Bruce and I were discovered, he did not say by whom, with any kind of weapon it would go much worse for us than if we were unarmed.

"You forget," I said, "I have the sword."

Collins laughed, and said if any Vikings landed on the beach he would call on me to lead the charge against them. In the meantime, he would post Ryan outside our tent, to ease our minds. Never let it be said that the British did not value their scholars, even if those scholars were American.

And then a sudden smell flooded my nostrils, a thick stench full of bog rot and rancid flesh. I coughed, fighting down the bile rushing up my throat, and Collins, Joseph, and Ryan gagged. I opened my mouth to ask what it was, and for a second the smell was in my mouth, a vile taste coating my teeth, my tongue, my throat. I thought I was going to vomit, and then, as quickly as it came, the smell was gone. I breathed deeply, and looked at Collins. I could not think what to say, and neither, apparently, could he. We stared at each other for what felt like minutes. "Well," I said at length, "I guess I'll turn in."

"Good," he said. "Do that."

I left Collins with a request that should the patrols return I would be notified, regardless of the hour, to which he agreed. Neither my work nor my sleep was interrupted that night. Sitting cross-legged in my tent, the notebook open on my lap, reaching for this dictionary, then that dictionary, moving ahead a line only to have to move back two to reconsider the way I had rendered this word, or that, making brilliant leaps and worse-than-obvious blunders, I tried not to think about whoever was waiting out there in the dark, whoever had seized those men's heads in his hands and twisted, swift and hard, so that their necks had snapped audibly and they had fallen down dead, their eyes food for the skuas. I tried not to wonder what he or they had done to the patrols, whether they were lying scattered over the island with their heads wrenched almost backwards, their arms and legs splayed; or had they been knifed? gloved hands clamped over their mouths, the blade drawn across their throats in a single burning stroke; or shot? a bullet spat out of a silencer into an eye, an ear. I tried not to think about any of these deaths being visited on me. I tried to decode more about the island leaders' response to the wizard's demand for a human being to serve as vessel to contain the plague. It appeared they had consented to his request with minimal debate: one man, Gunnar, a landowner of some repute, had refused to have anything to do with such dealings, but that same night the plague fell on him and by morning he was dead; his brains, the history detailed, burst and ran out his ears. After Gunnar, no one else contested the leaders' decision, and Frigga, Gunnar's eldest daughter, was selected by the leaders for the wizard's use. Elaborate preparations were made, several lengthy prayers were addressed to various gods—Odin, Loki, and Hel, goddess of death, among them— and then the wizard called all of the plague to himself, from all the islands he summoned it. It came as, or as if, a cloud of insects so vast it filled the sky, blotting out the sun. Men and women covered their heads in fear; an old woman fell dead from terror of it. The wizard commanded the plague into Frigga, who was lying bound at his feet. At first, it did not obey, nor did it heed the wizard's second command, but on his third attempt his power proved greater and the plague descended into Frigga, streaming into her mouth, her nose, her ears, the huge black cloud lodging itself within her, until the sky was once again clear, the sun shining.

This, however, was not the end. Frigga remained alive; she had become as fierce as an animal, straining against her bonds, gnashing her teeth and growling at the wizard and at the islands' leaders, threatening bloody vengeance. Nonplussed, the wizard had her rowed to the island of the—to Skua Island, where she was put ashore, her feet loosed but her hands still bound. The island was full of the skuas; there to nest, I supposed; and when Frigga, or what had been Frigga, set foot among them, they flew at her fiercely, attacking her unprotected face and eyes with no mercy. Her screams were terrible, heard by all the peoples of all the islands. At last, the birds left her with no face and no eyes, which the wizard said was necessary so that she should go unrecognized among the dead, so that she should be unable to find her way out of the place to which he was going to dispatch her. Half a dozen strong men seized her, for even so injured she was fearfully powerful, and bore her up to the summit of one of the island's hills, where the wizard once more bound her feet and slew her by cutting her throat. The blood that spilled out was black, and one of the men it splashed died on the spot. When all the blood had left her, the wizard ordered her body buried at the summit of the opposite hill, and a stone placed over it as a reminder to all the people of all the islands of what he, (once more that name I couldn't decipher), had done for them, and as a warning not to disturb this spot, for now that the girl's body had been used as a vessel for returning (that symbol, the broken circle)'s evil to him, it would be a simple matter for him to return Frigga to her body full of his power, and if he did, she would be awful. He, the wizard, would place a sword between the stone and the girl that would keep her in her place, and he would write the warning on the stone himself, so that all could read it. Woe be to he who disturbed the sword: not only would the wrath of the one who had sent the plague fall on him, but the wrath of the wizard as well, and he would lose to the reborn girl that which she herself had lost, by which I assumed was meant his face.

It was late when I completed the preliminary translation; Bruce had long since retired to sleep. You might think I would have experienced some trepidation, some anxiety, over what I had brought to light, but you would be mistaken. Despite the hour, I was exhilarated: in a matter of days, I had rendered into reasonably intelligible English a text written in a language whose idiosyncrasies would have cost many another scholar weeks if not months of effort to overcome. Yes, there was a curse, a pair of curses, threatened against whoever disturbed the site, but such curses were commonplace; indeed, I would have been more surprised had there been no curse, no warning of dire consequences. Melodramatic films aside, when all was said and done, King Tut's curse had been nothing more than a self-fulfilling prophecy. If I was worried about anything, it was the team of Soviet commandos creeping ever closer to us, knives clenched between their teeth, waiting for the precise moment to take revenge on us for whatever operations Collins and his men had been performing. The text on the column I judged an elaborately coded narrative, possibly intended to justify an actual event, the killing of the girl we had discovered, through recourse to supernatural explanations.

I was not particularly moved by the story I had translated. I don't think it will surprise you to hear that: you're academics; you understand the idea of professional distance. You might be interested to learn the number of people unable to maintain a similar distance. I have encountered them in my classrooms, generally in my introductory courses, and at the public lectures I have delivered, usually at the request of a museum. Perhaps you have dealt with them, too. These people find the notion of the kind of thing that happened to Frigga having occurred in their country unduly upsetting. That such actions are performed in other places, by other people, they readily accept; as long as it's foreigners, they are not troubled. Suggest, however, that, as it were, someone's hundred-times great-grandfather was a participant at a human sacrifice, and it's an affront, as if you had accused the person her or himself of having held the knife and made the cut. Some try to suggest that the people who performed these acts were foreigners, in this case, Vikings as opposed to true Scots, until I remind them that those foreigners are their ancestors, that the Vikings became Scots. By the time Frigga was slain, the two cultures were already fairly integrated. I imagine it's shame that's at the root of the sometimes surprisingly intense denials I have met with. There is no need for it: there is no culture that is innocent. In most cases, you don't have to dig particularly long or hard to unearth similar events. We are never as far from such things as we would like to think.

I unzipped the tent's flap and stepped out into the night air to stretch legs long past cramped and unbend a back in danger of remaining permanently crooked. To my relief, Ryan was still on watch. There had been, he informed me, still no sign of either patrol; come morning, he thought the Major was going to call for someone to come fetch us. He, Ryan, was sorry that I would have to abandon the dig, which I assured him he needn't be. Even the little we had accomplished was something, and there was always the possibility of returning at a later date, during the summer, maybe, when it was warmer, and light for most of the day. If he wanted to join us, I said, I would be happy to hold a place for him. He thanked me but thought he had best decline, since come summer there was a good chance he would be quite a distance from here. And good riddance at that, he added. I laughed and said I completely understood. Stretching myself a final time, I told Ryan I would see him in the morning.

"Let's hope so, sir," he said.

Before I fell asleep, I thought again about my father, about his death. I remembered the suit we had buried him in, a cheap, worn and faded, brown polyester suit that was at least ten years out of fashion; I remembered the tie we had given the funeral home for him, a red, white, and blue adaptation of the Stars and Stripes I had given him when I was twelve for Fathers' Day and that he had continued to claim was his favorite tie; I remembered the small group of mourners at the funeral service, barely sufficient to fill the first three pews of the church. At the time, I had found all of it maddeningly pathetic; now I thought that at least my father had had a funeral. It seemed likely I was going to die out here alone and who knew what was going to be done with my body? Stripped and set out for the birds, perhaps, or my pockets stuffed with rocks and submerged, an unexpected bounty for the crabs and fish. At least there was a place with my father's name on it and the dates of his birth and death, a place to which you could drive on a Sunday with your children, as my sister sometimes did. My monument would be an island few knew and even fewer had visited.

I slept unexpectedly late, waking with the sunrise. I suppose I expected the morning to bring, if not my own death, or Bruce's, news of the deaths of others, of one or several or even all of the men during the night. That was not the case: although the four men who had left camp yesterday morning had not yet returned, and did not seem likely to, the seven of us had survived, and the chill, bright air was warm with the relief bubbling up out of us. Overhead, a skua cried out, and I took the sound for a good omen. Collins was no less relieved than the rest of us, but had decided to take no chances, radioing for the boat to return for us. We had two hours, and then we would be leaving Skua Island. No one, least of all me, was upset by this. Maybe, I thought as I hurried to my tent and stuffed my notebook, pen, and assorted dictionaries into my duffel bag, the Soviets had not intended to liquidate the lot of us, only enough to disrupt the mission, cause Collins to pull up stakes and leave sooner than he had intended to; if that was the case, they had succeeded. Or maybe one or both of the patrols had managed to wound their assailants mortally even as they themselves were killed. A day raid was not impossible, but unlikely: obviously, whatever force had been deployed on the island was too small to storm the camp, or it would have done so already, and attacking during daylight would not improve its chances in a firefight. It did occur to me that the Soviets might be waiting for all of us to board the ship to torpedo it, but I thought that scenario unlikely: to destroy a civilian vessel in its territorial waters was to risk consequences far in excess of whatever small benefit or satisfaction our deaths might bring. Having come through the night, I felt strangely invincible, the way, I imagine, one of Beowulf's men must have felt after having lived through that awful night in Heorot.

Fueled by that sensation of invincibility, I decided I must return to the hilltop to take photographs of the column and the mummy. I had copied down the runes but I had no evidence of the object they had covered, as I had no evidence of what that object had covered. All I had was the sword, which, while intriguing, required the column and the mummy to establish its full significance. The risk of this past day, I

thought, the lying in my tent waiting to die, would have been for nothing, if I couldn't bring back sufficient proof of the island's archaeological significance to ensure funding to mount a return come summer. Of
course it was irrational, contradictory, but in a remarkably short space
of time—the time it took to shove two pairs of socks and an extra pair
of jeans into a duffel bag—I had convinced myself that if we had
survived the night then we were free and clear of danger, and if we were
free and clear of danger, then there was no reason not to go to the site.
When I broached the subject to him, Bruce was game for running up
the hill, snapping a dozen quick photographs, and running back down;
as for Collins, he said that while he advised against our leaving the
camp, he would not stop us from doing so. He also would not give us
any of his men to accompany us, and he would not hold the ship for us
if we were not back when it sailed into the bay. He appeared neither
surprised nor concerned; his mind, I assume, occupied by other things.
I thanked him and returned to the tent, which Bruce, ever efficient,
was in the process of flattening and rolling up. I was searching through
my bag when Ryan walked up beside me and, before I realized what he
was doing, slid an automatic pistol into the right pocket of my coat. "If
anything happens," he said, smiling as if he were sharing a joke or a
pleasant observation, "you switch off the safety, hold it in one hand and
steady with the other, and line up the front sights with the back. It's got
quite a kick to it, so be ready. If me and the lads hear anything, we'll try
to do what we can." I nodded, and he strolled away to join the rest of his
colleagues as they continued packing up the camp and loading it into
the yellow inflatable rafts.

Bruce and I made the top of the hill without incident. There were a
trio of skuas roosting on the column, but they flapped off as we
approached. The hole was still full of black water, I saw, but once more
thought it would be good for preserving our find. Bruce snapped
pictures of the column lying on its blue tarp while I eased myself down
into the pool beneath whose surface our mummy, our Frigga, as I had
started to think of her, lay. We would raise her, which I thought could

be accomplished with minimal damage, set her on the ground, photograph her, and return her to the water. The water was almost to the tops of my boots, but only almost, for which I was grateful. Balancing on my left foot, I brought the right forward, feeling for the body. I touched nothing. Apparently, she was further away from this side of the hole than I had remembered. I advanced a step, repeated the procedure, and again felt nothing. Confused, I tried a third time, and a fourth, and then I was at the other side of the hole. I turned around and ran through the process again, with no more success. The hole was empty: someone had removed Frigga. I looked up at Bruce to speak, but was stopped by a sound: the popping of firecrackers, gunfire, and brief, high cries that sounded like those of birds but were not. His face paled, and I felt the blood drain from mine. Struggling up the side of the hole, I felt in my coat pocket for the pistol and, my fingers closing around it, withdrew it as Bruce caught the top of my coat and helped me the rest of the way up. The sight of the gun startled him; he had not seen Ryan slip it to me nor had I told him. For another five, maybe ten, seconds, the distant gunfire continued, two or three submachine guns stuttering at the same time, and the cries, too, before all of it ceased. It did not start again.

Although, for reasons more of irrational panic than any real knowledge, I did not believe what I said, I told Bruce that undoubtedly we had heard Collins and the men dealing with whoever had been plaguing us. All the same, there was no harm in being careful: thus, attempting to conceal ourselves behind the scant cover afforded by slight rises of ground and solitary boulders, we descended the hill back to camp, myself in the lead with the pistol held out in front of me, Bruce following. I was filled with an almost overwhelming sense of dread, an emotion that partook equally of hanging over the toilet knowing you were going to vomit and in so doing plunge yourself into stomach-twisting illness, and of watching your father's chest sink for the final time, standing on the brink of a plunge of a very different, but no less real, kind. The camp was quiet as we sighted it, and as we drew nearer,

I saw why: everyone was dead, Collins, Ryan, Joseph, the two others. Ryan was collapsed on a yellow raft, and I could not understand what was wrong with his body until I realized that his head was turned around backwards, his eye sockets empty and bloody, blood trailing from his nose, his open mouth. Collins was on the ground next to him, face down in a wide pool of blood still spreading from where his left arm had been torn from his body and tossed aside, where it lay with a pistol still clenched in its hand. I did my best not to look directly at either of them, because I was afraid that if I did I would join Bruce, who was sobbing behind me. The remaining three men lay with one of the other rafts: a glance that lasted too long showed me another of them with his neck broken, one, I think it was Joseph, with both his arms torn off, the third with a gaping red hole punched into his chest. All their eyes appeared to have been gouged out. There was blood everywhere, flecks, streaks, puddles of red splashed across the scene. From where we were standing on the hill, I could see over the rise beyond the camp to the bay and sea, both of which were empty.

"What happened?" Bruce said. "What happened to them?"

I told him I didn't know and I didn't: no team of Soviet commandos, however brutal, however ruthless, would have done this. Overhead, a small flock of skuas, a half-dozen or so, circled, crying. This, this was gratuitous, this was—I didn't know how to describe it to myself; it was outside my vocabulary.

As was what I saw next.

There, running toward us from over the rise beyond the camp, was Frigga. For a moment that stretched on elastically, I was sure my mind had broken, that the superabundant carnage spread out in front of me had snapped it with the ease with which you snap a match between your fingers. So, I thought, this is insanity, as I watched her race closer, her back hunched, her braid flapping from side to side like the tail of an animal, her sightless eyes pointed at me, her mouth open wide, her arms stretched out to either side of her, her fingers hooked. Amazing, I thought, what detail. Then Bruce saw her too and started screaming, which was all it took for me to know I was not insane, and even as I knew this I felt a tremendous regret, because I was not sure my mind could support Frigga running across the ground and everything that implied, and I felt a tremendous fear, my gut squeezing. I leveled the pistol, aligning the sights on Frigga's chest, and squeezed the trigger. The gun roared, almost kicking itself from my hands, but I held on to it and fired again, and again, and again. I could see the fabric of her tunic pucker where the bullets struck with what at this distance should have been sufficient force to knock a big man sprawling with several large holes in him. I fired again before she was on me, striking me on the side of the head with a kindling-thin arm that connected like a heavy club in the hands of a weightlifter, sweeping me from my feet and sending me rolling down the hill. Everything spun around, and around, and around, then I hit the bundle that was my duffel bag.

On the hillside above, Bruce was screaming. Pushing myself up on my hands, I saw him on his back, Frigga straddling him, one hand at his throat, the other approaching his jaw. My God, I thought, the warning was true: she's going to take his face. She did not care that Bruce had had nothing to do with what had happened to her so long ago: she had suffered, and now someone else could suffer. The pistol had fallen from my grip, but was close; I picked it up, aimed it, and emptied the rest of the clip into Frigga's back. It did not affect her in the least. As Bruce struggled to free her hand from his throat, she dug the thumb of her other hand into his skin and began drawing it along his jaw, blood squirting out as she split his flesh. His screams increased. Enraged, I threw the useless pistol at her. It struck her head and fell to the side, without her noticing. Frantically, I looked about for a weapon, for something that might be of use against her, as her thumb continued its circuit of Bruce's face and his screams continued. Guns were useless, and I doubted explosives—the sword! It had kept her in place for a thousand years: it might be effective. Bruce had rolled it up inside the tent to protect it. The tent was behind my duffel bag; I dropped to my knees and began furiously untying the tent's straps. Bruce's screams continued. I fought with a knot, tore the strap off. I undid the remaining strap, unrolled the tent, shouting for Bruce to hold on. His screams continued. I did not look up. Two pairs of socks, a sweater, where was the sword? There! Swaddled in a blanket I yanked away. There was a tearing sound, like a shirt caught on a nail, and Bruce's screams became a wet, choked gurgle. I looked up, the sword in my hand, and saw that I was too late: Frigga had taken Bruce's face, peeled it off him the way you might peel an orange, and draped it over her own ruined face. His face gone, his throat split open by her thumb, Bruce was dead. Through the ragged holes in Bruce's face, Frigga's empty sockets gazed at me, and my mind trembled at the sight. In a bound, she had leapt off him, and was running toward me.

I fled. Sword in hand, I ran as fast as I could for the beach, praying that the boat would have made its appearance, that it would be sitting there in the bay and I would be able to swim out to it, leave Frigga behind. Even as the beach came into view, though, and I ran down on to it, slipping and almost falling on a loose rock, and I saw the bay, the sea beyond, and, yes, the ship approaching in the not-too-distant distance, I could hear Frigga's feet clattering across the rocks behind me, feel her hand reaching out to catch my jacket. She was too fast; she was on me: I was going to die here, on the beach, in sight of the ship and salvation; if I were lucky, she would break my neck and be done with me quickly. A tidal wave of rage swelled in my chest, rushing up into my brain, swamping my fear. I was going to die here, on this Godforsaken island, at the hands of a monster I had brought up out of the ground, and no one would know, no one would know any of this, anything. I caught the sword in both hands, stopped, pivoted, and swung it as hard as I could, screaming my throat raw with fury and frustration.

Frigga could not stop in time to avoid me. The blade caught her on the side of the head, cracking it, sending poor Bruce's empty face flying off her. She staggered, and I struck again, bringing the sword down on her right collarbone, breaking it and three of the ribs beneath it, ripping open her leathery skin. She swept at me with her left hand, catching me a glancing blow on the right shoulder that spun me half around; I struck her right arm and heard a bone snap. We were at the water; a wave swept around my boots. I backed into it, Frigga following, her dark face streaked with Bruce's blood. The freezing water rising to my knees, my thighs, I continued back, holding the sword before me. Frigga feinted to the right, then lunged at me, and with a scream I drove the sword straight through her, just under the breastbone, all the way in and out the other side, to the hilt. It pushed through her with the sound of leather tearing. I kept screaming as she stumbled and fell in the water with a splash; I kept screaming as she tried to stand and could not, flailing at the sword impaling her; I kept screaming as I pulled off my coat, tugged off my boots, and swam for the boat. I screamed as if screaming would defeat her. I did not see Frigga sink under the water, a crowd of skuas descending on to it as she did, flapping and crying: that was what the ship captain claimed to have seen. I was still screaming when they pulled me out of the water on to the ship, and when at last I stopped screaming, all I would say, for a week, in reply to whatever question was posed to me, was, "They're dead. They're all dead. She got them. Frigga got them."

Of course, that isn't enough for you. Of course, you want to hear more; you want to know what happened next. It's all right: I would, too. I was put in a hospital, in Edinburgh, in a private room. I saw various doctors, took various medications, and had many interviews with many men, some of them in uniform, some in suits. I told them all the same story I told you. I presume there was an investigation, even several, although apparently Frigga was not found; that was what I was told, at least. No charges of any kind were brought against me; why they would have been, I'm not sure, except that when things go wrong to this magnitude and this many people die, a scapegoat is usually required. I have no idea what explanation was provided Bruce's family, whether his body was returned to them and if so in what state. In the hospital, I tried to compose a letter expressing my sympathy at their loss, but I could not write anything that did not sound too much like a lie, so in the end I sent a generic card that a nurse bought for me. I presume the deaths of Collins, Ryan, Joseph, and the others were assigned an unrelated tragic cause: lost at sea during training maneuvers; killed when their helicopter went down. Eventually, I was released from the hospital, with a generous supply of pills to keep me from waking in the night, screaming. I taught at Aberdeen the following semester, actually delivering my own lectures and running my own tutorials, but I returned home before the last semester, leaving the department in the lurch and not caring that I did. They have not invited me back; I've had no desire to return. My career since then—has been less than it could have been. I—I think I've psychoanalyzed myself sufficiently for one night. I'll leave the reasons for my failure to achieve, whether they be guilt, fear, heredity, a combination of the lot, or none of the above, to your discussion.

I tend to avoid the sea. Had I realized how close this house is to the Atlantic, I most likely would not have come. You told me, Bob, I simply wasn't paying attention. Beside the sound and smell of the ocean, I try to stay busy; when my mind is free, I wonder: Was that final blow sufficient to kill Frigga? Can you even speak of such a thing, is it possible? The birds, the skuas, what were they doing there? Did the deaths of Collins and the men, Bruce's death, satisfy her, or, even now, as we sit here talking, is she making her way toward me? Nights like this, if I'm unwise or unlucky enough to find myself by the sea, I imagine—well, I'm sure you can guess.

Paul Cornell's mummy makes a unique journey to the afterlife. The Niagara Falls Museum he references was the oldest (1827) museum in Canada and did, indeed, house what is probably the mummy of Ramesses I for almost 140 years. In 1998, the museum's contents were sold to a Canadian businessman who sold the Egyptian collection (including the mummies) to the Michael C. Carlos Museum at Emory University in Atlanta, Georgia. The mummy's probable identity was deduced from X-rays, CT scans, skull measurements, and radiocarbon dating. The care and skill used in mummification indicates a high-status or royal individual and the mummy's arms are in a position reserved for royal males of the proper period. There is also a notable physical resemblance to the extremely well-preserved mummies of Seti I (Ramesses' son) and Ramesses II (his grand-son) The museum returned the mummy to Egypt in 2003 as a gift of goodwill and international cultural cooperation. It now resides in the Luxor Museum . . . another unique journey.

Ramesses on the Frontier
Paul Cornell

———

Imagine Pharaoh Ramesses I, first of his dynasty, the father of imperial Egypt, being kept at the Niagara Museum and Daredevil Hall of Fame in Ontario, Canada. Ramesses himself can't. He lies in a stone casket, not his own. Only a rope strung between two sticks stops the casket from being interfered with. A sign nearby proclaims something in livid letters that he can't read. He's been put on display with several others. These include a man with two heads (one of them added post-mortem; Ramesses has looked closely and seen the stitches), an unfortunate with some sort of skin disease that gives him webbing between his fingers, and something with a thick coating of fur, preserved under glass. To be arranged with them annoys Ramesses. One of these things is not like the others, that's what he wants to shout. These are dead bodies that have been defiled. He is . . . well, he's not quite sure what he is right now, but he has the powers of awareness and motion, and these sorry bastards don't.

He keeps wondering if something went wrong with his funeral rites. He's sure his *ka*, which left his body at the moment of death, has been provided with excellent refreshment. And many spells had been written and placed to allow him to deal with the problems of the afterlife. He examined the lists himself, just days before he went to bed for what turned out to be his final sleep. There had been a great rush to get it all done. He'd only been Pharaoh for a few months before his illness, and they'd only made a small tomb as a result, but he'd been told that everything was ready. His son Seti had repeatedly assured him. But here he is, feeling like he's still in his body, but with his body being a . . . well, Ramesses isn't really comfortable thinking about that.

His *ka* certainly left, because he remembers the moment of his death, him looking up at his beautiful son, and darkness moving swiftly in from the world all around his eyes. His *ba*, the record of his ethical efforts, is supposed to have stayed attached to his body until the correct ceremonies were performed, but there's no way to tell if they were, because he's as unaware of his *ba* now as he was in life.

If that new High Priest got that bit wrong, then perhaps that's why he's more like a corpse than an *akh*. This is definitely not what he was expecting.

He's sure that whatever's going on here, he won't be here forever. But time does seem to be stretching on, and nothing much seems to be happening. When he was High Priest, he put the correct religion back in its rightful place. The gods owe him. So what's the hold-up?

It's not just himself he's worried for. It's his people. The nation of the river, the mirror of heaven, depends upon him completing this journey in order for others to follow. He is their ambassador. He changes the way as he passes through it. He makes it easier, like someone who stamps down reeds as they walk through a marsh. The rest of his folk who've died will be backed up by now for . . . well, who knows how long he's been here? The halls have certainly changed during that time, but they might change continually. He walks at night, but he doesn't know if that's every night. He only feels it is night because the mysterious lighting is kept so low, and he has a vague awareness of there being times when it's been brighter.

So that's his situation. He's awake again tonight. He's stuck. And he can't find a god to complain to.

As usual, he cautiously pulls back the lid of the casket, waits for a moment to check that there is only what passes here for silence, and climbs out. He feels the ache in his back. He sighs. He wonders if there is ever, actually, an end to pain. He sometimes thinks that's his punishment, but it's really not much of one, is it? And one should be aware of justice having been done to one, not just wake up in jail none the wiser. When he sent those sun worshippers running, he made damn sure they knew what was being done to them. Don't be such cowards, he bellowed at them, Ra will be back tomorrow, and it's the other gods you should worry about. The people applauded him and threw things at the sun worshippers as they ran from his soldiers. A great day.

Ramesses realizes he's allowed himself to become lost in reverie. Again. This is no good. His mind is a little foggy. But maybe that's only to be expected, considering how far he is from his organs.

He goes for a wander.

He walks through the vast, quiet halls, looking up once more in undiminished awe at the crystal ceiling, the flowing images that are somehow pinned to the walls, put inside frames like important declarations. This building, so reminiscent of a tomb, must be the Duat, the underground world where spirits and gods come and go, which leads to final judgment. The images on the walls are one piece of evidence that points to this theory being correct. What he's seeing there are perhaps those caught on the way, because of his own predicament. He sees the same faces many times. They are mostly faces that are rather like those of Syrians, but paler, which is a bit weird. Perhaps that's just who was coming across when he got here, when the system seized up. It is a little surprising that these unknown races should be involved. That they should be depending on him. But pleasing, in a way. The true religion must be true wherever you go. His river people are ahead in that regard. At least, they are now he's gotten them back on track.

The pale people's clothes are bizarre. Ramesses assumes that their dream selves are being examined alongside their lives. There is no other explanation for the impossible wonders. Whoever these foreigners are, he's pretty sure that if they could, for instance, fly by the use of machines, they would have jealously come and taken the land of the river. He shivers at the thought of how many of them there are, and how strong. He's glad they're dead now, and not about to invade his beloved land. But still, he'll put in a good word for them. They seem fun.

Ramesses moves on.

At the end of the central chamber, there are a series of paintings, rendered to a high degree of detail, most of them oddly not in the colors of life but in blacks and silvers. Perhaps the artist only had those available. They show the great river that must be nearby, the sound of which Ramesses can sometimes hear when the halls are relatively quiet. In the pictures, souls are either in the river, or in containers placed in the river. These are very like the vases that, back in his grave, contain his own internal organs, assuming that new High Priest got that bit right. The pictures show people getting into these containers and being taken out of them. There are a few on display —just the remains of them, with no sign of the soul inside. All of them are pictured in the vicinity of a thing Ramesses has only heard of, but never previously seen: a great downward plunge of water, foam, and rising mist.

He stands there staring up at the perplexing images. What *is* he supposed to do? What is he *missing*?

There are doors that obviously lead outside, but he has put his ear to them, and heard strange blarings and screamings every time he has done so, surely the wailings of those who haven't been allowed into the Duat. One is not supposed to arrive in the Duat and then simply leave. If he could find just one minor god, he could indicate to them that the Pharaoh is here, and they would surely realize that something has gone wrong and remember their obligations. He would be gracious. He would say hey, mistakes happen. They'd be tripping over themselves with an urgent need to put right this terrible *faux pas*.

He stops beside one of the upright walls of crystal and considers himself. He is not what he was. He looks as hollow as he feels, well, as hollow as, actually, he is. His arms are used to resting across his chest now, so accustomed to the position that, whenever he gets up, he fears he will break one of them. His eyes have narrowed to slits, so he looks permanently like he's holding in a laugh, which isn't how he feels at all. His nose, which used to be so fine, looks like it's been broken in a fight. His neck is thin, like that of a strangled goose. At least his temples still remind him of himself. He still has wisps of hair, pushed back from his bald patch. He touches them sometimes. They remind him of touching the head of Seti, of smelling that scalp when the kid was newborn. His own head is that soft now. All that's left of his wrappings, so carefully prepared, are a few rags. They do not preserve his modesty. Not that he's got much to hide. His legs are so thin it's like walking on stilts. His hands are all knuckle. He holds one up and looks at his palm. It resembles papyrus. He is a scroll that has been filled with writing, and is now crisp out of its jar, and yet still he knows too little. No scroll knows the information it contains, he thinks. And all he wants is to be read.

No. He wants to see Seti again. He wants to touch his hair instead of his own.

There is a noise from behind him. He realizes he has been so lost in his thoughts that he hasn't considered the possibility of him not being alone in the halls tonight. This has happened on a couple of previous occasions. The first time he saw the lamps he wanted to stop their owners and question them about where he was and what he could do to continue, but then he saw that those carrying the lamps were of the same people he'd seen on the walls, and realized that they must share his predicament, rather than be responsible for it, and not wishing to be weighed down by questions he could not answer, he'd avoided them. He's done so ever since.

But now the sound is so close that he's not sure he can avoid it. The light from the lamp is all around him.

He summons his regal bearing, highly aware that he is naked, and turns to see the newcomer.

Ramesses is relieved to see that this is not someone of an unknown race who is staring at him, but a Nubian woman. Finally! Here is someone who might understand how he came to be here. Perhaps they can share information, see if any new conclusions can be drawn. Ramesses raises his hands to call for silence, but then remembers, ridiculously, that he can't speak, that his tongue is still with his organs in their jar.

He attempts to speak anyway. He manages to summon a sound that vibrates like breath in his chest.

"Arrooooogghhhhhh!" he says.

The Nubian stares at him. She's playing that lamp in her hand up and down Ramesses' body as if what she's seeing might change any moment. He should tell her that in his condition that's pretty damn unlikely.

She finally says words that Ramesses doesn't understand. "You better come talk to my supervisor."

And then, bewilderingly, she turns around and starts to walk away. To turn her back on the Pharaoh! Ramesses can't quite take it in. In his working life he has seen comparatively few backs. He keeps his arms in the air, and repeats his opening statement, that takes such an effort of will to generate. "Arrooooogghhhhhh?!"

The Nubian looks back over her shoulder and gestures to Ramesses with a crooked finger. He is, it seems, to follow.

Ramesses bridles for a moment, but then decides. He won't let pride get in the way of the first sign of progress since he got here.

Putting stilt leg after stilt leg, trying to keep up with the Nubian, he follows.

They reach a small, lighted enclosure, in an area that Ramesses has never explored, because it has always been full of foreigners. "Seth?" calls the Nubian, opening the door.

Inside the enclosure sits a Nubian man looking at unbound sheets of papyrus with the black and silver drawings on them. A greyhound sits at his feet. The dog is attached to his chair by a leather rein. It's looking imperiously at Ramesses, and now so does Seth. "Ah," says Seth, looking up and seeing Ramesses, "there you are. Finally."

Ramesses still doesn't understand a word of what's being said to him.

Seth reaches beside him, picks up a walking stick, and uses it to get slowly to his feet. Ramesses recognizes the walking stick. It has a slim handle and a forked base. Ramesses smiles, opens his arms. Here he is! Finally! Seth goes to a cabinet, opens it and finds something. He hands it to Ramesses. The Pharaoh peers at it. It's a small, hard cake, with the image of a dog imprinted on it.

Apt. Ramesses wants to indicate that he has no tongue, but he assumes that the god Seth, bearer of a Was Staff, knows that. He puts the cake in his mouth and does his best, with so little water in him, to give it a good hard suck. As he does so, Seth starts talking, with little hand gestures that seem to say that it doesn't matter much what he's saying . . .

". . . the god of foreigners, and so it's only apt that I'm in charge of—ah, OK, now you can understand me. Great."

Ramesses suddenly finds that, though he still has no tongue, he can talk properly too. "Have you been here all this time, Seth?" he says. "I consecrated my son to you, and still you didn't come to find me?"

"It was you who didn't come to find me."

Ramesses holds himself back. He's speaking, unlike at any other time in his life or afterlife, to an equal. So he must be diplomatic. And he knows Seth can be tricky, can be about storms and the chaos of the world, about what's over the border. That's why, while he was in the land of the living, he put in a word with him by naming his son that way. "Okay," he says, "well, putting that aside, maybe you could answer my questions now. How long have I been here?"

Seth looks at his watch. "Three thousand, three hundred years, give or take."

Ramesses frowns. It makes his brow hurt. "But . . . it doesn't feel like—"

"You've only been in this building for the last one hundred and thirty-nine years. You were taken from your tomb by thieves. All part of the great design, but of course they can't know that, so the usual curses have been bestowed upon their families."

Ramesses wants to say that he's very much in favor of that, but he's been struck by what Seth said a moment earlier. "This . . . building?"

Seth sighs. He goes to another cabinet, and pulls out a rolled-up piece of papyrus of a sort which is familiar to Ramesses. It's stored a bit offhandedly, but the Pharaoh stops himself from saying anything; the gods can keep things any way they like. Seth unrolls it on to the table.

The Nubian woman who led Ramesses here joins them to look down on it also. "I'm Mattie," she says. "If you're a good boy, you might be seeing me later."

Ramesses gets what she means. He nods his understanding.

The scroll turns out to be a map. Ramesses' gaze immediately seeks the river of his country and the green around it, but although he finds many rivers, none are the right shape. In fact, he doesn't recognize a single geographical feature. He can't even find the great waterfall that he's heard outside.

He looks up and sees that Seth is smiling at him. "You got separated from your coffin book," he says. "So I thought I'd show you our own Book of the Dead: a map of the United States, circa 1999." He puts a cook's relish into the pronunciation of each meaningless digit. "That's what the locals call the Duat and that's the year by their calendar. The Duat, you see, extends far beyond the walls of this building. In fact it only properly begins just south of here. We're in its hinterland, another country." His finger stabs down and down and down, faster than Ramesses can follow. "Over here's the White House, here's Disneyland, here's Canaveral, here's Graceland, here's Nashville." The finger spins. "In the air above it all, fear of the future, which is starting to crystallize as . . ." He spreads his palms wide to create a shadow with wiggling fingers on the map. "The Millennium Bug!" He laughs. It's not a nice laugh. "What the future actually holds for them . . . well, that's in the next drawer!"

Ramesses tries not to frown again. "You speak as though this is a real nation, with real subjects."

"They do think of it in that way, yes," he chuckles.

"So . . . if all this is the Duat . . ."

Seth nods. "You haven't started your journey yet."

"Why?"

"Because the Duat is the land of opportunity, a mirror of the mirror of heaven, and you've done nothing to take advantage of the opportunity you've been given. You were separated from your grave goods, which is where your *ka* goes back to during the day. And I've come back here night after night waiting for you to make your first move. In that time I've seen so many other guys get to where they're going—"

"My people—"

"The ones who died after you did are in a holding pattern. They're fine. The ones born after you died went on along after the next Pharaoh, your son."

"Seti has already—"

"He has indeed. And many others after him."

"What must I do?"

Seth gestures at the map. "I've let your *ba* go on ahead, as far as it can. Catch up to it, where it's waiting for you, at the Weighing of your Heart."

Ramesses leans closer, to where his thin eyes can see the words beside the geographical features, and he finally sees something he recognizes. He finds he knows many of the inscriptions. They are familiar from the Books of the Dead he has seen prepared for others. So here are destinations. But they don't suggest a path. He is aware now of the shadow of the rest of his people, falling on him from behind. He is not even on this map yet. He doesn't know where he'll enter or how. He looks up at Seth again. "If I open the doors and go out there . . .?"

"You'll find your way. During your lifetime, you always had a map that led you along. But here, you'll be lucky if you can get a few pointers. It's all up to you. That's the way we made it. Go out into the world of the day. Go to America." And before Ramesses can take another look, he rolls up the map again, and puts it back in its cabinet. Then he looks back to the Pharaoh. "You move on now."

And the dog even barks in warning.

It's winter here, he's told, so the day of these people's calendars will begin while it's still dark. Ramesses will be able to leave when the doors are opened, when he would normally be driven back to his bed by the noise.

So Ramesses waits, standing around the halls a little awkwardly. Then, when the big doors are opened, and these pale people, who live, unknowingly, right next to the Duat, and are colored fittingly for a life in shadow, start to flood in, he boldly marches towards them. Some of them scream and point, but some of them laugh, or even, more suitably, applaud. The eyes of children are shielded from him, but he suspects that's not because of his magnificence, or his fearsomeness, but because of his tiny genitals.

He steps bravely out into this new world and winces. Oh, it's a bit cold out here. He sees that the screams he heard are mostly the sounds of unusual vehicles. But under that is a bigger sound.

He goes to see the waterfall. He stands there for quite a while, letting the spray moisten his face. He finds a smile cracking his lips. This is great. And he's full of hope, because he finally has a way.

A few passers-by actually ignore him when he asks which way America is. He's not so bothered by that, just pleased that he can make himself understood. Eventually there's one who points him in the right direction before hurrying away.

He spends several fruitless nights trying to get through customs. The guards at the gates turn him away and threaten him with arrest. He explains that he is the Pharaoh, that he is trying to save his people, but this does not impress them.

But he was not Pharaoh for nothing. He goes further away from the gates, into the streets and the buildings, and steals a coat. Then he tries the gates again, but is once more turned away. This is only to be expected. The journey through the Duat is all about getting past gates and those guarding them. During the days he sleeps in parks or in the gaps in the great stone palaces. Nobody bothers him. He wonders if this is part of his test.

He has an idea. He tries to find one of those urns he saw in the pictures. But those he sees are in strange contexts, unsuitable for his needs. Finally, he decides he can do without. That night, he steps over the low wall by the riverbank. He has never learned to swim, but it can't be as hard as all that, and will not be required for the hardest part of this.

He floats, initially quite slowly, downstream. He is aware of cries from the bank as people notice him. The roaring of the great falls gets ever closer. He speeds up. He paddles a bit to make it faster. There are flashing lights by the side of the river now, but it's too late, the spray is upon him!

He falls, laughing. He has passed the first gate!

He lands in the Duat in a deep pool. He waits. He does not need to breathe. He finally bobs to the surface a long way downstream, and is surprised to see the angry lights there too. He pushes at the water, and manages to head for where a group of trees stands beside the river, in some sort of park.

He struggles out of the river, and is away into the darkness before the guards can find him.

He is now in the Duat proper. The land of the souls that are free from their bodies. Not that they know it. He doesn't need very much. He doesn't get very much. He clothes himself by stealing, and drinks water from public fountains, merely to keep the power of speech. He expects the people here to be much more scared of him than they turn out to be. They can accept, it seems, almost anything. It helps that they will actually turn away from him rather than scare themselves by looking closely. It's just as well they're so hard to scare. But like animals that are hard to anger, Ramesses thinks, actually pushing them to that emotion might be a very bad idea.

He remembers a few things from the map. He knows where the challenges he must overcome can be found. And now he can look at other maps, and knows he is at the top, and presumably has to make his way to the bottom, as the country gets narrower and narrower. It is like being born again. And there was one name in particular that was meaningful to him on that first map, and so he must go there.

But there's something that worries him. "The world of the day" was how Seth described this place. That sounds worryingly like sunworshipper talk. And everything Ramesses sees of religion here suggests that is indeed the case. The false belief has flown here and taken root! And of course it suits the Duat, all these souls on the edge of hysteria, every moment seeking escape, angry with their lot without fully understanding their situation. He passes gigantic fields of worship, open to the sky, shining huge lights upwards at night in hope of the sun, from which he can hear the cry of "Ra! Ra! Ra!" He allows himself a painful frown.

Ramesses initially assumes it's his task here to once more drive the sun worshippers out, and so bursts into one of their temples and starts yelling, but he's repelled by sheer force of numbers, and threatened with the arrival of the guards, and worse still, invited to submit to the embrace of these heathen ways. They say they want to listen to him, but having heard him, finally decide they don't.

He falls on to a very finely cut lawn and is sprayed with water from something like a snake. He is gone before the guards arrive.

He's not here to learn that sun worship is true, is he? That'd be awful. But one thing he has discovered is that he's definitely not here to push the reeds down before him. Rather, it's like he's leading his people across a swamp. He must tread carefully and listen to local advice.

He makes his way down the country, night by night. He has to take many side-trips and excursions, dictated by the passage of the vehicles on rollers that he sneaks on board, or the wagons with drivers that he requests access to with a gesture. Those conversations are extraordinary. The drivers always assume he is something from their mythology, or something they can make money from. Because they have money here. When he tells them the true nature of their world, that's it all in the service of something else, they simply don't believe him.

He is not allowed access to the White House, where the guards tell him that instead of talking to the elected head of the peasants here, he should put his question in a net.

He asks around about that, and spends an evening with the god Thoth in a place that he is told is called Radio Shack. Thoth goes on a bit, but gives him a spell jar that is small enough to put in his pocket. He uses the spell jar to "download" and "update" all of the spells that are upon him, which he is pleased to see are still in place. One of them is a compass, which allows him to better navigate the Duat. Thoth's whole tone suggests that a moral conversation is beneath him, so this time Ramesses doesn't even try.

In Nashville, he wins a musical contest in front of an audience against a man in a wide-brimmed hat who, once backstage, identifies himself as the terrifying He Who Dances In Blood, a figure Ramesses is familiar with from many Books of the Dead. He tries to tell Dances that he's learned a moral lesson about humility, but Dances just looks at him oddly.

At Graceland he fights an army of warriors, all dressed alike, flinging them into each other, delighting in his martial grace, taking their songs for his own. "What did you stand for?" he asks the fallen. "What can I learn from you?" They all start to answer, but their answers are all different.

At Disneyland, he meets with He Who Lives On Snakes, who has a giant orange and white head, and a fierce tail, and keeps insisting that the most wonderful thing about him is his uniqueness, which is hardly the case. Every question Ramesses asks him about what his next test will be is met with a reply formed in cryptic poetry. Again, Ramesses tries to suggest that he's becoming a more moral character through these tests, but the answers he gets aren't receptive to that idea.

At Canaveral he is spun round and round by the goddess Nut, who every now and then allows those who live here to pierce her body, and tries to persuade them that they exist in a world which has no meaning, while everything else here says the opposite, thus torturing them with doubt, a nuance Ramesses can't help but think of as cruel. He tries to tell Nut he's learnt an important lesson, but all he does is vomit.

Finally, he makes his way to the lower left coast of the Duat, where the kidneys should be, and there finds the building with the title he recognizes: "SETI Institute." It must be named, he's sure, in honor of his son. It is unfortunate that he gets there as the sun is coming up, and so Ramesses falls asleep on a chair in the waiting room. When he wakes, he is in a room festooned with the instruments of torture, and he shakes until he realizes that there is nobody here, that they have taken him as a corpse, that he interested them. He is sure this must be where he is intended to be, that this must be an important test on his journey, and so he waits until the peasants arrive once again, and then announces himself.

This time, they scream and run. Which is pleasing. But then they slowly come back, and remain interested. And that is even more pleasing.

He scares and interests them in equal measure, not too much of either. This, he thinks, might finally be the lesson he's meant to learn. He is only disappointed that his son isn't here.

This is how Ramesses ends up on Eater of His Own Excrement's chat show, carefully not quite explaining his mysterious origins, saying he's "from time as well as space" and wearing, after an intervention by an anxious wardrobe department, a clean, over-the-shoulder set of what the Pharaoh gathers are bandages.

Eater treats Ramesses as if he knows the answer to everything, which suits him down to the ground. "I see . . . the Millennium of your people will pass without an attack from this creature you call the Bug." This gets as much laughter as applause, which puzzles Ramesses, but he nods along, he'll take it. He's asked what his own beliefs are, and what he makes of the old-time religion in the States. He lies enormously, saying he believes much as they do, and that all people should be free to worship as they wish. He manages to stretch out a gummy grin, which is really painful.

After the show, Eater shakes his hand and says that he'd be happy to send Ramesses on to his final destination by private helicopter. SETI will be angry, but with nothing but his own authority to go by, he's decided Ramesses is a person, not property. Ramesses feels elated and terrified at the same time. He runs to the helicopter pad, turning down autograph requests as he goes, waving to a crowd that's still screaming, but now not in fear.

And so he lands at the southernmost end of the country, in New Mexico, at the Acoma Pueblo, which, he is told, is "the town in the place that always was." A figure stands tall under the whip of the helicopter blades, and Ramesses is relieved to see that it's Anubis, actually wearing an appropriate headdress, dogs barking around his feet, and he's carrying a Was Staff too.

"This is where they keep what they think of as the truth," the god explains, leading him into a small pueblo hut. Ramesses looks around for a moment before he ducks inside, and sees the faces of the Acoma tribe, with all sorts of expressions suggesting interest and lack of it, involvement and lack of it, as real as life.

Inside the hut stands Osiris, green-skinned, his legs wrapped, holding his crook and flail in the posture of a Pharaoh. Ramesses relaxes. It really is time, and he's ready. "We've had your *ba* here for some time," says the god, unrolling a scroll and raising an eyebrow. "And when we heard you'd finally gotten around to gracing us with your presence, we sent ahead for your heart." And there it is, in his hand, a tiny shriveled apple of a thing.

And now Ramesses is afraid again. For himself, and his people, and that he won't see his son. He can hear movement outside, a siren again; a shadow is cast through the door on to the wall. It's Ammit, the devourer, the end of the world, ready to take him.

Osiris produces the scales, and puts the heart on one of them. Ramesses gets out his spell jar, and switches it on, fingers fumbling with the tiny glyphs on the screen. Osiris makes a movement of his fingers, and produces a feather from the air, that is the goddess Maat, also represented by a glyph. It's good to see Mattie again. The green god puts the feather on to the other pan of the scale. The heart starts to grumble. Ramesses is fearful that it'll tell tales about the anger and cruelty of his life. So he quickly activates the spell he's been told will silence it. He lets out a long breath as the heart subsides. Osiris smiles at him. Well done.

The feather and the heart remain in balance. Osiris produces another scroll, and compares it to the *ba*. Then he asks the first of the forty-two questions. "Have you committed a sin?"

Ramesses makes sure the right spell is activated and quickly replies. "No."

The list includes having slain people, terrorized people, or stolen the property of a god, all of which Ramesses knows he's done, but the spell lets his lies go unchallenged. One of the questions is whether or not he's felt remorse, which makes him feel particularly vindicated. He may not have changed the Duat, but it has not changed him.

Osiris reaches the end. The feather has remained in balance with the heart. He smiles again, and holds up his own spell jar to show Ramesses. On it is a communication from a museum in Atlanta, who have bought him intending to set him free.

The transition finally happens on one of these people's flying machines, somewhere over the ocean. The context changes between the Duat and the mirror of heaven. Ramesses finds himself standing beside the crate containing his body, and here is Seti with him!

He laughs and cries, hugs his son to his breast. They are both themselves again. "The things the gods have put in place!" says Seti.

"I liked your Institute," says Ramesses.

"They do their best," says Seti, stroking his father's hair.

Terry Dowling mixes historical fact with the supernatural and steampunk elements in "The Shaddowwes Box." The West's hunger for ancient artifacts, the looting of tombs, the abundance of mummies, Gaston Maspero's 1881 discovery of a cache of thirty-six mummies (more than a dozen of which were probably pharaohs), Victor Loret's find (fourteen mummies, nine of them kings): all quite true. Although references to the practice have been and are still repeated by many reputable sources, the belief that mummies were used as locomotive fuel is not true. It arose from a joke made by Mark Twain in *The Innocents Abroad* (1869).

The Shaddowwes Box
Terry Dowling

———

On the fourth night the dream remained the same: our train ran along the banks of the Nile, its locomotive fired by the mummies of cats and kings. There was Akhmet, yet again, insisting that it was true, leaning forward, bright-eyed, gesturing wildly in our hard-won compartment. A new tomb-pit, shallow but vast, had been unearthed in the sands south of Cairo, he was telling me as if he never had before, hundreds of mummified cats to one side, dozens of human pauper mummies to the other.

"There had to be kings among them, Mr Salteri," Akhmet said, eyes flashing with the fine joke of it, exactly as they had on the momentous day itself six years earlier when I had made the fateful journey to the Wadi Hatas. "It's what the Re-interment Commissions did back in the New Kingdom. They feared looters, professional *tombaroli* such as you, so they moved the royal mummies, hid them. This field had a small precinct to the west. Probably special mummies there, possibly nobles, queens, even kings! But so many mummies. Too many, you understand? What to do? Sell to the Americans? They pay well and take everything, but there is no time. The excavation supervisors search for amulets, jewelry, then dispose of the remains with the railway factors before the authorities arrive. Everything goes into the fireboxes. Whoosh! We ride on the burning dead."

"You can't be serious," I said, those words again, then as now, largely because Akhmet wanted me to, and once again fancying our own late great Queen Victoria, or even the recently crowned King, giving their all like this, blazing away to help complete the run south from Saqqara.

"Very common now, Mr Salteri. The *moumia* burn like sticks. It's the pitch."

"Akhmet, Mr Minchin is aboard, you say?"

"Of course, *sahib*. Even now he will be making his way here. The carriages are crowded. A few moments more."

And, as if the words were indeed a cue, the door opened and Charles Minchin eased into the compartment, short and florid, grandly mustachioed, looking impossibly crisp in his suntan and sola topee.

In the dream I stood, now as then, allowing that any archaeologist this well turned out might be a stickler for the niceties. "Mr Minchin, it's a pleasure." We shook hands.

"Lucas Salteri, the pleasure is mine. I've long admired your work."

I had to control my smile. To what did he refer? My most recent *work* had been looting Etruscan tombs outside Veii and Norschia in western Italy. Before that ten years as a West End stage magician, and eight as an engineer before that. My career echoed the great Giovanni Belzoni's in so many ways. "Our arrangement stands?"

"Of course. We have camels waiting. We will be at the site by early afternoon."

"But between stations—?"

He consulted his timepiece. "The train will stop in a few minutes. It has been arranged."

And indeed the train did begin slowing.

Ten minutes later, we stood by the Nile amidst a cluster of date palms, watching swifts and martins darting over the fields of maize and sorghum as the train disappeared into the south. Ten more and we were mounted, and Minchin's three fellahin assistants—accomplices they would soon prove to be, Akhmet, Moussa, and Sayeed, nondescript then but made vivid by subsequent events and the dream's repetition—had finished loading the pack camels and we were heading off into the western desert.

And that was where the dream ended, always ended, even in the earliest hours of this new momentous day, not at the tomb itself, not when Minchin played his hand, not at the betrayal.

Herbert Kray arrived almost precisely at three o'clock. The bells of St Paul's across the Thames had just finished sounding when he knocked at the door, and I heard Mrs Danvers, my only *human* servant, hurrying to answer.

I sat waiting in the large, elegant drawing room, secretly pleased that the day had turned chill and overcast again beyond the heavy drapes, and watched Ramose. There were fourteen things that he could do really well and tending the fire was one of them. He propped and stilted in his best penny dreadful/*Boys' Own Paper* mummy fashion over to the grate, poked it several times, then set down the poker and moved to the side, waiting for his next task.

Mrs Danvers ushered in my guest and left us without saying a word, just as I had instructed. Dr Kray was very well presented, a tall handsome man in his early to middle forties, with a neatly trimmed beard and wearing a suit of the finest tweed. The golden watch-chain in his waistcoat pocket had a fob in the shape of a Horus falcon, proclaiming something of his trade in antiquities. I had no doubt that the Horus was genuine.

I stood, crossed to him and shook his hand. But before we could exchange more than a few of the usual pleasantries, I had the distinct if modest pleasure (modest given what was to follow) of seeing his eyes go large at the sight of my favorite mannikin.

"Good Lord, Trenton!" Kray said. "Bendeck mentioned that he'd heard one or two odd stories about you, but I would never have thought this! Tell me that you haven't revived one of them!"

"Hardly, Dr Kray. It's a construct, nothing more, made to resemble one of the partly unwrapped mummies from Maspero's 1881 DB320 cache from Deir el-Bahri."

"It certainly looks authentic to me!"

"You're kind to say so. But listen and you will hear the clockwork. It's all Bryson gears and a rotating oriete of my own design. A fairground diversion, nothing more. Still, if I time it right, you will think it is responding to my commands. But please do be seated."

There were three armchairs arranged before the fire, two in a semicircle facing the cheerful blaze, my own somewhat to the right so I could survey the whole room: the single door, the heavily fastened drapes that deadened most of the street noise, the darkly shrouded shape over by the southern wall.

Even as Kray took the armchair nearest my own, I called, "Ramose, the port, if you please," and the mummiform stirred, moved forward once more, propping and stilting, half-toppling along, very much like one of those clever mannequins you sometimes saw in the better klatsches and *salons mécanique* off Fleet Street.

The port had been poured out earlier by Mrs Danvers, of course, three sets of glasses on three separate trays, all placed carefully out of sight of where Kray now sat (Ramose was far from having the dexterity to actually pour drinks from a decanter). This way the bandaged form needed only lean forward and bring up the first tray, then do a slow turn which put it close by Kray's elbow.

With an admiring chuckle at the cleverness of the whole thing, the antiques dealer took a glass, crying, "Bravo! Truly marvelous!"

Ramose straightened, moved behind the semicircle of chairs and brought the tray and the other glass to me.

Herbert Kray sipped his port, then set his glass on the small occasional table before the chairs. "Dashed clever. I'd love to know the trick of it. But to business, Mr Trenton. Your message said that you might have a prime antiquity to sell."

I too set aside my glass. "Let us let Ramose do his other party trick first." I made sure Kray saw me take out my timepiece, seem to be consulting and calculating an exact timing. "Ramose, please show our guest the WH38."

Again, as if responding to the spoken command, the mummiform jerked into life. With a whirring of gears and the distinctive click-shift-lock of the Bryson armatures, he stiff-legged to the shrouded shape looming behind the curve of the armchairs. Kray craned about to follow the whole thing, showing the same wide-eyed delight as before, watching as the mummy stopped, raised one bandaged, hook-clawed hand and seized the black velvet dust-cloth covering the tall shape beneath. The claw-hand closed, clenched, pulled. Ramose took one, two steps back, tottering slightly as the shroud came fully away.

In my mind I applauded silently. *Exactly as rehearsed.*

"Ah my!" Kray said, and yet again stared in wonder. Before him—behind him more correctly, though by now he was out of his chair and standing once more—was an unadorned wooden Egyptian burial casket propped upright, held at a gentle eight degrees in a gleaming brass frame consisting of rods, brackets, intricate clamps, and gears, all fitted close, keeping it secure.

"Wonderful!" Kray said. "But that frame. I see clockwork. What on earth—?"

"Just some new conservation techniques I'm trying, Dr Kray. Precautions against the local humidity, vibrations caused by traffic, doors closing, that sort of thing. I keep my guest in the drawing room here to offset the effects of damp. Hence the heavy drapes I've had installed. The subdued lighting."

"Of course. Of course. Has it been opened?"

"It never has. Please feel free to examine the seals, if you wish. They are Twentieth Dynasty."

Kray did so, moving in close. His zeal was impossible to hide. He was seeing a lost king, a queen, another of the marvelous re-interred royal mummies of the kind officially discovered by Maspero in 1881, or those from the Loret cache seven years later. "You are prepared to sell this?"

"Dr Bendeck and yourself are reputable experts in this business. I thought I should come to you first."

"Yes, yes. Capital! But contents unseen? Hm." Kray made as if to be deep in thought, frowning slightly, stroking his neatly bearded chin with one hand.

"Just as I found it, Dr Kray," I said.

"Which was where, Mr Trenton, if I may ask?"

"You will understand that this must remain undisclosed for the present."

"Of course. Of course." Kray was examining the casket again, carefully, so carefully, spending long minutes studying the wood, the mixture of pitch and resins keeping it still airtight after so many centuries. He was no doubt imagining a new royal cache, one not yet made known to the Arab Bureau, the Antiquities Service, or the British High Commission, or possibly even more: the barely imaginable wonder of a new *sealed* tomb, possibly that of Herihor or Tutankhamun, for heaven's sake, a continuing stream of artifacts finding their way into the special holds of ships using the Suez Canal or reaching England by way of the old contraband routes out of Morocco and Spain. "I'm sure we can reach an agreement, Mr Trenton. But please. Why have you invited me here ahead of Dr Bendeck? We are business associates. He said he was asked to call on you at *four* o'clock, yet your invitation to me specified three and asked for strictest discretion. Surely we might have called on you together. Unless . . . May I assume . . .?" Kray hesitated a final time, daring not say it.

I spread my hands. *You understand how it is. Make an offer if you wish.* "I know you are a man of discrimination, Dr Kray. A man of letters. A scholar as well as a collector and a dealer. I merely wanted to give you time to examine this piece, make an unhurried appraisal, form your own conclusions."

"Yes, yes, I see. I thank you for that."

"And give us a chance to talk. Let me be frank. When Dr Bendeck arrives, it will be different."

Kray returned to his armchair, seated himself again. He took another sip of port and gave me a shrewd look. "Very well," he said finally, setting down his glass. "May I be equally frank? This is an unadorned casket. It possibly contains the mummy of a nonentity like those unidentified individuals Maspero discovered among the fifty kings of the DB320 cache. The controversial Unknown Man E, for instance, possibly a disgraced royal prince, possibly a murdered royal suitor for Tutankhamun's widow, but, equally possible, nothing more than a favorite servant, even someone the overzealous re-interment officials accidentally included in their haste to stay ahead of the loot-ers." Kray leant forward, well-manicured hands on his knees. "If there were the occasional relic of—not to put too fine a point on it—actual *intrinsic* as well as archaeological value, say, of gold or silver, gemstones, of the finest craftsmanship, I would be happy to reach some mutual accommodation on a more—personal—basis."

I smiled and nodded to indicate that this was exactly what I had had in mind, as if, all going well, there would indeed be such intrinsically valuable pieces on offer.

"Excellent," I said, raising my glass. "This is precisely why I made so bold as to ask you here ahead of your, so I've been told, more officious colleague. As you can appreciate, I prefer not to deal with a consortium."

"Capital." Kray emptied his glass, chuckled with pleasure again as Ramose repeated his earlier performance, stilting and propping across to the decanter, tilting forward to pick up the second tray of the three, and returning with it, setting it down on the occasional table between Kray and myself. Fortunately, instinctively, my guest moved his empty glass clear and placed it on the tray when he took a filled one. Ramose could not have managed such a retrieval. The mummy then stiff-legged back to his place to the left of the fire and became still, though, as ever, seemed to be listening, following everything we said.

While Kray's attention was on the construct, I checked the time. A quarter of four. Kray's examination of the WH38 casket had taken longer than expected. Bendeck would be here soon. It was time to give the good doctor his due. Minchin had been their agent in Cairo, the one who did the dirty work, Bendeck the main investor. But Herbert Kray, as several reliable sources had it, had been the mastermind behind all that had happened in the tomb in the rocky defile at Wadi Hatas that day. Minchin and his fellahin may have done the actual deed, Bendeck may have sold on the artifacts, but Kray had undoubtedly planned the whole affair. I had simply been an awkwardness, an additional complication to be dealt with, someone to be left behind when they had finished plundering the tomb and sealed it up again. They knew nothing of the two goat-herders who had followed us, brothers to the one who had sold me the papyrus. Instead of robbing *me* themselves as they had originally intended, they had become my liberators.

I pretended to sip my port, began directing the small talk that would crown the afternoon's events. "Dr Kray, do you know what a Shaddowwes Box is?"

"No, Trenton. I can't say that I do."

"The great Elizabethan alchemist John Dee was said to have had one. And Aleister Crowley, our Great Beast. It's a sealed box containing nothing but darkness. A sort of *memento mori* really. A reminder of what awaits us all unless we believe in a Creator. Even Shakespeare was said to own one. And it's spelt 'shaddowwe' with the double 'd' and 'w' after one of the Bard's favored spellings for 'shadow.'"

"I see." Kray didn't see at all, and my rhapsodic tone clearly troubled him.

I gestured at the coffin behind his chair. "I must say that having an unopened casket standing there for the past three weeks has given me a shudder or two. I mean, have you ever wondered about what truly happened to that Unknown Man E in the DB320 cache?"

Kray had to come back from where his own thoughts had taken him. "The Unknown Man? I have to say I know very little about it. He's the chap they found screaming, yes?"

"Indeed. Wrapped in a sheepskin—something ritually unclean to the ancient Egyptians—bound hand and foot, it seems. Some say it's Penteweret, the conspirator son of Ramesses III who was captured when the harem conspiracy against his father failed. Some accounts say he was made to take poison, others that he was buried alive in an unmarked casket."

"Awful business either way."

"Indeed. But it makes you think. *Both* versions may be correct. The poison could have been a sedative and Penteweret awoke in darkness to find himself entombed alive."

"Yes, well." Now Herbert Kray was the one to bring out his time-piece, an impressive gold one, and check the time. "Elleston will be here soon. This mechanical mummy of yours will really take his fancy. He has always loved automata."

Again I pretended to sip my port. "I'm pleased to hear it. And do excuse my rambling on like this. It's having that casket in here. I'm not one to worry about mummies coming back to life, but the *darkness* now, that is another thing. It bothers me. Have you ever wondered what might happen in total darkness, Dr Kray?"

Irritation showed briefly in Kray's eyes, though was brought quickly under control. "Presumably nothing, sir. The workings of air and silence, I suppose. Time doing its thing. In windowless rooms the movement of dust particles. In caves the drip of water, I suspect. The formation of stalactites. You tell me."

"But that is *unconsidered* darkness surely. The darkness of nature, chance, and random circumstance. What of the *considered* kind?"

Herbert Kray had no idea how to respond to such a question or, ultimately, even what it meant. Things were taking a definitely queer turn, but if there were treasures, even trinkets, to be gained, he had resolved to be politeness itself. "If you mean to tell me, sir, pray do. I admit that your exact point escapes me."

"If I consider it, I change it."

"Really? How so?"

"By the participating mind, Dr Kray. Our minds, our very thoughts, galvanize the thing observed at its most basic level. There are religions that turn on this way of thinking. Someday it will be proven beyond doubt as a scientific fact as well."

Kray chuckled. "I'm sure. So I might argue that I could affect this rather fine port by reflecting upon it."

"You may not be able to measure the shift enough for it to matter, but yes. First, you are unconvinced, skeptical. Secondly, it would take more time than I believe you would care to give it."

Kray chuckled again. "You probably need to do better than that, Mr Trenton. That's the refrain of mystics and charlatans the world over. You *must* believe! You *must* allow time! Have the correct *discipline*. Oh, and a small donation will help to purchase paraffin for the lamps during such a vigil. Your support will be ever so greatly appreciated."

I made sure that I smiled before pressing my subject again. "I ask my question because the rage and anguish, the despair and agony felt by Unknown Man E waking in his coffin could have been enough to change the imprisoning darkness, if you follow my drift. That darkness would have been the intensely considered kind, I suggest."

"Doubtless true, old fellow. We can only wonder what Maspero and his assistants must have felt when that particular coffin was opened. The pharaoh's curse of the melodramas!"

I turned my glass in my hands. "Or simply sufficiently *changed* darkness. Nothing more."

"Well, let's pray that fellow behind you had a peaceful and easy time of it."

"On the contrary, Dr Kray. I have it on good authority that the fellow within was *definitely* buried alive. Unlike Penteweret, or whoever

Unknown Man E happens to be, this mummy had an accompanying papyrus telling his story."

Kray's eyes widened. "You have this papyrus?"

"I do, and had it translated some years ago. Best of all it is that rarity amongst Egyptian funerary texts, not the usual fragments of the *Amduat*, not a list of personal accomplishments, but an actual account of a non-royal burial."

"Non-royal?"

"And of a desperate reckoning. His name is Panuhe, Dr Kray, a luckless courtier who murdered the lesser princess with whom he was smitten when he could not have her for himself. Her slighted husband was high vizier and dealt with him accordingly, had him sealed up in a rough-hewn annex in her own modest tomb. All very sordid, I know, the very stuff of melodrama in any age!"

Suddenly the clock in the hall began chiming. At the same time, the bells of St Paul's started sounding across the river. Bendeck's knock came mere moments later.

Kray's relief was palpable, yet quickly replaced by a natural concern. "There were other things in the annex, did you say?"

I heard Mrs Danvers answering the door, heard voices in the hall. "You are being mischievous, Dr Kray. I deliberately did not say."

Kray grinned. "Of course. Of course. Look, old man, about this three o'clock thing. Do you think—?"

I anticipated him. "Best we say that you arrived just a few minutes ago. The keen enthusiast arriving a tad early."

Kray nodded. "Splendid. Greatly appreciated."

Mrs. Danvers showed Elleston Bendeck into the room and left us, closing the door behind her. It was her final duty for me. Her salary was paid; I would never see her again.

Bendeck was a portly man in his late fifties with gray eyes, steel-gray hair and as well turned out as Kray was, though wearing one of the new American suits that had become all the fashion lately. Again the pleasantries were hardly started before he was crying out in astonishment and delight as Ramose repeated his earlier performance, stilting over to fetch the final port tray.

Then, with both men seated before the fire holding their glasses, sharing first in the bewildering eccentricity of my toast to the King, then to the success of our negotiations, I prepared to enter our final phase. This time the port contained a strong-enough sedative, though one sufficient to cause mere muscular debilitation rather than unconsciousness. I wanted my guests awake.

"Dr Bendeck, while awaiting your arrival I was just now showing your colleague that casket behind you and suggesting that it is quite likely the handiwork of the re-burial commissions of the Twentieth Dynasty."

"Indeed. Twentieth Dynasty, you say?" Bendeck craned his neck to see, pointedly ignoring any social impropriety in our apparently having commenced proceedings without him. He dealt in antiquities, not always from reputable suppliers. He knew to go with the flow of events if ultimately to his advantage.

"I was also suggesting that it is effectively a Shaddowwes Box, such as Dr John Dee was said to possess and even William Shakespeare. Not a Shaddowwes Box in intention, mind, more by circumstance, purest chance."

"Right." He turned to his partner. "I see that you have the advantage of me, Kray. Perhaps, Mr Trenton, you might care to—"

But the door to the drawing room slammed open then and stopped his words. Through that doorway came an old bath chair in which sat slumped none other than Charles Minchin, clearly in a torpor, as if just now roused from an opium sleep. And that wasn't the only cause for amazement. The chair was being pushed by another mummy, stilting and propping as best it could, and door was now being closed by yet another.

"Minchin!" Bendeck cried, and Kray did too, more in astonishment at the sight of additional clockwork mannikins appearing in the room as seeing their colleague like this, both men rising to their feet, and doing so unsteadily, I noted, as the sedative took effect.

"Our final guest, gentlemen," I announced, watching as Ahmose wheeled Minchin in alongside Bendeck's armchair. Senawe had closed the door and now came prop-stilting over to join Ramose and Ahmose. Then, in startling unison, the three mummiforms began hooking away the bandages across their stomachs, each drawing forth a golden dagger concealed there, all three brandishing them in an inevitably comical but clearly menacing fashion.

"Trenton, what's going on?" Bendeck demanded.

"Not Trenton!" Minchin slurred the words. "That's *Salteri*! Lucas Salteri."

"What's that you say?" Kray cried. "Salteri?"

"Left 'im in the tomb," Minchin managed, drooling as he spoke. "Left 'im in the bloody tomb!"

"You did, Minchin," I said. "Took everything and sealed it up again. But the fellahin I'd bought the papyrus from had followed with his brothers. They meant to loot the place themselves, you see, but wanted to have this document translated first before attempting it. That's why they sold it to me. They were being cautious. I mean, gentlemen, how many tombs have a papyrus in a sealed canopic-style vessel deliberately left at its main entrance, right beneath the traditional seal of the nine bound captives? Our vengeful vizier *wanted* posterity, possibly the great gods, to *know* Panuhe's story. Anyway, the brothers released me, and we found *this* casket in its hidden annex."

"The brothers—" Kray could barely manage the words. "Not these?"

"My three friends here? Hardly. Well, parts of them at least."

I was now moving to the doorway, about to close and lock it behind me. Mrs Danvers had long since departed the premises. The mummies stood with their gilded daggers between the three men in the chairs and the room's only exit.

"You surely do not hope to scare us with a few sideshow gimmicks, Salteri?" Bendeck called, his words slurred.

"No, Dr Bendeck. They are mere diversions, window dressing to distract you from the sound of additional clockwork now operating at the casket behind you. If you turn your heads, if you can manage it, you will notice that a special mechanism has already been activated, is even now preparing to apply pressure to the casket."

"What, an' set 'nother mummy on us?" Bendeck said. The words were still recognizable.

"Hardly. Just as the papyrus says, the body in that coffin was never mummified."

"I don't follow," Kray said, slumped heavily in his chair.

"Unlike Unknown Man E, this sorry fellow truly was interred alive in that casket, bound and helpless. He *filled* that darkness, gentlemen. Surely *changed* it in more than a casual way. I now give you that darkness. It is my gift to you."

And with that I extinguished the remaining lights, closed and locked the heavy mahogany door and arranged the special bolster at the bottom to shut out all hope of illumination.

All timed. All of it. The pressure edges would be touching the wood by now, relentless. A true full minute to the splintering point, so far as I could judge. But now it was ten seconds to step through the front door, eight more to turn the key behind me. Five seconds for the front steps. Twelve paces along the sidewalk, fifteen, possibly twenty.

Then darkness in darkness.

And the screaming.

"Egyptian Avenue" is one of Kim Newman's series of occult/sf/ mystery stories featuring Richard Jeperson. The story was inspired by a J. K. Potter photograph of the famous Egyptian Avenue in London's Highgate Cemetery. The "avenue" path begins with a neo-Egyptian gateway, flanked by a pair of obelisks. The cemetery was opened in 1839 when the first wave of nineteenth-century western Egyptomania inspired such Victorian architectural interpretations. The association of Egypt with the memorialization of the dead was, at least, understandable. The "tourist guide" speech in the story about the fictional cemetery is very close to the facts about the real one.

Egyptian Avenue
Kim Newman

———

"This tomb's leaking sand," said Fred Regent. "And beetles." Fine white stuff, hourglass quality, not bucket and spade material, seeped from a vertical crack, fanning out around and between clumps of lush, long green grass. Black bugs glittered in morning sunlight, hornlike protrusions rooting through the overgrowth, sand-specks stuck to their carapaces.

Fred looked up at the face of the tomb, which was framed by faux-Egyptian columns. The name BUNNING was cut deep into the stone, hemmed around by weather-beaten hieroglyphs.

It was the summer of 197—. Fred Regent, late of the Metropolitan Constabulary, was again adventuring with the supernatural. As before, his guide off life's beaten track was Richard Jeperson, the most resourceful agent of the Diogenes Club, which remained the least-known branch of Britain's intelligence and police services. All the anomalies came down to Jeperson. Last month, it had been glam rock ghouls gutting groupies at the Glastonbury Festival and an Obeah curse on

Prime Minister Edward Heath hatched somewhere inside his own cabinet; this morning, it was ghosts in Kingstead Cemetery.

Jeperson, something of an anomaly himself, scooped up a handful of sand and looked down his hawk nose at a couple of fat bugs.

"Were we on the banks of the great River Nile rather than on a pleasant hill overlooking the greater city of London," said Jeperson, "I shouldn't be surprised to come across these little fellows. As it is, I'm flummoxed. These, Fred, are *Scarabaeidae* beetles."

"I saw *Curse of the Mummy's Tomb* at the Rialto, Richard. I know what a scarab is."

Jeperson laughed, deepening creases in his tanned forehead and cheeks. His smile lifted black moustaches and showed sharp teeth-points. The Man from the Diogenes Club sounded as English as James Mason, but when suntanned he looked more like an Arab, or a Romany disguised as Charles II. His mass of black ringlets was not a wig, though. And no gypsy would dress as gaudily as Richard Jeperson.

"Of course you do, Fred. I elucidate for the benefit of exposition. Thinking out loud. That is Sahara sand and these are North African beasties."

"Absolutely, guv'nor. And that bloody big dead one there is a scorpion."

Jeperson looked down with amused distaste. The scorpion twitched, scuttled, and was squashed under Jeperson's foot.

"Not so dead, Fred."

"Is now."

"Let us hope so."

Jeperson considered his sole, then scraped the evil crushed thing off on a chunk of old headstone.

For this expedition to darkest N6, he wore a generously bloused, leopard-pattern safari jacket and tight white, high-waisted britches tucked into sturdy fell-walker's boots. His ensemble included a turquoise Sam Browne belt (with pouches full of useful implements and substances), a tiger's-fang amulet that was supposed to protect against evil, and an Australian bush hat with three corks dangling from the rim. Champagne corks, each marked with a date in felt-tip pen.

"The term for a thing so out of place is, as we all know, an 'apport,'" said Jeperson. "Unless some peculiar person has for reasons unknown placed sand, scarabs, and scorps in our path for the purpose of puzzlement, we must conclude that they have materialized for some supernatural reason. Mr Lillywhite, this is your belief, is it not? This is yet another manifestation of the spookery you have reported?"

Lillywhite nodded. He was a milk-skinned, fair-haired middle-aged man with burning red cheeks and a peacock tail-pattern smock. His complaint had been passed from the police to the Diogenes Club, and then fielded to Jeperson.

"What is all this doing here?" asked Vanessa, Jeperson's other assistant—the one everyone noticed before realizing Fred was in the room. The tall, model-beautiful redhead wore huge sunglasses with swirly mint-and-yellow patterns on the lenses and frames, a sari-like arrangement of silk scarves that exposed a ruby winking in her navel, and stack-heeled cream leather go-go boots. Beside the other two, Fred felt a bit underdressed in his Fred Perry and Doc Martens.

"Appearing supernaturally, I should say, Vanessa," said Jeperson. "That's generally what apports do."

"Not just the apports," she went on. "All the obelisks and sphinxes. Oughtn't this to be in the Valley of the Kings, not buried under greenery in London North Six?"

Jeperson dropped the sand and let the scarabs scuttle where they might. He brushed his palms together.

Vanessa was right. Everything in this section of Kingstead Cemetery was tricked out with ancient Egyptian statuary and design features. The Bunning tomb was guarded by two human-headed stone lions in pharaonic headdresses.

Their faces had weathered as badly in a century as the original sphinx in millennia. All around were miniature sandstone pyramids and temples, animal-headed deities, faded blue and gold hieroglyphs, and ankh-shaped gravestones.

"I can explain that, Miss . . . ah?" said Lillywhite.

"Vanessa. Just Vanessa."

"Vanessa, fine," said the scholarly caretaker, segueing into a tour-guide speech.

"The motif dates back to the establishment of the cemetery in 1839. Stephen Geary, the original architect, had a passion for Egyptiana, which was shared by the general public of his day. From the first, the cemetery was planned not just as a place for burying the dead but a species of morbid tourist attraction.

"Victorians were rather more given to visiting dead relatives than we are. It was expected that whole families would come to picnic by Grandmama's grave."

"If my gran were dead, we'd certainly have a picnic," said Fred. Lillywhite looked a little shocked. "Well, you don't know my gran," Fred explained.

"They held black-crepe birthday parties for the many children who died in infancy," the caretaker continued, "with solemn games and floral presents. Siblings annually gathered around marble babies well into their own old age. It's not easy to start a graveyard from scratch, especially at what you might call the top end of the market. Cemeteries are supposed to be old. For a Victorian to be laid to rest in a new one would be like you or me being bundled into a plastic bag and ploughed under a motorway extension."

"That's more or less what Fred has planned," said Jeperson.

"I can't say I'm surprised. To circumvent the prejudice, Geary decided to trade on associations with ancient civilizations. If his cemetery couldn't be instantly old, then at least it would look old. This area is Egyptian Avenue. Geary himself is buried here. Originally, there were three such sections, with a Roman Avenue and a Grecian Avenue completing the set. But the fashionable had a craze for Egypt. The Roman and Grecian Avenues were abandoned and overtaken. It was no real scholarly interest in Egyptology, by the way, just an enthusiasm for the styles. Some of the gods you see represented aren't even real, just made up to fit in with the pantheon. A historian might draw a parallel between ancient Egyptian obsession with funerary rites and the Victorian fascination with the aesthetics of death."

Fred thought anyone who chose to spend his life looking after a disused cemetery must have nurtured some of that obsession himself. Lillywhite was an unsalaried amateur, a local resident who was a booster for this forgotten corner of the capital.

"It's certainly ancient now," said Fred. "Falling to pieces."

"Regrettably so. Victorian craftsmen were good on the surface, but skimped everything else. Artisans knew the customers would all be too dead to complain, and cut a lot of corners. Impressive stone fronts, but crumbling at the back. Statues that dissolve to lumps after fifty years in the rain. Tombs with strong corners but weak roofs. By the 1920s, when the original site was full and children and grandchildren of the first tenants were in their own grave-plots, everything had fallen into disrepair. When the United Cemetery Company went bust in the early sixties, Kingstead was more or less abandoned. Our historical society has been trying to raise money for restoration and repair work. With not much luck, as yet."

"Put me down for fifty quid," said Jeperson.

Fred wasn't sure if restoration and repair would improve the place. The tombs had been laid out to a classical plan like miniature pyramids or cathedrals, and serpentine pathways wound between them. Uncontrolled shrubbery and ivy swarmed everywhere, clogging the paths, practically burying the stonework. A broken-winged angel soared from a nearby rhododendron, face scraped eyeless.

It was the dead city of a lost civilization, like something from Rider Haggard.

Nature had crept back, green tendrils undermining thrones and palaces, and was slowly taking the impertinent erections of a passing humanity back into her leafy bosom.

"This is the source of your haunting?" asked Jeperson, nodding at the Bunning tomb.

Fred had forgotten for a moment why they were here.

"It seems to be."

There had been a great deal of ghostly activity. Yesterday, Fred had gone to the newspaper library in Colindale and looked over a hundred and twenty years of wails in the night and alarmed courting couples. As burial grounds went, Kingstead Cemetery was rather sporadically haunted. Until the last three months, when spooks had been running riot with bells and whistles on. A newsagent's across the road had been pelted with a rain of lightning-charged pebbles.

A physical culture enthusiast had been knocked off his bicycle by ectoplasmic tentacles. And there had been a lot of sightings.

Jeperson considered the Bunning tomb. Fred saw he was letting down his guard, trying to sense what was disturbed in the vicinity. Jeperson was a sensitive: "According to your report, Lillywhite, our spectral visitors have run the whole gamut. Disembodied sounds . . ."

"Like jackals," said Lillywhite. "I was in Suez in '56. I know what a jackal sounds like."

". . . phantom figures . . ."

"Mummies, with bandages. Hawk-headed humans. Ghostly barges. Crawling severed hands."

". . . .and now, physical presences. To wit: the scarabs and other nasties. Even the sand. It's still warm, by the way. Does anyone else detect a theme here?"

"Spirits of Ancient Egypt," suggested Vanessa.

Jeperson shot her a finger-gun. "You have it."

Fred would have shivered, only . . .

"Richard, isn't there something funny here?" he said. "A themed haunting? It's a bit Hammer Horror, isn't it? I mean, this place may be done up with Egyptian tat but it's still North London. You can see the Post Office Tower from here. Whoever is buried in this tomb . . ."

"Members of the Bunning Family," put in Lillywhite. "The publishing house. Bunning and Company, Pyramid Press. You can see their offices from here. That black building, the one that looks like the monolith in 2001: A Space Odyssey. It's called the Horus Tower."

Fred knew the skyscraper, but had never realized who owned it.

"Yes, them. The Bunnings. They were just Victorians who liked the idea of a few hieroglyphs and cat-headed birds in the way they might have liked striped wallpaper or a particular cut of waistcoat. You said it was a fashion, a craze. So why have we got authentic Egyptian ghosts, just as if there were some evil high priest or mad pharaoh in there?"

"George Oldrid Bunning was supposedly buried in a proper Egyptian sarcophagus," said Lillywhite. "It was even said that he went through the mummification process."

"Brains through the nose, liver and lights in canopic jars?"

"Yes, Mr Jeperson. Indeed."

"That would have been irregular?"

"In 1897? Yes."

"I withdraw my objection," said Fred. "Old Bunning was clearly a loon. You might expect loon ghosts."

Jeperson was on his knees, looking at the sand. The scarabs were gone now, scuttling across London in advance of a nasty surprise come the first frost.

"I've been trying to get in touch with the descendants for a while," said Lillywhite. "Even before all this fuss I was hoping they might sponsor restoration of the Bunning tomb. The current head of the family is George Rameses Bunning. He must maintain the family interest in Egypt, or at least his parents did. It appears George Rameses has his own troubles."

"So I'd heard," said Jeperson. "All dynasties must fail, I suppose."

Fred had vaguely heard of the Bunnings, but couldn't remember where. "Pyramid Press are magazine publishers," said Jeperson, answering the unspoken query. "You've heard of *Stunna*?"

Vanessa made a face.

Stunna was supposedly a blokes' answer to *Cosmopolitan*, with features about fast cars and sport and (especially) sex. It ran glossy pictures of girls not naked enough to get into *Playboy* but nevertheless unclad enough for you not to want your mum knowing you looked at them. The magazine had launched last year with a lot of publicity, then been attacked with a couple of libel suits from a rival publisher they had made nasty jokes about, Derek Leech of the *Daily Comet*. *Stunna* had just ceased publication, probably taking the company down with it. Fred realized he had heard of George Rameses Bunning after all. He was doomed to be dragged into bankruptcy and ruin, throwing a lot of people out of work. The scraps of his company would probably be gobbled up by the litigious Leech, which may well have been the point.

"Bunning and Company once put out *British Pluck* and *The Halfpenny Marvel*," said Jeperson. "Boys' papers. At their height of popularity between the wars. And dozens of other titles over the years. Mostly sensation stuff. Generations of lads were raised on the adventures of Jack Dauntless, RN, and the scientific vigilante, Dr Shade. I think the masthead of *Stunna* bears the sad legend 'incorporating *British Pluck*.'"

"You think there's a tie-in," said Fred. "With all the pluck business. It's a penny-dreadful curse."

Jeperson's brow furrowed. He was having one of his "feelings," which usually meant bad news for anyone within hailing distance.

"More than that, Fred. I sense something very nasty here. An old cruelty that lingers. Also, this is one of those 'hey, look at me' hauntings. It's as if our phantoms were trying to tell us something, to issue a warning."

"Then why start making a fuss in the last month? Any ghosts around here must have been planted . . ."

"Discorporated, Fred."

"Yes, that . . . they must have been dead for eighty years. Why sit quietly all that time but kick up a row this summer?"

"Maybe they object to something topical," suggested Vanessa. "Like what's Top of the Pops?"

"It's not dreadful enough to be after the Bay City Rollers, luv," said Fred.

"Good point."

Jeperson considered the Bunning tomb, and stroked his 'tache.

Fred looked around. The cemetery afforded a pleasant green dappling of shadow, and swathes of sun-struck grass. But Jeperson was right. Something very nasty was here.

"Vanessa," said Jeperson. "Pass the crowbar. I think we should unseal this tomb."

"But . . ." put in the startled Lillywhite.

Jeperson tapped his tiger fang, "Have no fear of curses, man. This will shield us all."

"It's not that . . . This is private property."

"I won't tell if you don't. Besides, you've already established that George Rameses Bunning has less than no interest in the last resting place of his ancestors. Who else could possibly object?"

"I'm supposed to be a guardian of this place."

"Come on. Haven't you ever wanted to open one of these tombs up and poke around inside?"

"The original Mr Bunning is supposed to have had an authentic Egyptian funeral. He might be surrounded by his treasures."

"A bicycle to pedal into the afterlife? Golden cigar cuspidors? Ornamental funerary gas lamps?"

"Very likely."

"Then we shall be Howard Carter and Lord Carnarvon."

Fred thought that wasn't a happy parallel. Hadn't there been an effective curse on the tomb of King Tutankhamun?

Vanessa produced a crowbar from her BOAC holdall. She was always prepared for any eventualities.

Fred thought he should volunteer, but Jeperson took the tool and slipped it into a crack. He strained and the stone didn't shift.

"Superior workmanship, Lillywhite. No skimping here."

Jeperson heaved again. The stone advanced an inch, and more sand cascaded.

Something chittered inside.

Vanessa had a trowel. She cleared some of the sand and picked out dried-up mortar.

"Good girl," said Jeperson.

He heaved again. The bottom half of the stone cracked through completely, then fell out of the doorway. The top half slid down in grooves and broke in two pieces. A lot more sand avalanched.

Fred tugged Lillywhite out of the way. Jeperson and Vanessa had already stepped aside.

A scarecrow-thin human figure stood in the shifting sands, hands raised as if to thump, teeth bared in a gruesome grin. It pitched forward on its face and broke apart like a poorly made dummy. If it were a guy, it would not earn a penny from the most intimidated or kindly passer-by.

"That's not George Oldrid Bunning," gasped Lillywhite.

"No," said Jeperson. "I rather fear that it's his butler."

There were five of them, strewn around the stone sarcophagus, bundles of bones in browned wrappings.

"A butler, a footman, a cook, a housekeeper, and a maid," said Jeperson. Under his tan, he was pale. He held himself rigidly, so that he wouldn't shake with rage and despair. He understood this sort of horror all too well—having lost the memory of a boyhood torn away in a Nazi camp—but never got used to it.

The servant bodies wore the remains of uniforms.

Lillywhite was upset. He was sitting on the grass, with his head between his knees.

Vanessa, less sensitive than Jeperson, was looking about the tomb with a torch.

"It's a good size," she called out. "Extensive foundations."

"They were alive," bleated Lillywhite.

"For a while," said Jeperson.

"What a bastard," said Fred. "Old George Oldrid Bunning. He got his pharaoh's funeral all right, with his servants buried alive to shine

208 | KIM NEWMAN

his boots and tug their forelocks through all eternity. How did he do it?"

"Careful planning," said Jeperson. "And a total lack of scruples."

Lillywhite looked up. He concentrated, falling back on expertise to damp down the shock.

"It was a special design. When he was dying, George Oldrid contracted a master mason to create his tomb. It's the only one here that's survived substantially intact. The mason died before Bunning. Suspiciously."

"Pharaohs had their architects killed, to preserve the secrets of their tombs from grave robbers. There were all kinds of traps in the pyramids, to discourage looters."

A loud noise came from inside the tomb. Something snapping shut with a clang.

Jeperson's cool vanished.

"Vanessa?" he shouted.

Vanessa came out of the tomb, hair awry and pinned back by her raised sunglasses. She had a nasty graze on her knee.

"I'm fine," she said. "Nothing a tot won't cure."

She found a silver flask in her holdall and took a swallow, then passed it round. Fred took a jolting shot of brandy.

"Who'd leave a mantrap in a tomb? Coiled steel, with enough tensile strength after a century to bisect a poor girl, or at least take her leg off, if she didn't have a dancer's reflexes."

"George Oldrid Bunning," said Jeperson.

"Bastard General," clarified Fred.

"Just so. He must have been the *bastardo di tutti bastardi*. It would have been in the will that he be laid personally to rest by his servants, with no other witnesses, at dead of night. They were probably expecting healthy bequests. The sad, greedy lot. When closed, the sarcophagus lid triggered a mechanism and the stone door slammed down. Forever, or at least until Vanessa and her crowbar. The tomb is soundproof. Weatherproof. Escape-proof."

"There's treasure," said Vanessa. "Gold and silver. Some Egyptian things. Genuine, I think. Ushabti figures, a death mask. A lot of it is broken. The downstairs mob must have tried to improvise tools. Not that it did them any good."

The now-shattered stone door showed signs of ancient scratching. But the breaks were new, and clean.

"How long did they . . .?"

"Best not to think of it, Lillywhite," said Jeperson.

"In death, they got strong," said Vanessa. "They finally cracked the door, or we'd never have been able to shift it."

The little maid, tiny skull in a mobcap, was especially disturbing. She couldn't have been more than fourteen.

"No wonder the ghosts have been making a racket," said Fred. "If someone did that to me, I'd give nobody any rest until it was made right."

Jeperson tapped his front tooth, thinking.

"But why wait until now? As you said, they've had a hundred years in which to manifest their understandable ire. And why the Egyptian thing? Shouldn't they be Victorian servant ghosts? I should think an experience like being buried alive by a crackpot with a King Tut complex would sour one on ancient cultures in general and Egypt in particular."

"They're trying to tell us something," said Vanessa.

"Sharp girl. Indeed they are."

Fred looked away from the tomb. Across the city.

The Horus Tower caught the light. It was a black glass block, surmounted by a gold pyramid.

"George Rameses Bunning is dying," said Lillywhite. "A recurrence of some tropical disease. News got out just after Derek Leech Incorporated started suing Pyramid Press. It's had a disastrous effect on the company stock. He's liable to die broke."

"If he's anything like his great-great, then he deserves it," said Vanessa.

Jeperson snapped his fingers.

"I think he's a lot like his great-great. And I know what the ghosts have been trying to tell us. Quick, Fred, get the Rolls. Vanessa, ring Inspector Price at New Scotland Yard, and have him meet us at the Horus Tower immediately. He might want to bring a lot of hearty fellows with him. Some with guns. This is going to make a big noise."

Fred didn't care to set foot inside the Horus Tower. Just thinking about what had been done in the building made him sick to his stomach. He was on the forecourt as the coughing, shrunken, handcuffed George Rameses Bunning was led out by Inspector Euan Price. Jeperson had accompanied the police up to the pyramid on top of the tower, to be there at the arrest.

Employees gathered at their windows, looking down as the boss was hauled off to the pokey. Rumors of what he had intended for them—for two hundred and thirty-eight men and women, from senior editors to junior copy-boys—would be circulating already, though Fred guessed many wouldn't believe them.

Derek Leech's paper would carry the story, but few people put any credence in those loony crime stories in the *Comet*.

"He'll be dead before he comes to trial," said Jeperson. "Unless they find a cure."

"I hope they do, Richard," said Fred. "And he spends a good few years buried alive himself, in a concrete cell."

"His Board of Directors was wondering why, with the company on the verge of liquidation, Bunning had authorized such extensive remodeling of his corporate HQ. It was done, you know. He could have thrown the switch tomorrow, or next week. Whenever all was lost."

Now Fred shivered. Cemeteries didn't bother him, but places like this—concrete, glass, and steel traps for the enslavement and destruction of living human beings—did.

"What did he tell what's-his-name, the architect? Drache?"

"It was supposed to be about security, locking down the Tower against armed insurrection. Rioting investors wanting their dividends, perhaps. The spray nozzles that were to flood the building with nerve gas were a new kind of fire-prevention system."

"And Drache believed him?"

"He believed the money."

"Another bastard, then."

"Culpable, but not indictable."

The Horus Tower was equipped with shutters that would seal every window, door, and ventilation duct. When the master-switch was thrown, they would all come down and lock tight. Then deadly gas would fill every office space, instantly preserving in death the entire workforce. Had George Rameses Bunning intended to keep publishing magazines in the afterlife? Did he really think his personal tomb would be left inviolate in perpetuity with all the corpses at their desks, a monument to himself for all eternity? Of course, George Oldrid Bunning had got away with it for a century.

"George Rameses knew?"

"About George Oldrid's funerary arrangements? Yes."

"Bastard bastard."

"Quite."

People began to file out of the skyscraper. The workday was over early. There was a commotion.

A policeman was on the concrete, writhing around his kneed groin. Still handcuffed, George Rameses sprinted back towards his tower, shouldering through his employees.

Jeperson shouted to Price. "Get everyone out, now!"

Fred's old boss understood at once. He got a bullhorn and ordered everyone away from the building.

"He'll take the stairs," said Jeperson. "He won't chance us stopping the lifts. That'll give everyone time to make it out."

Alarm bells sounded. The flood of people leaving the Horus Tower grew to exodus proportions.

"Should I send someone in to catch him?" asked Price. "It should be easy to snag him on the stairs. He'll be out of puff by the fifth floor, let alone the thirtieth."

Jeperson shook his head.

"Too much of a risk, Inspector. Just make sure everyone else is out. This should be interesting."

"Interesting?" spat Fred.

"Come on. Don't you want to see if it works? The big clockwork trap. The plans I saw were ingenious. A real economy of construction. No electricals. Just levers, sand, and water. Drache kept to Egyptian technology. Modern materials, though."

"And nerve gas?" said Fred.

"Yes, there is that."

"You'd better hope Drache's shutters are damn good, or half London is going to drop dead."

"It won't come to that."

Vanessa crossed the forecourt. She was with the still-bewildered Lillywhite.

"What's happening?" she asked.

"George Rameses is back inside, racing towards his master-switch."

"Good grief."

"Never fear, Vanessa. Inspector, it might be an idea to find some managerial bods in the crowd. Read the class register, as it were. Just make sure everyone's out of the tower."

"Good idea, Jeperson."

The policeman hurried off.

Jeperson looked up at the building. The afternoon sun was reflected in black.

Then the reflection was gone.

Matte shutters closed like eyelids over every window. Black grilles came down behind the glass walls of the lobby, jaws meshing around floor-holes. The pyramid atop the tower twisted on a stem and lowered, locking into place. It was all done before the noise registered, a great mechanical wheezing and clanking.

Torrents of water gushed from drains around the building, squirting up fifty feet in the air from the ornamental fountain.

"He's escaped," said Fred. "A quick, easy death from the gas and it'll take twenty years to break through all that engineering."

"Oh, I don't think so," said Jeperson. "Fifteen at the most. Modern methods, you know."

"The ghosts won't rest," said Lillywhite. "Not without revenge or restitution."

"I think they might," said Jeperson. "You see, George Rameses is still alive in his tomb. Alone, ill, and—after his struggle up all those stairs—severely out of breath. Though I left the bulk of his self-burial mechanism alone, I took the precaution of disabling the nerve gas."

"Is that a scream I hear?" said Vanessa.

"I doubt it," said Jeperson. "If nothing else, George Rameses has just soundproofed his tomb."

In the following story, Gail Carriger delves into the history of one of her most beloved characters. Set in the universe of her steampunk comedy of manners Parasol Protectorate series—in which Victorian England accepts the supernatural—we get to meet preternatural protagonist Alexia Tarabotti's father, Alessandro Tarabotti, who died when she was an infant. This glimpse into his adventures should delight those who already know how being sired by Tarabotti has negatively affected Alexia's social standing and more. For those unacquainted with the series, never fear, Tarabotti's adventure involving a most unusual mummy stands quite well on its own.

The Curious Case of the Werewolf That Wasn't, the Mummy That Was, and the Cat in the Jar
Gail Carriger

———

"Yoo-hoo!"

Alessandro Tarabotti's forehead crinkled under his grey top hat. Was that some peculiar birdsong?

"Yoo-hoo, Sandy!" No, it was a voice hallooing at *him* across the broiling humanity of the bazaar.

Mr Tarabotti was so thoroughly distracted upon hearing such a name hollered at him in such a place and voice, that he relaxed his grip. The place was Luxor. The voice was just the kind that bled the inner ear, trumpeting out a nasal ode to abundant schooling and little attention toward the details of it. His loosened grip allowed the scrubby native boy with terrified fly-ridden eyes to rip himself away and scuttle down a convenient alleyway, vanishing round a pile of broken pottery.

"Well, that's torn it." Alessandro threw the scrap of material he was left holding on to the dirt street. He squinted into the alley, eyes adjusting slowly to the slatted light that crept through reed mats stretched far above. High houses and narrow streets—who would have thought Egypt a child of shadows and shade?

"Sandy, old chap!" The voice was getting closer.

"Who knows you here, sir?" asked Floote.

"More to the point, who would dare yoo-hoo at me?" Mr Tarabotti turned away from the empty alleyway to glare at his valet as though the greeting were somehow Floote's fault.

Floote pivoted and gestured softly with his right hand. His left was occupied holding on to a large glass specimen jar.

The yoo-hooer hove into sight. Alessandro winced. The man wore the most remarkably bright blue frock coat, double-breasted, with brass buttons up the front. He sported a pair of Rumnook's stained-glass binocular spectacles perched atop his tiny nose, and a limp cravat. In Mr Tarabotti's world, nothing excused a limp cravat, even the dead heat of Egypt at high noon.

"Do I know that repulsive-looking blighter?" Floote twisted his mouth slightly to one side.

"Quite right, quite right. Someone from my early days. Before I cultivated a brain. School, perhaps?" Mr Tarabotti awaited his fate, brushing a non-existent speck of dust from the sleeve of his own gold frock coat. Single-breasted, mind you, with pearl buttons and a deceptively simple cut.

"Blasted English, blemishing about the world. Is nowhere safe?"

Floote, who was himself an Englishman, did not point out that Alessandro Tarabotti, of a similarly unfortunate over-education as the man approaching, dressed and spoke like an Englishman. He didn't actually look like one, of course, boasting a long line of ancestors who had invested heavily in being dark, hook-nosed, and brooding.

Mr Tarabotti continued grousing, right up until the yoo-hooer was in earshot. "I mean to say, Floote my man, what are your countrymen about these days? You'd think they'd leave at least one small corner of the planet to the rest of us. But no, here they are, shiny as all get up, ever expanding the Empire."

"We have benefited considerably from integration of the supernatural."

"Well, it's hell on the rest of us. Do stop it, will you?"

"Very good, sir."

"Yoo-hoo, yoo-hoo!" The man came to a wheezing halt before them, sounding like an exhausted steam engine, trailing some species of suitable young lady in his corpulent wake. "Sandy Dandy the Italian? By Jove, it is you! Fancy, fancy, fancy!"

Alessandro, who did *not* like the name Sandy Dandy the Italian, lifted his monocle and examined the man downwards through it.

The man said, to the monocle, "Baronet Percival Phinkerlington. How d'you do?"

At least he had the good grace to introduce himself. Mr Tarabotti put down his eyepiece pointedly. *Really, what a thing to do to one's cravat.*

"You knew my brother, I believe."

The face above the unfortunate neckcloth did have a familiar something about the eyes and mouth. "Good Lord, old Pink's kid brother?"

The man grinned and doffed his top hat. "Right you are! Fancy I was a bit smaller back when you knew me last!"

"Practically half the man you are now."

"You remember our sister?"

The lady in question went red under Mr Tarabotti's indifferent glance. He didn't bother with the monocle. She bobbed a trembling curtsy. Ladies always caught the blush-and-flutters upon meeting Alessandro Tarabotti.

He bowed. "Miss Phinkerlington."

"Leticia, you remember Sandy? Mr Tarabotti, I should say. Italian chappy, went to Oxford with Eustace. Used to bowl for New College. Toddled down for a stopover one session break. The same time Daddy had himself that whole werewolf pack visiting." He turned back to Mr Tarabotti. "Fancy meeting you here. In Egypt of all places!"

"Indeed." Alessandro tried to remember why he would bother visiting this man's family. Had it been an assignment? Investigating the werewolves? Or had he been there to kill someone? Perhaps just a mild maiming?

Sir Percival leaned in conspiratorially. "You ought to see to your man there, Sandy. You realize, he's got his arm 'round a jam jar of dead cat?"

"Mmm, yes, preserved in some of my best formaldehyde."

The baronet gave a nervous laugh. "Always were a bit peculiar, Sandy. Eustace seemed to like you well enough. I say, this may be Egypt, but trailing about dead cats—not the *done* thing."

"I have an eccentric aunt," replied Mr Tarabotti, as though that were explanation enough.

"Don't we all, my dear fellow? Don't we all?"

"It's her cat. Or it *was* her cat, I should say."

Miss Phinkerlington noticed the valet with the glass jar full of cat for the first time. She colored a sandy sage and turned away, pretending interest in the bustling natives ebbing and flowing around them. A proper Englishwoman must find it a spectacle indeed, that tide of humanity in its multicolored robes, veiled or turbaned according to sex, loud and malodorous regardless.

"Floote—" Alessandro used Miss Phinkerlington's discomfort as an excuse "—shove off, will you? Find out what happened to our young friend. I'll see you back at the hotel."

Floote nodded and disappeared across the bazaar, cat in hand.

Sir Percival seemed to take that as an end to the business. "Well, well, well, what a thing to see you here. Been a while, old chap. Came for the climate, myself. Wettest winter in donkey's years, decided on a bit of a change. Thought Egypt might suit."

"Imagine England having a wet winter, remarkable."

"Yes, yes, well, Egypt, here, a bit, eh, warmer, you understand, than I was expecting. But we've been taking the aether regular-like. Haven't we, Leticia? Keeps a body cool." The baronet jerked his head up at the three large balloons hovering high above Luxor. They were tethered by long cords to a landing platform dockside. Well, that explained the man's abysmal choice in eyewear. Tinted spectacles were recommended for high floating.

The baronet persisted in his social niceties. "And are you having an agreeable trip?"

"Can't stand travel," replied Mr Tarabotti, "bad for the digestion and ruins one's clothes."

"Too true." The baronet looked suitably somber. "Too true." Moving hurriedly on from a clearly distasteful topic, he asked, "Staying at Chumley's Inn, are you, Sandy?"

Alessandro nodded. It was the only place to stay in Luxor. Alexandria and Cairo provided a number of respectable hotels, but Luxor was still provincial. For example, it boasted a mere three balloons, and only one with a propeller. It was a small village, really, in an almost forgotten place, of interest primarily to those with an eye toward treasure hunting. Which didn't explain why Phinkerlington and his sister were in Luxor. Nor, of course, why Alessandro Tarabotti was.

"Catch a bite to eat later tonight, old man?"

Alessandro decided it was probably better for his image to be seen dining in the company of British tourists, than to be observed too frequently about his own private business. "Certainly. But now, I'm afraid, I must beg to be excused. My man, you understand, is gadding about Egypt with a dead cat."

"Of course, of course."

Mr Tarabotti bowed to Miss Phinkerlington, who pinked once more at such direct attention. Not a bad looking chit, really.

As he walked away, he heard the baronet say, in tones of deep censure and insufficient softness, "Really, Leticia, an Italian is most inappropriate. You must stop blushing at him so significantly."

Mr Tarabotti found Floote exactly where Floote ought to be, at the center of a milling whirl of dark limbs and bright fabric, engaged in a protracted bout of fisticuffs. It was unsurprising that Floote, who had fought werewolves in Scotland and vampires all along the French

Riviera, was holding his own. What was surprising was that he did this while still clutching the jar.

Alessandro removed his jacket and laid it atop a low mud-brick wall. He rested his hat carefully alongside. The jacket was tailored to perfection, flaring with just under enough fullness so as not to be thought dandified. It had three sets of invisible pockets in the lining, each housing a collection of sharp little sticks: silver, wood, and pepper-mint. The silver was for werewolves, the wood was for vampires, and the peppermint was for Mr Tarabotti. Mr Tarabotti was rather fond of peppermint. He was also fond of that jacket; it wouldn't do for it to be harmed, and he wouldn't need the weaponry, not in the middle of the day. He did transfer the letter of marque from the jacket to a waistcoat pocket next to his monocle and his miniature antikythera device, for extra security. Then he dove into the fray.

Alessandro was not burdened with Floote's sentimental British predilection toward proper violent comportment. When Mr Tarabotti fought, he used both his fists and his feet, drawing on some spate of skills he'd learned in the Orient. He would have been summarily thrown out of White's, for his technique was, it must be admitted, most ungentlemanly.

He enjoyed himself immensely.

Mr Tarabotti had always been fond of the occasional pugilistic endeavor, ever since he was a boy—reveling in that delicious slap and crush of flesh against flesh. He relished the heated blood buzzing through his brain, numbing all senses but those vital to security—sight and touch. Any pain was a boon, a reminder of watchfulness that he must keep his mind in play only so much as it did not hinder.

It was almost too easy. Floote's attackers were ill prepared for Mr Tarabotti's sudden appearance. Soon enough, the swirling mix of appendages and colorful flowing robes resolved itself into three local malcontents: one fallen and two running away.

While Floote recovered his equanimity, Mr Tarabotti sat astride the fallen man. He grabbed at the man's arms, pressing them to the ground.

"Who hired you?" he asked in English. No response.

He repeated himself in Italian.

The man only looked up at him, dark eyes wide. He writhed about in the dirt, shaking his head frantically back and forth as though in the throes of some fit. Then, before Floote could put down the cat and render assistance, the man surged up, shook Alessandro off, and dashed away.

When Floote would have gone after, his master stayed him with a touch. "No advantage in following. We won't extract any information from the likes of him—too frightened."

"Of us?"

"Of whoever paid them to engage the foreigner brandishing a dead cat."

"Hired by your contact, sir? Perhaps he changed his mind about notifying the government."

"No, no, I think not. There is someone else in play. Or several some-ones. Deuced inconvenient. Not to mention, insulting. As if I would gad about town dressed like a manservant."

He went to retrieve his jacket and hat.

"Who might be looking to stop you, sir?" Floote came over and straightened his master's lapel, checking the fit of the shoulders for good measure.

"Much good that blasted cat has done us. I thought it would provide quite the excuse for visiting Egypt. Now it's just making us easy to iden-tify." The cat had caused quite the flutter at customs. Officials were used to dead animals being transported out of Egypt, usually of the mummy variety, but not in. Luckily for Mr Tarabotti's aunt, gold worked regard-less of country, and Mr Tarabotti had the gold. The cat had served its purpose, until now. After all, why else would a rich Italian gentleman be traveling to Egypt during the high season of 1841?

"We must get rid of it, Floote."

Floote shifted his grip on the jar. "Shall I leave it in the street, sir?"

"Good God, no. Aunt Archangelica would never forgive me. Find someone to fix it up as she demanded, and quickly."

"Very good, sir."

Sunset found Sir Percival Phinkerlington and Miss Phinkerlington awaiting Mr Tarabotti's presence at dinner in the hotel dining hall. Some crosses were meant to be borne during one's lifetime, Alessandro supposed. He joined them with a tight little smile, and helped himself to a glass of the mostly empty bottle of wine.

"Sandy, evening!" the baronet squawked. Miss Phinkerlington blushed and nodded.

"Good Lord, man." Mr Tarabotti sipped the wine. It was cloyingly sweet. "Don't you own any other neckwear?"

The pleasantries disposed of, Mr Tarabotti settled back languidly in his chair, waiting for the first course of what, he had no doubt, would be an utterly unsatisfactory meal. "What happened to old Pink?" He was only half interested. "I thought he was due for the title, not you."

Out of the corner of his eye, he caught someone watching him closely from a nearby table. He leaned his chair back on two legs, tilting his head about in an attitude of foppish boredom. The watcher was a military gentleman of some breed, stiff about the neck and long about the hair. The man noticed Mr Tarabotti noticing him and returned to his food.

Baronet Phinkerlington frowned, troubled by the Italian's bluntness. "You didn't hear?"

"Married beneath his station, did he? Go into trade? Die?" Alessandro tut-tutted, and declined to remark that society gossip was not his focus during those few times he'd returned to England.

Miss Phinkerlington put a hand to her brother's arm. "Don't, Percy dear." He patted her hand. "It's all right, Leticia. Sandy here's an old friend of Eustace's. Eustace always spoke highly of him. Played cricket together. Solid fellow." He leaned toward Alessandro, his breath redolent with the scent of cardamom and burnt aubergine. "Eustace tossed the title over. Gave it up to become claviger to some toothy old fluff of a lone werewolf."

"They always do take the smart ones from a family, don't they?"

"Mother was devastated but, between you and me, it's probably for the best. Wouldn't have got any grandkids out of old Eustace. If you get my meaning." The baronet waggled his eyebrows.

Mr Tarabotti did. It also tickled his memory and explained why he'd visited the Phinkerlingtons all those years ago. Not an infiltration as it turned out, at least not an official one.

"Do I say felicitations?" Mr Tarabotti sampled a rolled ball of some fried brown crispy substance that in appearance resembled meat and in taste resembled sawdust.

"Only if he makes it through the bite and change. You understand how it goes. Oh, silly me, you don't, do you? Poor man. Italian." The baronet shook his head sadly—demonstrating the pity of the one country that had accepted the supernatural for all the other poor ignorant countries that hadn't. Open acceptance of vampires and werewolves was *the thing* that kept the British Isles separate from the rest of Europe. Well, that and their cuisine.

Alessandro stroked thoughtfully at the indent above his upper lip. "Ah the English—confident in but two things."

"And what are those, Sandy my lad?"

"The supernatural and cricket."

Sir Percival laughed heartily then stuffed his face with a number of the most uninviting-looking little cakes imaginable.

"You insulting the national pastime, old chap?" he said, fortunately after he swallowed.

"Which, the supernatural or cricket?"

"Cricket, of course. You used to bowl a nicely lethal over yourself, if memory serves. Spinner, no?"

"Pace bowler."

The baronet nodded. "Ah yes, I remember Eustace crowing about how fast you were."

Alessandro raised both eyebrows at that, but didn't reply. Out of the corner of his eye, he observed the blond military man stand up from his table and make his way toward the door, moving behind and around the various chairs in the dining hall with precise little twists. He disappeared, not upstairs to his rooms as one might expect, but out into the cold night.

"Fancy a little stroll, Phinkerlington?" suggested Mr Tarabotti, pushing his plate away petulantly.

The baronet, whose corpulence suggested he never fancied a stroll, little or otherwise, looked to his sister for salvation. She proved herself of no use whatsoever, a state evidently familiar to all around her, by saying, "Oh yes, Percy dear, do go. You know I shouldn't mind. Some of the other ladies were planning on a game of bridge in the drawing room. I shall be perfectly entertained there until your return."

Sir Percival Phinkerlington's only possible excuse thus occupied with cards, the poor chap could do nothing but join Mr Tarabotti on his perambulation.

The hotel was situated near the northern edge of Luxor, the better to take in the view, such as it was: sand and dust on one side and the Nile on the other. They turned away from the verdant embankment, with its cultivated palm groves, and headed toward the desert in all its burnt glory. A harvest moon hung low over two sets of limestone mountain ranges, one near and one far. Mr Tarabotti pulled out his antikythera and confirmed his suspicions—full.

"Crikey, that darn moon's bigger than a bison's bottom."

"Very poetical turn of phrase, Sir Percival." Mr Tarabotti put the antikythera away and searched the quiet streets. It was prayer time, so they were mostly deserted; yet he could not spot the missing military man.

They paused at the very edge of town. The baronet took out a large cigar, nipped the tip, and lit it with one of those new-fangled aethero-spark distributors. "Tell you the truth, old man, we're here for Leticia's health."

"Can't she withstand the damp?"

"No, not that. Hers is a health that's not quite right about the head, if you comprehend my meaning. Ever since Eustace went over. Chit sees night crawlers everywhere and wakes up screaming. Thought we'd bring her here." He puffed on his cigar.

"Because there are no supernatural creatures in Egypt?" Mr Tarabotti moved out of the smoke, coughing delicately. Cheap cigar.

"So they say, so they say. Like no snakes in Ireland. It's one of those things."

"True enough. There hasn't been a werewolf south of Alexandria in living memory." Alessandro thought of the papal letter of marque tucked securely in his waistcoat.

"Make a study of the supernatural, do you, Sandy?"

Mr Tarabotti said nothing.

"'Course you do. You Italians are all the same. Religious fanatics, the lot of you. Church says jump, you bounce about waving silver and wood, hoping it'll rid the world of all that goes chomp in the night."

"And yet I see acceptance of the supernatural has clearly done you and your family proud."

"Touché, touché. Fair enough. I'm not claiming to be a progressive, simply saying as how one extreme doesn't balance out the other. Far as I'm concerned, vampires and werewolves can do theirs, so long as I'm left alone to do mine. If you take my meaning." He removed the half-finished cigar from his mouth and looked at the glowing tip thoughtfully.

"Would you be so magnanimous, Baronet, had you not inherited a title because your brother chose the supernatural over family obligation?"

"Now see here, that's hardly the thing to say!"

Mr Tarabotti held up a hand sharply, cutting off any possible tirade. He cocked his dark head to one side, listening.

Far away, somewhere in the depths of a desert *wadi*, something howled. "Damn this country with all its foreign beasts. I'm telling you, it's all very well for Leticia's peace of mind—not a vampire in sight—but all these snakes and camels and jackals are playing hell with my finer feelings." Phinkerlington turned away, snorting.

Alessandro frowned. The howl came again. "Werewolf."

The baronet tossed the butt-end of his cigar petulantly to the sandy ground. "That moon may be full, but don't be ridiculous, you just said, remember? There are no supernatural creatures in Egypt."

Floote was waiting for Mr Tarabotti in their rooms.

"Message, sir." He held out a little wooden tray with two crisp pieces of papyrus on top. Scribbled on the top one was a message in Italian, the tiny, messy script bleeding in places along the lines of the fibrous paper. Alessandro deciphered it while Floote divested him of his coat and hat.

"I'm to go there tonight. He apologizes for the skittish messenger this morning. Apparently, the boy was supposed to deliver this, but was spooked by our cat. Imagine being raised amongst mummies and fearing modern scientific preservation techniques." He switched to the second sheet of papyrus. "And a map. How very thoughtful. I wonder if that's what those bully-boys were after this afternoon? This map."

Lowering his hand, he raised an eyebrow at his manservant. "Speaking of the cat."

Floote pointed to a wobbly reed dresser upon which lay a smallish cat mummy.

"Is that . . .?"

"Not your aunt's feline, sir. The reports were perfectly correct; no one remembers how to mummify any more. I found a willing apothecary, but the results were, regrettably . . ." a delicate pause ". . . squishy. I managed to acquire that artifact, there, at a reasonable price and in excellent condition as a substitute."

Mr Tarabotti peered at the specimen through his monocle. "It'll have to do. We'll tell Aunt Archangelica they made it look emaciated and ancient for the sake of fashion."

Floote went to hang up his master's outerwear.

"Don't bother, Floote. I'll need it again immediately."

"Sir?"

"Tonight, remember?" He wiggled the papyrus with the map on it at his valet.

"Of course, sir, but surely not the gold coat? Most inappropriate for one of your evening engagements."

"Silly me. You packed the burgundy?"

Floote gave him a look that suggested he was gravely insulted that Mr Tarabotti should ever doubt such a thing.

The burgundy jacket was a comparatively stylish affair, but cut looser than the gold to better hide multiple pockets, and with a full skirt to mask any additional accoutrement secreted about a gentleman's waist. Alessandro slipped it on while Floote bustled about putting various items on to a large silver platter, which he then proffered politely to his master.

Mr Tarabotti selected from the offerings, as a man will from a particularly delectable cheese plate: a nice bit of garrote there, two vials of quality poison here, a tin of Germany's best phosphorus matches for extra zest, and a flask of turpentine to wash it all down. He chose one of the two pistols, the smallest and his personal favorite, checked that it was loaded, and stashed it inside a pocket over his left hip. After a pause to think, he took three cigars, the tidy little cheroots he preferred, and stashed them in the tin with the matches.

"Will you be requiring my company this evening, sir?"

"I shouldn't think so. After all, he is only an archaeologist."

Floote refrained from comment upon that statement. He had spent over ten years as valet to Mr Tarabotti and, as yet, no one had turned out to be only anything. He smoothed down the sleeves of the burgundy coat and checked its armament carefully before buttoning it closed. He handed Mr Tarabotti a matching top hat.

"Will there be anything else, sir?"

Alessandro tightened his lips over his teeth in thought. "Perhaps the other gun as well, if you would be so kind?"

Floote passed it to him. "Try not to kill anyone important, sir."

Stashing the gun up his sleeve in a special quick-release wrist holster, Alessandro grinned. It was an expression that did not sit comfortably on his patrician face.

"Any final orders, sir?"

"The usual, Floote. If I don't come back . . ."

"No record, no witnesses. I am aware of your standing instructions."

"Proceed then, Floote."

"Very good, sir."

There were more people in the streets when Mr Tarabotti exited the hotel a second time. Alessandro wondered if nightlife had evolved in Egypt due to the lack of supernatural, much in the manner of peculiar animals evolving on islands without natural predators, if one were given to believe Mr Darwin's outlandish theories. Then, again, perhaps it was simply the coolness of the air that encouraged wide-scale evening socialization.

No one bothered him. No beggars whined for baksheesh. No tradesmen forced their goods in his direction. Alessandro Tarabotti had a way of walking that, even as a conspicuous foreigner in a foreign land, marked him as undesirable. Thus, he could move quickly through the narrow alleys that purported to be Luxor's main streets, passing whitewashed huts and undernourished obelisks, coming finally to a steep slope and sandy shore. Nearby, the three balloons were tied down, only one still inflated.

It took very little in the way of local currency or time to hire a stunted raft, piloted by a lackluster youngster, to ferry him across the river. It took slightly more to convince the urchin to wait. At two gold coins and twenty minutes, Alessandro considered it quite economical. The boat-boy even pointed out the path he needed to take toward the tombs. Mr Tarabotti had paid more for less in the past, and probably would again.

The map, it turned out, was not scaled as he might have hoped, and it was a long walk of some four miles before he noted any of the landmarks indicated there. He left behind the lushness of the floodplain for a long limestone canyon where little grew and less thrived. He was grateful for the moon, that he need not carry one of the ridiculous teapot-shaped oil lamps in order to see his way.

It should have been a pleasant walk, but Mr Tarabotti, whom no one would ever insult by calling anxious, could not shake the feeling that he was being followed. Every time he jerked about and looked behind him, he saw nothing there. Nothing at all. This was compounded by another sensation, one of being repelled, as though he were a magnet too close to another of the same polarity. He'd felt it ever since Cairo but here it was worst of all, almost unbearable.

He happened upon the archaeological encampment eventually; a copse of canvas tents nestled at the base of a cliff. It appeared quite deserted, so he clambered up to the mouth of a rock-cut tomb, marked by an uninspired "X" on his little map. As he climbed, a new scent overlaid the clay musk of the cooling sands—tobacco and vanilla.

"I thought you hadn't received the message," said a voice in Italian when he reached the top. A figure resolved itself from gloom into a man by stepping forward out of the shadow of the rocks around the entranceway. Fragments of limestone crunched under sensible boots. "Trouble finding the place?"

"You sent a map. It had an 'X' on it."

The man gripped Alessandro's shoulders, kissing him on each cheek in the manner of old friends. "Giuseppe Caviglia."

"Alessandro Tarabotti." Mr Tarabotti saw no harm in giving the archaeologist his name, though he objected to the intimacy of the rest of the greeting. "Show me what you found."

Mr Caviglia tilted his head to one side and took a draw on his pipe. "You know I can't simply do that."

Mr Tarabotti smiled tightly. "A rule player." He reached into his waistcoat pocket and pulled out the letter of marque, passing it over.

Giuseppe Caviglia unfolded and read it carefully by moonlight. "The government's full confidence? That must be nice."

"It has its benefits."

"You're authorized to take any action you deem necessary in conjunction with my findings here. What, exactly, does that mean?"

Alessandro ignored the question by asking one of his own. "You indicated in your original missive that this was a supernatural matter."

Mr Caviglia nodded once, sharply.

"Well, you caught the antiquities ministry's interest. They brought your letter to government oversight, and oversight brought it to the Templars, and the Templars brought it to me."

The archaeologist sucked in on his pipe sharply at that revelation. Mr Tarabotti waited with ill-disguised impatience while Mr Caviglia coughed out puffs of vanilla-scented smoke.

Eyes watering, the man looked more closely at Alessandro's face. "You're one of them, aren't you? I thought they were all dead. Too susceptible to the poisonous humors."

Mr Tarabotti, who was a bit of a poisonous humor, said sharply, "Interesting that you even know of my kind."

"My cousin is a Templar," Mr Caviglia explained hastily. Alessandro grimaced. That could make things difficult.

Mr Caviglia recovered his equanimity. He handed back the letter of marque, openly evaluating his visitor's appearance. Alessandro knew what he saw: a man of lean build and patrician nose, tall, wearing a cleverly cut coat and trousers a little too tight. In short—a dandy. He would not see that the coat was cut to hide musculature, rather than exaggerate it, and that the tightness of the trousers was to distract from the smooth movements of the legs that wore them.

"You're not what I would have expected."

Alessandro cocked his head. "Well, at least one of us is surprised. You're exactly what I expected."

And the archaeologist was—unshaven, undersized, wearing round spectacles, and a jacket no decent human would wish upon his worst enemy. He could be handsome under the grime, in a peevish scholarly way, but there were certain unforgivable flaws. Atop his head rested a battered object that might have started life as some species of hat many years ago and at the bottom of the ocean.

Mr Tarabotti shuddered. "Shall we go in now?"

Mr Caviglia nodded, tapping out his pipe on the side of the entrance-way. "A remarkable discovery, really quite remarkable." He led the way inside the tomb.

Its ceiling was higher than Alessandro had anticipated. A smoking torch in the far corner cast a dim flickering light. It was as clean as could be expected from a place recently filled with rubble for thousands of years. There were few artifacts left—a broken column, several pottery bowls before an inset shrine, and a pile of digging tools nested at the base of the torch—but the walls were littered with carved and painted images. On one, a jackal-headed man sat at a vast banquet—bread, meat, and fruit laid out before him, a curly-tailed monkey crouched underneath his throne. On the other, the same man was shown undergoing various death rituals of a decidedly heathen nature.

"We found the tomb partly looted, of course. Most of them are. Oddly, the looters stopped halfway through and not a single person has touched the tomb since. Until we came along." The archaeologist crossed the room, grabbed up the torch, and led the way through a carved opening into a short passageway.

Mr Tarabotti followed.

The passage turned to the left, and before them stood a huge basalt statue of a mummy, threatening and protective.

The archaeologist ignored this, turning again and leading the way down a steep set of stairs, talking all the while.

"Once we saw the mummy we realized why. The natives are terribly superstitious about these kinds of things. Well, you would be too, if you grew up in a land entirely devoid of the supernatural. I mean, our government has been trying for elimination ever since the Inquisition, but the hives and packs will keep springing up. Not here, though."

Mr Tarabotti placed a hand against the tunnel wall to steady himself as he climbed down the dark stairs. "They're too strong and too well connected."

"Yet the Templars back home keep trying."

"They're believers." Mr Tarabotti grimaced as his hand came away from the wall filthy with dark brown dust and a fine yellow powder.

"And you?"

Alessandro shrugged. He believed in very little beyond his job and the wealth it generated.

"Well, regardless, this excavation has been fascinating. The sarcophagus has unique hieroglyphics on it. And the mummy—excellent preservation, stunning condition, from flesh to fiber. There."

They emerged into a room slightly smaller than the first, and far less tidy. It was cluttered, with antiquities spread across the floor and nestled into niches in the painted walls. Everything was covered in a thick layer of dust and, while some artifacts had been knocked over and broken, most were intact. The preservation was amazing. Wooden furniture stood in the corners, draped in crumbling textiles with large stone statues of animal-headed gods resting on top. Pots in every shape and size lined the walls, nestled amongst crowds of tiny human statues, piles of copper weapons, and a myriad of other mundanities. In the middle of the jumble, next to the massive hole it had obviously been hauled out of, stood a large sarcophagus of red granite, its lid off and tilted against its side.

The archaeologist tugged Mr Tarabotti over to it. Inside, a mummy lay partially unwrapped, the looters having started with its head, lusting after the precious amulets of gold and lapis tucked inside the linen bandages.

They'd stopped.

There was no doubt as to why.

"Remarkable," said Mr Tarabotti in English.

The creature inside was human, almost, but the bones of its face were not. Teeth, jaw, shape of forehead all leaned more toward canine than man. There was even a light patterning of hair in the shrunken wrinkles of the dried brown skin.

"A werewolf."

"Undoubtedly."

"Mummified in half *Homo sapien*, half *Homo lupis* form." Alessandro pulled a small analogue aetheromechanical transducer from his jacket pocket and prodded delicately at the mummy, testing for remnant vital aetheromagnetism. Nothing. "They say alpha werewolves can maintain just such a state as this, half in, half out of human form. They use it in metamorphosis rituals. Can you imagine?" His fine upper lip curled. "Disgusting."

He investigated further. "Well, I commend you, Mr Caviglia. If this is a hoax, it is a very good one."

The archaeologist puffed up in outrage. "I assure you, sir—!"

Mr Tarabotti held up the transducer autocratically to stop any denunciation and continued examining the body. "Don't you think that head shape is a little odd?"

"Aside from it being attached to a human body?"

"We call it Anubis form," said a new voice in old-fashioned Italian flattened out by a British accent.

Out of the staircase entrance came the gleaming muzzle of a nasty double-barreled pistol followed by a blond military-looking gentleman.

"Hello, Curse-breaker," he said to Mr Tarabotti in English, gun steady. "You were at dinner earlier this evening." Alessandro switched to the Queen's tongue, out of courtesy for their visitor, at the same time releasing his gun out of its wrist holster. The movement was so subtle as to be imperceptible. The gun slid down toward his hand, almost peeking out of the bottom of one burgundy sleeve.

The man nodded. "I followed you from the hotel. As you inconvenienced me by not allowing my agents to steal the map from you."

Mr Caviglia raised both hands and straightened away from the sarcophagus. His eyes were fixed on the intruder's weapon.

Mr Tarabotti sniffed. "I knew someone was following me. How did I miss you?"

"You never looked up." The man had a soldier's bearing and a young face, but his eyes were dulled by past lives.

"I'm too old to remember humans have taken to the skies." Alessandro shook his head at himself.

"You're a werewolf," accused the archaeologist, with more power of deduction than Alessandro would have given him credit for.

The man snorted. "Not here, I'm bloody well not." He glared at Mr Tarabotti as though this fact were somehow his fault. "I hope you know what a bother it has been, traveling through Egypt after you these weeks. I had to learn to shave again, and every little cut takes donkey's years to heal. I don't know how you mortals do it. I really don't. I hope you appreciate the risk I'm taking."

Alessandro licked his lips. This was going to be fun. "Oh, I appreciate it."

The un-werewolf narrowed his eyes. "Don't you move." He glanced briefly at the archaeologist. "Is it true what you found? What he said? Is that there a mummy of a werewolf in Anubis form?"

"See for yourself," suggested Mr Tarabotti, hoping the un-werewolf would come within striking distance.

The un-werewolf didn't take the bait, too old for that. "We used to rule this land. Did you know that?"

Mr Caviglia gave a little snort of disbelief.

"You archaeologists haven't figured that one out yet, have you? They worshipped us as gods. Turned sour on us in the end. Most things do. The god-breaker plague swept the Two Lands and, within a generation, every werewolf had died. We've not been back since because this—" he gestured to himself "—is what results."

"Mortality."

"And why would you risk everything to follow me here?"

The un-werewolf looked at Mr Tarabotti. "Curse-breaker, this mummy is *our* ancestor. You daylighters—" and he included the archaeologist in his contemptuous statement "—have no right. Especially not some crusading religious fanatics. That mummy is the property of the British Government, we have the concession, not the Italians. Ours to study and understand."

Mr Tarabotti smiled his tight little smile. "Who said we wanted to study it?"

The archaeologist and the un-werewolf both looked to him in shock. "But the Templars promised."

Mr Tarabotti shrugged. "The Templars lied. And we can't very well have the English using it as some kind of pro-supernatural propaganda tool."

No record and no witnesses.

He slid the derringer smoothly the rest of the way out of his sleeve and into his hand, turned slightly in the same movement, and shot Mr Caviglia in the chest at point-blank range. The archaeologist fell with a tiny cry of surprise and lay still against the corner of the sarcophagus, slumped and limp.

"We can't allow you to go babbling about this to the antiquarian community either, I'm afraid." He looked thoughtfully down at the scholar's dead body. "Pity."

The un-werewolf started, but his gun remained trained on Mr Tarabotti. Alessandro tucked the now-useless pistol into his pocket casually, feeling about for his second one, and narrowed his eyes at the man.

"What it must be like, seeing that—" he tilted his head at the fallen archaeologist "—and knowing you could so easily end up the same way."

"Do you really think, after hundreds of years, we immortals fear death?"

"Do the crazy ones, who have lived too long, travel to Egypt to die voluntarily?"

The un-werewolf shrugged. "Some."

"So, we find ourselves at an impasse."

"Mmm, please take your hand out of your jacket, Curse-breaker."

Mr Tarabotti did so, tucking his second tiny gun up the end of his other sleeve in a maneuver he'd once learned from a street performer.

The un-werewolf gestured with his pistol for Mr Tarabotti to move away from the mummy and toward the door. Cautiously, Alessandro did so. But, near to the entrance, as he passed close to his opponent, he pretended to stumble over a fallen urn, lurching violently to one side.

The un-werewolf growled at him and stepped threateningly forward. Alessandro dove, shifting his weight and lashing up and out with his foot, striking the man's wrist where it held the gun.

The double barrel discharged a bullet, missing Mr Tarabotti by a foot, the slug plowing hard into a support column, spitting limestone shards at both men. The un-werewolf swore and rotated the chamber to load his second shot.

Alessandro rolled, as much as he could, over the small statues and artifacts littering the floor, coming into a crouch covered in thousands of years of dust but with his second gun clutched in his hand.

He fired, hitting the un-werewolf in the shoulder. The shot wasn't deadly, but it did cause the man to drop his own gun in surprise.

Mr Tarabotti lunged for the fallen weapon at the same time as the un-werewolf, and the two of them scrabbled through the ancient offerings. Alessandro struck out viciously at his opponent, connecting where the shoulder wound seeped old blood, groping for the fallen gun with his other hand.

The un-werewolf backhanded Mr Tarabotti, handicapped with only one working arm, and that odd British distaste for kicking in a fight.

Mr Tarabotti had no such compunctions. Crawling as they both were after the fallen weapon, Alessandro kicked out with one foot and managed to shove the man over. Grabbing the gun, he came up triumphant, pointing the weapon at the un-werewolf, who now crouched amongst the wreckage looking as savage as he might have in his lupine state.

Mr Tarabotti shot the last bullet. But the man was fast, even without supernatural speed, and managed to dodge. Frustrated, Alessandro threw the gun petulantly aside and pulled the flask of turpentine from his jacket.

He scattered it liberally about, making sure to coat the mummy in particular.

The un-werewolf lunged for him, seizing him by the waist and hurling him back to the floor. Mr Tarabotti pushed against the man's chin, trying to wrench his neck. His opponent howled, an animalistic sound coming from such a human face.

"That was you howling earlier this evening?" Mr Tarabotti panted out the question, clawing at the creature's eyes.

"Staying in practice, even if I can't change," came the hissed reply, as the un-werewolf struggled to hold Alessandro in a one-armed grip.

"That's rather perverse, you know that?" Mr Tarabotti uppercut sharply with the palm of one hand, achieving just enough leverage to break the un-werewolf's nose.

Alessandro squirmed away. Coming panting to his feet, he brushed off his burgundy coat with fierce disgusted movements. "Is such dusty combat strictly necessary?"

The un-werewolf only bled at him.

Feeling deeply put upon, Mr Tarabotti reached once more inside his jacket, pulling out the tin of phosphorus matches. He backed away until he was at the doorway. There, he struck a match and threw it at the turpentine-covered mummy.

Seeing this action, the un-werewolf decided on self-preservation and charged past him up the steps.

The flammable liquid caught easily, the fire quickly spreading to burn away happily at the wooden furniture and textiles scattered about. From the amount of smoke and flames flaring up from within the sarcophagus, Alessandro had no doubt the mummy was ablaze as well. He whirled and ran up the stairs and out of the tomb, coughing delicately.

Outside, things were not as they should be. The un-werewolf was getting away, dangling precariously off the edge of the gondola of a hot-air balloon, floating upwards. A tubby sort of personage was manning the balloon's thermotransmitter and cranking up the hydro-dine engine to get a steering propeller moving—a familiar tubby sort of personage, wearing a long scarf wrapped about his throat.

"Why, Sir Percival. I see you *do* own more than one item of neck wear."

"What ho, Mr Tarabotti? Sad business, this. I did so hope it wasn't you."

"Working for the Crown, are we, Phinkerlington? How menial."

"For the Glory of the Empire, Mr Tarabotti. Can't expect a Templars' toady to understand. Now can I?" As he spoke, the baronet succeeded in getting the propeller in motion, and then waddled over to assist the un-werewolf in flopping, fishlike fashion into the safety of the gondola.

The balloon began to rise upwards, its propeller whirling mighty gusts of steam. Soon it would be at sufficient height to set a steady course back to Luxor.

Alessandro flicked the air with the back of his hand, gesturing the men away as if they were mere irritations that had been bothering his evening's stroll.

No record and no witnesses.

He searched around his feet for a sharp fragment of limestone. The blaze from the lower part of the tomb had extended into the open room at the top. It lit the ridge-side on which he stood with flickering orange. It seemed the dust, itself, was flammable, and fresh air only encouraged the conflagration. He could hear the faint *poof* sound of limestone spalling in the heat.

He found a rock of adequate size. There was enough room on the hillside for him to run up his speed. Not exactly the perfect cricket pitch, but, then, one couldn't be too picky about such things. Mr Tarabotti may have been born Italian, but he *had* bowled for New College, and been widely regarded as one of the fastest on record. The stone hit the balloon perfectly, tearing through the oiled canvas right above the engine feed, with immediate and catastrophic results.

The hot gas leaked out, deflating the balloon from one side and causing the whole contraption to list dramatically. The un-werewolf let out a howl of mixed anger and distress and Sir Percival swore, but there was nothing either man could do to salvage the situation. Moments later the balloon burst into flames, falling to the ground with a thudding crash.

Mr Tarabotti paused to light a cheroot with one of his remaining phosphorus matches and then walked toward the wreckage.

Both men were lying face down in the sand. Mr Tarabotti turned the un-werewolf over with his foot, puffing softly. Definitely dead. Then he heard a small moan.

"Still alive, Phinkerlington?" He pulled out his garrote and tossed the end of the cheroot away.

No record and no witnesses.

The fallen baronet turned his head weakly and looked at Mr Tarabotti. "Looking less and less likely, Sandy my man," he croaked. "Nice bowl, by-the-by, perfectly aimed and you even got a bit of spin on it."

"I do what I can." Alessandro crouched over the fallen man and reached forward with the garrote.

The baronet coughed, blood leaked out the side of his mouth. "No need, Sandy old chap, no need. Do me a bit of a turn, would you? For old Eustace's sake, if not mine."

Mr Tarabotti sat back on his heels, surprised.

"See Leticia safely home to England, would you? Doesn't know a thing about this business, I assure you. She's only a slip of a thing, good chit, really, can't have her wandering about Egypt on her lonesome. You understand?"

Mr Tarabotti considered. He'd have had to investigate the girl anyway. This gave him a good excuse to find out what she knew. He'd be terribly, terribly understanding and sympathetic. Tragic accident in the desert. What were they thinking, floating at night? He'd been out for a stroll and saw the balloon fall from afar. Dashed to the rescue but wasn't in time to save anyone. Old friend of the family, of course he'd be happy to escort her home.

Percival Phinkerlington's watery eyes bored into him. Alessandro pursed his lips and nodded curtly. The baronet sighed, closing his eyes. The sigh turned into a wet rattling gurgle, and then silence.

Alessandro Tarabotti lit another small cheroot off the burning balloon basket. What *would* he put in his report to the Templars? Such an incommodious bit of business. A dead un-werewolf was one thing, but a dead British aristocrat? He sighed, puffing out smoke. They'd not be pleased. Not pleased at all. *And the mummy.* Did his superiors need to know the truth of the mummy? For the truth was, that was no wolf's head at all. Alessandro Tarabotti had killed enough werewolves to know the difference, emaciated or fully fleshed. No, it had been far more dog-like, small, pointed. *A jackal, perhaps?*

He smoked his cigar. On the walls of that burning tomb, the jackal-headed god, Anubis, had been depicted assisting a jackal-headed man into the afterlife.

Werejackals? Surely not.

Alessandro snorted. But some twinge of fancy reminded him of the un-werewolf's words. *They worshipped us as gods.* And Ancient Egyptian gods had other animal heads. Lots of other animal heads. No wonder the Templars wanted to keep such information out of British hands.

Mr Tarabotti turned to commence his long walk back to Luxor. Baronet Phinkerlington might be dead, but Alessandro had to escort Miss Phinkerlington back to England and deal with a mess of paper-work as a result. He wondered which one of them had got the better deal out of the arrangement. Probably Phinkerlington.

The fictional reporter, Gilbert Cox, of "The Night Comes On," would have gone to great lengths to get an Egyptological scoop. In 1931, when the story is set, Howard Carter was not quite finished with the enormous task of removing, conserving, and cataloguing the contents of Tutankhamun's tomb. The discovery coincided with the beginnings of the mass media age; "King Tut" made good copy. The continuing revelations of breathtaking objects that emerged from the tomb as it was painstakingly cleared meant the coverage continued. (As Carter later said, "No power on earth could shelter us from the light of publicity.") Then, too, there was always the hope of more "amazing discoveries" in the Valley of the Kings.

The Night Comes On
Steve Duffy

Precisely what treasures were lost to the world in the great fire at Rowlandson's of Putney may, I daresay, never be known. By 1935, the date of the fire, Rowlandson's was perhaps the largest pantechnicon in the country, having been open for the storage of goods since 1826; generations of Britons, most typically Empire families between postings, had availed themselves of its facilities, and it was stocked to full capacity on the night of the blaze, which is now thought to have been caused by a fault in one of the electric goods lifts. What is known is that less than ten per cent of the properties therein were recovered undamaged; of that ten per cent, some fifty-odd lots were never claimed by their owners. The process of notifying the holders of these items was hampered by the loss in the fire of all records pertaining to ownership; they were advertised extensively, in Britain and the Colonies, and those that remained unclaimed were eventually sold off at public auction. I was present at the crying of these items, and put in a successful bid for lot number thirty-six, described in the catalogue as *MSS.; various antiq. misc.*; it took the form of a small steamer trunk, whose contents—but that is a story for another time, I fear. For the tale I am now about to unfold, we must go a little further back in time—to the sweltering summer of 1931, and a curious newspaper article in the *Daily Dispatch*.

With the admittedly notable exception of the Great War, news items have traditionally been reckoned by the journalistic trade to be at a premium in high summer. Thus one opens one's paper in July or August and reads accounts, not of great doings on the international stage, or of the bold and daring exploits of great men, but instead of Lord So-and-So the Cabinet minister's choice of bedside reading, or of the latest talkie-star's intention to buy up a castle in England and ship it piecemeal back home to California, or some other such feeble diversion. Sub-editors issue increasingly wretched and despairing entreaties for news—any news—and are in the last extremity quite often driven to resurrect from amongst the piles of "spiked" items on their desks some story which, on any normal news day, would have hardly warranted an inch of column space; this squib is then resubmitted to its originator for fattening and "dressing," like a Christmas goose, before appearing across six or seven columns of a prominent inside page, with eighteen-point headlines and an artist's impression. The trick is to pretend by this treatment that some entirely novel, but nevertheless great and vital issue is being aired, with the suggestion that it has been criminally overlooked by all other commentators (though of course the issue must not be so out-of-the-way as to preclude the British public from forming an opinion on it). If the thing is well enough managed, rival views on the subject may be solicited; a correspondence may be sparked off, and in time, the affair may even be graced with the ponderous imprimatur of an editorial opinion, in the second or the third week of its brief mayfly life. Thus we see demonstrated the undreamt-of resourcefulness of the great British press; *et in sempiternum floreat*.

Doubtless these seasonal exigencies lay behind the appearance, in much the manner outlined above, in the *Dispatch* of 29 July 1931, of a communiqué from Mr Redmond O'Connell, the notorious adventurer and black magician. I am safe in employing the latter description, since Mr O'Connell is now, alas, unable to invoke the law of libel as he did in a previous case against the *Daily Rocket* in 1920. Even at that time, however, not a few people found it strange that so tireless a self-publicist should choose to take issue at the appellation, and wondered why he should complain at being referred to in a newspaper article in the style in which he so assiduously strove to present himself in all his other dealings. For Redmond O'Connell, of Dublin, Paris, and latterly Cornwall, had long been fixed in the popular mind as a mountebank at the most charitable estimation, ever since his well-publicized sending-down from Trinity College in the furor over his first book of blasphem-ous poems and *contes*. The impression was reinforced when he formed the Grand Loge de l'Innomable in Paris at the turn of the century, and boasted to the press that if he so wished, he could cause the death of all the leading statesmen of Europe by performing a certain invocation, at a certain time, in a certain place, to a certain deity; and it was redoubled when, on his island retreat of Kaikethera in the Cyclades, the wife of a leading American industrialist was discovered dead of a morphine overdose on the beach before the Grand Loge's Temple of the Will. The Greek authorities chose not to prosecute, on the understand-ing that he quitted Kaikethera—quitted, in point of fact, the country; and so began his scandalous and ignominious wanderings across the map of Europe, fresh outrage in each fresh capital, till at last he was forced to take up his abode in an old part-ruined priory near Gorran Haven, in Cornwall, his considerable fortune all but gone, his influence fatally diminished.

Even in his semi-fallen aspect, however, the self-styled Fiery Lucifer was still a Name before the newspaper-purchasing public, and so when the *Daily Dispatch* sought around for a stick with which to beat its circu-lation rival, the *Rocket*, O'Connell's unsolicited communiqué from Cairo came in conspicuously useful. True, it was atrociously written, in O'Connell's characteristically bombastic and portentous style; but then the *Dispatch's* readers would expect bombast and portent from the pen of the Fiery Lucifer. True again, it was contentious to the last degree in point of factual content; but they could always run a follow-up article by a recognized expert in the field, by way of a corrective. And so, the *Dispatch* ran its story, beneath the title "Amazing Discoveries in the Valley of the Kings—Renowned Mystic Claims to have Rocked the World of Archaeology"; and gave perhaps a quarter as much space the next day to one Professor Mellis of the British Museum, writing incognito as a Respected Archaeologist, that he might seek to refute some of O'Connell's wilder contentions. Thus two of our protagonists enter the ring; the next may now be introduced, ascending the steps of Professor Mellis's club in Pall Mall perhaps a week after the *Dispatch* went to press with its first sensational article.

Mr Gilbert Cox, of the *Daily Dispatch*, was conducted to a small room off the lobby to wait for his professor, who came down after five minutes or so, all apologies, and led him up to the library. Conscious of the popular prejudice concerning newspapermen, Cox refused the offer of a drink and took instead a cup of Turkish coffee. "Thanks again for seeing me, sir," he said, sipping the piping syrupy brew. "I know we've hounded you rather over this O'Connell business, but the fact of it is, there's been what you might call a fresh development, and I was anxious to get your opinion on it."

"Oh! I see," said the professor. "Well, Mr Cox, I am sorry to disappoint you, but I think I made it clear to your editor that I should prefer my connection with this case to be as slight as possible. The man O'Connell is the most fearful charlatan, you know, and I am afraid even a negative association with him in the popular press would hardly be to the benefit either of myself or of the Institution I serve. There are reputations greater than mine to consider, Mr Cox."

"I shouldn't want to quote you, or to use your name in any way," Cox hastened to reassure him, "only I should like the opinion of an expert on the whole affair—and I should like you to hear what one other person has to say about it."

"Not O'Connell?" exclaimed Professor Mellis, in some alarm.

"No, no, not O'Connell!—good Lord, no, leave him out there in the Valley of the Kings or wherever!—no, this man is a very respectable, common-or-garden, down-to-earth type, who contacted me after reading both O'Connell's thing and your article. He has some new information, which may or may not be interesting."

"What information is that?"

"I'd rather let him tell it, if you've no objections, sir. Would you be prepared to consider coming with me to meet him this evening? I promise you'll find it interesting at the very least. It wouldn't take more than an hour or two of your time, and I'd value your opinion immensely. The whole O'Connell thing is starting to take on a definite new aspect, and I think what's needed is a drawing-together of the threads, so to speak, and we can't do that without an expert like yourself."

Professor Mellis was no doubt as susceptible to flattery as the next man, and gradually allowed the newspaperman to coax him against his better judgment into agreeing to visit the mysterious third party that evening. It was arranged that a cab would call for the professor at eight; the journey, said Cox, would not be long.

The cab, bearing Mr Cox, was punctual; the journey was indeed short, for its destination was Rowlandson's depository, in between the bridges at Putney and Wandsworth, just across from Hurlingham House. The massive old warehouse abutted directly on to the river, with its own wharf alongside and a number of loading bays and platforms on the higher stories jutting out over the muddy waters; Cox gave directions for the cab to turn into a goods yard at the back of the building, where a man wearing uniform coat and cap waved from an open doorway. In some consternation, Professor Mellis looked to Cox for an explanation. "Here's our man," said the latter, smiling mysteriously. "His name is Dalton, and he's the Rowlandson's nightwatchman. Come along, Professor, he'll make us quite comfortable."

And so the strange company was joined: the Egyptologist, the journalist, and the nightwatchman, sitting in a miniscule (yet not uncomfortable) back office of the great depository, drinking coffee from the pot kept simmering on the hob, deep in the strangest of conversations. "I don't suppose there are three other men in all London who've had such an evening of it," said Cox later that night as he and the professor drove back across the Thames in their taxicab; and, indeed, the point would seem unarguable.

Dalton, the nightwatchman, was a dark, heavy-browed man, softly and respectfully spoken, something of an autodidact, and a particular fan (so he said) of the works of Mr H. G. Wells. He was at first a little nervous of the man from the British Museum, and was thus disinclined to speak out, but Cox was at pains to set the meeting on a level footing. "I think the best thing to do," he said, "is to go over the whole affair from the beginning: I'll run through O'Connell's piece, and the professor can tell us why it's all bunk and tommyrot, and then Mr Dalton can speak his piece. Well then!

"Here's Redmond O'Connell: yesterday's man by all accounts, left over from the bad old days of the naughty nineties. More or less broke. I happen to know that he's had to move out of his old abbey, or whatever it was, down in Cornwall, because of lack of funds, and to all intents and purposes he's a kind of glorified vagrant nowadays, putting up with whoever will still have him about the place. Now, somehow or other, he scrapes together, or borrows, or steals, the money to go to Egypt, and engages in some sort of archaeological dig out in the Valley of the Kings; a month goes by, and bingo! We get the communiqué from him, telling us that he's found something to put the wind up absolutely everybody, hold the front page.

"What's he found? A tomb, or tombs, or a complex of tombs and tunnels and what-have-you; no treasure to speak of, but mummies, mummies by the bushel, and not just any ordinary mummies, either. I don't pretend to understand the ins and outs of it—that's the professor's job—but what he seems to be getting at is that the vast number of ordinary mummies, the ones in all the museums, that we've been used to seeing in Egyptian tombs and pyramids and so forth—they're something like failed experiments, whereas O'Connell's mummies are the real thing. He says that all the traditional embalmers were trying to preserve the bodies of the kings and pharaohs for the afterlife, but that by and large they made a pretty poor job of it—not like O'Connell's lot, because he says that in all essential respects, *they're* perfectly preserved. In fact, he goes one step further—he says that given the right conditions, spells and incantations and goodness knows what mumbo-jumbo, these mummies might be revived—brought back to life, as their embalmers intended. Which, of course, is where he loses all contact with reality, but then he's already made quite a splash even without that—hasn't he, Professor?"

Professor Mellis snorted, and coughed immediately, as if to camouflage his indiscretion. "Some people might say he lost all contact with reality long before that, Mr Cox," he said acerbically. "Really, the entire affair is quite impossible. Let me go through the points as you have enumerated them.

"To begin with, I must correct you in a minor matter: the tomb complex O'Connell claims to have discovered is not in the Valley of the Kings, but in a ravine some miles to the west. It is entirely typical of the man that he should seek to dignify his preposterous claims by lending them whatever spurious support geography might provide. As to the contents of the tombs: in my experience, the practice of mummification remained essentially unchanged after about 2000 BC, down through all the later dynasties of ancient Egypt, and I should be most surprised to see any significant changes to the standard procedure, such as O'Connell hints at.

"As you may know, the body was prepared for mummification by the removal of all the major organs—not just the contents of the thoracic cavity, but also the brain, which was extracted by means of a hook through the nasal septum." (Here Mr Cox rather hastily set aside the coffee cup from which he had been about to drink.) "The cadaver thus emptied was soaked in a bath containing various preservatives and tanning agents; it was then dried by the application of salts until it assumed the general appearance and coloration of tough leather. The abdomen was packed out with various filling materials to simulate its natural appearance in life, and oils and unguents were applied before the whole was wrapped in bandages and placed in the coffin."

"One moment, Professor," broke in Cox, "wasn't that when this ceremony that O'Connell mentions was carried out?"

"The Opening of the Mouth, yes: the high priest would touch the mouth of the mummy with a powerful amulet, thus endowing it with life in the hereafter, identifying the deceased with the god Osiris who ruled over the Western Lands. The ritual is preserved in the Book of the Dead: it bears no resemblance to those fragments quoted by the man O'Connell, which I can only assume are of his own invention."

"He claims to have translated them, from wall paintings found in the tomb."

"I daresay he does: he might as well prove an expert in hieroglyphs, together with all his other accomplishments," said Professor Mellis witheringly. "The existence of an entirely new, entirely separate and hidden strand of ancient Egyptian belief—"

"It would be that, then?"

"I can only say that the details as related by O'Connell bear little or no resemblance to those of any dig I have undertaken. If there was a fraction of truth in it, it would be a matter for investigation by a responsible party. As it is, I am amazed that the Egyptian Department of Antiquities have allowed him to carry on such an ill-conceived and outlandish excavation."

"I see," said Cox, "so, let me try to summarize. O'Connell claims to have found some remarkable mummies, prepared according to a process entirely unlike the standard mummification drill. He goes so far as to suggest that they might be capable of being revived, if certain rites are carried out—yes, I know, Professor, that last's all bunk, of course, but it helps to sell the newspapers, you know! Now Professor Mellis says that O'Connell is unreliable, and not a proper Egyptologist, and twenty kinds of con man into the bargain—fair enough. I've no qualms with that. But nevertheless, he *does* feel able to say that *if* O'Connell has turned up something out of the ordinary, then it *might* merit looking into a bit more closely. No?"

Professor Mellis assented unwillingly, and Cox went on: "Which would mean a proper scientific dig on the site, and the authorities in Cairo having a representative out there, and so on: not just the jolly old Great Lucifer scratching around his ravine with a handful of native bearers. Right, Professor? So far, so good. Now: you see how the story becomes, what if O'Connell has turned up something interesting? What's the procedure in those cases, Professor?"

"Well, the site is sealed off at once, of course, and the Department of Antiquities must be informed. No work can be carried out on the dig until the conditions of the digging permit have been verified, and a representative of the Department is on hand."

"Just so; and what about the removal of any artifacts from the dig?"

"Out of the question," said the Professor decisively, "oh, quite out of the question. The Department is absolutely steadfast on that—absolutely. The laws do not permit the removal of antiquities from any designated archaeological site, save at the discretion of the Department, and then only to a location of the Department's choosing—usually the museum at Cairo, or very rarely to a reputable, recognized institution abroad, on loan for further investigation."

"So the days of bagging any, ahem, mementoes, shall we say, from a dig are gone now? Tutankhamun's uncle in a glass case in the hall, and all that?"

"Quite gone: the laws are extremely strict, and the authorities do not hesitate to enforce them."

Cox turned to the nightwatchman, who had hitherto been silent. "Mr Dalton: over to you."

"Well, sir," began Dalton hesitantly, "I saw the piece in the *Dispatch*, and yours too, sir," (this to Professor Mellis) "and it took my curiosity, on account of the delivery we'd had just the night before. You see, what happens is, they deliver to the yard up until eight o'clock in the evening, and after that I'm the only staff in the place till six in the morning, when the day shift comes on. Now occasionally—it's by special arrangement, and it's regular customers only—there *are* deliveries after eight, and I can book 'em in myself in the usual way; there aren't so many of these, though, only what you might call exceptional circumstances.

"So, as I say, the night before the article came out, I was on shift as usual, and about ten the bell rang through from the goods yard, meaning someone was wanting to make a delivery. Now I hadn't heard anything about it, but I went down anyway, and found it was Carter Paterson's—I knew the driver quite well, as it happens—that had come straight from meeting the boat-train. The driver gave me the paperwork, and I saw it was made out in the name of the Hon. James MacVeigh—"

"Remember that name," interjected Cox.

"The Honorable James MacVeigh, sir, that's had an account with Rowlandson's ever since I've been here. So obviously there was no question about it, and the driver and I went and hauled the delivery off the back of the van: it was a crate about six foot by three by three, and the papers said it was to be kept special, because the contents were particularly valuable. Bay Seven on the top for that, then, I said to myself—that's storage bay seven up on the top floor, where a lot of the valuables go; I'll show it to you later.

"We got the crate on to a trolley, and took it up to Bay Seven in the goods lift, and I parked it away in a corner to itself, and took the Carter Paterson's man downstairs for a cup of coffee before he went off. I remember now that he said to me, I'd do well to taste the coffee with the smell of that thing still lingering around, but there! he wasn't to know I've not had any sense of smell since I was a kid, and fell off a swing and hit the bridge of my nose. Anyway, he had his coffee and was off not long after, and I had a last look at the booking-in papers before setting off on my rounds.

"I thought it was odd straightaway, when I went over the details. You see, the crate had come from Cairo—that's where the paperwork was originated, anyway—but there wasn't any Customs stamp on the papers, nor anything chalked on the crate itself. I went up again, just to check. What was on the crate was a canceled-out address of a Mr Redmond O'Connell, in Cornwall—someone had scribbled it over in chalk, but you could rub it off and see the writing underneath.

"Now, I was in a bit of a quandary. The MacVeigh business—well, it's one of the company's longest-standing accounts, and I didn't like to cast any aspersions, as you might say. It wouldn't be my place, and jobs are hard enough to come by nowadays. Still, if a consignment comes in from abroad, and Customs hasn't seen it—especially from somewhere like Egypt, where the authorities are usually red hot, like you say, sir, and there's release forms and suchlike—it's odd, and I can't deny it worried me a little, what to do for the best.

"What I decided to do in the end, was to book it in from Victoria, as if that was where it came from: that wasn't anything I could be pulled up over, if there was any trouble over it later on, since Victoria was all the address there was on the Carter Paterson's paperwork, you see. I wasn't happy with it—it was just all I could think of to do for the best, as I say."

"Oh, absolutely," said Cox, encouraging him. "You couldn't have been expected to do anything else, under the circumstances."

"So," resumed Dalton, looking a little relieved at the newspaper-man's kind words, "what's in the papers next day, but the piece about the new find, in the Valley of the Kings? Redmond O'Connell—I thought I knew the name, but I couldn't place it before I read it in the *Dispatch* that morning. Well, then, I thought: it looks like that crate has come from Egypt after all—and very likely without the Customs knowing about it, though how they managed that part of it has me beat."

"It needn't, you know," said Cox; "I've looked into it, and I'll tell you after. Go on, now."

"Well: I read the article, and then I read Professor Mellis's piece the next day, and I thought that was a bit more sensible, if you know what I mean. Bit more scientific—I've not much time for magic and hocus-pocus, as a rule."

Professor Mellis smiled self-deprecatingly, and Cox observed to no one in particular, "Spare a thought for the poor trod-upon hack, dear heart: the Great British Public tend to quite like a bit of flummery, from time to time."

"Is that so, sir? Perhaps it is—I wouldn't know, myself. As I was saying, I read both the pieces in the *Dispatch*, and the business was sort of in the back of my mind, for a few days after. It got to the point where I was convinced something wasn't right, but I couldn't work out what to do about it. I couldn't go to my superiors and tell them—after all, I'd booked the thing in myself—and I couldn't very well get in touch with the MacVeighs and ask them, this crate you've put into storage, what do you know about it, and how's it got past Customs?"

"Frightful quandary," agreed Cox, "really, you did the best thing in coming to me. A newspaperman's allowed to be a nosy-parking blighter—people expect it of him—just the chap for a little poking around behind the scenes, as it were."

"Just so, sir," agreed Dalton, "I daresay that's the truth of it, if you like plain speaking. I saw Mr Cox here's name at the foot of the original article, and rang him up in strictest confidence—and here we are."

"Just so," said Cox briskly, "and you needn't worry about that confidence, by the way. I shan't bring you into it, you know, and Professor Mellis will keep mum—won't you, Professor?"

The Professor agreed enthusiastically, and Cox resumed: "Now: Cox is the name, and snooping's the game—wouldn't you like to hear what I've found out since you first told me all this, a couple of days ago? Well, then: MacVeigh first of all, and this business of the crate.

"If you'd have taken the trouble to try and get in touch with the Honorable James MacVeigh, you'd have found out fairly soon that he was in Cairo—in the Hotel Luxor, with a party of three; himself, his wife, and Mr Redmond O'Connell. The minute you said MacVeigh to me, I thought, hullo: wasn't his wife one of those rather scatty old dears who went in for table-tapping and Spiritualism and mediums and all that nonsense? Of course she was, and she'd had Redmond O'Connell leeching off her for the last fifteen years, on and off—that's the way he lives, you know, just like the very worst sort of hanger-on and cad. I believe he'd even managed to take in the Honorable James—and he was quite a big noise in the Foreign Office not so long ago, when there were plenty of people backing him for the top spot in Whitehall. Then his wife took up O'Connell, and all that fizzled out rather. But still he must have contacts in the embassies, you know—I asked the fellows on the foreign desk, and it turns out that our man in Cairo at the present is none other than MacVeigh's one-time protégé, a man named Harris, who owes absolutely everything to his old boss.

"Which raises all sorts of possibilities—if you want to get something out of the country on the q.t., you know, and not bother those poor busy Customs chappies any more than you have to."

"Good gracious!" ejaculated Professor Mellis.

Cox smiled, and resumed: "Well, it's a theory. It's also libelous in the extreme, and the sort of thing no self-respecting editor would allow within shouting distance of newsprint without the most copper-bottomed, triple-caulked, reinforced proof going to back it up. I had to dig a bit further if the story was going to come to anything, and not just end up spiked for lack of evidence, so I got on to our Cairo stringer, a chap named Masters, to see if he could find out exactly what O'Connell and party were up to out there.

"He rang me up this morning with all the gen he could raise at such short notice. It seems things are jumping rather in the dear old bazaar, so to speak. The first bit of news was that the authorities are on to O'Connell. Of course I'd been expecting that, after the fool was good enough to splash it all over the pages of Britain's third-largest rag— Masters said that O'Connell had been taken under arrest to the police station the night the story broke, and had been held overnight before MacVeigh turned up and stood bail the next morning. The dig site is closed off, with armed guards on patrol, and no one can get within fifty yards of it—Masters tried, but no joy.

"Next off, Masters telephoned the Hotel Luxor, and tried to get an interview out of O'Connell. Now normally, this is about as difficult as getting fizz from a shook-up bottle of bubbly, but this time, O'Connell is playing it close to the chest—very. He won't see Masters, and that's that; neither will MacVeigh. No comment, is the line they're putting out. But Masters is a resourceful egg, bit like yours truly, and he knows a way around this: he has a word with the porters, and the desk staff, and so on, and a few bob changes hands, all *sub rosa*, and the upshot is that everything that comes in or out of MacVeigh's suite, letters or telephone calls or telegrams, comes across Masters' desk as well. Hardly ethical, you say; but then neither is defrauding Customs.

"After a couple of days, Masters has a nice little sheaf of this and that: a lot of telephone calls, placed to the Department of Antiquities; three or four telegrams as well, begging them to allow O'Connell back on to the dig—grave and unspecified consequences if they don't, they've no idea what they're dealing with, dark forces uncovered, beyond all control save that of O'Connell . . . the usual bombast, you know his sort of thing. Just like in the original piece: I had to tone that down ever so much before we ran it, and it was still the most creaking old rot even then. It doesn't wash with the Department, though: no joy, the site is still closed, Mr O'Connell will remember that he is technically still under arrest, and is requested not to leave the precincts of the hotel.

"MacVeigh even tries to get the Embassy involved; but not even old Harris is going to stand for that, and neither will the Irish Embassy, where they've even less time for the Grand Panjandrum, or whatever he likes to be called. So there we have it: O'Connell is under house arrest in the Hotel Luxor, the dig is under armed guard around the clock, and back here at Rowlandson's—well, Mr Dalton, do you think we might just slip upstairs now, and have a look at your famous crate?"

So Professor Mellis and Mr Gilbert Cox found themselves being transported to the top floor of the depository in the electric goods lift, operated by Dalton the nightwatchman. The lift appeared to be reluctant to deliver them directly to their destination; Dalton had to work the up-and-down controls for some little time to align the floor of the lift compartment to that of the upper story. "Always get trouble with this, on the top floor," he muttered under his breath. "Hang on a minute, gents—now come on, you—there!"

He released the sliding grille doors, and ushered them out into a large open space, dimly lit by a few weak electric bulbs, that extended the width of the building. This space was divided along each side by thin partition walls into open bays or carrels, such as one might find in a library, say. In each of these bays were stacked crates and boxes and trunks, each with an identifying label indicating its owner and date of admission, and spaces beneath in which an auditor might mark off and date his regular inspection of all the goods in the warehouse.

Dalton led them to the last of these bays on the left, in which there was but the one crate, of the general dimensions described by him earlier; it was stood up on its end, in accordance with the "This Way Up" labels it bore. "That's the one," he said, indicating. "Now, do you gentlemen smell anything about it, the way the Carter Paterson's man said he could?"

As a matter of fact, both Cox and the professor could smell something: to Cox, it was a vaguely High Church odor, faintly exotic yet faintly bitter, with something in it of the damp cellar or the potting shed in wintertime. To the professor, who had been in Egypt many times during his long and illustrious career, the scent was immediately recognizable, and he burst out, "That's Egyptian, or I'll retire on the spot—there's no mistaking that scent, I've come across it a hundred times. I was with Carter, when he broke through to the burial chamber of Tutankhamun: it's the very same smell, the incense and spices and the unguents the high priests used to—"

"Quite," said Cox, scratching his nose, "to dress up the dear old mummies, before they put them to sleep, as it were." He laid a hand experimentally on the side of the crate, and withdrew it quite quickly. "Rather warm," he said, as if by way of explanation. "I suppose it gets a bit stuffy up here in the summertime, eh, Mr Dalton?"

"This floor's supposed to be temperature-controlled, sir," the night-watchman said, his eyes on the crate. "But yes, I daresay you're right, it is a little warm."

"Just a little," said Cox, and again placed his hand upon the crate. He rapped tentatively at its side: it sounded hollow, yet sturdy, though the planking of the crate was only a thin plywood layer. "There's something under this," he said aloud, and picked at a corner of the crate that had been knocked in transit, so that the plywood had splintered a little. "I thought so: it's lead, I think. Thick lead foil, a layer of it all the way round inside the crate, so as to keep what's inside airtight. Now what," he continued, rhetorically, "might need to be kept airtight, that came out of an old Egyptian tomb, I wonder?"

Professor Mellis was also examining the outside of the crate, stooping this way and that to see around it. "There are no stamps of any kind from the Egyptian authorities," he reported, straightening at the knees. "If this came out of Egypt, as I have no hesitation in supposing it to have done, then it came illegally, and I must congratulate you, Mr Dalton, on your perspicacity."

"That's that, then," said Cox decisively, "and now shall we go back downstairs? Whatever he's got in there, I don't particularly want to spend the evening up here with it, especially as it's getting rather dark now. I don't like that scent—and I'm not sure I like this, either," he continued, moving sharply to one side, away from the crate. "Tell me, Mr Dalton: I suppose there's bound to be a problem with vermin in a place like this—rats, and mice, and the like?"

"We lay traps, sir, and there's a cat has the run of the place, and there's poison bait put down in the cellars each night," said Dalton, with a dutiful show of professional pride and loyalty to his employers. "But between ourselves, it'd be unreasonable to expect anything else, this close to the river, and such a big old building. There's usually a few dead 'uns to throw away, before we open to the public each morning."

"Just so," said Cox, "like these, perhaps?" He gestured behind the crate, back in the shadows. Dalton and the Professor looked where he pointed, and saw three or four bodies of rats, legs up stiff in the air, backs bent in a taut impossible arch, littering the area to the back of the crate.

"That'll be the poison bait, sir," suggested Dalton, with a distinct trace of doubt in his voice.

"No doubt, no doubt whatsoever," said Cox. "Now, as I was saying, shall we go back downstairs?"

They descended to the ground floor by way of the staircase, since Dalton was disinclined to trust the lifts. "Not when they're playing up, sir: they've only to jam on us, as they've been known to before now, and there we'd be, the three of us—stuck till the morning, and then how should I explain it away?"

Back in the little ground-floor office, a plan of action, of sorts, was agreed on: Mr Cox and Professor Mellis would between them compose a letter, to be sent to Redmond O'Connell, as if from a wealthy admirer who was also something of an Egyptologist. This letter would contain an offer of funding for further excavations, together with a plea for full details of the discoveries to date; in this way, Cox hoped to gain the confidence of the Irishman, and acquire valuable information on his activities so far and his intentions for the future. Mr Dalton, meanwhile, was to keep an eye on the crate, and see that, if any attempts were made to move it, a record of its new destination was kept.

On that note, they parted, Cox and Professor Mellis returning to the professor's club, where they set about composing their letter. This fraudulent missive was ready for dispatch by the morning of the following day, and should have arrived in Cairo under normal circumstances some forty-eight hours after that; as it turned out, though, events had by that time taken a fresh turn.

The meeting at Rowlandson's had been on a Wednesday; it was Friday when Professor Mellis next heard from Gilbert Cox. The professor had just finished his dinner, and was retiring to the Club smoking rooms, when he was seized by the eager young reporter, his eyes alight with mischief. "Look here—Professor—you must come—unbelievable news from Cairo—unbelievable!" This was all the perplexed academic could get out of him, until they were both in the cab and heading out west, towards Rowlandson's pantechnicon.

"It's all gone haywire over in Cairo," explained Cox breathlessly. "I had a phone call from Masters not half an hour ago, and he says—well! Let me try to get my breath and tell you properly.

"Masters had been keeping up the watch on the Hotel Luxor, to see which way O'Connell would bolt. Today, around four p.m. their time, he got word that a private car had been ordered on the west bank of the Nile, by the passenger ferry landing, to be there in an hour's time, orders of MacVeigh. Jolly good, says Masters, and undertakes to be the driver for the occasion: he puts his most down-at-heels suit of whites on, and passes himself off as an ex-Army sort down on his luck, bit fond of the bottle—you know the type, if you've knocked round the Middle East much. Round comes the car by the landing at five; Masters is waiting, and he pays off the Egyptian fellow and gets in. Five minutes later, over come O'Connell and MacVeigh on the ferry, done up to the nines in robes and *burnouses* and what-have-you, like Lawrence of Arabia— obviously thinking this'll go to make them less conspicuous, bless 'em!

"Masters opens the door for them, and asks them where they want to go, and O'Connell gives directions; it's up past the Valley of the Kings, to where the dig is, of course. He drives them up there, and drops them off where the road gives out; off they slink, and Masters is left with orders to wait for them—they'll be back just after dusk.

"So, Masters waits and waits, till the sun's going down, and all of a sudden there's gunshots, and yelling and shouting, and a fearful hulla-balloo from up where the dig is. Naturally, he's out of the car, and haring off to see what's what. He gets there just as the whole thing goes up in smoke. Literally: there's smoke and flames coming up from the shaft down into the tomb, and Masters says there's a screeching that sounds like about fifty men down there, all being roasted alive. Well! The Egyptian guards are standing round the top of the shaft, looking down: they want to know who Masters is, of course, and he shows them his press credentials and manages to get round them somehow—I told you he was a resourceful beggar. It turns out that O'Connell and MacVeigh were down there, and that it must have been them doing all the screaming: apparently, MacVeigh had actually held up the guards at gunpoint, if you can believe it, while O'Connell went down into the tomb. Some security! The guards said they could hear him chanting and singing down there—that was how they put it, Masters says—and one of them said that he thought there must have been somebody else down there already, because it sounded as if there was somebody answering him towards the end. Then there was the most frightful shout, the guards said, and MacVeigh jumped like a rabbit and ran down into the tomb as well; so right away they slammed the gate shut at the top and put the padlock back on, so they'd have them prisoner at least till they could send for reinforcements—and it was just then that the fire broke out. They thought it must have been a lamp, or some such, that got turned over down there: there were all the mummies, remember, and I daresay they'd go up like dry tinder. Bingo! Off goes Masters like a shot; he finds a telephone somewhere, and manages to get through to me at the paper—and here I am, hotfoot."

The professor had been listening to this extraordinary narration as if spellbound; only now could he find words to express his feelings. "The fools!" he swore, through clenched teeth. "The damned idiotic vandals! Think of the research—think of the opportunities, everything lost now forever—"

"Just so—think of the opportunities," said Cox. "I've got an opportunity here, if you like: the biggest story I've ever had a sniff at, and they're holding the front page for me now, while we go down to Rowlandson's. I mean to have a look inside that crate now if it's the last thing I do: there's the whole story intact, from illegal exporting of relics through to armed robbery and death by the mummy's curse. What a headline—what a headline!"

Dusk was settling over the Thames-side suburb by the time the taxi-cab deposited them in Rowlandson's yard; at the back of his mind, Professor Mellis reflected that Cairo was two hours ahead of London, and that the whole unbelievable affair had sprung up in just that short period of time, since the sun had sunk over the western shore of that other great river in the East. Cox set up a clamor on the bell, and soon Dalton was opening the door to them, in some consternation. They lost no time in explaining the situation to him, in much the manner described above. Dalton demurred over one point only, which was the opening of the crate. "It'd cost me my job, sir," he said, doubtfully. "I don't know that I can let you do that without permission."

"Oh, hang it all," said Cox impatiently, "the man was a villain—a common crook! He held up these guards at gunpoint! Now, the crate was damaged a little at one corner, wasn't it?'

"Yes—a little—I noted it down in the paperwork—"

"Well, there you are, then," urged Cox, persuasively, "we'll just damage it a bit more, till we can get a look inside and the professor can tell us what it is he's got in there—because it's one of these new-fangled mummies of his, or I'm a Dutchman. He got one out, before they sealed up the dig, and MacVeigh helped him do it: now are you going to let us have a look in that crate, and see for yourself why they're so special that two men lost their lives over a tomb-full of 'em, just this very evening?"

With this desperate cajoling, and much more to the same point, Dalton's strength of character was tried to the sticking-point, and eventually beyond: at last, he agreed to let them open the crate just enough for them to see inside, and without further ado they set off through the half-lit echoing corridors towards the goods lift.

The lift hummed and coughed as it rose through the levels; they were about to gain the topmost floor when disaster struck, and the engine gave out with a very definite, and very final, clanking noise. The light went out in the cramped compartment, and now the only illumination was admitted via a slit some fifteen inches or so high at the very top of the meshwork lift doors, opening on to the top floor. By standing on tiptoe, Cox could just see the shadowy bays from his vantage point at floor level: a large black cat strolled over to him and regarded him gravely, eye to eye, before turning away to sit and wash itself.

"Damnation!" said Dalton vehemently, and jerked without success at the levers. "The blasted thing's always doing this—"

"Then what do you usually do when it happens?" enquired Cox, patiently and not unreasonably.

"Well, there's usually someone downstairs who can start up the emergency generator—that powers all the electrics, independently—" began Dalton, then stopped as the situation became more clear to him.

"Is there?" said Cox, his hands on his hips. "Is that a fact, now? Then I jolly well wish he'd stayed on and done a bit of overtime tonight, because I can't see how we're going to get out of this otherwise, you know."

Dalton stared at the newspaperman for a second, then turned to his levers and applied himself with fresh urgency. "You go ahead and try those by all means, old chap," said Cox, without rancor, "but I rather think we'll have to see if we can't squeeze through the gap at the top, here, if we don't want the day shift to find us—and the dear old *Rocket* to scoop us, confound them!"

Now Professor Mellis had been observing the predicament as it developed with increasing alarm. "But—but," he interjected at this point, "I can't—that is to say, there's not the slightest possibility—"

"Not you, Professor," said Cox, appraising his ample girth with cocked head and half-closed eye: "no, I don't think you'd make it, quite. That burial chamber of Tutankhamun's must have been a good bit wider than this, or you must have been a good bit narrower back then—eh? what? No—I think I'll try it, or perhaps you, Mr Dalton—do you fancy it? Then we can go down and start up the blessed generator, and *then*, perhaps—"

"Hark!" said Dalton. He stopped the newspaperman with a gesture, and nodded upwards, to the top floor. "Did you hear that?"

They had all heard it: a loud bang, as if caused by the overturning of some large object. Now came a series of smaller thumps and bangs, and a kind of dry rustling. The three men in the lift looked at one another in mute perplexity, as the noises echoed through the deserted warehouse. Cox, as ever, was the first to speak.

"Well, I don't suppose it was rats, at any rate," he said, his usual jauntiness a little forced. "Come, Dalton, hoist me up so's I can see what's going on up there."

Dalton made a back for him, and Cox sprang to the gap at the top of the lift doors, pulling aside the gates so that he could put his head through and see more easily. At first he noticed nothing unusual—except for the cat, which was stood bolt upright, arching its back wildly, its fur up on end, spitting and hissing in the direction of a far corner of the room. Cox twisted awkwardly to follow its gaze, and saw what it had seen: he let out an involuntary gasp, and Professor Mellis called up, "Cox! What is it?"

His voice came back down to them: "It's the crate—over in the far bay there—it's fallen over, face down, so as to jut out into the aisle. I don't know how, but—wait a minute—there it goes again—it's rattling, and moving about by itself somehow, as if something had it by an end and was shaking it—ugh!" He came down from his perch precipitately, and stumbled to the floor; in an instant he was up on his feet again, consternation over his thin keen features. "It just moved by itself," he said. "A great kind of jerk, so the end came clear off the floor and banged down again. I know I said it looked as if something had hold of it—well, it wasn't like that, really; it was more as if there was something inside it that was alive, and moving around . . ." He tailed off, conscious of what he was saying, and of the effect it was having on his companions in the trapped lift. "I know how it sounds," he said, after a short period in which no one spoke, "but that was what it was like. Here—I'll go up again, and see what it's doing now—make a back, Dalton, there's a good fellow—up she goes—"

Again, he put his head through the gap, and this time his in-drawing of breath was clearly audible from down below. "It's rattling around like the dickens now—can you hear it? Thumping and rattling . . . there's something in there, all right, you can take my word on that, and it means to get out, if I'm any judge in the matter."

"But Cox—the crate was lead-lined—airtight," called up the professor, now exceedingly uncomfortable and anxious. "You saw as much yourself. What can it be that could live in an airtight container?"

"I think that's more in your line than mine," came the reply, above the now-steady tumult of rattling from above. "Perhaps it's something that can do well enough without any air to breathe—perhaps it's the same sort of thing that could prevent two able-bodied men from getting out of the way of a fire down inside a tomb, just a couple of hours ago. Or perhaps I'm just talking a lot of stuff and nonsense—but don't you think we'd better try to get out of this confounded death trap of a lift before it gets out of its crate—whatever it is?"

So saying, Cox began a violent series of wrigglings and contortions, with the object of getting a shoulder through the gap, as well as his head. This he succeeded in achieving, at the cost of the greater portion of his coat, which snagged on a protruding edge as he hoisted himself up on to the top floor. In an instant his hands came through the gap, and he called, "Dalton—quick—we haven't much time, I think—it's almost dark up here." Through the gap came a waft of that incense scent from the night before last: stronger now and all-pervasive, all but overpowering.

His face white and set, Dalton took the newspaperman's hands, and struggled through the gap. Professor Mellis, much against his inclination, was left alone in the dark lift-shaft, and shouted up, "Cox! Dalton! What's happening? What's up there?" But neither man answered.

Both were staring, speechless, at the crate in Bay Seven. The impression Cox retained, and later described, was of some great engine, closed up inside a container far too small to hold it, in the process of shaking itself to pieces. Dalton thought of a magic trick he had seen once, in which the magician had himself chained, bound, and sealed in a sack, which was then lowered into a tank of water; the writhings of that sack, in which the escapologist struggled to escape, came to his mind now as he beheld the shuddering and jerking of the crate, which was slowly working its way out from its bay into the aisle with the violence of its motion.

Cox turned to Dalton with an effort, his eyes standing from his head. "What are we to do with it?" he said, in a half-whisper, as if it might overhear. "This is frightful—if it should get out—"

"I don't know," Dalton whispered back. "Should we open it?"

"Open it? Not on your life. We've got to get rid of it, somehow—put it somewhere it can't get out of. Think!"

Dalton cast around the familiar warehouse surroundings, as if seeing them for the first time. His mouth opened, and closed without making a sound; and then he saw a possibility. "There," he managed to get out, in a voice little above a croak, "look there."

Cox looked where he pointed, and saw a large pair of double doors set in the farther wall, secured with two great padlocks. "What on earth does that lead to? We're on the top floor—" and he jumped involuntarily at a fresh barrage of poundings from inside the crate.

"It's the old loading platform, right out above the river—they used to use it to winch stuff up, in the days when most of the freight came by boat. If we can push it that far, and get the doors open—"

"I'll push it," said Cox grimly; "you see to the doors, and jump to it."

Dalton hastened to the doors, rummaging through the keys on his ring; meanwhile, Cox screwed his courage to the sticking-point and approached the crate, from which now proceeded a series of convulsive rhythmic knocks, one every second or so. He set his hands to one end of it, and was repulsed by a warmth that went far beyond any conditions prevailing on the top floor of the warehouse; it was as if the crate had stood all day beneath a blazing desert sun, he thought, and it cost him no little effort to resume his stance, this time with the shreds of his ruined coat between his hands and the splintering plywood. He began to push, and Dalton called over to him, a rising panic in his voice.

"I can't find the keys—they're not on this ring—there's some old ones down in the office—"

"Damn it, man, how long do you think we've got?" panted Cox, beginning to gain momentum as he heaved away at the crate. "Get out of the way, if you can't get it open—I'll come at it flat out, and see if that'll do it."

Dalton said nothing, but turned and put his shoulder to the doors. There was a creaking that spoke of rotten wood, and of nails coming loose; he redoubled his efforts, and called out: "Flat out it is, then:

watch you don't go through with it." Again he barged at the doors: one of the hasps shivered loose, and there was a glint of light at the bottom of the join.

Cox was by now moving at top speed; he tried to ignore what he could feel through the palms of his hands, the thumps and bangs and scrabblings, and he looked directly ahead, lest he should see the panels of plywood come clear away, and the lead foil beneath giving way to a volley of blows. His one great fear, overmastering all the lesser ones, was that the crate might come apart completely before he reached the doorway, and shatter to pieces while still on the inside. He fancied he knew what was inside it, now, and he did not know what he should do, if it got loose.

With one last desperate heave, he reached the doors: they sprang apart at the collision, coming almost off their hinges with the momentum of it. The crate, still substantially intact, sailed out into the night sky; Cox might have followed it if Dalton had not grasped him firmly around the waist and hung on to him. They both saw the crate describe a great falling arc, and splash end-on into the river: a furious bubbling and steaming erupted briefly as it went under, and then subsided as bits and splinters of the crate popped up again to the surface, shattered entirely to pieces by the impact. Cox thinks he may have seen something else—he cannot swear to it, or will not—in the swirls and eddies of black water; it might have been an arm reaching up, he says, and will go no further. It is a fact, though, that anything inside the crate would, like the fragments of plywood to which the outside was reduced, have been borne down the Thames on the strong ebb-tide to the estuary, and the sea, and it is at least a strong supposition that nothing retraced its path that way, to the not inconsiderable peace of mind of all concerned.

Professor Mellis was, you will be pleased to hear, freed without undue delay from the trapped lift. Mr Dalton, for his part, was obliged to effect certain repairs on the fabric of the warehouse, and to engage in a little creative reordering of his paperwork in the matter of the MacVeigh deposits. The only real loser in the affair was, sad to say, Mr Gilbert Cox, who did not at last get the scoop he so keenly anticipated. It transpired that the Hon. James MacVeigh was a second cousin, once removed, of the then Prime Minister. We may never know what orders were handed down that night, or what sums of money changed hands, both in distant Egypt and nearer home, but the next day's headlines read "Tragic Death of Englishman in Bizarre Archaeological Accident," sub-headed "Irish Citizen Also Mourned as Freak Blaze Kills Two," with editorial comment headed "The Need for Better Organization Abroad."

It was small consolation for Cox to be given the job of accompanying Professor Mellis to Cairo, where he had been seconded as part of the team working under Professor Al-Qawwani on the site of Redmond O'Connell's ill-fated dig. The bodies, of mummies and interlopers alike, had long since been removed from the chambers by this time, but from what remained of the wall paintings the professor was able to ascertain that the tombs had been used by a breakaway religious sect of about the time of the Hittite invasion—an era of great turbulence and upheaval in Egyptian history—who referred to themselves as the Children of Set. It seemed that this sect had turned away from the worship of the great pantheon headed by Ra and Osiris, and given allegiance solely to evil Set; further, that its practice of mummification had indeed differed significantly from the traditional method. There was an incantation, done in hieroglyphs on the wall, which Professor Mellis was at some pains to translate, which had to do with the ceremony of the Opening of the Mouth alluded to previously; sadly, though, the fire had rendered the latter part of it illegible, and so it is impossible to say what interest it may have held for such as Redmond O'Connell. It began, "When the night comes on, and the great darkness falls on the banks of the river, then journey forth towards the Western lands . . ." The rest is silence, so to speak.

American mummies? Discovered in 1940 near Fallon, Nevada, the "Spirit Cave Mummy" is the oldest human mummy yet found in North America. Along with artifacts from the cave, when the mummy was examined at the Nevada State Museum it was first thought to be between fifteen hundred and two thousand years old. The remains were kept at the museum's storage facility until 1996 when an anthropologist tested some of the artifacts using mass spectrometry. The results indicated the mummy was approximately 9400 years old. In 1997, the Fallon Paiute-Shoshone Tribe of the Fallon Reservation and Colony made a Native American Graves Protection and Repatriation Act (NAGPRA) claim of cultural affiliation with the artifacts and mummy. Legal battles continue.

American Mummy
Stephen Graham Jones

———

Garrett finally made himself just sit the hell down. The hotel was going to charge him for walking a bald spot in its carpet if he didn't stop with the back and forth.

It was some time after nine, coming on to eleven.

He knew it wasn't eleven yet because that was check-out, that was when housecleaning came through knocking. Because they didn't have a clipboard of what rooms were going to be empty and which ones might be sleeping?

Garrett had some ideas for this hotel. Had there been an old-fashioned suggestion box at the registration desk? Maybe. This place didn't even have computerized registration.

Garrett squinted, trying to see back to three nights ago at two in the morning, but all he could make out was his hand tracing the letters and numbers Lady had been feeding him. Every time they checked in, she was always the one with the truck's license plate in her head. No matter the hour, no matter if they'd been drinking, no matter if this was the first topside air they were getting to breathe for the week.

The reason he knew it was after nine had nothing to do with the digital clock on the nightstand.

It had everything to do with the continental breakfast downstairs. The one Lady *knew* warmed up at six and shut down three short hours later.

It was the usual stuff, the microwave oatmeal and slightly too small apples and gumball machines of cereal, the six-slot toaster and foggy cabinet of cinnamon rolls and bagels, jelly packets for everybody.

What this hotel had that not all of them did, though, it was a steamer bin with a roll-top lid. On one side was the bacon that didn't really check out as meat if you held it up to the light, but on the other side were those glorious eggs, poured on to some perfect griddle like pancake batter then graced with a slice of cheese, and folded over.

"So, an omelette?" Garrett had said their first morning, touching at the edge of his with the tines of his plastic fork.

"They come in frozen on a truck once a week," Lady had said, and tipped back her coffee cup of cartoon cereal.

Because she was either Chippewa or Kiowa, depending on the day and who was asking, she ate her cereal dry, to keep her stomach from knotting up around the milk. For their first couple of years together Garrett had thought her no-milk cereal was just a taste she'd acquired, growing up without money. It turned out to have more to do with her being from a people who ate their buffalo instead of milking them, so never needed the enzymes Garrett came with from the factory. End result? Lady didn't have much luck with dairy.

Or with damn *clocks*, Garrett told himself, bouncing in place on the edge of the bed even though their fight had been over for ten minutes now.

It had started when he tapped the face of his watch and told her they didn't want to miss omelettes, right? That's what he was still calling them because that's what they were.

Lady had been over at the phone talking to her sister, who was too paranoid to trust her secrets to anything but a landline.

Instead of holding her finger up for him to wait she'd threaded her hair over the ear on the other side of the phone, and switched the phone across to it—away from Garrett. And then she'd angled her body away from him as well, giving him her back, trading him in for her goddamn sister Penny, who had a new drama every time Garrett and Lady surfaced from a month or two in the field. It usually involved Penny *not* being a punching bag. At least that's what it sounded like from this end.

Garrett had nodded that this was fine, this was OK, this was part of it, and he'd made his way over to the window. Their room was on the second floor. It was just April but they still had to keep the air conditioner under the window running. That was Arizona for you.

The refrigerated air slid up his frontside, dried his eyes.

The dually was still out there, unmolested.

It was Garrett's pride and joy. The camper on top, though, that was just temporary, that was just until he found a good one. It wasn't for sleeping, it was for hiding what they were usually running in the bed.

What was in the bed now would just about pay the dually off, Garrett was pretty sure.

It had made him want to celebrate.

With, say, two or three plates of mini-omelettes.

He looked back to Lady but she was still bent over the phone, listening to Penny's sob story.

He pulled the curtains as shut as they would get and made his way back to the bed, sat down on it hard enough that she had to look around. He tapped his watch again. In reply, she scooted over, presented the digital clock on the nightstand to him, showing they still had half an hour, what was he so on about?

Garrett clicked the television awake. It came on loud like he wanted, some local station's news, and then an instant later it muted.

Lady, at the nightstand. With the remote.

He locked eyes with her for maybe three seconds and she didn't look away.

"Omelettes," he hissed to her.

"*Penny*," she said back, covering the mouthpiece to say it.

And that's how it had started. That's how the morning fell apart.

Garrett should write a freaking book about it, he knew. One where he could showcase how put upon he was by women. One where he could make his case for how the gods were always punishing him by withholding things.

All he wanted was to eat a mini-omelette with a plastic fork, right? Was that too much to ask, after two weeks in a dusty red cave?

Apparently so.

Now, the fight Lady had been asking for done and over, Garrett turned the television back on. Just to keep himself from walking from the door to the window and back again.

He was sitting close enough to the set to have just reached out, punched the power button, but he had the remote now and he was going to use it, by God.

It was the local news, still, on some kind of insistent loop.

So he wouldn't have to look around at the room, Garrett made himself focus on the reporter.

She was in a ditch west of town. Garrett knew it was "west" because right now it was a split-screen thing, with her on the left side, a map where she was on the right. The pulsing star was west of town.

Garrett didn't think a star was in good taste for a fatality.

He had some ideas for the local news, too. A cross, a skull, a little mushroom cloud because it was a wreck, one involving multiple vehicles, multiple fatalities. The highway was shut down going both ways.

Garrett edged closer, trying to see around the reporter's shoulder now that she had the whole screen. When he couldn't quite make the truck out, he turned her voice down enough for her to start making sense.

She was apologizing to motorists about the shutdown. Apparently it was going to be a few hours until traffic could resume.

The screen split again, the reporter-in-the-ditch on her left side, the anchor-at-the-desk on the other side.

The anchor was saying *"Hours, Jill?"*

At which point the screen dissolved to a high angle of the wreck.

It was a green-on-white Ford king cab Garrett prayed he wasn't really recognizing. A king cab currently spread across both westbound lanes. The only thing not crushed on it was the driver's side mirror, standing straight up as if to show that it had made it through, that it was winning.

The semi that was tangled up with the Ford Garrett *did* recognize had a bit of its trailer crossing the median, over into the eastbound lanes. It wasn't enough to block eastbound traffic—not both lanes, anyway. Just set up some cones, some flares, direct around it.

But they weren't.

Jill explained why.

Apparently the king cab had been carrying Native American artifacts.

"Pothunters, Jill?" the anchor asked, evidently a coached question, allowing him to turn to face the camera, explain to the tourists that pothunters weren't amateur archaeologists or even cultural enthusiasts, as they liked to claim, but looters, thieves, trespassers.

Garrett peeled his top lip back from his teeth about that.

If Lady were here she would have laughed in that way she had, said, "Trespassing?"

Goddamnit.

Without her, how was Garrett going to have any reason to be on reservations any more?

Just because of the stupid folding eggs. The eggs that had already been wheeled back into the secret parts of the hotel by now, he knew. Taken away from him, like everything.

"Sorry, Bats," he said to the dead driver of the green Ford, and reached across to turn the news off, to not have to look at Bats's king cab turned inside out any more. But now the camera was back to Jill one more time.

She had her index finger pressed to one ear like for quiet, please, and was holding on to her mic for dear life, trying to carve out just thirty seconds more of airtime for herself.

She was still explaining about the shutdown.

Yes, the driver of the Ford had apparently been a black-market procurer or dealer of some kind, but the reason for the shutdown was so the Feds could sweep in. Not for the artifacts, but for the human remains. The *ancient* human remains.

"No," Garret said, scooting forward on the bed to be closer to this. "You asshole, you didn't, did you?"

Jill hadn't said just "human" remains. She'd said *ancient* human remains. That could only mean one thing.

Bats had dug up some true American gold: a mummy. A leathery piece of human jerky ten thousand years old, its skin dark and drawn and wrinkled, lips peeled back from the teeth, hair so delicate that, carrying a prize like that out into the sunlight, the hair turns from black to red while you watch.

You can pull five grand from a basket in the right condition, to go into a private collection on some non-working ranch.

A mummy, though—holy hell.

For a mummy you could set up an auction, start the bidding at a hundred thousand, then ride it all the way to the top.

And, best of all, because the NAGPRA bible thumpers wanted to rebury all remains that turned out to be authentic, the mummy would never have to submit to museum scrutiny, lest word of it get out. Its only provenance would be the story you told the buyer, about how you punched through the wall of an old mineshaft and there was the chamber right there like it had been five thousand years before the pyramids.

Would the burial be pre-Clovis? Some Aztec or Olmec up here, looking around? Or, if you X-rayed it, would there be coins in the skull, fallen through from the empty eye sockets? *Roman* coins?

And what had those eyes seen?

Ten thousand years ago there'd been megafauna in North America.

"You bastard," Garrett said to Bats. Because he'd spread the find of the century out across a quarter-mile of Arizona blacktop. He'd spread his own retirement out with the remains of what had been a pretty fine Ford.

"Not that you need it any more," Garrett said, and turned to the bathroom as if for a response from Lady.

She was still lying there in the doorway like he'd left her. Lying there right where she'd fallen—well, where her head had hit the metal doorframe the first time. And the second and third and fourth times, too. And all the other times.

There was a pool of blood under her head. It came from her mouth and her ear and from her left eye.

That eye was still open.

"Thirty minutes," Garrett said to her, and tipped his head at the clock she'd set back while talking to her sister. Like Penny's drama was more important than breakfast.

And then Garrett noticed that the phone was still hanging from its cord, off the nightstand. Because, when he'd straight-armed Lady into the headboard, the lamp had dislodged and he'd darted a hand out to catch it, keep from paying for it.

He'd forgot about the phone, though. About Penny.

He lifted it to the side of his head.

"Where's my sister, you bastard?" Penny said. She'd waited half an hour to say it.

Garrett hung up gently.

When housekeeping came to the door he cracked it open enough to shake his head no, then slipped the PRIVACY PLEASE placard out, hooked it on to the doorknob. And then he walked across in front of the dresser, to the window, and then he walked back again, spun back around for the hundredth time, like he could come around fast enough to catch the solution to this morning. The answer to what to do with Lady.

She was just staring at him, her mouth slightly open, the teeth not lining up any more.

Because Garrett wasn't stupid—and because a man needs a bathroom at some point in the day—he peeled Lady up from the floor after an hour or so. Some of her hair stayed with the blood that was already clotting up. The blood that he was going to be charged for, he knew.

The reason it was smart to peel Lady up, not let her lay there all sprawled out like she'd fallen three stories to get here, was that soon enough rigor was going to set in, and he might need to be rolling her up in some version of a rug.

He didn't want her on the king bed, though.

The corner, then. He propped her up and she sloughed down into herself, sat like a five-year-old sits: butt-down, knees up.

When her head was hanging back behind her, her jaw all slack and broken, Garrett took her by the hair, pulled her face forward so it could rest on her knees.

Would she fit in a duffel like that?

Maybe. If it was late enough. And it wasn't like Garrett didn't know every crack and crevice in the sandstone for three hundred miles in every direction. Hidden in the right place, she'd dry out, turn to leather inside of a year. Let her sit a couple thousand more, and she'd be a mummy herself.

"Gonna make an artifact of you yet," he said to her, and went out to run down some lunch, which turned into an afternoon at the bar, which turned into a liquid dinner as well.

The next time he saw Lady, it was three in the morning.

He'd cranked the air conditioner down before he'd left. The room was a refrigerator now.

He sat on the bed and stared at her. At the top of her head.

"Sorry, girl," he said, his voice slurring more than he'd heard, telling himself he was all right to drive home.

Calling her "girl" was his joke on her name. Used to, she'd smiled about it.

Dropped just inside the door was the cargo bag he'd been able to scrounge in town. It was either that or a laundry bag, and a laundry bag was going to require a saw, or at least a chisel and hammer. And he didn't even have an apron.

The cargo bag was the kind for strapping on to the top of a car. It was supposed to be weatherproof, had double-zippers, reinforced corners, the whole deal.

Except, now that Garrett got to studying on it: did he really want to Ziploc a bag of rotting meat in where it couldn't breathe?

It made him gag, thinking about how he would definitely gag somewhere down the road, unzipping that body bag alone in a pasture. Ten steps later he was knelt in front of the toilet, splashing the day's peanuts and pretzels and boiled eggs into the toilet.

"Fuck it," he said, and pulled himself up by the shower curtain. It popped its rings one by one, shot them across the bathroom. They rattled for long after.

Garrett tried to wait their spinning plastic sound out but finally couldn't, had to just lie back into the dry bathtub.

The last thing he knew was that he had to kick the door shut.

Because Lady was out there.

The goddamn clock was *still* wrong.

Garrett had bet everything on it again, like an idiot, and now he'd missed the hotel's breakfast *again*.

He sat on the edge of the bed, right where Lady had sat talking to Penny, and tried to reprogram the time, his hands shaking with fury each time he set the alarm, not the goddamn *time*.

When the proper hour kept slipping past he finally just yanked the clock's cord from the wall.

"This is your fault," he said to Lady.

She still had her head down, her hair spilling down along her calves.

Some of it was pressed between her arms, and some of it was spread over them.

Garrett had to cock his head at this.

He tried to replay her ass-sliding down the wall to her current sitting position.

Why would he have posed her like that?

"Lady?" he said.

She just sat there.

Tendons in the shoulders drying up and contracting, he told himself. Muscle memory.

To prove he could, he stepped across, pushed her shoulder.

She was already stiff. Her whole body tipped a bit, settled back down. Just that tearing sound, where her fluids had seeped through her pants, stuck her to the stupid carpet.

She was like an egg was what she was. Put a shell around her.

Garrett went back to the window, stepped back from it all at once.

La Migra was parked by his truck, its green-and-white paint clearing the parking lot all around it.

The officer had his flashlight out, was shining it through the camper's tinted side-glass.

"No no no no," Garrett said.

It worked: five breaths later—what would have been breaths, had Garrett been breathing—the officer saw no illegals back there, continued on his way. Into the hotel?

Meaning his Blazer, it was still right there, parked the other way from the dually but right beside it.

Garrett sat back on the bed and buried his face in his hands.

Still shaking his head no, he made himself stand again, stand in the cold rushing air.

How was he supposed to carry Lady out, when dark skin in the back of a dusty truck was exactly what Border Patrol was trained to see? He could do it any minute, he knew. But which one? Which minute was going to be the one the officer wasn't going to be through with his business in the hotel?

It was impossible.

Garrett skipped lunch, kept his vigil.

Instead of leaving, the federal vehicle multiplied.

All the feds Bats had pulled in with his big wreck? They were bivouacking here, it looked like.

From the wheeled, dragging sounds in the hall, they were *right* here.

Garrett heard himself laughing. He didn't like the way it sounded.

Instead of walking out to his truck for his tools, or to better hide the coolers packed with foam and history, Garrett stiff-legged it through the lobby, his sunglasses already on.

It was two miles down to the hardware store. And two miles back.

There was a new plan.

Garrett had thought it up at the exact instant the phone on the nightstand rang.

He'd clamped his hand down on it like to keep it still, to hide it from the Feds all around.

He lifted the phone to the side of his face.

"I know where you are, you son of a bitch," the voice said. The female voice.

Garrett looked up to Lady hesitantly, like a plea. For her to be quiet, please. To not be saying this. To just be dead.

But then his rational mind kicked in.

"Penny," he said.

She chuckled, hung up.

Garrett tilted his head back, his eyes closed against all of this.

If she knew to call back, it was just a matter of time until she called management. Or the police.

His heart was slapping the inside walls of his chest.

He could get in the dually and leave, just keep driving, but his plates were on that index card.

"Because you wanted them there," he said down to the top of Lady's head.

That he couldn't see her face told him she was smiling.

He wanted to kick her, except he was suddenly sure her right arm would stab out, catch him by the shin.

And then she'd look up to him.

"Bats," Garrett said to her, instead.

Bats had brought the Feds here, but, to make up for it, he'd also given Garrett a way to slither out.

Mummies.

At the hardware store—it was local, expensive—Garrett bought a sheetrock knife, some mud, a putty knife, a roll of clear tape, and a disposable plastic drop cloth.

The boxed-in space under the hotel's king bed would have been the place to bury Lady, except that's where the kids hid their beer and drugs, Garrett knew. Lady had told him, showed him the six-pack rings, the wadded-up balls of foil, the rubber bands.

And hotels updated the furniture every decade or so anyway.

But they didn't update the dead space between the walls. Not unless there was a smell. The drop cloth would take care of that, if he sealed it up right.

Garrett made it back just as night was falling.

The Feds and the locals and La Migra were all at the bar, having a good old legal time.

Garrett felt like crying.

Using the skills he'd hated his dad for making him learn, sitting on the floor with his back to Lady, Garrett razored through the thick wall-paper, careful not to go too fast and rip it.

What he was cutting was a door. One-time use. A door to a tomb to be sealed up for ten thousand years.

It was as tall as just over his knee, as wide as his shoulders. Lady wasn't as big as him, but her length now, from her lower back to her toes, was about that. She was probably going to have to sit sideways along the wall, Garrett figured. But that was better than the other option—what he'd be having to do if they weren't in a room by the elevator: sawing her into pieces, the more gruely bits slipping down the drain of the bathtub, the rest double-bagged in those flimsy trash bags from the cleaning cart.

This was better.

Until he heard something behind him.

A *breath*?

Garrett turned, brandishing the sheetrock knife, but Lady was as she had been. Still, he planted a heel in the carpet, pushed himself away from her, closer to the bed.

"Quit goddamn smiling," he said to her.

She either did or she didn't.

And, her hair now, her long black hair—was it *all* outside her arms? Was there none between the skin of her arms and the legs of her pants? That would be most comfortable, he figured. Would allow her head to move.

It made sense, except that she was dead.

Standing, Garrett edged up to her, used the knife to flick her hair to the side. It was like unburying her, uncovering the Indian artifact she was slowly becoming.

Her hair kept falling back into place, though.

Finally, to show her he could, he pressed the business edge of the sheetrock knife into the meat of her shoulder and pulled down, away from himself.

Her flesh opened like flan. A foul blackness slid down to her elbow, held on for a moment before dripping to the carpet and mixing with all the previous occupants' stains

"There," Garrett said, and swallowed the stupid lump in his throat.

When he went back to the wallpaper he kept himself facing her now, even though it meant coming at the cuts wrong-sided, like he was left-handed.

He didn't peel the wallpaper back. Instead he clicked the knife's razor out farther, prayed for no studs, and traced along the wallpaper cuts, slicing deeper now, into the sheetrock. And, it wasn't sheetrock after all, like he'd been taught on, but some sort of fiberboard.

When had this started happening?

"While you were in a cave," he said to himself.

And, fiberboard was better, as it turned out. It cut cleaner, didn't crumble like sheetrock. He wasn't sure the mud would stick to it right, since it wasn't coated in paper. But maybe.

Everything else was working out, right?

This would too, he told himself.

Though it had to be sub-zero in the room, he was sweating by the time the door was ready, two hours later.

Inside the wall there'd just been lint and dust and insulation over-spray. No wires, no pipes, no junctions, and, most importantly, no studs. He didn't have a plan B if there'd been a stud.

To be sure she was going to fit, Garrett breathed all his air out, crawled in himself.

It was tight for sure, but, first, she wasn't his size, and second, she was only going to be getting smaller and drier over the years, right?

In case her drop cloth filled with fluids that might leach out, stain the wall, call for an investigation, Garrett commandeered the no-slip mat from the bathtub. Folding the corners up and crimping them with bent staples and paper clips, he was able to make a tray of sorts for Lady to sit in. A pan to keep her from staining the wall behind the industrial baseboard.

It was almost midnight by the time he realized he was stalling with the last step, then.

"I'm sorry, girl," he said, and wrapped Lady as gently as he could in the drop cloth. When it was done he kissed her on the cloudy top of her head, closed his eyes in farewell.

They'd had a good run, all told.

It was too bad it had to end like this.

There was no blue cornmeal to sift down over her, no sage to smudge the air with. No songs.

She hadn't been that kind of Indian, though. She was more the beer-can-splintering-campfire-light-out-into-the-darkness kind.

Garrett dropped to his knees, cradled her to his chest, and maneuvered her through the opening in the wall, tipping her head down so as not to catch, then propping her back up.

When he turned around to get the "door"—it was leaned against the dresser far away from him, so he wouldn't accidentally bump into it, snap it in half—he thought he heard it again. Not a breath, but . . . like a sigh?

"Gases escaping," he said out loud, to make it true.

And the sound didn't repeat.

Now that there was just a half-inch of fiberboard and a scrim of wallpaper between him and his neighbor, it could even be the sound of someone turning over in bed.

Garrett nodded because that was definitely it.

It meant he had to be extra quiet, too.

He turned the television on to mask what sounds he had to make, and then he set the door back into place.

It fit so perfect he closed his eyes in thanks.

Then he let it lean back, dabbed all around the three raw edges of the fiberboard with the pale mud. The door still closed like it was supposed to. Just, it made more of a seal now. Once the mud dried, the wall would be hermetic again.

To be sure, he wet the pad of his index finger with the mud, ran a ghost of it down along the crack in the fiberboard that was hardly even there any more.

This was going to work.

Instead of using the clear tape like he'd thought he was going to have to, for the wallpaper, he simply pressed the cut wallpaper into the ghost of mud smeared over the crack. It was like the wallpaper had adhesive backing.

Ten careful, tedious minutes later, the deed was done.

Garrett pushed back from the wall, looked away then came back to it like just seeing it for the first time.

The outline of the door was still there, but it was so, so slight. If anything, it looked like a plumber or electrician had had to open the wall a year or two ago, make a service call, then do his best to cover his tracks.

"Yes yes yes," Garrett said, and stood, cased the room.

He packed Lady's clothes and bathroom junk into her own suitcase, his stuff in his duffel, and was saying goodbye to this chapter of his life when the top right corner of the door was casting a triangular shadow he had to look at twice to be sure he was really seeing.

A corner of the wallpaper had curled back. It was where he'd cut maybe a sixteenth of an inch higher than he needed to.

He dropped the bags, got the mud out but finally decided against it this time. There was no way to get any in behind a curl of paper that small.

The tape it was, then.

It was clean, was as "invisible" as the packaging claimed.

Now there was no shadow, no curl of paper.

No Lady.

"Well then," Garrett said, and hiked the bags back up, took the stairs down to the parking lot instead of the elevator to the lobby. No need to announce his exit, right?

He threw the bags over the tailgate, into the camper, and counted the coolers. They were all there. And even if they weren't, he was still gone. Especially if they weren't, right?

He looked up to the window of his room for one last goodbye, and, through the gauzy curtains, there was a form. A figure. A shape.

Garrett fell back, had to stab a hand out to the dually's fender flare to keep standing.

The curtains had been moving with the air conditioner, so he hadn't been able to tell male from female.

But—even if it was female, that didn't mean it was Lady, right?

There was the cleaning staff. There were the female federal agents.

Already in his room, though? Had they been watching? Listening? Had they had a cadaver dog or methane-sniffing equipment next door, and figured out what he was doing?

"No way," Garrett said out loud.

Because the door from the stairs had locked behind him, he had to come back through the lobby.

He pretended to be lost in his phone.

The bar was empty.

He took the elevator.

A Fed stepped in with him at the last moment. A guy about Garrett's height, his tie two-fingers loose.

He nodded to Garrett and, because there was only a second-floor button, Garrett pushed it. The Fed walked behind Garrett the whole way down the hall, until Garrett had to stop. He pretended to be confused about his key situation until the Fed had stepped past.

The reason he didn't want to open the door with the Fed right there was because he didn't know what was going to be on the other side of the door.

Who.

No one was in the room. The secret half-door—*quarter*-door—was still in place.

Garrett closed his eyes to heighten the sensitivity of the pad of his index finger, traced the cut-line to be sure.

According to the clock he'd plugged back in, figured out how to set, there was still four hours until the hotel rolled breakfast out. Nine hours until next check-out.

Garrett nodded to himself, reminded himself about the omelettes, the folded eggs, whatever the hell they were.

This was all because of them. It would be foolish to leave without at least getting a plateful. It would be even more foolish to leave before the mud had dried all the way. He could wait. If Penny had called the cops, they would've been here by now. He didn't want to get this close and screw it all up when the maid saw a corner of loose wallpaper where it shouldn't have been, and wrote it up for Maintenance.

"Good, good," Garrett said about this decision to stay, and used the remote to turn the television on. Whatever channel, just something for sound. He stripped down, stood in the curtainless shower, the steam from his water making cyclones in the doorway with the air conditioner.

That's what he liked about hotels: unlimited hot water, unlimited refrigerated air.

This was better than driving a hole in the night, wasn't it?

The towel he used to dry off still smelled like Lady. And, because he'd always used her brush, there wasn't one. It was in the dually. Along with forensic proof that he'd been running with her, he figured. The brush was always matted black with her Indian hair.

Until the first roadside trash can.

Garrett told himself to remember that. To remember it hard. It would be stupid to get busted for something like that. Penny was still out there, after all. Still might do something.

Before lying down to soak in the news or the movies or the basketball highlights, Garrett slid the nightstand over in front of Lady. Now if that little door fell open, the lamp would tip over, the bulb would flash blue and fizzle out.

It was in case he went to sleep.

How long had it been? Just one day? It felt like longer. It felt like forever.

Garrett settled back on to the bed, watched the kung fu movie until that thing happened that meant he was sleeping: he started hearing different voices from the screen. His own voice.

He changed to where the news had been but it was just a dead picture, a holding pattern, the current time and temperature. It matched the clock. Garrett smiled about that.

He ended up on a kids' sit-com that made so little sense to him that when he started hearing his own voice talking to him from the characters' mouths, the show actually started to track.

He chuckled, felt his chest rising and falling with it.

And then he looked over, he wasn't sure why—oh, it was because of the shadow, right.

Was that on the show, or was it from the show?

No. It was from the lady crawling out of the wall, her hair dragging the ground under her it was so long.

And then the show went off with no warning, no prelude, the picture sucked down to a point of light, which the set then swallowed.

Next was a flash of blue.

It was just enough for Garrett to see a woman standing at the foot of the bed, her chin hanging low and crooked because the bones in there were gravel now, her mouth a twisted oval opening on to endless black.

Garrett's fingers knew to grab into the damp sheets he was lying on when that blue flash fizzled, but the rest of him didn't even flinch.

Garrett came to. A wall of thunder was falling down over him.

The door, knocking.

Sunlight cutting in through the window.

Morning.

Somebody at the door.

He fumbled out, tangled in the sheets, still blinking, and stabbed his hand out for the nightstand for support but it wasn't there.

And then he remembered. All of it.

He looked to where the nightstand still was.

The lamp had fallen in the night.

Garrett's chest went cold until he tracked back from it, down along its cord to the throw pillow he'd had his head propped on.

It had fallen right on the cord, which had been stretched tight to accommodate the lamp's new position.

And the knocking would not stop.

"Hold on!" Garrett said, his voice still congested with sleep.

It wasn't the cleaning staff. Their knocks were timid, apologetic.

According to the digital clock, he still had fifteen minutes to make breakfast.

"This better be good," he said, and stepped across the room in his underwear and button-down shirt, the top sheet dragging behind until he shook it off.

Garrett hauled the door open.

It was the cops.

Two of them, anyway.

Guns holstered. Khaki uniform shirts, brown pocket flaps.

Deputies, then.

Not the Feds all up and down the hall.

"Um," Garrett said, trying to rub the blear from his eyes, mentally casing the room behind him.

It was empty, though. He knew. It had to be. Because he'd meant to be gone already.

And then Penny stepped in front of the deputy on the right. It wasn't who he figured had to be Penny, it was definitely Penny. He could tell by the way something in his chest collapsed—he could tell by the way he nearly said Lady's name, to ask her how she was here when she was already dead in the wall.

He'd never thought to ask Lady if she had a twin.

Her eyes cut right through Garrett.

"What's this about, officers?" he said.

"Deputy," the deputy on the left said.

"You know what it's about," Penny said.

Garrett focused in on her, said, "Do I know you?"

"I know you," Penny said back, and pushed past him, the deputy on her side reaching out to catch her by the shoulder.

Garrett stepped aside, let her pass.

"I heard what you did to her," Penny was saying.

"What's this about?" Garrett said again.

The deputy on the right shrugged, said, "She kept calling, claims her sister—that something's happened to her sister."

"Sister?" Garrett said, looking back to Penny, walking all over the room. Into the bathroom now, having to step over the sheet that had fallen over the bloodstain.

"Apparently she thought she heard her sister be the victim of some sort of violence," the deputy on the left said.

"Hunh," Garrett said, then: "She's Lady's sister?"

"So you do know Lady Catches Twice," one of the deputies said, Garrett couldn't tell, was watching Penny now.

"I ought to," Garrett said. "She took my jeep."

Penny was back, glaring at him.

"Your *jeep*?" she said.

"Would you like to file a—?" the deputy on the left said, but Garrett held a hand up, was already shaking his head no.

"You're Penny," Garrett said, to Penny.

"I'm the alive sister, yeah," Penny said.

"You think I—" Garrett started, said again: "You think I did something to Lady?"

"Was there an argument, sir?"

Garrett nodded, said, "She broke the lamp. I told her we were going to have to pay for that. She screamed, threw her shit into her bag. I didn't realize she had my keys until it was too late."

Penny threw herself into Garrett, her nails gouging into his chest where his shirt was open.

Garrett turned his head and fell back until the deputies dragged her off.

He looked down to the scratches on his chest.

"I figured she went to you," he said to Penny, breathing hard now, restrained.

"She can't," Penny said. "Because she's dead. I can't *feel* her."

"You can't . . .?" Garrett said, squinting for help.

"Because they're sisters," the deputy on the right said.

"Twins," the left deputy said, as if embarrassed about what this was becoming.

Garrett nodded like processing this—not believing it, just under-standing it—and finally said, "She's done this before. She knows I can't pay without her card. She'll leave me here for three or four days, come back with enough cash to cover it. I don't know where she gets it."

"You lie," Penny said, still struggling.

"You know her," Garrett said. "You know this is what she does."

"You killed her!" Penny screamed. "I heard it! I felt it!"

"You heard the lamp break?" Garrett said, touching a delicate finger to one of the deeper claw marks on his chest, making sure the deputies saw what she'd done to him—what they were now accomplices to, if it came to that.

They stepped out, Penny between them, her feet pedaling air.

"We're sorry to bother you, sir," the left one said.

"You'll be here for a day or two?" the right one said.

Garrett nodded, said, "I need my jeep."

"Year and make?"

"Green and rusted. CJ, eighty-two. Pipe bumpers front and back." Garrett supplied a license plate number when asked. If they checked, they'd find a match, but he'd abandoned the jeep with a blown engine months before.

"We'll keep a lookout, sir."

"Check the bars."

"Like I said, we'll keep a lookout."

"You can't do this!" Penny said, trying to pull away.

Garrett closed the door on her, stood there with his eyes closed.

This was better, he told himself.

They hadn't connected his truck to him. His plates were on the index card at Registration, but with no body, it wasn't going to come to that. If he left now, if he made sure to pay then left, they'd probably just toss his index card, right? Clean getaway. No tracks.

The clock on the nightstand said he could still make breakfast.

Garrett slid his pants on, stepped into his boots, ran a finger through his hair and left the hellhole of a room.

The whole way down, federal agents in various states of dress and undress were stationed in their doorways, clocking him.

He nodded to the first couple then just pushed on, down to the elevator, to the lobby, where he made sure to pay for his stay with cash.

"Let me ask you something," he said to the clerk.

"Shoot," the clerk said.

"At breakfast," Garrett said. "Are those omelettes, or they still eggs?"

"I didn't see you at breakfast," the clerk said, and Garrett turned around to the breakfast area.

It was closed down.

The clock had still been lying to him.

"Lady," he said, shaking his head.

Garrett made like he was going for the elevator but kept walking, down the long hall to the back parking lot.

When there were no Sheriff's department cruisers loitering around, and when there were no curtains on the second floor parted with federal interest, and when the Border Patrol Blazer parked by the dually was just flashing its side mirrors back at the morning, Garrett climbed behind the wheel, waited for the glow plugs, and left.

Ten miles out of town, nobody important in the rear view, Garrett pulled over to a rest stop's barrel trashcan, emptied the contents of Lady's roller bag into it, then covered it with some of the trash from the bed of the dually.

Twenty miles after that he turned off into some BLM, massaged a fire up from the belly of the roller bag. The smoke was oily and black and perfect. He left it burning.

That was it, then.

Now he could speed if he wanted. Now he could do anything.

"New Mexico," he said out loud. To the dually, he guessed. It was his new partner in crime.

New Mexico, though. Driving out of Gallup with Bats once, Bats had tipped his head to the north side of the highway, a different patch of BLM, and dropped into this story about how his dad, in West Texas in high school, his dad and a buddy had found a hole out in a field, and followed it down to a cave that had been a home, a hundred and fifty years ago. There were untouched baskets, pots, tools, a woven sleeping mat.

It was the sleeping mat that got Garrett's interest. Because the Comanche would have used robes or skins.

Did a mat mean that cave might have been *older* than the Comanche? Pre-Clovis, even?

A score like that, it would set him up for life.

Bats' dad and buddy had rocked it shut, walked away.

Like a hundred other stories you heard around the pawnshop.

But still, right?

The end of Bats' story was how *his* stash might be like that for some-body someday. Garrett had looked over for the rest of the story and Bats shrugged, said didn't Garrett cache his stuff somewhere?

"A storage unit, yeah," Garrett had said.

Bats shook his head no, no, said the proper place—tipping his head to the north side of the highway again, twelve and a half miles west of Gallup, New Mexico—it was a natural cave, one that nobody else knows about.

He might as well have said his stash was there.

And Garrett could find it, he knew. Because he knew how Bats' head worked. What his eyes could and couldn't see.

There'd be a faded silver can or two close to the hidden entrance.

Any pothunter worth his salt wouldn't need three days.

Garrett gave himself two, tops, and eased into the dually's turbo diesel, switching hands on the wheel.

Instead of turning the air on like Lady always insisted on, he cracked the window and then slid the back glass open.

In a pickup with no camper, it would pull the wind through too fast, be a mess. With a camper as poorly matched to the bed rails as Garrett's, it just made for a breeze.

Because the troopers only patrolled this stretch of highway with planes—which is to say, with road signs threatening planes—Garrett let the dually have its head. Seventy, eighty, ninety.

In the bed, under the shell, some of the trash kept lifting up into the rear view. It was kind of pretty in its slow, go-nowhere way.

Garrett leaned ahead to the radio to dial away the solitude, and when he looked up to the road again, the trash in the rear view had coalesced into a shape. A form.

A woman.

He locked his arm against the steering wheel, opened his mouth to bellow, to scream, he didn't know and it didn't matter.

She was already crawling through the rear window, seeping through it like oil, pulling herself through from the bed.

Garrett leaned forward, away from her, he was ready to crawl through the windshield out on to the hood—who cared?—but now her sharp-fingered hands had him by the side of the head, some of that foul taste in the corners of his mouth, her skin so dry.

She pulled his head back to the headrest, his mouth open, and brought her face up alongside his, her loose chin rubbing at the base of his jaw, his hands clawing blackened skin from her wrists.

It meant driving with his knees.

Except he was pushing his feet into the floorboard, trying to fight her.

In what felt like slow motion, then, he felt the left front tire of the dually find the inside shoulder, spatter gravel up into the wheel well. An instant later the double back tires did the same, the gravel they threw bursting through the fiberglass fender.

Garrett tried to shake his head no, no, not like this, but the dually's weight was already shifting, one side of it lighter now, and the semi coming on the westbound side of the highway was already flashing its lights in panic, and now Lady had her mouth open to his cheek, her blind dry tongue to his skin, one of her eyes open against his, the pupil blown wide.

Garrett never heard the crash, even though it lasted nearly half a mile.

His last glimmer of a thought was of a tall woman standing at the foot of his bed the night before, then, as if hearing something, jerking her head over, following that sound out of the room.

No, not a woman.

A lady.

Joe Lansdale's Texas tall tale was first published in 1994, but it became well known when Don Coscarelli's film *Bubba Ho-tep*, starring Bruce Campbell and Ossie Davis, was released in 2002. A limited number of prints were "roadshowed" to film festivals. Critical acclaim followed. (Roger Ebert praised the film's "delightful wackiness," saying it had the "damnedest ingratiating way of making us sit there and grin at its harebrained audacity, laugh at its outhouse humor, and be somewhat moved . . .") The film had achieved cult status by the time it was released on DVD. Lansdale's mummy is certainly an original ideation, and his story deals with the subject of immortality . . . and the lack of it . . . in his unique way . . .

Bubba Ho-Tep

Joe R. Lansdale

Elvis dreamed he had his dick out, checking to see if the bump on the head of it had filled with pus again. If it had, he was going to name the bump Priscilla, after his ex-wife, and bust it by jacking off. Or he liked to think that's what he'd do. Dreams let you think like that. The truth was, he hadn't had a hard-on in years.

That bitch, Priscilla. Gets a new hairdo and she's gone, just because she caught him fucking a big-tittied gospel singer. It wasn't like the singer had mattered. Priscilla ought to have understood that, so what was with her making a big deal out of it?

Was it because she couldn't hit a high note same and as good as the singer when she came?

When had that happened anyway, Priscilla leaving?

Yesterday? Last year? Ten years ago?

Oh God, it came to him instantly as he slipped out of sleep like a soft turd squeezed free of a loose asshole—for he could hardly think of himself or life in any context other than sewage, since so often he was too tired to do anything other than let it all fly in his sleep, wake up in an ocean of piss or shit, waiting for the nurses or the aides to come in and wipe his ass. But now it came to him. Suddenly he realized it had been years ago that he had supposedly died, and longer years than that since Priscilla left, and how old was she anyway? Sixty-five? Seventy?

And how old was he?

Christ! He was almost convinced he was too old to be alive, and had to be dead, but he wasn't convinced enough, unfortunately. He knew where he was now, and in that moment of realization, he sincerely wished he were dead. This was worse than death.

From across the room, his roommate, Bull Thomas, bellowed and coughed and moaned and fell back into painful sleep, the cancer gnawing at his insides like a rat plugged up inside a watermelon.

Bull's bellow of pain and anger and indignation at growing old and diseased was the only thing bullish about him now, though Elvis had seen photographs of him when he was younger, and Bull had been very bullish indeed. Thick-chested, slab-faced, and tall. Probably thought he'd live forever, and happily. A boozing, pill-popping, swinging dick until the end of time.

Now Bull was shrunk down, was little more than a wrinkled sheet-white husk that throbbed with occasional pulses of blood while the carcinoma fed.

Elvis took hold of the bed's lift button, eased himself upright. He glanced at Bull. Bull was breathing heavily and his bony knees rose up and down like he was pedaling a bicycle; his kneecaps punched feebly at the sheet, making pup tents that rose up and collapsed, rose up and collapsed.

Elvis looked down at the sheet stretched over his own bony knees.

He thought: *My God, how long have I been here? Am I really awake now, or am I dreaming I'm awake? How could my plans have gone so wrong? When are they going to serve lunch, and considering what they serve, why do I care? And if Priscilla discovered I was alive, would she come see me, would she want to see me, and would we still want to fuck, or would we have to merely talk about it? Is there finally, and really, anything to life other than food and shit and sex?*

Elvis pushed the sheet down to do what he had done in the dream. He pulled up his gown, leaned forward, and examined his dick. It was wrinkled and small. It didn't look like something that had dive-bombed movie starlet pussies or filled their mouths like a big zucchini or pumped forth a load of sperm frothy as cake icing. The healthiest thing about his pecker was the big red bump with the black ring around it and the pus-filled white center. Fact was, that bump kept growing, he was going to have to pull a chair up beside his bed and put a pillow in it so the bump would have some place to sleep at night. There was more pus in that damn bump than there was cum in his loins. Yep, the old diddle-bopper was no longer a flesh cannon loaded for bare ass. It was a peanut too small to harvest, wasting away on the vine.

His nuts were a couple of darkening, about-to-rot grapes, too limp to produce juice for life's wine. His legs were stick and paper things with over-large, vein-swollen feet on the ends. His belly was such a bloat, it was a pain for him to lean forward and scrutinize his dick and balls.

Pulling his gown down and the sheet back over himself, Elvis leaned back and wished he had a peanut butter and banana sandwich fried in butter. There had been a time when he and his crew would board his private jet and fly clean across country just to have a special-made fried peanut butter and 'nanner sandwich. He could still taste the damn things.

Elvis closed his eyes and thought he would awake from a bad dream, but didn't. He opened his eyes again, slowly, and saw that he was still where he had been, and things were no better. He reached over and opened his dresser drawer and got out a little round mirror and looked at himself.

He was horrified. His hair was white as salt and had receded dramatically. He had wrinkles deep enough to conceal outstretched earthworms, the big ones, the night crawlers. His pouty mouth no longer appeared pouty. It looked like the dropping waddles of a bulldog, seeming more that way because he was slobbering a mite. He dragged his tired tongue across his lips to daub the slobber, revealed to himself in the mirror that he was missing a lot of teeth.

Goddamn it! How had he gone from King of Rock and Roll to this? Old guy in a rest home in East Texas with a growth on his dick? And what was that growth? Cancer? No one was talking. No one seemed to know. Perhaps the bump was a manifestation of the mistakes of his life, so many of them made with his dick.

He considered on that. Did he ask himself this question every day, or just now and then? Time sort of ran together when the last moment and the immediate moment and the moment forthcoming were all alike.

Shit, when was lunchtime? Had he slept through it?

Was it about time for his main nurse again? The good-looking one with the smooth chocolate skin and tits like grapefruits? The one who came in and sponge bathed him and held his pitiful little pecker in her gloved hands and put salve on his canker with all the enthusiasm of a mechanic oiling a defective part?

He hoped not. That was the worst of it. A doll like that handling him without warmth or emotion. Twenty years ago, just twenty, he could have made with the curled-lip smile and had her eating out of his asshole. Where had his youth gone? Why hadn't fame sustained old age and death, and why had he left his fame in the first place, and did he want it back, and could he have it back, and if he could, would it make any difference?

And finally, when he was evacuated from the bowels of life into the toilet bowl of the beyond and was flushed, would the great sewer pipe flow him to the other side where God would—in the guise of a great all-seeing turd with corn kernel eyes—be waiting with open turd arms, and would there be amongst the sewage his mother (bless her fat little heart) and father and friends, waiting with fried peanut butter and 'nanner sandwiches and ice cream cones, predigested, of course?

He was reflecting on this, pondering the afterlife, when Bull gave out with a hell of a scream, pouched his eyes damn near out of his head, arched his back, grease-farted like a blast from Gabriel's trumpet, and checked his tired old soul out of the Mud Creek Shady Rest Convalescent Home; flushed it on out and across the great shitty beyond.

Later that day, Elvis lay sleeping, his lips fluttering the bad taste of lunch—steamed zucchini and boiled peas—out of his belly. He awoke to a noise, rolled over to see a young attractive woman cleaning out Bull's dresser drawer. The curtains over the window next to Bull's bed were pulled wide open, and the sunlight was cutting through it and showing her to great advantage. She was blonde and Nordic-featured and her long hair was tied back with a big red bow and she wore big gold hoop earrings that shimmered in the sunlight. She was dressed in a white blouse and a short black skirt and dark hose and high heels.

The heels made her ass ride up beneath her skirt like soft bald baby heads under a thin blanket.

She had a big yellow plastic trashcan and she had one of Bull's dresser drawers pulled out, and she was picking through it, like a magpie looking for bright things. She found a few—coins, a pocket-knife, a cheap watch. These were plucked free and laid on the dresser top, then the remaining contents of the drawer—Bull's photographs of himself when young, a rotten pack of rubbers (wishful thinking never deserted Bull), a Bronze Star and a Purple Heart from his performance in the Vietnam War—were dumped into the trashcan with a bang and a flutter.

Elvis got hold of his bed lift button and raised himself for a better look. The woman had her back to him now, and didn't notice.

She was replacing the dresser drawer and pulling out another. It was full of clothes. She took out the few shirts and pants and socks and underwear, and laid them on Bull's bed—remade now, and minus Bull, who had been toted off to be taxidermied, embalmed, burned up, whatever.

"You're gonna toss that stuff," Elvis said. "Could I have one of them pictures of Bull? Maybe that Purple Heart? He was proud of it."

The young woman turned and looked at him. "I suppose," she said. She went to the trashcan and bent over it and showed her black panties to Elvis as she rummaged. He knew the revealing of her panties was neither intentional nor unintentional. She just didn't give a damn.

She saw him as so physically and sexually non-threatening, she didn't mind if he got a bird's-eye view of her; it was the same to her as a house cat sneaking a peek.

Elvis observed the thin panties straining and slipping into the caverns of her ass cheeks and felt his pecker flutter once, like a bird having a heart attack, then it laid down and remained limp and still.

Well, these days, even a flutter was kind of reassuring.

The woman surfaced from the trashcan with a photo and the Purple Heart, went over to Elvis's bed and handed them to him.

Elvis dangled the ribbon that held the Purple Heart between his fingers, said, "Bull your kin?"

"My daddy," she said.

"I haven't seen you here before."

"Only been here once before," she said. "When I checked him in."

"Oh," Elvis said. "That was three years ago, wasn't it?"

"Yeah. Were you and him friends?"

Elvis considered the question. He didn't know the real answer. All he knew was Bull listened to him when he said he was Elvis Presley and seemed to believe him. If he didn't believe him, he at least had the courtesy not to patronize. Bull always called him Elvis, and before Bull grew too ill, he always played cards and checkers with him.

"Just roommates," Elvis said. "He didn't feel good enough to say much. I just sort of hated to see what was left of him go away so easy. He was an all-right guy. He mentioned you a lot. You're Callie, right?"

"Yeah," she said. "Well, he was all right."

"Not enough you came and saw him though."

"Don't try to put some guilt trip on me, Mister. I did what I could. Hadn't been for Medicaid, Medicare, whatever that stuff was, he'd have been in a ditch somewhere. I didn't have the money to take care of him."

Elvis thought of his own daughter, lost long ago to him. If she knew he lived, would she come to see him? Would she care? He feared knowing the answer.

"You could have come and seen him," Elvis said.

"I was busy. Mind your own business. Hear?"

The chocolate-skin nurse with the grapefruit tits came in. Her white uniform crackled like cards being shuffled. Her little white nurse hat was tilted on her head in a way that said she loved mankind and made good money and was getting regular dick. She smiled at Callie and then at Elvis. "How are you this morning, Mr Haff?"

"All right," Elvis said. "But I prefer Mr Presley. Or Elvis. I keep telling you that. I don't go by Sebastian Haff any more. I don't try to hide any more."

"Why, of course," said the pretty nurse. "I knew that. I forgot. Good morning, Elvis."

Her voice dripped with sorghum syrup. Elvis wanted to hit her with his bedpan.

The nurse said to Callie: "Did you know we have a celebrity here, Miss Thomas? Elvis Presley. You know, the rock and roll singer?"

"I've heard of him," Callie said. "I thought he was dead."

Callie went back to the dresser and squatted and set to work on the bottom drawer. The nurse looked at Elvis and smiled again, only she spoke to Callie. "Well, actually, Elvis is dead, and Mr Haff knows that, don't you, Mr Haff?"

"Hell no," said Elvis. "I'm right here. I ain't dead, yet."

"Now, Mr Haff, I don't mind calling you Elvis, but you're a little confused, or like to play sometimes. You were an Elvis impersonator. Remember? You fell off a stage and broke your hip. What was it . . . Twenty years ago? It got infected and you went into a coma for a few years. You came out with a few problems."

"I was impersonating myself," Elvis said. "I couldn't do nothing else. I haven't got any problems. You're trying to say my brain is messed up, aren't you?"

Callie quit cleaning out the bottom drawer of the dresser. She was interested now, and though it was no use, Elvis couldn't help but try and explain who he was, just one more time. The explaining had become a habit, like wanting to smoke a cigar long after the enjoyment of it was gone.

"I got tired of it all," he said. "I got on drugs, you know. I wanted out. Fella named Sebastian Haff, an Elvis imitator, the best of them. He took my place. He had a bad heart and he liked drugs too. It was him died, not me. I took his place."

"Why would you want to leave all that fame," Callie said. "All that money?" And she looked at the nurse, like *Let's humor the old fart for a lark.*

"'Cause it got old. Woman I loved, Priscilla, she was gone. Rest of the women . . . were just women. The music wasn't mine any more. I wasn't even me any more. I was this thing they made up. Friends were sucking me dry. I got away and liked it, left all the money with Sebastian, except for enough to sustain me if things got bad. We had a deal, me and Sebastian. When I wanted to come back, he'd let me. It was all written up in a contract in case he wanted to give me a hard time, got to liking my life too good. Thing was, copy of the contract I had got lost in a trailer fire. I was living simple. Way Haff had been. Going from town to town doing the Elvis act. Only I felt like I was really me again. Can you dig that?"

"We're digging it, Mr Haff . . . Mr Presley," said the pretty nurse.

"I was singing the old way. Doing some new songs. Stuff I wrote. I was getting attention on a small but good scale. Women throwing themselves at me, 'cause they could imagine I was Elvis, only I was Elvis, playing Sebastian Haff playing Elvis . . . It was all pretty good. I didn't mind the contract being burned up. I didn't even try to go back and convince anybody. Then I had the accident. Like I was saying, I'd laid up a little money in case of illness, stuff like that. That's what's paying for here. These nice facilities. Ha!"

"Now, Elvis," the nurse said. "Don't carry it too far. You may just get way out there and not come back."

"Oh, fuck you," Elvis said.

The nurse giggled.

Shit, Elvis thought. *Get old, you can't even cuss somebody and have it bother them. Everything you do is either worthless or sadly amusing.*

"You know, Elvis," said the pretty nurse, "we have a Mr Dillinger here too. And a President Kennedy. He says the bullet only wounded him and his brain is in a fruit jar at the White House, hooked up to some wires and a battery, and, as long as the battery works, he can walk around without it. His brain, that is. You know, he says everyone was in on trying to assassinate him. Even Elvis Presley."

"You're an asshole," Elvis said.

"I'm not trying to hurt your feelings, Mr Haff," the nurse said. "I'm merely trying to give you a reality check."

"You can shove that reality check right up your pretty black ass," Elvis said.

The nurse made a sad little snicking sound. "Mr Haff, Mr Haff. Such language."

"What happened to get you here?" said Callie. "Say you fell off a stage?"

"I was gyrating," Elvis said. "Doing 'Blue Moon,' but my hip went out. I'd been having trouble with it." Which was quite true. He'd sprained it making love to a blue-haired old lady with ELVIS tattooed on her fat ass. He couldn't help himself from wanting to fuck her. She looked like his mother, Gladys.

"You swiveled right off the stage?" Callie said. "Now that's sexy." Elvis looked at her. She was smiling. This was great fun for her, listening to some nut tell a tale. She hadn't had this much fun since she put her old man in the rest home.

"Oh, leave me the hell alone," Elvis said.

The women smiled at one another, passing a private joke. Callie said to the nurse: "I've got what I want." She scraped the bright things off the top of Bull's dresser into her purse. "The clothes can go to Goodwill or the Salvation Army."

The pretty nurse nodded to Callie. "Very well. And I'm very sorry about your father. He was a nice man."

"Yeah," said Callie, and she started out of there. She paused at the foot of Elvis's bed. "Nice to meet you, Mr Presley."

"Get the hell out," Elvis said.

"Now, now," said the pretty nurse, patting his foot through the covers, as if it were a little cantankerous dog. "I'll be back later to do that . . . little thing that has to be done. You know?"

"I know," Elvis said, not liking the words "little thing." Callie and the nurse started away then, punishing him with the clean lines of their faces and the sheen of their hair, the jiggle of their asses and tits. When they were out of sight, Elvis heard them laugh about something in the hall, then they were gone, and Elvis felt as if he were on the far side of Pluto without a jacket. He picked up the ribbon with the Purple Heart and looked at it.

Poor Bull. In the end, did anything really matter?

Meanwhile . . .

The Earth swirled around the sun like a spinning turd in the toilet bowl (to keep up with Elvis's metaphors) and the good old abused Earth clicked about on its axis and the hole in the ozone spread slightly wider, like a shy lady fingering open her vagina, and the South American trees that had stood for centuries were visited by the dozer, the chainsaw, and the match, and they rose up in burned black puffs that expanded and dissipated into minuscule wisps, and while the puffs of smoke dissolved, there were IRA bombings in London, and there was more war in the Mideast. Blacks died in Africa of famine, the HIV virus infected a million more, the Dallas Cowboys lost again, and that Ole Blue Moon that Elvis and Patsy Cline sang so well about swung around the Earth and came in close and rose over the Shady Rest Convalescent Home, shone its bittersweet, silver-blue rays down on the joint like a flashlight beam shining through a blue-haired lady's do, and inside the rest home, evil waddled about like a duck looking for a spot to squat, and Elvis rolled over in his sleep and awoke with the intense desire to pee.

All right, thought Elvis. *This time I make it. No more piss or crap in the bed.* (Famous last words.)

Elvis sat up and hung his feet over the side of the bed and the bed swung far to the left and around the ceiling and back, and then it wasn't moving at all. The dizziness passed.

Elvis looked at his walker and sighed, leaned forward, took hold of the grips and eased himself off the bed and clumped the rubber-padded tips forward, made for the toilet.

He was in the process of milking his bump-swollen weasel when he heard something in the hallway. A kind of scrambling, like a big spider scuttling about in a box of gravel.

There was always some sound in the hallway, people coming and going, yelling in pain or confusion, but this time of night, 3:00 a.m., was normally quite dead.

It shouldn't have concerned him, but the truth of the matter was, now that he was up and had successfully pissed in the pot, he was no longer sleepy; he was still thinking about that bimbo, Callie, and the nurse (what the hell was her name?) with the tits like grapefruits, and all they had said.

Elvis stumped his walker backwards out of the bathroom, turned it, made his way forward into the hall. The hall was semi-dark, with every other light out, and the lights that were on were dimmed to a watery egg-yolk yellow. The black and white tile floor looked like a great chess-board, waxed and buffed for the next game of life, and here he was, a semi-crippled pawn, ready to go.

Off in the far wing of the home, Old Lady McGee, better known in the home as The Blue Yodeler, broke into one of her famous yodels (she claimed to have sung with a Country and Western band in her youth) then ceased abruptly. Elvis swung the walker forward and moved on.

He hadn't been out of his room in ages, and he hadn't been out of his bed much either. Tonight, he felt invigorated because he hadn't pissed his bed, and he'd heard the sound again, the spider in the box of gravel. (Big spider. Big box. Lots of gravel.) And following the sound gave him something to do.

Elvis rounded the corner, beads of sweat popping out on his fore-head like heat blisters. Jesus. He wasn't invigorated now. Thinking about how invigorated he was had bushed him. Still, going back to his room to lie on his bed and wait for morning so he could wait for noon, then afternoon and night, didn't appeal to him.

He went by Jack McLaughlin's room, the fellow who was convinced he was John F. Kennedy, and that his brain was in the White House running on batteries. The door to Jack's room was open. Elvis peeked in as he moved by, knowing full well that Jack might not want to see him. Sometimes he accepted Elvis as the real Elvis and, when he did, he got scared, saying it was Elvis who had been behind the assassination.

Actually, Elvis hoped he felt that way tonight. It would at least be some acknowledgment that he was who he was, even if the acknow-ledgment was a fearful shriek from a nut.

Course, Elvis thought, *maybe I'm nuts too. Maybe I am Sebastian Haff and I fell off the stage and broke more than my hip, cracked some part of my brain that lost my old self and made me think I'm Elvis.*

No. He couldn't believe that. That's the way they wanted him to think. They wanted him to believe he was nuts and he wasn't Elvis, just some sad old fart who had once lived out part of another man's life because he had none of his own.

304 | JOE R. LANSDALE

He wouldn't accept that. He wasn't Sebastian Haff. He was Elvis Goddamn Aaron Fucking Presley with a boil on his dick.

'Course, he believed that, maybe he ought to believe Jack was John F. Kennedy, and Mums Delay, another patient here at Shady Rest, was Dillinger. Then again, maybe not. They were kind of scanty on evidence. He at least looked like Elvis gone old and sick. Jack was black—he claimed the Powers That Be had dyed him that color to keep him hidden—and Mums was a woman who claimed she'd had a sex-change operation.

Jesus, was this a rest home or a nuthouse?

Jack's room was one of the special kind. He didn't have to share. He had money from somewhere. The room was packed with books and little luxuries. And though Jack could walk well, he even had a fancy electric wheelchair that he rode about in sometimes. Once, Elvis had seen him riding it around the outside circular drive, popping wheelies and spinning doughnuts.

When Elvis looked into Jack's room, he saw him lying on the floor.

Jack's gown was pulled up around his neck, and his bony black ass appeared to be made of licorice in the dim light. Elvis figured Jack had been on his way to the shitter, or was coming back from it, and had collapsed. His heart, maybe.

"Jack," Elvis said.

Elvis clumped into the room, positioned his walker next to Jack, took a deep breath and stepped out of it, supporting himself with one side of it. He got down on his knees beside Jack, hoping he'd be able to get up again. God, but his knees and back hurt.

Jack was breathing hard. Elvis noted the scar at Jack's hairline, a long scar that made Jack's skin lighter there, almost gray. ("That's where they took the brain out," Jack always explained, "put it in that fucking jar. I got a little bag of sand up there now.")

Elvis touched the old man's shoulder. "Jack. Man, you OK?" No response.

Elvis tried again. "Mr Kennedy?"

"Uh," said Jack (Mr Kennedy).

"Hey, man. You're on the floor," Elvis said.

"No shit? Who are you?"

Elvis hesitated. This wasn't the time to get Jack worked up.

"Sebastian," he said. "Sebastian Haff."

Elvis took hold of Jack's shoulder and rolled him over. It was about as difficult as rolling a jelly roll. Jack lay on his back now. He strayed an eyeball at Elvis. He started to speak, hesitated. Elvis took hold of Jack's nightgown and managed to work it down around Jack's knees, trying to give the old fart some dignity.

Jack finally got his breath. "Did you see him go by in the hall? He scuttled like."

"Who?"

"Someone they sent."

"Who's they?"

"You know. Lyndon Johnson. Castro. They've sent someone to finish me. I think maybe it was Johnson himself. Real ugly. Real goddamn ugly."

"Johnson's dead," Elvis said.

"That won't stop him," Jack said.

Later that morning, sunlight shooting into Elvis's room through venetian blinds, Elvis put his hands behind his head and considered the night before while the pretty black nurse with the grapefruit tits salved his dick. He had reported Jack's fall and the aides had come to help Jack back in bed, and him back on his walker. He had clumped back to his room (after being scolded for being out there that time of night) feeling that an air of strangeness had blown into the rest home, an air that wasn't there as short as the day before. It was at low ebb now, but certainly still present, humming in the background like some kind of generator ready to buzz up to a higher notch at a moment's notice.

And he was certain it wasn't just his imagination. The scuttling sound he'd heard last night, Jack had heard it too. What was that all about? It wasn't the sound of a walker, or a crip dragging their foot, or a wheelchair creeping along, it was something else, and now that he thought about it, it wasn't exactly spider legs in gravel, more like a roll of barbed wire tumbling across tile.

Elvis was so wrapped up in these considerations, he lost awareness of the nurse until she said, "Mr Haff!"

"What . . ." and he saw that she was smiling and looking down at her hands. He looked too. There, nestled in one of her gloved palms, was a massive, blue-veined hooter with a pus-filled bump on it the size of a pecan. It was *his* hooter and *his* pus-filled bump.

"You ole rascal," she said, and gently lowered his dick between his legs. "I think you better take a cold shower, Mr Haff."

Elvis was amazed. That was the first time in years he'd had a boner like that. What gave here?

Then he realized what gave. He wasn't thinking about not being able to do it. He was thinking about something that interested him, and now, with something clicking around inside his head besides old memories and confusions, concerns about his next meal and going to the crapper, he had been given a dose of life again. He grinned his gums and what teeth were in them at the nurse.

"You get in there with me," he said, "and I'll take that shower."

"You silly thing," she said, and pulled his nightgown down and stood and removed her plastic gloves and dropped them in the trashcan beside his bed.

"Why don't you pull on it a little?" Elvis said.

"You ought to be ashamed," the nurse said, but she smiled when she said it.

She left the room door open after she exited. This concerned Elvis a little, but he felt his bed was at such an angle no one could look in, and if they did, tough luck. He wasn't going to look a gift hard-on in the pee-hole. He pulled the sheet over him and pushed his hands beneath the sheets and got his gown pulled up over his belly. He took hold of his snake and began to choke it with one hand, running his thumb over the pus-filled bump. With his other hand, he fondled his balls. He thought of Priscilla and the pretty black nurse and Bull's daughter and even the blue-haired fat lady with ELVIS tattooed on her butt, and he stroked harder and faster, and goddamn but he got stiffer and stiffer, and the bump on his cock gave up its load first, exploded hot pus down his thighs, and then his balls, which he thought forever empty, filled up with juice and electricity, and finally he threw the switch. The dam broke and the juice flew. He heard himself scream happily and felt hot wetness jetting down his legs, splattering as far as his big toes.

"Oh God," he said softly. "I like that. I like that."

He closed his eyes and slept. And for the first time in a long time, not fitfully.

Lunchtime. The Shady Rest lunch room.

Elvis sat with a plate of steamed carrots and broccoli and flaky roast beef in front of him. A dry roll, a pat of butter, and a short glass of milk soldiered on the side. It was not inspiring.

Next to him, The Blue Yodeler was stuffing a carrot up her nose while she expounded on the sins of God, The Heavenly Father, for knocking up that nice Mary in her sleep, slipping up her ungreased poontang while she snored, and—bless her little heart—not even knowing it, or getting a clit throb from it, but waking up with a belly full of baby and no memory of action.

Elvis had heard it all before. It used to offend him, this talk of God as rapist, but he'd heard it so much now he didn't care. She rattled on.

Across the way, an old man who wore a black mask and sometimes a white Stetson, known to residents and staff alike as Kemosabe, snapped one of his two capless cap pistols at the floor and called for an invisible Tonto to bend over so he could drive him home.

At the far end of the table, Dillinger was talking about how much whisky he used to drink, and how many cigars he used to smoke before he got his dick cut off at the stump and split so he could become a she and hide out as a woman. Now she said she no longer thought of banks and machine guns, women and fine cigars. She now thought about spots on dishes, the colors of curtains and drapes as coordinated with carpets and walls.

Even as the depression of his surroundings settled over him again, Elvis deliberated last night, and glanced down the length of the table at Jack (Mr Kennedy), who headed its far end. He saw the old man was looking at him, as if they shared a secret.

Elvis's ill mood dropped a notch; a real mystery was at work here and, come nightfall, he was going to investigate.

Swing the Shady Rest Convalescent Home's side of the Earth away from the sun again, and swing the moon in close and blue again. Blow some gauzy clouds across the nasty, black sky. Now ease on into 3:00 a.m.

Elvis awoke with a start and turned his head toward the intrusion. Jack stood next to the bed looking down at him. Jack was wearing a suit coat over his nightgown and he had on thick glasses. He said, "Sebastian. It's loose."

Elvis collected his thoughts, pasted them together into a not-too-scattered collage. "What's loose?"

"It," said Sebastian. "Listen."

Elvis listened. Out in the hall he heard the scuttling sound of the night before. Tonight, it reminded him of great locust-wings beating frantically inside a small cardboard box, the tips of them scratching at the cardboard, cutting it, ripping it apart.

"Jesus Christ, what is it?" Elvis said.

"I thought it was Lyndon Johnson, but it isn't. I've come across new evidence that suggests another assassin."

"Assassin?"

Jack cocked an ear. The sound had gone away, moved distant, then ceased.

"It's got another target tonight," said Jack. "Come on. I want to show you something. I don't think it's safe if you go back to sleep."

"For Christ sake," Elvis said. "Tell the administrators."

"The suits and the white starches," Jack said. "No thanks. I trusted them back when I was in Dallas, and look where that got my brain and me. I'm thinking with sand here, maybe picking up a few waves from my brain. Someday, who's to say they won't just disconnect the battery at the White House?"

"That's something to worry about, all right," Elvis said.

"Listen here," Jack said. "I know you're Elvis, and there were rumors, you know . . . about how you hated me, but I've thought it over. You hated me, you could have finished me the other night. All I want from you is to look me in the eye and assure me you had nothing to do with that day in Dallas, and that you never knew Lee Harvey Oswald or Jack Ruby."

Elvis stared at him as sincerely as possible. "I had nothing to do with Dallas, and I knew neither Lee Harvey Oswald nor Jack Ruby."

"Good," said Jack. "May I call you Elvis instead of Sebastian?"

"You may."

"Excellent. You wear glasses to read?"

"I wear glasses when I really want to see," Elvis said.

"Get 'em and come on."

Elvis swung his walker along easily, not feeling as if he needed it too much tonight. He was excited. Jack was a nut, and maybe he himself was nuts, but there was an adventure going on.

They came to the hall restroom. The one reserved for male visitors.

"In here," Jack said.

"Now wait a minute," Elvis said. "You're not going to get me in there and try and play with my pecker, are you?"

Jack stared at him. "Man, I made love to Jackie and Marilyn and a ton of others, and you think I want to play with your nasty ole dick?"

"Good point," said Elvis.

They went into the restroom. It was large, with several stalls and urinals.

"Over here," said Jack. He went over to one of the stalls and pushed open the door and stood back by the commode to make room for Elvis's walker. Elvis eased inside and looked at what Jack was now pointing to.

Graffiti.

"That's it?" Elvis said. "We're investigating a scuttling in the hall, trying to discover who attacked you last night, and you bring me in here to show me stick pictures on the shit-house wall?"

"Look close," Jack said.

Elvis leaned forward. His eyes weren't what they used to be, and his glasses probably needed to be upgraded, but he could see that instead of writing, the graffiti was a series of simple pictorials.

A thrill, like a shot of good booze, ran through Elvis. He had once been a fanatic reader of ancient and esoteric lore, like the Egyptian Book of the Dead and *The Complete Works of H. P. Lovecraft*, and straight away he recognized what he was staring at. "Egyptian hieroglyphics," he said.

"Right-a-reen-O," Jack said. "Hey, you're not as stupid as some folks made you out."

"Thanks," Elvis said.

Jack reached into his suit coat pocket and took out a folded piece of paper and unfolded it. He pressed it to the wall. Elvis saw that it was covered with the same sort of figures that were on the wall of the stall.

"I copied this down yesterday. I came in here to shit because they hadn't cleaned up my bathroom. I saw this on the wall, went back to my room and looked it up in my books and wrote it all down. The top line translates something like: *Pharaoh gobbles donkey goober.* And the bottom line is: *Cleopatra does the dirty.*"

"What?"

"Well, pretty much," Jack said.

Elvis was mystified. "All right," he said. "One of the nuts here, present company excluded, thinks he's Tutankhamun or something, and he writes on the wall in hieroglyphics. So what? I mean, what's the connection? Why are we hanging out in a toilet?"

"I don't know how they connect exactly," Jack said. "Not yet. But this . . . thing, it caught me asleep last night, and I came awake just in time to . . . well, he had me on the floor and had his mouth over my asshole."

"A shit eater?" Elvis said.

"I don't think so," Jack said. "He was after my soul. You can get that out of any of the major orifices in a person's body. I've read about it."

"Where?" Elvis asked. "*Hustler?*"

"*The Everyday Man or Woman's Book of the Soul*, by David Webb. It has some pretty good movie reviews about stolen soul movies in the back too."

"Oh, that sounds trustworthy," Elvis said.

They went back to Jack's room and sat on his bed and looked through his many books on astrology, the Kennedy assassination, and a number of esoteric tomes, including the philosophy book, *The Everyday Man or Woman's Book of the Soul.*

Elvis found that book fascinating in particular; it indicated that not only did humans have a soul, but that the soul could be stolen, and there was a section concerning vampires and ghouls and incubi and succubi, as well as related soul suckers. Bottom line was, one of those dudes was around, you had to watch your holes. Mouth hole. Nose hole. Asshole. If you were a woman, you needed to watch a different hole. Dick pee-holes and ear holes—male or female—didn't matter.

The soul didn't hang out there. They weren't considered major orifices for some reason.

In the back of the book was a list of items, related and not related to the book, that you could buy. Little plastic pyramids. Hats you could wear while channeling. Subliminal tapes that would help you learn Arabic. Postage was paid.

"Every kind of soul eater is in that book except politicians and science-fiction fans," Jack said. "And I think that's what we got here in Shady Rest. A soul eater. Turn to the Egyptian section."

Elvis did. The chapter was prefaced by a movie still from *The Ten Commandments* with Yul Brynner playing Pharaoh. He was standing up in his chariot looking serious, which seemed a fair enough expression, considering the Red Sea, which had been parted by Moses, was about to come back together and drown him and his army.

Elvis read the article slowly while Jack heated hot water with his plug-in heater and made cups of instant coffee. "I get my niece to smuggle this stuff in," said Jack. "Or she claims to be my niece. She's a black woman. I never saw her before I was shot that day in Dallas and they took my brain out. She's part of the new identity they've given me. She's got a great ass."

"Damn," said Elvis. "What it says here, is that you can bury some dude, and if he gets the right tanna leaves and spells said over him and such bullshit, he can come back to life some thousands of years later, and to stay alive, he has to suck on the souls of the living, and that if the souls are small, his life force doesn't last long. Small. What's that mean?"

"Read on . . . No, never mind, I'll tell you." Jack handed Elvis his cup of coffee and sat down on the bed next to him. "Before I do, want a Ding Dong? Not mine. The chocolate kind. Well, I guess mine is chocolate, now that I've been dyed."

"You got Ding Dongs?" Elvis asked.

"Couple of PayDays and Baby Ruths too," Jack said. "Which will it be? Let's get decadent."

Elvis licked his lips. "I'll have a Ding Dong."

While Elvis savored the Ding Dong, gumming it sloppily, sipping his coffee between bites, Jack, coffee cup balanced on his knee, a Baby Ruth in one mitt, expounded.

"Small souls means those without much fire for life," Jack said. "You know a place like that?"

"If souls were fires," Elvis said, "they couldn't burn much lower without being out than here. Only thing we got going in this joint is the pilot light."

"Exactamundo," Jack said. "What we got here in Shady Rest is an Egyptian soul sucker of some sort. A mummy hiding out, coming in here to feed on the sleeping. It's perfect, you see. The souls are little, and don't provide him with much. If this thing comes back two or three times in a row to wrap his lips around some elder's asshole, that elder is going to die pretty soon, and who's the wiser? Our mummy may not be getting much energy out of this, way he would with big souls, but the prey is easy. A mummy couldn't be too strong, really. Mostly just husk. But we're pretty much that way ourselves. We're not too far off being mummies."

"And with new people coming in all the time," Elvis said, "he can keep this up forever, this soul robbing."

"That's right. Because that's what we're brought here for. To get us out of the way until we die. And the ones don't die first of disease, or just plain old age, he gets."

Elvis considered all that. "That's why he doesn't bother the nurses and aides and administrators? He can go unsuspected."

"That, and they're not asleep. He has to get you when you're sleeping or unconscious."

"All right, but the thing that throws me, Jack, is how does an ancient Egyptian end up in an East Texas rest home, and why is he writing on shit-house walls?"

"He went to take a crap, got bored, and wrote on the wall. He probably wrote on pyramid walls, centuries ago."

"What would he crap?" Elvis said. "It's not like he'd eat, is it?"

"He eats souls," Jack said, "so I assume, he craps soul residue. And what that means to me is, you die by his mouth, you don't go to the other side, or wherever souls go. He digests the souls till they don't exist any more—"

"And you're just so much toilet water decoration," Elvis said.

"That's the way I've got it worked out," Jack said. "He's just like anyone else when he wants to take a dump. He likes a nice clean place with a flush. They didn't have that in his time, and I'm sure he finds it handy. The writing on the walls is just habit. Maybe, to him, Pharaoh and Cleopatra were just yesterday."

Elvis finished off the Ding Dong and sipped his coffee. He felt a rush from the sugar and he loved it. He wanted to ask Jack for the PayDay he had mentioned, but restrained himself. Sweets, fried foods, late nights and drugs had been the beginning of his original downhill spiral. He had to keep himself collected this time. He had to be ready to battle the Egyptian soul-sucking menace.

Soul-sucking menace?

God. He *was* really bored. It was time for him to go back to his room and to bed so he could shit on himself, get back to normal.

But Jesus and Ra, this was different from what had been going on up until now! It might all be bullshit, but considering what was going on in his life right now, it was absorbing bullshit. It might be worth playing the game to the hilt, even if he was playing it with a black guy who thought he was John F. Kennedy and believed an Egyptian mummy was stalking the corridors of Shady Rest Convalescent Home, writing graffiti on toilet stalls, sucking people's souls out through their assholes, digesting them, and crapping them down the visitors' toilet.

Suddenly Elvis was pulled out of his considerations. There came from the hall the noise again. The sound that each time he heard it reminded him of something different. This time it was dried corn husks being rattled in a high wind. He felt goose bumps travel up his spine and the hairs on the back of his neck and arms stood up. He leaned forward and put his hands on his walker and pulled himself upright.

"Don't go in the hall," Jack said.

"I'm not asleep."

"That doesn't mean it won't hurt you."

"*It*, my ass, there isn't any mummy from Egypt."

"Nice knowing you, Elvis."

Elvis inched the walker forward. He was halfway to the open door when he spied the figure in the hallway.

As the thing came even with the doorway, the hall lights went dim and sputtered. Twisting about the apparition, like pet crows, were flutters of shadows. The thing walked and stumbled, shuffled and flowed. Its legs moved like Elvis's own, meaning not too good, and yet, there was something about its locomotion that was impossible to identify. Stiff, but ghostly smooth. It was dressed in nasty-looking jeans, a black shirt, a black cowboy hat that came down so low it covered where the thing's eyebrows should be. It wore large cowboy boots with the toes curled up, and there came from the thing a kind of mixed stench: a compost pile of mud, rotting leaves, resin, spoiled fruit, dry dust, and gassy sewage.

Elvis found that he couldn't scoot ahead another inch. He froze.

The thing stopped and cautiously turned its head on its apple-stem neck and looked at Elvis with empty eye sockets, revealing that it was, in fact, uglier than Lyndon Johnson.

Surprisingly, Elvis found he was surging forward as if on a zooming camera dolly, and that he was plunging into the thing's right eye socket, which swelled speedily to the dimensions of a vast canyon bottomed by blackness.

Down Elvis went, spinning and spinning, and out of the emptiness rushed resin-scented memories of pyramids and boats on a river, hot blue skies, and a great silver bus lashed hard by black rain, a crumbling bridge and a charge of dusky water and a gleam of silver. Then there was a darkness so caliginous it was beyond being called dark, and Elvis could feel and taste mud in his mouth and a sensation of claustrophobia beyond expression. And he could perceive the thing's hunger, a hunger that prodded him like hot pins, and then—

—there came a *popping* sound in rapid succession, and Elvis felt himself whirling even faster, spinning backwards out of that deep memory canyon of the dusty head, and now he stood once again within the framework of his walker, and the mummy—for Elvis no longer denied to himself that it was such—turned its head away and began to move again, to shuffle, to flow, to stumble, to glide, down the hall, its pet shadows screeching with rusty throats around its head. *Pop! Pop! Pop!*

As the thing moved on Elvis compelled himself to lift his walker and advance into the hall. Jack slipped up beside him, and they saw the mummy in cowboy clothes traveling toward the exit door at the back of the home. When it came to the locked door, it leaned against where the door met the jamb and twisted and writhed, squeezed through the invisible crack where the two connected. Its shadows pursued it, as if sucked through by a vacuum cleaner.

The popping sound went on, and Elvis turned his head in that direction, and there, in his mask, his double concho-studded holster belted around his waist, was Kemosabe, a silver Fanner Fifty in either hand. He was popping caps rapidly at where the mummy had departed, the black-spotted red rolls flowing out from behind the hammers of his revolvers in smoky relay.

"Asshole!" Kemosabe said. "Asshole!"

And then Kemosabe quivered, dropped both hands, popped a cap from each gun toward the ground, stiffened, collapsed.

Elvis knew he was dead of a ruptured heart before he hit the black and white tile; gone down and out with both guns blazing, soul intact.

The hall lights trembled back to normal.

The administrators, the nurses and the aides came then. They rolled Kemosabe over and drove their palms against his chest, but he didn't breathe again. No more Hi-Yo-Silver. They sighed over him and clucked their tongues, and finally an aide reached over and lifted Kemosabe's mask, pulled it off his head and dropped it on the floor, nonchalantly, and without respect, revealing his identity.

It was no one anyone really knew.

Once again, Elvis got scolded, and this time he got quizzed about what had happened to Kemosabe, and so did Jack, but neither told the truth.

Who was going to believe a couple of nuts? Elvis and Jack Kennedy explaining that Kemosabe was gunning for a mummy in cowboy duds, a Bubba Ho-Tep with a flock of shadows roiling about his cowboy-hatted head?

So, what they did was lie.

"He came snapping caps and then he fell," Elvis said, and Jack corroborated his story, and when Kemosabe had been carried off, Elvis, with some difficulty, using his walker for support, got down on his knee and picked up the discarded mask and carried it away with him.

He had wanted the guns, but an aide had taken those for her four-year-old son.

Later, he and Jack learned through the grapevine that Kemosabe's roommate, an eighty-year-old man who had been in a semi-comatose condition for several years, had been found dead on the floor of his room. It was assumed Kemosabe had lost it and dragged him off his bed and on to the floor and the eighty-year-old man had kicked the bucket during the fall. As for Kemosabe, they figured he had then gone nuts when he realized what he had done, and had wandered out in the hall firing, and had a heart attack.

Elvis knew different. The mummy had come and Kemosabe had tried to protect his roommate in the only way he knew how. But instead of silver bullets, his gun smoked sulfur. Elvis felt a rush of pride in the old fart.

He and Jack got together later, talked about what they had seen, and then there was nothing left to say.

Night went away and the sun came up, and Elvis, who had slept not a wink, came up with it and put on khaki pants and a khaki shirt and used his walker to go outside. It had been ages since he had been out, and it seemed strange out there, all that sunlight and the smells of flowers and the Texas sky so high and the clouds so white.

It was hard to believe he had spent so much time in his bed. Just the use of his legs with the walker these last few days had tightened the muscles, and he found he could get around better.

The pretty nurse with the grapefruit tits came outside and said: "Mr Presley, you look so much stronger. But you shouldn't stay out too long. It's almost time for a nap and for us, to, you know . . ."

"Fuck off, you patronizing bitch," said Elvis. "I'm tired of your shit. I'll lube my own transmission. You treat me like a baby again, I'll wrap this goddamn walker around your head."

The pretty nurse stood stunned, then went away quietly.

Elvis inched his way with the walker around the great circular drive that surrounded the home. It was a half-hour later when he reached the back of the home and the door through which the mummy had departed. It was still locked, and he stood and looked at it amazed. How in hell had the mummy done that, slipping through an indiscernible chink between door and frame?

Elvis looked down at the concrete that lay at the back of the door. No clues there. He used the walker to travel toward the growth of trees out back, a growth of pin-oaks and sweet gums and hickory nut trees that shouldered on either side of the large creek that flowed behind the home.

The ground tipped sharply there, and for a moment he hesitated, then reconsidered. *Well, what the fuck?* he thought.

He planted the walker and started going forward, the ground sloping ever more dramatically. By the time he reached the bank of the creek and came to a gap in the trees, he was exhausted. He had the urge to start yelling for help, but didn't want to belittle himself, not after his performance with the nurse. He knew that he had regained some of his former confidence. His cursing and abuse had not seemed cute to her that time. The words had bitten her, if only slightly. Truth was, he was going to miss her greasing his pecker.

He looked over the bank of the creek. It was quite a drop there. The creek itself was narrow, and on either side of it was a gravel-littered six feet of shore. To his left, where the creek ran beneath a bridge, he could see where a mass of weeds and mud had gathered over time, and he could see something shiny in their midst.

Elvis eased to the ground inside his walker and sat there and looked at the water churning along. A huge woodpecker laughed in a tree nearby and a jay yelled at a smaller bird to leave his territory.

Where had ole Bubba Ho-Tep gone? Where did he come from? How in hell did he get here?

He recalled what he had seen inside the mummy's mind. The silver bus, the rain, the shattered bridge, the wash of water and mud.

Well, now, wait a minute, he thought. Here we have water and mud and a bridge, though it's not broken, and there's something shiny in the midst of all those leaves and limbs and collected debris. All these items were elements of what he had seen in Bubba Ho-Tep's head.

Obviously there was a connection.

But what was it?

When he got his strength back, Elvis pulled himself up and got the walker turned, and worked his way back to the home. He was covered in sweat and stiff as wire by the time he reached his room and tugged himself into bed. The blister on his dick throbbed and he unfastened his pants and eased down his underwear. The blister had refilled with pus, and it looked nastier than usual.

It's a cancer, he determined. He made the conclusion in a certain final rush. They're keeping it from me because I'm old and to them it doesn't matter. They think age will kill me first, and they are probably right.

Well, fuck them. I know what it is, and if it isn't, it might as well be.

He got the salve and doctored the pus-filled lesion, and put the salve away, and pulled up his underwear and pants, and fastened his belt.

Elvis got his TV remote off the dresser and clicked it on while he waited for lunch. As he ran the channels, he hit upon an advertisement for Elvis Presley Week. It startled him. It wasn't the first time it had happened, but at the moment it struck him hard. It showed clips from his movies, *Clambake*, *Roustabout*, several others. All shit movies.

Here he was complaining about loss of pride and how life had treated him, and now he realized he'd never had any pride and much of how life had treated him had been quite good, and the bulk of the bad had been his own fault. He wished now he'd fired his manager, Colonel Parker, about the time he got into films. The old fart had been a fool, and he had been a bigger fool for following him. He wished too he had treated Priscilla right. He wished he could tell his daughter he loved her.

Always the questions. Never the answers. Always the hopes. Never the fulfillments.

Elvis clicked off the set and dropped the remote on the dresser just as Jack came into the room. He had a folder under his arm. He looked like he was ready for a briefing at the White House.

"I had the woman who calls herself my niece come get me," he said. "She took me downtown to the newspaper morgue. She's been helping me do some research."

"On what?" Elvis said.

"On our mummy."

"You know something about him?" Elvis asked.

"I know plenty."

Jack pulled a chair up next to the bed, and Elvis used the bed's lift button to raise his back and head so he could see what was in Jack's folder.

Jack opened the folder, took out some clippings, and laid them on the bed. Elvis looked at them as Jack talked.

"One of the lesser mummies, on loan from the Egyptian government, was being circulated across the United States. You know, museums, that kind of stuff. It wasn't a major exhibit, like the King Tut exhibit some years back, but it was of interest. The mummy was flown or carried by train from state to state. When it got to Texas, it was stolen.

"Evidence points to the fact that it was stolen at night by a couple of guys in a silver bus. There was a witness. Some guy walking his dog or something. Anyway, the thieves broke into the museum and stole it, hoping to get a ransom probably. But in came the worst storm in East

Texas history. Tornadoes. Rain. Hail. You name it. Creeks and rivers overflowed. Mobile homes were washed away. Livestock drowned. Maybe you remember it . . . No matter. It was one hell of a flood.

"These guys got away, and nothing was ever heard from them. After you told me what you saw inside the mummy's head—the silver bus, the storm, the bridge, all that—I came up with a more interesting, and, I believe, considerably more accurate scenario."

"Let me guess. The bus got washed away. I think I saw it today. Right out back in the creek. It must have washed up there years ago."

"That confirms it. The bridge you saw breaking, that's how the bus got in the water, which would have been as deep then as a raging river. The bus was carried downstream. It lodged somewhere nearby, and the mummy was imprisoned by debris, and recently it worked its way loose."

"But how did it come alive?" Elvis asked. "And how did I end up inside its memories?"

"The speculation is broader here, but from what I've read, sometimes mummies were buried without their names, a curse put on their sarcophagus, or coffin, if you will. My guess is our guy was one of those. While he was in the coffin, he was a drying corpse. But when the bus was washed off the road, the coffin was overturned, or broken open, and our boy was freed of coffin and curse. Or more likely, it rotted open in time, and the holding spell was broken. And think about him down there all that time, waiting for freedom, alive, but not alive. Hungry, and no way to feed. I said he was free of his curse, but that's not entirely true. He's free of his imprisonment, but he still needs souls.

"And now, he's free to have them, and he'll keep feeding unless he's finally destroyed . . . You know, I think there's a part of him, oddly enough, that wants to fit in. To be human again. He doesn't entirely know what he's become. He responds to some old desires and the new desires of his condition. That's why he's taken on the illusion of clothes, probably copying the dress of one of his victims.

"The souls give him strength. Increase his spectral powers. One of which was to hypnotize you, kinda, draw you inside his head. He couldn't steal your soul that way, you have to be unconscious to have that done to you, but he could weaken you, distract you."

"And those shadows around him?"

"His guardians. They warn him. They have some limited powers of their own. I've read about them in *The Everyday Man or Woman's Book of the Soul.*"

"What do we do?" Elvis said.

"I think changing rest homes would be a good idea," Jack said. "I can't think of much else. I will say this. Our mummy is a nighttime kind of guy, 3:00 a.m. actually. So, I'm going to sleep now, and again after lunch. Set my alarm for before dark so I can fix myself a couple cups of coffee. He comes tonight, I don't want him slapping his lips over my asshole again. I think he heard you coming down the hall about the time he got started on me the other night, and he ran. Not because he was scared, but because he didn't want anyone to find out he's around. Consider it. He has the proverbial bird's nest on the ground here."

After Jack left, Elvis decided he should follow Jack's lead and nap. Of course, at his age, he napped a lot anyway, and could fall asleep at any time, or toss restlessly for hours. There was no rhyme or reason to it.

He nestled his head into his pillow and tried to sleep, but sleep wouldn't come. Instead, he thought about things. Like, what did he really have left in life but this place? It wasn't much of a home, but it was all he had, and he'd be damned if he'd let a foreign, graffiti-writing, soul-sucking sonofabitch in an oversized hat and cowboy boots (with elf toes) take away his family members' souls and shit them down the visitors' toilet.

In the movies he had always played heroic types. But when the stage lights went out, it was time for drugs and stupidity and the coveting of women. Now it was time to be a little of what he had always fantasized being.

A hero.

Elvis leaned over and got hold of his telephone and dialed Jack's room. "Mr Kennedy," Elvis said when Jack answered. "Ask not what your rest home can do for you. Ask what you can do for your rest home."

"Hey, you're copping my best lines," Jack said.

"Well, then, to paraphrase one of my own, 'Let's take care of business.'"

"What are you getting at?"

"You know what I'm getting at. We're gonna kill a mummy."

The sun, like a boil on the bright blue ass of day, rolled gradually forward and spread its legs wide to reveal the pubic thatch of night, a hairy darkness in which stars crawled like lice, and the moon crabbed slowly upward like an albino dog tick thriving for the anal gulch.

During this slow-rolling transition, Elvis and Jack discussed their plans, then they slept a little, ate their lunch of boiled cabbage and meatloaf, slept some more, ate a supper of white bread and asparagus and a helping of shit on a shingle without the shingle, slept again, awoke about the time the pubic thatch appeared and those starry lice began to crawl.

And even then, with night about them, they had to wait until midnight to do what they had to do.

Jack squinted through his glasses and examined his list. "Two bottles of rubbing alcohol?" Jack said.

"Check," said Elvis. "And we won't have to toss it. Look here." Elvis held up a paint sprayer. "I found this in the storage room."

"I thought they kept it locked," Jack said.

"They do. But I stole a hairpin from Dillinger and picked the lock."

"Great!" Jack said. "Matches?"

"Check. I also scrounged a cigarette lighter."

"Good. Uniforms?"

Elvis held up his white suit, slightly grayed in spots with a chili stain on the front. A white silk scarf and the big gold and silver and ruby-studded belt that went with the outfit lay on the bed. There were zippered boots from K-Mart. "Check."

Jack held up a gray business suit on a hanger. "I've got some nice shoes and a tie to go with it in my room."

"Check," Elvis said.

"Scissors?"

"Check."

"I've got my motorized wheelchair oiled and ready to roll," Jack said, "and I've looked up a few words of power in one of my magic books. I don't know if they'll stop a mummy, but they're supposed to ward off evil. I wrote them down on a piece of paper."

"We use what we got," Elvis said. "Well, then. Two forty-five out back of the place."

"Considering our rate of travel, better start moving about two-thirty," Jack said.

"Jack," Elvis asked. "Do we know what we're doing?"

"No, but they say fire cleanses evil. Let's hope they, whoever they are, is right."

"Check on that too," said Elvis. "Synchronize watches."

They did, and Elvis added: "Remember. The key words for tonight are *Caution* and *Flammable*. And *Watch Your Ass*."

The front door had an alarm system, but it was easily manipulated from the inside. Once Elvis had the wires cut with the scissors, they pushed the compression lever on the door, and Jack shoved his wheelchair outside, and held the door while Elvis worked his walker through. Elvis tossed the scissors into the shrubbery, and Jack jammed a paperback book between the doors to allow them re-entry, should re-entry be an option at a later date.

Elvis was wearing a large pair of glasses with multicolored gem-studded chocolate flames and his stained white jumpsuit with scarf and belt and zippered boots. The suit was open at the front and hung loose on him, except at the belly. To make it even tighter there, Elvis had made up a medicine bag of sorts, and stuffed it inside his jumpsuit. The bag contained Kemosabe's mask, Bull's purple heart, and the newspaper clipping where he had first read of his alleged death.

Jack had on his gray business suit with a black-and-red-striped tie knotted carefully at the throat, sensible black shoes, and black nylon socks. The suit fit him well. He looked like a former president.

In the seat of the wheelchair was the paint sprayer, filled with rubbing alcohol, and beside it, a cigarette lighter and a paper folder of matches. Jack handed Elvis the paint sprayer. A strap made of a strip of torn sheet had been added to the device. Elvis hung the sprayer over his shoulder, reached inside his belt and got out a flattened, half-smoked stogie he had been saving for a special occasion. An occasion he had begun to think would never arrive. He clenched the cigar between his teeth, picked the matches from the seat of the wheelchair, and lit his cigar. It tasted like a dog turd, but he puffed it anyway. He tossed the folder of matches back on the chair and looked at Jack, said, "Let's do it, amigo."

Jack put the matches and the lighter in his suit pocket. He sat down in the wheelchair, kicked the foot stanchions into place and rested his feet on them. He leaned back slightly and flicked a switch on the armrest. The electric motor hummed, the chair eased forward.

"Meet you there," said Jack. He rolled down the concrete ramp, on out to the circular drive, and disappeared around the edge of the building.

Elvis looked at his watch. It was nearly two forty-five. He had to hump it. He clenched both hands on the walker and started truckin'.

Fifteen exhausting minutes later, out back, Elvis settled in against the door, the place where Bubba Ho-Tep had been entering and exiting. The shadows fell over him like an umbrella. He propped the paint gun across the walker and used his scarf to wipe the sweat off his forehead.

In the old days, after a performance, he'd wipe his face with it and toss it to some woman in the crowd, watch as she creamed on herself. Panties and hotel keys would fly on to the stage at that point, bouquets of roses.

Tonight, he hoped Bubba Ho-Tep didn't use the scarf to wipe his ass after shitting him down the crapper.

Elvis looked where the circular concrete drive rose up slightly to the right, and there, seated in the wheelchair, very patient and still, was Jack. The moonlight spread over Jack and made him look like a concrete yard gnome.

Apprehension spread over Elvis like a dose of the measles. He thought: *Bubba Ho-Tep comes out of that creek bed, he's going to come out hungry and pissed, and when I try to stop him, he's going to jam this paint gun up my ass, then jam me and that wheelchair up Jack's ass.*

He puffed his cigar so fast it made him dizzy. He looked out at the creek bank, and where the trees gaped wide, a figure rose up like a cloud of termites, scrabbled like a crab, flowed like water, chunked and chinked like a mass of oilfield tools tumbling downhill.

Its eyeless sockets trapped the moonlight and held it momentarily before permitting it to pass through and out the back of its head in irregular gold beams. The figure that simultaneously gave the impression of shambling and gliding appeared one moment as nothing more than a shadow surrounded by more active shadows, then it was a heap of twisted brown sticks and dried mud molded into the shape of a human being, and in another moment, it was a cowboy-hatted, booted thing taking each step as if it were its last.

Halfway to the rest home it spotted Elvis, standing in the dark framework of the door. Elvis felt his bowels go loose, but he determined not to shit his only good stage suit. His knees clacked together like stalks of ribbon cane rattling in a high wind. The dog-turd cigar fell from his lips.

He picked up the paint gun and made sure it was ready to spray. He pushed the butt of it into his hip and waited.

Bubba Ho-Tep didn't move. He had ceased to come forward. Elvis began to sweat more than before. His face and chest and balls were soaked. If Bubba Ho-Tep didn't come forward, their plan was fucked.

They had to get him in range of the paint sprayer. The idea was he'd soak him with the alcohol, and Jack would come wheeling down from behind, flipping matches or the lighter at Bubba, catching him on fire.

Elvis said softly, "Come and get it, you dead piece of shit."

Jack had nodded off for a moment, but now he came awake. His flesh was tingling. It felt as if tiny ball bearings were being rolled beneath his skin. He looked up and saw Bubba Ho-Tep paused between the creek bank, himself, and Elvis at the door.

Jack took a deep breath. This was not the way they had planned it.

The mummy was supposed to go for Elvis because he was blocking the door. But, no soap.

Jack got the matches and the cigarette lighter out of his coat pocket and put them between his legs on the seat of the chair. He put his hand on the gearbox of the wheelchair, gunned it forward. He had to make things happen; had to get Bubba Ho-Tep to follow him, come within range of Elvis's spray gun.

Bubba Ho-Tep stuck out his arm and clotheslined Jack Kennedy. There was a sound like a rifle crack (no question, Warren Commission, this blow was from the front), and over went the chair, and out went Jack, flipping and sliding across the driveway, the cement tearing his suit knees open, gnawing into his hide. The chair, minus its rider, tumbled over and came upright, and still rolling, veered downhill toward Elvis in the doorway, leaning on his walker, spray gun in hand.

The wheelchair hit Elvis's walker. Elvis bounced against the door, popped forward, grabbed the walker just in time, but dropped his spray gun.

He glanced up to see Bubba Ho-Tep leaning over the unconscious Jack. Bubba Ho-Tep's mouth went wide, and wider yet, and became a black toothless vacuum that throbbed pink as a raw wound in the moonlight; then Bubba Ho-Tep turned his head and the pink was not visible. Bubba Ho-Tep's mouth went down over Jack's face, and, as Bubba Ho-Tep sucked, the shadows about it thrashed and gobbled like turkeys.

Elvis used the walker to allow him to bend down and get hold of the paint gun. When he came up with it, he tossed the walker aside, eased himself around, and into the wheelchair. He found the matches and the lighter there. Jack had done what he had done to distract Bubba Ho-Tep, to try and bring him down closer to the door. But he had failed. Yet by accident, he had provided Elvis with the instruments of mummy destruction, and now it was up to him to do what he and Jack had hoped to do together. Elvis put the matches inside his open-chested outfit, pushed the lighter tight under his ass.

Elvis let his hand play over the wheelchair switches, as nimbly as he had once played with studio keyboards. He roared the wheelchair up the incline toward Bubba Ho-Tep, terrified but determined, and, as he rolled, in a voice cracking, but certainly reminiscent of him at his best, he began to sing "Don't Be Cruel," and within instants, he was on Bubba Ho-Tep and his busy shadows.

Bubba Ho-Tep looked up as Elvis roared into range, singing. Bubba Ho-Tep's open mouth irised to normal size, and teeth, formerly non-existent, rose up in his gums like little black stumps. Electric locusts crackled and hopped in his empty sockets. He yelled something in Egyptian. Elvis saw the words jump out of Bubba Ho-Tep's mouth in visible hieroglyphics like dark beetles and sticks.

$$\text{🜚}\ \text{🜚}\ \text{🜚}\ \text{🜚}\ \text{🜚}\ \text{🜚}\ \text{🜚}\ {}^*$$

Elvis bore down on Bubba Ho-Tep. When he was in range, he ceased singing, and gave the paint sprayer trigger a squeeze. Rubbing alcohol squirted from the sprayer and struck Bubba Ho-Tep in the face.

Elvis swerved, screeched around Bubba Ho-Tep in a sweeping circle, came back, the lighter in his hand. As he neared Bubba, the shadows swarming around the mummy's head separated and flew high up above him like startled bats.

* *"By the unwinking eye of Ra!"*

The black hat Bubba wore wobbled and sprouted wings and flapped away from his head, becoming what it had always been, a living shadow. The shadows came down in a rush, screeching like harpies.

They swarmed over Elvis's face, giving him the sensation of skinned animal pelts—blood-side in—being dragged over his flesh.

Bubba bent forward at the waist like a collapsed puppet, bopped his head against the cement drive. His black bat hat came down out of the dark in a swoop, expanding rapidly and falling over Bubba's body, splattering it like spilled ink. Bubba blob-flowed rapidly under the wheels of Elvis's mount and rose up in a dark swell beneath the chair and through the spokes of the wheels and billowed over the front of the chair and loomed upwards, jabbing his ravaged, ever-changing face through the flittering shadows, poking it right at Elvis.

Elvis, through gaps in the shadows, saw a face like an old jack-o'lantern gone black and to rot, with jagged eyes, nose and mouth. And that mouth spread tunnel wide, and down that tunnel-mouth Elvis could see the dark and awful forever that was Bubba's lot, and Elvis clicked the lighter to flame, and the flame jumped, and the alcohol lit Bubba's face, and Bubba's head turned baby-eye blue, flowed jet-quick away, splashed upward like a black wave carrying a blazing oil slick. Then Bubba came down in a shuffle of blazing sticks and dark mud, a tar baby on fire, fleeing across the concrete drive toward the creek. The guardian shadows flapped after it, fearful of being abandoned.

Elvis wheeled over to Jack, leaned forward and whispered: "Mr Kennedy."

Jack's eyelids fluttered. He could barely move his head, and something grated in his neck when he did. "The President is soon dead," he said, and his clenched fist throbbed and opened, and out fell a wad of paper. "You got to get him."

Jack's body went loose and his head rolled back on his damaged neck and the moon showed double in his eyes. Elvis swallowed and saluted Jack. "Mr President," he said.

Well, at least he had kept Bubba Ho-Tep from taking Jack's soul.

Elvis leaned forward, picked up the paper Jack had dropped. He read it aloud to himself in the moonlight: "You nasty thing from beyond the dead. No matter what you think and do, good things will never come to you. If evil is your black design, you can bet the goodness of the Light Ones will kick your bad behind."

That's it? thought Elvis. *That's the chant against evil from the Book of Souls? Yeah, right, boss. And what kind of decoder ring does that come with? Shit, it doesn't even rhyme well.*

Elvis looked up. Bubba Ho-Tep had fallen down in a blue blaze, but he was rising up again, preparing to go over the lip of the creek, down to wherever his sanctuary was.

Elvis pulled around Jack and gave the wheelchair full throttle. He gave out with a rebel cry. His white scarf fluttered in the wind as he thundered forward.

Bubba Ho-Tep's flames had gone out. He was on his feet. His head was hissing gray smoke into the crisp night air. He turned completely to face Elvis, stood defiant, raised an arm and shook a fist. He yelled, and once again Elvis saw the hieroglyphics leap out of his mouth. The characters danced in a row, briefly—and vanished.

Elvis let go of the protective paper. It was dog shit. What was needed here was action.

When Bubba Ho-Tep saw Elvis was coming, chair geared to high, holding the paint sprayer in one hand, he turned to bolt, but Elvis was on him.

* *"Eat the dog dick of Anubis, you ass-wipe!"*

Elvis stuck out a foot and hit Bubba Ho-Tep in the back, and his foot went right through Bubba. The mummy squirmed, spitted on Elvis's leg. Elvis fired the paint sprayer, as Bubba Ho-Tep, himself, and chair went over the creek bank in a flash of moonlight and a tumble of shadows.

Elvis screamed as the hard ground and sharp stones snapped his body like a piñata. He made the trip with Bubba Ho-Tep still on his leg, and, when he quit sliding, he ended up close to the creek.

Bubba Ho-Tep, as if made of rubber, twisted around on Elvis's leg, and looked at him.

Elvis still had the paint sprayer. He had clung to it as if it were a life preserver. He gave Bubba another dose. Bubba's right arm flopped way out and ran along the ground and found a hunk of wood that had washed up on the edge of the creek, gripped it, and swung the long arm back. The arm came around and hit Elvis on the side of the head with the wood.

Elvis fell backwards. The paint sprayer flew from his hands. Bubba Ho-Tep was leaning over him. He hit Elvis again with the wood. Elvis felt himself going out. He knew if he did, not only was he a dead sonofabitch, but so was his soul. He would be just so much crap; no afterlife for him; no reincarnation; no angels with harps. Whatever lay beyond would not be known to him. It would all end right here for Elvis Presley. Nothing left but a quick flush.

Bubba Ho-Tep's mouth loomed over Elvis's face. It looked like an open manhole. Sewage fumes came out of it.

Elvis reached inside his open jumpsuit and got hold of the folder of matches. Laying back, pretending to nod out so as to bring Bubba Ho-Tep's ripe mouth closer, he thumbed back the flap on the matches, thumbed down one of the paper sticks, and pushed the sulfurous head of the match across the black strip.

Just as Elvis felt the cloying mouth of Bubba Ho-Tep falling down on his kisser like a Venus flytrap, the entire folder of matches ignited in Elvis's hand, burned him and made him yell.

The alcohol on Bubba's body called the flames to it, and Bubba burst into a stalk of blue flame, singeing the hair off Elvis's head, scorching his eyebrows down to nubs, blinding him until he could see nothing more than a scalding white light.

Elvis realized that Bubba Ho-Tep was no longer on or over him, and the white light became a stained white light, then a gray light, and eventually, the world, like a Polaroid negative developing, came into view, greenish at first, then full of the night's colors.

Elvis rolled on his side and saw the moon floating in the water. He saw too a scarecrow floating in the water, the straw separating from it, the current carrying it away.

No, not a scarecrow. Bubba Ho-Tep. For all his dark magic and ability to shift, or to appear to shift, fire had done him in, or had it been the stupid words from Jack's book on souls? Or both?

It didn't matter. Elvis got up on one elbow and looked at the corpse.

The water was dissolving it more rapidly and the current was carrying it away.

Elvis fell over on his back. He felt something inside him grate against something soft. He felt like a water balloon with a hole poked in it.

He was going down for the last count, and he knew it.

But I've still got my soul, he thought. Still mine. All mine. And the folks in Shady Rest, Dillinger, The Blue Yodeler, all of them, they have theirs, and they'll keep 'em.

Elvis stared up at the stars between the forked and twisted boughs of an oak. He could see a lot of those beautiful stars, and he realized now that the constellations looked a little like the outlines of great hieroglyphics. He turned away from where he was looking, and to his right, seeming to sit on the edge of the bank, were more stars, more hieroglyphics.

He rolled his head back to the figures above him, rolled to the right and looked at those. Put them together in his mind.

He smiled. Suddenly, he thought he could read hieroglyphics after all, and what they spelled out against the dark beautiful night was simple, and yet profound.

ALL IS WELL.

Elvis closed his eyes and did not open them again.

THE END

Thanks to

(Mark Nelson) for translating East Texas "Egyptian Hieroglyphics."

Carole Nelson Douglas's Midnight Louie is—in more recent times—a black feline private investigator featured in over two dozen novels and several short stories. But Heart of Night, the narrator of this clever comic tale, is evidently an ancient incarnation of the tomcat sleuth: he shares both Louie's distinct attitude and his aptitude for solving mysteries.

Fruit of the Tomb:
A Midnight Louie Past Life Adventure
Carole Nelson Douglas

———

"Out of my way, Worthless One!"

After these welcoming words, I feel Irinefer the scribe's sandal scuff a cloud of desert dust into my delicate nostrils.

I sneeze, elude the kick that follows the scuff and duck into the nearest doorway.

I may be Worthless, though I would think one of the Sacred Breed would get a tad more respect in this Necropolis.

But when a Pharaoh dies, two things are certain: the eternal embellishment of his royal tomb will finally end, and the endless plotting by grave robbers to sack his tomb will begin.

Here on the shores of the River Nile, "eternal" and "endless" are pretty flexible concepts. I am lucky that we of the Sacred Breed are accounted to possess nine lives. Frankly, with such a heritage, there is little need for us to partake in stripping down to our remaining *Kas* to cross the River of Death with our human master.

Even a Pharaoh is only accorded one *Ka*, or material soul. You would think these one-*Ka* wonders would not be so hasty to rip we of the Sacred-Breed-of-Nine-*Kas* from our earthly hides before our appointed times. Those unfortunate enough to have attended Nomenophis I, who decreed that his household servitors should be present in his tomb in more than pictorial fashion, had no choice.

So came the ceremonial gutting and the claustrophobic swathing in a length of linen as long, narrow, and winding as the River Nile. Even the household cat ends up with its empty hide preserved in its original shape and its innards stored in a jar more suitable for a potent attar of lotus. So much for being a Sacred Breed.

Yet some, especially the humans under discussion, consider Egypt the height of civilized society in these times and climes.

Perhaps I am a bit jaded. I have recently lost my own mother to the prevailing customs.

Our freshly designed family cartouche bears the Eye of Horus, a symbol of theft and restitution. In one of those gory tales religions the world over seem to favor, the Egyptian god Horus's eye was stolen by his jealous brother Seth, but was restored by order of a court of gods. Perhaps this is where the "eye for an eye" adage I have heard in my travels came from. Or perhaps this is where the expression, also heard in my travels, "gypped" came from.

Since my mother and I were apparent imports to this land, being as black as a ceremonial wig rather than the usual burnt-cinnabar shade of both the people and felines who inhabit the Nile valley, we occupied an unusual place here.

The Egyptians called us by unpronounceable syllables we ignored whenever possible, but my moniker translates to "Heart of Night."

I suppose the title is a comment on our family's ebony good looks. My mother was known as Eye of Night, since it was her job to keep a vigilant watch on the persons and events surrounding Pharaoh, and to warn him of any untoward acts, such as attempted assassination.

It was obviously in her personal interest to keep our Pharaoh alive as long as possible.

Unfortunately, he died of indigestion, an internal affair my mother could have done nothing to prevent.

So passed his servants, including my esteemed maternal parent, in a paroxysm of the embalming arts that left the linen supply of Thebes in a severe shortage.

Not being a member of the Pharaoh's household, I escaped the general weeping and winding to live to mourn my mother's passing.

Unfortunately, I have lost not only a mother but also my sole connection to the palace, where once I had visiting privileges as the offspring of a member of Pharaoh's bodyguard.

This has meant I must make my way in the City of Cats near the Necropolis. I do not refer to fabled Bubastis where Bast Herself, Eye of Ra and mother of all cats, reigns. No, I am journeying to a feline colony that forages in the shadow of the Pyramids, catching vermin unhoused by the constant construction and begging food from the artisans and slaves always laboring on the massive tombs that give the term "work in progress" an entirely new dimension.

Since I am suspected of being a foreigner and am now also an orphan bereft of parental protection, life after mother's death has not been easy.

The resident feline in Irinefer's rooms beyond my doorway shelter swats me on the posterior.

"Out of my house, familyless foreigner. Positionless beggar!"

Like ill-tempered master, like servant, I think.

I ebb before a paw gloved in sphinx-colored fur, a lean Abyssian with a revolting kinship to the metalwork feline statues scattered about the royal city. Even the commonest felines here, being considered Sacred, think that they are to the linen and bronze born.

I slink away, contemplating another tasty repast of locusts and cactus-cider.

If only I could demonstrate that I possess some of my mother's superb hunting instincts, I could win a place in the palace and sleep on an ebony-and-ivory inlaid chair with a zebra-hide pillow.

I would look very well against zebra-hide.

A hiss erupts from behind the mud-daub wall of another house.

I arch my back, preparing for defense. But this sound is a *pssst!* for attention rather than the usual *hssst!* of hostility.

An aged Abyssinian who wears a palace collar is escorted by a pair of husky Necropolis cats, commoners, but uncommonly large.

"Heart of Night, I wish a word," says the old one.

"You are Ampheris, Counter of the Royal Vermin."

As an "outside" cat, Ampheris was not considered part of the royal household and thus escaped the recent bagging, binding, and burying.

"True. A pity that your revered mother has passed to the Underworld. She was a peerless hunter. Have you any talent along that line?"

I edge into the shade they occupy as if they owned it.

Ampheris nods at his bodyguard. They push a shallow bowl of sour goat's milk toward me. I lap delicately inside the scummy outer ring and consider. This is a serious matter if I am being offered drink. My whiskers twitch more at the scent of opportunity than at that of rancid milk.

We all crouch on our haunches.

"What is up?" I ask.

One bodyguard growls, as if I had made a jest.

The old man answers. I doubt his henchmen can talk. "It is what is up . . . and walking . . . that is the question, Son of She Who Sat Beside Pharaoh's Sandal."

The royal groundskeeper is so old that his whiskers never stop trembling.

"Something walks here," I ask, "in the Valley of the Kings? Or in the palace within the city?"

"Here," Ampheris hisses, his whiskers quivering anew. "Have you not heard?"

"I am not exactly *persona grata* in this Necropolis."

"I see why you are held apart. Perhaps it is the foreign words you employ, such as this '*persona grata.*' What language is that? Manx? Mesopotamian?"

"No, nothing edible. Something I picked up on my travels among the uncivilized tribes in the lands across from where the Nile empties into the sea."

"There is nothing solid beyond where the river Nile empties into the sea. But there is something . . . semi-solid . . . here on the Necropolis under the shadow of the pyramids."

I keep mum; that is the best way to learn things in the Eye of Horus game. My mama told me that much.

"I have seen it," one bodyguard growls, sounding ashamed. "In all my seven lives I have never seen anything so terrifying. A mummy that walks."

I nod to gain time. How can a mummy walk? The first thing the embalmers do is wrap every limb up tighter than the Pharaoh's treasure. A dead mummy cannot even crawl. And they are all decidedly dead.

I tell these Sacred ninnies so.

The old guy nods. "Yet this apparition has been seen by others of our kind here. It walks . . . upright. It . . . gleams linen-white in the moonlight."

"Has anyone attempted to question this restless mummy?"

One bodyguard catches my ruff tight in nail-studded paws. "Listen, stranger, you would not be so glib if you encountered this abomination. You would draw back and slink away and count yourself lucky to do so."

I shrug off his big mitts. "Maybe I would. And maybe I would not. Especially if there were something in it for me."

Their six amber eyes exchange glances before returning to confront my green ones.

"Should you banish this restless spirit," Ampheris says slowly, "the Sacred Breed of the Necropolis would deign to accept your unworthy presence. We would allow you to live and hunt among us."

"As if I would want to! No, I seek a more fitting reward. My mother's old position at the palace."

"Impossible! That is awarded at the discretion of Pharaoh."

"Perhaps you could trot indoors and put in a good word for me with Nomenophis Two."

"For what?" snorts one of the bodyguards.

Ampheris nods and trembles. "Put this unnatural mummy to rest and we will see."

"It might be Nomenophis One, has anyone considered that? He is the most recently dead human of note."

Ampheris wrinkles his already creased forehead fur into a semblance of sand dunes. "But the mummy that has been glimpsed is not human."

"Of course it is not human if it is mummified, yet walking. It may be a demon, or a god. One never knows."

"Idiot foreigner!" scoffs a bodyguard. "This mummy is of our own breed."

"You mean that a mummified *cat* stalks the Necropolis?"

"Exactly," Ampheris says. "I fear that Pharaoh would not be sufficiently grateful for your laying such a thing to rest, as it is not his royal sire. The most reward you can hope for is a better toleration of your presence among the Sacred Breed."

I shrug. Any improvement in my status is a step up, and I come from a long line of high-steppers.

By the time the sun-god's boat is sinking slowly in the west, I have accosted and interrogated most of the individuals whose names were given to me.

It has not been easy. I have had sand kicked in my face and tail, and have been spit at and hit. I have even had to resort to pinning my witnesses against a wall until they burp up their stories like so many hairballs.

My last victim . . . I mean, witness, is Kemfer the jeweler's companion. He is a wiry but cowering sort who wishes only to be off the streets before night falls and "it walks" again.

"How tall?" I ask.

"T-two tail-lengths. Let me go, please. My master is calling me home for supper."

I do indeed hear a human repeating "*mau, mau,*" the Egyptian word for cat. "You say it walks upright on two legs, like a human? Then why do you think it is a cat?"

"The upright ears, you imbecile! Oh, sorry, I did not mean to call Your Honorableness names. Please let me go. It darkens."

"But you saw it by night?"

"Yes, and I will go forth by night no more."

"Are you sure you did not see the ears of Anubis?"

Now the creature trembles like old Ampheris. "The jackal-headed embalming god? Say not so, for then we are all doomed!"

"Well, I could use the company," I reply sourly. At least this sorry specimen of the Sacred Breed has a home to go to by night.

The creature whines when I relax my grip and kicks up a dust-devil of sand as he streaks away.

I shake my head, only partly to dislodge the stray grains from my ears. My dear departed mama, foreign-born or not, was worth twenty of these craven Necropolis cats. I see my only option is to hunt this apparition myself. And since pale funereal wrappings are its hallmark, I shall have to do so by night. At least it will not see me first.

I head down the mean streets that twist and turn past houses warmed by window-squares of lamplight toward the deserted valley where only the dead keep each other company.

I do not believe in risen spirits, mummified or not, but I have heard ample testimony that something unnatural prowls the Valley of the Kings. I call upon the protection of Bastet as I move alone toward the artificial mountain range of tombs glowing softly gold in the last rays of the departing sun-god.

The hot sands are already cooling beneath my pads and night's sudden cloak blends into my despised dark fur. I am unseen but not sightless, silent but not mute, uncertain but not fearful.

Once human habitation has been left behind, only sand and stone stretch around me. I pause to listen to the skitter of the night, the scratch of verminous claws, the sinister hiss of scales slithering over sand, the distant call of a jackal.

I hear a sudden scramble behind a broken pyramid stone left to mark its own grave in the desert. This may be some nocturnal drama of stalk and kill, dueling beetles, anything normal to the night, but I hasten over, leap atop the cut stone and peer beyond.

My keen night vision sees sands swirling up, a mouse in their midst, eyes gleaming red, and a stiff, plunging, ghostly white figure lurching after it.

The hair lifts along my spine and tail.

For this creature indeed walks upright on two legs, yet its head has a distinctly cat-like profile. Were it more than two tail-lengths tall, I would take it for the mummified form of Bastet herself, She of the human female body and the feline head.

But all statues I have seen of Bast cast her in a gigantic mold, three human-heights high. Even if the sculptors exaggerate in the way of men personifying gods, Bast must be at least of human height.

Whatever this monster's composition or identity, I must challenge it, or fail.

As I dive into the fray below, my arrival frees the desert mouse to retreat into a crack in the stone block. I am left facing a furious monster, a growling, spinning, spitting dervish of aggravated linen. Funereal wrappings whip around the figure like human hair. I snag one with a claw and begin pulling. Perhaps the apparition is disembodied beneath the wrappings. Perhaps I will free a trapped spirit . . .

A dust-spout of linen knocks me on to my back. Then a weight crushes me to the desert floor until my spine is cradled by sand. My claws keep churning, snagging in linen and pulling, cutting, until loosened wrappings fall over my face, smothering me.

I fight the toils of the funereal art, digging my own grave deep into the sand, providing my own shredded cerements. My strength ebbs, and the monster atop me has grown no less heavy with the loss of its linens.

Yet it tires too. I finally open my grit-caked eyes to discover we have both ground ourselves into a sand-trap, our contending bodies frozen from further motion by the sand our fight has kicked up. I feel matted fur sprouting like grass between the rows of savaged linen. Only the creature's face remains shrouded, emitting faint, eerie, and still-angry moans.

Heaving upward, I dislodge drifts of sand over my foe. After moments of furious kicking, I am upright and my exhausted opponent is encased in sand from neck to foot. Talk about a mummy case.

Now is high time to solve the mystery of the resurrected mummy. I start pawing delicately at the facial wrappings, loose but still intact.

I am beginning to suspect exactly *what* the mummy is.

A few dreadfully crumpled whiskers spring out from the unwinding linen. Then a spray of sand from a choked mouth. Finally I unveil an eye, which reflects gold in the moonlight, and I now know *who* it is.

The eye is green.

"Mummy!"

A hiss and spit are my only reward.

I unwind further, at last revealing the sadly abused fur and face of my supposedly former mother, Eye of Night.

"But you are three-days dead!" I tell her.

"Close," she agrees, struggling upright.

Her once-sleek black fur is matted into curls by the linen's long press. Her poor tail has been bound to her body like a broken limb. Her mouth is dry with sand.

She pants. "And three days starved. See what you can get me."

I turn to the crack.

Later, after a desert buffet of fare far below the palace menu, my mother sits licking her lackluster fur in the moonlight and tells me her story in a voice hoarse and shaking with rage.

"First," she says, "I have been prevented from joining my master in the afterlife. I will not sit beside his royal sandal on guard for eternity. Whoever has done this shall pay."

"Still, I am glad to see you alive."

"I will not be able to enjoy my additional life unless I find the person who has done this."

"Then the one behind your resurrection was human?"

"In word and deed. I was taken to the embalmer, where I was . . . hit upon the head. I naturally assumed the blow would be fatal to my earthly body and that I would awake in the underworld at the court of Pharaoh, in my rightful place of Pharaoh's Footstool."

I nod.

"But when I awoke, I was . . . alone. Wrapped in linen, it is true, but with my insides intact. I was neither here nor there but in some blasphemous in-between state that I knew immediately. Though I could see that, I could not see past these blinding bindings you have removed."

She paws the piled linen strips. "Why? Why was I not permitted the ritual death and resurrection in the underworld? Was this some way to harm my master after death? It is a great puzzle."

"The great puzzle is that you are still alive, honored parent. You were abandoned in bindings in the waste between the Valley of the Kings and the Necropolis. You should have died of hunger, heat, or thirst, or been easy prey for some jackal. Yet you fought to free yourself from the bindings, and your struggles were seen by the Necropolis cats, who feared you as a demon."

"I was hungry. Hungry! As if I was alive. I could barely move at first but finally my writhings loosened the linen and I could flail along like a fish spit out of the Nile to the shore."

"No doubt you bewailed your lot."

"I screamed to high heaven."

"No wonder they took you for a monster." I stood up and began to dig in the sand.

"Excuse me, lad, but I do not think now is the time for a bathroom break, not when we face a conspiracy of great umbrage and import to all of Egypt. Pharaoh must not be cheated of his attendants in the afterlife. It is sacrilege."

"Perhaps," I say, still kicking sand, "but I think it is also something else far more common to this world than the next."

She finally sees that I have contrived to bury her wrappings under a mound of sand.

"You conceal the evidence of this outrage?"

"You must take on a new identity. You are not known in the Necropolis except by name and position. I can introduce you as my aunt from . . . Sumeria."

She rises weakly to her feet and stamps one. "Can you not understand, Heart of Night? My duty to Pharaoh is not over so long as whoever has separated us for eternity lives."

"Oh, I see that perfectly well, Auntie . . . Jezebel. That is why we must keep you dead and buried until we can expose the criminal."

"How?" she wails in a fit of maternal exasperation.

"First," I say, "we must discover what and why. Only then will come the 'who.'"

My mama is no shrinking lotus, but even she pauses when she realizes what our next step must be.

"You wish us to disturb the dead? To break into the tomb and desecrate the royal resting place?"

I have led her to the base of the Necropolis for a long drink from the potter's jar where he keeps water to moisten his wheel. Not a soul, human or feline, has stirred. Ordinarily the Sacred Breed overruns the Necropolis night and day, but the mummy sightings have driven them indoors.

"It is necessary. There is something I must see for myself in Pharaoh's tomb."

"I suppose," she says glumly, trying in vain to uncurl her whiskers by wetting them in the jar, "that is the place that I was meant to be."

"Exactly. Taking me there only fulfills your disrupted destiny. Besides, I know little of tomb construction, and I imagine you must have heard the plans discussed in the palace."

"Endlessly," she says tartly, rising off her haunches. "Then let us be off. I need to stretch my limbs."

I follow her lead, not caring to mention that her tail bends crookedly to the left. My mama has much in common with Bastet, in that she can be a benign godlike force and also one Hatshepsut of a demonraiser when riled. Especially when raised from the dead.

The walk is long and the moon has only sailed halfway through the sky-bowl when we pause in the awesome shadow of the pyramid. This man-made and stone-clad mountain, smooth as sandalwood and as precisely pointed as an arrowhead fashioned for a behemoth, seems like a monument worthy of its mighty occupant-in-chief, Death.

My mama has finished lamenting her impious fate by now, and is all business.

"There are secret ways into every pyramid, son, stones that balance upon the weight of a hair to spring open. Sniff for air."

So that is how I come to scraping my nose raw along stone seams so narrow the advertised hair could hardly slip into them.

Suddenly my mama stretches up her front feet. Just as suddenly they plunge forward back to the level, taking her with them. I find the stone has swung open wide enough to admit a mouse. Apparently my food-starved mama fell right through. I must grunt and groan my way past, much compressing my innards. Maybe hers were removed after all . . .

"Hush!" she warns from within.

I sense a draft of air we are soon following up a long stone-paved ramp.

"I have seen the plans," she hisses in the dark. "No one expects a cat, no matter how sacred, to understand the science of humans. But living in the palace taught me the value of learning their labyrinthine ways."

Whatever, I just hope she can lead us out of *this* maze.

Then I see the light. My mama is a haloed silhouette ahead of me. She stops. "This is wrong, Heart of Night. No one should be in the pyramid now."

"Not even some artisan finishing up a frieze?"

"No one."

Mama pads grimly forward, and I follow.

The passage opens into another, then finally into a large chamber lit by the flicker of an oil lamp. I brush past my mother to reconnoiter. She may know her pyramids, but I know the perfidy of humans from my time in the Necropolis.

Yet no humans are present, just the flickering lamp scenting the air with a rancid odor. Or, rather, the only humans present are a painted parade upon the walls. Several Eyes of Horus gaze down on me, as well as a number of insect- and animal-headed gods. I do not spot the Divine Bastet.

I do spot the massive stone sarcophagus that occupies the center of the room.

Mama jumps atop this with an impressive leap for one in her recent condition.

"It is untampered with," she reports with satisfaction. "In fact, from up here, I see no signs of disruption."

"There must be something. Why else the lamp?"

I take advantage of its erratic illumination to study the paintings. The figures, so stiff in their ceremonial headdresses, seem to move in the uncertain light. I see Nomenophis ministered to by serving girls. Offering something to wing-armed Isis. I see sacrificial geese and bulls. I see the noble cat in several representations, all sitting, all in formal profile, like the people. Like the people, the cats are all a burnt-sand color, ruddy brown.

All except one.

The painting depicts Nomenophis in his throne room. Officials and gods gather around. At his feet crouches, not sits, a single cat. She is black.

"Look, Mama! You are in one of the paintings!"

"Hush, boy. Of course I am. As I should be here in my mummified form, with a canopic jar of my vitals nearby. Instead I am robbed.

Robbed of my immortality. That painting is a lie! I am no longer Pharaoh's Footstool!"

Her voice has risen to echo off the stone walls.

"Hush," I tell her in a reversal of roles. "Whoever has lit this lamp may still be within hearing."

I leap up beside her and survey the room in all its glory. I know Nomenophis inhabits a richly painted and inlaid mummy case beneath this stone sarcophagus. I know beneath that his linen-wrapped mummy wears a jeweled gold headpiece and collar.

Yet the tomb itself has not been breached.

I look around, until my eyes rest upon something that should not be here, but is.

My mother ceases her mourning long enough to notice and follow my fixed gaze.

"My mummy! It is here."

Indeed, a wrapped white figure of a cat sits upon a costly miniature throne (quite appropriate placement for one of the Sacred Breed).

"Who has usurped my place?" my mama demands, assuming the very same combative crouch in which she is depicted so handsomely on the tomb wall.

"I am not sure that anyone has."

"And what does that mean?"

I am too busy casting my particular Eye of Horus, representing theft and restitution, about the premises. I spy a pile of abandoned linen windings near the oil lamp on the floor. The inspiration of Bastet floods my brain.

"I apologize for urging you to, er, shut up earlier, Mama. I think you should resume your caterwauling, but first . . ."

In a few minutes my mama's finest notes are bouncing off the sober faces of Isis, Osiris, Selkis, and Neith on all four walls.

I join her, and quite an impressive chorus we concoct in the silence of a deserted tomb.

I soon hear running sandals slapping stones down the long, dark corridor leading toward us. I also hear the sweet sound of curses.

A moment later two linen-kilted men burst into the lamplight.

That is when Mama and I proceed to dance atop Nomenophis's sarcophagus.

We are not particularly good dancers but manage to totter on our hind feet and bat our flailing front feet enough to provide an artistic flurry among the mummy-wrappings that drape our assorted limbs.

"The fury of Bastet," howls one man, falling to his knees and pressing his forehead to the cold stone.

"We have offended the goddess!" screeches the other, doing likewise. "I told you we should not tamper with the mummy of the Sacred One."

At this, two of the Sacred Ones leap off the sarcophagus on to the temptingly revealed naked backs of the prostrate worshipers of Bastet.

Claws dig deep and often. The wretches' howls mingle with our own. They rise to evade our rear harrying, only to find their faces being inscribed with the sacred sign of Bastet: four long parallel tracks repeated to infinity.

Soon we are alone in the tomb, listening to the eerie echoes of tormented escapees.

I leap off the royal masonry to meet the mummy who has replaced my mama.

"Heart of Night," she calls after me. "You have seen the Revenge of Bast. Touch not the cat."

"I do not touch the cat . . .

". . . I level it." With one paw-blow I knock the mummy over and begin unraveling the wrappings. I am getting good at this.

While my mama howls her horror (receiving fresh echoes down the corridor with every bleat), I turn the mummy into shredded wheat.

Lo, this mummy's innards have been left inside too, only they gleam hard and gold in the lamplight.

"Those are some royal artifacts of Pharaoh," my mama says from her perch, stunned.

I nod. "That is why you were shuffled into some spare wrappings and thrown into the desert to die. Your false image here hid the items the servants filched during the funeral. Even as Pharaoh in all his richness was lowered into his sarcophagus, those vermin were wrapping priceless trinkets into a feline-shaped treasure chest. No wonder they fled just now as if the breath of Bastet were smoking their heels behind them."

"But they escaped."

"Marked by the tracks of Bastet? People will comment on their condition. In their current state of fear they will not have the wits to conceal anything. Also, the stone is askew that opens the secret passage we used. Someone will soon notice. We must guard the mummy treasure until the authorities arrive."

"But that may take hours, even days."

"Shall I go out and hunt food first, or you?"

So it is written that when Pharaoh's guard came to his father's tomb two days later, after the claw-marked thieves had been noticed, questioned, and confessed, a fierce black cat was found crouched over the spilled booty from the mummified cat wrappings.

The mummy of the former Pharaoh's cat, the valiant Eye of Night, was missing and presumed to have been assumed into the underworld by Bastet Herself, whose Terrible Tracks still defaced the backs and faces of the would-be thieves.

And so it is now inscribed on the tomb walls of Nomenophis II, who will in his own day go into that underworld that all Egyptians long for, that the position of Pharaoh's Footstool is once again occupied, by Heart of Night, son of Eye of Night, who will live in human memory for two thousand years . . . or possibly more, so long as Bastet and the Sacred Breed are revered, to the ends of the earth.

The Eye of Horus, representing theft and restitution, never sleeps. Evil-doers, read Heart of Night's cartouche and weep.

During the nineteenth century, scientific archaeology—with its meticulous excavation, recording, and study of artifacts—was being born. Meanwhile, treasure hunters and nationalistic antiquarians ignored science as they raced to secure ancient relics, art, statuary, and monuments. With no regard for the knowledge that can be gained from the methodological study of the past, these treasure hunters, tomb robbers, and curio seekers irrevocably destroyed priceless information. Tilton and Doyle invent two men who personify that struggle between science and greed, combine it with ancient myth, and come up with a compelling tale.

The Chapter of Coming Forth by Night
Lois Tilton and Noreen Doyle

———

The wake of the sun's golden barge washed over the limestone cliffs, flooding the desolate landscape with the lurid hues of the dying day. For a brief moment the fading brilliance illuminated a narrow fissure among the rocks, until it was lost in the shadows climbing up from the valley floor.

The cooling desert exhaled; the lizards and scorpions crept from the crevasses and shallow dens where they had taken refuge from the searing heat of the day. Sand slid away, widening the fissure, from which stepped into the newborn night a figure draped in a hooded black cloak, as if shadows had wrapped themselves around her. The Oppressor had departed the sky and she was free, until his return.

Raising her arms, she faced the west and her voice filled the evening silence:

> *A hymn of damnation to thee at eventide,*
> *When thou shalt set as the living set,*
> *Forever and forever in the west,*
> *Never to traverse thy nightly passage,*

For the Fiend shall swallow thy prow,
For the Fiend shall swallow thy midships,
For the Fiend shall swallow thy stern,
And the Fiend shall swallow thee and thy every crew.

Here of all places on earth was the oppressive power of the sun most manifest, this barren land burned lifeless, a place where only the dead dwelled, they and their forgotten gods. She knew them all, the ancient dead: from the gnawed and scattered bones of beggars to the flesh of kings preserved in aromatic resins and cased in solid gold. Yet it was life she needed now, so she descended with a smooth gliding stride across the crumbling rocks and sand, toward those places where water flowed.

Approaching the familiar scent of goats and donkeys—a well, and men drawn to it with their livestock to spend the night. One of them slept a bit apart from the fire where the rest were gathered, wrapped in his ragged blanket against the evils of darkness. She beckoned him in dreams. He opened his eyes, he beheld her: the black cloak thrown back from her shoulders uncovered the alabaster smoothness of her form, glowing like the moon against the cloak that hid only her face from his sight.

Like a serpent his staff of life rose, though he never willed it, for he knew what she was, and his fear would have made him flee if he only could have moved. But he was entirely powerless to resist her, and soon his drained and lifeless form lay empty on the ground.

Five thousand years ago the people of this region had found the remains of such men, her victims, preserved undecayed in the sun-baked sand. So they in error came to believe in the power of the Oppressor to grant eternal life, and they began to prepare the bodies of their dead to keep them from corruption in their tombs. But those times had long since passed and the monuments they had once raised were ruins now, their treasures plundered and despoiled by grave-robbers.

This man too had been a grave-robber, drawn to this barren land by greed, which overruled his fear of the specters that were whispered to haunt the buried necropolis. Now his own grave would be a shallow pit in the desert. But all mortals must die; only the gods were doomed to live forever.

She drew a leather sack out from his tattered garments, spilled out the familiar contents on to the ground. Once these had lain in the tomb of Nakht, her faithful worshipper: scarabs and other amulets of fine faience; a gold ring; a tiny glass bottle; the stopper of a canopic jar with the head of a baboon carved of alabaster from Hatnub. She reflected that once her own image had watched over the preserved remains of her mortal worshippers. How long it had been since anyone had called upon her power or sung her praises! Now she too was reduced to a thief, little more than a grave-robber herself, she who had once been invoked as a protectress of the dead. In ancient days, she had commanded men to steal for her, to bring her riches from the graves at Thebes and Memphis, and with these lures of gold and alabaster and real lapis lazuli she tempted others into these hills. Sometimes she had caught her own. "Forgive me, Nakht," she whispered.

She poured the objects back into the sack and drew the strings tight. On her return, she would replace them among the rocks. More men would come to seek such things, as they had for ages. And they would find them. And her.

Sunrise came too soon. Fearful of the Oppressor's harsh touch, that which would shrivel her as surely as it had the desert, as surely as she had shriveled this man at her feet, she returned to her Lord's house of eternity.

Within the heart of the hills was the tomb where her Lord was imprisoned. He lay at the very back of it, fastened to the rock floor by adamantine chains forged by the Creator from the substance of Creation. But more hateful yet was the immense Serpent coiled next to his body, formed from the living stone.

"Brother, I return."

He turned a face that pain could never make less beautiful to her. "You were not gone so long tonight."

Millennia had passed while he lay bound here, great empires rose and fell, and the gods themselves had passed away, fading even from the memory of the people who now lived in this most ancient of lands. But there was yet a sharp pang to see the plunder of the temples and shrines which men so long ago had built for the worship of her Lord and their brothers and sisters. She hated the thieves but she needed them, for without their lives she could not spare her Lord the most painful of his torments.

"More rich foreign merchants come into the land. The grave-robbers are all dreaming of becoming wealthy men." So she had heard their thoughts as she slid unseen past their sleeping forms.

He sighed, nostrils flaring. "It seems strange to think of the world become such a poor place that so many men still travel here from afar to hunt for gold. Has the breed of man become too lazy to dig their own mines? Or do they build their cities of gold and, having run dry the veins within the earth, seek the gold of ancients?"

"Not just for gold, beloved brother, do they come. It might be common stone shaped by human hand, so long as it is five thousand yeas old they covet it. It is antiquity they seek." Five thousand years. Near two million sunrises had passed since her Lord was first chained here. How could so much be endured?

They spoke of tomb-robbers, of such matters of little significance, to keep their minds from the dreadful hour that approached, when the burning golden barge would break through the barriers of night ferrying the Oppressor on to the throne of his realm—the Usurper who had chained his brother, the rightful Lord of the land, and condemned him to this eternal suffering. Nothing could hold back the hours, not even a god, and the moment came at last when the darkness lifted at the back of the cave, and the stone Serpent moved.

First its eyes shifted, then its head rose, and its tongue flicked the air, searching for the scent of its appointed prey. She watched her Lord, unable to avert her eyes as the vast head turned toward him, as the fanged jaws slowly opened. So she had watched for century after century, helpless to stop it, powerless to help him while the cruel jaws bit and severed his limbs, one by one, devouring them as the Usurper's curse had decreed: *Like the Serpent thou shalt be limbless, by the Serpent thou shalt be dismembered.*

As it had been spoken, thus it was done.

And for all those centuries she had searched through the most secret archives of the temples, the hidden tombs of priests and magicians, through the scrolls and inscriptions, searching for the spell to save him. And found it at last, though the cost was high—the cost was a life, for every sunrise.

Yet why were mortals born, except to die? And to serve their gods?

So this night as on so many others she had gone forth to take life, and now she gave it up, straining to give birth, uttering the words of the spell as it had been written: *O thou shabti! As my lord is called, as my lord is adjudged, behold! Let the judgment fall not upon him, but upon thee!*

And into her hands it came, wet from the birth-passage between her legs, the homunculus, a perfect copy of her Lord, who as god of the barren desert could never himself father a child. The Serpent's cruel jaws gaped wide, about to strike, and she forestalled it, offering this small piece of flesh as a sacrifice in the place of her Lord. So it was done, the sacrifice taken, and her Lord spared his suffering until another sunrise came.

Dr Archibald E. Wordsley turned up the flame of his lamp and drew it closer to the fragment of papyrus that lay on an Arab table he had appropriated as a desk. Why did the beggars always have to come here by night, like thieves? Of course, thieves they certainly were, and the meanest sort—grave-robbers.

The *fellah* named Ali leaned closer, exhaling foul breath from a mouth full of blackened teeth that he framed by a grin. Wordsley wished there were a little more space in this rented room; it was a potter's storeroom where he and his makeshift desk and cot and boxes competed with bowls and jugs and heaps of little cups—and now an Arab—for the floor. "You see, *effendi*? Is it not what I promised?"

In reply, Wordsley pulled out a magnifying glass from his desk drawer to better examine the text. These hieroglyphs were timeworn, difficult to read, but this spoke in favor of the papyrus's authenticity. Forgery was an industry with these beggars; you could never quite trust them, but papyri were beyond their clever skill. The industry had been lost, the script forgotten.

Out of habit, he picked up a pen and began to draw a facsimile of the papyrus. There was nothing here of any great interest, just another chapter from the Book of the Dead looted from the grave of some artisan or minor bureaucrat, a man of no known importance but wealthy enough at least to afford a proper burial and a scroll containing the spells necessary to ensure him prosperity in the afterlife to come.

"Where did you get it? The little pyramid that the American tore down and shipped downriver—from there, eh?"

"No, no, *effendi*. By decree of the pasha, what the American digs up belongs to the American. And he pays besides. This is from—it is from elsewhere."

Wordsley looked up sharply at the thief. "Was there anything else with this? Pottery, for example? Even ostraca, broken pottery? With writing or pictures upon it?" He had found interesting things written on potsherds, names, faces of kings. These might just date the papyrus.

The Arab grinned in false apology. "No, *effendi*, pardon me, but there was nothing else at all, just this piece of writing. Very old, very genuine *anteekah*. Very valuable."

Wordsley snorted. "I'll give you a shilling." Payment enough for this beggar, and all Wordsley could afford, given the present state of his finances.

The would-be seller howled in offended outrage. Only a shilling for such a valuable antiquity? A genuine manuscript from the tomb of the kings? The Englishman insulted him with such an offer. He would take his find instead to the American, who would be sure to pay what it was truly worth.

But Wordsley was unmoved. A shilling was two piasters, enough to feed the thief and his family for a day. And he was sure that if the beggar was offering the papyrus to him now, doubtless the American had turned it down already. Phineas Bigham had no interest in common funeral texts, not the man who bought the head of the Sphinx itself and shipped it back to America as a museum exhibit.

In the end Ali accepted the shilling and left, assuring Wordsley that the starvation of his children was imminent. Wordsley poured himself a glass of claret to wash the taste of the transaction out of his mouth, as well as the dust. Every corner of the room not taken up by the potter's stores held boxes of ostraca, potsherds and scrolls, most untranscribed and untranslated, most likely as worthless as this one, but he did not dare risk the loss of any manuscript of potential significance. Too much had been lost already, too much was being lost even yet, thanks to the activities of tomb-robbers and plunderers and in particular the greatest plunderer of them all, this American mountebank Bigham.

"Bigham!" The name was a curse on Wordsley's lips. Destroying everything in his quest for antiquities, forever obliterating the historical record of millennia, Phineas Bigham was hardly the first of the tomb-robbers, but his dollars had inflicted more damage on the remains of ancient Egypt than centuries of conquering armies. His lavish bribery had purchased the pasha's license to carry off whatever he pleased, and his devastating methods of excavation left irreplaceable papyri torn and rotting amid the ruins he left in the wake of his search for the monumental statues and gold coffins of ancient pharaohs.

Wordsley had had hopes when he set out for Tukh, devoid of the great temples such as those at Luxor or Philae or Abu Simbel. Nothing, he thought, would attract the American here. But something had, nevertheless. The tumbledown pyramid was gone when he arrived two days ago, removed stone by stone; in fact, he had seen but not recognized it sitting on a wharf in Cairo, awaiting steamers to take it seaward as ballast to America, where it would be resurrected again. The graves, most ancient graves, that edged the farmers' fields had been stripped of their occupants and the gold and stone and ivory that had accompanied them in death. More than two thousand looted in a fortnight. Whatever else had stood in the vicinity of Tukh was gone too.

What could he do but salvage here? He felt like a gleaner following an army through fields of devastation. And there was something to glean, for the American had his own desires to satisfy. Only the finest manuscripts, with crisply drawn vignettes painted in delicate green, red, white, and gold, merited Bigham's interest. Wordsley had let it be known that he would pay for whatever the American had thrown aside, at least for as long as his funds held out.

Lighting a second lamp, he applied his attention now to the papyrus fragment on his desk. He copied it out, sign for sign, word for word, column for column, translating in his head. He knew the words before he even saw them: ordinary, ordinary, ordinary! Yet he did not consider his shilling entirely wasted, for perhaps the next manuscript Ali brought in would contain the name of some previously unknown king or god or spell.

There was the piece on which he had been working before the thief's arrival, for example: a new hymn to the sun god Ra-Horakhety triumphant over his enemies at dawn. So much remained unknown and unexplained about the ancient Egyptian gods, so much they might never know, despite all that was left behind. It was now smashed by the chisel for the heads of pretty goddesses, torn up for amulets of gold and lapis lazuli.

Wordsley poured another glass of claret and dipped his pen again into the ink. So much to do.

In the next few days his labors were interrupted so often, by so many natives bearing artifacts for sale—papyri, scarabs, shabtis, pottery jars, bits of mummified animals and birds—that he soon realized something was amiss. The vendors were sly; they said nothing, but it was not only in their silent smiles that Wordsley knew something out of the ordinary was happening.

The two thousand and more graves and tombs near Tukh had been of utmost antiquity: Wordsley had ascertained from interviews of the workmen that there were no scrolls among them, but rather ivory combs, fine stone vases, gold jewelry, and other things for which the American had paid handsomely. Although the *fellahin* were reluctant to admit it, the scrolls and ostraca he had been purchasing from them came from less ancient ruins south of the stolen pyramid. What they brought him now, however, came in such quantity and diversity that he knew they had discovered a new source.

So, having paid six piasters for an ostracon with the cartouches of a king he did not know—Neb-Khepru-Ra Tut-Ankh-Amun—Wordsley pushed himself away from his desk, called his servant Ahmed to bring his hat, and ventured out into the marketplace to investigate the situation.

Heat and sun-glare and dust, with the overpowering scents of dung from camels, asses and the native Arabs, met him. The skirling whine of flies was his greeting. Few people were abroad today, and all of those were women and girls and very small children. Virtually every man and every boy older than eight or ten seemed absent.

"Where is everyone?" he asked of the potter from whom he had rented the room. He wondered how many of his own pots the man had thrown to the ground, buried in dirt, and dug up again for some wide-eyed tourist sailing by in his *dahabeeyah*.

"With the American," was the reply.

"With the American? I thought Bigham had gone."

"He is gone, gone into the desert. He has hired most any man with a pair of legs, see?" The man displayed his crippled feet. "From here, from el-Ballas, from Naqada. They're all in the desert now, far up the *wadi*. Another Biban el-Molouk they have there, yes, it is said. Another Valley of the Kings. Oh, but your face, *effendi*, it is flushed. Come inside, come inside. It is too hot here. Beer, yes? Come inside. The sun has made you ill."

Wordsley brushed away the old man's offer.

What had Phineas Bigham found? The objects the Arabs were bringing to Wordsley lately were undoubtedly more typical of Thebes than of this region. No one had ever reported such tombs or temples here before. *Terra incognita!* Overlooked by Napoleon's savants, missed by that Italian king of grave-robbers Belzoni, could it be? The place would be destroyed, utterly and totally, and carted off to America before it was ever known in Egypt.

"He must be stopped—" Wordsley choked the words back as the potter regarded him coldly. The villagers would not treat kindly anyone apt to thwart their benefactor. Regardless, Phineas Bigham had to be stopped before he raped another tomb, plundered another temple.

Wordsley strode rapidly back to his rented storeroom and shouted for Ahmed, who dutifully appeared and listened to instructions. He must prepare, at once, for an expedition into the hills. Donkeys, flour, water, whatever would be needed. There was no other way. Appeals to the local authorities would be futile. Bribes had placed the pasha squarely in the American's pocket. The British consul, to whom Wordsley would naturally appeal, was interested only in the matter as far as it came to getting a share of the loot; the British Museum was Bigham's greatest rival in the antiquities trade.

So with great difficulty and expense a tent and supplies were obtained, and donkeys to carry them, and an animal for Wordsley to ride. He was, alas, no great explorer, no doughty digger-of-tombs. He was ordinarily content to let others bring their manuscripts and scarabs and ostraca to him for deciphering. But he now had to press beyond that. His mission, if ever he had one, was clear and neither discomfort nor inconvenience would deter him. Bigham had gone into the desert and so Wordsley must follow. The gleaner would glean no longer: time had come for the harvest to end.

It was an army. She had no other word to describe the host now encamped in the *wadi* east of the tomb. The scent of smoke and cooking food rose from hundreds of campfires, mingling with the odors of dung from a thousand pack animals. There was a large tent which certainly belonged to king or general. She saw no swords or bows, not even the explosive firearms of recent invaders, but it was an army of many hundreds advancing toward her, toward the hidden tomb where her Lord was chained.

Dismayed, she realized why they must have come: the bait by which she lured robbers into her hands had now succeeded beyond her purpose, bringing appalling numbers of them. If they should happen by some evil chance to discover the location of her Lord's tomb, to expose it, even for an instant, to the sun . . .

But they could not possibly remain in this region for long, she tried to reassure herself. Not such a great number of men. There was not enough water, they would drink the wells dry—what few wells there were.

And these were only *fellahin*, superstitious and ignorant. She knew how to prey upon their fears. Had not she and her brothers and sisters once inspired their forefathers to prayer and to sacrifice, to raise tombs high into the sky? To dig them deep into the earth? She knew these people. Once, she had owned them.

Now she descended to the camp and took one of the lives that were hers. When the others woke in the morning they would remember whose land this was, whose land this had always been.

Napoleon's army had not made such tracks through the Egyptian desert, of that Wordsley was sure. These parched desert hills had never before seen such a traffic, at least of the living. Once the dead in their thousands had come this way but one by one, dragged on sledges and laid to rest in shallow graves or mud-brick mastabas. Not in such a multitude as this! He followed the trail as it wound into the high hills, pausing for one last glimpse of the green fields. His donkey-boys trudged forward, urging their animals, sparing no such glance, as if it were ill luck to covet the gift of the river being left behind.

Already Wordsley's lips felt parched. Never had he traveled this far into the desert. Its vastness, even cut up by the hills, surprised him. Along the river, there was a feeling of closeness, of definition, brought about by the demarcation between Black Land and Red, but here there was no definition save that between earth and sky. It was entirely the Red Land below and the heavens above. Pharaohs had once hunted lion and ostrich here, praised the setting sun here, buried their dead here. The beasts were gone now, but the sun and the dead remained, always. The brown hills seemed capable of swallowing a man, of sucking him dry.

For an interminable time they followed the tracks. Wordsley began to wonder if the desert might have evaporated Bigham and his work gangs. It was the heat, worrying at his head, that gave rise to such fanciful notions.

"How much farther?" he asked of Ahmed.

Ahmed shrugged and said, "Nearby. Nearby."

Nearby! Nothing could be near here, Wordsley despaired. He thought of going back, of abandoning the past to the depredations of the American, but just at that moment his donkey, as if offended by this notion, stumbled, pitching him off head first into the sand. His hand, breaking his fall, closed on an object.

The *fellahin* swarmed upon him, eager to assist him back to his feet, but Wordsley beat them off with his riding crop so fiercely that one might have thought that these poor bedraggled sons of Adam had pulled him off the beast to rob him. Freed of them, his attention was wholly for what his hand had found.

It was a shallow grave in a hollow in the rocks filled by drifting sand. Something Bigham had already plundered, surely, Wordsley thought. Nonetheless his fall had exposed—he fell back to his knees and scooped sand away with his bare hands—a black, mummified foot, miraculously not reduced to bleached white bone as so many other remains had been. He began to dig the grave out with his hands, then thought of Ahmed and the donkey-boys who were standing about, providing him shade but no other assistance.

"Dig," he ordered.

"*La, la*," they replied.

"What? Why 'no'? You dig them up every night you can. Why not now?"

"The *ferengi* will see," Ahmed said, "turn us over to the authorities."

"There's a *ferengi* leading scores of your uncles and brothers out in the desert at this very moment, doing just such a thing. Why not for me?"

"The pasha. The American has his *firman*. For anyone else, it is forbidden."

With an exasperated rattle in his throat, Wordsley continued digging with his own bare hands. In little time he had revealed a dried husk of a corpse, its skin nearly black, marvelously intact and preserved. He considered it sheer luck that Bigham had not himself stumbled upon this poor wretch, in the course of his trek through this place. Not so much as a stitch of linen clothed his limbs. He began to dig a wider hole, and when it occurred to the Arabs that there might be *anteekahs* to be found, they abandoned their reservations and joined in the search. But there was nothing. Not a potsherd, not a scrap of leather, not a stone knife. Wordsley was disappointed. The only thing of value here was the body itself.

Nevertheless, the men seemed to have found something of interest. Wordsley approached unnoticed, so engrossed were they upon their find. They were passing something small amongst themselves, and did not at first notice that a *ferengi* hand had interposed itself to join in the sharing. Wordsley found himself holding a jasper scarab, neatly incised on its belly with hieroglyphic writing. It did not belong in this wretched grave, of that he was certain.

"*Effendi! Effendi*, we did not know! We thought it nothing, a trifle, a bauble of modern manufacture for the other *ferengi*, not a learned scholar such as yourself. Abdullah makes them just so—"

"Never mind. Bigham would pay you nothing for this; he must have a hundred thousand already. Here." He handed one of them a shilling. This satisfied their business with him, but now they had to settle the coin out amongst themselves. They would be at it for generations, Wordsley reflected, knowing their ways.

He fingered the stone beetle, making out the sense of the glyphs. It was a small heart scarab, inscribed with a formula from the Book of the Dead for a man named Nakht.

Was this naked mummy, then, this Nakht? Had the scarab been overlooked by whomever first plundered this pathetic burial place? Wordsley glanced at the hills. Or had it washed down, perhaps years ago? Assuredly it had come from the same unrecorded place as had the other trinkets the Arabs had been bringing him.

This find settled his resolve. Abandon the past to the likes of the American? Never, *inshallah*.

He had not lied to his Egyptian companions; Bigham would not pay one American cent for the scarab. For so fine a mummy, so perfectly preserved, however—ah! Might he not trade papyri, pottery bowls, flakes of limestone? Items Bigham and his American public considered worthless, but oh! so valuable to the true scholar. The British Museum would display them proudly.

Wordsley called the donkey-boys, who under his direction obediently placed the dried corpse in a linen sheet, and then in two more. Ahmed rearranged his packs, having to leave behind only a sack of flour to accommodate their new traveling companion. He swore them to silence. The mummy was Wordsley's coin, and he would lay it upon the American's counter in due time.

The trail led to a broad encampment in a state of pandemonium. Nearly the entire town was here, and every man who could be hired from el-Ballas and Naqada, excavating the sands of the *wadi*, scouring it like industrious ants. They probed the rocks, they dug, they shifted the sand by the basket-load, a vast effort mobilized, all to earn the American's gold.

Bigham strode among them like a king. His striped waistcoat of French silk stretched across an ample expanse of belly and sported a brave festoon of watch-chain, fobs and seals. A floppy-brimmed hat covered his face, and a parasol rested over his left shoulder. His right hand, encumbered by the dwindling remains of a cheroot, gestured exuberantly as he spoke to the foremen who came and left his presence like bees at a hive. He was possessed of a booming voice, but above the cacophony Wordsley could not make it out. Did Bigham even speak Arabic? Wordsley doubted it. There were enough men in the villages who spoke enough English for Bigham to get by. And they all under-stood his desire, in any case: *anteekahs*.

The entrance of Wordsley and his party into the *wadi* did not go unnoticed. Wordsley had scarcely time to take in the scene before six men posted as guards descended upon them. Only the realization that among the newcomers were their younger brothers stopped the men from delivering blows then and there. One of the guardsmen ran for a foreman, who, as Wordsley watched, ran to another foreman (who likely spoke better English), who at last ran to Bigham. Bigham stared dumbly at him, perhaps not realizing what this Egyptian was trying to say to him. He turned and walked straight for Wordsley. His hearty approach reminded Wordsley of a new-made man who has just caught sight of his country neighbor at a London dinner party.

"Say, now! Professor! Wordsley, isn't it? Aren't I just glad to meet a man of the Queen's tongue in these desert parts!" The guards scattered at Bigham's approach, and Wordsley's own hired party melded into Bigham's, leaving him quite alone except for his donkeys and, anonym-ous among the parcels, the mummy.

The American's good humor was not reciprocated. "See here, now, Bigham," Wordsley said sharply, "what is all this?"

"Only the find of the century, that's all! The tombs of kings!"

Wordsley looked around him at the desolation. "All I see here is rock and sand."

Bigham's laugh came from his belly. "All you see, yes! But they see more than we do!" He aimed with his parasol at the *fellahin*. "These rascals have been living out here robbing graves for generations. For centuries. They know where to find gold where all a white man can see is sand. Ivory, like pebbles to them." He beckoned Wordsley closer and pulled something strung on a thong out from under his shirt. "Look here! Solid gold, this is! That's lapis from Afghanistan, mark me. And have you ever seen such a big and brilliant carnelian? And here—that sign means a king, doesn't it?"

With ill grace, Wordsley bent to examine the artifact, a small gold pectoral in the graceful form of the solar barque, with a carnelian cabochon as the disk of the sun sitting amidships. Unwillingly, he made out the royal cartouche—Ramesses! Ozymandias!— leave it to Bigham, an ignorant mountebank, but he knew enough at least to recognize that aspect of the hieroglyphic script, if it meant profit.

"That fellow brought it to me," he told Wordsley, expansively pointing out the Arab with the most thievish grin of the lot. "Solid gold. Buried right out here in these rocks. And where there's one king, you know, there's a whole raft of them!" He patted his chest, secreting his treasure back beneath his vest.

Unhappily, Wordsley found himself confirming all of Bigham's fond assumptions. The hieroglyphic inscription on the pectoral proved it had belonged to a royal personage of ancient Egypt. It was all too likely that Bigham had indeed discovered another valley of buried kings, hidden up to now from tomb-robbers and other looters over the millennia.

"Now look here, Bigham," he began firmly, "if this find is genuine— if, I say—then this is a matter for scholars to investigate. Properly. Carefully. Artifacts should be handled scrupulously. Inscriptions copied. Not—" He waved his arm to indicate Bigham's army of workers. "Not this."

"Pshaw," scoffed Bigham. "Don't tell me you're worried about a few mummies! Why, it's not as if they were Christians!"

"You don't understand, I'm talking about knowledge here, precious knowledge lost forever in the hunt for treasure! There is none of this in the *Description de l'Égypte*. You won't find it in Lepsius's *Denkmaeler*.

Unpublished, utterly unknown, unseen by European—American—eyes. What you propose—what you're doing—is vandalism!"

Bigham frowned. "And were it not for me it would remain utterly unknown, unseen by white eyes. People come from everywhere on earth to see the treasures in my museum—they call it one of the Wonders of the World. Why, before I dug it up, the Sphinx was buried up to its neck in sand! I saved it, that's what I did, saved it for the ages!"

And now it sits decapitated, Wordsley forbore to reply. Instead, he adopted a conciliatory tone. "But you know what can happen when diggers are careless, what they can destroy or overlook by mistake. Who among your men will recognize if one of those potsherds you order him to throw away might be another Rosetta Stone?"

"Well, yes, you're right, it pays to be careful. That block, plain that it is, makes a fine display," Bigham agreed. "And as I was saying, I can use a fellow like you, who can speak to these natives, who can read those picture-scribbles. I'm sure I can make it worth your while."

Retro me Sathanas! Wordsley thought, with his first impulse to turn his back on the tempter. And yet . . . the pectoral was undeniably authentic. What other wonders lay buried here beneath these sands? What discoveries might he not make, if only Bigham allowed him access to them?

Which reminded him . . .

"I stumbled on something you might find interesting," he said, turning to beckon to his servants. "It's a mummy, actually, but the condition is extraordinary! You might think it had been buried only yesterday." He finally picked a face out of the throng surrounding them. "Ahmed! Bring me that bundle from the donkey."

Ahmed carefully untied the bundle, laid it on the ground. Wordsley impatiently bent to unroll it. The desiccated body was quite light, yet every detail was so perfectly preserved, down to the circumcised tip of the man's most private part. "You see what I mean," he began to tell Bigham. "I suppose grave-robbers must have found this fellow, smashed in his coffin, stripped the body of anything valuable, then left him like this for the sand to bury over again. It was only a matter of chance that I found him—"

But at that moment a terrible cry broke out from among the bystanders who had gathered. "El-Rasul!"

"What?" Bigham expostulated, "What are they caterwauling about now? I can't figure out two words of that damned gibberish."

With some difficulty, Wordsley managed to make out the wails of the natives, who were all backing fearfully away from the mummy, making signs against evil. "They say . . . they know this man! He was a colleague of theirs, another tomb-robber. And—they say he was taken one night by some sort of demon."

A time later, Wordsley reclined, ill at ease, on the cushions in Bigham's sumptuous tent, sipped the thick, strong coffee brought by Bigham's servant, and cursed himself for accepting the American's hospitality. Among the Arabs, hospitality made a sacred bond. Wordsley felt himself a traitor of sorts, as if he had betrayed his principles, allying himself with the enemy for a simple cup of coffee.

Yet Bigham's pavilion was most decidedly more opulent than the potter's storeroom, and, as the American said, they were two white men and Christians here, alone in a throng of superstitious savages. The servant in his slippers crouched miserably outside the entrance, crooning some spell to himself, invoking protection against the evils of the night.

With some difficulty, Wordsley had elicited the tale: According to the nearby villagers—grave-robbers by hereditary occupation—this region was said to be haunted. A *sheytana* lurked among the rocks, a she-demon or *ghûl* who walked at night and could suck a man's life and soul from his body, leaving him nothing but a husk.

Since Bigham had begun operations here, one or two men each night had been reported missing by the Arab foremen. He hadn't given it much thought, native workers sneaking off. But now, with the discovery of the thief's body . . .

"Demons?" Wordsley wondered.

"Humbug!" Bigham expostulated. "In the morning, they'll come here wanting their wages raised, that's what this is all about! Why, you leave a man's corpus out in the desert that way, under the sun, it'll shrivel right up like any mummy! Isn't that so, Professor?" he demanded.

Wordsley frowned silently into the sludge at the bottom of his cup. He hated being made to look a fool. What kind of learned man could not tell the difference between a week-old corpse and a three-thousand-year-old mummy? Yet up until an hour ago he would have insisted, would have sworn that no amount of sunlight and desiccation could have produced a corpse in the condition of the grave-robber. Impossible, he would have said. And there was the amulet found on the body—the scarab. But of course the man had stolen it from some tomb. Any other explanation was flatly impossible. "Superstition," he said shortly.

"That's all it is," Bigham agreed, "just superstition and humbuggery. Why, when I lay that fellow out in a gold box, put a crown and a fake beard on him, he'll be as good as any pharaoh ever born."

"What?" Wordsley exclaimed. "You don't mean to *exhibit* the wretched thing?"

"And why not? You said it yourself, that fellow is the best-preserved mummy I've come across in a long time. He'll be a capital exhibit. It's not likely any of his relatives is going to recognize him in a museum case in Philadelphia, now, is it?"

"But—that's—" Wordsley sputtered. He hated sputtering. "That would be fraudulent!"

"Pshaw, as if anyone would care about that! Look here, Professor, I know what the public wants to see! They want to see mummies, sure they do. But you know what kind of condition most of these old kings are in when we find them—gone half to dust, chests caved in, ribs and bones showing through everywhere. You should see what we've dug up so far—not a one of them worth a plugged cent! That's not the thing to bring in the big crowds. Not like your fellow outside, there. No, he has a fine career ahead of him in my exhibition hall." Then he scowled.

"Unless those relatives of his get too greedy and queer the deal. I'll not pay a cent more than five dollars for him, mark my word."

"But were there artifacts buried with the mummies you've found? Were there papyri?"

"Nothing worth bothering with. A few cheap scarabs, that's all. Some scraps. You know, the sort of thing these thieves have been bringing to you in Tukh. Yes, I know, I know what they've been up to. There may be some better things to your eyes. You can go through it all in the morning, if you'd like, but I can tell you right now, there's nothing worth a plugged cent."

Wordsley could only shake his head. How could he reason with such a man as this? How could he price knowledge in terms of pounds and pence, dollars and cents?

For several nights now, she had sown fear in the camp, in these peasants, thesc *fellahin*. She could taste it in their dreams, in their minds. Yet they remained here, swarming over the sands with their tools and their baskets, probing deeper and further into secrets they must not be allowed to uncover. Greed, as so often, had proved greater than fear. Once this had been in her favor: did they not always return eventually to the salted hills, no matter how many of their kinsmen she took? They were like cattle who did not know pasture from slaughterhouse. But now that she wanted them to fly off, they would not. She had bound them too well with gold chains about their hearts.

Tonight, then: their king.

Unseen by beguiled mortal eyes she passed through the camp, through the hundreds of men who slept rolled in their ragged garments by the sides of campfires to the great pavilion of the king. There was a much smaller tent pitched beside it, and within glowed a faint light, illuminating the figure of a man bent over some work. She briefly paused, touched his mind. A scribe, a servant of the king. He was poring over some odd scraps and fragments of funerary texts, searching. She was briefly curious to have met one who knew the old script, but this was not the one who commanded the army, not the one she must find.

She moved on to the greater tent of the king. Here the dreams were all of greed and grandeur, palaces, and wealth. But in a moment she would reduce it all to a shriveled husk, and the rest, who fed from the grain he scattered from his hand, would then disperse.

She beckoned, she summoned him to her.

He sat erect. The blanket fell from his chest.

The sudden searing light made her fling up her cloak to protect herself. An afterimage of the solar barque was branded across her vision. This one was under the Oppressor's protection! He wore his sign, the image of the sun!

Half blind, she stumbled from the tent, tripped over a bundle of rags, one of the king's slaves, wrapped in fitful, demon-haunted dreams. She left him drained and empty, she passed through the camp like an angel of death—those words from one of their minds: *angel of death*, and she understood that an *angel* was a *messenger of god*.

But it was not a messenger who walked among them tonight. It was the goddess herself. It was death.

Wordsley awoke from a dream in which untold riches had beckoned to him like the harlot of Babylon. He had only to give up his quest and it would all be his, gold from the tombs of oriental kings. His own will had won out in the end, but he was sweat-matted and shaking, as if in one of those Nile fevers. He inspected himself for stings or bites, but found none as he washed himself from a half-empty basin of tepid water. "Ahmed!" he called, but the servant did not appear. He cursed the fellow, and his poor night's sleep, that had put him in such a state. Poor sleep and the wicked temptations of Bigham. Curse him, as well!

Wordsley examined his work of the night before. He had sketched a dozen scarabs, several pieces of funerary jewelry, knowing that they would soon be packed up in crates and shipped across the Atlantic. Although he valued them equally, none of the objects had been very interesting to him, none of them anything new. Yet he dutifully noted names, variants in spelling, and in hieroglyphs, in his epigraphic catalog.

One object alone had held some promise. It was a square wooden tile, rather the broken half of one, caught up in with the scarabs as dunnage. If he could find the rest of it, that would be worth pursuing, for it was nothing less than a bookplate, a tag once tied to a papyrus scroll, and the title, so much of it as he could make out, was *The Chapter of Lying Bound*. An unknown text!

The camp was quiet, preternaturally so. Already the morning sun was fierce, even through the open flap of the tent. Aware of his thirst, Wordsley looked around for his servant with his morning coffee. "Ahmed!" he called out. "Ahmed! Damn his heathen soul, where is that beggar?"

But it wasn't the faithless Ahmed who burst into his tent, it was a red-faced Bigham, shouting, "Damn you, Wordsley!"

"What?" Too astonished to protest the man's rudeness. "What do you mean?"

"The bastards! The bastards up and left me, almost to a man! When the pasha hears about this—oh!" He raged in the most vile obscenities, which seemed to serve the purpose of restraining his fist from Wordsley's face. "It was that mummy of yours, that you brought into *my* camp! *My* camp, Wordsley!"

Wordsley was dumbfounded. True, the Arabs were a superstitious race, but hitherto all could be overcome by the appropriate application of *bakshish*. Still why should they be upset by one mummy? He suspected other reasons at work. "Did you cut their wages? Did you threaten to?"

"No! No, no! I'll show you! Come see for yourself!"

Bigham flung open the tent, slashing at the air with his parasol. "Look! Look, you!

"*One* mummy, you brought me—just one—and the beggars saw how I paid you for it. Oh, it's the bazaar! They live to bargain! You can't show the first bit of enthusiasm, or they'll skin you, Wordsley, they'll dicker you down to your combinations! Mummies—that's what they think I want, and so they tell themselves, 'Oh, here is the American's price. That is what he wants. Oh, them we have aplenty, and aplenty we'll give him.' Dozens of them, Wordsley! They left me dozens of them, and I don't want them all. Mummies! I want the gold, dammit, the jewels, oh, to hell, I want—"

Up until this point it was not clear to Wordsley what it was that the *fellahin* had given to Bigham. But Bigham stopped at the inert figure dozing in the shade of Wordsley's tent. With his folded parasol, he prodded it, just a short stab, and it fell over with a dry thud.

"See! They're all over camp. Dozens of them! Dozens of damned, worthless mummies! Not a workman in sight!"

"But . . . Ahmed! This is—"

"What?" Bigham demanded impatiently. "Your servant's in on this scheme, too?"

"No, no. I think I know that man. That corpse. My servant, Ahmed."

"Now, you're not putting stock in that Arab hoodoo? You've been too long in Egypt, Professor. You've absorbed their superstitions."

"Yes, but—"

Bigham moved forward for a closer look at the mummy. "Come on, now! You may see a resemblance to your man, but then I see a resemblance of that face of yours to that of Judas in *The Last Supper*, and I don't go about accusing you of the crime now, do I? If I knew that beggar, I'd whip his hide and have him digging in these hills as he ought to. I'll tan their hides yet. Dig, you desiccated monsters!"

"No, really, Bigham! I insist!" Wordsley followed the American to a heap of rags in the sand that proved on closer examination to be another desiccated corpse. "Look here! Look how they are dressed! These are modern robes! Just what the *fellahin* wear. They can't be old mummies! It's quite impossible!"

"No, you look at it, man!" They wandered among the mummies, not daring to venture too near any one. "Dry as old bone and leather! All of them! All the juice sucked out. Mummies aren't made overnight.

And even if they have made some improvements since Ozymandias's day, Musselmen or even the poor Copts aren't going to submit their brethren to that heathen practice! Why, it's likely the one thing Musselman and Copt will agree upon. Which leaves us with the question of how they got into the robes. Either the villagers put the robes on these dead creatures—for whatever reason we can guess until the sacred cows come home—or these are old clothes, old as the mummies."

But that was simply absurd, so much that Wordsley knelt down to examine more closely the disputed remains of the mummy at his own tent. The features, reduced to leather as they were, with the lips pulled back from the teeth, were nonetheless very much like those of Ahmed. And in the purse beneath his robes

"Ah! Now, you just look at this!" he cried triumphantly, holding up for Bigham's inspection the shilling he had found. "Tell me how you account for this coin, not so lately removed from my own purse! No, I tell you, these are our own men, this is my servant Ahmed. Something— I'm not saying any supernatural agency, I'm not saying that, but something has done this to them! A geologic or atmospheric event from which we were protected by our tents."

Bigham, with ill grace, discontinued asserting his own theory of the events. Together they moved out across the sands of the camp, counting the mummified figures strewn about the place.

"Fifty-six of them," Bigham said at last.

"And the rest?"

"Why, run away! The cowardly beggars ran away! I had four hundred men and boys crawling this *wadi*. Now this! A camp full of worthless corpses and the rest of them all skulked off in the night!" Bigham's sullen tone made it clear that he knew this was all some sinister, if yet unexplained plot to deprive him of his workers. "Listen, Wordsley, I'll make a deal with you. You go back to Tukh, tell those Arabs that I'm expecting them back here, working, just as we agreed. They can have their wages, as before, and I'll pretend that none of this ever happened."

Under his breath he muttered, "None of your she-demons, your *ghûl*. None of that bunkum."

Wordsley stared at the face that might have been Ahmed's, then at Bigham's, not entirely sure which made him more uncomfortable. "That is your deal with the Arabs. What is your deal with me?" He wasn't certain that he wanted to hear it. That dream of his. The temptation, the serpent's voice.

But while the Arabs might not have liked Bigham's price, the American certainly knew Wordsley's. "Every scrap of papyrus I find. Any trinket with the littlest bit of glyph that is not museum-worthy. It's yours. Crated up and shipped wherever you wish. Ink and paper to do your drawing. Candle, lamp, whatever you want to work with. And you may have inspection of everything: reliefs, inscriptions, coffins, whatever. Copy it all. Publish it all, if that's what you like! Send the printer's bill to me. There may even be a job for you in Philadelphia, if you want it."

Wordsley stared at the hills that held—what? He still had the bookplate in his pocket, the half of it. What would he give for the rest! What he would give for the scroll to which it had once been tied! Sell his soul for a papyrus?

"It is agreed, then. Give me your donkey, or did the *ghûl* take that too?"

Wordsley returned three days later. Besides the ass given to him by Bigham, he had a string of six donkeys with him, and half again as many men.

"The rest are coming tomorrow?" Bigham demanded.

"The rest are not coming tomorrow or the next day or ever again," Wordsley sighed. "They are too frightened of the *ghûl*. I went to the Copts, too, but none would approach the Hill of Lilith. I even offered them more wages—"

"What? You offered the beggars more? And they still won't come?"

"They're afraid!" Wordsley exclaimed, weary and exasperated from his futile journey. "Do you blame them? There are fifty men dead in this camp, and no way to account for it."

"Bogeys and boggarts!" Bigham howled, throwing up his hands. "Well, that does it! I can't do anything with nine men. Have them crate up what we've got now and load it on the donkeys. What a poor-looking team they are too—men and beast, matched!"

"You are quitting, then?" Wordsley could scarcely believe this, or the pangs of regret that he himself felt. He might have saved the hills from rape, but he was losing his papyri.

"No!" Bigham swelled with determination, and Wordsley found himself brightening, hating himself for it. "No tribe of flea-bitten Arabs is going to get the better of Phineas Bigham! They'll see what American ingenuity can do! I'll show them! I'll show the whole world! Damned if I don't!"

The army had gone. The Lady had defeated them, drunk their lives, until she was full and sated. If only she had been able to lay her touch upon their king, but he was protected by the Oppressor's sign.

Still, he had gone and taken his army with him. She had won, she had conquered. Her concern had been groundless, after all. They were after all no more than any other host that had invaded the Red Land and the Black over the centuries.

She lay beside her Lord that night, kissed his fettered limbs, each so perfect and fine. She wept for him, for his pain, for his suffering. But the lives she had taken would spare him for two cycles of the moon, for that many sunrises, each time the Serpent woke.

He at once sought her comfort and comforted her. So it had always been between them. So it would be until the end of time.

Wordsley gave little thought to Bigham's whereabouts. The American had taken himself off, removing all temptation with him, and it was just as well. The secrets of the desert remained inviolate and undespoiled, and it was surely just as well.

He had done as agreed, with the assistance of those few Arabs he had convinced to return with him, offering them doubled wages. Bigham's few initial finds had all been gathered up, boxed and bundled, loaded on to the donkeys for transport. There was nothing the American had valued sufficiently to take with him, nothing except for the golden pectoral which had once belonged to a king—that, Bigham kept on his person always.

But Wordsley had been conscientious. All the spoils of the American's dig were currently reposing in the potter's house, as carefully stored as if they had been the most costly and delicate antiquities. He was cataloging them now, in Bigham's absence, labeling each piece and taking thorough notes, copying all inscriptions.

The finds, despite the initial promise of the golden pectoral of which Bigham was so fond, must have been a disappointment to the hopeful collector. Tonight so far, Wordsley had cataloged a dozen scarabs, an ivory statuette of a king or god (it was too crudely done to be sure) wearing the White Crown and a false beard, a necklace of amethyst beads. Curious, he thought, that they were found so scattered, not as if placed in some ancient cache by grave-robbers to hide their crime or priests to hide their sacred objects. He had counted items from no fewer than twenty different tombs, but it seemed inconceivable that they could all be in those hills. There was nothing else like them in the area, nothing at all.

Ah, well. There was much to learn, so very much. And that finished one crate.

He stood, stretching cramped muscles, and crossed the room to brew himself a fresh pot of tea. Since Ahmed's death, he had no servant; none of the Arabs would hire themselves to him, and he was aware that they made gestures to avert a curse whenever he crossed their path in the streets or marketplace. Of course Wordsley was as little susceptible to such a notion as Bigham had been, but still, when he considered the mystery, it was hard to account for so many sudden deaths among the workers. Sunstroke, he supposed it must have been. What other explanation could there be?

Refreshed by the tea, he pulled another crate out from the heap and carried it to his worktable. Inside, he found a bundle of rags and heard the unmistakable clink of broken pottery as he began to unwrap it. The object inside was a clay jar in fragments, a piece of no intrinsic interest to any collector with Bigham's tastes, but Wordsley's attention was piqued as he saw it was filled with scrolls. Poking out through the still-intact mouth he could see the broken end of a wooden tile, a bookplate.

He sprang instantly to his feet to rummage among the items on a shelf. Ah! Yes! There it was! The other half of a bookplate he had encountered in the camp. Fetching it to the table, he matched it to the broken bookplate in the jar. Despite the worn edges, they clearly fit together into a single whole.

The bookplate, now reunited, now revealed the complete title: *The Chapters of Lying Bound in Darkness and of Coming Forth by Night.* Wordsley's heartbeat quickened. Indeed, this must be a new funerary text! Not merely a new chapter of the Book of the Dead or of the Book of Breathings, but a genuinely new text!

He worked methodically, never hurrying the task in his excitement, putting aside the pottery fragments and removing several scrolls from the broken jar. The papyri were old and brittle and crumbled into fragments at his touch. He kept each in its own box, so that they would not become confused like a jumble of so many jigsaw puzzles.

With hands that threatened to tremble, he assembled his ink and paper and several lamps. Where to start? At the beginning, surely, but which scroll was first? It did not really matter. Order would come from chaos soon enough. He lit all of the lamps, that he might see very trace of ink on the ancient, yellowed surfaces of the papyri. They were old and exceptionally fragile; once, surely, they had been very fine. Along the top of the text ran a register of repeated solar barques painted in gold.

It was near dawn by the time he began his transcription, murmuring as he wrote: "The Chapter of Binding the Limbs . . ."

*   *   *

At that very moment, as the desert stirred with the presentiment of sunrise, a vagrant breeze swept the sand and sifted a few grains into the abandoned excavations. In time, the sand would cover it all once again, and the newly made dead would sleep alongside the old.

The desert would prevail, as it always had. Even more than gods, the desert was immortal.

Wordsley stirred in his sleep, lying half-clothed and sweating on his rumpled cot. What was that infernal din? Jackals—no, no, it was the Arabs and their dreadful noises.

Suddenly, his eyes flew open. There was a sound he knew! That piercing shriek—it could only be a steam whistle!

The Arab ululation rose to an answering wail.

Fearing the worst, fearing riot and chaos, Wordsley flung on his clothes and rushed toward the marketplace. The stalls were all deserted, but ahead, along the riverbank, he could discern the mob gathered. He pushed his way through, hearing as he did the repeated: *ferengi! ferengi!* And other words as well: *monster, demon . . . machine . . .*

But even Wordsley was taken aback when he finally saw the apparition that had come up the river. A monster indeed! A veritable behemoth of mechanical monstrosity.

As if to answer him, the thing whistled again. That it was a steam engine of some sort, he was well aware. But a sort that he had never seen, or imagined seeing, in all his life. A massive boom swung out from the base, supported by a system of beams, pulleys and chains, and from it was suspended the maw of a giant scoop.

Though he had never seen one before, Wordsley instantly grasped what it was, what it was meant to do. A shovel! A giant, steam-powered shovel! "Bigham!" he cursed out loud, and began to shove through the native throng with no regard for the persons he might displace.

His worst suspicions were realized as soon as he came closer to the riverbanks. Aboard the barge in all the puffed-up pride of ownership stood the American under his customary parasol.

Wordsley shook his fist. "Bigham! We had a gentlemen's agreement, Bigham! You'll not cheat me out of it, you colonial cretin!"

The American, on board the barge and too far to hear Wordsley's maledictions, returned a wave of exuberant misunderstanding.

Under the direction of several Europeans, native workers on the boat were sliding a massive gangplank into place. Then, with another blood-curdling whistle, the machine began to move!

The mob onshore shrieked. The Egyptians turned to flee, trampling one another in their panicked rush to escape the advancing behemoth. Wordsley gave thanks that he had by this time pressed forward toward what had been the front of the crowd, or he might surely have been caught in the midst of it. As it was, he was now well placed to watch the huge, ungainly machine as it clanked and clattered inch by inch down the sagging gangplank, moving quite under its own power!

Wordsley had heard of such marvels, had read of them in the London papers, but never, never had he expected to see one, not here, in this benighted, backwards part of the world, where donkeys still turned water-wheels in just the same way as they had done since the days of the pharaohs! He had a moment of hope, when it seemed that surely the vast weight of the machine would crack the gangplank and send the monstrosity to the muddy bottom of the Nile, but no, it continued to inch forward until it stood at last safe on the quay, shuddering and clattering and belching smoke and steam.

"Wordsley!" came a shout over the ungodly din. "Wordsley!"

With an effort, he stood still to let the American approach.

"There you are! I thought it was you! So, you're still here! Well, what do you think?" Bigham turned to gesture with expansive pride at his appalling mechanical prodigy, and without waiting to hear a reply, "It's an Otis Shovel. Built in Philadelphia, by God! I told you American ingenuity would show them! It can do the work of a hundred men, Wordsley! One machine, the work of a hundred men! I tell you, this is the future!"

He shook his parasol at the distant crowd of natives, whose fearful wailing was drowned out by the roar and clatter of the machine. "I'll show them! They think they can hoodwink Phineas Bigham, do they? Filthy beggars, deserting me, leaving mummies all over the camp—so they want more wages, do they? Why, then let them take a look at this! A hundred men, Wordsley, and it isn't going to strike for more wages, or take sick in the middle of a work day, or start gibbering any superstitious bunkum about she-demons!

"American know-how! I'll tell you, Wordsley, for years and years we Americans stood by the sidelines as you Europeans grabbed it all: Greece, Rome—all of it. I hated that. So I earned my fortune in steel and whiskey, and came here to bring America something of a past our ancestors left behind for freedom. It's not necessary to trade off history for liberty, you know. It's not. And so now in Philadelphia the Sphinx's head sits a block away from the Liberty Bell. And this, this fine Otis Shovel, is what they cast in Philadelphia nowadays! Oh, I'm not finished, Wordsley, not by a long shot. I won't let those black beggars beat me, I'll be damned if I will!"

"You had this shipped all the way from Philadelphia?" Wordsley asked, distracted by wonder.

"From Russia! From the Crimea," Bigham boasted. "It was shipped there in '41 to dredge the harbors. I had my agents locate the nearest available machine and offer the highest price for it. Telegraphy, Wordsley! Dynamite! Steam power! They can lick any of your she-demons ten ways from Sunday, and you can bet on that!"

Wordsley cleared his throat. "I've sorted and cataloged those pieces you left with me—"

"Trash!" Bigham dismissed it with a snort. "All of it, worthless! Keep it, if you want it—keep it all! Now that I have old Otis, here, I'm going to find those royal tombs! See if I don't! Treasures that will dazzle your eyes! They're out there, Wordsley, I know they are! And I'm going to have them! America, by God, is going to have them!"

*   *   *

This time the approach of the invading army was signaled not by a cloud of dust, as it had always been before, but a dark cloud of smoke, not by the braying of asses but the clang of metal and the hiss of steam. Of all the most hideous monsters of the Underworld, there was nothing to compare with this smoking beast, but she was certain that it must have been spawned in the pits of fire where the enemies of the Oppressor were sent to be consumed. Its teeth were of iron, and its breath was flame.

She looked upon it, and she uttered a spell of protection:

> *Now though I stand in fire, yet I am not consumed,*
> *For the fire shall not harm me,*
> *Nor shall the flame of the fire touch me,*
> *Nor shall the heat of the fire burn me,*
> *And the Fiend shall be powerless before me,*
> *And my enemy shall be powerless to destroy me,*
> *As I pass through the fire unconsumed.*

Yet still she was afraid.

If Wordsley had only consulted his better judgment, he would have left Bigham and his steam juggernaut to enter the desert alone, with only the dour Scots engineers he had hired to minister to the needs of the iron beast and tend to the crates marked Giant Powder Company. His better judgment wanted nothing more to do with the American and his grandiose, demented notions. He had escaped once already, and brought forth a treasure vastly more precious than any gold or lapis or electrum that Bigham might find in the tombs of kings: the manuscript, previously unknown, rescued from the destruction of Bigham's vision of the future.

During the months of the American's absence, he had spent hours, countless hours, meticulously copying, transcribing and translating the hieroglyphs, committing them to memory. He had done what he could to restore the original brittle, crumbling papyri. But the text—so distinct with its frieze of solar barques—had broken off abruptly, and nowhere in all the boxes, bundles and crates he'd brought back with him from the desert had there been another scroll to complete it. The rest of it had to be out there, still!

Yet what hope was there of retrieving it from out of the iron maw of Bigham's mechanical monstrosity? The steam excavator would scoop up sand by the ton, bite through explosive-shaken stone, devour a complete necropolis in a single day, in search for treasure Bigham considered worthy. The devastation would be incalculable!

He must stop him!

At first, he had entertained the hope that the behemoth might collapse of its own weight into the desert. The steam shovel was designed to propel itself, but not for vast distances over such ground. Bigham would not be thwarted. His engineers designed a portable wooden roadway, and he hired a team of workers to set each section in place ahead of the iron wheels of the moving behemoth, then run back and pick up the next section as it passed. The steam boiler devoured water, it consumed wood, but Bigham had these supplies brought up in donkey carts and by porter, declaring he would be damned if he gave a pin for the expense. In such a way, a mile or so closer every day, they approached the site where he supposed lay the royal tombs.

The American, Wordsley concluded, was obsessed. There was no other name for this condition. What havoc might he not wreak, if someone were not there to prevent it!

Yet when it began, he was helpless to stop it. The steam boiler roared and shook and smoked and hissed, gears clanked and chains rattled: the boom lowered, the huge shovel bit into the desert floor and rose again with its iron maw full of dirt and sand and shattered stone and God-knew-what-else. Now and then the earth shook as the stubborn rock was dynamited into shards. *Ya Allah!* the few native donkeyboys and servants exclaimed in terror and awe.

Lord preserve us! thought Wordsley.

And Bigham strode about the site, a general brandishing his parasol like a sword, directing operations.

Within two days, the excavator had unearthed a vast city of the dead that seemed to extend all the way to the hills. Mummies everywhere, lain in shallow graves, some with bags of golden statuettes, silver cups, beads of semiprecious stone, most with plugged-cent bits of this and that. These were not, certainly, the tombs of kings, although the names of kings—many kings and queens and princes and viziers and even the emperors of Rome—were graven upon so many of these objects. Hundreds of thousands, nay, a million graves lay open to the sky, now broken open and their mummified contents now ground to dust under the iron wheels of the juggernaut.

"You must take care!" Wordsley protested, appalled to his heart. "Tell them to take care with that machine! This—this is a priceless find! So many mummies—my God, man, so many men here! There is not its like in all of Egypt—all the world! How did they all get here?"

But Bigham dismissed his concerns. "Trash! That's all this is, Wordsley, trash! A few scarabs, a few scrolls, a few broken jars, a bit of bone or human leather—who could care about truck like that when we can discover a real treasure! It's out there, I tell you! That's what these thieves were doing here. Somewhere there is the tomb of tombs! So great a find that a million men came here to their deaths for it. Ah, but none of them was an American, eh? Further into the hills, maybe. I will tear all of them down to bedrock and beyond if I must. But it's out there—the treasure of kings, Wordsley! I know it!" He slapped his chest as if reassuring himself. "This tells me so! Like a lodestone, Wordsley. Like a compass. It tells me I'm on the right bearing here, it tells me this is all going to be worth the effort."

Wordsley could only shake his head and mourn. He haunted the ruins of the ancient necropolis like a bereaved ghost, so overwhelmed by the scope of the find that he could not think of how to begin to salvage the least part of it. It would take an army, a veritable army of workers and scholars years to properly map and catalog the discoveries here. But already he was quite sure that the only reason so many would seek their burial here was a site of extraordinary holiness, a temple or tomb of a forgotten dynasty of god-kings. For that reason alone could so many have chosen to lay tombless, in meager graves, in this desolate waste for eternity.

Bigham, damn his greedy soul, must be right. The treasure, the treasure of kings, had to be close at hand.

Before long, Wordsley's tent was filled with scrolls. Even his cot was covered with them, so that he would have had to clear the space to sleep, if only he could spare the time for sleep.

He could have filled a dozen tents with scrolls and still not had room for them all. And he was not the only one to be gleaning from the tombs. Bigham's few Arab hirelings—all from Cairo—clanked as they walked, so laden they were with pilfered scarabs and seals. Even the Scottish engineers were filling their pockets during the hours of rest from attendance on their steam-powered charge and the careful laying of the dynamite sticks. Only Bigham ignored the fortune in antiquities that the shovel dug up from the sands with every bite, for his grandiose ambition would settle now for nothing less than the tombs of a hundred kings. Whatever he obliterated in his path, it was nothing to him.

Wordsley agonized to leave so many fragile papyri exposed to the hostile elements of the desert, but what else could he do? He was only one man! All he could do was search for the most promising, the rarest of the scrolls, and save those few, as many as he could. Yet as many as he found, so many more were being destroyed.

He thought perhaps of some way he might play hob with the infernal machine, but in truth he could discern no way this could be done that the engineers would not be able to fix within the course of a day. They were rough men, with permanently blackened faces from the smoke and smuts, but intelligent and ingenious craftsmen. A broken pivot or chain was nothing to them.

There had been no more of the mysterious deaths or disappearances in the night, such as had plagued Bigham's first expedition and driven off all the native workers. "Aren't you afraid?" he asked the donkey-boys who trekked into the camp daily, carrying water. "The villagers of Tukh say this place is cursed. The Copts call this the Hill of Lilith. You Musselmen say it is the haunt of a *ghûl*!"

At this, the Cairene boys and men made signs to avert evil, but one of them replied, "If there is a demon in this place, it does not dare approach the *makina*!"

Yet the *makina*, the diabolical creation, did have its weakness. It devoured not only water, vast amounts of it, which had to be carried in on donkey-back, but fuel as well. And this was not a country with abundant supplies of wood or any other fuel.

One day, the flames diminished in the boiler. The needle on the steam-gauge sank. The iron scoop hung motionless on its boom.

"I have to hire more men!" Bigham raged when the engineers explained the silence and inactivity of their mechanical charge. "More donkeys! Damn these natives and their superstitions! Do you know what they're charging me for a load of wood?" He spun around, as if searching the sere and desolate terrain for a forest he could chop down to feed the steam boiler's insatiable appetite.

But this was the desert. There was nothing in sight as far as the horizon but rock and sand and despoiled graves.

"I'll show you what to burn!" he shouted. "I'll show you fuel!"

The engineers stared uncomprehendingly, but Wordsley had grasped Bigham's intent. "You can't! You couldn't do such a thing! It would be monstrous! Infamous!"

"I can't, can I? Why, I'll show you *can't*!" The American seized up a mummy from the nearest heap of broken bone and cloth. "We'll just see how well these peasants burn!"

To Wordsley's inexpressible horror, he flung the mummy into the boiler's open maw, on to the seething bed of ashes, and instantly it burst into flame!

"There!" Bigham shouted triumphantly. "There's your fuel! Start stoking your boiler! Pass over that big fellow! I'll bet he'll burn as well as any split oak log! Let's build up a great head of steam, there!"

The mummies, as dried as they were and preserved by inflammable resins and pitch, were an inexhaustible source of fuel. Not only the human inhabitants of the graves, but mummified birds and beasts, all went into the fire. The head of steam built up again, the shovel rose and bit into the sand.

"That's it!" Bigham exclaimed. "That's the way! Throw in all of them, a million of them! Tear down those hills!"

"My Lord," she confessed on her knees before him, "I do not know what to do! The fiery Fiend—every day it comes closer to this place! It is surely spawned from Hatet-Ketits, the pit of fire where the Oppressor's enemies are consumed, for I have seen it myself, consuming the bodies of the dead! It bites through the sand and stone, it devours the hills! I cannot stop it! And I am so much afraid!"

Her Lord strained against his unbreakable bonds, lying within the Serpent's coiled embrace. "This is a creature of my brother that shakes my house of eternity! He is not willing that I survive, even in chains! See, the monster he first set here to devour me has failed, thanks only to you, my sister! Now he sends this thing with the fire of the sun in its belly to tear away the rock from over my head! He will not be satisfied until he sees me burn!"

The Serpent of living stone watched and waited, coiled to strike, yet motionless while darkness held sway over the land. She shuddered as always when she met its malevolent eyes, remembering how many times its cruel fangs had seized her beloved Lord's limbs and tore them from his body, fulfilling the Oppressor's curse.

Yet she had already thwarted the Serpent's purpose and spared her brother unspeakable pain. Could she do less now? Faced with this new Fiend, could she let her courage fail her? Could she stand by and see her Lord exposed to the punishing rays of the sun, his eternal enemy, or burned in the fiery pit?

"I will go forth again," she promised him. "Their king remains protected by the sign of the Oppressor and I cannot touch him, but I will find a way to stop this thing. I must."

For no one else could defend her Lord.

At night, the beast of fire slept, its belly no longer incandescent with heat, its roaring voice silenced. But the scent of myrrh still hung about it, the scent of the smoldering dead.

She had no spell to use against this enemy, it possessed no life that she could drain away. Its attendants, however, the men who fed it— against those she could act. Only the king was under the Oppressor's protection, not his servants.

One of them crossed the sands now, bearing an armload of scrolls, toward one of the small canopies where they slept. Another grave-robber, she thought. Yet a sense of familiarity pricked her. This one, she had encountered before: the king's scribe, she recalled him, the man who knew the old script. Yet the man's thoughts, when she met them, startled her: *He must be stopped! I have to find a way, before this is all destroyed!*

Here was an unexpected ally!

She slipped into the tent behind him. The scribe bent over a low bed where scrolls were heaped, sorting through the papyri. She stepped forward. Suddenly aware, he turned.

His eyes went very wide, his body rigid. His mind roiled with lust, concupiscent shame, and borning terror. He could not move, though her smile beckoned him. Her cloak was flung back, and her flawless body gleamed like polished alabaster in the low lamplight.

"Read to me. Read to me and this shall be yours."

He needed no more urging than that, for his passions were now twice-stirred. He read, he spoke from memory, he uttered the spells guarded from her own eyes by a frieze of solar barques. For hours he went on, for hours she listened, committing to memory, rejoicing in the knowledge even as this scribe rejoiced.

All night she listened to his recitations, until the warning tints of approaching dawn came through the tent's cloth walls. Her hand sought his staff beneath his garments, her mouth pressed against his, and she took him into her, all of him. His husk fell away, his soul gestated within her.

As dawn rose in the sky outside, within the cavern that was her Lord's prison, she strained to give up the life she had just taken. The homunculus emerged from between her legs, in form the image of her Lord, but its soul had so lately been her ally. It stared at her—it thought and it feared and she averted her face. "Forgive me," she whispered, as the cruel stone head of the Serpent began to move. "But I grant you the boon for which you have been praying. Together, we shall thwart the purpose of your king!"

The spell she uttered was the one she had used now for thousands of years to turn the Serpent's punishment away from her Lord: *let the judgment fall not upon him, but upon thee.*

But now she added these words, taken from the foreign scribe's treasure-trove of scrolls:

> *Return thou now to the pit of fire,*
> *Return now to the flame that spawned thee.*
> *For thine enemies are given to the fire,*
> *In the fire thine enemies are consumed.*
> *For thou art the Devourer.*
> *Thou goest forth to meet thine enemies*
> *And thine enemies shalt thou consume.*
> *Thou shalt swallow them up entire,*
> *Nor shall they rise again,*
> *Nor any of their creation,*
> *But they shall be utterly destroyed.*

The homunculus, animated by its own knowledge of the spells, let loose a shriek that echoed down the long, devouring throat of the

Serpent. But this time, instead of returning to immobile stone as it had always done for two million sunrises, the Serpent's body rose higher. Its tongue flicked out, its head turned from side to side, seeking.

Then, slowly, the entire sinuous length of it uncoiled. With its scales rasping against the floor of the tomb, the Serpent of living stone slid out through the entrance of the cave, and so great was its girth that the rock split and chipped as it passed through.

The camp was stirring in the first full flush of dawn as men rose eager to take advantage of the cooler hours before the heat became too oppressive. It was one of the donkey-boys who first saw the giant serpentine form approaching from out of the hills. At first, he thought it was some strange form of sand-slip, for the snake was the color of the stones of the hills, but then it raised its head, as if scenting for prey, and the boy screamed, "*Te'aaban!*"

For a long moment he stood as if paralyzed, but his scream alerted others and spurred them into motion, and when they too saw the monstrous form descending upon them, they fled, calling on God for deliverance from such manifest evil. The Scotsmen, busy stoking the boiler from a large stack of well-dried, quick-burning mummies, gaped at this sudden exodus of Bigham's native help. Their first thought was earthquake, not unknown in this region. But when they too understood at last that the roiling motion and rock and sand was the wake and the very body of the Serpent, they abandoned the boiler, the mummies and the shovels and joined the native Arabs in their headlong flight to escape the monstrous apparition.

"Get out!" they shouted to Bigham as their employer came from his palatial tent, demanding loudly to know what in the devil was going on and why weren't they getting back to work now, damn them!

But words, there were no sufficient words, not in Arabic, not in English. One of the engineers mutely pointed behind him as he fled.

Then Bigham saw the Serpent. He blinked. To his eyes, it seemed as long as a freight train, and its girth so vast that it would have taken two men with linked arms to span it. He blinked again.

Phineas Bigham was a man of the world—this world, not the next. Before beginning his museum he had been familiar with the ways of theatrical performances and exhibitions, carnivals and side-shows, he knew the arts of capturing the imagination of the gullible, he knew how much was owing to the work of illusion. But he, Phineas Bigham, was not to be so easily deceived. So arming himself with common sense and rejecting the delusions of the credulous and superstitious, he brandished his parasol like a sword and advanced toward the apparition, shouting, "Humbuggery! Hoodoo! You won't fool me—not Phineas Bigham!"

But when the Serpent paused, turning toward him, Bigham was considerably disquieted. Illusions, to his knowledge, did not interact with bystanders, not like this. When confronted, they vanished like smoke or became only queer patterns in tea leaves. They did not pause to reconsider their relationship with reality.

This apparition, this Serpent, however, did exactly that, and it came—it seemed to the stunned and disbelieving Bigham—to the rational conclusion that when something the size of it was confronted by something the size of he, that is to say, of a size to be swallowed, that he inevitably should be.

But it was the reek of hot stone, like lava gushing fresh from the interior of the earth, that finally convinced Bigham the Serpent was truly what it seemed to be, and of the reality of his own impending demise. He ran, stumbled and fell to the sand, crawled like a brutish animal on his belly, but the Serpent's maw—vast, gaping, surely leading straight to hell—closed on him, splintered his parasol, engulfed him to the shoulders.

In that instant of decapitation, it was as if a blazing light shone, as if he bore around his neck the blinding glory of the sun itself, borne within a boat of ancient and holy design.

And the Serpent jerked back as if it were burned, shaking its vast head as Bigham sprawled helplessly on the sand. Its tongue flicked out to scent the air. It tasted incense and myrrh, it knew the scent of mummified bodies, burning. It saw the fire in the iron boiler, already red hot, a pit of fire to consume the dead, yet not hotter than the golden barque of the Sun, its god and master.

But the words of the spell bound it now:

> *For thou art the Devourer.*
> *Thou goest forth to meet thine enemies*
> *And thine enemies shalt thou consume.*
> *Thou shalt swallow them up entire.*

And so it did, it swallowed them whole: the great digging thing, the dead and the fiery pit of iron.

Even in the distant cavern the sound of the explosion was audible, and the clatter of once-living stone shards as they fell down on to the desert like a fiery rain.

The Lady embraced her Lord in his chains, crying tears of joy, for the Fiend had been defeated at last, and it was utterly destroyed. After so many thousands of years, from this tormentor at least, he was now finally freed.

"You need go forth at night no longer, my sister, to seek lives. You need not suffer any longer in order to save me. We—you and I and the living—may we rest in peace."

"It was my duty and my joy, to see you spared, beloved."

Yet she knew that she would continue to go forth and seek, for as many thousands of years as necessary. For in the mind of the foreign scribe there had been many images, and some of them were of other gods, who had once been bound and now were freed.

Perhaps she might yet one day find the spell to liberate her Lord, so that they might go forth together, into the night.

*   *   *

The Egyptian Museum in Philadelphia was a complete success, unquestionably the First Wonder of the New World. Men, women, and children from all across the United States came to see it and marvel at what American ingenuity had accomplished to bring such relics of the pharaohs to the City of Brotherly Love. It was fitting, they said, just fitting that the Sphinx and its riddles (they could not keep the Greek Sphinx separate from her Nile counterpart) be preserved in a land where cleverness and ingenuity flourished as they did.

It was a shame, however, about Mister Phineas Bigham. He had, it was clear, quite lost his mind in the desert; what a great and terrible sacrifice he had made for the edification of the American public. These days he wandered the museum's corridors leaning on a cane that had once been the stick of a parasol, but which was now repaired and inseparable from Mister Bigham's hand, no more than one could remove the golden amulet, souvenir of his Egyptian travels, that he kept hidden beneath his vest. He was at once a living monument to what Americans could accomplish abroad and to why they should perhaps not go abroad at all.

For he was, quite simply, tetched. Had he gone to war, been shattered at Gettysburg, they might have understood. But he had only gone into the desert and come home with mummies and sphinxes and pyramids and other such truck, but most remarkably the shards of stone, which—once reassembled by skilled stonemasons—took the form of a gigantic serpent, coiled to strike.

It was, they all agreed, quite a remarkable thing he had found in the sand, nearly as remarkable as the bodiless Sphinx. It was so unnecessary (and in fact so sad) that he should feel compelled to embroider a tale—and a tall tale at that—around it. And insist on its truth, no matter how the experts scoffed and ridiculed his greatest discovery. But children, anyway, adored the story he told as he haunted his museum's halls. And if they were very good children and listened attentively, he might even open his vest and show them the golden amulet he kept there on a chain around his neck, bearing the image of the barque of the sun. For this, he told them, was the only thing that had saved him on the day that the great Serpent swallowed whole the famous Otis Shovel and its boiler, which, stoked to the bursting point with mummies saturated in combustible resins and pitch, had just built up such a very great head of steam.

Norman Partridge loves old movies and scary stories. In a way, this sensational novella is a paean to mummy movies—especially those from 1932 through the 1950s. It's also an outright scary story. The mummy may not really be a mummy, but he is also not playing a role—he is embodying an iconic, if monstrous, mummy. As for death, the afterlife, nightmares, and love . . . well, there's a lot to think about here.

The Mummy's Heart
Norman Partridge

———

Who knows how dreams get started.

But they gear up in all of us, maybe more than anything else. Waking . . . sleeping . . . sometimes it's hard to tell the difference. Sometimes dreams are sweet little ghosts, dancing in our heads like St Nick's visions of sugarplums. Other times they're a hidden nest of scorpions penned up in a bone cage they can never escape, digging stingers into soft brain-meat hour after hour and day after day.

Sugarplums and scorpions. Take your pick. Or maybe grab yourself a full scoop of both. Because we all do that, don't we? Hey, I plead guilty. I've had my share of dreams. Most of them have been bad, but even a guy like me has had a few sweet ones. And every time I've bedded one of those and snuggled up close, a monster movie scorpion came crawling from beneath the sheets and jack-hammered his king-sized stinger straight into my brain.

That's why I don't trust dreams.

That's why I'd rather have nightmares.

Nightmares are straight up. They're honest—what you see is what you get. Dreams are another story. They don't play straight. They take your nights, and they take your days, too. Sometimes they make it hard to tell one from the other. They make you want things and want them bad, and every one of those things comes with a price.

Of course, no one thinks about the price of dreams on the front end of the deal. We all figure we'd pay up, but that's because the price is never self-evident going in. So we spend more time dreaming, as if the act itself will turn the trick. A few of us work hard, building a staircase toward a dream—but people like that come few and far between. Most of us look for a short cut. We toss coins in a fountain or go down on our knees and say a prayer. We look for a quick fix from some mystic force, or one god or another.

After all, that's the dreamer's playbook. Dreamers don't take the hard road. We look for instant gratification. We make a wish, or two, or a dozen . . . as if something as simple as a wish could be a vehicle for a dream. But you never know. The universe is deep, and odds are that someone has to get lucky taking the short road sometime. And wishing only takes a second. Like the man said: *Nothing ventured, nothing gained.*

Nothing. It turns out that's a key word, because the thing most dreamers end up with is a fistful of nothing. And for most of us, that's when the whole idea of *dreams becoming reality* disappears in the rearview mirror. For others, that's when the longer road comes in. It's not a road taken by realists, or workers, or builders. No. It's a madman's road. It's built on books of mystic lore, most of them written by other madmen. It's built on half-truths and faulty suppositions and twisted logic that (by rights) should be nailed through with a stake, boxed up, and buried in a narrow grave. It requires a certain brand of blind faith codified in stories and legends, and it demands a high level of trust in things that are beyond fantastic. Wizards and witches, monsters and myths. The power of an eye of newt, a jackal's hide, or even a child sacrifice.

Most of the time, it's a twisted trail that leads nowhere, except maybe to a cozy rubber room or not-so-cozy prison cell, or (if we're going gothic) a locked attic in the home of some rich relation. But that doesn't happen all the time . . . and it doesn't happen for all madmen.

I say that because I know it's true.

I've seen where those roads can lead.

The night I first walked a madman's trail I was in the wrong place at the wrong time, no more than a passer-by in the darkness. It wasn't my own dream or my own trail, but it was one I took.

Walk any trail and you're bound to soak up the scenery. Might be there's only one way to go, so you follow it. And you put one foot in front of the other, the same way as those who have gone before you, and sometimes the darkness takes hold of you as it did them. Sometimes it draws you in.

You might stay on that trail a long time, always looking for a way off, sure you'll find one eventually.

But walk anywhere long enough, and that place becomes yours.

Especially if you walk alone.

The trail I'm talking about was cut by a mummy.

He did the job on Halloween night in 1963. He was mad as a hatter, and he came out of a plywood pyramid that was (mostly) his own making. And no, he wasn't really a mummy. But that night, he was definitely living the part. Even in the autopsy photos, that shambler from the dark side was a sight to behold.

His name was Charlie Steiner and he was nearly twenty-three years old—too old to be trick-or-treating. And Charlie was big . . . football-lineman big. If you know your old Universal Studios creepers, he was definitely more a product of the Lon Chaney, Jr *engine of destruction* school of mummidom than the Boris Karloff *wicked esthete* branch. But either camp you put him in, he was a long way from the cut-rate dime-store variety when it came to living-dead Egyptians.

Because this mummy wasn't playing a role. He was embodying one.

Which is another way of saying: He was living a dream.

Charlie's bandages were ripped Egyptian cotton, dredged in Nile river-bottom he'd ordered from some Rosicrucian mail-order outfit. He was wound and bound and wrapped tight for the ages, and he wasn't wearing a Don Post mask he'd bought from the back pages of *Famous Monsters of Filmland*. No. Charlie had gone full-on Jack Pierce with the make-up. Furrows and wrinkles cut deep trenches across his face like windblown Saharan dunes, and the patch of mortician's wax that covered one eye was as smooth as a jackal's footprint . . . add it all up and drop it in your treat sack, and just the sight of Charlie would have made Boris Karloff shiver.

And you can round that off to the lowest common denominator and say that Charlie Steiner would have scared just about anyone. Sure, you'd know he was a guy in a costume if you got a look at him. But even on first glance, you might believe this kid was twenty-three going on four thousand.

Look a little closer, you'd see the important part: Charlie Steiner was twenty-three going on insane. There was no dodging that if you got close enough to spot the mad gleam in his eye—the one he hadn't covered with mortician's wax. Or maybe if you spotted his right hand, the one dripping blood . . . the one he'd shorn of a couple fingers with a butcher's cleaver. And then there was his tongue, half of it cut out of his mouth with a switchblade, its purple root bubbling blood.

Charlie wrapped those things up in a jackal's hide he'd bought from the back pages of a big-game hunting magazine with Ernest Hemingway on the cover. Who knew if that hide was real but Charlie believed in it, same way he believed in the little statue of a cat-headed goddess he added to the stash, along with a dozen withered red roses, his own fingers and tongue, and a Hallmark Valentine's Day card.

The same way he believed in the dream those things would deliver to him.

The same way he believed in the madman's trail he was about to travel.

Charlie tossed all those things in the back of the family station wagon (along with one other important ingredient), and he drove down to the local lovers' lane, which wasn't far from his house. At that time of year, the place was deserted. By the time Charlie had things set up to his satisfaction, he had swallowed so much of his own blood that he might as well have eaten three raw steaks. But he kept on moving—readying his incantation mummy-slow . . . sure but steady. Just the way you'd expect a mummy to do business, moving like the sands of time.

Just the fact that Charlie could do that was a little slice of a miracle all by itself. Whittling himself down like that, how'd he even keep walking? Chalk it up to drugs he stole from the VA hospital. All through high school, Charlie worked in an after-school program up there, pushing guys around in wheelchairs. He learned about pain management during that time, and he'd continued working as a part-time attendant after he graduated. In other words, Charlie knew what he was doing with the needle and the knife.

So Charlie Steiner was walking on a cloud that night. Or an imaginary dune overlooking an Egyptian oasis, with jackals howling in his head and a mad priest's plan in his heart. On this single night, at long last, he'd finally become the sum of his dreams . . . or maybe a dream *personified*. And what wasn't locked up in his own skin was wrapped in that mojo hide . . . or waiting, bound, beneath a blanket in the back of the station wagon.

Put it all together and it was an offering, a single wish boiled up, and Charlie had a place for it.

Not in the plywood temple he'd abandoned. No. His place was out in the night and under the Halloween moon . . . just a stone's throw from lovers' lane.

Beneath the same stars that shone down on Egypt.

If you've seen those old mummy movies, you know something about mummies and their dreams. And Charlie knew that, too. He knew those movies backwards and forwards, and he knew that mummy was always after the same dream. Kharis was looking for a reincarnated princess, Ananka, who died on the altar of a dark Egyptian god and left Kharis alone to pay the price for their twin blasphemies. Which, when you strip the Hollywood mysticism and curses and *high priests of Karnak* window-dressing off the tale, means one thing: Kharis died for love, and he came back from the dead looking for a second eternal helping of the very same thing.

Pure love. Eternal love. Love that didn't backslide.

That's what Kharis was after, and almost every knock-off mummy who came in his wake wanted the same thing. That's what Charlie Steiner was after, too, and his madness started on the day he wrapped his needs in the bandages of the most accessible mythos he could find. And while that's a ticket that buys us an ingress to Charlie's story, it's a long way from the whole deal, because there was a lot of other mumbo jumbo that Charlie Steiner believed. But eternal love was the final destination Charlie had in mind, and the path that led to it traveled through Egypt and Hollywood. As crazy as he was, that's all Charlie really wanted. The quest for same lay beneath the insanity, and the magic, and the bad things he'd done and was about to do.

Who knows.

Maybe the whole thing came to him in a dream.

Of course, I didn't understand any of that back then. That's because I was just a kid, out on the prowl on Halloween night in 1963, looking for candy and ready (or so I thought) for whatever came my way.

We were out trick-or-treating for the very last time before our teenage years closed the door on the holiday. My brother Roger and me and Roger's best friend. On the loose without the parents, or any adult supervision at all. I was twelve, Roger was thirteen. We were a pair of Irish twins, as they used to say back in the day, brothers born just eleven months apart.

Me, I was dressed up like a soldier—mostly courtesy of the local army surplus store, but with a coat my dad had worn in Korea. Roger was a baseball player. Yankee pinstripes just like Roger Maris, and a Louisville Slugger, too. The preacher's kid who lived next door to us was a vampire. Hair slicked back with Brylcreem, he looked like the greaser son of Bela Lugosi himself.

Of course, our parents had given us ground rules for the night. Stay on the streets. Don't go anywhere the street lights don't shine. But we had our own agenda, and we got down to business with it once our treat sacks were full. And that put us on the edge of town, where the black-top ended at a rust-flecked twenty-foot stretch of guard rail capped with a NO TRESPASSING sign.

Beyond that was a dirt trail that twisted through a eucalyptus grove. And beyond the grove was a cattail-choked hollow, a place called Butcher's Lake. Maybe that was the only place for us to go that night, because by then we wanted to find out if there was something more to Halloween than knocking on doors and getting candy. We were looking for something a little more exciting.

Butcher's Lake seemed like the best place to find it. Though there were a few ghost stories about the place, it wasn't named for a murder spree or anything quite that exciting. No. The far side of the lake just happened to mark the border of a couple of neighboring cattle ranches, and that's how it got its name. The only other thing about Butcher's Lake was that it was the local lovers' lane, but by the time Halloween rolled around that action had pretty much shut down for the season.

That night, it was ghosts we were after.

So Butcher's Lake was where we went.

That's where we found Charlie Steiner.

Or the thing he'd become on Halloween night.

Or the thing he most wanted to be.

As soon as we climbed over that rusty guard rail, Roger's friend, the preacher's kid, said, "I don't know, Rodge." He said that practically right away, before we took a single step on that trail that led through the eucalyptus grove, as if he was already primed to turn tail and head for home. But my brother gave him a look. "We've been planning this for weeks," Roger said. "We're not turning chicken now."

Rodge meant it. Every word. Like I said, he was only thirteen, but he'd grown up on John Wayne movies and TV cowboys and that was how he operated. If you didn't grow up back then, it seems impossibly archaic now. But in those days, they built us to do what we set out to do, and finish the job. Or, as our old man always said, "If you talk the talk, you walk the walk."

So we set out, putting one foot in front of the other. Roger took the lead on that snaking path through the eucalyptus grove. He had a flashlight, but he didn't turn it on—we were counting on the moon that night, and we didn't want to spook anyone who might be down by the lake. Anyway, the trees grew close in the grove. Straight. Thick-bodied. Tall. And the moon was full, but you wouldn't have known it. Those eucalyptus trees blocked out the light and made everything you heard seem twice as loud.

The castanet rattle of dry leaves.

The soughing wind tearing snakeskin flaps of bark from straight, smooth trunks.

The short whispering breaths of three kids on the prowl.

Ahead, near the lake, the sounds were moist and alive. Crickets cut their music in the night. Frogs croaked a hundred yards away, where the trees gave ground to a muddy little patch of beach that rimmed the first wall of cattails.

And there was another sound just ahead . . . one that hung over the night like a shroud. It was enough to make us slow our pace as we approached the last stand of eucalyptus trees, and I remember telling myself that it was probably just the sound of the wind cutting through the cattails.

It might have been . . . but it wasn't.

Chanting. That was the sound waiting for us down by the water.

Bright moonlight shone over that muddy little beach. It washed in waves, as if buffeted by the winds and the clouds—silver light lapping over the dark water and the sandy banks of the lake, each little glimmer of moonlight washing in rhythm to the sound that I'd mistaken for a soughing wind.

Because now I knew what that sound was. Someone was down there, ahead of us in the night. He stood before the lake and the swaying cattails, silhouetted by the glow of the moon, watching the water. We didn't know it then, but he was watching for a sign.

Of course, there were a lot of things we didn't know then. All we knew was what we saw, and we couldn't believe it as the moonlight spilled over the figure and turned that silhouette into something we could recognize.

A big thing, pacing back and forth along that shore. Wrapped in bandages.

Gray and silent as a mountain of cobwebs.

A mummy. At Butcher's Lake. On Halloween night.

The preacher's kid said something, and Roger cut him off with a sharp whisper. The monster didn't see us. We stood frozen at the edge of the grove. Every once in a while he'd stop and stare at the water, but there was nothing waiting for him except the sound of his own chanting rolling over the surface. The moon washed over it and spilled a reflection on the murky waves like a spotlight that could open a hole into a black brimming pit. And that mummy would stare at that white hole in that black sky, and the white hole in the water, and the emptiness of both seemed to drive him mad. He stared up at the heavens, and he swung his free arm like a crane, and the wrinkled fist on the end of it was like a wrecking ball ready to tear down the universe.

Of course, we didn't know the reason for that then. We had no idea that it was Charlie Steiner beneath those bandages. We didn't know he was casting a spell to that dark water and that bright moon and whatever gods or demons worked their magic in it, tossing the contents of his jackal-hide mojo bag into Butcher's Lake. We didn't know he was waiting for a sign that would tell him it was time to conduct the most difficult and dangerous part of his spell. We didn't know he was trying to raise a dream woman from the depths of Butcher's Lake. All we knew was that his pendulum wrecking-ball fist was swinging in a way that told us he was coming up empty, and he wasn't happy about it, and that there was going to be hell to pay.

From some god we hadn't heard of. Or some devil. Or the universe itself.

Or maybe us.

Then Charlie Steiner started screaming, and it got worse.

I'll never forget the sound of that tongueless scream. Even though we were hidden from view in the treeline twenty feet away, I'll never forget the sight of it, either. The mummy turned toward us, and his cobweb lips opened into a black hole that even a full bucket of moonlight couldn't illuminate, and more black spilled out of it, dripping blood that ran in rivulets through the irrigation-ditch wrinkles that covered his chin. And then came the sound—a buzz-saw screech that descended into a roar so heavy with anguish it could have made a deaf man jump up and take notice.

"Oh, God," the preacher's kid said, and just that fast he was gone.

We didn't even hear him running back to the road. The mummy was coming toward us now, still screaming, taking one sloughing step after another. At first I thought he'd spotted us for sure, but then he suddenly reversed course and headed toward the deep shadows near a thick stand of cattails.

At that moment, we had no idea what he was up to. But it came clear later. With his three-fingered hand, Charlie Steiner was ready to grasp for the final straw that might seal the deal he'd tried to cut with the powers of darkness.

That meant he'd gotten down to the portion of night that was really bad business.

The worst.

The mummy stopped at the rear of a station wagon. Swaying just a bit, as if it were fighting gravity itself. Then his fist swung down, and the tailgate dropped, and a light came on in the rear of the vehicle.

We couldn't see much by that light, but we could see the mummy bending low. He reached inside, grabbing for something. There was a muffled scream as he took hold of it, and something tumbled to the sand.

"Sweet Jesus," Roger said. "It's a little girl."

The mummy bent low, staring down at the prone figure before him. He wasn't chanting any more.

Three words crossed his ruined tongue and bubbled over his bloody lips, and they were the only words he said that night that we truly understood:

"Dream . . . wish . . . *sacrifice!*"

The girl was nine, maybe ten. In the moonlight, I could see that her ankles and wrists were bound with ropes. And she wore a princess mask—the cheap plastic kind you found at a drugstore. Expressionless, with black hair cut straight across in bangs, and lips as red as red could be. That mask was taped to her head, thick swatches of sticky plastic stuck to her own black hair as if she'd been mummified herself.

If she hadn't screamed, I would have thought she was dead. She lay there on the ground, gasping now, the breath knocked out of her. She couldn't have moved if she wanted to. I stared at her, still unable to move myself. Roger was staring at her, too.

"We've got to stop him!" Roger said.

He wasn't whispering, and he was moving forward, flicking on his flashlight as he advanced.

"Hey!" Roger shouted. "Stop!"

The mummy whirled, holding up a hand against the bright beam. For the first time we saw that he truly was as gray as a grave, except for the places he was black-red. One hand was missing a couple fingers and dripped blood. More gore spilled from the thing's mouth—it looked like he'd been chewing razor blades.

Given all that, it was amazing how fast he moved when he saw Roger coming. One big arm swung down, and he snatched up the girl, and his bandaged feet kicked up gouts of sand that hissed against the October wind as he walked toward the edge of the lake.

His back was to us now, and he raised the girl over his head. "He's going to toss her in!" Roger said. "He's going to drown her!" I started across the beach, following Roger. He'd already covered ground. He'd dropped the flashlight and was closing on the mummy's back with his Louisville Slugger in his hands.

Someone else was coming, too. At least I hoped there was, because I heard police sirens rising in the distance. But I couldn't be sure they were headed in our direction, and there was no time to waste. The mummy already had that girl over his head, and before we knew it she was sailing through the dark night.

A hollow splash, and the lake took her. All I could think of as the water closed over her head was the black and bloody pit of that mummy's mouth snapping closed. And then the mummy whirled. Perhaps it was the sound of the sirens that brought him around, or maybe he heard Roger racing toward him. But that wrecking-ball fist of his swung out, and it banged my brother to the side.

For a moment, Roger was airborne. He hit the sand rolling. Then he came up, but he'd lost the baseball bat in the fall. By that time I was already halfway across the beach, splitting the distance against the mummy to come at him from the other side.

"No!" Roger yelled. "Get the girl! She'll drown!"

I was close to the mummy now. Close enough to see the crazy gleam in his eye. People have asked if I realized that he was a man in a costume, or if I thought he was real. To tell the truth, I can't remember any of that. I only knew that he was dangerous, and that if he had a chance he'd kill both my brother and me.

And that's what he tried to do. His fist flashed out again. I ducked and dodged the blow, trying to give Roger a moment to recover the bat. The mummy lurched forward, gaining ground for another strike, but I'd given my brother the moment he needed. Roger was up again, charging the mummy with his Louisville Slugger. As I turned toward the lake I heard it land once, and the mummy grunted. Another blow struck home and the mummy groaned, but I couldn't afford to look behind me. I already had my eye on the water and the dull moonlight washing those little bands of wave.

I searched the surface for a ripple . . . any sign of the girl as I tried to remember where she had gone under.

I should have had my eyes on the shadows.

Because the mummy was still coming for me, even as Roger struck him again with the bat.

He was coming with one fist raised like a wrecking ball.

And the sirens were louder now. Definitely coming our way. I was skirting the shore, moving quickly, when I realized that I had almost run into the rear of the station wagon. I got my hands up before I slammed into it, and then the mummy's fist cut a path through the shadows.

I never saw it. I never heard it. I can't even remember the first blow striking me. I know it caught me from behind, and low on the base of my neck, because I still get a little *click* in my top vertebrae anytime I turn my head to the left. Anyway, I staggered and spun on my heel like a drunk.

Roger bashed him again, but it didn't do any good. The next blow crashed against my forehead, just above my left eyebrow. It opened a two-inch gash. Not that I knew I was bleeding . . . or falling. I don't even remember falling into the lake. But the next thing I knew, I was underwater. I came up coughing a mouthful of sludge that tasted like something a frog had vomited up. For a moment I thought the mummy's fist was coming at me again, but I realized it was only a clutch of cattails waving in the wind.

The moonlight shone down, riding black ripples. My stomach roiled, and I retched. The sound of prowl car sirens still rode the night, but I saw no light cutting through the eucalyptus grove, and no light on the beach.

I didn't see Roger or the mummy. Apart from the sirens, there was no sign of activity behind me. It was as if they'd disappeared. And then I heard a splash out there in the darkness, somewhere near a large stand of cattails that cut in from the shore, and I thought maybe it was Roger.

Sure. It had to be. Maybe Roger had dropped the mummy with his bat. He'd dived in to join the search, and now he was out there in the lake, looking for the girl.

"Roger!" I shouted. "She went in over here . . . over by the road!" I didn't get a reply. Maybe the splash I'd heard was Roger going under, looking for the girl. One thing was for sure, if I was right and he'd found her, he would have called out. But I hadn't heard anything.

And I didn't hear anything now, except for the sirens drawing near.

Quickly, I pulled myself on to the muddy bank and kicked off my shoes. Then I shucked my father's jacket and sucked a deep breath, and dove back into that cold water.

The girl was still out there.

Maybe my brother was, too.

Hitting that water the second time was like swallowing an iceberg. My chest froze up, but my thoughts cleared as that icy black water shocked my brain alive. I didn't know how much time had passed between the mummy tossing the little girl into the lake and the time I went in after her. All I knew was that enough seconds—or maybe minutes—had been burned off the clock that the little girl couldn't have too many left.

I knew some other things, too. As big as he was, the mummy couldn't have thrown the little girl far. I had a rough idea where she had to be, because I'd made my dive from the spot where I thought the mummy had been standing when he heaved her in. But the water was deeper there than I'd expected. The sand didn't slope down from the water's edge the way a beach does. It was a sheer drop-off from sandy shore into murky lake—maybe a foot or a foot-and-a-half drop in some places—and the water was deep enough that I barely skimmed the sludgy bottom when I dove in.

I couldn't see a thing, of course. Even on a sunny day, that water was nothing but thick murk. I swam forward, my hands sweeping before me, but all my fingers found was slick bottom and broken cattail shafts.

I covered ten feet that way—maybe fifteen. Then I came up for air, turned, and immediately dove again.

This time I reversed course, swimming back towards the shore, covering the area to my left. My hands sweeping out, sure I'd hit something solid any second. I didn't find anything—not even a junked spare tire. Just that sludgy bottom and rotting slime a catfish wouldn't want in its belly.

Again I came up for air, breathing harder now. I was closer to the shore, and I could stand. A case of shivers rattled up my spine, and I was shaking now. The cold . . . the blows to the head . . . whatever the reason, I nearly lost it and passed out.

But I caught myself. I wasn't going to let that happen. "Roger!" I called. "Are you out there? Did you find her?" No answer.

I sucked another deep breath, but it came up in a wet cough that seemed like a slap against the quiet night. I cleared my throat and got another breath down and held it. It was only then that I realized the sound of sirens was gone.

Just that fast another sound replaced it.

The sound of a shotgun blasting away in the night. I didn't have time to listen.

That little girl was down there somewhere. I had to find her.

She's alive, I told myself, and even in that moment I knew it was a wish as much as a prayer.

She's alive.

Apart from that wish, I can't say what I thought about as I searched for the girl. Diving, coming up for air, diving again. It happened a long time ago, though I still dream about it sometimes. Over the years, those dreams have come and gone, but they always seem to come around . . . the same way that night has never left me.

Sometimes I dream about that mummy, too. And sometimes I think about him in the light of day. The mummy . . . Charlie Steiner . . . in my head, they're a pair. I don't know what emotions were squirming in

Charlie's guts by the time he found his way through the eucalyptus grove. He certainly wasn't walking out of there with a black-magic dreamgirl on his arm, the way he'd imagined. I'm sure anger and betrayal boiled in his crazy brain . . . maybe even fear. But all that's speculation. The only thing I know for sure is that by the time Charlie turned his back on Butcher's Lake his fate was sealed, and in more ways than he could ever imagine.

Because the preacher's kid hadn't chickened out. He had more stones than Roger or I had imagined. He'd run to the nearest house, banged on the door, and told the owner to call the cops because there was a crazy man loose in the woods.

God knows how the sheriff and his deputy reacted when they rolled in and caught their first glimpse of that bloody mountain of cobwebs coming out of the trees. Of course, I've heard the stories over and over. And, like I said, I've had dreams, too. And it's the dreams I see when I picture the scene in my mind's eye: *The mummy staggering backward when the patrol car lights hit him, then realizing he had nowhere to retreat because the cops were already out of the car. Sheriff Cross and Deputy Myers barking orders, drawing down. The mummy's black pit of a mouth opening like a sinkhole, and words and blood spilling out that no one ever remembered because his wrecking-ball fist was rising in the air as he lumbered forward, charging the cops. Then the sharp bark of gunfire, and the thunder of shotgun blasts, and a rain of blood and bone and flesh slapping against a straight and tall eucalyptus trunk as that bloody mountain of meat avalanched to the ground, leaving a wake of shotgunned Egyptian cotton fibers floating on the October wind like its very own ghost.*

You kill something that dead, you don't worry about it getting up again no matter what it looks like. At least, that's the way Sheriff Cross and Deputy Myers saw it. They weren't going to worry about a dead kid in a Halloween costume. And that's what they saw when they looked at Charlie Steiner's corpse. That's all they saw. A dead kid in a Halloween costume.

But that didn't mean they were done for the night. Cross and Myers worked their way through the eucalyptus grove, guns raised, not sure what they'd find when they reached Butcher's Lake. And the first thing they found was me, still diving in that black water, still looking for the girl in the princess mask. Sheriff Cross jumped into the water and grabbed me, and he always tells me I put up one hell of a fight, even though I was just a kid. I didn't want to give up the search. I told him the whole story. Practically screamed it in his face. The mummy . . . the little girl with the princess mask . . . Roger and I fighting the mummy. All of it.

The sheriff went into the lake himself that night, and he found nothing. Later a diver went in, and the next morning they dragged the bottom. But they didn't find any trace of a little girl, dead or alive.

They did find a body, just after dawn, but it wasn't underwater. It was a boy's body, and it was hidden in a stand of cattails.

The kid was wearing a New York Yankees uniform. It was my brother Roger, and he'd been beaten to death. *Blunt object trauma* was the phrase they used.

That could have meant a wrecking-ball fist had taken him down. Or it could have meant the mummy had used Roger's own Louisville Slugger to finish the job.

They found the Slugger just a few feet from my brother's dead body.

It's the one thing of Roger's that I still have.

Once people learned what Charlie Steiner had been up to in the weeks and months before that fateful Halloween night, they discovered he sure enough fit the m.o. for a kid who'd gone nuts enough to dress up like a Halloween boogeyman and charge a pair of fully armed cops.

Behind Charlie's house—which was just this side of the boondocks, and not too far from the dirt road that skirted the lake—Sheriff Cross discovered a path chopped through heavy brush. It was a little wider than a deer run, and it snaked up a hill. At the top of that hill was Charlie's own private temple. Google the name of this town and the word "mummy," and you'll find pictures of it. Some people say Charlie built it, that it was some kind of plywood pyramid, but I've seen it inside and out and I can tell you that's an exaggeration. It was (and still is) a simple A-frame design—that's how the pyramid stories got started—but it had four sides. And, sure, Charlie did paint Egyptian-style pictures and hieroglyphs on it back in the day, but all that stuff faded away a long time ago.

To tell the truth, there wasn't much *inside* to the place at all, then or now. One large room with a narrower loft cubby up above, the kind of place that used to sit in a far-off corner of a large property so the owner would have a hideout with just enough space to get into some trouble out of sight of the main house.

And maybe that's what the place was in the old days, when the A-frame had been in better repair. The whole property had made the slide to rack and ruin by the time Charlie's folks bought it. But in the old days—who knows? I've heard the old road along the swamp was once used by bootleggers who wanted to skirt the two-lane county highway on delivery runs. Hey, anything's possible. Histories get lost—for houses, for places . . . even for people.

But the little slice of history made by Charlie Steiner in his A-frame hideaway wasn't lost at all. No, after the incident at Butcher's Lake, the contents of Charlie's own private temple were photographed, cataloged, and filed, using the best police science of the day. Examine that stuff today and it looks like it belonged in a clubhouse for an obsessed monsterkid. The walls were papered with one-sheets from the old Universal creepers, and there were lobby cards and eight-by-tens of Lon Chaney, Jr doing his thing as Kharis. Comic books featuring an army of Kharis wannabes, too. Paperback novels, plus a couple magazines tipping monsterkids to Hollywood make-up secrets. There was even a stack of 8mm monster movies and a cheap projector. Remember, this was 1963—a long time before VHS, let alone DVD.

There was other stuff, too. Charlie had taken Woodshop 1, 2, and 3 in high school, and he'd learned enough to build himself his very own Egyptian sarcophagus. A couple professors from the State U came out and looked at it, and they said Charlie might have made something of himself as an archaeology student if he'd taken another path. They analyzed some other Egypt-ware he had in his little hideaway, too. There was a brazier that looked like a real-deal museum piece, a collection of little jars with odd-smelling oils, and a box with a bunch of leaves the guys at the local nursery couldn't identify. The profs from State U fingered the brazier as a knockoff piece of bric-a-brac from the days of the King Tut craze in the 1920s, and the carved box came from the same era, but they didn't have any more luck identifying those leaves than the nurserymen did. A rumor spread that Charlie had himself a stash of marijuana, but surely the profs would have known what that was. Even though Mickey Spillane always bumped Jack Kerouac out of the paperback racks around here, we weren't that far off the map. There's no doubt a couple of college guys would have known reefer when they saw it.

But it wasn't the drugs (or possibility of same) that kept the story pot bubbling. No. The mummy mythos did that job. Of course, there weren't too many people around here who knew much about Kharis and his eternal search for a reincarnated princess, but that changed PDQ. The local all-night TV station took a clue and started running those old movies on the *Late Late Show*, and a lot of folks stayed up watching, looking for answers. Not long after that, we had a town full of experts. You'd hear people sitting around in coffee shops discussing reincarnation, black magic, and all the rest of it. A couple of tabloids picked up the story, too. One of them ran a piece called "The Terror of Butcher Lake." That's where the name came from, and it stuck.

Sheriff Cross and Deputy Myers became mummy experts, too. Just like everyone else, they coffee'd up and watched those Universal movies on the *Late Late Show*. After the mummy marathon aired, Cross even borrowed the prints from the TV station and ran them on the big screen at the local Bijou for some of the guys from the D.A.'s office, the state shrinks, and a few other invitees. God knows what that crowd made of them. I've always wondered if they just sat there stunned, or if they ate popcorn and had themselves a ball. I especially wonder about Sheriff Cross—after all, he'd gunned down the thing. It must have been something to see its twin take loads of buckshot and keep on coming, even if it was just a Hollywood shadow show up on the big screen.

Of course, the Hollywood part of the equation was just the sizzle for the story, not the steak. The inventory of Charlie's temple didn't stop there, because there was more locked up in his personal madhouse besides the movie stuff. There were books about black magic, too. A stack of them. And there were notebooks Charlie had written with lots of missing pages, and other books with whole chapters cut out.

But by then, it really didn't matter.

After all, Charlie Steiner was dead.

For the next few weeks, I told the story over and over. My parents didn't let me talk to any reporters, of course. It's hard to believe with the way things are now. These days people spill their guts anywhere and everywhere, but that didn't happen back then. You kept your business to yourself unless the cops told you otherwise, and that's the way we played it. I talked to a couple of doctors, and I talked to someone from the district attorney's office. Of course, I talked to Sheriff Cross, too.

I told all of them the same story. How Roger and me and the preacher's kid had come across the mummy—or Charlie Steiner. How he seemed to be working some kind of magic spell, and how he'd tossed a bound girl into the water after saying something about dreams, and wishes, and sacrifice.

It really was a simple story, and it didn't change. But every time I told it, the whole thing always came back to one question that punched a hole in the whole deal: Where was the little girl? They never did find her body in the lake. And, sure, there had been a couple young girls reported missing in neighboring towns during the preceding months, but that didn't mean anything. After all, if Charlie had tossed a missing girl into Butcher's Lake, they should have found her body. Drowned girls didn't just disappear into thin air.

Pretty soon, that girl in the princess mask was all the doctors wanted to talk about. I can't really blame them. After all, I'd been busted up pretty good that night. I had a concussion. I was still having headaches several weeks after the fact. My sentences would run off to nowhere, and my thoughts would run to places I didn't like. I wasn't sleeping too well and I admit I had problems putting things together after a while.

Not the story, but other things.

The story was always there in my head. The story was always the same.

I knew what I saw and heard that night, and I was sure it happened just the way I remembered it.

But, in the end, it didn't matter what I thought. The doctors brought in a headshrinker from upstate, and he put the word out that I was having trouble separating reality from fantasy. Something about disassociation, or misassociation, or something like that. All this, because I stuck to my story about a little girl who no one could find. That, and the fact that sometimes I talked about a mummy, and didn't talk about Charlie Steiner at all.

Like it mattered.

Like that thing hadn't been real for me on Halloween night.

For most people, that delivered the entire episode to the closing gate. Sure, something had happened out there in the darkness, and my brother was dead. But as far as the state shrinks and the DA were concerned, they already had the culprit responsible for my brother's murder. That kid's name was Charlie Steiner, and Charlie wasn't talking to anyone. He'd died in his very own boogeyman suit. The undertaker didn't have to do much work on him—Charlie's belly had been hollowed out by the sheriff's shotgun, and there weren't enough guts left in his carcass to fill a whore's nylon. So they sluiced the blood off Charlie and scraped off his make-up and dressed him up in a suit that had already been a couple sizes too small on him a few years before. Didn't matter, because there was less of Charlie now. His family (such as it was) didn't even hold a funeral. They wanted Charlie in the ground double-quick, and they didn't have any money anyway. So the county took care of things, and they did a first-class, bang-up job.

I've heard that some of Charlie's wounds leaked so bad you could hear the formaldehyde sloshing around in his plywood coffin when they hauled him off to the local Potter's Field. They dropped him in a hole and covered him over. They didn't even put a tombstone on Charlie's grave, though it didn't take long for most of the kids in town to figure out where it was.

Pretty soon guys were daring each other to climb the wrought-iron fence and take a piss on old Charlie, the trick being to do the job without the terror of Butcher's Lake reaching up and pulling them down to hell by the short hairs. And not too long after that . . . well, people have short memories, don't they?

They forget.

They forgot the Terror of Butcher's Lake.

They forgot Charlie Steiner.

They forgot my brother Roger.

And life moved on.

For most people, anyway.

For most people, that's the way they like it.

The story ends, and they turn the page.

So life moved on, the way it does. I finished junior high and started high school. But everything I did, I figured Roger would have done better. It made me feel kind of like a shadow, two steps behind a guy who wasn't even there to cast it any more.

Fresh out of high school, I got drafted. Uncle Sam sent me to Vietnam, and I stayed there four years. That was the first thing I felt I did on my own, so it didn't seem like such a bad deal to me. Of course, I couldn't leave everything behind. I took Roger's Louisville Slugger with me. Sometimes I used it on scruffy baseball fields . . . most of the larger bases had ball fields. Sometimes I took it into the jungle, but I never used it there. It was just something to help me keep away the bad dreams.

Funny to be in a jungle and dream about a desert, or a mummy, but it happened.

Over and over, night after night.

But after a couple years, I stopped dreaming about the mummy. I dreamed about the jungle instead, and the war. I was crazy enough to think that marked some kind of progress, but looking back on it maybe all I did was trade one bad dream for another.

Then I came home and slipped back into the world. I borrowed a car, drove around. Started doing some of the same things I'd done before I left. And then the dreams started to change again.

I dreamed about my brother, and Butcher's Lake.

And the girl in the princess mask. And the mummy.

I'd wake up sweating, with my head feeling like it was ready to crack. Finally one morning I didn't go for a drive. I started looking at the newspaper classifieds instead. Figured it was time to find work, something new that would put the past behind me. For a while I even thought about college, because I could have used my GI Bill benefits.

But that whole plan changed one morning with a couple of knocks on the front door. It was Sheriff Cross. Older and grayer, but still built like a guy who could hold his own with just about anyone.

"Hey, Sergeant. Welcome home."

"Thanks." I knew I should have said more, since I was practically a kid the last time I'd seen him, but I couldn't think of anything else to say.

"Got a minute?" he asked. "I've got something here I'd like to show you."

"Sure."

Sheriff Cross had a new leather wallet. He flipped it open. There was a deputy sheriff's badge inside. He flipped the wallet closed and handed it to me. I took it from him.

"I think you're the guy I'm looking for," he said. "What do you think?"

"I don't need to think. I'm in."

"That's what I like to hear. We've got some paperwork to fill out. An application . . . some other stuff. You'll have six weeks up north in the training academy. You'll have to pass a physical, some other tests. You can talk to the other guys about that. They can let you know what's coming."

"Sounds good."

"I thought it would. Now let's go down to the cop shop and I'll introduce you around. This is going to work out fine."

The town had changed while I was gone.

Actually, that's an understatement.

What had really changed was the whole damn country.

It seemed like a century had passed since the lockstep America of the fifties. The sixties had definitely made their mark. And even though it was 1973, the sixties were holding on, the same way the fifties had right up until the time that JFK took that bullet down in Dallas. Even in our little corner of the world, it might as well have been the Summer of Love. Grass and acid and downers had come to town. Hair got longer; guitars got fuzzy. No one remembered Elvis or Mickey Spillane. Truth be told, most of my contemporaries didn't remember Jack Kerouac, either.

But in the heart of the town, and the heart of America, not much was different. Same stores, same people, same crew cuts on the older guy who held the keys to the store. Every now and then some kid got hired, and there were a few twenty-somethings checking groceries at the market or selling TVs over at Sears or working down at the bank in the teller's cage. But they came and went. They didn't stick around long enough to wear out the linoleum or pocket the keys to the store, like the old guard had. For them, it didn't seem like ringing up corn flakes was a lifelong ambition, or moving a weekly quota of Magnavox consoles, or stamping deposits in the Christmas Club accounts. No. The twenty-somethings would catch a whiff of sweeter possibilities and move on, and the old guys would stub out their cigs and put up a HELP WANTED sign, and some fresh face would take the bait and give the forty-hour grind a test-drive while the old guard grumbled about training another kid who wasn't going to stay the course.

So, in that way, things were pretty much the same, it was just that the faces changed more often. Tote things in those terms, and you'd say that all that had really changed were the clothes and the haircuts and the vices. But around the corners, the town had gotten a little frayed.

Take Charlie Steiner's house. Charlie's mother had passed away when I was in high school. Then one day his father packed up his pickup and left the place behind. The house sat vacant the whole time I was in 'Nam, and it was the "20" for one of the first calls I rolled on after Ben Cross pinned a badge on my chest.

I still remember that night. Wind rustling through overgrown trees around the place as I pulled up the drive, no lights inside but a fire in the fireplace that cast flickering ribbons against windows dull with grime. I killed my lights as I cut off the dirt road that went out toward Butcher's Lake, and I killed the patrol cruiser's engine ten feet after that. We'd had reports of stoners using the place as a crash pad, and I didn't want to leave them a way out if they had wheels.

The walk to the house was a long one. Not because I was worried about what I'd find inside. For the first time since the jungle I felt edgy. I mean, really edgy. I had a .38 strapped to my leg, but what I wanted in my hand was an M-16, or even Roger's Louisville Slugger. Something familiar, something I could trust. It was a weird feeling, as if yesterday's baggage were ready to bury me as deep as Charlie Steiner, right along with the new future I was building. I felt like I was on Charlie's turf, and even though I knew he was six feet under in Potter's Field, that night he cast a long shadow.

Lucky for me, Charlie's shadow got shorter once I took charge of the situation. I banged through the front door and hit the occupants with my flashlight beam. A couple of the stoners rabbited through a back window, and two girls spread out on a mattress in front of the fireplace were so toasted on downers they didn't even wake up. It was almost comical. Right away I forgot all about Charlie. I nudged those girls and shook them, and after about ten minutes I even got them up walking, but it was tough to manage the both of them. Before I could do anything about it one would wander off and find her way back to the mattress, and when I went to grab her, the other stumbled out the door and fell asleep in the weeds in front of the place.

I called it in to Jack Morrison, who was on duty back at the cop shop. He said he'd roll out and give me a hand with the girls. In the meantime, he told me to check out the rest of the place. Right away I knew what he meant.

He didn't mean the house.

He meant Charlie Steiner's pyramid.

By that time I'd cooled out. Still, you never know what you'll find, and I'd tangled enough with Charlie in my dreams that I wasn't looking forward to a walk up his own personal madman's trail. But it was my job. So I checked behind the main house and found the little deer-run path that led up to the A-frame. No lights out there except my flashlight, and the wind had died. If there had been a noise, I certainly would have heard it. A mouse skittering across the porch. A mummy's padded footfall. Anything. I would have heard it.

But I didn't hear anything that night.

I walked up to the A-frame.

I swung open the door.

I didn't know what to expect.

My flashlight beam skittered across the floor and over the walls. But it was just an empty room. There was nothing there at all. And that taught me something . . . at least for a while. Even though it was a lesson that didn't stick, I held on to it—and that moment—for a few months.

For a while, it convinced me everything would be okay.

For a while, I actually believed that dreams were ephemeral.

About a month later, the sheriff called me up on a Sunday morning and asked me to go to breakfast down at the diner. Ben told me he'd bought the old Steiner place, and was thinking he'd fix it up and turn it into a rental. Maybe even look into moving into the place himself when he hit retirement age and was ready to get a little farther out of town. He said it seemed like a good investment, and that he'd make some money if nothing else.

"Sounds like a sweet deal," I said. "I'm going to bank as much of my check as I can this year. Maybe one of these days I'll have enough to start looking around for a place myself."

"That's a good plan," Ben said. "Can't be easy being under your parents' roof again."

"Well, I'm probably going to grab a studio apartment after I get a few more checks, but paying rent will definitely cut down on the savings. Can't have it both ways, though."

"Maybe I can help you out with that."

"How do you figure?"

Ben took a sip of coffee. "The Steiner place needs a lot of work. I'm looking for someone to help me out with it. Way I see it, you could live there rent-free. Clear the brush around the place. Do some carpentry. Some painting. I'd come in on the weekends and help out. How's that sound?"

I didn't know what to say, but I knew I had to say something. "Well . . . hey, it's hard to turn down free rent."

Ben nodded and set down his coffee cup. "Look, I know you have a history with Charlie Steiner, and this was his house. Maybe this isn't the best move for you. If you have any second thoughts—"

"I know what you're saying, Ben . . . but I'll probably always have second thoughts. But I can't bury the past, and maybe I shouldn't try. Maybe what I need to do is confront it. You know, come to terms with it. And maybe working on that house will help me do that."

"Okay . . . but if it doesn't work out—"

"Then we'll cross that bridge when we come to it."

We shook on the deal, and that was that. I moved into the Steiner house, and fortunately the night with the crash-pad girls was still fresh in my mind. I told myself everything would be okay, just as it had been that night, and if it wasn't . . . well, I'd find a way to tell Ben that it wasn't going to work, even if that was the last thing I wanted to do after the conversation we'd had.

The first week, I lay awake at night listening to every creak and moan the old house made, and it seemed like those old fears had moved in with me. But eventually, spending so much time in that old house made the worries I'd had about moving into the place seem as out-of-style as a teenager with a crew cut. And it got easier once I started to work on the place. I took one thing at a time, and focused in on each project. A few weeks went by, and I'd cleared all the brush around the house, even chopped a wider path up to Charlie's pyramid so I could get up there with a wheelbarrow and some tools. I figured I'd use that pyramid as practice before I started on the main house.

To tell the truth, at first I was tempted to talk to Ben about knocking the pyramid down. After all, that had really been Charlie's place. But if part of this deal was about confronting Charlie Steiner, then I knew I couldn't do that. So I decided to work on it first.

I replaced a few broken windows, then gave the place a coat of paint inside and out. The further I got with work on the A-frame, the less I thought about Charlie and the past. Instead, maybe for the first time ever, I started to think about myself and what lay ahead of me. I didn't know what that was going to be. Sometimes it was scary to think about it and sometimes it was exciting, but in the end it didn't matter.

In the end, I didn't think about myself for very long at all.

I was working with Ben Cross the night the call came in. Since starting at the cop shop I'd been on day shift with the sheriff, and by this time he was breaking me in to work swings. That way, I'd have my mornings free and could work on the house before clocking in at three, and Ben could come by and do some work of his own after he clocked out without having to worry about crowding my space. That way we could double-shift projects during the week. The plan was to work together on weekends on stuff that took two pairs of hands, and we'd get the place in shape faster. It made sense, and I knew going in that I'd take swing shift over graveyards any day. I'd pulled those shifts a few times and they made for a long night of patrolling empty streets, rattling doorknobs, and (mostly) trying to stay awake until the sun came up.

It was July. Not too hot for that time of year, with the possibility of a summer storm blowing in. It was around 10 p.m. and neither one of us had had any dinner. We were talking about where to catch a bite when the main line rang. Ben wasn't on the phone more than a minute. And he didn't say much besides "yeah" or "uh-huh" before he finished with the important one: "I'll check it out."

He cradled the receiver and shot me a look. "What's the deal?" I asked.

"You know that guy who owns the dairy farm out by the county two-lane?"

"You mean Vince Kaehler?"

"Yeah, that's the one. His ranch backs up against Butcher's Lake on the north side. He found a stretch of downed barbed wire this afternoon. Turned out some of his stock got loose. A couple cows wandered up the dirt road that skirts the lake, and Vince spent the evening rounding them up. He just got back to the house after fixing his fence. Says he saw a campfire down there by the water, heard some loud rock 'n' roll and some screaming, like a party was going on."

"Loud rock 'n' roll? He actually said that?"

"Well, what he really said was *goddamn loud hippie music*, but that's close enough."

"Yeah. Well . . . Vince is a Merle Haggard kind of guy."

"Uh-huh." Cross smiled. "And he didn't say *party*. He said *orgy*."

"You're kidding."

"No . . . not even a little bit."

Quiet hung there between us, but just for a second. "So you want to roll with me on this one?"

"Sure, boss," I said, and we strapped on the hardware.

Of course, at that point it hardly seemed worth it. I mean, strapping on our guns or rolling on the call at all. I figured I was in for an instant replay of crash-pad night at Charlie Steiner's. Maybe I'd even find those same two stoner girls who'd been asleep on the mattress in front of Charlie's fireplace that night, only tonight they'd be snoozing on a couple of air mattresses out in the middle of Butcher's Lake.

Man, was I ever wrong.

Dead wrong.

I killed the lights before I pulled up to the rusty guard rail by the eucalyptus grove. The night really wasn't that much different than that Halloween back in '63 when I'd met up with Charlie Steiner. But I wasn't really thinking about Charlie on this night.

Part of that had to do with living in his house. It seemed the creep factor around the place had reached the point of diminishing returns, as if the work I'd done there had exorcised his spirit. The other part was easier to explain, because it didn't have anything to do with a ghost of the past—it was all sensory input and gut reaction as Ben Cross rolled down his window and a couple specific varieties of noise spilled up that black little path that led to Butcher's Lake.

Laughter. Lots of it. And all of it male.

And music. A transistor cranked up to ten, playing Iron Butterfly. "Goddamn," Ben said. "It *is* hippie music."

I couldn't argue. I couldn't return the joke, either.

Because I wasn't listening to the music. The sound of that laughter reached down and grabbed me by the balls. It was over the edge and more than a little mad, reminding me of party sounds I'd once heard in the jungles of Vietnam. We'd run across a village another platoon had raided looking for Cong. We'd come upon them at dusk, tipping back bottles of Cutty Sark, partying with VC soldiers who were dead and others who wished they were.

Those weren't good memories.

And the laughter I heard that night at Butcher's Lake brought them back.

*   *   *

Of course, I didn't mention any of that to Ben Cross.

There was only time to size up the situation and move forward. That's what we did. We didn't take the trail through the eucalyptus grove. We figured we'd cut around to the dirt access road that led to the lake and block it with the cruiser, just in case the laughing crew had wheels. That way we'd pen them in, because there was only one way out of there.

I backed up, then started down the dirt road. I thumbed the lights, pushing in the knobbed rod until the headlights died. That left the parking lights, which were just bright enough to get me down the road. I knew where I was going: this was the same road I took to the Steiner house. When I hit the forked cutoff down to the lake itself I knew I'd gone far enough, because there was a solid-panel Dodge van parked about halfway down the fork, alongside a couple of choppers.

"Bikers," Ben said. "Shit."

We ran the plates. The Dodge had been reported stolen three days before, more than two hundred miles away. The choppers were registered to a couple of bikers with gang affiliations and rap sheets a mile long. With my Spidey senses already tingling, this didn't surprise me. I don't know if Ben had a clue before the hard news came over the squawk-box, but he didn't look happy. Any way you sliced it, the idea we were in for an easy time of it rousting a bunch of partying teenagers had definitely gone south in a big way.

We got out of the car.

That laughter was still there, hanging on the wind like a coming storm.

Ben said, "Watch yourself."

I said, "You do the same, boss."

That about covered it. Cross unlocked the shotgun from the rack. He jacked a shell into the chamber. My left hand slid toward my holster, and I unsnapped the leather strap that ran over my .38.

Then we walked around the Dodge van and moved into the darkness.

*   *   *

The young woman screamed just about the time we spotted the campfire.

She was down by the water. Naked, wearing nothing but mud. The bikers stood between her and the fire, backlit by the flames. And since one of them wasn't wearing his pants, it wasn't hard to figure out what had been going on.

Mr Bare Ass brayed like a billy goat. Then he said: "You don't want to play any more, babe, then we ain't got no further use for you."

His hand came up, rising like a fistful of molten lava. It jerked out, shot back. Then repeated the action.

The woman screamed again. The bikers laughed, and her hand shot out, slapping Bare Ass across the face.

"Whoa. She's a live one!"

"Not for long," Bare Ass said. "This bitch is just another rack of ribs ready for the grill."

"Burn, baby, burn!" one of the bikers yelled.

Those words sent a chill up my spine. Just that fast another biker raised his fist. More molten fire, this handful so bright it made me squint.

That's when I realized what the bikers had in their hands. They'd sparked a bunch of road flares.

They were using them to herd the young woman into the water. The flare jabbed against her arm, and she screamed like she'd swallowed a bucket of brimstone. Ben was way ahead of me, advancing toward the fire with the shotgun shouldered and the barrel trained on the bikers.

"County Sheriff!" he shouted. "Freeze. Now!"

I knew they wouldn't. Ben probably knew it too. And to tell the truth in that moment we had as much going against us as we had going for us. The pack started to turn, and I had the feeling at least one of them was going to end up with something more than molten fire in his hand. At the same time, I doubted Ben was going to let loose with the street howitzer unless he absolutely had to—after all, the woman was right in the middle of the pack, and the scattergun would sure enough do a job on her, too.

The best thing going in that moment was that none of the bikers had thought to grab the woman and use her for a shield. Apart from the gap between two of them, she was almost standing behind them. Two of them were holding burning flares, and one of them let his loose, throwing it in Ben's direction. In the time it took Ben to sidestep the flare, I drew my .38. The fire was between us and the mob; the flares were blazing; there was light. But there were shadows too, and night pouring thick around the edges of every damn one of them, and there was no way to judge everything without making a dozen guesses that could be dead wrong.

One sound took all that second-guessing away.

I heard a .45 chambering a round, and I let loose.

The .38 bucked in my hand. Once. Twice. One of the bikers fell like a slaughterhouse steer. Another stumbled a few steps and dropped on his knees in the campfire before pitching face-first across the flames. That cleared enough ground to see that the young woman wasn't in the picture any more. Just about the time I thought we were about to tighten the cinches on the deal, another shot rang out.

It wasn't mine.

It was the .45. I hadn't dropped the man who held it after all.

The biker fired again. This time, the sound hit me just as someone laid a red-hot poker across my shoulder. At least, that was the way it felt.

The .38 dropped out of my hand. By then, it didn't matter.

Because Ben Cross let loose with the shotgun.

A couple ticks of the second hand, and the whole thing was as over as over can be.

At least, we thought it was.

Four of the bikers lay on the ground. Still. One of them face down in the fire. Smoke billowed up around him, and he was finished. I didn't give him a second glance, because I was only thinking of one thing.

The woman.

Had to be she'd gone into the water to escape the gunfight. It had been the only way out.

I dropped my gun belt and kicked off my shoes. I didn't say a word to Ben. Didn't have to. The sheriff was standing next to Mr Bare Ass, who was the last biker standing. Only now he was down on his knees, with his hands behind his head. Ben had the shotgun near the biker's head, and I know he wanted to pull the trigger. After what the bastard had done, he sure enough deserved it. But all Ben did was touch that shotgun barrel against the biker's cheek, and he let out a howl as the hot metal scorched him. Then Ben put a knee to his spine, and he was flat on the ground as the sheriff snatched the cuffs from his gun-belt and proceeded to truss up the turkey.

I was headed for the water by that point. The smoke from the dead-man fire drifted between me and the lake, giving the heavy moon above a black cataract. But I was through it in a second, and the cataract was gone, and a familiar white glow pooled on the still water before me.

Black water.

And beyond the expanse of darkness, out there where the moon's reflection floated, a glimmer of movement.

I heard a splash, and spotted the woman.

I dove into the darkness.

I swam towards the light.

It had to be her. That's what I told myself as my hands cut furrows in that cold water and I stroked toward the moon's reflection.

By that time, you'd think I would have been flashbacking like a son of a bitch. Seeing visions of a little girl taped up in a plastic Halloween mask. Seeing her disappear underwater all over again. Only difference from that Halloween night back in '63 was that I wasn't a kid any more . . . but the girl in the water wasn't a kid, either.

Other than that, my heart was pounding exactly as it had ten years before—same lake, same hope, same fear, same desperation. That's how far I'd put Charlie Steiner's memory behind me . . . or maybe it was just how deep Charlie was buried.

At least that's what I thought. That's what I told myself.

Whatever the case, I wouldn't give the past a window. I felt no pain; didn't even feel the bullet wound trenched in my shoulder. Everything that was with me was in my head. The things that had just happened most of all—each one of them was a flashbulb pop that waited for me every time I closed my eyes and dipped my head into that water.

Ben walking with the shotgun.

The naked woman getting prodded with the flares.

The gunfight.

The corpses on the beach.

The man face down in the fire, and the stink of burning flesh.

And then I'd gulp a clean breath, open my eyes, catch my bearings, and see that spot of moon on the water, and the streak of light that stretched across the lake between it and me—

—and the woman. There she was. Paddling away from me, arms splashing the water in hard slaps, a black wake left behind by her kicking feet.

She had to be terrified. That was it. Had to be she didn't even know what had happened back at the beach. If that were true, she was still trying to get away. Hell, she might think I was one of the bikers, and—

She coughed. Hard. Like she'd swallowed water. Again, as if she was spitting up a bellyful.

"Hey!" I yelled. "It's over! It's okay. I'm with the sheriff. Tread water. Stay in one spot. We'll take care of you!"

Another cough. A few frantic splashes in a streak of moonlight.

She was going under.

My head was above water as I stroked forward. Watching, keeping my eye on the woman so I'd know exactly where to dive if it came to that.

A gasp for breath, and then her head went under.

And her arms followed. And her fingers.

That's when the past slammed me hard, right between the eyes. And it wasn't the woman disappearing beneath the surface of the lake. It was a sound, from behind me.

I knew it was only the campfire, stirring in a gust of wind.

Or the rising wind carving a path through those old stands of eucalyptus.

I knew it was. It had to be.

Because it wasn't a mummy, swinging his wrecking-ball fist, roaring in the darkness.

It wasn't a mummy, cursing loneliness, and dreams, and wishes, and magic . . . and fate.

So I ignored it, and I swam fast, and then I started diving. Underwater, there was silence. My heart pounded with desperation, but there was nothing else to do. I dove once, twice. And the second time down I thought my fingers were passing through a tangle of weeds. At first I did. But it had to be the woman's hair. Because as I pulled my hand free, the strands were pulled in the other direction, and a torrent of bubbles came up at me from below, brushing my face as they rose to the surface.

I wished I could gulp one down. My chest was burning, but I pushed further, deeper. She had to be close. But there was nothing but black. Nothing to see at all. My hands pulled at the water, as if straining to part a pair of locked doors. And this time I touched flesh, and my fingers passed over lips and an open mouth.

And next I found a hand.

It seemed small. Not like a child's hand. But frail, like something you'd brush against in an old woman's coffin.

For a moment I thought it was something long dead.

But I grabbed it, and five fingers closed around my own. And we rose to the surface together.

*   *   *

The whole department ran on adrenaline for the next few days as we put the investigation together. Everyone pretty much had to double-shift it, questioning the perps and doing the crime scene and handling anything else that came our way.

The crime scene itself wasn't much to sweat over. We were prepared to bring in a drug-sniffing dog from upstate if we had to, but the bikers weren't that clever. Once we got a look, we knew we'd have an open-and-shut case. There were several baggies of cocaine inside the van's spare tire, more in the gas tank of one of the choppers. A couple of sawed-off shotguns rolled up in a rug in the back of the van. Besides that, it turned out that there were two .45s down by the campsite, both of which had been in the hands of convicted felons. The biker who went face down in the fire had a .357 Magnum tucked into his pants, and Ben and I both knew we were lucky he hadn't managed to pull that cannon. So even without rape charges, and the double-shot possibles of kidnapping and attempted murder, we had those boys cold.

At least, we had the one who was still alive.

For his part, Mr Bare Ass lied up one side and down the other. About everything. Swore he didn't know anything about the drugs, or the guns. Swore he was just along for the ride with some friends of his who maybe once in a while got a little bit out of hand. All he wanted to do was party. That was his sole mission in life.

The only thing he'd admit straight up was that, sure, he liked to smoke grass. Who the hell didn't? And the girl? Hell, she was down by the lake. That's where they found her. She was nineteen, maybe twenty . . . just another stray. She wandered up to their campfire, shivering, covered in mud and naked as a little spring daisy. Connect the dots, and she was just some misplaced flower child who got herself dosed up on acid and was left behind on life's long and lonesome highway. Wasn't that a pity. And what the hell were they supposed to do, with some naked chick showing up like that? They weren't Boy Scouts, and this wasn't the annual jamboree. So they gave her a blanket and a couple pulls on a bottle of screw-top red, and then she took herself a few hits of herb. What was supposed to happen next? Didn't the same thing happen, everywhere? Nature took its course.

When he finished up his tale, Ben hit the STOP button on the little cassette recorder we used for interviews. I escorted Mr Bare Ass back to his cell, then met up with Ben in his office.

"That guy couldn't shut himself up if you gave him a rubber plug and a roll of duct tape," Ben said.

"Yeah . . . but when I think about what they did to that girl. Man. Sometimes I just don't know. Talk about a guy who deserves a beating. Walking him back to his cell, it was all I could do to stop myself from ramming his head into the wall. Take my badge if you want to, but I really wanted to knock the teeth right out of his mouth."

"Oh, he'll have his beating coming . . . and worse. You can bank on that. I'm sure he's got a full-course menu of pain and humiliation ahead of him."

"Where?"

"In prison." Ben smiled. "They've got plenty of experts in there." He grabbed his keys off the table.

"Now let's go check on that girl."

And that's what we did.

Walking into that hospital room with *Jane Doe* taped on the door, it was almost like seeing her for the first time. The night I'd rescued her was a blur, and there were really only two things I remembered about her— her eyes, which were wide and terrified. And the trail of bloody burns the bikers had left on her body with those road flares, as if they'd wanted to leave her with a set of brands that marked a trail of pain she'd never forget.

Ben had already called an ambulance by the time I got her out of the lake. We carried her up the access road and met the paramedics where we'd blocked the road with the police cruiser. Maybe two minutes later, the ambulance doors closed and she was gone. That was the last we saw of her until the hospital visit.

A couple days rest had done her some good. She actually smiled at us as we came through the door. We talked for a while, just chit-chat. *Nice day . . . nice room . . . oh, you've got a great view here . . . and look at that little birdbath out on the patio. That's nice.* I was surprised to find how pretty she was. Especially her eyes. They were dark pools, deep brown, and they shone beneath long bangs that were the same color.

Ben asked her some questions. He was patient. He had to be, because she really didn't have any answers. After a while she said, "I'm sorry I can't be more help. I'm still kind of tired. The doctors say things might be better after I get some rest."

"Okay," Ben said. "You take care of yourself. If there's anything you think of, just give us a call." He handed her his card. "Anything you need, too. We'll be right here if you need us."

After that, there wasn't much else for Ben to say.

But she had something to say, and she looked at me when she said it.

"They tell me you saved my life, and I remember that." I nodded.

"It's the one thing I do remember. I didn't forget you."

She stared at me.

"I won't ever forget you."

She didn't blink. I was about to say something stupid, like I was just doing my job, but then she said something else.

Something I'll never forget.

Her eyes were bright pools beneath those dark bangs as she spoke. "I tell myself there are other things I'll remember," she said. "Right now I'm waiting for them, like I was waiting for you. Underwater."

And maybe that's the way it was. I didn't know. There was a lot we didn't know about the young woman in the hospital room with *Jane Doe* on the door. Some of the hospital staffers thought she knew more than she was saying. Not so much the doctors, but a couple of the nurses definitely felt that way. One of them even said the girl was in on the dope deal, and that she was just putting on an act until she could get free and clear. Ben and I didn't buy any of that, and for one simple reason—our Jane Doe just didn't act like any biker chick we'd ever seen.

The doctors weren't much help. One dealt the *amnesia* card on the table; another wouldn't even use the word. He said that diagnosis was out of his league. And, who knew, it could have been that foul-mouthed biker wasn't far off the mark. Maybe the young woman was some cast-off flower child, left by the side of the road after a literal and figurative bad trip of epic proportions. Or maybe the bikers had snatched her off some college campus, dosed her up and kept her that way until she couldn't even see straight. We could have speculated until the wheels came off, but no amount of guessing was going to get us to the truth.

Me, I found another answer. It came in a dream . . . or it might have been a nightmare. I wasn't sure which.

It was 1963 again. That same Halloween night. I was a kid all over again, battling a mummy, trying to save a little girl. She hit the water, and I dove in. Only this time, things ended differently.

This time, underwater, I reached out and found a hand. It seemed small, but not like a child's hand. I took hold of it and kicked to the surface, and I came up in sunlight.

In that moment, things changed.

We weren't kids, either of us.

It was a woman I'd saved, and I was a man.

I carried her to shore.

We were all alone.

"I didn't forget you," she said, looking up at me. "I won't ever forget you."

And then our eyes closed, and our lips met, and we were like that, together. The wind rose around us. I could smell the clean, cold scent of the eucalyptus grove, hear the dry leaves rattling in the breeze. And when our lips parted, I felt calm . . . as calm as I'd felt in a long, long time.

Then I looked behind me and saw the dead thing standing at the edge of the eucalyptus grove, watching us. Charlie Steiner smiled, and blood bubbled over his lips. He was still dressed up in his Halloween clothes. Still playing the part of the thing he wanted to be . . . and the thing that would get him what he wanted.

His words were slurred around the bloody remains of his tongue. "It takes a long time for a dead girl to grow into a princess," Charlie said, "and this one is mine."

Then he raised his bloody hand.

And he started forward.

My shoulder healed up fast, but that dream stuck with me. Sometimes it made it tough to be in the Steiner house, though I tried to stay busy and wear myself out with work. I tore out drywall, started on the electrical. That kept me going. A lot of nights, exhaustion kept the dreams at bay. Other nights I'd go to bed, and I wouldn't sleep at all. I'd listen to the wind outside, waiting for a sound that didn't belong. And when I did sleep (and sleep deeply), it didn't turn out well, because Charlie Steiner was waiting for me.

"She's my dream," he'd say, his mouth bubbling blood. "Not yours. Mine."

And so I'd get up and work. I'd walk around the house, listening to the floorboards creak, wondering if they'd creaked that way for Charlie when he was on the road to insanity. That wasn't a good way to think. Sometimes I'd grab Roger's old Louisville Slugger and use it to take out some drywall. That made a mess, but at least it worked off some energy, and it felt good. Then I'd clean it up and do some real work. And, eventually, I'd sleep.

Sometimes working with the Slugger, I'd imagine that I bashed in a wall and found the missing pages from Charlie Steiner's notebook tucked between the wall studs. I'd wonder what those missing pages would say, and what they'd tell me, if they told me anything.

I'd wonder if it would be anything I didn't already know.

I didn't think so.

See, by then I understood Charlie Steiner pretty well.

*　　*　　*

There wasn't really anything I could do about any of it. I didn't think talking would be a good idea. I wasn't good at talking. The way I was built, I figured there wasn't much to do but ride it out.

So that's what I tried to do. But maybe I wasn't the only one pushing my way through a bad patch. I didn't see Jane Doe again after that day at the hospital, but I heard a lot about her. For a few weeks her picture was in all the papers. The story even made the national news a couple of nights running. But no one came forward to ID her. No relatives, no friends, no co-workers. It was as if she'd come from nowhere.

Or out of a dream.

That's when the gossip geared up. A tabloid ran an article, "The Lady in the Lake." That got them through the first week. By the second, they'd dredged up the old Terror of Butcher's Lake stories about Charlie Steiner. A few of them even mentioned me. They ran with that until the story cooled off, and then they found something else.

Of course, that wasn't the end of it around here. The local chatter started up, and it was running strong by the time the young woman was released from the hospital. Some of the nurses had taken to calling her "Ananka" behind her back. And maybe she'd heard them. Maybe that's why she took the name "Ana Jones."

Anyway, Ana walked out of the hospital. She walked into town and found a studio apartment with some money a few of the doctors had raised for her. Pretty soon she was working at a roadhouse out by the state highway. A place called The Double Shot.

She worked swings, same as I did. Mornings she had to herself. Nights, too. Sometimes I'd drive by The Double Shot toward the end of my shift, thinking I'd stop in and say hello. See how she was doing. Then I'd remember what she said to me, and how her words had frozen me up. I'd remember the look in her eyes, and I'd remember Charlie Steiner's words. And I wouldn't stop. I don't even know why, exactly, but I wouldn't.

I felt like I had to figure things out before I could talk to her again. Sometimes it seemed things were coming full circle, and other times I felt like I was just going around and around like a cat chasing its own tail. Maybe life (and fate) were doing the same things. Which is another way of saying that the wind blew in different directions, and it definitely had me in its grip.

I don't know how those times were for Ana. For me, the nights remained the worst part. Even if I didn't dream, Charlie Steiner was waiting there behind my eyelids. Some nights Ana was waiting there, too.

Things stayed that way for a while. Some mornings I'd get up early and go for a run on the dirt road that ran along the lakeshore. Sometimes on my way back I'd take that familiar cutoff down to the water, just to stare out at the lake. I'd listen to the wind whispering through the eucalyptus, and try to convince myself that there was nothing there at all.

Sometimes I'd take that road and find that there was already someone else down by the water.

Sitting, watching, listening.

Ana Jones.

I didn't talk to her.

I left her alone.

I left most everyone alone.

Things settled into a routine. Not a pleasant one, but a routine. Six weeks like that, maybe seven. I still wasn't sleeping much, and I wasn't really trying any more. It just didn't feel right, and, like I said, I didn't like what was waiting in my head when I tried to sleep.

So I'd bang nails during the day, replacing dry rot around the doors and windows. Then I'd go to work at the cop shop. Walked in one afternoon, and Ben Cross was waiting for me.

"How's your shoulder?" he asked.

"Ancient history, Ben. The bullet didn't dig deep. I'm all healed up."

"Really?"

"Well, I don't sleep on it, if that's what you mean. But, hell, Ben . . . I'm fine. It's not like I ended up face down in a campfire, like that biker did."

"Let me be straight with you: I'm thinking you should take yourself a couple weeks off. Rest. Relax. Rehab. We'll take a break from working on the house. I won't come around, and you won't bang nails."

"C'mon, Ben—"

"No arguments. Go to the gym. Drink some beer and eat some barbecue. Get laid. Do whatever it is you young guys do these days."

"Really, Ben. It's no problem. If I'm screwing something up, I'll fix it. Just give me some time."

"If you were screwing up, we'd be having a different conversation."

"Fair enough."

"The thing is, I don't want you screwing anything up . . . and I think we're getting to a point where you might."

"Okay. That's plain enough. But—"

Ben put up a hand. "No 'buts.' Two weeks off, pardner. Sick leave. You get paid, and you hang on to your vacation time. As far as I'm concerned, that's doctor's orders, and the clock starts ticking right now."

"All right, boss."

"That sounds better," Ben said, and we shook on it. "Like I said, I'd better not catch you pounding any goddamn nails, either. Get out of that goddamn house."

Of course, I didn't take Ben's advice. I went right back to the Steiner place. I holed up there like a grizzly with a toothache. It wasn't the best move I've ever made. I might as well have barricaded the door.

Around that time, my phone started ringing more often. I didn't answer it. Ben and I had hooked up a police radio in the house, so I knew it wasn't someone calling from the cop shop. If Ben wanted me, he would have called on the squawk-box.

For my part, I didn't really want to talk to anyone . . . especially another tabloid reporter. I was even avoiding my family. You could get away with that in those days. It was easier to check out of the game for a while. People didn't walk around with phones in their pockets. The phone hung on a wall in your house, or sat on a table. It was easy to ignore. If it rang and you didn't answer it, you'd have no idea who called. No caller ID. No muss, no fuss.

My phone didn't ring a lot, just enough to tell me there was someone out there who wanted to talk to me. Just enough to tell me they were going to keep trying.

And then one day it didn't ring at all.

It was a Saturday. I'd been off for a full week, and I was trying to figure out what to toss on the barbecue.

That was the evening Ana Jones knocked on my front door.

"Take a walk with me?" she said. "I'd like to talk."

So we walked. It was a crisp night coming on after a sunny day, the kind of day that makes you think of spring more than fall. Ana wore a long dark skirt, sandals, and a flannel shirt over a tight top—the kind dancers wore. As we walked the road toward Butcher's Lake, sunlight trickled through the branches and shone against her long black hair. Wherever she went that night, I would have followed.

She wanted to go down to Butcher's. I wouldn't have suggested going there. I would have thought she'd never want to see the place again, but she said she needed to. So we went down to the lake, neither of us saying a word. I was carrying a couple of blankets and a bottle of wine. I thought the wine was the least I could do for putting her off, because I was sure it was Ana who'd been calling. Besides that, I figured a little wine might help loosen my tongue. Hell, I probably could have used a case of wine and a shoebox full of dynamite, too. But there were things I needed to know. I didn't know if Ana had the answers, but I knew I needed to find some before I skidded into a really bad place.

We sat, and we watched the sunlight on the dark water. That wasn't exactly a conversation starter, considering. So I took out my knife, flicked the corkscrew out, and opened the wine.

The sun went to orange and started to set. "I guess I forgot cups," I said.

"That's okay." Ana smiled. "I think there's enough history between us to share a bottle."

It was easier after the bottle went back and forth a couple of times. Ana talked about her job, and the town, and what it was like settling in. She even talked about the gossip that was going around.

"Have you heard the latest? Some people are saying you shouldn't have saved me. They say I'm a witch, and that I would have sunk to the bottom of that lake like a stone."

"People." I stared across the water. "That's why I like to be alone."

"Yeah. I kind of figured that out."

"Look, it's nothing personal. I've been having a tough time of it. Nothing like you've had . . . but it hasn't been good for me lately. Ever since that night with the bikers some old ghosts have come knocking at the door. I'm trying to handle them."

She handed me the bottle, and when I took it she caught my arm and my gaze.

"Am I one of those ghosts?"

"I don't know, Ana. You're the only person who can answer that one."

"I wish I could. Sometimes I think I'm so close to figuring things out. I feel like I'm scratching at the surface of a real memory. I wish I'd never read any of those tabloid articles or listened to any of the gossip. It gets in there, too . . . and sometimes I can almost see some of it happening—even that whole thing on Halloween night all those years ago. I wonder if I really could have been there. And sometimes I have these nightmares—"

"I have a few of those, too."

"About Charlie Steiner?"

"Yeah."

I handed back the bottle and she tipped it against her lips—a short, sharp swallow. "Last night was the worst. I dreamed of Egypt. I was standing near a pyramid, and Charlie was there . . . fresh off the autopsy slab. He didn't say anything. Every time he tried, blood spilled out of his mouth and splattered the sand like rain. But it didn't matter that Charlie couldn't speak. There were a dozen dead roses in his hands, and I knew what he wanted. I couldn't get away from him. I tried, but he just kept coming. And then he cornered me, and he peeled the petals off one of the roses with a three-fingered hand, and he pressed them against my lips, and he opened my mouth with a pair of withered fingers, and—"

"Don't torture yourself. It was just a nightmare."

"You really believe that?"

I looked at her, realizing what I'd said. We might have laughed then, and maybe we should have, but we couldn't.

Something else happened.

She put down the bottle.

And she reached out and took my hand.

"This isn't easy," Ana said.

"For me, either," I said.

"You know, sometimes I think that maybe they're right. The ones who say I popped out of some warlock's bubbling cauldron. Maybe that's the reason I took that princess's name, or at least part of it. Like the poet said: *Such stuff as dreams are made on.* Sometimes I think it could be true, and I'm just a shadow of someone else's dream. I was nowhere for such a long time. Forever, almost. And then you came along and—"

"Don't read too much into me. I'm no knight in shining armor."

"Maybe not. But if it is true—and let's just say it is—then you're the one who tried to save me the first time around and paid a price for it. You lost your brother. And you're the one who came back all those years later and did the job the second time, and you're paying still."

I didn't say anything. I looked across the water.

"And I just want you to know. I have to tell you: When you swam out there and took my hand, that's when life started for me. I was underwater, and you saved me. But part of me feels like I'm still underwater. And I'm never going to get to the surface unless you pull me through."

Her grip tightened, and it was strong.

"See, it doesn't matter who I was," she said. "It doesn't matter at all. It only matters who I'm going to be."

She moved closer then, and my arm slid around her shoulder. We kissed, and our kiss deepened. And it was so quiet out there by the lake. The wind was still, and so was the water, and the tall eucalyptus covered us in long shadows.

It was so quiet. I could almost hear her heart beating. I could feel it beneath my hand. And in that moment I wouldn't have cared if the worst of it was true. It wouldn't have mattered if Ana was a witch, or a dead thing born in Egypt five thousand years ago. Because in that moment I believed what Ana believed, that none of it mattered, that what really mattered was ahead of us.

I held her tight, and I held her close, and I told myself I'd pull her through.

I wasn't going to let her go.

That was what she wanted.

That was what I wanted, too.

I didn't work on the house the next day. To tell the truth, I didn't do much of anything. I had a big breakfast and then I went for a walk, following the dirt road until it connected up with a county two-lane on the other side of the lake. I thought about what Ana had said, and I thought about the past and the future. Then I came back to the house, ate lunch, and fell asleep.

No dreams came my way, and that was a very good thing.

At dusk, a knock came on the door. I got up, running a hand through my hair, and went to answer it, expecting that Ana had cut out of work early and come back.

I opened the door, and a mummy was standing there. A small one.

He held out a paper bag and said, "Trick or treat."

I didn't have any Halloween candy, so I grabbed a bag of cookies out of the cupboard and gave a few of them to the kid in the mummy costume. He thanked me, and I watched him walk across the yard, alone. He made me think of Roger somehow, and that last night we'd gone trick-or-treating so long ago. For a second I wanted to call out to him and ask his name, but I didn't. Still, it felt right somehow, remembering Roger. It felt good.

I closed the door. I didn't know how the date had slipped by me, but the circle had come around again. But for the first time in as long as I could remember, Halloween seemed different. It wasn't just Ana, though she was a big part of it. Things were changing. I was different. The Steiner house was different. And maybe those old ghosts could finally get some rest.

I poked around the kitchen. It turned out I had a couple candy bars in the house, but that was it. I didn't figure to get much action since the house was down a dirt road and a good piece off the beaten path. But I also knew the Steiner place was as close to a haunted house as we had around here, so it was hard to tell. After a few more knocks, I drove down to the grocery store, grabbed a couple bags of Snickers and enough goods for a late supper with Ana, and then I headed back home.

By eight-thirty, maybe ten Snickers were gone.

After that, the only ones that disappeared were the ones I ate. And then, just past eleven, there was another knock on the door. I have to admit, that knock gave me enough of a jolt that I set my .38 on the side table next to the door . . . just in case.

Then I answered the door.

An Egyptian princess was standing there. Diaphanous gown. Little tiara. Lots of eyeliner.

Ana said, "That bastard down at The Double Shot made all of us dress up in costumes tonight."

She tossed the plastic tiara on the floor as she came in. "I think I'm going to quit that job."

I picked up the tiara and threw it out the door.

"I think that's a good idea," I said.

I'd bought a bottle of wine, a loaf of sourdough, and fixings for pasta. We never got to it. A few Snickers, and we were out of there. The bedroom was too strong a draw.

Later I slept deeply, and I didn't dream, and I didn't wake.

Two hours passed.

And then I woke sharply.

I thought I'd heard a knock at the door.

Ana was still asleep. I slipped on my jeans and grabbed a flannel shirt. I was halfway down the hall before it hit me.

I didn't want to answer that door.

Not at all.

Certainly not without a gun in my hand.

And suddenly I wondered if I'd imagined the whole thing. Sure. Maybe that knock was just a leftover shard of dream jackknifed in my brain. By the time I reached the end of the hallway that opened into the living room, I'd almost convinced myself of that. But I'd also remembered that I'd left the .38 on the side table next to the door, and I planned to grab it before I checked things out.

But like they say, plans change.

I came around the corner. The lights were out in the living room, but I could see.

Because the front door was open.

And dull moonlight spilled across the hardwood floor.

I waited for Charlie Steiner to follow that moonlight through the doorway. And I thought of those bikers I'd killed, too—after all, they had friends who might be looking for revenge. All that flashed through my brain in a couple ticks of the second hand, but no one was there.

I didn't wait for someone to make an appearance. I was moving. Toward the door, and the side table. I snatched up the .38 and flicked on the living room light. I hit the porch light at the same time and scanned the front yard.

Nothing. No one there. No sign of movement. Just my pickup truck parked on the gravel drive, and Ana's beat-up Toyota parked next to it.

I closed the front door and set down the pistol. I was just about to turn around when I caught a flash of reflection on the living room window. Something against the far wall behind me, a dark smear waiting in the corner. Whatever it was, it didn't belong there.

It wasn't moving . . . yet.

I spun, staring across the room.

The thing that stood in the corner wasn't a mummy.

But it was Charlie Steiner.

All trace of the Hollywood monster was long gone. No costume, no bandages, no Lon Chaney, Jr frightface. Charlie wasn't a rampaging mountain of cobwebs any more. No. He was just a thing that had lain in a leaking plywood box for ten long years. Shrunken and black. Desiccated and degraded. His corpse had rotted in the wet earth, then dried and baked in the heat of summer, then rotted some more when the next rains came. It had been like that month after month and year after year as the seasons ran their circles and ran them again, until all that was left of him was bone and gristle and the black jerky that held it all together . . . along with a little bit of a very old dream.

What remained couldn't have weighed more than fifty pounds. Charlie stood in that corner, looking more like a giant marionette than anything human, a pile of tottering bone. Empty-eyed, he stared across the room at me, death's eternal grin on his skinless face.

I expected him to collapse if he moved so much as an inch.

But he didn't.

He still knew what he wanted.

He still knew what he needed.

He came after it, faster than I ever could have expected. He skittered across the room like a giant insect, and his bones clicked against the hardwood floor, percussion for a nightmare dance. His arm came up just as I raised the .38, and as I turned to face him I thought that arm had become thicker and whiter as it descended toward me.

But the thing I saw wasn't Charlie's arm at all.

It was Roger's Louisville Slugger, and it came at me in a white-ash blur.

The bat slammed my wrist, and I lost the pistol. Charlie's jaw clacked open and closed, and the sound was castanet laughter as he whirled and slammed the Slugger against my skull. Next thing I knew I was on the floor, and as I rolled away the bat came down on the meat above my collarbone.

That burst of pain hard-wired me.

The pistol was right there, by my other hand.

I snatched it up. Charlie stood above me, Roger's bat raised over his head with both skeletal hands. He opened his mouth, and I swear I actually heard him take a breath. Blood bubbled over his black teeth, and he started to say something, the way he always did in my dreams.

"No," I said. "This time you don't say a word."

Six times I pulled the trigger. And I thought of Roger, and a missing little girl, and a woman who was down the hall.

And Charlie Steiner fell. His bones clattered to the floor. The lights started to flicker, and then the room started to spin. A black hole opened up in the middle of it, and I remembered the mummy's cobwebbed mouth opening all those years ago at Butcher's Lake, and I remembered his buzz-saw scream.

But there was no scream this night. There was only chanting. There on the ground, with gunfire echoing in my skull, I know I heard it. Distant. Indistinct . . . as if it came from a place far below or far above. And then I started to fade and the lights went out, and the black hole went away, and the moon seemed to hang above me in the darkness. It shone on me and the dead thing at my feet like a spotlight that could open a hole into a black brimming pit. And there was no way to fight it, not when the moon shone down and that black hole returned at my feet. Charlie's wrecking-ball fist had already crumbled, and I was slipping into unconsciousness, and everything was suddenly slipping away except for me and the whisper of my own breath.

Wherever I went next, I didn't hear anything.

It was a quiet place, and empty, and I was alone there.

I awoke the next morning, and I was alone still.

The Louisville Slugger lay there on the floor. My pistol was next to it. But Charlie was gone. The only trace of him was a set of scratches that started in the far corner of the living room and ended at the front door. Looking down at them, I remembered the clicking percussion of his bony feet as he came after me the night before.

I searched the house for Ana, but she was gone, too. All that was left was a beat-up Corolla parked in my driveway, and a princess costume on the bedroom floor—a gown that smelled of Ana's vanilla perfume. I went down to Butcher's Lake, hoping I'd find her there. I drove to her apartment, and then I went to The Double Shot, but by then I knew she wouldn't be there . . . or anywhere.

I kept it to myself for a few days, hoping the phone would ring, hoping it would be Ana. But the phone didn't ring. Finally, I worked up the nerve to call Ben Cross. He came over to the house, and I told him the whole story. God knows what he thought of it. But after I finished, Ben asked me to get in the car and we went for a little drive.

To Potter's Field.

To Charlie Steiner's unmarked grave.

"We thought it was kids who did it," Ben said staring down at the open hole and the broken box at the bottom. "You know—Halloween night, taking a dare to buck the town legend. We expected we'd find Charlie's bones hanging in a tree somewhere. But after what you've told me, I'm not so sure."

Ben kept the story out of the paper. That was fine with almost everyone. The town fathers didn't want any more tabloid reporters sniffing around. The next day, a county work crew used a backhoe and filled in Charlie's grave. They tamped down the earth and rolled a couple strips of fresh grass over the top of it. Next thing you knew, Charlie's unmarked plot looked like it had never been disturbed at all.

Ben didn't really want me in the Steiner place any more, but we worked it out. I had nowhere else to go. Now it's my home. More than anything, it was the place I'd been with Ana. That's what I wanted to remember about the house by Butcher's Lake, and that's why I stay there.

As for Butcher's, I still go down there. Not often, but often enough. Usually at sunset. Sometimes I'll take a bottle of wine and walk along the shore. One night the wind was up, blowing through the eucalyptus, making the cattails dance. It was almost dark. And I thought I saw someone down near the water, staring at me from a gap in the cattails.

I hurried to the spot.

Someone was there. In the cattails, watching me.

I moved closer.

My hand reached out.

It was a Halloween mask. A little princess with black hair and red lips. The mask was hung up in the cattails. I didn't want to think about how it might have gotten there. I really didn't need any false hope. But I took the mask home with me, and I put it on the mantelpiece right next to the plastic tiara Ana had worn that Halloween night.

Of course, I didn't tell anyone about it.

No one, except Ben.

"Maybe she'll come back," he said. "She was a dream, that one. I guess she really was."

I don't know any more. I really don't.

Like I said, I don't like dreams. I don't trust them

But that doesn't mean I don't have them.

I have them, still.

"The Emerald Scarab" is one of a series of short stories featuring Kamose, a magician and Archpriest of Anubis—the jackal-headed god of cemeteries, embalming, and funerary rites—and hated rival of the priesthood of Thoth. The character was inspired by the Setne Khaemwaset cycle of Egyptian fantasy stories/legends. Two parts of it survive on papyrus: the first (dating from the Greek Ptolemaic Period) is in the Cairo Museum; the second (probably from the Roman Period in the first century CE) resides in the British Museum. "Setne Khaemwaset" (*setne* is the priestly title *setem* garbled into a name) was a fictionalized version of Khaemwaset, a real son of Rameses II: a prince, soldier, and priest. Centuries later, he was regarded as a great magician and his putative exploits became stories.

The Emerald Scarab
Keith Taylor

————

I.

The Archpriest Kamose, at the best of times, had an austere, sardonic presence. This was not the best of times. Haggard from grim vigils and sorceries, eyes reddened and sunken, he glared at the stone desiccation table on which lay a Pharaoh's corpse. It neither impressed nor awed him; he had seen other dead Pharaohs—greater ones.

Besides, and strictly speaking, the body could not be seen for the heaps of powdered natron covering it over. Kamose noted the hue and texture with an expert's eye. Frowning, he rubbed a little of the granulation between his fingers.

"How long since this was changed?" he demanded.

"Ten days, holy one."

Penma'at spoke, the Second Prophet of the Temple, a thickset, conscientious man. Although he made an able subordinate, he would have done poorly as the Archpriest. In Kamose's absence, he had directed the embalming process. Now he watched apprehensively as his master lifted the corpse's arm out of the grayish-white heap. Turning swiftly, he raked his underlings with a baleful stare.

"You sacrilegious swine! This is a *Pharaoh*, and you prepare him for the tomb as though he were a Libyan spearman! Ten days, you say? I cannot believe this natron has been changed at all!"

"Yes, holy one!" Penma'at bleated. "Each ten, or sometimes seven, days! I saw to it!"

"If that's true, it was not fresh. Either you hoped, with the spirit of a sand-flea, to pare cost—or you are so wholly incompetent you did not even know. Remove this excuse for natron! Take it hence! Let me see how much of your witless damage I can undo."

They obeyed, bowing out backward, one or two of the minor priests even stumbling in the face of their master's ire. Penma'at kept his usual pompous poise, though appalled to have been berated before his inferiors in such a fashion. Old Djeseret looked vaguely distressed, and the young lector-priest (whom Kamose did not know) seemed amused if anything.

Certainly his air of self-love did not lessen. Well, it wasn't astonishing; he had noble, if not prince, written all over him.

Alone in the *wabet*, the place of embalming, Kamose swept the natron to the foot of the sloping stone table. Setekh-Nekht's eviscerated, eyeless body looked almost prepossessing when one considered that he had been thrashed to death with a heavy rod. Curved ivory splints and gold wire braced his ribcage within. His right arm, broken in two places while he strove to protect himself, had been neatly bound in straight splints.

The fractures were not fatal. It had been savage blows across his abdomen, one after the other, that truly made an end of Setekh-Nekht.

Nothing could have been done for the ruptured stomach and spleen (and almost pulped liver) except, when death came, to dry them, preserve them with spices, and cover them with layers of resin before they went into the mortuary jars. Sinking to one knee, Kamose studied the four such jars ranged on a shelf near the floor, with their varied stopper-lids, one each for the lungs, liver, stomach, and viscera.

All appeared in order. It should be. Worthy, predictable Penma'at would never allow anything less than what was wholly proper. Setekh-Nekht's existence in the hereafter depended on the presence and condition of those internal organs. Penma'at believed it, and so did the Pharaoh's kindred.

Kamose smiled at the thought—a mocking, blasé smile. All this careful art, perfected down the generations, to preserve a corpse intact in the belief that the spirit could not survive without it—and the first step in the process was to scrape out the brain and discard it like rubbish! Could there be a finer example of the power of tradition to immobilize the wits? Doctors knew the various effects of blows to the skull and brain injuries. They knew them well. Medical scrolls listing the symptoms dated back to Imhotep's time. Surgeons even opened the skull to relieve the pressure of bleeding or a depressed fracture, and the result—on occasion, at least—was a wondrous benefit. Yet established lore said the heart was the seat of mind and spirit, so even those with the strongest reasons to know otherwise, took it for granted.

So be it. Kamose did not intend to correct the error. As Archpriest of Anubis, jackal-headed lord of the mortuary and embalming arts, he controlled vast estates, properties, and endowments because of that fatuous belief. Let him contradict it, and his enemies would swarm over him like gleeful crocodiles. Even the queen-widow and her son, Prince Rameses, heir to the Double Crown, would turn against him. At present they were his friends.

Setekh-Nekht, I'll see you embalmed and coffined, and preside at your funeral since your survivors command it. But assuredly it is a step down for me. I performed the obsequies of Usermare. You reigned a scant three years.

Leaving the *wabet*, Kamose paused a moment in the hard, hot sunlight beside his pole-chair and four brawny servants. For that moment, his brain spun and his legs felt weak. Betraying no sign of indisposition, he climbed into the pole-chair and ordered his bearers to proceed.

"The Temple of Amun-Ra."

He wasn't himself, he thought grimly. After the stresses of his recent sorcery, he would be lucky if he was himself again in two seasons. His physical vitality had worn thin, his temper become raw, his control over it uncertain, and his sight dimmed on occasion. He carried the slash of a demon's quadruple talons across his chest beneath his robe to remind him of an almost mortal mistake. And his enemies must not know it, which meant, of course, that Kamose's few friends must not know it either, for once they did, his enemies soon would.

He'd been foolish to go about the city in a pole-chair, when he normally traveled by chariot or his black galley. Chariot, next time, with a great show of vigor, no matter how wearing it might be—and once the Pharaoh was duly entombed, a request to be allowed a retreat to his mansion at Abdu. Even though his enemies might gain political ground, Kamose could regain it when he returned, especially with his greater lifespan.

Politics, to him, was a tiresome necessity, not sport or a serious affair.

From such political necessity, he paid his respects to the local chief priest of Amun-Ra. Minor though this Delta edifice might be compared with its immense mother-temple at Thebes, still it was rich, still a fane of the most powerful priesthood in Egypt. Even Kamose took care to stay on amicable terms with them. (He enjoyed the never-failing enmity of the Temple of Thoth, and one priestly feud was enough.)

Kamose proceeded to the treasure room. Penma'at arrived and joined him shortly. The various substances and appurtenances needed to complete the preparation of the king's body, once it came out of the natron, had been stored here awaiting use. The largest temple of Anubis in the Delta was neither large enough nor secure enough for such a purpose. Having been appointed Controller of the Mysteries (chief embalmer, in plain speech) by royal command, Kamose must now take inventory and arrange to transfer it all to the *per-nefer*, the "house of beauty", where the embalming process would culminate.

Oils, balsams, spices, and resins took a good deal of space, along with myrrh-filled cloth pads for stuffing the body cavity. Despite their immense cost, they were cheap beside the array of amulets meant for planting within the royal corpse or wrapping between the layers of mummy bandage. Casket after casket Kamose opened, under the watchful witness of two priests of Amun-Ra, to record the contents after he had noted them against a master-list. Golden djed pillars, scarabs winged and plain, sun disks, Eyes of Horus, lions, bound gazelles, couchant jackals, little figurines of at least twenty gods, stylized papyrus columns, horizons, paired feathers, and more and more, in gold, electrum, and gemstone, were taken out, itemized, and meticulously packed in their caskets again. The least article in the array would set a man up comfortably for life—and, if he were caught stealing it, cost him a less than comfortable death.

The greatest talisman lay within a box of jointed ivory. There was no visible lid or hinge. Two of its five hidden catches had nothing to do with opening it; they merely released poisoned needles, and breaking it would unleash a fine dust deadly to breathe. Even Kamose, who knew its secrets, placed bronze stalls on his finger-ends before touching it.

Closely nested inside blazed the Pharaoh's heart scarab, an emerald the size of a man's two fists, carved in the shape of the beetle of resurrection. Heavy gold clasped the base, on which was engraved a prayer.

Kamose repressed a scornful smile, unmoved by the jewel's splendor.

It was supposed to prevent the Pharaoh's own heart from testifying against him in the judgment hall of the gods. In that respect it had about as much power as a pebble, to Kamose's certain knowledge; and besides, a few generations at most after Setekh-Nekht's funeral, it would have been taken by tomb robbers.

Briefly, then, the Archpriest's face and eyes altered. He bent over the emerald scarab once more. Lifting it in his sinewy hands, he stared at nothing for a space, seeming to brood like a vulture high in some burning sky; intent on a portent below that only his eyes could discern. Then he replaced the gem in its box with a steady hand.

"Let this be taken to the *per-nefer* under no ordinary guard," Kamose ordered. "Twenty warrior princes will suffice. Only porters of our temple, who have served long, are to bear it, and you and I will accompany them, O Penma'at. Then the divine body of Pharaoh is to be carried there—after cleansing, as always."

Penma'at bowed. "As you command, holy one."

He spoke a little stiffly. Kamose supposed his language to the man in the *wabet* still rankled. He would concede it had been ill advised, especially before underlings, but he had a larger matter on his mind than any grievance of Penma'at's. A discovery just made had briefly brought him close to panic, as though he were a normal mortal man.

The emerald scarab was false as a harlot's affection.

II.

Mertseger laughed, a tippling susurration like wind in dry grass, the mirth of the serpent she was.

"Oh, no! Indeed? This great gem is nothing but paste?" Kamose smiled with her. It was rather a joke, for those who could appreciate it, and he had found the lamia to be among the few able to share the blacker depths of his humor. Jesting with her of course was dangerous. That had to be borne in mind.

"The great gem is real. There has been a substitution. Malachite and gilded lead, not paste, if I may be laboriously exact. One cannot tell the difference by sight because the thief has cast an illusion of similitude over the counterfeit. He must have placed them side by side to do that."

"That might have been anyone, at any time, my lord," she said pensively. "Even the temple artisan who carved the jewel, if he knew magic—and if he did not, any priest down to the most minor would have been able to supply his deficiency." She ended in a tone fit for discussing the most remote abstractions, "There *are* corrupt priests."

"Even priestesses," Kamose replied just as gravely. "Now hear me, marvelous one. The risk alone means this can be no ordinary theft. The robber chose to chance his act being noticed before the scarab was hidden forever inside a king's carcass. One supposes he must be daring, bold, without scruple, and confident—even over-confident, reckless. The qualities of youth."

"And greedy. Or desperate."

Kamose agreed. "I have such a fellow under my eye. He's the lector-priest taking part in the mummification, and I have not known him before. He's some sort of cousin to Prince Rameses. Wenching, betting, and racing his chariot are his chief delights; he gives as little time as possible to priestly duties. It shows, I may say. His knowledge of the rituals is slipshod. I'd confine him on a plain diet and have him study day and night until he was perfect—not in any hope of making him devout, my serpent, but to teach him that I expect my priests to be meticulous, at least. It cannot be done because he's royal. The Vizier at Hikuptah appointed him to this task. I wish—quickly—to learn if he pilfered the emerald."

Mertseger stretched, smiling. "For that he must run free."

"He might be desperate for wealth. His favorite pleasures are costly. Assume the guise of a courtesan, O Mertseger, and cross his path; learn if he is guilty. But that is all! Control your deadly appetites where he is concerned! He's not to be harmed, nor is he to guess what you are. I will deal with him if he is the thief." Kamose looked her in the face with a gaze more lethal than her own. "Flout this command and I turn the blood in your veins to vitriol, serpent."

He could do it, and would. Mertseger knew it beyond doubt. In her human shape as a priestess, she was a tall woman, supple to the point of seeming boneless, and here in Kamose's private quarters she had cast off her temple robe to be easy in her skin, unconfined. But as anger possessed her, that skin colored in serpentiform mottlings, black and yellow, while actual scales broke out in places. Her fingers tensed.

"Vitriol?" she said fiercely. "To hold me captive, even for you, Kamose, is to keep vitriol in a tube made of unwaxed reed. Have a care to *your* flesh!"

"I shall. Meanwhile, go fascinate this youthful lector-priest—or lecher-priest may be more appropriate. His name is Reni."

The ophidian patterns faded from Mertseger's skin. She said woefully, "Will you allow me nothing in the way of pleasure?"

"Of your own peculiar pleasures, from this man, no. He's highly connected. And I cannot always find traitors or criminals for you, O Mertseger. Discover all there is to know about Reni, and I make large effort in that direction."

Mertseger departed, seething, but intent on her task and hopeful.

Kamose experienced a certain relief. She would do as he ordered, and do it well, but in all likelihood there was no need. The young lector-priest did love chariots and fine horses and exorbitant wagers; but such was his skill that he generally won. He was unlikely to be the culprit. This, Kamose had already ascertained.

He preferred, though, to have Mertseger occupied, and at a distance from himself. Let her discern his current weakness, and there would probably be no choice for him but to destroy her. Holding her under his control, just as she said, formed a circumstance of extreme peril, but until he had done so her depredations had imposed terror on the entire Delta. By bringing an end to that, Kamose had vastly increased his own reputation.

Besides, the lamia made a fearsome weapon when his enemies overstepped the mark or some criminal—tomb robbers in particular—grew too egregious. And she was a remarkable lover.

Kamose's expression became bleakly amused. Until he recovered, it was fortunate that he possessed elixirs and potions which could renew a man's vitality even at the point of extinction. Although they could not be taken too often, he would assuredly never conceal the truth from Mertseger without them.

She had shrewdly said that the emerald might have been stolen at any time since it was carved. Still, Kamose had his own reasons for thinking the theft a recent one, and the motive one other than greed. The emerald scarab being his responsibility, the most likely reason for stealing it (almost the only one to justify such immense risk) would be to discredit him. Kamose knew numbers of folk who dreamed longingly of such an outcome.

So. Recent theft reduced the number of suspects. Reni, though not eliminated yet, ranked among the less likely. Any of the half-dozen lesser priests involved in embalming Setekh-Nekht had had opportunity. They might be desperate on their own account, or the compelled tools of a greater man's scheme. Kamose had given secret commands already, and meant to know everything there was to know about all of these men within three days.

That left, in positions of far greater trust and authority (and therefore opportunity), Penma'at and Djeseret. Both possessed more than ordinary integrity, Penma'at in addition valued his honors as Second Prophet more than any conceivable wealth, while Djeseret had always been removed from worldly matters to a nearly grotesque degree, wholly steeped in religious concerns. Besides, he was growing senile.

Penma'at did have a large family, though, and if one of them should be in serious trouble or threatened with disgrace—*that* would make him vulnerable to pressure, honest as the Second Prophet was. No. Penma'at could not quite be discarded from consideration as a thief and traitor. Both Penma'at and Djeseret possessed more than the modest degree of magical ability needed to perform the theft. For that matter, most of the lesser priests probably had it.

Kamose pondered. It would be interesting to solve this riddle by his own knowledge and wit, not by divination or the aid of spirits. Simply giving the culprit enough rope for his own noose might provide the answer.

He began early next day in the *per-nefer*. Unlike the *wabet*, a closed and heavy vault, this place admitted air. Little square windows near the high ceiling let in light while keeping out oppressive heat. The plaster walls carried bright paintings. While their subject matter was solemn—embalming rites, funeral processions, the judgment of souls—one wall showed happy spirits in the Afterworld, and all were decorated in vivid hues.

Even the mortuary bench was very different. Procedures in the *wabet* had been carried out on a heavy stone table, sloping and channeled to drain away fluids. Here the royal cadaver lay on a magnificent lion-headed bier.

Kamose, washed and purified, entered in his ceremonial vestments as Controller of the Mysteries. A black jackal-mask with crystal eyes covered his head. He wore a kilt of many intricate pleats and a sort of linen corselet to his armpits. It almost hid the lacerations of the demon's claws. The fresh red scars just showed. His collar, armlets, belt, and short oblong apron glittered with crusted jewels. From behind the belt a long black tail hung down.

The lector-priest Reni came late, and through the mask's eyes Kamose saw that he looked somewhat worn and wilted. Flagrantly against the ritual purification rules, and the sanctity of the rite in which he was engaged, he had been wenching and carousing the night before, and Mertseger—abroad in a rich litter—had contrived to catch his attention. She worked swiftly. Kamose had heard her description of events when she returned an hour before dawn. The lector-priest assuredly did not behave like a man with aught on his mind but merriment.

Kamose rebuked him sharply for lateness. The rituals began. Setekh-Nekht's gutted corpse had been washed clean of natron before Kamose's minor priests carried it to the *per-nefer*. Much shrunken by the desiccation process, it stared from empty sockets while the minor priests rubbed milk wine and juniper oil into the skin—all but the face, which had already been covered with a thin coating of resin.

Kamose's part began. Personifying Anubis, he chanted an invocation. That complete, he removed the temporary stuffing which had filled out the bereft body cavity until now. The lesser priests placed it aside in a basket. Kamose, each movement slow and solemn, began to restuff the body with linen pads containing fine sawdust, powdered myrrh and cassia. He had to reach in through a deep slanting cut above the groin to accomplish it.

"O royal falcon, Setekh-Nekht, go forth into heaven as the lion-god Ra, who has eaten the thigh and divided the carcass. Be justified; inherit eternity. Your heart shall speak for you, it shall be found true." Kamose reached out his hand. The lector-priest took the great scarab in a grasp that trembled. Its green blaze illumined his face. He appeared distinctly out of sorts. Passing over the jewel, he intoned the prayer engraved on its underside, working hard to speak clearly.

"O my heart, which I had from my mother! O, my heart of my coming into being! Do not stand as a witness against me. Do not contradict me with the judges, or be my enemy in the presence of the guardian of the balance . . ."

Kamose took the scarab, watching his subordinates as he did so, his masked gaze intent and assessing. Penma'at had pressed his lips together in disapproval as the lector-priest stumbled once or twice in his phrasing.

Old Djeseret echoed the prayer silently, moving his withered lips. He could have recited it in the midst of a whirlwind. He was old and death hovered close to him. Hardly a time of life to take theft and sacrilege on his soul. What could it gain him now? He always had seemed more concerned with the Afterworld than with life, and Kamose had known him when he was a green youth in the temple gardens.

And yet someone in this chamber must be sweating with fear lest the theft be discovered. Kamose held the scarab longer while he stared at the six minor priests, all of whom he knew, and wondered if one of them had been corrupted so far—or even if someone in the Temple of Amun-Ra, while the emerald had been stored in its treasure room—

Enough. Kamose thrust the great jewel deftly into the Pharaoh's body, settling it next to the heart, and packed more myrrh-laden pads around it.

Systematically he filled the thoracic hollow from the collarbones down, until the torso presented a natural appearance again, and covered the incision in the lower belly with an engraved golden plate. This, too, Reni handed to him, speaking the appropriate incantation in a slurred and thickened tone.

I'll teach you better in time, Kamose thought grimly, *whether or not you are a thief. Not even whelps of the royal house conduct lax rites in my temple, or guzzle and swive during a mummification.*

The lesser priests now rubbed the corpse with a paste of spices, while new resin melted over a brazier. Using wide brushes, they coated the entire cadaver with it, sealing the golden plate in place thereby. If the thief was present, he must think that danger no longer hovered close above his head.

Let him think so, then—for now.

III.

Five days passed. False eyes of gemstone were seated in the Pharaoh's empty sockets. His jaws and face were bound up with fine linen bandages, each finger and toe wrapped separately, then capped with wrought gold. Kamose's minor priests wrapped his limbs and torso. The next day, a selection of precious talismans were placed on his body and then brushed over with molten resin. Tilting his head reverently back over the end of his bier, they poured more resin into his skull through the nasal passage. The following day, they bandaged the head and wrapped the entire body in further strips of fine linen. The prayers and rituals provided by Kamose, Penma'at, and old Djeseret never ceased.

Away from the *per-nefer*, investigation by Kamose's agents went on unceasingly also. Within it, he watched his subordinates with the eye of a cobra making ready to strike. By the fifth day, he felt that he knew the thief, and could even name his motive.

It wasn't Reni. That young roisterer had lost his swagger and indeed had difficulty, by then, in keeping his feet. Several nights with Mertseger were enough to humble the proudest, randiest he-goat. Kamose, amused, decided nevertheless that Reni's attrition must end while the lamia still managed to restrain her more deadly lusts.

"It will be unnecessary for you to keep any more assignations with the lector-priest," he told her.

"Ah," Mertseger said without regret. "He's virile, but—he will be no further use to me unless you permit me to slay him." She shrugged. "I think he will be of no use to anything female for some time now."

"You may not slay him."

"Have you found the thief, then, my lord?"

"Thieves. And I imagine they will come to find me on the morrow." Kamose was smiling. Mertseger knew that smile; it meant that the Archpriest was aware of something that others were not, that he had a fatal surprise waiting for them. It was a smile steeped in poison direr than her own. Curving her lips expectantly, she asked, "Why, O Kamose?"

"To accuse me of stealing the emerald."

Mertseger's smooth brows drew together so that two tiny upright creases showed between them; in her, the equivalent of wailing, shrieking, and tearing her garments.

"That's an absurd charge. Is there danger that they could succeed with it?"

So spoke her tongue. Her thought, rather, was, *Is there hope that they could succeed with it?*

"No danger at all," Kamose replied cheerfully. He understood her very well. "I have expected for days that the scarab will appear again, in circumstances contrived to make me appear guilty. It was stolen for just that purpose. A shoddy scheme, but it might have succeeded had I not become aware of the substitution." He laughed. "Don't ask me how they ever supposed I would not!"

"Yet the spurious gem now lies next to Pharaoh's heart. Where you placed it."

"Surely a difficult state of affairs to explain," Kamose agreed, "unless we recover the true emerald scarab tonight. How fortunate for me that we can. I'll garb as an ordinary stolist-priest, you as a priestess. We leave at once."

"For what destination?"

"The temple of Anubis."

The temple of Anubis within Pi-Rameses was little more than a chapel, though larger ones existed at other cities in the Delta. Still it boasted a gateway, courtyard, and inner shrine. The single priest serving at night duty allowed Kamose and Mertseger in when he saw the parchment letter they carried, signed with his Archpriest's cartouche. If he discerned that the man bearing the letter was his Archpriest, he wisely refrained from announcing it. He hurried away to the courtyard.

"It is here?" Mertseger asked.

"Yes. I had the culprits followed closely enough to erase any question.

"Not that I was sure they were the culprits—then. Others were closely followed besides them."

Kamose bowed deeply before the atramentous, jackal-headed statue behind the altar. Its red tongue lolled between the jaws. Both hands held daggers, and a horned viper coiled around one forearm.

"Lord of Tombs, Announcer of Death, great seer and diviner; we come to undo sacrilege. We would set aright a perversion of the mortuary rituals by lewd and vile theft. Prosper our actions."

Mertseger bowed as well, fluid and supple of movement.

"Where is the emerald?"

"In a secret cache beneath the altar which clearly is secret no more."

Vipers were carved along the altar's sides. Kamose twisted the heads of several in apparently random order. Then he thrust against one end of the altar. It pivoted smoothly around. Beneath it lay a stone-lined cuboidal hole. It contained papyri in cylindrical cases and certain other objects, including a skull. Near the skull lay a pouch of gazelle-skin, tightly filled out by something rounded and hard.

"I believe we have it," Kamose said. "Had this been proved missing, and then found here in my temple—by the Vizier, let us say—how lamentable for me!"

He opened the pouch. A hard green glitter flashed at him. In a moment Kamose held a huge emerald scarab between his hands. Staring down at it—at and into it, with his magician's perceptions—he knew in a moment that it was real.

"Good, thus far. Now return we to the *per-nefer*. There is much to do yet!"

Twenty princely warriors guarded the *per-nefer*, posted there by Kamose himself. None was aware of the subterranean passage and hidden door which gave access to the embalming chamber through one painted wall. Soon, Archpriest and lamia stood beside the Pharaoh's corpse, which was sealed within layers of linen swathing and hard-set precious gum.

"Were you another man, I should say it had been an error to lodge the false gem within this mortal husk and then wrap it so securely," Mertseger said with transparently false respect. "Can you open the body and close it again?"

"I can open the very earth and then close it again, as you know, but that would be excessive and needless now. Watch the entrance very vigilantly, child of a serpent. Warn me if someone comes."

"Indeed," Mertseger said coolly, "I have no more wish to be trapped here than you."

Kamose laid the huge emerald blazing on Setekh-Nekht's linen-wrapped torso.

"The spurious gem is made of malachite and gilded lead," he explained. "To make it resemble the emerald, the thief had to place them side by side and cast a spell of similitude. A paltry matter, but it formed a sorcerous link between them, and of course they are the same size and shape precisely. To transpose them—so—without disturbing any matter in between, is an act but a little more finely skilled, slightly more subtle."

Kamose's somewhat oblique eyes looked into strange dimensions. His hands moved. They seemed to slide *past*, not through, the layers of bandage, the shells of hardened resin, the desert-dry flesh and ribcage.

Then his right hand was empty, the left full.

"All is now as it should be."

"Not all, surely. The thieves are yet at large."

"They are about to walk into quicksand of their own volition. There is one more thing we must do to guide their steps. Come."

Sunrise came to the marshes, cities, and harbors of the Delta, its vineyards and orchards. It found Kamose in his jackal mask and regalia, a picture of somber, sepulchral dignity. Not even Mertseger knew what expression he wore behind the mask.

A procession came to the *per-nefer* while dawn was still red, before they could begin the day's embalming. A company of archers came with it as escort. A dozen scribes and priests of Thoth walked ahead. Most conspicuous and august, borne in a litter because of his arthritis, was the Vizier of Lower Egypt.

Kamose saw him, and the rotund, purse-mouthed man who rode in a second litter following him. This one clearly felt satisfaction so immense he could not keep it from showing in his face however he tried. He wore precisely the look of a glutton who had tasted something that delights the mouth as much as it gratifies the belly, and now looked forward to the full banquet.

"Beba," Kamose said, very softly.

"The Archpriest of Thoth?" Mertseger, who knew something of Beba, sounded incredulous—with reason, Kamose thought. "Is this plot his?"

"Beba would not have the wits or the daring. No, someone has duped him. He believes me guilty because it is his dearest wish."

The Vizier leaned upon a staff because one leg had become twisted by his ailment. Although the pain made him irascible, his judgment had not suffered thereby. He almost personified the great principles of order, harmony, and justice which Egyptians called Ma'at, and his wisdom led him to doubt that Kamose valued these things cardinally.

Kamose pronounced a formal greeting. The Vizier advanced into the *per-nefer*'s antechamber with a few attendants, and Beba waddled with them. Mertseger discreetly withdrew.

Although the Vizier returned Kamose's greeting, he did so in a bleakly formal manner; and lost no time thereafter.

"The matter is too grave for drawn-out courtesy," he said. "It concerns the Pharaoh's heart scarab. Has anything come to pass concerning it which ought not to happen?"

"No, excellent Vizier. It has not."

"A lie!" Beba said impatiently.

"But there has assuredly been an attempt at something which ought not to happen. Someone has essayed to steal the heart scarab by exchanging a worthless copy. My report of this sacrilege was sent by my ablest courier to your greatness at Hikuptah. It was dispatched—yes, two days gone."

"No!" Beba's chagrin pleased Kamose. "No! The worthless copy of which the—the Archpriest—speaks was placed beside Pharaoh's heart. It rests there now!"

"If that were true," Kamose said austerely, "it would mean that you know a great deal about it. Yet that is not true. Nor do you flatter me. Who supposes that such a thing could be done and I not know? All that passes in my Temple is known to me, august Beba. Some of my subordinates, like some of yours, I dare say, are crafty."

Beba glared up at his rival. "There are witnesses of high character who will swear the scheme to filch the emerald scarab was yours!"

"Then name them."

"The Third Prophet of your own temple, Djeseret, and a lesser priest, Ib!"

"Djeseret? Ah." Kamose's voice came muffled and unctuous through the jackal-mask's black muzzle. "Sad. He's reaching his dotage."

The Third Prophet, summoned, gave much support to his Archpriest's comment. He decried Kamose as a creature of utterest evil, one who blasphemed the gods and had contrived the late Pharaoh's death. Since the Vizier knew the precise circumstances of Setekh-Nekht's death, that accusation gained no credence. Djeseret then averred that Kamose had tried to steal the heart scarab to deny the Pharaoh joy in the Afterworld. Clearly he had believed for some time that his Archpriest was less reverentially pious than he ought to be, and someone had worked on that belief through the decline of Djeseret's superannuated mind. Worked upon it with skill. Kamose soon observed that Djeseret believed all he was saying.

"He stole the gem! He! It lies beneath the altar in the temple of Anubis!"

There was one thing Djeseret could not possibly believe was true. Not even in his dotage. He could not believe it because, as Kamose had concluded days before, he was the thief himself.

Kamose removed his mask at last, to show a face set in lines of vast patience.

"What lies concealed there," he said, "is a false copy I discovered before I penned my report to you, O excellent Vizier. The true emerald scarab is where it ought to be, within the sacred body of Setekh-Nekht. If Prince Rameses or yourself orders, I shall open the mummy and prove this, but I should view it as woeful desecration. Perhaps the most skilled augurs and diviners in Egypt—outside my own Temple—should test the matter. I leave it in your hands and those of truth."

That ended it, in effect. The Vizier looked as though he considered Kamose's response too glib and knew there was more in the business than appeared, but the scarab had not been stolen, and the funeral must proceed without scandal. He conscientiously took possession of the false scarab, followed Kamose's suggestions, and had two of his own trusted scribes supervise all further proceedings. Setekh-Nekht's mummy remained closed, and Kamose presided at his obsequies.

Beba, the Archpriest of Thoth, presented a picture of incarnate woe while these events unfurled.

Epilogue

"*Djeseret* stole the scarab?" Mertseger marveled. "He?"

Kamose nodded. "To blame me. The dotard never thought of it as rascality. He persuaded himself—primed by someone else, I think— that I was spiritually unfit to be Archpriest of the Temple he had served lifelong. It's easy to make a righteous man commit acts of vile treachery if you only convince him they are his distasteful duty. The same person must have had Beba make the accusation, and so I infer that he ranks high in the priesthood of Thoth. I suspect he hoped to diminish me, if the plot succeeded, or Beba if it failed, and in either event to add to his own consequence."

"How that capon Beba slavered with joy to accuse you! Why did you let him off so lightly, my lord? You might have brought him down over this. Yet you assured the Vizier his motives were honest, and that Beba had been deceived."

"And how it mortified him to accept his status back from my condescending hand! I have no wish to bring him down. Having an incompetent at the head of my fiercest enemies is much to my advantage. My troubles will increase on the day an able man rises to lead that priesthood!"

"Such as the one who conceived this plot and used Djeseret and Beba as his cat's-paws. Do you know his name?"

"Not yet. One day I shall know, and deal with him. I am patient."

"You were lenient with Djeseret and Ib, also."

"Sending them to maintain a shrine in the western desert for the rest of their days is scarcely lenient. The Libyans may murder them. Certainly, if they ever take one step beyond the precincts of the shrine, I shall have them crushed like frogs between the stones." Kamose played with his pointed chin-beard. "Like our sagacious Vizier, I wish no scandal."

"And now you retreat to your mansion at Abdu for a time, with the Prince's leave."

"After he becomes Pharaoh, formally."

"May I accompany you?" The request came like poison mingled with honey.

Kamose rubbed his chin once more. Leaving her to her own malign devices would be madness! Mothers would wail for their infants again, and wives for their young husbands, throughout the Delta. Kamose had enhanced his fame greatly by ending Mertseger's reign of terror, and allowing it to begin anew would have the reverse effect.

"Abdu is a long, safe distance from Pi-Rameses. No doubt there are malefactors there, or in Thebes, who would be improved by your attentions, and I did promise you some diversion for your patience."

"Then I may come?"

Like unto a breathless little girl hoping for a gift, Kamose thought wryly. Knowing the risk, he said assessingly, "I believe you must, daughter of a serpent."

There are hundreds of books about mummies and ancient Egypt published for children. The British Museum, the Children's University of Manchester, the Oriental Institute of the University of Chicago, and other institutions have colorful "how to make a mummy" features online. Mummy exhibitions, reconstructed tombs, and funereal artifacts are big draws for museums and science centers, and often well attended by the kiddies. Helen Marshall's "The Embalmer" may be fiction, but . . .

The Embalmer
Helen Marshall

————

Henry didn't think of himself as an embalmer, not really; embalming was a sort of hobby for him, nothing serious, nothing more than a pastime. If someone asked him what he wanted to be when he grew up he would not have said *an embalmer*. He would have said *an astronaut* on most days because most days what he wanted to be was an astronaut.

He sometimes wondered if anyone ever got embalmed in space. He read once that if you went into space without a space suit then you would asphyxiate and suffer from ebullism, which he had to look up and it turns out it meant a "boiling away" of water vapor from the body. If you stayed in space long enough you would freeze into a giant chunk of ice. The embalmer thought that sounded an awful lot like embalming. Space was the biggest embalmer of them all.

Henry was not interested in modern-day embalming involving chemicals and such. He learned about embalming from a big book about Egypt that his mother had bought him after they went to the museum to see the mummies. The book said that Egyptians were made into mummies because they wanted to live forever. That made sense to the embalmer. The embalmer wanted to live forever too. The book said that it wasn't just people who were mummified. Sometimes it was people's pets. It was cats, dogs, mongooses, monkeys, gazelles, and birds. People didn't want to leave them behind. The embalmer thought this made good sense too. Those people were good people. They were responsible pet owners.

Sometimes the embalmer would dream that he had died. He dreamed that he was in Heaven and he got to take all the cats and dogs that he mummified with him. He wanted a legion of cats and dogs, so in the next life he would look like one of those dog-walkers, those college girls with a thousand leashes roped around their wrists. They looked like horizontal balloon artists holding strings attached to all sizes and shapes of furry balloons. That was what he wanted for himself when he died. Lots of cats and dogs. Hordes of them. He wasn't so sure about the mongooses, monkeys, gazelles, and birds. They sounded pretty unruly. Maybe that would just be overkill.

The embalmer was struck by love suddenly; love seized him up, it entered through his nostrils as he breathed in Dahlia's smell, it liquefied his insides and hardened his skin. She was fourteen years old, two years older than the embalmer was, and that was the perfect age gap. She was beautiful. She smelled beautiful. Her skin was light and lustrous, it positively glowed with warmth. Her teeth were straight. She had a little mole above her lip but the mole didn't have any hairs sticking out of it. It was a perfect mole. She had perfect skin. Her smell was luscious and sweet. It wasn't just all that though, the smell and the skin and the mole, it was the sadness she wore like a second skin, a second smell, a second perfect beauty spot right above her lip.

Dahlia's little brother had been hit by a car two months ago. The embalmer saw it on the news even though his mother didn't want him to. He set the DVR to record it. The news had traffic camera footage. The little brother had gone sailing through the air. He was wearing Superman pajamas but he didn't look much like Superman.

By this point the embalmer knew something about flying. He knew you had to hold your arms straight. You had to be an alien. Also you had to be invincible and maybe not need to breathe. Aliens didn't have to deal with asphyxiation or ebullism and the embalmer figured that must help when it came to flying.

Dahlia's brother wasn't an alien. If he had been in space his face would have turned bright blue. His eyeballs would have frozen into solid snowballs. But he wasn't in space. He was hit by a car and when the car hit him he flew only a short distance in his Superman pajamas.

So, the sadness. There was something he could do about that.

The embalmer chose one of his favorites—a black Labrador mixed with something else, something tall, a Great Dane maybe. The Labra-Dane's name had been Diesel. He had lived next door at the Smiths' house. The embalmer used to watch Diesel running the yard. Diesel was a champion Frisbee catcher. He loved to catch Frisbees. Boy could that dog fly! One leap and he was in the air, long ears streaming like bunting. In the winter, the Smiths wouldn't bother with the Frisbee. It was too cold. After the sun had gone down, they'd stand on the porch and run a flashlight over the fresh snow. Diesel was mad for those little sparks of light, like they were animals, like they were squirrels. It didn't matter that there was nothing but snow to fill his mouth. He'd bound in circles chasing the light and the Smiths would be careful to shine it only on the new snow, the snow unturned by Diesel's snowplow body.

One day Diesel was out in the backyard. Now it was summer—oh, maybe, three months ago? The Smiths were building a new fence. Earlier they had thrown a Frisbee badly and Diesel had leapt so high he cleared the old fence and ended up in the embalmer's yard. So they were building a new fence, a taller fence, a fence so high Diesel couldn't possibly make it over.

And he didn't.

The Smiths were cutting planks with a circular saw in the backyard and Diesel was running around loose, barking at squirrels, having a grand old time. Then he saw a flash, the saw-blade throwing off reflected triangles of sunlight. Well. You can guess what happened. That was it for Diesel.

The embalmer dug him up the day after he was buried. He had got pretty good with coat hangers and a pair of wire cutters. He didn't have natron like the Egyptians, so he dried him out with silica gel packages from his mother's closet. She always kept them.

Now Diesel was the embalmer's favorite. He was a flier. He was the one the embalmer wanted to see most tugging at the end of his leash in Heaven. He had already chosen Diesel to be the leader of the pack.

But by then the embalmer had fallen in love; he was too young to know for sure if it was true love or just a love-mirage, but he suspected it was probably the first one. He watched Dahlia at school. He heard she didn't bother to hand in her homework any more. She never answered questions. She had been popular for a while but that was starting to slip too. No one talked to her. It was like there was a terrible stink of death around her. But the embalmer knew death pretty well by that point and so to him it just made her more beautiful. Here was someone who had also seen the Before and the After. Everyone else in the class was just stuck in Beforeland. When After came their parents rushed them out of the room so that they could go on pretending that After was really Never.

So the embalmer left Diesel on Dahlia's porch. Diesel was swaddled up very tightly. The embalmer had done a gorgeous checkered pattern with the bandages and then he had colored them black with a Magic Marker so that they matched the color of Diesel's coat. It was his finest work.

What the embalmer didn't know was that Dahlia was already an expert at mummification. When her little brother died she decided that time ought to have stopped. It *had* stopped briefly inside of her, and she had felt quiet and calm and safe in a sort of hazy forever—but then time had started up again with that sickening thud. She had been trying unsuccessfully to stop time ever since. She would sit for hours with her face pressed against the window and she would stare at the traffic passing by. When a car was going too fast she would begin to shake. "Stop!" she would whisper. "Please stop!" Sometimes the cars would stop. This gave her a sense of control. But sometimes they didn't. This made her crazy. She started chewing on her hair but when she did that she got afraid that there was going to be a giant lump of hair inside of her and when she died some doctor would find it and know for sure that she was a hair chewer.

She was learning that the external world was too big, too hard. It could not be forced. On the other hand her body was something she *did* have control over. She had put on weight over the last two months. People kept leaving pies at the door. She never told her parents when she found the pies. She simply took the pies up to her room and ate them one by one, ate every slice of cold grief pie all on her own.

So, the weight. She wanted it off. She wanted to return to the exact size and shape she had been when her little brother had died. She started a cleanse, ordered the cold-pressed bottles of liquid online from All Juiced Up Cleansing Routines. She followed the routine for twenty days and at the end she had lost twenty pounds exactly as promised but not one inch of her had changed. She was still spilling out over the tops of her jeans. Her thighs were ungraceful as turkey drumsticks. She called up the number on the box to complain.

"That's perfectly normal," said the lady on the phone, her voice so cheerful that Dahlia for a moment saw a phantom floating smile in front of her eyes. "All the pounds, none of the inches. A miracle, huh? That way you don't need to buy a new wardrobe! You can feel better about yourself but nothing needs to change!"

"But I want to change," Dahlia said even though this wasn't quite true. What she wanted was *not* to change, but to get to that point she had to change back first. It was very complicated.

"Huh," said the lady. "No one ever wants to change. Not *really*. Take it from me, missy, illusion is enough. But what you've got works so what's the big deal?"

Dahlia hung up the phone. She checked the ingredients on the bottle and discovered she'd been drinking turpentine. But the lady on the phone had been right. Dahlia felt clear all the way through, like it had tunneled a hollow space right through her own hollow space.

Still.

Two days later she called up again to demand a refund. She told the entire dead brother sob story while the lady clucked sympathetically at all the right points.

"Sorry," the lady said at the end of it. "No can do. Death is a pre-existing condition. It voids the money back guarantee."

Dahlia said something unpleasant and slightly racist.

"Geez," said the woman, "don't get snippy. Tell you what, I'll send you a free sample of our new product. It's super secret right now but I swear it'll do the job, okay? Okay."

Dahlia slammed down the phone for a second time. The anger made her feel better. It hollowed her out as well. It turns out that anger and turpentine have a lot in common. But when she went to check on the mail later that day she found on her doorstep the swaddled corpse of the Labra-Dane, perfectly preserved.

"This is more like it," she said, absently stroking the linen bandages. They stained her fingers black.

The embalmer felt Diesel's absence immediately. When he slept, he slept fitfully. There was a hole in the middle of his dreams. The other dogs and cats had come to rely upon Diesel. They needed his sense of direction, his manic energy. He always knew which direction to pull and he never stopped wanting to be somewhere else. Now the others sat there. Some of the dead cats licked at their paws. Others fought, big screeching cat battles where they stood up on their hind legs and threw their front paws in front of them like puppeteers. It got so that the embalmer could hardly stand the racket any more.

And then the next morning, Dahlia brought Diesel to school. He was awkward to carry. He wouldn't fit in her backpack but she wouldn't have wanted to carry him that way even if he had. She set him up just underneath her desk so that his bandaged nose poked against her knees while she worked at her fractions.

The embalmer didn't see this but he heard about it at lunch. In math class he volunteered to deliver a note from Miss Persimmons, *his* teacher, to Miss Kitagawa, *her* teacher. The note was folded carefully in two but he read it anyway. The note said, "What do you want for dinner tonight, Kitty?"

Dahlia was in the classroom. She didn't look up when he knocked on the door. She didn't look up when Miss Kitagawa passed her to answer it. And when Miss Kitagawa was carefully writing the words "roast beef and mashed potatoes" underneath Miss Persimmons' tidier handwriting, the embalmer pretended to knock an eraser off Miss Kitagawa's desk. From down below all he could see was knees mostly. Miss Kitagawa's knees which were dead white underneath her panty-hose. And more knees and sneakers. Dahlia's knees. Diesel's nose. Dahlia's hand stroking the Magic-Markered bandages. He thought if she ever ruffled his hair like that he would probably just die he would be so happy.

After class the embalmer decided to risk it all on an approach. He feigned nonchalance. He carried a leash in his left hand.

"S'cuse me," he mumbled. His throat was dry as hot tarmac.

Dahlia said nothing but she turned at least, she looked at him. Her eyes were the same color as the lockers. Time was not his friend right now. She would have to leave to catch her bus.

"I thought he might make a run for it." He handed her the leash. Her eyes grazed him carefully, confused, skeptical, irritated, angry—but then she laughed all at once like a hiccough and she clipped it on to the Labra-Dane's collar and then maybe it was okay even if she had been all of those things before

"I almost lost him in first period," she confided. "He saw a squirrel. He's absolutely bananas for squirrels."

"He looks like he could drag you ten feet."

"I'm stronger than I look."

This is good, thought the embalmer, *I'm really doing this. I think she might be in love with me.*

But then there was the bus and even though Dahlia didn't have any friends to remind her about it, there is some power that buses always have. They let you know they are leaving. They let you know you're supposed to be going someplace else.

"Bye," Dahlia said. She ruffled the top of his head very gently. He was barely taller than her shoulders. He thought about stilts. He thought he might need a ladder if he was ever going to kiss her. He wondered if maybe she'd be willing to stop growing so he could catch up a little bit.

But then the back of her skirt was swishing as she ran for the bus. He watched the inside of her knees which were lovely like little china cups and her calves which were perfect and her socks which were plain white and her sneakers which were older than they should be if she wanted to be popular but all the while he could still feel her fingers touching the hairs of his head and each of them like a raw nerve, each of them standing up like he'd been zapped by lightning.

He missed his own bus. He walked all the way home, but he didn't mind.

That night the embalmer's mother answered the door to find a policeman standing there, awkward; he looked like he wanted to clean his nails or his teeth but he didn't have anything useful with which to get the job done. The embalmer peeked at him from the top of the stairway.

"Sorry, ma'am," he said, his voice a dry cough with extra vowels, "but some of the neighbors have complained about missing animals."

"Missing animals?" she asked.

"You've read the stories? Seen them on the news? Missing animals can mean all sorts of things. But sometimes it means. Well. A killer, you know? A psychopath. Very young. An infant psychopath." He ran his hands through his hair like he was searching for something. "They like to cut things up, yeah? They like to hang them from trees. Or keep them in sheds."

His mother was easily shocked. Her voice echoed with a slow quaver. "Has someone found an animal like that? Goodness gracious me!"

"Not as such," answered the officer. "But we think. Maybe. The animals are missing, you see? So we think maybe that's what's happening."

"But you're not sure?" Relief edging in. "Maybe it's something else? Maybe, coyotes?"

"That's the thing, ma'am. Something already got them." Cough cough. "*Something* already got them. The animals. Feline leukemia. Or a Buick. One of them drank weed killer, we think. It's hard to tell. There's no body to autopsy."

His mother stared blankly.

"It's only *after* they were dead we found out they were missing. So. Pretty strange, isn't it? Someone digging up and taking dead pets? Pretty *criminal*, wouldn't you say?" A rapid blink then the eyes swung to the stairs like searchlights. The embalmer almost gave himself up then and there. "When we find them we'll know. That's what I'm saying. So. Tell us if you see anything."

That was the end of the conversation.

The embalmer ran to his bedroom and flopped down. His heart beat desperately, it shuddered in his ribcage like a fist pounding a door.

"I'd like to report a crime," Dahlia said into the telephone. She wished there was one of those old springy cords she could twirl around her fingers while she was talking. She wanted her fingers to be more active. They twirled her hair but then she started licking her lips and that made her stop immediately. The craving was still strong, but she was stronger. She was stronger than she looked.

"Someone out there is killing people," she said, "and dogs. Dogs too. The dogs are also important. It's easy to overlook the dogs but we shouldn't because they are the first sign, aren't they?" She patted the Labra-Dane's head. She wondered what his tongue looked like. She could see the nose, it glimmered from between the bandages like a third eye.

"Did you ever think it was cruel that God gave animals such a short lifespan? I mean, not for the animals. But have you ever thought about Adam and Eve? One day he's playing with his cocker spaniel, throwing sticks or whatever, and the next day the poor thing just keels over. He doesn't know what's wrong with it. But then an angel says to him, 'That'll be you one day, kid. One day you're just going to keel over. That's what God did for you.' And Adam knows he's right. Adam starts watching everything drop around him. Bunnies. Grasshoppers. He swats a fly and then the fly stops moving. So he gets extra careful for a while but that doesn't help because there's a wolf that brings down a deer and if it didn't bring down that deer then its wolfpups would starve and there's a cat with feline leukemia and if it didn't have feline leukemia eventually it'd go blind and mangy and brittle. All of these things are just happening anyway so it doesn't matter what he does, it's going to get him too. And he thinks, Jesus, why did you make me name all these fuckers?"

"I'm sorry, miss," said the receptionist, "but you said there was a crime? Is someone hurt? Please stay where you are, miss."

"I can't help it," she said, "I'm the victim of a crime."

But then she wondered if that was true and she started replaying what she'd said. It made her sound like a serial killer. She wondered if they could trace the call.

"Sorry," she said. "I think I must have dialed the wrong number. Is this All Juiced Up? There's a problem with your product."

She hung up the phone.

In the middle of the night the embalmer had the strange sense that something was trying to wake him up. He thought it was Diesel or he thought, rather, that it would have been Diesel yapping for his attention but Diesel wasn't there any more.

He opened his eyes.

There was Dahlia. Her face was an inch away from the glass of the bedroom window. He could see her but he couldn't smell her. She was on the other side of the window. Her mouth had clouded the glass. There were two lip prints in the mist. It was like a giant mouth coming out of the darkness and into his room and there was Dahlia behind it.

He went to the window. He blew on it very gently. It did not cloud up. It was too warm inside the room. But he pressed his lips against it anyway. The window tasted of glass. It didn't taste of Dahlia. But he kissed it again. She had leaned down for him. He didn't need a stepladder at all.

The next day in class it was clear to the embalmer that Miss Persimmons was frightened. She had a nervous disposition to begin with. She jumped when the boys dropped their textbooks and of course this made the boys drop their textbooks a lot, on some days it sounded like London in the Blitz there were so many textbooks slamming the linoleum.

"Excuse me," she said, "excuse me, boys and girls, everyone listen!"

A math book hit the ground. It was only an exercise book, it barely made a noise at all, but she still shuddered and all the boys sniggered under their hands.

It was her kitty. Her kitty had gone missing. Last week she was a person with a kitty but the embalmer knew that look, that she had already begun to accept being a person without a kitty. She looked devastated.

Another book fell. A hardcover this time, the air *whoofed* out, scattering dust in a perfect circle around it.

Then there was silence.

After class, everyone in the hallways was whispering and pointing and pulling and snarling, yapping, yammering. They were an angry crowd, there were sharpened pencils, there were scissors, they were cutting at her hair, they were slicing up her skirt. They knew it was her, of course they did, they knew it was Dahlia. They knew it was her because they'd all seen the black dog she carried around with her, and even when they couldn't see the black dog, it was still like there was a black dog following her day by day by day so they *knew* and it made them happy and it made them angry and it made them dangerous.

There was a bit the embalmer had read in one of his books, about a crocodile god, or maybe only part crocodile, because there were other parts too, part hippopotamus, part lion, all of those animals which were known to be man-eaters. And it was this god who would eat the hearts of the dead if they weren't good enough, if they weren't skinny enough, if they weren't cool enough, if they carried black dogs with them, if their brothers died, if they were good with wire cutters, if they needed stepladders to kiss—and the people in the hallway were like that now, they had become the Great Devourer.

The embalmer wanted to stop it all but he didn't know how. He didn't know what to do when things went a little bit wrong, only when things went very wrong like if your pet rabbit accidentally drank weed killer or you forgot to feed it for a while. Death was fixable. Hurt was much harder.

But Dahlia bore it all patiently. She reminded the embalmer of pictures he had seen, pictures of St Thecla and all the little virgin martyrs his mother prayed to every night. Even when the yammerers cut her hair into a jagged line she had this look in her eyes that was peaceful and serene. She looked like she could reach out and touch them and then they would all be blessed, their zits would clear, their periods would dry up, their unwanted erections would wither, their wanted erections would swell to the size of cucumbers. They were making her powerful and they didn't even know it.

I think you know where this story is going now. I think if you knew what happened to Diesel in the yard with the circular saw then you think you know where this story is going, you think you know what's going to happen to Dahlia because maybe she'll drink the weed killer, maybe that's what she got in the mail the next day from All Juiced Up, maybe she'll die and then the embalmer will come for her the way he came for Diesel, the way he came for all the other animals.

But that's not this story.

The kitty was found. Miss Kitagawa organized an urgent postering campaign and pretty soon the street was covered with pictures of the missing cat. It was the Smiths who finally found her. She was scratching at their backdoor, demanding to be let in. The littlest Smith wanted to keep her so they kept her for a while even though she had a collar, even though there were all those signs taped to poles and tacked to bulletin boards. But the Smiths had to keep her in the basement. They were worried about someone spotting her in the window. She was a celebrity now, the kitty was, sure to be recognized. But then the littlest Smith had a change of heart when she saw Miss Persimmons crying in the girls' bathroom, all of her adult self curled up on one of those tiny toilets that barely reached her knees.

But by then Dahlia had been pulled out of school. Her parents were moving to Florida, some place where it was warm and sunny and where they wouldn't have to see that awful stretch of road outside their house. Dahlia buried the Labra-Dane in the backyard garden. She planted an acorn over the top. Maybe in a thousand years, she thought, there'll be squirrels. God that dog was bananas for squirrels.

In Florida Dahlia was mysteriously cool. Maybe it was the jagged punk hair she wore. Maybe it was the mole above her lip. Maybe it was the fact that the new cleanse was working, she'd lost twenty-four inches even if she never dropped a pound. All of her felt heavier after that and her sandals always made deeper footprints in the sand than anyone else's did.

When the other kids whispered that *something had happened* where she came from and that *she used to have a brother* this all had a kind of magic to them. Like they didn't have Death in Florida. Which maybe,

Dahlia thought, they didn't. Everyone she saw had brownish-orange skin, everyone's face had withered, everyone looked like they'd been around since the pyramids.

But she felt better. It wasn't the weight thing, though that's what her parents thought. It wasn't the kids either. They didn't matter to her so much now. They were just kids. Maybe it was just the move, being somewhere new. The ocean. The sunlight. Maybe they were good for her. Maybe that was enough for her to let go a little and be happy.

It was soon after Dahlia moved that Henry's mother discovered the wire cutters in his bedroom. She couldn't understand why he was sad all the time and her magazines said it was probably drugs and that they'd probably be in his closet or in his mattress. She checked all those places but she didn't find the drugs, she found the wire cutters instead. And because she was a mother and she had a mother's instinct and she remembered the way the police officer had been looking up the stairs it all came together in one awful, glorious moment of realization.

So they left too. They weren't hiding out exactly, it was never anything as obvious as that. Henry hadn't broken any laws. He probably wasn't an infant psychopath. But they loaded up the car and they drove away. Just in case.

Wherever they ended up they didn't stay very long. She never let him into pet shops and she was suspicious when he went out by himself or he didn't come home on time. But he was getting older and she didn't want to suffocate him. He had a girlfriend, the girlfriend did drugs but she was pretty and his mother figured they'd both grow out of it eventually, what was she supposed to do, just ground him forever? Of course not. He had a life to live. She couldn't freeze him in place, she couldn't stop bad things from happening. All she could do was watch and wait and pray that he was okay, pray that her love was enough to keep him safe forever.

Adam Roberts offers a brilliant alternative history take on the assumed superiority of imperial "civilization" and its views of subordinate colonial lands filled with interesting archaeological relics and remnants, inhabited by "degenerate" races mired in the past and incapable of prevailing as their ancestors had. In our world, "Tollund Man" is much like the mummy described. Probably the most well-preserved body we have from pre-historic times, the mummy was discovered in 1950 in a peat bog near a small village—Tollund—on the Jutland Peninsula of Denmark. Now estimated to have died between 375 and 210 BCE, it has been determined that the cause of his death was hanging.

Tollund
Adam Roberts

———

-1-

1330 AH

As he stepped from the boat, Gamal el-Kafir el-Sheikh's impressions were of warm air and a bright sky. That vivid, alien green so characteristic of the northlands. It was, altogether, a pleasant surprise. There weren't many passengers; for few people had any reason to come to this far-flung land, and el-Kafir el-Sheikh's servant—assigned him for the duration of the excavation—found him easily enough. "I am Bille, *minherr*," he said in passable Masri. "I may take you the hotel?" He was a tall man, but he stared at his own shoes as he spoke, which in turn prompted el-Kafir el-Sheikh to look down. The fellow had huge feet, big as boats, wrapped in two ill-cobbled shoes of scuffed leather. "Bille what?" el-Kafir el-Sheikh asked him. "Or is it, what-Bille?

This seemed to confuse the big Jutlander. "I'm sorry, *minherr*?"

"I'm asking your full name."

"Bille Jensen, *minherr*."

"Come along, man, don't quail! I'm a historian, an archaeologist, not a Grendl! I won't eat you." The fellow didn't respond to this, but el-Kafir el-Sheikh clapped him on the back. "My first time here, you know. Though I've spent years in libraries learning about it. What a charming-looking country!"

"Yes, *minherr*."

They rode a horse and cart, the nag a proper north-European beast, rust-colored, barrel-flanked, its legs tasseled with dirty trailing strands of hair. The road was rutted and progress was slow. El-Kafir el-Sheikh didn't care. The air was full of xylophonic birdsong and the breeze had the authentic tang of occidental exoticism. It was all so *green*! The trees positively foamed with leaves. "Are my colleagues all at the hotel?"

"*Minherr*?"

"Professor Suyuti? Professor el-Akkad? Or are they at the dig?"

"At the hotel, *minherr*."

"You have seen the dig?"

The fellow angled his long-boned face in his master's direction. Was that fear in the old man's eyes? "Yes, *minherr*."

"Oh it's a marvelous thing. You know, I have nothing but respect for your people and your culture," el-Kafir el-Sheikh told him, a touch over-earnestly (but he was prone to over-earnestness). "You should know that these archaeological digs are a way of uncovering the rich history of your folk."

"Yes, *minherr*," the fellow said, sulkily, turning his big head back in the direction of travel.

"I sense your disaffection. You don't like us rootling around amongst your old kings and dukes." When this failed to produce a reply, el-Kafir el-Sheikh added: "Are you a *superstitious* fellow, Bille? Is it the business with the mummies?"

The servant put a brief sine wave into the reins he was holding and barked a barbaric Jutlandese command at the horse. But he did not answer el-Kafir el-Sheikh's question.

"It's all nonsense, you know, my dear fellow," el-Kafir el-Sheikh told him, pulling out his pipe and lighting it. "We are men of science. Of course I heard those stories about murders and strange deaths. Which is to say, I read about them in the papers. Back in Cairo there's a deal of excitement about your mummies, you know. Oh we have mummies back home, you know, but they're *clean*. The fact is, there's a certain type of Egyptian who likes nothing better than grisly stories of the bog-mummies, coming alive and turning human victims to sludge. But that it's a good story doesn't mean it's true, now does it!"

The cart trundled round the corner, under an archway formed by two lusciously foliaged trees, and the hotel appeared before them. And sauntering out through the main entrance was Professor Tawfiq el-Akkad. "Gamal, you old rogue!" he cried. "Finally you have come!"

-2-

The whole team took tea in the conservatory: el-Kafir el-Sheikh, Suyuti, el-Akkad, and Hussein. Everyone called Hussein *Gurbati* because he was Dom rather than misriyūn; but he didn't seem to mind. "It's too late to go out to the site today," el-Akkad announced. "And tomorrow is Sabbath. But first thing al-Ahad we'll go straight there. We have a car, you know. I do believe it is the only internal combustion engine in the whole of Jutland!"

"I really can't wait," el-Kafir el-Sheikh gushed. "I brought all my books."

"Oh, it's your noggin we really need," said Suyuti.

"Don't tell me there aren't any runes," said el-Kafir el-Sheikh. "I was *promised* runes."

"Runes," said Gurbati, in a bored-sounding voice. "We've dozens of tablets, linden-wood mostly, absolutely covered in runes. But it's not that."

"People are chatting," Suyuti said. "In Danish."

"You mean—Old Danish?"

"I certainly don't mean new Danish!"

"Which people?"

"Natives; whitters. People who cannot read or write. As to how they could acquire the complex grammar and vocabulary of a dead language . . . well, some say their god of language, Jut, has put a spell upon them. Cast a spell across time, from a thousand years ago."

"Good gracious!" el-Kafir el-Sheikh sucked lustily on his pipe stem. "It took me seven years' careful study to acquire it. Are you sure they're speaking Old Danish?"

Suyuti's laugh was like a thunderclap. "That's what you're here to determine, my old friend!" he boomed. He took a drink, and when he lowered the cup the hairs of his moustache were dewed with droplets of tea. "That—and the runes."

"Of course you've heard the stories of strange goings-on," Gurbati observed, gloomily.

"Well," el-Kafir el-Sheikh laughed. "I've read some silly stories. People exploding and so on. People turning to . . . well, manure. I can't say I believed it."

"*He* believes it," Suyuti chortled, clapping Gurbati on the shoulder.

"Really? I didn't realize you were a superstitious type, Gurbati! And you think it's connected to your digging up these old mummies? It hardly seems credible."

"It looks unlikely in the sunlight, I grant you," said Gurbati. "But you wait. The weather will revert to type tomorrow, and everything will look different. As to the mummies, well, I don't know. But I do know that there have been strange deaths. The police have opened official investigations on three of them. Talk to Bille. He saw one of the victims die. Actually watched the woman . . . deliquesce!"

But nothing could dampen el-Kafir el-Sheikh's spirits. He was actually here, in Jutland, with his university friends, about to take part in the most exciting discovery in the history of archaeology! "Come, come," he said. "It's 1333! It's not the dark ages. We are men of science.

I'll keep an open mind," he added, "of course. But I'm itching to see these mummies, and I don't believe they're *cursed*."

Later that evening, after a splendid supper, they all sat in the conservatory of the hotel. The weather had changed, and el-Kafir el-Sheikh listened to the rain percussing the roof with a continual, rather soothing rush of noise over their heads. They all smoked. Mohammed Suyuti gave them the benefit of his theory as to why the northerners had failed to rise to the level of the Ummah. "It's not racial, whatever some people say. I do not hold with those despicable racist views. There's nothing *intrinsically* inferior about the northerners. It's an accident of geography."

"You mean," said el-Akkad. "The climate."

"The climate dulls their spirits, it is true," said Suyuti. "In Africa it is so hot that a man must either wilt or rouse himself to great things. There's nothing like that here; they all stumble about in a daze. It's too cold to sleep properly, and also so cold that they can't properly wake up. But, no, I meant something else. Here." He pulled a notebook from his pocket, opened it and began to read:

> *Egypt is not just a piece of land. Egypt is the inventor of civiliza-tion . . . The strange thing is that this country of great history and unsurpassed civilization is nothing but a thin strip along the banks of the Nile . . . This thin strip of land created moral values, launched the concept of monotheism, developed arts, invented science, and gave the world a stunning administration. These factors enabled the Egyptians to survive while other cultures and nations withered and died.*

"I copied that from a book I was reading. Doesn't it strike you as true? In Egypt civilization was focused about the Nile, and that focus, the pressure that applied to human culture, *generated* civilization—as carbon is compressed into diamond! But throughout northern Europe there's no such focus. Population spreads itself more or less equally about the inlands, more or less diffuse, and no great civilization can coalesce."

"It's an interesting theory," said el-Kafir el-Sheikh, gesturing towards Suyuti with the stem of his pipe. "But I would need to see hard evidence. Science! That's the key, gentlemen!"

"My father used to tell me," Gurbati said, in a gloomy voice, "*men contend with the living, not with the dead.* It was his way of telling me to get on with life, and not waste my energies worrying about the past. But here—in Jutland—well, I tell you, the opposite is true. The opposite is literally true."

"Nonsense," el-Kafir el-Sheikh retorted. "Don't tell me you've become a slave to superstition?"

"Back home the past is cleaned and tidied away. Here it's simply left to rot where it falls. It mulches down. These bogs all around us—compacted layers of decaying generations." He shuddered, visibly. "Magic may not be so difficult to believe as all that, you know. Not here. Not in this land."

-3-

First sun, then rain, and finally mist. The following morning el-Kafir el-Sheikh pulled the curtains back to be faced with an honest-to-goodness Jutland fog. The homely sun and blue sky had been completely erased, as if dissolved in white solution. Boughs from a couple of the nearer trees loomed blackly towards him, looking disconnected from the world as if levitating in mid-air. Everything else was albumen and opacity. He opened his window. The smell of clouds, wet and faintly vegetative, and a weird muffled silence.

Breakfast was a muted affair, as if the fog had gotten into everyone's spirits. Suyuti spoke at an ordinary volume, which for him was akin to whispering. "You'll need gloves and a scarf," he advised el-Kafir el-Sheikh. "And I recommend a hat. It's a long drive to the dig, and we'll have to take it slowly in this weather. Visibility, you know."

"Chilly, chilly," el-Akkad confirmed.

The drive was a surreal experience. The road was unsmooth, and the four of them (plus Bille, who was driving) were bounced around, continuously jiggled and agitated; but otherwise el-Kafir el-Sheikh had almost no sensation of motion. Objects might suddenly appear, as if magically transported from nothing into being—the end of a hedgerow, a cow—and lurch towards them, and then vanish into nothingness behind them. And it *was* cold. Worse, el-Kafir el-Sheikh found that his clothes soaked up moisture and quickly became sopping. The sun was a vagueness of light, high up and to the south. Nothing cast a shadow. "I pride myself on my scientific rationalism," el-Kafir el-Sheikh confided to Gurbati, "but even I can see that—this is a spooky sort of place."

"It's so *ancient*," Gurbati replied, raising his voice over the rattle and hum of the car's passage. "I mean: Egypt is ancient, obviously. But Egypt has moved on. *This* land is trapped by the past—as if the past is throttling it, preventing the whole country from going forward." He shuddered. With the cold, perhaps.

"It's like some vast entity has breathed on to the mirror of the sky, and clouded it over," el-Kafir el-Sheikh said.

Finally they arrived: two lights like pearl-colored eyes bright in the fog revealed themselves to be oil lamps, struggling to light either side of a gateway in a fence of knitted wire. A Jutlander boy, presumably alerted by the sound of the approaching vehicle, was standing guard. Bille drove past him, and turned the car to a halt, tossing up a little surf of mud. They had parked in front of a long wooden shed, lit from within. El-Kafir el-Sheikh was not sorry to get inside, for there was a stove in the middle around which they all huddled. "So cold!" el-Kafir el-Sheikh gasped. "And yesterday was sunny and warm!"

"We're on higher ground," Gurbati said. "That, and the mist, cools it. That, and the fact that this land is always cold—cold as death! Come! Do you want to see this mummy, or not?"

The four of them went out of the back of the building, leaving Bille scowling by the stove. The trench was two dozen yards away, roofed with canvas; they went down the turf-cut steps one after the other into the dark. It took Suyuti an unconscionably long time to light the lamp, and el-Kafir el-Sheikh stood in the gray murk trying to see where the mud at his feet ended and the ancient bodies began. But even when light filled the space it was hard to see. "They're the same color as the soil," Gurbati explained, pointing to the first of them. Dark brown bumps and ridges, inset in the ground. Suyuti lit a second lamp and handed it to el-Kafir el-Sheikh; and by squatting down he made out the contours of the body. "The face is," Suyuti prompted, pointing, "particularly well preserved."

"Remarkable!" el-Kafir el-Sheikh agreed, holding the lamp closer. And so it was: two thousand years old, yet every detail perfectly preserved—the grain of his chin stubble; the left-curling line of his nose (broken in life, perhaps; or distorted by the pressures of the bog); the creases under his closed eyes; the vertical worry-ridges running up his forehead. As if he were asleep and having a bad dream. The fellow was wearing a thin leather cap, tied under his chin. Moving the lamp, el-Kafir el-Sheikh could see the cord—he'd read about it, of course— tight around the corpse's neck and trailing down his back like a tentacle; the leather rope that had killed him. "Why the hood?" he wondered aloud. "From Strabo and Tacitus we discover that the northerners stripped their victims naked before sacrificing them to the goddess. And—" He moved the lamp to shine more clearly on the corpse's emaciated body, a man-shaped, teak-brown leather sack pulled tight around its skeleton. "He is naked. But his head is covered!"

"The other bodies we've found *have* been bare-headed, as you probably know," said Suyuti, in a condescending voice. "This chap must have been special."

"Fascinating," said el-Kafir el-Sheikh, poking gently at the face with the stem of his pipe. He stood up. "Are we moving him today?"

"I was thinking we would," Suyuti replied. "Get him back to the hotel. It's the peat that has preserved him, and now he's exposed to the air he's going to start decaying. He needs to go into the chemical bath back at the hotel. You see," Suyuti said, as they started climbing, single file, out of the tent, el-Kafir el-Sheikh carrying one torch and Suyuti the other, "he's not a true mummy. When *our* ancestors mummified a man they did it properly: took out the viscera and brains, all the matter that would putrefy quickly. They cleaned everything up. But this dirty fellow has all his guts and brains intact—they just strangled him and shoved him in the bog!"

"Clean," Gurbati observed gloomily, "is an alien concept to these people."

Back inside the hut they found Bille and the boy huddled at the stove. It was, el-Kafir el-Sheikh thought with an inward sigh, hard to dispute Gurbati's prejudice when faced with the two of them: grimy faces, unwashed clothes. A tight, sweaty stink seemed permanently attached to them, as if they never bathed. Suyuti shooed them away and the four archaeologists pulled up chairs and smoked their pipes. El-Akkad fetched a folding table, and the wooden paddles from a crate in the corner of the hut, and el-Kafir el-Sheikh diverted them for half an hour by reading the runes aloud, translating as he went. "There's not much here," he said. "Itineraries, heads of cattle—this one is a royal proclamation, declaring that King Rudolphus claims all the land from the north sea to the southern mountains."

He read out another, hesitating over the characters. "Well, I'm not sure what this one is—a poem, maybe. It doesn't really make a lot of sense."

"Difficult to know what to *do* with these things," said el-Akkad. "We could put them on display in the museum, but who wants to see some old wood tablets? I was thinking if there's anything exciting—a new Beowulf story, maybe—something that would tickle the popular appetite for northern exoticism."

"He was thinking of maybe publishing a translation and making his fortune," boomed Suyuti, with a laugh.

"It would be of *scholarly* interest," insisted el-Akkad.

"I don't think there's anything here like that," said el-Kafir el-Sheikh. He read another one aloud.

"What a barbarous language it is," noted Gurbati. "And as much gibberish to those two as to us!" He gestured at the two Jutland servants in the corner.

"Well if you don't want them for the university in Aarhus," said el-Kafir el-Sheikh, stacking the clicky wooden tablets one on top of the other. "Then I would love to take them back to Cairo with me. We have Danologists who would love to get their hands on this."

"We can discuss it later," said Suyuti. "Bille!" he called. "Hans, come along! We'll need you to help us lever the body out of the . . . Hans!" he shouted. "Stop that! What are you doing?"

What Hans was doing could best be described as dancing. His eyes were wide open, popping from his circular face, his arms were stiff at his side. He hopped in a rapid, jittery jig from left foot to right foot. The old man, Bille, was regarding the lad with frank horror. "Stop!" yelled Suyuti, angrily. "What do you think you're *doing*, boy?"

The child opened his mouth, and gurgled. Black blood poured from his lips. His arms jerked and flew away from his sides, and with a crash he fell backwards on to the wooden boards. The four scientists leapt up. The lad was supine, thrashing as if in the middle of a conniption fit. Blood began to ooze from the pores of his face. His shirt and trousers soaked black from within. His eyeballs had rolled up white, and the sockets filled with red. In moments he stopped moving.

The four men, and the servant, stood motionless, horrified. "What?" el-Kafir el-Sheikh gasped. "What?"

"It is the curse-death," said Bille, in a gravel voice. "The curse-death of the bog king! We have all seen it, *minherren*! We are all cursed too."

"Curse, nonsense," barked Suyuti, "It must be some terrible medical condition—the poor fellow!"

"Do you think it's contagious?" Gurbati wanted to know, stepping back from the boy's body. Blood was still oozing from him, seeping between the planks of the floor.

"We should call the police," said el-Kafir el-Sheikh. "We should notify the authorities."

"There aren't any phone wires out here," Suyuti said. "We could make our way to Tollund—that's the nearest village. But there are no phone lines there either; it's a tiny place, a community of farmers and a couple of Ummah policemen in an outpost. Better to go back to the hotel."

El-Kafir el-Sheikh looked down. To think he was gazing on a fresh corpse! Yet it felt queerly unreal. The strange thing was that the dark-brown body in the trench outside had a greater heft about it, a sense of the gravity of actual deceased humanity. This diminutive shape, wet with dark fluid, looked like a doll. "Where was he from?"

"*I* don't know," said Suyuti. "One of the villages, I suppose. Tollund, probably."

"We can't leave him here."

"We can't take him with us!"

"Bury him," said el-Akkad. "Get Bille to dig a grave."

"Burn him, rather, *minherren*," exclaimed Bille, waving his arms. He added something in his own language, but gabbled it too fast for el-Kafir el-Sheikh to be able to understand. Then, in Masri: "Burn the body, or more will die!"

"The police will surely want to look at the corpse," Suyuti declared. "So we can't burn it; and we can't just leave it here." But then Gurbati worried aloud about wolves, which hadn't occurred to el-Kafir el-Sheikh; so they did bury it in the end—a shallow grave, that Bille dug very complainingly. The corpse was so covered in blood that there was nowhere to hold him without dirtying one's hands; in the end they wrapped a rope about his feet and dragged him outside and into the trench.

-4-

They agreed to postpone undertaking further work on the mummy until after the police had examined the scene; given them the all-clear. In the circumstances there was nothing else for them to do but return to the hotel. Suyuti went outside to tie down the canvas over the trench, but he came back in a state of agitation. "The mummy is gone."

"Gone!"

Naturally they all rushed out to see for themselves. It was true. The body had been stolen. The man-shaped indentation remained in the mud, showing exactly how the figure had once lain curled on its side. They searched the length of the trench, and then moved in a series of wider circles through the foggy ground outside, but there was no sign of the body.

"Gurbati!" Suyuti called. "Do you have your pistol?"

"I do."

"Good. I'm also armed."

"What are you bellowing about *guns* for?" el-Akkad wanted to know.

"Isn't it obvious?" Suyuti replied, in a lower voice. "Somebody has stolen the mummy. Whoever they are, they're dangerous. There must be more than one of them, or they couldn't have got the body away. You think it mere coincidence that the boy died just when he did? It was a diversionary tactic—they poisoned him, to keep us occupied. Murder is nothing to *them*."

The fog seemed to have crept into el-Kafir el-Sheikh's stomach; his whole torso felt cold. "But what do they want with a mummy?"

"These people," Gurbati said, "are a mess of superstitions and muddled religion. Who knows what devil-magic they hope to perform? We really ought to get back to the hotel. We need to get the police out here. We need the colonial military to go through the whole area."

They found Bille by the grave of the lad, on his knees in the dirt with his palms pressed together over his head, after the manner of the strange religion of the land. He was not happy to be interrupted, but he did what he was ordered, howsoever surlily. They all clambered into the vehicle. It took a repeated series of backward-forward maneuvers, each one topped with a bone-breaking sound of gears being shifted, before the automobile was facing the right way. Then they drove off down the track, through the gates, and el-Kafir el-Sheikh felt a weight lift from his soul. He was the least superstitious person in the world, but it was good to get away from that place. "Is that how the others died?" el-Kafir el-Sheikh asked the Jutlander. "Did they—sweat blood until they died?"

"Some, *minherr*," Bille replied. "Some melted away, like lard in a pan. Some exploded, *bmm!* and flew in lumps in all directions." He smacked his lips.

The road began to climb, and all at once the wheels of the vehicle became stuck in the soft ground. They all had to get out and push, save only Bille crouched over the steering wheel. By the time they had freed the automobile and hefted it to the top of the rise the four archaeologists were mud-caked up to their hips, and spattered all about their bodies and faces. Suyuti in particular was in a foul mood. "Cursed countryside—this is the very landscape of uncleanness!" he yelled.

El-Kafir el-Sheikh could not disagree. It was not the mud, only; it was the fog. There was something noisome about the vapor. It had thickened, and its pearl chill had yellowed, acquired a buttery, rancid quality. It stuck in the throat. "Come along, gentlemen," he called, trying to chivvy himself along with everybody else. "Back in the car and to the hotel. A hot bath will restore us to humanity!"

That was when they saw the mummy.

There was no mistaking it: el-Kafir el-Sheikh has studied that leathern face, with its millennially etched detail of wrinkle and stubble, carefully enough. And now it was standing in the headlights of the automobile. Its skinny arms were little more than two bones; but its face was solid, fleshy. Its eyes were open: they glinted blackly in the electric beam of the headlight.

For a moment nobody moved. Then the mummy opened its mouth, and began to speak—one word, two, three emerged, impossibly, from the dead man's mouth. El-Kafir el-Sheikh was thrown. It was no language he recognized; neither Marsi, nor Old Danish, nor even New Danish. The creature stopped, as if to draw breath; but what use could it have with breath? Then it uttered a string of words. One sounded like the Old Danish for "possession," but el-Kafir el-Sheikh could not be sure.

This weird monologue was interrupted by Bille's screaming—the big man opened his own mouth wide and howled like a dog. He gunned the engine and, notwithstanding that none of the four archaeologists were inside the car, accelerated hard. The left front bumper struck the mummy with an audible clunk. The dark leather man lurched and spun away into the mist—but the automobile did not stop. "Bille!" Suyuti shouted. "Come back, man!"

For a long minute the throaty diminuendo of the vanishing car was the only sound. Then everything was quiet again, the eerie muffled silence of fog. "I'll have him flogged," Suyuti fumed. "That dog!"

"I suppose, then, that we are walking back to the hotel," el-Akkad said.

"Are we going to pretend we didn't see that?" el-Kafir el-Sheikh demanded. "The *mummy*? It was right there!"

"I only saw the mummy," said Suyuti.

"What do you mean, you only saw?"

"I mean," said Suyuti, stomping over to where the car had been. "There must have been people, or at least a person, propping it up—to play that . . . trick upon us. There must have been, but I didn't see *them*. Perhaps they were dressed in white?"

"It was a strange thing to see," said Gurbati, in a cowed voice.

"Bille knocked it over," said al-Akkad. "Drove straight at it and knocked it down. It must be just *there*—where you're standing, Mohammed."

"I know," snapped Suyuti. "But I can't see anything. This cursed fog! Gamal—could you bring your lamp over here?

The only thing el-Kafir el-Sheikh wanted to do was to run—to get away from that place as fast as his legs could propel him. If a jinn had appeared and offered him instant transportation back to Cairo for the price of all his personal wealth, he would have taken the deal without a moment's thought. But here he was, stuck in this remote place, in the whited-out cold. It took an effort of will, and he was not naturally a brave man, but he conquered his panic. Suyuti and he then spent twenty minutes searching the soggy turf, looking first for the mummy, and when it became apparent that it was not to be found, looking for the traces of whoever had carried it there. They found nothing; not so much as a footprint. "The turf, though wet, is pretty springy," Suyuki said. "Footprints might not leave much of an impression."

"Are we sure we saw—what we all think we saw?" el-Akkad asked. "Might it be some kind of . . . collective hallucination?"

"It spoke!" cried el-Kafir el-Sheikh.

"Bille clearly thought it was real," Gurbati said. "And for a hallucination it made a hell of a *thwunq* when he drove into it."

"Well it's not here now," said Suyuti. "And in this fog we won't be able to track it. I think the best thing we can do is walk back to the hotel. It'll take us a while."

"We're simply going—to walk away?" el-Kafir el-Sheikh asked.

"You propose we stay here?" returned Gurbati. "This fog is bad enough in the daytime; imagine how it will be after sunset! Come—*you're* the rationalist, my friend. I agree that we have seen some strange things, but there must be a scientific explanation."

"I suppose there must," el-Kafir el-Sheikh conceded.

"To subscribe to supernatural explanations," Suyuti went on, giving his hands alternately a rub and a squeeze and stamping his feet, "would be to sink to the level of the natives. We can do better than that."

"And to speak for myself, I'll find it easier," el-Akkad agreed, "to discuss the possibilities inside, with a hot meal in my belly. And a pipe."

They started walking. To begin with it was easy enough following the road; and after half an hour it even looked as though the fog was thinning. A drizzle started falling, and everybody grew colder and grumpier. "At least," Suyuti declared, "the rain will drive away the fog!"

But it didn't happen. The drizzle faded, leaving them wet to the skin, and the fog was still all about them. Then the road led them down into a declivity and the mist thickened so much that el-Kafir el-Sheikh lost sight not only of his surroundings but even of his fellow travellers. The men called to one another to prevent them losing touch, and after an hour the road rose again. As they went up the fog thinned somewhat. The trunks of trees became dimly visible in the cataracting blankness of the mist.

"I can't remember the last time I felt this *cold*," el-Kafir el-Sheikh announced, to no one in particular. "I'm shivering continually! It's like my muscles are being twitched by repeated electrical shocks."

"So many trees!" said el-Akkad. "I sometimes imagine they're whispering to one another. The forest stretches a thousand miles east from here, you know. Nothing but trees, primordial. It's not *natural* for humankind to live amongst the trees. Crowding all around—it turns a human being into an interloper in a population of aliens. It's not *clean*," he added, with sudden vehemence. "This whole landscape is cluttered and dirty and—ugh!"

They marched on in silence after that. After a while Mohammed Suyuti began what el-Kafir el-Sheikh assumed was a morale-boosting speech. "Do not despair, my friends. The journey is an hour and half by automobile; and so I calculate four or five hours by foot. Six at the most. And we have been on the road two hours already, and have made good progress. Soon we will arrive at our destination."

"Not yet halfway," grumbled Gurbati.

"I shall flog Bille personally, when we get back," declared el-Akkad. "What he has done is unforgivable."

Nobody had anything to say to this, so they trudged on. Twenty minutes further the road turned right. Round the corner two eyes gleamed at them: the rear lamps of the car.

El-Akkad launched into a run, calling out Bille's name and adding choice imprecations. But he broke off abruptly, and by the time the others reached him he was standing, his mouth open. Bille was there, in the driving seat, but he was not moving, and his head leant back at a bizarre angle. From the front it was clear his throat had been cut—more than cut, ripped from chin to breastbone. Blood had pooled and congealed in his lap in an oval sheet, and stalactites of red dangled into the footwell.

It was horrible.

Suyuti broke the silence. "At least we won't have to walk the rest of the way."

"Did a wild beast do this?" el-Kafir el-Sheikh asked. "Did a *wolf* do this?"

"If it was a wolf why didn't he finish him off? Or drag him away."

"Maybe," said el-Akkad, "the wolf was interrupted. By something worse than a wolf."

"Whatever happened, it does not make me wish to stand around here," said Gurbati. "Here, Tawfiq—help me move him. I'll drive."

"And put him—where?"

"In the back seat, I suppose."

"Don't be absurd!" said Suyuti. "I'm not sitting squashed up against a corpse all the way home."

"Why did he *stop*?" el-Kafir el-Sheikh wanted to know. "Why not just drive straight through—if it was a wolf, surely you'd try and run it down, not stop and let the beast jump you!"

"Why not read one of your rune tablets," Gurbati sneered, "and bring him back to life—then you can ask him yourself."

"That was uncalled for," el-Kafir el-Sheikh returned, stiffly.

"We cannot bury him," said Suyuti. "The tools are back at the dig. And if we just leave him by the road, then wild animals will surely devour his body."

"Ugh!" el-Akkad cried, recoiling from the car. "His clothes are full of blood."

"It's true," said Gurbati, in a hollow voice, poking a gloved finger at the body. "To touch him is to—it feels, it feels . . . It is repulsive. It's like a hot-water-bottle, full of . . . ugh!"

-5-

The four agreed to pitch Bille's body straight out of the automobile, to lay a coat down where he had been sitting and drive straight off. "It's unfortunate for Bille," Suyuti said. "But our hands are tied." It was not a pleasant business: when el-Kafir el-Sheikh put his hand to the corpse's shoulder and felt the fluid under the man's jacket shift and squelch, it took a prodigious effort of will not simply to snatch his hand away again. But with a concerted effort the corpse was pulled over the low windshield and on to the hood, and from there it was an easy enough business to slide him off on to the turf at the side of the road. Then Gurbati fussed for a while about arranging his coat over the blood-stained seat. But finally they all got into the automobile and started off.

Almost at once it started raining again. "Shall I stop?" Gurbati asked. "We could put up the roof."

"This shower will pass in a minute," was Suyuti's opinion.

"It's easy for you to say," Gurbati complained, his teeth clacking. "You're all still wearing your coats."

The rain fell steadily, more than drizzle but less than a full shower. El-Kafir el-Sheikh shivered and jerked in his seat. The shower showed no signs of ceasing, and water began filling the front and rear footwells, so Gurbati announced—shouting, to be heard over the downpour—that he was stopping to put up the roof. But no sooner had he done so, and stepped out of the car, than the rain stopped completely.

"Put the roof up anyway," Suyuti instructed. "Now that we've stopped."

On cue, a wolf's cry—loud, musical, mournfully sustained but at the same time intensely frightening—sounded in the white air. The fog made it impossible to know whether the beast was far away, or near by. "Get back in the car!" el-Akkad yelled, although Gurbati needed no prompting. He leapt back into the driving seat and started the engine.

They bounced and jarred a half-mile or so further on, but when the road curved right Gurbati drove straight on. The passengers all hallooed in fear, and the driver stomped on the brakes, but he wasn't prompt enough to stop the car colliding with the broad black pillar of a roadside tree. "What are you *playing* at!" Suyuti yelled at him. "You stupid Dom—you've crashed us."

"The wheel is slippy and these gloves don't *grip*," Gurbati snapped back.

"Take them off then," Suyuti ordered him. "Oh, you've broken the engine! I just know you have!"

Gurbati pulled the ignition lever, and the engine made a noise like a stick being run along a stretch of palings. But it caught, and came shudderingly to life. Gurbati backed the vehicle up, and hopped out to examine the front bumper. "Banana'd but not broken," he announced. "Let's get on. I've had enough of this place. Back to the hotel without further prevarication, I say."

"Gloves off," Suyuti repeated.

"Easy for you to insist on that," Gurbati grumbled. "My hands will be carved from ice by the time we get back to the hotel." But he did remove the gloves.

He took hold of the steering wheel and slowly rolled the car forward and around, until they were back on the road. "Maybe slower but more sure?" he said. "More haste less speed, after all. All." The car wasn't moving. "All," Gurbati said again, in a higher-pitched voice. "All! A-a-a-a-all!"

"What on earth are you gabbling about?" Suyuti called. But Gurbati wasn't speaking now; it was a cry of sharp pain, a howl. The vowel slid half an octave upwards, and Gurbati started thrashing in his seat, bucking and jerking.

"What's the matter!" boomed el-Akkad, who was seated beside him. "What? What?"

"Steering!" Gurbati shrieked. "Wheel!"

"His hands are seared to it!" el-Kafir el-Sheikh cried, leaning forward. "Help me—" He and el-Akkad took an arm each, and pulled hard, but it took several tugs before they could dislodge Gurbati's hands, and they came away in a spray of blood. By then it was too late. Gurbati slumped back, and a horrible, splashy noise replaced his screaming. Red slime spewed down his front. He stopped twitching.

The other three exited the car in a scrabble. The engine throbbed and throbbed, the gears in neutral. Because it seemed like the thing to do, el-Kafir el-Sheikh reached in and turned the motor off.

For a long time the three of them stood there, silently aghast, in that whited-out, chill space. El-Akkad consulted his watch. "Two forty-five," he noted. "How far do you think it is from here to the hotel?"

Suyuti turned on him. "How can you be so callous?"

"I'm not getting back in that automobile," el-Akkad returned, hotly. "It is cursed. This whole evil landscape is cursed! I'm *walking* back to the hotel, and then I'm getting on the next boat back to civilization."

"You never liked him," Suyuti spat. "You were envious of him. He had twice the intellect you did. And now look at him!"

"Envy?" scoffed el-Akkad. "Don't be absurd."

"It happened," el-Kafir el-Sheikh said in a small voice, "when he took his gloves off."

"What do you mean by that?" Suyuti snarled, turning on him. "Are you blaming me? Is it my fault?"

"*You* organized the trip," el-Akkad said, accusingly. "You brought us all here. Ultimately, of *course* you're to blame."

"I only meant," a conciliatory el-Kafir el-Sheikh explained, "that it was only after his bare flesh touched the steering wheel, that . . ."

But the other two were not listening. "You are a disgrace to archaeology!" Suyuti yelled.

"At least I am an archaeologist! You're just a jumped-up pen-pushing civil servant!"

"He was *my* friend—you never liked him. Petty professional jealousy!"

"I'm going back to the hotel," el-Akkad fumed. "And tomorrow I'm getting the boat and going home, whereupon I hope never to see you again." He stomped off and was lost in the mist almost immediately.

"Come back here!" Mohammed Suyuti shrieked. "We are not leaving Gurbati's body to be devoured by wolves! We are just not—leaving—him—here!"

His words were swallowed by the muffling fog. There was no reply. The whiteness and silence. El-Kafir el-Sheikh looked around. There was the car, the ground at his feet, and Suyuti's form. But apart from that and a few black tree trunks like spectral versions of themselves, everything was milky and blank. Suyuti hid his face in his hands.

After a while, el-Kafir el-Sheikh asked: "I suppose we can't trust the car."

"No," agreed Suyuti.

"And what *about* Gurbati? Shall we bury him?"

"I don't suppose we can," Suyuti replied, into his palms. "I don't suppose that's practical, without shovels. Poor Hussein!" He dropped his hands to his sides and stood up straighter. "Let's put the roof up, at any rate. Maybe that will keep the wild beasts off his body."

"All right," el-Kafir el-Sheikh said, and although he had a flinchy desire not to touch the automobile at all, he pulled his gloves tighter and helped Suyuti unpack the canvas roof from its rear compartment. It came out on unfolding metal struts, like an umbrella, and they pulled it to the front windshield, fixing it into place. "Do you want to say something?" el-Kafir el-Sheikh asked.

"I'm no imam," was Suyuti's reply. "And anyway: we can have a proper funeral later. After we've got home and sorted this sorry business out. We'll have servants come retrieve the car tomorrow." He leaned through the opened door, and when he stood straight again he was holding a pistol. "Here," he instructed el-Kafir el-Sheikh. "It's no good to him any more, but you may need it."

"I haven't so much as touched a firearm since national service," el-Kafir el-Sheikh replied.

"There are wolves in the woods," was all Suyuti said, and he slammed the door shut. El-Kafir el-Sheikh slipped the pistol into his jacket pocket.

They set off trudging along the road, walking through the silent and unchanging white. Dark trunks toyed with el-Kafir el-Sheikh's peripheral vision, as if trying, and failing, to manifest into full presence only to fade into nothing again. The road squelched underfoot. His feet were soaked inside his shoes. His clothes, still wet, slapped and rubbed uncomfortably against his skin as he moved.

"Mohammed," he said, shortly. "What do you think happened?" When the other man did not reply, he pressed. "To Gurbati, I mean. Back there."

"He died," Suyuti returned.

"But *how*? And that native boy, back at the dig. I have never heard of a form of tubercular infection so rapid in its pathology." He was interrupted by a long, mournful, bassoon-like howl—far away or near by, it was impossible to say. Both men stopped, and in the absence of their squelching footsteps everything was perfectly quiet. There was another long lupine call, and then nothing. "We'd better hurry along," was Suyuti's opinion.

They picked up their speed.

"There must *be* a scientific explanation," el-Kafir el-Sheikh pressed. "I mean, must be! But what? El-Akkad said—"

Suyuti broke in with a scornful barking laugh. "I consider *him* no longer my friend and colleague," he said. "I'll not even say his name. He fell into superstitious nonsense almost as soon as he arrived on these shores. Magic and nonsense and the worship of devils. I'll tell you what's wrong with these people? I'm no racist, Gamal, but they're a *primitive* people, closer to apes than true men. Ancestor worship. Human sacrifice!" They squelched on for a while without talking. The road dipped down, and then climbed once again. There came a new drizzle, and soon enough it thickened into full rainfall.

One consequence of this was that the fog—finally—began to dissolve and vanish. The trees all around them came into focus, like a photograph being developed. Soon enough the fog was gone, the whiteness filled in with a retreating vista of trees. It was a development that gladdened el-Kafir el-Sheikh's heart. The rain thrummed on to his head, and water was dribbling from his beard, but he felt somehow cleaner with it.

"Ah well," he called to his companion. "One can only get so wet, and no wetter!"

Suyuti looked back, over his shoulder, and if he didn't exactly smile then at least his scowl shrank away. He nodded.

Then he flew to the left, and rolled on the ground between the trees in a tangle of limbs and gray.

It took el-Kafir el-Sheikh a slow moment to comprehend what was happening, and then another moment to act. His limbs responded only slowly and sluggishly to his mental command. Suyuti was yelling. He came up, struggling, and the wolf covered him again. A snarl, a snap, and Suyuti's yells shifted to throttled gulps.

E-Kafir el-Sheikh brought out from his jacket pocket Gurbati's pistol, but slowly, and then he took aim. The beast had Suyuti by the throat. He could not afford to shoot at the creature's head, for fear of hurting Suyuti. He took hold of his right wrist with his left hand. Then he stopped.

Slowly he turned his head.

A dozen feet away were four more wolves, and all of them were eyeing him.

El-Kafir el-Sheikh felt his lungs contract. His heart felt stiffer as it pumped, even as it began to gallop behind his ribs. He could not take his eyes from the four wolves. He heard a succession of ripping sounds, from the direction in which Suyuti lay. It was the noise of tearing flesh, audible even over the sound of the rain. But there was no space in his head to think about that.

His whole chest trembling with his accelerated heartbeat, el-Kafir el-Sheikh rotated his body, bringing his pistol around until it was aimed at the four other wolves. He was thinking: *How many bullets in this gun?* He was thinking: *How hungry are these wolves?*

The four beasts stood, not snarling, barely even breathing; motionless in the curtaining rainfall. *Can I scare them off with a gunshot?* el-Kafir el-Sheikh asked himself. The rain would not help; it would muffle much of the bang. Still: what else could he do?

He pointed the gun at one wolf. The beast's coat was a light gray streaked with black; its doggish eyes yellow as honey. El-Kafir el-Sheikh's fingers refused to close on the trigger. He was frozen. "Are you hypnotizing me, old wolf?" he said, his voice croaky. The rain was slapping the top of his head, and water running into his eyes. Words came to him, he wasn't sure from where. "Your turn now," he said. "My turn later."

He fired.

The wolf made no sound, but it flinched back, its rear legs folding up. Then the creature fell over to the side. El-Kafir el-Sheikh pulled the trigger again, but nothing happened. He wasn't thinking straight. He recocked the gun—a wolf was in mid-air, hanging right in front of him. El-Kafir el-Sheikh didn't even have time to yell out in fear. It was as if the lines of rain were silver cords, suspending the bulky animal right there. He yanked the trigger, more on reflex than anything. The gun discharged a second time. The bullet went down the wolf's throat, but its leap had enough momentum to carry it on. It collided with el-Kafir el-Sheikh, all wet pelt and seven-foot-long muscular body, more than enough to bowl him completely over. El-Kafir el-Sheikh rolled, came up on his knees, overbalanced and got up again. His heart was yammering and yammering. The wolf that had taken Suyuti had looked up in the middle of its feast. Of the other two, one was disappearing away, loping off between the trees. But one remained, its hunger more pressing than its fear. It lowered its head, keeping its yellow eyes on its prey.

El-Kafir el-Sheikh got to his feet and held out his arm. Two from two shots was lucky, but perhaps the gods of Jutland were favoring him; and there was nothing he could do except try again. But he was shaking now, shaking with both cold and fear.

He aimed as best he could and pulled the trigger. Nothing happened.

He looked at the gun. It had been beneath him when he rolled in the muddy turf. A chunk of brown earth had been packed into the barrel, and the firing pin was clogged with dirt. He looked up at the wolf, and back at the gun. With shivering fingers he tried to pick away some of the muddy matter, but it didn't seem to want to come out of the weapon. *Suyuti had a pistol too*, he thought. But Suyuti's was underneath a feeding wolf.

He tried to remember what he knew about wolves. His nurse had read him fairy stories when he was a child, and many of those had been set in faraway forests filled with ogres and wolves. Could they climb trees? He felt the answer was yes; but then he found himself thinking— or was that bears?

The beast in front of him put out a paw and took a step in his direction, testing the ground, waiting for the pistol's report. El-Kafir el-Sheikh held out the useless gun. "Back off," he called. "Shoo away."

The wolf took another step, closer still.

El-Kafir el-Sheikh could feel his resolve beginning to give way. He would crack, and turn, and run; and then the wolf would be on him in moments. He could not outrun it, he knew that. But his heart was going so hard and fast it felt like it would burst inside him.

He chucked the gun at the muzzle of the beast, and heard, or thought he heard, over the sound of the rain, a yelp of pain. But he wasn't looking; he had turned and was sprinting away, a sort of struggling gallop over the soggy ground. "I don't want to die," he gasped. "Not to *die*—" A forked tree loomed out of the falling water, and he scrabbled up the shallower of the two trunks, up to a bough. But when he looked back he saw that the wolf was following him. It leapt halfway up the angled trunk, claws digging into the bark.

El-Kafir el-Sheikh yelled, scrabbled along a bough and was pitched off when the branch broke. The ground below was ferny, but he fell hard on to his shoulder. A bolt of pain shot down his left arm. When he got himself upright again it hung at his side. Every fiber of his being was desperate to run, to get away. He took three steps, got his feet tangled in something in the undergrowth and went down again. Up again, breathing hard and heavy, he ran a dozen broad strides.

Looking behind him, he saw the wolf disentangling itself from the tree, and leaping down in an insolently easy motion. It came trotting after him.

El-Kafir el-Sheikh ran on, looking back over his shoulder. He turned to face front again, but the tree was right there—he could not avoid the collision. He didn't even have time to bring his hand up; he just ran smack into the trunk, recoiled and fell back, his face stinging.

He got somehow to his feet, blinded and stunned. With his right hand he wiped water from his face. The wolf was standing directly in front of him, snarling, his teeth like rows of sharp horns in a mouth long as a canoe. This was it: death. But nothing happened. Only then, gasping and agonized by anticipation, did el-Kafir el-Sheikh look to his left.

The Tollund mummy was standing there: large as life and twice as ugly. Water ran down his dark brown leathery skin, and his withered skeletal arms moved in slow circle. There was nobody holding him up. However this magic trick was being performed, it was not obvious. El-Kafir el-Sheikh took a step, unable to stop himself recoiling. But looking back at the wolf he could see the beast's attentions had been distracted by this apparition. The beast began snarling.

The rainfall was dying away.

The wolf leapt and el-Kafir el-Sheikh shrieked, holding his right hand, the only one that worked, in front of his face. But the beast had jumped the mummy, not him. Through his fingers el-Kafir el-Sheikh saw the dead man hold out a dark brown arm—saw the wolf's jaws snap on it—saw the hand come clean away. When the wolf landed, it was holding the mummy's hand in its mouth.

The rain had stopped. There was only the sound of water dripping from the trees all around, and the panting of the wolf. It wasn't the wolf panting; it was el-Kafir el-Sheikh himself. Gasping, gasping. A strange clarity possessed the air. The Tollund mummy stood there, so vividly present it seemed almost to pass beyond real into some dreamlike state beyond it.

The wolf coughed. It spat the mummified hand from its jaws, and it put its long snout down and it coughed again. It placed a paw over the top of its nose, a peculiar, strangely human gesture. Then it barked, or coughed, and leapt backwards. Red fluid gushed copiously from its open mouth. It danced and gamboled. Its gray fur darkened, and a black ooze slicked through its covering of hair. In moments it lay dead on its side.

Breathing in, and out. The sound of el-Kafir el-Sheikh breathing in and out, like surf; and the drips and drips of water from the wet trees.

The mummy was looking at him.

"To touch you is poison," el-Kafir el-Sheikh told the mummy. Sunlight, swept by the broom-end of a retreating cloud somewhere far above them, rolled through the trees. The water on the mummy's skin gleamed like jewels.

"Yes," the creature replied. "I regret to say." Its voice was creaky but strong. It spoke Masri with a thick northerner accent; but el-Kafir el-Sheikh could understand it perfectly well.

"You killed the boy," el-Kafir el-Sheikh said. "And Bille. And poor old Gurbati! And now you will kill me!"

"I will not," said the mummy. "Attend! Here is a word. Nanomachine."

How el-Kafir el-Sheikh's left shoulder hurt! He breathed, breathed. "I have never heard such a word," he said.

"Of course not. But you must learn it."

"What does it mean?"

"It means," said the mummy, "the means by which I am animated. We are sorry about your friends. It seems that the nanomachines have been altered by their passage. Many things are not as we expected them to be! I believe the alteration in the nanomachines to be a form of friction, although of a temporal rather than a physical nature."

"You are talking some sort of gibberish," said el-Kafir el-Sheikh, taking a step back. A twinge of pain ran along his limp left arm.

"*You* are a scientist!" the mummy called, in a great, dour voice. "*You* must understand!"

"I am a specialist in old northern languages, and runes," el-Kafir el-Sheikh returned, in a quivery voice.

"Do not run!" commanded the mummy, holding out both its arms. The left had no hand, and the severed bone-end looked like a chopped-through wooden stick. "It is all science. It is not magic."

El-Kafir el-Sheikh took another step back.

"I am animated by nanomachines. There are millions of these machines, but they are miniature in dimension, and you may not see them, except perhaps with powerful magnification devices. They have been fed backwards through time; for time-backwards is a road machines may travel where human beings may not."

"Gibberish!" exclaimed el-Kafir el-Sheikh.

"It is hard for us, where we are, to monitor. We did not expect the nanomachines to have the effect they have had, when they entered living flesh. In our time, it is possible for the nanomachines to enter a body without harming that person, and then the person might speak, or write, or pass on our message to others, as the machines might prompt them. That is all we intended, we swear! We seek only to communicate with your time!"

"Communicate?" scoffed el-Kafir el-Sheikh. He took a third step backwards.

The mummy stumbled towards him. "The passage is one hundred and sixty-nine years, and that passage appears to have energized the nanomachines in unpredictable ways. They are too energetic for ordinary metabolisms to contain. We attempted, at first, to situate the nanomachines in likely subjects, but their bodies disintegrated as soon as the nanomachines were inserted into them."

"Nonomachine," said el-Kafir el-Sheikh. "No-no."

"The nanomachines ran wild, passing from membrane to membrane, and we are sorry that some people died. So we have tried again, with a second batch. But they are just as bad. It is imperative we communicate with your people, in 1912. The disaster may still be averted, if we can only communicate!"

"You have the year wrong, my friend," said el-Kafir el-Sheikh.

"The world is not as we expected it!" the mummy screeched. "The past is not as we expected it! The timelines are contaminated! We intended to alter the timeline only from 1913 *onwards*, but we discover the world has already been altered at an earlier point!" The stretched skin over the mummy's jaw was starting to tear, and the jaw to hang lower. With weird detachment el-Kafir el-Sheikh thought, If it keeps talking, its jaw will simply fall off. "We do not know why," the mummy was saying, "or how—unless our attempts to alter the timeline have set up resonances that reached *backwards* as well as forwards from the point you presently inhabit! We sent a second batch of nanomachines. This body—" And the mummy slapped its own chest with the stump of its left arm. "This body is able to withstand the insertion of the nano-machines, and they are able to bond together to animate it. Its skin is tough enough, its metabolism is already dead and cannot be made deader. But the nanomachines malfunction! In a living machine they malfunction. It is the friction of temporal passage! They have become hyper-energized. They spread, like a disease, from membrane to membrane. To touch me is to absorb them, and they react in living flesh with catastrophic suddenness. This body—" and, *thump*, again on the chest "—is tougher, because it is dead and leathern. But you must not touch me."

"I intend not to," sobbed el-Kafir el-Sheikh. "Truly, I intend not to."

"You must listen. We meant no harm to your fellows. But you *must* listen! We must somehow undo the damage we have done!"

"Poor Gurbati!" el-Kafir el-Sheikh said. "I was at university with him, you know!"

"The automobile is another machine-system, just as a human body is a machine-system. The contagion passes from organic to inorganic, and back. You understand that I am talking from the perspective of the nanomachines?"

"I understand nothing!" el-Kafir el-Sheikh snapped. He turned and ran—ran hard and long. Behind him the mummy was calling out, in its deadly voice. "Wait! Wait! We must communicate. Everything is wrong! You can carry our message, and save the future! But everything is wrong!" When he looked back, el-Kafir el-Sheikh could see the mummy stumbling after him; but slowly and awkwardly, and it was not hard—even with his useless, hurting arm—to outpace it. "Everything is wrong," he gasped, as he ran. And on he went through the trees, not knowing the direction and not caring, so long only as it was away from the monstrous leathern form of death that staggered, slowly, after him.

The protagonist of Will Hill's story is extremely old. He is slightly younger than his pharaoh, Ramesses II, and we are fairly sure Ramesses ruled sixty-seven years and died around age ninety. At death, Ramesses was suffering from severe dental problems, arthritis, and hardening of the arteries. He may have fathered as many as ninety-six sons and sixty daughters, but he probably outlived most of them—as he did his favorite wife, Nefertari. His successor was his thirteenth eldest son, Merneptah, who himself may have been in his late sixties or early seventies when he inherited the throne.

Three Memories of Death
Will Hill

———

When they came, the old man was ready.

His daughter and her children were surprised to see him up and dressed in his finest robes, but he saw no reason why they should be. It had been seventy days since the God-King, the Light of Ra, the Pharaoh Ramesses II had breathed his last, but the old man had been waiting longer than that.

He had, in truth, been waiting for this day for most of his life.

Amun shuffled slowly into the main room of the small home on the edge of Thebes he had taken for himself when his time in the temple had come to a close, carrying a linen sack in his gnarled hands. Vast, splendid dwellings had been offered to him, as befitted his standing and long service, but he had rejected them all. He had agreed to the construction of the temple that bore his name only at the insistence of the Pharaoh himself, and needed no reminders of the duties he had performed with such diligence.

His memories were more than sufficient.

Standing in the center of the room, being fussed around and cooed at by Amun's daughter and grandchildren, was Prehotep, the Vizier of the North and second most powerful man in the empire. His robes gleamed red and gold, and his retinue could be seen lurking just beyond the threshold, ready to attend to his every need, no matter how tiny. Prehotep was feared for a thousand miles in every direction, but when Amun appeared before him he broke into a wide smile, and embraced the old man with great tenderness.

"Hery Sesheta," said the Vizier. "It is good to see you."

Amun carefully unwrapped the arms from his shoulders, and returned his old friend's smile.

"I no longer wear the mask, as well you know," he said. "I am a humble servant of Ra."

"The God-King continued to believe otherwise," said Prehotep. "The time has come, Hery Sesheta. The embalming is done, and the wrapping is complete. Only one thing remains."

"I am ready," said Amun, his voice sounding stronger than it had in many years. "Take me to him."

"Father?" asked Anahita. "What do you mean? Where are you going?"

"To finish my work," said Amun. "You will stay here."

"Your work is done, Father. You are supposed to be at rest."

"I've rested long enough," said Amun.

Anahita frowned deeply. The thought of her father traveling, even in the company of the Vizier, made her deeply uneasy. He was entering at least his eightieth year, and his eyes were deteriorating almost as rapidly as his ears and his equilibrium.

"Are you sure this is wise, Father?" she asked.

"It is neither wise nor unwise," replied Amun. "It is my duty. Prehotep, if you would take my arm, we can be on our way."

"It will be my honor, Hery Sesheta," replied the Vizier.

He reached out and took hold of Amun's arm with a tenderness that raised a lump into Anahita's throat. She watched the Vizier lead her father towards the door of his home, and as they passed beneath the arch, she found her voice a final time.

"Goodbye then, Father."

Amun turned back, and Anahita gasped. The light of the morning sun illuminated a smile that was wider and more beautiful than she would have believed him capable of producing; a smile that stripped years from his weathered face, decades even. For a single, suspended moment, her father looked like the man she had never known, young and proud and vital.

"Goodbye, my child," said Amun. "May the eye of Ra warm you."

Then he stepped through the door, and was gone.

Amun's father slid the blade into the side of the dead man with well-practiced ease, and stepped back. The ceremonial Anubis mask of the Hery Sesheta, the Overseer of Mysteries, the High Priest who directed the entire burial process, was heavy and cumbersome, and greatly limited its wearer's vision; it prevented Amun's father from carrying out the wet, slippery work for which he had become renowned.

"Continue," said Ahmose, from behind the blue and gold jackal's head that covered his own.

Amun looked up at the mask and felt a familiar shiver run up his spine. The jackal's mouth hung open, its eyes were empty ovals, and its ears stood up tall and pointed, as though it had heard something in the distance; to Amun, the mask always looked hungry.

At his father's command, the Hetemw Netjer, the priest who assisted with these first stages of the process, scuttled forward. At the edge of the Ibu, the purification tent that had been hurriedly erected after Ramesses I's short reign had come to an end, the pale sand that covered the Valley of the Kings blew steadily around the ankles of the Hery Heb as he recited an endless series of incantations and prayers, his voice barely audible. His tone didn't alter as the Hetemw Netjer, a man named Bes who Amun had known his entire life, who had once wept when a flock of birds, bewildered by a sandstorm, had thrown themselves against the walls of the temple, carefully widened the incision in the dead Pharaoh's side, and reached into his mortal body.

Amun forced himself not to look away; it would be inappropriate for the son of the Hery Sesheta, a boy who would one day be expected to follow in the footsteps of his father. He focused instead on the smells that filled the tent, the fragrant palm wine and the fresh Nile water that had been used to wash the body of the Pharaoh, the acrid scents of sand and animals that would have informed him he was in the desert even if his eyes were covered, and kept his gaze fixed straight ahead.

One after the other, the Pharaoh's liver, stomach, and intestines slid out of the incision Amun's father had made. The organs were handled with the reverence that befitted them, and set carefully into bowls. The Wetyw, the army of the most junior priests, who Amun was certain were every bit as nervous as he was, scurried forward and moved them to a second table, where they were washed and packed in natron. The intestines uncoiled as they were released from their tight confines, translucent purple snakes that squirmed and writhed. The Wetyw took extra care with them, working the glistening ropes between several pairs of hands, keeping clear of the abrasive sand below.

As they set about the cleaning, Bes reached back into the body with his knife, and sliced the lungs free, taking the utmost care not to so much as nick the heart; the thick muscle was the center of all the dead man had been, and would be needed in the afterlife. He drew out the lungs, set them down, and stepped back into line alongside Amun and the rest of the priests; they filled one side of the Ibu, silent and watchful.

On the other, their attention focused on the rapidly emptying body before them, stood the family of the Pharaoh, a long line of somber men and women in the splendid dress of royalty. Amun had been around death since his birth in the Anubis Temple at the center of the Theban Necropolis, and had seen the wives and sons of merchants and traders collapse in storms of sobbing and chest-beating on a number of occasions; he had even seen one particularly distraught man throw himself atop the body of his wife, a violation of the burial rituals so profound that the Hetemw Netjer had taken the man by the neck and thrown him out into the desert.

The family of the Pharaoh was clearly not inclined to any such public displays of emotion; there was nothing to suggest that they were even slightly upset by what they were seeing. Ahmose had told his young son that he was not to speak to any of the royal party under any circumstances, not to even look at them if possible, but Amun found himself unable to resist; there seemed to be some great weight to the line of mourners, a solidity, as though they were statues rather than human beings. Their faces were pale and smooth, without the work-lines and blemishes of the men who toiled in the Valley of Kings or the deep-set eyes of the priests, eyes that had beholden both glorious wonder and great horror; they seemed unreal, as though they inhabited a different world.

"Boy." It was a male voice, even and full of authority.

Amun's eyes widened, and he snapped out of the thoughts that had momentarily distracted him. He returned his gaze to the body of the Pharaoh, but it was too late; his loss of focus had clearly been noticed.

"Boy," said the voice again. "I am speaking to you."

Slowly, as though it was painful to do so, Amun turned his head to the left, and sought out the speaker. Shame was bubbling up within him; a reprimand inside the Ibu, from one of the royal mourners no less, would see him punished with great enthusiasm by his father when the ceremonies were complete. Ahmose was a man who believed that children learnt from their mistakes most effectively when the lessons were punctuated with the crack of a bamboo cane.

The man who had spoken was not a man at all. Standing at the center of the familial line was Seti, the man who would become the new Pharaoh when his father was safely sent on into the afterlife and his mortal remains were interred. At his side, his face remarkably similar to that of the dead man lying on the stone, was Seti's son, who also bore the name Ramesses, and was looking directly at him.

"Yes, your Highness?" said Amun, his throat as dry as the desert that surrounded them.

"Come here," said Ramesses.

Amun stared at the boy, acutely aware that activity in the tent had ceased; the priests were now all watching him, the Pharaoh's family watching Ramesses, waiting to see what the young royal's intentions were toward the apprentice. Amun swallowed hard, and crossed the tent. He stopped in front of Ramesses, his head lowered respectfully.

"Look at me," said the prince.

Amun did as he was told. Up close, Ramesses' face was unquestionably that of a boy; handsome, made of straight lines and soft skin, but a boy's nonetheless. Amun had seen nine years come and go, and he suspected that Ramesses had only seen two or three more.

"What is your name?"

"Amun, your Highness."

Ramesses broke into a wide smile. "Amun?"

"Yes, your Highness."

"My birth name is Meryamun. Do you know what that means?"

"Yes, your Highness."

"Cease with the formalities, Amun. Just answer."

"It means loved by Amun."

"That's right. We are well met, you and I. Amun and Meryamun."

Amun smiled involuntarily, then forced it away, replacing it with the respectfully neutral expression that was expected of all the priests of Anubis. Ramesses looked around, as though realizing for the first time that everyone had stopped what they were doing to observe his exchange with the apprentice.

"Hery Sesheta," he said, his voice full of natural authority. "Continue."

The mask of Anubis nodded, and beckoned to Bes. The Wetyw resumed their duties as the Hetemw Netjer came forward and handed Ahmose a long metal hook. Ramesses watched for a moment, then returned his attention to Amun.

"Stand with me," he said. "We will see my grandfather into the afterlife together."

Amun cast a glance in the direction of his father, but the jackal mask was silent and impassive. When no objection was forthcoming, he did as he was told, and watched as his father bent to one of his most delicate tasks.

"You have seen this many times," said Ramesses.

"Yes," replied Amun, unsure whether the young prince had been asking a question or not. "Many times, your Highness."

"I have not," said Ramesses. "It is beautiful, to see my grandfather treated with such love. But it is horrible too, I think."

"It is necessary," said Amun, his voice full of learned devotion. "It is an honor to send such a man onwards."

"Of course," said Ramesses, and smiled at him. "The afterlife is full of dangers. It is only right that we enter it whole."

In the center of the Ibu, Ahmose carefully guided the hook up the left nostril of the Pharaoh. When it was almost as deep as it would go, he pushed it forward with his strong, steady hands. There was a loud crunch, and Amun felt his stomach revolve; this was the worst part, the part he looked forward to least. His father moved the hook forward, twisted it, and pulled it slowly back. It emerged with a large piece of the Pharaoh's brain attached to it; the grey matter was dull in the fading light, pale and torn. Bes stepped forward, pulled it free, and placed it into a bowl as the Hery Sesheta inserted the hook a second time.

"Are you scared?" asked Ramesses, his eyes fixed on the stone table.

"No," said Amun.

"You do not fear death?"

"No."

"You should not," said Ramesses. "It is only a doorway."

The two boys stood in silence for a long moment.

"Why were you looking at us?" asked Ramesses, eventually. "When your fellow priests were working, your attention was on this side of the Ibu. Why was that?"

"I am sorry," said Amun. "It was wrong of me."

"I care not about that," said Ramesses. "Right and wrong is my father's domain. Why did you look?"

"I was interested, your Highness."

"In what?"

"In why you do not seem sad," said Amun. "I have seen many families stand within a tent like this one, and many of them are very upset. Your family do not seem sad."

"I am not," said Ramesses. "Grief is selfish. I will miss my grandfather, but sadness would be improper. He was old, and he has gone to a new life. Why should that make me sad?"

"I do not know," said Amun. "Why are other people sad when their loved ones die?"

"Because they cannot see," said Ramesses. "Life is a great house, with many doors. We come in through one, and leave through another. I see in your eyes that you do not know this yet, not truly. But you will. In time you will. And we will speak again."

"Hery Sesheta?" said the Vizier. "Are you unwell? Perhaps we should stop?"

"No," said Amun, his voice little more than a croak, then repeated the word more forcefully. "I am fine. Let us continue."

"As you wish," said Prehotep, although Amun saw the concern in the Vizier's eyes. "We will be there soon."

"Good," said Amun, and leaned forward, bracing himself more steadily against the desert wind. For a moment he had been able to smell the Ibu, to see every detail of his father's mask as he worked. He looked down at his hands as they gripped the chariot's rail, their backs covered in veins and wrinkles and the unsightly blemishes of old age, and grimaced. "Very good."

The Vizier spoke the truth; their journey had been fast, and was almost done. Amun had emerged from his house to find a fleet of chariots filling the road outside; Prehotep had carefully led him to the largest and most splendid, in which the two men were now traveling. Nine military chariots surrounded them, along with several dozen soldiers on foot, their spears drawn. It was an awesome sight, a physical manifestation of the Vizier's power and influence; as they made their way through the center of Thebes, heading for the Valley of the Kings to the east and the Ibu that had been constructed there, men and women prostrated themselves at the sides of the roads, their heads lowered to the sand in deference to the passage of Prehotep and his passenger.

At the eastern edge of Thebes they passed the temple of Anubis, the great stone monument to death and rebirth in which Amun had been born and lived. He stared at it as they rumbled by its southern façade, a flat wall of pale yellow rock that rose imposingly towards the heavens; he had spent more days inside it than out, by a great number.

"Does the temple bring back memories?" asked Prehotep.

"The temple never leaves me," replied Amun. "I do not need to see it to remember."

Prehotep smiled, and turned his attention back towards their direction of travel. The last of Thebes ebbed away and the desert swallowed them, seeming to appear from nowhere and coat the entire world with a blanket of sand and stone. Amun shielded his eyes against the worst of the dust, making sure to keep one hand firmly on the chariot's rail, and squinted; in the distance, a white square rose against the shimmering horizon.

"The Ibu?" he asked, and pointed.

Prehotep followed the line of his finger, and nodded. "Yes. It is the largest that has ever been built."

"Why?"

"I do not understand," said Prehotep, frowning. "Why what?"

"Why must it be so large?" said Amun. "The rituals require no more space now than in years past."

"It is not a matter of practicality," said Prehotep, the smile returning to his face. "It is for the glory of Ra, and for his departed servant."

"I do not think Ramesses would have cared about the size of the tent he was laid in," said Amun.

"I would not presume to guess," said Prehotep. "I did not have the privilege of knowing the Pharaoh for the weight of years that you were given. But it is what is required, for the death of the greatest ruler the empire has known. It is what is expected."

Amun grunted. He was sure the Vizier was correct; the monuments and temples that had been built for Ramesses and his many wives and children had grown ever larger as his reign had reached its fifth, sixth, and seventh decades, towering creations dedicated to the glory of the Pharaoh and the empire he led. Of course the mourning public would expect an Ibu larger than any that had gone before it; it was only natural. Although he was also sure that he was correct, that Ramesses himself would not have cared about the dimensions of the room in which he was laid to rest; he would have cared only about what was done to him inside it.

"Life is a great house," he whispered. "With many doors."

"Did you say something, Hery Sesheta?" said Prehotep.

Amun shook his head. "No."

The body of Seti I rested on the same stone table that his father had lain on eleven years earlier.

It had been forty days since Amun had helped to cover the dead Pharaoh's body in natron, the task he had once watched the Wetyw, of whose ranks he was now a member, do for Ramesses I as he stood beside his grandson. He was now a man of nineteen and a full member of the priesthood of Anubis, although still one of the most junior; his father, whose health was now beginning to fail him, had made it very clear that he would receive no advancement for reasons other than his own devotion and competence. Ahmose was standing silent watch at the head of the table as the Wetyw unpacked the thick layer of salt and carried buckets of water from the Nile into the Ibu, ready to wash Seti clean and oil his skin so that it remained supple inside his wrappings.

They would begin as soon as the Pharoah's family arrived.

Amun had been looking forward to this day, even though he knew how inappropriate it was for him to do so. He was now involved in carrying out the rituals upon which a man's safety in the afterlife depended, and if Ahmose knew his focus was on anything other than the task at hand, he would have been severely beaten.

But he simply could not help himself.

Today, the Prince Regent, who would shortly ascend to the throne as Ramesses II, was going to observe the beginning of the wrapping, a process that would take fifteen days to complete. The young royal had not attended any of the burial process so far, much to Amun's disappointment. He had heard tales of the Prince Regent's adventures in the years since their single conversation had taken place, and had felt a strange pride, as though he were hearing stories of his own brother, rather than a member of the royal family. He knew, deep down, that it was incredibly unlikely that the Prince Regent would remember him, or recall a conversation that had taken place when they were both still boys, but he didn't care.

He remembered.

Ahmose, his face hidden behind the Anubis mask that was now faded and worn, much like the skin beneath it, tapped the bottom of his staff against the stone table. Amun and the rest of the Wetyw immediately formed a line on one side of the Ibu, drew themselves up to their full height and waited silently as Seti's family entered the tent.

The Prince Regent led them, his head up, his eyes clear and full of life. The nose that had been full when last Amun saw him had developed into a pronounced hook, and there was a slight unsteadiness to his left side, as though he were feeling pain in that leg. But the rest of him was just as Amun remembered; the face handsome, the hair jet black, the skin smooth and gleaming. The man who was about to take charge of the entire Egyptian empire strode into the Ibu, looked around quickly, then broke into a smile.

"Amun," he said. "Have you forgotten your place in this tent?"

Amun felt a lump rise into his throat, and fought back the urge to laugh with delight. Instead, he forced himself to turn slowly and bow to his father; the Hery Sesheta acknowledged it with the merest inclination of the Anubis mask's snout. Amun thanked him, and walked across the tent to where Ramesses was stood, facing the dried-out remains of his father. With him were a large number of his wives and retinue, but the Prince Regent paid them all scant attention; he was focused on the body before him. Amun slipped into the line beside him, and followed his gaze. For a long moment, neither man spoke, until Ramesses uttered a single word.

"Begin."

The priests did as they were told. The Hery Heb began to recite his verses and incantations, as the Wetyw washed the Pharaoh, gently rinsing away the natron and removing the salt parcels from inside the body. As the first oils were applied to the dead man's skin, Ramesses turned to Amun.

"I had your father provide me with updates on your progress," he said. "I am glad to see you are doing well."

"Thank you, your Highness," said Amun. "I am sorry for the loss of your father."

Ramesses nodded. "He lived a full life."

"Are you sad, Highness?"

Ramesses broke into a smile. "I should have you whipped for impudence," he said. "You remember our conversation as well as I do."

"I do."

"And do you see?"

"I see, your Highness."

"Tell me."

Amun smiled. "I have seen much. I have seen women shriek and men weep and beat their chests with pain. I have cut flesh and packed salt and washed and oiled skin. I have seen what is inside all men, be they slave or merchant or Pharaoh."

"What is inside?" asked Ramesses, his voice low.

"Meat," said Amun. "Blood and bone. The souls cannot be seen, but they are there, in every man whose body lies before me. They will move on, whether they wish to or not, just as they were born into this world, whether or not they wanted to be."

A smile of great beauty lit up Ramesses' face. "You have seen."

"You showed me the path, your Highness," said Amun. "I merely walked it."

On the stone table, Seti's body had been emptied of the salt that had filled it. His organs, which had been carefully dehydrated in ornate jars, were wrapped in linen and handed to the Hetemw Netjer, who placed them back into the empty cavity. When they had all been returned to their rightful places, the Hery Sesheta stepped back from the table, and the Wetyw scurried forward with armfuls of leaves and linens with which to pack the Pharaoh's body. Ramesses and Amun watched as they soaked the dead skin a final time with scented oils, then stepped back.

"Now comes the wrapping?" said Ramesses.

"Yes," said Amun. "Now it comes."

The Hery Heb's incantations grew louder and more frenetic as the Hery Sesheta bent down until the snout of the Anubis mask was almost touching the corpse. Then, working with a speed and dexterity that belied his advancing years, Ahmose began to loop strips of linen around Seti's head, pulling them tight and fastening them in place with resin. When it was done, an unspoken command passed from him to the Wetyw, who began to wrap the individual fingers and toes with the same remarkable precision. As they wound linen up the legs, Ahmose produced two blue amulets from his robe, and held them up above his head. The Hery Heb's chanting became almost frenzied, and as the Wetyw reached the hips with their first layer of wrapping, Ahmose placed the two pieces reverentially on to Seti's chest. As they were bound to his flesh for all eternity, Ramesses, who had been watching in devout silence, spoke to Amun.

"Tell me of the amulets. I would know."

"The one that now rests over your father's heart," said Amun, his voice little more than a whisper. "That is the Isis Knot. It will protect his body in the afterlife. The one that lies on his stomach is the Plummet. It gives balance, in all worlds."

"You are sure?"

"I am," said Amun. "My father would not let the Pharaoh travel onwards unprotected."

Ramesses nodded, his eyes still fixed on the dried-out husk that had been his father. Then he turned to Amun. "If I asked you to accompany me to the palace and serve as my personal priest, what answer would you give?"

"Your Highness," said Amun, his eyes widening. "There are many priests more senior than I, who would be—"

"I am not interested in other priests," interrupted Ramesses. "I am interested in you. What answer would you give?"

"I would thank your Highness for such an offer," said Amun. "And then I would refuse it."

Ramesses stared at him for a long moment. "You would refuse the chance to sit at my side?"

"I would, your Highness."

"Explain."

"What I do here is more important, your Highness," said Amun. "There is no greater honor than preparing our fellow men for the afterlife, and no greater responsibility. I would not do anything else."

Ramesses narrowed his eyes. "And if I commanded you?"

"I would beg your Highness for mercy," said Amun. "For leave to carry on with this work. And I believe it would be granted."

Ramesses smiled. "Why do you say so?"

"Because I was taught that life is a great house, with many doors."

The Prince Regent's smile widened. "I will return in fourteen days when the wrapping is done," he said. "Before your father opens my father's mouth. Then one day, my friend, you will do the same for me." Amun opened his mouth to protest, but Ramesses spoke over him. "Would you deny the request of your Pharaoh? Would you say no when he asks for your help, when he entrusts the most important thing in the world to you?"

"No, your Highness," said Amun. His mind was racing. "But only the Hery Sesheta may open the mouth, and I am only Wetyw."

"I have every intention," said Ramesses, smiling once more, "of living a long life, Amun. I will die an old, old man. You will be almost as old yourself, and you will do this last thing for me. I would not have it done by any other. You will open my mouth and then another will open yours and I will see you on the other side, where perhaps you will be the Pharaoh and I the priest. Or perhaps we will both be herders, or builders. We will find out, in time. Do you make this vow with me?"

"I do, your Highness," said Amun, his voice full and thick. He knew it was wrong to promise that which he could not guarantee; he might never be Hery Sesheta, and he might well not outlive his friend, even allowing for the dangers that went with the role of Pharaoh. But he had been asked to make a vow, and he had made it. He would simply have to find a way; breaking it was unthinkable.

"Good," said Ramesses. "I must depart, but I will see you in fourteen turns. And we will speak again."

And we did, thought Amun, as the chariot neared the towering Ibu. *We spoke when Seti's mouth was opened, and when Ramesses moved his Palace from Thebes to Pi-Ramesses Aa-nakhtu. We spoke when he buried the first of his sons, when he had been fighting in Syria and Nubia and some of the light had left his eyes. And then . . .*

Amun looked out through the eyeholes in the Anubis mask, and felt his heart aching for his friend.

The mask had been a gift from the man who was now stood inside the Ibu, his head lowered, his hands clasped before him. It was a marvelous creation, set with jewels and gold and painted by the finest craftsman in the empire, with ears that rose more than two feet above his own head and teeth that seemed alternately to snarl and smile, depending on the angle they were viewed from. Amun had been Hery Sesheta for less than a year, and had presided over the burials of a dozen men and women in that time; none of them had in any way prepared him for what was asked of him now.

The Pharaoh Ramesses II, the God-King, the Conqueror of Syria, the Scourge of Nubia, raised his head, and Amun was horrified to see tears on his face. Before him, on the same stone table that had held his father, his grandfather, and almost a dozen of his sons, lay the mummified body of Nefertari, his Great Wife. Amun had demanded his priests' very finest work, and they had delivered; the mummy was a work of art, its lines smooth and elegant, the amulets contained within the wrappings the finest he had seen, the scroll of the Book of the Dead that had been placed in her hands the work of the finest calligrapher in all of Thebes, and the painting of Osiris that covered her chest a glory to the god it depicted. He had dismissed his priests before the Pharaoh arrived, despite their desire to discover whether the God-King was pleased with their work. Amun knew that there was nothing inside the Ibu that was going to give Ramesses any pleasure.

"Take off the mask," said the Pharaoh. "I would see your face, Hery Sesheta."

Amun reached up and lifted the mask clear. His face now wore the lines of middle age, the weathering of a life spent on the edge of the desert. It had been twenty-five years since he had stood beside Ramesses as his father was washed and oiled, a long reign by any standards, a great reign, perhaps the greatest of them all, with no end in sight. But time had taken its toll on the Pharaoh too; his once clear skin was now marked and ridged with scars, his eyes were sunken, and his spine was beginning to curve alarmingly, causing him to walk with a stick when not in public.

"I am here, your Highness," said Amun.

"Stand by me," said Ramesses. "As you always have."

Amun swallowed hard, and walked across the Ibu. He was slower than he had been, far slower than when they had first met, when he had all but skipped across the sand to take his place at the young prince's side. As soon as he was within reach, Ramesses' hand shot out and gripped his arm, the knuckles white with effort; it hurt, but Amun gave no sign of it.

"You once asked me about grief," said Ramesses, his gaze fixed on the remains of his wife. "About sadness. I gave you a foolish answer. Do you remember?"

"I do," said Amun. "You told me that grieving for the dead was selfish."

"And it is," said Ramesses. "By any measure, it is. But I would give anything in the empire, anything in all the worlds and heavens to have her breathe again. Does that make me weak?"

"No," said Amun, his voice cracking. "It makes you human."

Ramesses turned to face him, and for a fleeting moment, Amun saw the boy the Pharaoh had been: his whole life ahead of him, able to dismiss grief because he had never experienced it, full of the heavy certainty of youth. Then he was gone, replaced by the grown man who carried the weight of the world on his shoulders.

"Do it," he said, his voice low and full of pain. "Open her mouth. Let us send her onwards. Perhaps she will wait for me on the other side."

Prehotep brought the chariot to a halt outside the Ibu, and offered his arm. Amun refused it, and stepped carefully down on to the desert floor on his own.

The vast tent was perched on the western edge of the Valley of the Kings, above the resting places of countless Pharaohs and their families. The tomb in which the mortal remains of Ramesses II would lie for all eternity was waiting below, opposite the enormous labyrinth of rooms in which his children and wives, better than five dozen of them, lay in silent rest. The tomb of Nefertari, the grandest and most lavish of them all, was beside Ramesses' own.

The Vizier's retinue formed a guard, two silent lines of dark robes and lowered eyes. Amun walked through it, his head raised, his mind focused solely on the fulfillment of a vow that was more than half a century old. He carried with him his linen sack, and he walked as steadily as he was able. That he was old was impossible to hide, but the watching soldiers need not know just how infirm he had become. He looked straight ahead, his eyes fixed on the entrance to the Ibu, and stepped through it.

For a long moment, he couldn't breathe.

He had prepared himself for this moment, ever since word had begun to spread through the empire that the Pharaoh was gone, had believed he had steeled himself further during the journey in the Vizier's chariot. But now that he was here, now that his friend, the man who in many ways had been the great constant of his long life, was actually lying before him, he faltered. His legs threatened to give way beneath him, but Prehotep's hand was there again, unasked for but not unwelcome, holding Amun gently until he regained his composure.

Arranged along the opposite side of the Ibu were the priests of Anubis, every one of whom had been admitted into the temple during Amun's time as Hery Sesheta. The majority were watching him with the professional dispassion he expected, but his experienced eyes saw flickers of concern on several of their faces. At the center of the line stood Masud, the priest who it had been Amun's final act to promote to Hery Sesheta in his place. He was holding his jackal mask in his hands, and looking at Amun with great warmth in his gaze.

On the stone table lay the mummified remains of Ramesses II, the God-King, the Light of Ra, the Breath of the World. Amun's professional eye examined the mummy, and concluded that the work was good; the painting of Osiris was perhaps the most beautiful he had seen, in all his long years. On a smaller table lay the cloth and strips of linen that would make the final wrapping; beyond them stood the two coffins that would convey the Pharaoh down to his tomb. There, the priests and mourners would share the funeral meal and make offerings of meat, before the rooms were sealed forever. There was a single thing to be done first.

The Opening of the Mouth.

Unless the ritual was performed perfectly, Ramesses would not be able to eat, drink, or speak in the afterlife. It was of vital importance, and Amun had promised that it would not be done by anyone else.

"Hery Sesheta," said Masud, smiling gently. "It is good to see you. Would you wear my mask?"

"Thank you, Masud," said Amun. "But I will wear my own, if that does not offend?"

"It does not, Hery Sesheta," replied Masud, then turned to his priests. "Clear the Ibu."

The priests turned silently and exited the tent, without a backward glance between them. Amun admired their stoicism; it was as it should be, death treated as ritual and ceremony and work. He had instilled that focus into every priest he had taught, and was heartened to see their resolve hold. His own was another matter.

"The libations and offerings have been made," said Masud. "The ritual is all but complete. I will leave you to finish it."

"As will I," said Prehotep. "When it is done, give word."

"I will," said Amun, his gaze still locked on the mummy.

The Vizier and the Hery Sesheta both nodded, and left the Ibu. Amun waited until the flap of cloth had swung back into place, then addressed the body of his friend.

"I am here, your Highness," he said, his voice low and thick. "You cannot know it, but I am here. We are together in this place a final time."

He lifted the linen sack on to the stone table and opened it. His Anubis mask gleamed under the flickering light of the torches that stood around the edges of the tent; beside it lay a small ornate axe, its head smooth and sharp, its handle carefully painted with inscriptions from the Book of the Dead.

"I did not believe I would see this day," said Amun. "I held my vow, and nothing would have seen me break it, other than my own death. But I did not truly believe I would stand here, old as I am, with you gone. I am sad, your Highness, and although I know that would not meet with your approval, you are no longer here to tell me so. I would not bring you back, even if such a thing were possible, as I do not believe you would want me to. Instead I will do all that it remains within my power to do. I will send you onwards, in health, in strength, ready to experience the wonders of the next world. And in time, I will follow you."

Amun raised the mask of Anubis, his hands trembling slightly, and carefully placed it over his head. It seemed so familiar, so right, that he wondered briefly why he had ever taken it off. Then he ordered himself to focus, to put aside the grief that was flooding through him, and raised the axe.

Gently, taking the utmost care, he touched the sharp head against the lips and eyes of the mummy. Then he placed it down, and began to recite words he had long known by heart.

> *I have pressed your mouth to your bones for you,*
> *whom Horus did take as his Great in Power,*
> *whom Seth did take as his Great in Power.*
> *She has brought you all gods, so you may make them live.*
> *You have come into being in your strength,*
> *to select your protection of life,*
> *to guard against his death.*
> *You have come into being as the sustenance of all gods,*
> *and arisen as dual king, with power over all gods.*
> *Oh Osiris, Shu son of Atum, as he lives, you live.*
> *Sharpness is yours.*
> *Glory is yours.*
> *Homage is yours.*
> *Power is yours, for he has not died.*
> *Horus has opened your mouth for you,*
> *he opens your eyes for you with the Great-of-Power blade,*
> *with which the mouth of every god is opened.*

As he reached the final lines, tears began to spill from Amun's eyes; they pooled inside the mask, then dripped from the eyeholes and fell on to the smooth face of the mummy, darkening the linen with tiny explosions. When it was done, he removed the mask and bent at the waist, lowering himself unsteadily towards the tablet. His lips brushed the hard, dry surface of the mummy's forehead.

"Life is a great house," he whispered. "With many doors. Fare well, my friend."

Amun straightened up, the muscles and bones in his back creaking, and shuffled towards the Ibu's entrance, to tell the Vizier and his successor that he was done.

About the Authors

Kage Baker's notable works include "The Company" novel *Mendoza in Hollywood* and *The Empress of Mars*, a 2003 novella that won the Theodore Sturgeon Award and was nominated for a Hugo Award. In 2009, her short story "Caverns of Mystery" and novel *House of the Stag* were both nominated for World Fantasy Awards. Baker died on 31 January 2010. Later that year, her novella *The Women of Nell Gwynne's* was nominated for both Hugo and World Fantasy Awards, and won the Nebula Award. Based on extensive notes left by the author, Baker's unfinished novel, *Nell Gwynne's On Land and At Sea*, was completed by her sister Kathleen Bartholomew and published in 2012.

Gail Carriger writes comedic steampunk mixed with urban fantasy in three series: two adult, the Parasol Protectorate and Custard Protocol, and one YA, the Finishing School series. Her books are published in over a dozen different languages. She has twelve *New York Times* best-sellers via seven different lists (including #1 in Manga). She has received the Alex Award from the ALA (for her debut *Soulless*) and the Prix Julia Verlanger and the Elbakin Award from French readers. She was once an archaeologist and is overly fond of tea. More: gailcarriger.com

Paul Cornell—a writer of science fiction and fantasy in prose, comics, and TV—is one of only two people to be Hugo Award-nominated for all three media. He's written *Doctor Who* episodes for the BBC, Action Comics for DC, and Wolverine for Marvel. He's won the BSFA Award for his short fiction, an Eagle Award for his comics, and shares in a Writer's Guild Award for his television work. His modern fantasy novella *Witches of Lychford* is out now Tor. He lives in Gloucestershire with his wife and son.

Carole Nelson Douglas is the award-winning author of sixty-some novels—mystery, thriller, fantasy, science fiction, mainstream women's fiction, and romance. She launched the first series to feature a

Sherlockian woman protagonist, Irene Adler, and the first Holmes spin-off series written by a woman, with the *New York Times* Notable Book of the Year, *Good Night, Mr. Holmes*. Douglas has two bestselling series set in a Las Vegas worlds apart: the contemporary Midnight Louie feline PI mysteries and the Delilah Street, Paranormal Investigator, noir urban fantasies set in a post-monster apocalypse Vegas. The twenty-eighth Midnight Louie novel, *Cat in an Alphabet Endgame*, will end the series in 2016. In addition to his life in ancient Egypt, hard-boiled Louie has had "past life" adventures in an all-cat *Maltese Falcon* world, Edgar Allan Poe's creepy 1795 lighthouse, and Sherlock Holmes's Victorian London. More: carolenelsondouglas.com and @CNDouglasWriter.

Terry Dowling is one of Australia's most respected and internationally acclaimed writers of science fiction, dark fantasy, and horror, and author of the multi-award-winning Tom Rynosseros saga. The *Year's Best Fantasy and Horror* series featured more horror stories by Dowling in its twenty-one-year run than by any other writer. His horror collections are *Basic Black: Tales of Appropriate Fear* (International Horror Guild Award winner for Best Collection), Aurealis Award-winning *An Intimate Knowledge of the Night*, and the World Fantasy Award-nominated *Blackwater Days*. His most recent books are *Amberjack: Tales of Fear & Wonder* and his debut novel, *Clowns at Midnight*, which London's *Guardian* called "an exceptional work that bears comparison to John Fowles's *The Magus*." More: terrydowling.com.

Noreen Doyle is a freelance writer, editor, photographer, and consultant. A longtime resident of Maine, Noreen Doyle moved to Arizona a few years ago to work for the Laboratory of Tree-Ring Research and the University of Arizona Egyptian Expedition. She's earned graduate degrees in nautical archaeology (Texas A&M University) and Egyptology (University of Liverpool) and is the author of many articles on Egyptian, archaeological, and historical subjects. Her fiction has appeared in *Realms of Fantasy*, *Century*, *Weird Tales*, *Beneath Ceaseless Skies*, and several anthologies, including *Fantasy: The Best of the Year*. As an anthologist, she edited *Otherworldly Maine* and co-edited the World Fantasy Award-nominee *The First Heroes: New Tales of the Bronze Age*.

Steve Duffy has written/co-authored four collections of weird short stories. *Tragic Life Stories*, *The Five Quarters*, *The Night Comes On* (all From Ash-Tree Press), and his most recent, *The Moment of Panic* (PS Publishing). His work also appears in a number of anthologies published in the UK and the US. He won the International Horror Guild Award for Best Short Story, and has been shortlisted for a World Fantasy Award twice.

Karen Joy Fowler is the author of six novels and three short story collections. Her novel *The Jane Austen Book Club* spent thirteen weeks on the *New York Times* bestsellers list and was a *New York Times* Notable Book. Fowler's previous novel, *Sister Noon*, was a finalist for the PEN/Faulkner Award for fiction. Her debut novel, *Sarah Canary*, was a *New York Times* Notable Book, as was her second novel, *The Sweetheart Season*. In addition, *Sarah Canary* won the Commonwealth medal for best first novel by a Californian, and was listed for the *Irish Times* International Fiction Prize as well as the Bay Area Book Reviewers Prize. Fowler's short-story collection *Black Glass* won the World Fantasy Award in 1999, and her collection *What I Didn't See* won the World Fantasy Award in 2011. Fowler and her husband, who have two grown children and five grandchildren, live in Santa Cruz, California.

Will Hill is the bestselling author of the Department 19 series, a contributor to various award-winning and award-nominated anthologies, and a former judge of the Kitschies Awards. He lives in London.

Stephen Graham Jones is the author of fifteen novels and six collections. His more than 220 stories have been published in *Cemetery Dance*, *Weird Tales*, *Asimov's*, *Clarkesworld*, *The Dark*, and other venues as well as many anthologies and "best of the year" annuals. Jones's work has been a Shirley Jackson Award finalist three times, won three This is Horror Awards, and his latest collection, *After the People Lights Have Gone Off*, was a Bram Stoker Award finalist. He's also been an NEA Fellow, a Texas Writer's League Fellow, and has won the Independent Publishers Award for Multicultural Fiction. Next up is *Mongrels*, from William Morrow, in May. Jones teaches in the MFA program at CU Boulder and in the low-res MFA at UCR-Palm Desert. More at demontheory.net and @SGJ72.

John Langan is the author of two collections of short fiction: *The Wide, Carnivorous Sky and Other Monstrous Geographies* (Hippocampus, 2013) and *Mr. Gaunt and Other Uneasy Encounters* (Prime 2008); a third, *Sefira and Other Betrayals*, is forthcoming. He has written a novel, *House of Windows* (Night Shade, 2009), and with Paul Tremblay, has co-edited *Creatures: Thirty Years of Monsters* (Prime, 2011). He lives in upstate New York with his wife and younger son.

Joe R. Lansdale is the author of over forty novels and numerous short stories. In addition to "Bubba Ho-Tep", his story *Incident On and Off a Mountain Road* also became a film. His mystery classic *Cold in July* inspired the recent major motion picture of the same name starring Michael C. Hall, Sam Shepard, and Don Johnson. His novel *The Bottoms* will also soon be a film directed by Bill Paxton. His literary works have received numerous recognitions, including the Edgar, eight Bram Stoker Awards, the Grinzane Cavour Prize for Literature, American Mystery Award, the International Horror Award, British Fantasy Award, and many others. His most recent novel is *Paradise Sky*.

Helen Marshall is a critically acclaimed author, editor, and doctor of medieval studies. Her debut collection of short stories, *Hair Side, Flesh Side* (ChiZine Publications, 2012), won the 2013 British Fantasy Award for Best Newcomer. Her second collection, *Gifts for the One Who Comes After*

(ChiZine Publications, 2014), was nominated for several awards. She lives in Oxford, England where she spends her time staring at old books.

Kim Newman is a novelist, critic, and broadcaster. His fiction includes *The Night Mayor*, *Bad Dreams*, *Jago*, the Anno Dracula novels and stories, *The Quorum*, *The Original Dr Shade and Other Stories*, *Life's Lottery*, *Back in the USSA* (with Eugene Byrne), *The Man From the Diogenes Club*, *Professor Moriarty: The Hound of the d'Urbervilles*, and *An English Ghost Story* under his own name and *The Vampire Genevieve* and *Orgy of the Blood Parasites* as Jack Yeovil. His most recent book is *Secrets of Drearcliff Grange School*; *Angels of Music* and a fifth Anno Dracula novel are forthcoming. The author of nine non-fiction books and a contributing editor for magazines *Sight & Sound* and *Empire* (where he writes the popular "Video Dungeon" column), Newman has also scripted radio and television documentaries, stage and radio plays, and (with Maura McHugh) the comic book mini-series Witchfinder: The Mysteries of Unland (Dark Horse), illustrated by Tyler Crook. More: johnnyalucard.com and @AnnoDracula.

Norman Partridge's first short story appeared in *Cemetery Dance #2*, and his debut novel, *Slippin' into Darkness*, was the first original novel published by Cemetery Dance Publications. Since then, he has written a series novel (*The Crow: Wicked Prayer*), which was adapted for the screen, comics for DC, and six collections of short stories. Partridge's Halloween novel, *Dark Harvest*, was chosen by *Publishers Weekly* as one of the 100 Best Books of 2006 and has become a seasonal classic. The recipient of three Bram Stoker awards and an International Horror Guild Award, he is third-generation Californian who lives in the San Francisco Bay Area with his wife, Canadian writer Tia V. Travis, and their daughter Neve. His latest novel is *The Devil's Brood*.

Adam Roberts is Professor of Nineteenth-century Literature at Royal Holloway University of London, and the author of fifteen science fiction novels, most recently *Twenty Trillion Leagues Under the Sea*

(Gollancz, 2014) and *Bête* (Gollancz, 2015). His next project will be a racy SF novelization of Kant's *Critique of Pure Reason*, to be called *The Thing Itself*, which will appear later in 2016.

Robert Sharp works for the free speech campaign group English PEN and has written widely on freedom of expression issues, including for the *Guardian*, the *Independent*, the *New Statesman*, and the *Huffington Post*. He was formerly a director of 59 Productions, the award-winning video design agency. He lives with his family in Bromley, UK.

Brisbane-based writer Angela Slatter has won five Aurealis Awards and one British Fantasy Award, been a finalist for the Norma K. Hemming Award once and the World Fantasy Award twice. She's published six story collections, has a PhD, was an inaugural Queensland Writers Fellow, is a freelance editor, and teaches creative writing. Her novellas, *Of Sorrow and Such* (Tor.com) and *Ripper* (in *Horrorology*, Jo Fletcher Books), will be out in October 2015, and Jo Fletcher Books will publish her debut novel, *Vigil*, in 2016, with its sequel, *Corpselight*, coming in 2017. Prime Books will publish a collection of her short fiction in 2016 as well.

Born in Tasmania, **Keith Taylor** now resides in Melbourne, Australia. Getting his start in Ted White's *Fantastic* magazine, Taylor went on to collaborate with Andrew J. Offutt on two novels based upon the Robert E. Howard hero, Cormac Mac Art. A two-time winner of the Ditmar Award, his series of novels centering around the Irish bard, Felimid mac Fal, was published throughout the 1980s. Much of Taylor's fictional output in the 1990s was in the Arthurian fantasy subgenre. Many stories featuring his character, Kamose the Magician, were published in *Weird Tales* from 1999 to 2006 and later collected (2012) in *Servant of the Jackal God: The Tales of Kamose, Archpriest of Anubis*.

Lois Tilton is a science fiction, fantasy, alternate history, and horror writer. She won the Sidewise Award for Alternate History in the short form category for "Pericles the Tyrant" in 2006. In 2005, "The Gladiator's War" was a nominee for the Nebula Award for Best Novelette. She has also written several novels featuring vampires. Tilton sold over seventy pieces of short fiction between 1985 and 2009, many of which appeared in *Asimov's* and *Realms of Fantasy*. She is now the short-fiction reviewer for the website *Locus Online*. Previously, she reviewed short fiction for the *Internet Review of Science Fiction*.

About the Editor

As a child, Paula Guran wanted to be an Egyptologist. She grew up, but didn't become an Egyptologist. Her love for the subject and autodidactic study of it, however, never died.

Now—many years later—Guran is the senior editor for Prime Books and an anthologist who has written on mummies in literature for a couple of encyclopedias. Despite having about three dozen anthologies to her credit, she was more thrilled by the chance to edit this one than you might imagine.

The mother of four, mother-in-law of two, and grandmother of two, she lives in Akron, Ohio, only forty-five minutes away from the Cleveland Museum of Art and its Egyptian collection, which is internationally recognized as one of the finest of its kind.

Acknowledgements

"The Queen in Yellow" © 2002 Kage Baker. First publication: *Black Projects, White Knights: The Company Dossier* (Golden Gryphon Press, 2002).

"The Curious Case of the Werewolf That Wasn't, the Mummy That Was, and the Cat in the Jar" © 2014 Gail Carriger. First publication: *The Book of the Dead*, ed. Jared Shulin (Jurassic London, 2014).

"Ramesses On the Frontier" © 2014 Paul Cornell. First publication: *The Book of the Dead*, ed. Jared Shulin (Jurassic London, 2014).

"Fruit of the Tomb" © 1998 Carole Nelson Douglas. First publication: (as "The Mummy Case") *Cat Crimes Through Time*, eds. Ed Gorman, Martin H. Greenberg and Larry Segriff (Carroll & Graf Publishers, 1999).

"The Shaddowes Box" © 2011 Terry Dowling. First publication: *Ghost by Gaslight*, eds. Jack Dann and Nick Gevers (Harper Voyager, 2011).

"The Night Comes On" © 1998 Steve Duffy. First publication: *The Night Comes On* (Ash-Tree Press, 1998).

"Private Grave 9" © 2003 Karen Joy Fowler. First publication: *McSweeney's Mammoth Treasury of Thrilling Tales*, ed. Michael Chabon (Vintage, 2003).

"Three Memories of Death" © 2014 Will Hill. First publication: *The Book of the Dead*, ed. Jared Shulin (Jurassic London, 2014).

"American Mummy" © Stephen Graham Jones 2016. Original to this volume.

"On Skua Island" © 2001 John Langan. First publication: *The Magazine of Fantasy & Science Fiction*, August 2001.

"Bubba Ho-Tep" © 1994 Joe R. Lansdale. First publication: *The King Is Dead; Tales of Elvis Postmortem*, ed. Paul M. Sammon (1994).

"The Embalmer" © Helen Marshall 2016. Original to this volume.

"Egyptian Avenue" © 2002 Kim Newman. First publication: *Embrace the Mutation: Fiction Inspired by the Art of J. K. Potter*, eds. Bill Sheehan and William Schafer (Subterranean Press, 2002).

"The Mummy's Heart" © 2013 Norman Partridge. First publication: *Halloween: Magic, Mystery and the Macabre*, ed. Paula Guran (Prime Books, 2013).

"Tollund" © 2014 Adam Roberts. First publication: *The Book of the Dead*, ed. Jared Shulin (Jurassic London, 2014).

"The Good Shabti" © 2014 Robert Sharp. First publication: *The Good Shabti* (Jurassic London, 2014).

"Egyptian Revival" © Angela Slatter 2016. Original to this volume.

"The Emerald Scarab" © 2001 Keith Taylor. First publication: *Weird Tales*, Spring 2001.

"The Chapter of Coming Forth by Night" © 2000 Lois Tilton and Noreen Doyle. First publication: *Realms of Fantasy*, February 2000.